MW00887010

FROM GENERATION TO GENERATION

The Series

Book 1 of 7

In

"The Curse Must Be Broken!"

By

LSB

LEWIS - SMITH BOOKS

William C. Lewis / Jennifer R. Smith

FROM GENERATION TO GENERATION
"The Curse Must Be Broken!"

Book 1
of
A Fiction Series
Written Jan 2013
2nd Edition – November 2020

As a result of their parents' lifestyles, children from different walks of life inherit curses that make their adult lives, a living hell. This spiritual, high-energy, suspense, unfolds within families in Atlanta Georgia, as uncontrollable curses rule and seek to destroy them. The question is… *"Will The Curse Be Broken",,,,,,, or passed...*

FROM GENERATION TO GENERATION!

William C Lewis / Jennifer R Smith

<table>
<tr><td>

c/o Jonathan Lewis
CFO / Editor
1480 Bourdon Bell Drive
Conyers, GA 30013
jlinlithoniaga@yahoo.com
(678) 755-6103

</td><td>

c/o Donna D. Lowe
Admin / Editor
1139 Timberlake Ct.
Riverdale, GA 3029
Willdee1959@yahoo.com
(770) 899-5223

</td></tr>
</table>

Website: www.lewissmithbooks.com Email: lewissmithbooks@gmail.com
Manufactured in the United States of America

LSB

Lewis – Smith Books

ACKNOWLEDGEMENTS

FROM GENERATION TO GENERATION, this first novel of our 7-Book Series" has been a long time coming. Being handicapped by confinements, where there was no computer or typewriter made available for use, during the three months of writing and the nine months of rewriting, typing, proofing, editing, organizing, soliciting financial assistance then repeating the process numerous times, until this novel was ready to print. Nevertheless, it was joyous pushing the pen day and night until the publishing process was completed.

During the initial stages, God sent Myrtice Roberts, my closest friend and sister in the faith, to organize my writings, while providing her personal finances to spearhead the typing which helped to forward this novels success. Natalie Curry, who was also brought on board by Myrtice, worked many days and nights at her computer to insure the novel's continued progress, while Myrtice diligently helped to provide daycares over South Georgia with food supply and management assistance.

In later months, Satan attacked Myrtice and she became ill, and mostly bed stricken. Therefore, she was not able to continue the timely assistance she had faithfully provided for many months. Just as God sent Myrtice, he later opened the heart of Bobby "Big Brother" Head, his wife Darlene, and my son, Jonathan Lewis, whom all have always been there, picked up where Myrtice left off. Even Derrick Lee and Montaque Jackson, who were with me in my situation, assisted to keep the progress moving forward while Myrtice fought for her life.

Like Myrtice, Bobby and Jonathan faithfully provided funding and personal efforts to see this novel to completion. Natalie, Derrick, and Montaque stayed on board as Mitchell Williams and Donna D. Lowe, my friend and editor, helped to pick up the pieces, while Joseph Butts, author of *"When Nobody Brings You An Apple,"* provided his experience to help see the project through.

While laboring faithfully through finger cramps, calluses, backaches, watery eyes that sometimes were dimmed, restrictions, and hardships, this novel still would not be completed had it not been for much prayer, and God allowing the above named family and friends to share their personal love and unselfish efforts to assist me....the author....William Charles Lewis.

To all of you, I love you, and I thank you so much. It is my prayer that God richly blesses you with the desires of your heart while you're on this earth then presents you faultless before the presence of his glory, when you leave it. Until then, I dedicate this....my first novel, in your honor. Myrtice....Velvet....I love you, girl, and pray for your speedy recovery. God Bless.

Enjoy This Masterfully Written Generational Series!

This High Suspense Spiritual Series is one of the best fictional dramas of all times about hidden curses that seek to destroy family life for generations to come!

A generational curse within your family's bloodline could be the very reason for your sicknesses, rebellions, adulteries, loneliness, imprisonments, homosexuality, and numerous other failures, because somebody within your generations defiled the will of the living God and caused this curse to fall on you. Now the question is, Can This Curse Be Broken? Or will you allow it to linger and ruin your life, until it passes on to your kids? See what readers are saying about this enlightening series:

ANNETTE OWENS
Atlanta Georgia – Suspenseful; dramatic with unpredictable twists ....Looking forward to reading the rest of this outstanding series.

RAYMOND A. WESNER
Pittsburgh Pennsylvania - From Generation To Generation is one of those rare novels that have no specific genre; it's a bit of this and a pinch of that. All and all it's a "Recipe for a Masterpiece!" Kudos to William Lewis for a job well done!

CASSANDRA LAMBERT
Taylor Michigan – "A PICTURE IS WORTH A THOUSAND WORDS!" Author William Lewis can truly bring a story to life!

Don't allow generational curses that you don't know anything about to destroy the lives of you and your children. Break The Curse! Get this series now, and find out how!

Preface

High above the stars, huge blazes of colorful light flashed within the deep darkness of the universe. Each time a child is conceived and destined to live upon the earth, the windows of heaven opens and dispatch blessings and curses that will alter that child's life.

As Larry and Gladdis sexually conceived their daughter Cherlene, a huge streak of bluish-colored ice emerged from the darkness of the heavens and raced toward the earth. Afterward, a huge colorful streak of fire also emerged and trailed the ice. No matter which way the ice turned, the colorful ball of fire stayed on its trail.

Later, as Jennifer was conceived in Margit, the blue streak of ice split and became two streaks of ice racing side by side still toward the earth. Finally, as Keisha conceived Donna in her womb, the streak of ice split into a third piece of ice racing side by side, with the colorful ball of fire still following them.

As the streaks of ice neared the earth, the huge colorful ball of fire suddenly split into six balls of multi-colored fire all racing side by side but still trailing the streaks of ice wheresoever they went.

Chapter 1

"Stop!" yelled the store manager. "I know who you are and you can't get away!"

"Dad! Wait! It's me!!" But her dad kept running hard like he didn't hear her.

"Stop!" he yelled. "Or I'll shoot!"

"Bang! Bang!" sounded the gun.

"Aaah!" she screamed. Her eyes peered on as the gun fired many times and her dad fell to the ground.

****

Jennifer, being about 7 years old, held her mom's hand as they entered a large grocery store near Candler Road in Decatur, Georgia. In her other hand, she carried a small toy as her mom pulled her along.

"Jennifer, stay close," said her mom. "And don't touch anything." She let go of Jennifer's hand and proceeded down the aisle. Jennifer's mom, Margit Sweet, a tall, slender, sexy, white woman, is shacking with Jennifer's dad, who is also a tall, slender, energetic, educated, black man.

Jennifer is a very beautiful, light browned skinned child, with gorgeous brown hair, who loves family and family fun. She is very smart, and hopes to someday have a family of her own. Being a very inquisitive child, Jennifer watched closely as her mom opened her purse and pulled out two grocery bags. Then she laid them flat in the shopping cart and continued down the aisles. Jennifer had seen her mom do this many times, and she was bothered by it every time.

"Mom, why don't we ever pay for the grocery?"

"Don't ask me these questions, Jennifer. You know that your dad and I are doing all we can just to live. So the money we save, we can spend on you and other important things. Now let it go and help me get the items we need." She handed Jennifer the grocery list. Instead of taking the list, Jennifer disappointedly walked away and started putting the items in the cart.

She knew exactly what to get because they were the same items her mom steals every time, they came to that store – cigarettes, coffee, and cereal.

After they'd finished getting the groceries, Margit would move to a secluded aisle or place in the store, fill the bags with the groceries, and sit the bags upright in the cart. Then she would leave the store as if she had purchased them. Today would be no different as she looked for a suitable place to sack her items.

As she bagged them, she didn't notice the store manager watching her. He'd been suspicious of her for a while, but could never catch her. This time, he saw her bag the items and move toward the exit door. Margit looked back just in time to see the store manager waving to the security guard while he pursued her. With one hand pushing the cart, she grabbed Jennifer's hand and sped toward the exit.

"Stop!" yelled the store manager. "I know who you are and you can't get away!" After exiting the store, she quickly dashed around the corner and mixed into the crowd. She'd hoped to make it safely to her car, which was parked a little ways down the street.

This was the first time anyone had ever pursued her and she was scared. After awhile, she looked back and could no longer see her pursuers as she almost made it to her car.

Suddenly, as she and Jennifer were within yards of the car, the door of the pawn shop near them flew open and a tall black man, carrying a tote bag, came out running for his life! Margit lightly screamed as Pete Lockhart raced by, but Jennifer's eyes stayed locked on him because she recognized him and loved him. Being secured in her mother's arms, she yelled,

"Dad wait! It's me!!" But her dad kept running hard like he didn't hear her. With her dad still being in sight, she saw another man come running out of the same door she had seen her dad come from. It was the store's manager, and he was pursuing her dad ... with a gun!

"Stop!" he yelled. "Or I'll shoot!"

Within minutes, Jennifer had seen and heard two different store managers yell, "Stop!" and each time it was directed toward her parents, who were being pursued.

Except this time, she also heard... "I'll shoot!" Being unaware of what was about to happen, she watched the store manager kneel on one knee then shoot the gun in the direction of her dad.

"*Bang! Bang!*" sounded the gun.

"Aahhh!" she screamed. Her eyes peered on as the gun fired many times and her dad fell to the ground. "Daddy! Daddy!" she yelled. Then she broke away from her mom and ran toward her dad as the crowd gathered around him.

A woman nearby, who had been watching the whole thing, quickly grabbed Jennifer to prevent her from seeing her dad up close like that. As Jennifer struggled to free herself from the woman's grasp, her eyes briefly glanced in the direction where she'd left her mom, just in time to see the grocery store manager and a police officer cuffing her, and shoving her into the backseat of a police cruiser.

Tears and screams were many as Jennifer struggled in the arms of a stranger, while losing both of her parents.

Meantime, the streaks of ice followed by the balls of fire continued on their course toward the earth.

Chapter 2

A few months later, Donna being about 6 years old, is returning from a family vacation with her parents. Donna's dad, Mr. Antwaun Banks, is the Solicitor General for the State of Georgia. Her mom, Keisha Banks, is the anchorwoman for a local news broadcast in Atlanta.

Living in the Buckhead community, this somewhat arrogant, uppity couple, lives well above their income, while attempting to impress others that they are the ideal American family. In order to uphold this image, they'll do whatever necessary, whether moral or immoral, to present themselves luxurious and superior to their peers and subordinates.

Donna, a very vibrant child, doesn't think it strange to often see her parents meeting in secluded places with people she sometimes see on TV. Besides, her mom is on TV everyday, and sometimes, so is her dad.

Today, as they walked through the Atlanta airport, a heavy set, tall, Black man, and a pretty, young, Caucasian woman, walked up and faced-off with her parents. Both were dressed in trench coats and dark clothing while wearing lots of jewelry. The couple looks mean to Donna, but so do most of the people her parents meet with. Today, they all seemed very friendly as they greeted each other and talked.

"What's up, Mr. Solicitor General?" greeted the man. "How was your vacation in Jamaica?" Antwaun Banks pulled a small raw carrot from his pocket and bit it.

"Thanks to you and your kind, it was very nice and good for my family," he smiled.

"Me and my kind? What in the hell is that suppose to mean?" Donna saw something shiny within the man's coat when he placed his hands on his hips. It was a gun.

"No need to get hasty," said Antwaun.

"They're just words that don't apply to anyone in particular, but only to the business at hand. So please let's continue to handle this in a rational manner as we always have."

Antwaun nervously ate on his carrot while the man stared meanly in his face. Donna watched as her mom also seemed fidgety and very nervous. She quickly grabbed her mom's hand and held on. When both parties saw this, their attitudes and countenances changed to a calmer demeanor.

"I hope your words are about the business at hand and nothing else," said the man. "I'd hate to see your entire lifestyle changed because of 'me and my kind.'"

"My, my, my," laughed Keisha. "We don't want that to happen, now, do we?" She nudged her husband and signaled him to smile. After a pause, the man and the woman burst into laughter with the Banks also laughing with them.

"Ms. Keisha Banks! Anchorwoman!" yelled the pretty woman. "Why don't we step into the ladies room and powder up a bit?"

"Hee Hee! Ok," laughed Keisha. "I like the sound of that!" She took Donna's hand and walked into the nearby ladies room. Donna stood at the door playing with her toy and listening as the woman handed Keisha a thick envelope.

"Here is our next installment as promised," said the woman.

"I take it that it's all there, as we agreed, and I thank you."

"Yes, it's all there. You will get your final payment when our shipment clears customs and is in our control, also as agreed," said the woman.

"Well, my husband takes care of that part. I just take care of this!" She patted the envelope to her breast and placed it in her purse. They both laughed as they left the bathroom and rejoined the men.

"I take it that business is good my dear?"

"Yes, yes!" smiled Keisha while patting her purse.

"Then our business here is done," said Antwaun. He extended his hand to the couple and they left.

On the way home, Donna kept wondering about the envelope that caused her mom to hold onto her purse so tightly. Soon, they were home and began to settle in. Donna turned the TV on and heard her mom's replacement anchorwoman talking about Public Officials.

"Mommy, what's a public official?" yelled Donna.

"Those are good people who hold office in the city, county, and state government, like your daddy."

"Does Daddy take money from bad people?" The question startled her parents so shockingly; they ran into the den where Donna was watching TV to see what was going on. They heard the news woman on TV.

"In many of the cities around the state, GBI (Georgia Bureau of Investigations) have been undercover in an attempt to identify city, county, and state leaders involved with drug dealers, and other businessmen for personal profit or gain.

It is reported that dozens of public officials all over the state, have taken bribes, are involved with child pornography, or create passageway for the incoming drugs that occupy in many of our schools. Here is the latest report that identifies those state offices, where GBI have found corruption..."

As the news continues, Antwaun sees an unmarked police car pulling up to his house. When he opened the door, he was surprised to find the Mayor and the police chief, already standing on his porch, about to ring the doorbell.

"Mr. Mayor...Chief? What have I done to deserve such a special visit?"

"Antwaun," spoke the Mayor. "Do you mind if we come in a minute?"

"Not at all, Sir. What's this about?"

As they enter, the police chief waves a search warrant and quietly moves through the house. Antwaun reaches for a small carrot in the dish on the coffee table and bites it.

"Antwaun, I have some disturbing news," said the Mayor. "Your office has been under GBI investigations for months now. Since that time, many records and other documents from your office have connected you with...well, some *'not-so-good'* businessmen, if you know what I mean." The Mayor saw Donna walk into the room with her toy, so he curbed his words.

"No Sir, I have no idea what you mean," answered Antwaun.

"Ok, then," continued the Mayor. "Sources tell us that you took a family trip to Jamaica and spent thousands of dollars. Where did you get the money, Twaun?"

"Mr. Mayor, it isn't a crime to spend money while being on vacation."

"Where did you get the money, Antwaun?" About that time, the TV anchorwoman presented videos of dealers and other businessmen being arrested during a GBI bust.

"Daddy! Daddy!" yelled Donna as she pointed. "We're on TV!" A video was airing of the Solicitor General and his family at the airport, shaking hands with one of the most notorious drug dealers in the state. "Daddy, that's the man and woman we saw today!" The video showed the man and woman being arrested outside the airport.

About that same time, the police chief walked back into the room with Keisha in one hand, and the envelope full of money in the other.

"Antwaun, the envelope is full of marked bills," said the Mayor. "We were gonna get you at the airport, but I must be getting soft in my old age. I just couldn't arrest you in the public eye like that. But now, an unmarked cruiser awaits you outside. I won't cuff you if you come quietly, but you have to come now. It's out of my hands." Antwaun was shocked as he stared at Keisha and bit his carrot.

"Honey, I will be down in a few minutes to get you out of this mess. You are the Solicitor General for the State of Georgia! We will see what the Governor has to say about this!" argued Keisha.

"Well Keisha, you might do that later," stated the Mayor. "But right now, you're going down to the station, too--Governor's orders. You have been identified as an accessory in Antwaun's misdealing. Besides, the money was found in your purse."

"What! You can't arrest me! Antwaun, don't let them do this! What about my baby? My job?"

"Those things will be taken care of, Keisha. But right now, I need you to come quietly or I will place you in cuffs and drag you if I have to. Do you understand?" Keisha said nothing but quietly made her way outside.

As Donna watched her parents being escorted to jail, she didn't know what to think. Both cars drove away with her parents inside, and she was alone. As she watched, a third car pulled to the house and stopped. Donna saw the pretty woman get out of the car that she had seen at the airport, and again being arrested on TV.

"Hi Donna, remember me? We didn't get a chance to properly meet earlier today, because I was working. Anyway, my name is Agent Smith--Agent Rosa Smith, but you can call me Rosa, ok?"

"Rosa, can I go see my Mommy, now?"

"I'm sure you will get to see Mommy, soon. But, right now, we have to go in the house and get you some things. Then we're gonna take a ride, ok?" Donna nodded...

"Yes."

Meantime, the ice and the fire continued on their course toward the earth.

Chapter 3

While little 7 year-old Cherlene is sleeping soundly in West End, Atlanta, she is awaken by strange noises coming from within the apartment. Cherlene lives with her mom in a very high crime area of the city of Atlanta.

Before her dad went to prison, they were a family living in a nice Alpharetta neighborhood with other respectable families and kids. But now, things are hard as Cherlene and her mom, Gladdis Tullis, struggle just to find food from day to day.

Cherlene's dad is serving time for participating in child pornography and soliciting young women in a prostitution ring. Her mom, who used to be a prostitute, married her dad, and became a respectable house wife... that is, until her husband went to prison to serve a life sentence. Now, Gladdis and her daughter, Cherlene, were only hours away from eviction and homelessness, as Gladdis did all she could to find money for food and shelter.

As Cherlene heard the thumping noises get louder, she could also hear her mom in the next room. So she felt safe as she climbed out of bed and made her way to her mom. As she approached the cracked opened door to her mom's bedroom, she saw her mom in bed with her arms and legs wrapped around a man. They were rocking the bed really hard and causing it to make the noises that had awakened her.

"Uh!!! Uh!! Uh!! Oh God!" screamed her mom, as Cherlene gently pushed the door opened and stepped in. Cherlene sees her mom scratching the man's back and pulling on the covers while she screams and hits the man like she was fighting.

"Mommy!" yelled Cherlene. "Stop hurting my mommy!" Gladdis and the man with her turned sharply to look at Cherlene then laid motionless for a minute.

"Baby, go back to your room and lay down. Mommy will be there in a minute," said Gladdis being very friendly to her child.

"No, Mommy," Cherlene spoke softly. She didn't want to leave her mother with this strange man. "Come with me!" The man seemed frustrated and attempted to remove himself from between Gladdis legs, but she grabbed him and clamped to him.

"What's wrong?" she asked sweetly.

"This wasn't part of the deal, baby. I want you out of here in 2 hours or I'm calling the sheriff." Then he tried to remove himself again, but Galddis embraced him and held him close.

"We made a deal and I'm keeping my end of it, because I don't have anywhere else to go. So please, let's finish the deal."

"What about the kid?"

"Don't worry about her, "Gladdis said with tears in her eyes. "She'll be fine."

The man, seemingly having a cold heart, smiled at Gladdis then went back to work like Cherlene wasn't even there. As he pounded and screwed, Gladdis laid motionless as her teary eyes stayed locked onto her daughter, who was watching her as well.

Gladdis was very hurt and embarrassed to have her young daughter to witness such a sexual act. Even though she tried her best to show no emotions in front of her daughter, she couldn't deny the feeling created by the deep, hard hitting, pounding, that was penetrating vibrantly inside her. In an instant, when she felt the swelling and stiffening of his penis about to ejaculate, she screamed,

"Uh! Uh! Oh God!" Then she spread her legs wide and high, and again, clawed her nails into the back of the man, and onto the bed covers. Now, she too, like her sexual partner, completely ignored Cherlene, who stood in the doorway feeling confused and scared. After the orgasm, they laid there being exhausted and looking at Cherlene. Then the man got up, dressed himself, and patted Cherlene on the head.

"That bought you 7 days. I'll be back in a week expecting another payment or your ass is out." Then he left.

For the next couple of days, Gladdis could hardly live with herself as she cried and cried, and held Cherlene. She still didn't know what she was going to do when the 7 days were up. Would he want money this time, or could she just have sex with him again and get another week.

At the end of the 7 days, Gladdis found herself in bed with her landlord again, hoping to get more than 7 days this time. She could tell that he really enjoyed the sex with her and she too, loved the way he made her feel when he was deep inside her. This time, Cherlene stood outside her mom's locked bedroom door and listened. After the sex was over, they began to talk.

"Melvin, I need more time to find work and to secure my baby. I need at least a month, this time," she pleaded.

"I'm sorry, baby, but I can't help you. I've got to put money on my books by tomorrow."

"Tomorrow? How in the hell am I to get money by tomorrow?"

"Well, I've done you a favor. Later tonight, a friend of mine is gonna come by and visit you. Give him what he wants and he can help you. I've already told him that you are worth every dime."

"What are you saying,,, that you've pimped me out?" she asked angrily.

"I need my money and I don't want to put you out on the street. So take it or leave it."

"Get your ass out of my apartment!" she screamed while crying and pointing.

"No baby! It's my apartment and if you don't make this money, tonight, that I've set up for you then you get your ass out!" Then as usual, he left.

Gladdis knew that her whole life was about to take a turn for the worst. She wasn't worried about herself because she had been here before. But she was worried about Cherlene, her 7 year old daughter.

Gladdis didn't have anyone she could call or leave Cherlene with, in the event something happened. Now, Gladdis felt she was faced with a situation that would expose her child to the very lifestyle she had left behind, and trying to avoid.

That night, about an hour before Melvin's friend showed up, Gladdis decided that it was time to talk to Cherlene. So she went into Cherlene's bedroom and sat next to her on the floor. Cherlene was playing with her toys.

"Hi Mommy! Wanna play house with me?"

"Oh, I would love to play house with you baby, but we need to talk about something first, O.K.?"

"What do you want to talk about, Mommy?" she asked being attentive.

"Remember the other day....." Gladdis spoke slowly as she began to cry.

"Don't cry, Mommy," said Cherlene as she hugged Gladdis. Gladdis hugged her back, then continued.

"Remember the other day when you saw Mommy and Melvin in bed?" Cherlene nodded,

"Yes." Gladdis was struggling to talk as she tried to hold back the tears. Finally, beyond her control, she burst out with a loud cry as tears began to flow like a river.

"I don't know what to do," she cried as she lay back on the floor.

"Mommy, please don't cry. Everything's gonna work out just fine," she said. Through the tears, Gladdis burst into laughter as she hugged her daughter. "I love you so much... and you are so right! Everything's gonna be just fine." Then she sat up, wiped her eyes, and got herself together.

Cherlene's innocence to the situation had given Gladdis a new spark, and she was planning to take charge of her life again. Besides, she felt that what she was about to go through was old news and she knew it well from her past. Now that she was 26 years old, she felt more experienced, and she knew she had to take charge of her life. So she dried her tears and began to get herself together as she held Cherlene and spoke.

"Sweetheart, tonight I want you to go to bed early, ok? I'm gonna play some music for you so you can sleep good, ok?"

"Ok, Mommy."

"But I don't want you to leave your bed for any reason until I come to check on you, ok? If you need something, just wait until I come and I will get it for you. Now let's take our shower and go to bed because we have a big day tomorrow," she said playfully.

Cherlene was happy that her mom was back. She could tell that whatever was bothering her mom, wasn't bothering her anymore. So she enjoyed her bath with her mom, then she went to bed as Gladdis tucked her in.

Minutes later, just before Cherlene fell asleep, she had to use the bathroom. Forgetting her mother's words, she got up and went to the bathroom. As she passed her mom's bedroom, she saw her mom combing her hair and looking very pretty. She left the bathroom door open while she used the toilet.

Suddenly, there was a small knock on the apartment door. Cherlene suddenly remembered that she was not supposed to get up without calling her mother first. So she quickly cleaned herself then tried to hurry back to her bed without being noticed, but she was too slow.

Before she could get out of the bathroom doorway, her mom was already at the front door and opening it. So to keep from being caught, she quickly darted into her mom's bedroom, which was next to the bathroom, and hid in the closet. She could hear her mom talking to someone, but she couldn't hear what they were saying.

"Hi, Gladdis?"

"Yes, that's me."

"I'm Nard; that's short for Bernard," he smiled.

"Come on in, Nard." He entered and sat down.

"Well, I guess you know why I'm here," he gestured.

"No, I don't know why you're here, Nard, so why don't you tell me?" Gladdis spoke boldly. Bernard must have been about 38 or so, maybe just a little younger than Melvin. Melvin had really satisfied her in bed and even made her enjoy it and want more. Now, as she checked Bernard's very manly physique, he was built even better than Melvin. Melvin was about 5 feet 11 inches, medium built, weighing about 180 pounds, just right. But Bernard was about 6 feet 1 inch, weighing about 200 pounds .....perfect.

As Gladdis looked him in the eye, she begin to reminisce about the very pleasurable, sexual moments, she'd recently enjoyed with Melvin. Now, she hoped that what she was about to do with Bernard, would be even more unforgettable. She couldn't help but to blush as her eyes lowered toward his zipper. Gladdis wasn't bad herself. She was 26, thick, weighing about 155 pounds, at 5 feet 8 inches. Bernard was checking out every inch of her and he wasn't hiding it. He loved her nice, long black hair, and her baby face.

"Melvin told me that we both could find what we needed here tonight and..."

"And what is it that you need, Nard?" she asked while cutting in boldly.

"Look, is this some kind of game you're playing, cause if it is...,"

"No game, Nard. What did Melvin tell you?"

"He told me that you needed money, now, so what's up?" Gladdis paused.

"I need a drink! I really need a drink, right now," she pleaded. Bernard reached inside his jacket and pulled out a small flask and handed it to her.

"Here. This helps me to get through my rough days." She took the flask and drank from it.

"Nard, I need $700.00." Nard didn't say a word as he just smiled, eased from his chair, and headed toward the door. Gladdis quickly ran in front of him and stood with her perfumed lips close to his. "I have a daughter sleeping in the other room," she said humbly. "If I don't pay my rent and get some food, we will be put out tomorrow. You are my last hope and I really need this money."

Again, Bernard said nothing. Instead he reached inside her loosely fitting knee high pants and began to fondle her until she hissed. She quickly grabbed his hand and slowly led him to her bedroom, not aware that Cherlene was hiding in her closet.

Cherlene's eyes peered through the closet's louver door as Bernard and her mom undressed each other. He took three $100.00 bills, laid them on the dresser then fell face first between Gladdis' legs, giving her oral sex, until she moaned with pleasure. No one heard the front door slowly opening as Melvin walked all the way to the bedroom and picked up the money from the dresser.

"Don't y'all mind me," he said as Gladdis tried to cover herself. She saw him take her money and she knew she couldn't do anything about it. She was behind for 2 months rent at $500 a month. She had figured that if she could get $700.00, then she could pay 1 month, and use the rest for food until she could get more. But her plan was already failing.

"If only I had a little more time," she thought.

"This will get you two more weeks," Melvin smirked as he counted. Bernard was acting like Melvin wasn't even there as he pulled away the bed covers and exposed Gladdis' smooth body. As Melvin walked out, Bernard laid her on her back and began penetrating her. She quietly screamed and moaned with Cherlene watching through the closet doors.

Bernard was turning out to be all that Gladdis hoped he'd be. It had become pleasurable as she allowed him to have his way with her. She had no idea that Melvin was still in the apartment peeking at their every move, while undressing in the living room. As Bernard slid from between her legs and laid on the bed, he pulled Gladdis on top of him, then lowered her head to his penis for oral sex. He saw Melvin quietly entering the bedroom.

"Get on your knees, baby, so I can see your body," said Bernard as he smiled. Evidently, he and Melvin had planned this.

While Gladdis was on the bed, on her knees, giving Bernard oral sex, Melvin walked up behind her and penetrated her deeply. He locked his hands on her hips so she couldn't move, while Bernard took her head with both his hands and began slamming her mouth on his penis until she began to gag and choke.

Melvin began to spank her painfully as he slammed himself inside her until it hurt. She was scared, now, as she began fighting for her life, but the men were too much for her.

While Bernard was holding her head and thrusting himself in her mouth, Melvin was doing the same with her body. She was so scared as the tears came, but she knew that she was at the mercy of the men who had her in their grasps.

As both men approached climax, Gladdis, through tears, caught a glimpse of the closet door and saw Cherlene... watching. She could only see for a moment, but she knew Cherlene was there. The more she struggled to free herself, the tighter the men made their grip on her.

Realizing that her daughter was watching, Gladdis struggled harder to free herself as she choked on Bernard's semen, and hurt from Melvin's merciless thrusts to her body. Gladdis could handle the sex, but the fear of believing that these men would take her daughter and harm her, flooded her mind with a series of concerns that worked her brain harder than the men were working her body.

"Will they go after my child when they finish with me?" she panicked. *"Will they turn her out? Will they turn her on to porno and make her a whore like me? What can I even say to her? Lord, please, help me! And don't let them touch my child! I... uh... need... uh... my eyes... my mouth!"*

As Gladdis continued to think and struggle, her breathing became sporadic, her vision became blurred, and her mind-to-body coordination was completely out of sync.

"What's wrong with me?" she wondered. Suddenly, her arms began to tuck themselves and her mouth began opening and closing like a fish needing water. Even while still on her knees, her body automatically took the fetal position as her mind went blank.

As the men continued to sexually abuse her, they had no idea that Gladdis' mental and physical stresses were causing impaired circulation to her brain. Within minutes, Gladdis suffered a massive stroke to her brain and died, while her daughter watched from the closet. After awhile, Melvin and Bernard released her, only to learn that Gladdis wasn't moving.

As Rosa and the state social worker escorted Cherlene to a foster care home outside of Atlanta, Ms. Myrtice Roberts welcomed her and introduced her to the other young girls.

"Hi, Cherlene," she spoke friendly. "I understand that you will be staying with us a while. Here, let me introduce you to some friends." Two young girls about Cherlene's age came toward her.

"Cherlene, this is Donna Banks, who is 6 years old, and this is Jennifer Ramona Sweet, who is 7 years old. Girls, I want you to welcome Cherlene Tullis to our home. She is your new 7 ½ year old sister, and she will be staying with us."

"Hello, Cherlene!" said Jennifer and Donna as they held her hand. As the three girls walked away hand in hand, the streaks of ice and the balls of fire raced toward the earth.

Chapter 4

For the next few years, the girls went through a lot of drama and heartache as they remembered what they had witnessed concerning their parents. Therefore, they went to lots of counseling and psychological evaluations. They were sometimes ridiculed and made fun of by the other children, because they were foster children.

All during their junior years, they continued to wrestle with thoughts surrounding their past that caused them to fight each other and others. Sometimes, they would tear up their rooms, run away, or just cry. When the girls entered high school, memories of their parents began to fade from their minds.

Overtime, the girls learned to rely on each other for strength and to forget the past. Eventually, all they could remember about family was what they had experienced together, and how they had comforted one another when it was needed. They became so close, that neither one did anything unless the other two approved of it. They had become the best of friends.

One day, about 4 months before Jennifer and Cherlene's senior year graduation, Donna was sad.

"What's wrong with you?" Jennifer asked as they walked home from school.

"Nothing," said Donna as she shrugged her shoulders from Jennifer's hand.

"I saw Dapp talking to Tenisha earlier, and I know you saw him, too. Pissed you off, didn't it?" said Cherlene. Suddenly, Donna grabbed Cherlene by the throat, and started screaming and choking her, as they fell to the ground.

Jennifer fell with them in an effort to separate them, but they were fighting hard and Jennifer couldn't stop them. All three girls were about the same size and just as strong, so no one was winning. Soon, they were all fighting each other, all over the grass.

Then Cherlene began to get the best of them as Tenisha, an arch foe of the girls, came walking by with her two girlfriends. She suddenly reached down, caught Cherlene by the collar, and yanked her off of Donna and Jennifer. Cherlene went flying through the air then bumped her head as she landed hard on the ground.

"Girls, can't we all just get along?" mocked Tenisha. "Cuz' none of you have what it takes to get it on." Then she and her girls, laughed. "So don't let me tell you again!" she said while pointing her finger and mocking them as a mother would. Then she and her girls laughed again, and walked away.

Tenisha was a tall, slender, very lovely senior, who was very arrogant, like her parents, and acted like she was the goddess of all women. If you were a girl and didn't hang out with her crew, she would often belittle you or make you feel inferior to her, just as she was doing the girls today. When Jennifer and Donna saw Cherlene hit the ground, they ran to her to make sure she was ok.

Suddenly, the three girls ran and grabbed Tenisha and her crew and started fighting them. Within seconds all six girls were wrapped together on the grass, kicking and slugging it out. Before any real damage could be done, two parents came out of nowhere, and separated them. Tenisha and her crew went their way with threatening, and the three girls continued toward home being hugged together with laughter.

"Now that was fun!" said Donna. "That's what's up! Too bad it will soon be over," she spoke with her laughter being cut to tears. Now, the girls knew that it wasn't Tenisha talking to Dapp that made Donna sad.

"Dee, why have you been acting so sad, lately?" asked Jennifer.

"You guys are seniors and I will be left another year by myself, once you are gone. Where will y'all go? What will y'all do?"

"Yeah, I've been thinking about that, too," responded Cherlene. "This is definitely something we have to talk about."

"The school counselor has really been pushing me to make a decision about my future, and I don't know what to tell her," spoke Jennifer.

"I know, because I've been putting her off as well," said Cherlene.

As the girls walked home, they were quiet as they thought about the situation being seniors had put them in. That night, Cherlene is in the yard talking with her boyfriend, Terry Billingsly, who is also a senior.

Terry is a 6 feet, 190 pounds black guy, whose family have a lot of problems. But Terry is the family's go-to guy, because he is level headed and thinks about things before he acts. Terry doesn't know what his future holds, but he loves Cherlene, and he knows that he wants her in it.

"Have you made up your mind about what you will do after high school is over?" asked Terry.

"I don't know, yet. My sisters and I are talking about it but we just don't know, yet," responded Cherlene. "What about you?"

"Cherlene, baby, I want to be with you. It really doesn't matter after that."

"Yeah, but you need a way to take care of yourself. Have you thought about that?"

"I'm a go-getter. Right now, all I want to know is, if you will be with me. I'll get an apartment, then a better job, and worry about the small stuff later. But, right now, I'm waiting to make all my plans around you," begged Terry. "I really want us to stay together, Cherlene, so please talk to me." Cherlene leaned into Terry's arms and kissed him softly and sweetly.

"Let's talk about it later, ok? Right now, I have to talk with my sisters and work some things out. I promise that I'll let you know soon." Then she kissed him again and said, "Goodnight."

Terry was a very nice guy. Cherlene loved him, but she was not in love with him. As she walked back into the house, she knew what she had to do. So she called Jennifer and Donna to the bedroom.

"Ladies," she started. "It's time to move."

"Move?" shouted Donna! "You mean Terry's kiss did all that? What are you gonna do when you have sex?"

"Were you watching us again?" Cherlene asked surprisingly!

"You're damn right!" laughed Jennifer. "There wasn't anything on TV so it was better to watch you."

"What! You too?" questioned Cherlene. Then she grabbed a pillow and the pillow fight began. Moments later, they laid together in bed, talking.

"We can't separate, right now, so here is what we have to do," continued Cherlene. "Dee (short for Donna), you still have a whole year to decide what you want to do with your life. Therefore, Jenny and I will also take another year to decide, too. Meantime, me and Jenny will get a job and find us an apartment, so that we can move in together and get away from here."

"Cheryl, would you do that for me?" Donna asked excitedly!

"Dee, you are our sister and we love you. But I think it's a good plan and we're doing it for all of us," remarked Jennifer.

"Oh, I love you guys so much!" said Donna while crying and hugging them. "Wait a minute! What about Terry? Cheryl, he really wants to be with you and this may spoil his plans."

"I'll still see him, but family comes first. Eventually, we will get our own places and we'll see where Terry and I are, by then."

"So in other words, we still have a chance to see you and Terry do baby making practice," laughed Jennifer.

"Oh yeah!" screamed Donna as she clapped and laughed, too.

"I love you guys, but I don't know about all that," commented Cherlene. The girls just laid on their backs thinking for a moment. Then Donna asked,

"Didn't you say earlier that you saw Tenisha talking with Dapp?"

"Yep! And they were kinda close, too," said Cherlene.

"And it looked like Dapp was enjoying every minute of it," added Jennifer.

"Ok! Just wait! I've got something for that bitch, tomorrow!" said Donna.

"Dee, you can't just walk up to Tenisha and kick her butt cause her posse will be all over you," said Jennifer.

"I'm not talking about Tenisha; I'm talking about that bitch, Dapp!" Cherlene and Jennifer paused for a minute to think then they burst with laughter.

Chapter 5

Over the next year, everything went exactly as planned. Donna even got an after school job which really helped with the finances. The girls moved together in an apartment just outside of downtown Atlanta and they were very happy.

Things between Donna and Dapp didn't work out but Terry was still managing to hang in there with Cherlene. Donna became more and more interested in a lifestyle of being in the spotlight, while Cherlene was just the opposite. Cherlene liked working with kids and management, while Donna liked communications and photography. Jennifer was more of a private person, but she also liked glamour and owning worldly possessions.

Over the next 2 years, all the girls took night or evening classes in the field of their choices. As a result, they were able to take on more responsibility and get better jobs. But the better the job they got, the smaller and more crowded their apartment became.

"This is too much," said Cherlene one night. "It's time for us to move again because it's too crowded in here." For a minute, the other girls were quiet and looking suspicious. Cherlene noticed it. "What's wrong with y'all? Don't you think that this place is too small for the three of us?" After a pause, Donna spoke:

"Cherlene, Jenny and I have been talking and we know this place is too small for all of us."

"Ok, we will find a bigger one and move then. So what's the problem?" Jennifer slowly started backing up while she let Donna do all the talking. She knew how Cherlene was, and she could sense that the next words from Donna's mouth, might send Cherlene into a psychotic overdrive.

"Cheryl, we just think that no matter what place we find, it's not gonna be big enough for all three of us," spoke Donna.

"So what are you saying? Do you guys want to buy a house?"

"No," Donna continued cautiously. "We want to move out, but we want our own separate places now."

For a minute, everything was quiet. Then Cherlene placed her hands on her hips and slowly walked toward the kitchen table. Donna's feet were locked to the floor, but Jennifer knew better. Therefore, while Cherlene was making her way to the table, Jennifer was slowly backing toward the bedroom, while checking to make sure she had a clear path to run, when the time came. Just as Jennifer expected, Cherlene picked up the sugar dish from the table and threw it at Donna while screaming;

"You bitch!" Donna ducked. Then she took off running after Donna, and chased her all through the apartment while screaming and throwing things.

Jennifer had safely made her way into her bedroom and locked herself in. She was very smart and knew that Cherlene was not gonna take it kindly that she and Donna wanted to separate the family.

Truth is, they didn't want to separate the family, but they needed their own private space and they thought that this was the way to get it. As Jennifer stood at the door listening, she could hear Cherlene and Donna screaming at each other, while Donna attempted to outrun her.

"I can't believe you made me waste all my time and money trying to help take care of your selfish butt, when I've had many opportunities to leave! I should have left you in school when I had the chance! Now that your selfish ass have made it, you want to leave me here to pick up the pieces!" screamed Cherlene. "Bring your chicken-shit ass out here, Jenny!"

"Cheryl, it's not like that!" yelled Donna as she ran through the apartment, jumping furniture and hiding behind tables and sofas. "Cheryl, you've everything in your name and we have nothing in ours! Plus, I'm tired of hearing Terry or whoever bouncing your bed every night. I can't get a man to come home with me cause I've got sisters living here! I'm 17 and I've only had sex one time when I was 13! Please Cheryl, try to understand! I need more!"

"Oh, I understand," she yelled angrily! "I understand that you want to be sucked and stuck; is that it?" Cherlene grabbed a fork. "Ok then, I'm gonna stick you, slut!" About that time, Cherlene caught Donna and wrestled her to the floor, while cussing and trying to stick her with the fork. Jennifer knew that the situation had gotten too serious, so she ran out of the room and quickly attacked Cherlene and pinned her to the floor...with Donna's help.

"Let me go!" she demanded, but they would not. "Let me go, you bitches!" she yelled while struggling. Suddenly, she burst into tears and cried out;

"Mommy, why did you leave me...why did you leave me! Please, Mommy, come with me!" Cherlene was sounding a very deep, soul, painful cry. The girls were astounded by what was happening! They released Cherlene then laid down on the floor beside her and hugged her. They were all in tears as they listened to Cherlene cry for need of her mom.

"Cheryl, we are so sorry," cried Donna. "We never meant to hurt you. You've gotta believe that." Jennifer stood and got Cherlene a glass of water.

"I know," sputtered Cherlene as she laid on her back with Donna and Jennifer's hands in hers. Then in tears, she relived the experience of her mother's death as she told it to the girls.

"That first time Mom did it, I told her to get up and come with me to my bedroom, but she didn't. She stayed in bed with that man because it was all she had left to give just to take care of me. A week later, I saw my Momma die, while giving all she had, just for my welfare. Because of me, my mother's dead!" she said in tears. "And I will never forget it." By now, Jennifer's compassion was turning to anguish as she quickly jumped up and screamed.

"Stop it, Cheryl! Damn it, stop it! Do you think that you are the only one that's lost a mother or dad? Why do you think we're all here together?" Donna and Cherlene were really concerned because they'd never seen Jennifer snap before. She had always been the smart peaceful one. But right now, she was shouting, she was angry, and she was pacing the floor!

"I saw my Mom chased by the police, hand-cuffed, and thrown in a police car like a common criminal! While she was being cuffed, I saw a store manager chasing the only man I've ever loved, my dad, just to shoot him in the back over and over until he was dead. So stop your shit, Cheryl!"

She cried hysterically as Cherlene and Donna rushed to hold her. After Jennifer told her story, they all laid quietly on the sofa, all clammed up, wondering if Donna was gonna snap like Cherlene and Jennifer. Donna could feel the tension of them wanting to know.

"What? I don't remember anything." They knew that Donna was avoiding her pain and still holding it in but they didn't push her. They knew that when the time came, it would all come out, just as it had with them.

"Girls, you are right," said Cherlene as she came to herself. "It's really time for each of us to have our own places."

"No! No!" responded Jennifer and Donna. "It was a bad idea, Cheryl. We never should have brought it up."

"No, it's a good idea and I'm glad you brought it up. That's what we all need in order to grow. Besides, you weren't the only one thinking about moving out and being alone," smirked Cherlene.

"What! You too?" questioned Jennifer with a surprised look. "So why did you tear up the apartment and chase Dee, when you knew all along that you wanted the same thing?"

"I've been holding it inside for a long time, because I didn't want you to think I wanted to leave y'all. It kinda hurt when I heard it from Dee, because I felt like all my patience had been in vain."

"So how long have you wanted to get your own place?" asked Donna.

"Every since the first time Terry and I had sex about a year ago. He was hitting it so good that I wanted to scream. But I knew I shouldn't scream because it would give you two hussies something to mess with me about. I've been holding it in every since. But from now on when Terry and I have sex, I'm screaming my ass off! So if you don't want to hear it, you better move your asses out!"

As the girls ended their conversation, they began to play and pillow fight as they did when they were younger. Meantime, in the heavens the ice and the fire continued on its course toward the earth.

Chapter 6

A year later, Donna, Jennifer, and Cherlene, were well on their way in life, and things seemed to be looking up for them. Jennifer, now 20, was a manager in the lingerie department of Perimeter Mall. Cherlene, who was almost 21, had become a business manager with a very promising career at Childcare Enterprise and Daycare Center. Finally Donna, who had recently turned 19, hired as a secretary for the Atlanta Judicial Chronicle.

The girls had all moved into individual apartments in the Cobb county area. Therefore, they caught the transit daily to Joseph's Coffee Shop to get together before or after work.

After Cherlene moved into her own apartment, one of the streaks of ice in the heavens veered away from the other two, and went on its course toward the earth. Two of the colorful balls of fire also veered away and followed it.

After Jennifer moved into her apartment, a second streak of ice took its own course toward the earth. Again, two more of the colorful balls of fire followed it. The last streak of ice stayed on its course until Donna moved into her own apartment. Then, it veered away with the last two balls of fire following it.

It was a Saturday night as all the streaks of ice entered the earth's atmosphere. As it entered the Georgia area, the colorful balls of fire overshadowed the blue streaks of ice, veiled themselves then became three mighty rushing winds.

The girls were all sleeping soundly in their apartments when they suddenly became restless. They were all starting to have these urges they didn't understand. Suddenly, the mighty winds rushed through each of the girls' apartment and settled on them.

Cherlene felt herself becoming very horny. But she cast it off as just a desire for sex and decided to just hold out until Terry came over. Then she attempted to go back to sleep.

Jennifer, got from her bed, stood at her bedroom window, and stared down into the nearby department stores. She had never been into the stores, but now she was having an urge to know what was inside them. The urge became so strong, that she was tempted to go peek into the store windows just for the fun of it. The thoughts were so fulfilling that Jennifer quickly got dressed and sneakily made her way downstairs and to the store windows.

She had a very nice apartment and hardly needed anything. But as she stood at the window of this local retail store, she felt drawn to have this wonderful clock she saw on the store's sales counter. As she looked for a way to break in, she suddenly came to her senses.

"What in the hell am I doing?" she asked herself. *"This is crazy!"* While she stood there wondering and being surprised about her actions she heard someone whisper... *"The Curse Must Be Broken!"*

"Who's there?" she asked nervously! She paused and searched with her eyes but saw no one. She became afraid and ran back to her apartment. Then she sat in a dark corner of her bedroom all balled up on the floor, being confused about all that had just happened. She wanted to go back to the bedroom window, but she forced herself to stay away from it. Then she went back to bed...worried, and wondering, what did it all mean?

Donna, on the other hand, was also restless and couldn't sleep. She was suddenly feeling a strong urge to really get ahead in life; to be more than just a secretary but to be a prominent figure of the media and the world. So she made up her mind to become a journalist even if she had to make up a story or cheat to become one.

Tenisha, whom she despised in high school, was now an assistant journalist, working in the same department as she was.

"That's it!" she exclaimed to herself. *"I'll write a story telling how Tenisha performed sexual favors in order to become so popular in high school. Then I'll move up and take her job."*

Donna knew that Tenisha wasn't like that. But it gave her so much pleasure in thinking that she could move up in life by knocking someone else down. After she jumped out of bed, turned on the light, and began to write the story, she realized that even though this lie may help her to get ahead, it may also hurt somebody else and possibly ruin their life, and their career. She couldn't see herself doing that.

"What was I thinking?" she thought as she came to herself. As she tore up the paper and threw it away, she heard a voice whisper,,, *"The Curse Must Be Broken!"*

"Who said that?" she asked being panicked. She grabbed her mace then cautiously looked through the apartment, but found no one. Then she jumped in bed and covered her head.

As Cherlene lay in bed wrestling with her desire to have sex, she being unaware, started caressing her breast and between her thighs. It felt so good until she started believing that she could actually feel a man's penis inside her, while he kissed and sucked her breast. As she almost reached an orgasm, she forced herself from the bed and quickly stood to her feet, while panting and staring at the bed. She was perplexed about what was happening.

"Why am I going through this?" she spoke out loud. Suddenly, she heard a voice whisper from the dark.... *"The Curse Must Be Broken!"* Being strong willed, Cherlene quickly reached under her pillow, grabbed her pistol, and pointed it in the direction she thought the voice came from.

"*Bang! Bang!*" sounded the gun as she fired. Being inexperienced toward using a gun, the power of the .38 caliber handgun pushed her backwards as she tripped and fell to the floor. She quickly stood up, pointed the gun again, and waited.

"Terry, if that's you, you better show your face, right now!" she shouted. She eased through the apartment pointing the gun and watching. She knew that the voice she had just heard was not Terry's or anyone she knew. She found no evidence of anyone else being in the apartment so she lowered her gun. Then she went to bed wondering and doubting if she had heard anyone at all.

With it being 2:35 in the morning, she decided to call Terry and tell him to come over. Instead, she called Jennifer, who was already on the phone with Donna. The girls were relieved by being able to talk to each other in the late hours of the night, even though they evaded the real reasons why they were awake. Then, they decided to meet for brunch, as they hung up the phones, and wondered about their previous experiences of the night.

Chapter 7

As service neared an end at a Cobb County Baptist Church, Rev. Carl Simmons Sr., a black minister being about 41 years old, was delivering a very powerful sermon to his congregation.

Suddenly, he was briefly thrown off to see his son, Carl Simmons, Jr., better known as "Coldblood," ease in and sit near the back of the church. Carl Jr., 23 years old at the time, had become a very powerful gang member of the "Demon-bloods."

Many were afraid of him because he was very ruthless in his dealings, and he always valued his opinions, knowledge, and business, superior to all others. If he felt that you were smarter, more knowledgeable, or more experience in business than he, then he would devise a plan to weaken you, usurp your possessions, knowledge, and authority, then ruin your life so that you could never rise again. That's how he got the nickname..."Coldblood."

Coldblood was so indignant toward the world, that when he would see a young man with his head high, being proud of his life and his accomplishments, he would put a gun to his head, pistol whip him, then try to force him to walk with his head down, like a nigga suppose to do.

On the other hand, if he saw a man walking with his head down, he would treat him nice by giving him money and a gun, then force him to rob or steal and take what he wanted and be proud of his accomplishments. Carl Jr., was truly... "Coldblood."

One day when Coldblood was walking passed a neighborhood park, he saw some young boys playing together near a swing. The boys must have been about 10 years old, or so.

Coldblood's Memories #I
> Boy #1= Hey, here comes the new kid that showed up at school today. Man, have you ever seen anybody so stupid.
> Boy#2= Yeah, did you hear how he sounded when Ms. Rogers asked him to tell about himself?
> Boy#1= It's called a speech impediment, you idiot.
> Boy#2= A speech what?
> Boy#1= Never mind. Here he comes so be quiet and don't let him have your swing.

As the new kid slowly walked up, all was quiet as the two boys watched to see what he would do. There were only two swings in the swing set and they were guarding them like they were their own.

> Boy#2= What do you want? (he asked boldly.)

New kid= You wa... wa... want to pla... pla... play?

The boy was barely able to get his words out. The two boys just kinda looked at each other while Coldblood and his boys watched the whole thing.

Boy#1= What's your name?
New kid= My... Na... Na... name... is... Ra... R... Reggie... Ba... Ba... Brown.
Boy#1= Well, Ra...Ra...Ra Reggie Ba...Brown, we don't want to pa... pa... play with you. (This he said making fun of Reggie.)

Afterwards, they laughed so hard, they couldn't stand up straight. Then they started playing with the swings as Reggie stood and watched. That's when Coldblood and his guys walked over to them and caught them by surprise.
Coldblood= Hey kid, what up? Is this your swing?
Boy#1= No, it belongs to the park, but it's mine while I got it. (Coldblood quickly snatched the chains from his hands.)
Coldblood= Now that I got it, I guess that makes it mine, and I can do what I want to do with it. Here Reggie, you play with it. (Coldblood handed the swing to Reggie who seemed happier now.)
Boy#1= You big bully...I'm gonna tell my dad! (At that point, Coldblood and his crew pulled their pistols and pointed them at the boy.)
Coldblood= Let's get something straight. I ain't nobully, but I am a gangster. Today I might become a killer, if you call me a bully again.

The little boy panicked, and urine started to run down his leg and onto the ground. He was scared and nervous as he and the others completely froze. When the gangsters saw this, they put their guns away and laughed. Then they turned to the 2nd boy.

Coldblood= You were over here listening to a guy who pisses on himself when he sees a little sign of trouble. Now, I'm wondering how you would handle a little trouble if it came to you. (Suddenly, they all pulled their guns again, and pointed them at the second boy. The boy ran away screaming for his mother. Then Coldblood turned to Reggie.) The world ain't gonna give you nothing, son. You have to learn to take what you want or do without, you got that? (Reggie just sat in the swing being more afraid than ever, and wondering what would happen next. Then Coldblood and his men walked away while closely watching the little boy that urinated on himself. The boy was never the same again.)

(End of Coldblood's Mem #1)

After service was over, Rev. Simmons Sr. went to Coldblood and greeted him with a hug. Coldblood stood and hugged him back.

"It's good to see you, son. How've you been?" he asked proudly.

"I've been kinda busy, Dad. How're things with you?"

"You know, it's all about Jesus so I'm here minding the flock a lot."

"Yeah, yeah, the great Reverend Simmons, I almost forgot; there for everybody but his own wife and son," stated Coldblood.

"Is that why you came here today son--to ridicule me and remind me of my sins?"

"No, Dad. I was out back at Mama's grave site because today is the day she died 8 years ago. So I thought I'd stop by to see how you are doing before I took off. You do remember Mama, don't you, Dad?" Without thinking, Rev. Simmons slapped Coldblood very hard, almost knocking him over a pew. Coldblood's left eye started jumping and twitching as it often did, whenever he got really mad.

"Don't you ever imply that I've forgotten your mother? I loved her until the day she died, and you know that!"

"You mean until the day she was killed, don't you, Dad?" Rev. Simmons paused as he looked saddened and sat on the pew.

"Son, I really had no idea they were coming. It had been 16 years since I left that lifestyle and I didn't know they were looking for me."

"Dad I understand all that. But what I don't understand is that, when Mom took that drive by bullet that was meant for you, you did nothing. You sit behind your pulpit taking care of your so called flock, but you won't take care of these suckers that killed my Mom. I know that you know who they are and you won't tell me. Dad, that's wrong; she was your wife!"

"And you are my son!" Rev. Simmons shouted back.

"What's that got to do with you or me finding these guys and making things right, for Mom's sake?" Rev. Simmons paused again.

"Junior, sit down a minute son... please? I need to tell you something." Coldblood slowly sat down across from his dad. Then Rev. Simmons began to speak slowly and painfully.

"Twenty-five years ago, before you were born, I joined this street gang because I was young and stupid. As I became one of the leaders, we did a lot of terrible things including robbing, stealing, fighting, and even hurting people just because we could. I was 16 and it was the only life I knew. My mother was a drunk and I never even knew my dad, nor anything about him. So, I began to fit right in with the affiliation and they became my family.

After about 2 years of this ruthless lifestyle, we made a pact; an agreement; that once a gangster, always a gangster, and we could never get out of the brotherhood. That same year, I met your mother and we fell in love and started talking about making a family and everything.

Your mom wasn't with that gang stuff and she told me that she would be my family, if I would only give it up. I wanted to, but I didn't know how to tell the brotherhood that I wanted out. I was sure they would kill me, so I said nothing.

Your mom was so hurt and disappointed. When I tried to comfort her, she told me that she was pregnant with you, but she was going to abort the baby, because she could have no part of a gang member's lifestyle in her house. I didn't know what to do. I was so happy that I had a chance to make a family of my own, but I didn't know how to get out of the affiliation.

Then one night, me and your mom drove to this spot where we used to fool around at before she decided to cut me off and to abort our child. She hadn't told her folks, yet, so we went there to talk about everything.

After we drove there, we got out of the car and walked as we talked. After we had gone a small distance, we accidently walked upon this couple having sex in the backseat of this car. Being young, we decided to just have a little fun and peek in on them just enough to let them know that we saw them. As I got closer to the car, I saw that it was the car of Clay 'Big' Frazier, our gang leader.

I wondered as we crept closer to the car, who was he with? Big was high class and would never take his baby's mama to a spot like this, so I was curious to see who it was in the car. Evidently, I was not quiet enough because, Big suddenly jumped from the car and pointed his pistol in my face.

Reverend Simmons's Memories I

'Whoa! Whoa! Big, it's me!' I said quickly to avoid being shot.

'What are you doing here, man?' he asked. He was puzzled to see me and your mom! Before I could answer him the girl in the car turned and I saw her face.

'Lisa?' I spoke suddenly! Lisa was the wife of our second in command of the affiliation. His name is Derrick 'D-Lo' Logan. Earlier that day Big had sent D-Lo to Augusta to represent the brotherhood in some business that normally he would handle himself. At first, we didn't understand it. But now that I saw him with D-Lo's wife, Lisa, I knew what was up.

'What are you doing here, man?' asked Big again while pointing the gun. Before I could answer, two cars full of young kids, stopped near us while they were out having fun. Had it not been for them, I think Big would have killed me and your mom that night. When he saw the kids, he put his gun away, got in his car and drove off. Your mom and I ran back to the car and I speedily took her home.

'Where are you going?' she asked as I was leaving her at the house.

'I've got something I need to take care of right now; trust me baby.' Then I sped off in search for Big. I knew he'd be at the club on Moreland Ave., and that's where I found him...waiting for me as I drove up.

'What the hell was that all about, man?' Big asked while shoving me in my chest.

'Look Big, your business is your business and I won't get into it as long as you help me get what I want.' Big was so angry that he threw me against the car and placed his pistol in my face.

'Oh now you're gonna blackmail me, Dawg? Huh? Is that what this is?'

'Big, listen man! Stephanie and I are in love and we want to be together. She is pregnant with my child, and I want her to marry me!'

'So!' responded Big. 'What's that got to do with me?'

'I want out of the affiliation so I can go take care of her!' For a minute, Big stood with deep anger in his eyes, but saying nothing. After he calmed down and backed up, he spoke;

'You really love this girl like that, huh?'

'Yeah man, I do and she loves me. But she doesn't want to be with me if I'm still affiliated. I need out Big, and you're the only one that can help me to make that happen without repercussions. Please help me, Big; I really want this.' After a few moments of silence and thought, Big spoke again.

'You're gonna be a daddy, huh?' Smiles from us both changed the atmosphere.

'Yeah, man, and I really want it.'

'So what are you gonna do for me, man?'

'You name it, Big ... whatever you want.'

'I think you know already,' said Big. 'I need a code of silence about this thing you saw tonight. I'm telling you that this won't ever happen again. Can I trust you like that?'

'My brother and my leader, I promise that if you will do this for me, you will never hear from me again,' I assured him. I left that night feeling a bond between us even greater than before. A few days later, after I left the brotherhood, Big was found shot dead behind the liquor store on Columbia and Memorial. Word is that when Lisa confessed to

D-Lo, he burned her to death and later went after Big. D-Lo went in hiding afterwards.

    Two years later after you were born and we were a family; we were shopping at the mall, and ran into D-Lo's young and crazy partner, Carlton Hooks-better known as the 'Hookman.'

    'Hey brother!' He said greeting him. 'We were wondering what happened to you. D-Lo's been looking for you everywhere. What's up man?'

    'Hookman, I'm out, man,' I said.

    'What do you mean, you're out?'

    'I'm out of the brotherhood and I have a family now. Big was supposed to...'

    'Big?' he said cutting in. 'Big knew about this? Brother, I don't think D-Lo is gonna like the sound of this. Why don't you call him and talk to him. I'm sure he'll be happy to see you.'

    'No, it's over with, man! Tell D-Lo I'm out and that's that!' (End of Rev Sim's Mem I)

Then I walked away and never looked back.

    At first, I was a little nervous. But later, your mom convinced me to get involved and join the church. I became a respected deacon in the church and later an elder. From then on, I never looked back."

    "I remember that! I was 10 years old when I came to your ordination," injected Coldblood.

    "Prior to my ordination, the church did a routine background check on me to make sure they weren't putting trouble in the pulpit. To my surprise, one of the church mothers not only knew my mother, but she also knew my dad and what he was about. Turns-out, my dad was the leader of a mob gang that was sent on missions to do folks dirty work. When your mom found out about this, being a devout Christian, she immediately went to the word of God and put it all together.

Reverend Simmons's Memories II

    'Carl Sr., it may be that you have been cursed,' said Stephanie.

    'Baby, what are you talking about?'

    'Here, look at these scriptures,' she said as she handed me her bible. She showed me many scriptures and I understood them all.

    'Ok, Step, so what are you trying to tell me? How am I cursed?'

    'Carl Sr., your dad was involved in a mob gang and possibly committed sin that God have not pardoned. If that's the case, then when your dad died, it's possible that he's still being held accountable for his sin through you. That's why you also got involved in a street gang. You thought that it was your doing, but God have been in control all the time.

The generational curse is upon you, Carl Sr., and you must do all you can in the sight of God to break it, and keep it off of our son, Carl Jr. We have to train him in the Lord, and hopefully he won't depart from it.' (End of Rev Sim's Mem II)

As she read the scriptures and showed me more and more what she was talking about, I begin to see light in her words. Especially, when I read Exodus 34: versus 6 and 7 which reads:

> *"And the Lord passed by before him and proclaimed. The Lord, the Lord God, merciful and gracious, longsuffering and abundant in goodness and truth... Keeping mercy for thousands, forgiving iniquity and transgression and sin, and that will by no means clear the guilty; visiting the iniquity of the fathers upon the children and upon the children's children unto the third and fourth generation."*

Now that I was becoming a strong believer in God and his word, I knew that there was truth in what your mom was saying."

"Wait a minute, Dad!" paused Coldblood. "Are you telling me that because your dad was a gangster, you had to be a gangster, too?"

"No, son. But I'm saying that because my dad was never forgiven for the sins he committed as a gangster, those sins may have been placed on me, by God."

"That's not fair. You didn't do the wrong--your dad did. So why do you get the blame put on you?"

"Because God said that's how He does it," responded Rev. Simmons. "Our sins can follow us to our kids, up to the third and fourth generations of families."

"What kind of God is that?"

"He's a jealous one and he will not allow anybody to get over on him, son." After thinking about it all for a minute, Coldblood said, "Dad, that's crazy. Do you expect me to believe this?"

"It's right here in his word, son," he said while holding the bible. "But there's more, Junior, and I want you to hear me out before you conclude on anything. Your mom became more convinced than I was that the sins of my dad had been passed on to me. So she prayed and studied, and talked to our pastor to see what it would take for the Lord to have mercy on me, and relieve me of the curse. She found the answer in 1 Kings Chapter 21 verses 17 through 29.

This man King, named Ahab, and his wife, Jezebel, did so much evil, that God told them he would send much punishment upon him, his wife, and the people that he lead, because Ahab sin had corrupted them. Come on, Junior," he said as he handed Coldblood a bible. "Let's read it together, please?" Coldblood took the bible slowly, turned the pages and followed along with his dad as he read:

17"Then the word of the Lord came to Elijah the Tishbite, saying,

18arise go down to meet Ahab, King of Israel, who lives in Samaria. There he is in the vineyard of Naboth; where he has gone down to take possession of it."

19You shall speak to Ahab saying, "Thus says the Lord: Have you not murdered a man and seized his property?" Then say to him, "This is what the Lord says; in the same place where dogs licked up Naboth's blood, dogs will also lick up your blood—yes yours!"

20Then Ahab said to Elijah, "So you have found me, my enemy!" "Yes I have found you," he answered. "Because you have sold yourself to do evil in the eyes of the Lord,

21I am going to bring disaster on you. I will consume your descendants and cut off from Ahab every last male that's in Israel whether slave or free

22I will make your house like that of Jeroboam son of Nebat and that of Baasha son of Ahijah, because you have provoked me to anger and have caused Israel to sin."

23Also concerning Jezebel, your wife, the Lord says, "Dogs will eat the flesh of Jezebel by the wall of Jezreel.

24Dogs will also eat those belonging to Ahab who die in the city, and the birds of the air will feed on those who die in the country."

25There was never a man like Ahab, who sold himself to do evil in the eyes of the Lord, urged on by Jezebel, his wife.

26He behaved in the vilest manner by going after idols, like the Amorite people that God drove out the land before Israel.

Then Rev. Simmons paused before reading on.

"Ok, this Ahab guy and his wife did some really wild things and God punished him for it. I get that, Dad. But....?" He asked as if he wanted his dad to make his point.

"Read on, Son," said his dad. This time, Coldblood began to read.

27So it was that when Ahab heard these words that he tore his clothes and put on sackcloth and fasted. He laid in sackcloth and went around mourning.

28And the word of the Lord came to Elijah the Tishbite saying:

29"Have you noticed how Ahab has humbled himself before me? Because he has humbled himself, I will not bring the disaster in his days, but I will bring it on his house in the days of his son."

Being in deep thought, Coldblood paused for a minute then he began to read the last 2 scriptures again, very slowly as he wanted to be sure of his understanding.

"Are you telling me that after this dude, Ahab, did all these crazy things, God let him get away with it, then put the blame on his son, all because this guy, Ahab, changed his ways?" asked Coldblood.

"Almost, but not exactly," responded Rev. Simmons. "You see, Junior, God's word is so powerful that it cannot be changed. In one place, he said that when we do wrong or commit sin, we will pay for them even if he has to get us through our children. In another passage, His word says,

"If my people which are called by name, shall humble themselves, and pray and seek my face and turn from their wicked ways; then will I hear from heaven and will forgive their sin and will heal their land."

"Junior, because Ahab humbled himself before God, God forgave him, like He said He would. But the sin had to be passed on until somebody paid the price."

"So do you think that your dad humbled himself before God, and now you've got to pay the price?" asked Coldblood.

"I don't know what my dad did because no man can know another man's heart. But I do know that he was involved in some serious mob activities and so was I. Did God pass it on to me? I don't know. But like Ahab, I've repented of my sin and God has forgiven me."

"You said that when God forgives, the sin must be passed on until somebody pays the price. So if you repented of your sin, that means they would be passed on to your..." Both men paused as Rev. Simmons dropped his head and Coldblood stared at him. Coldblood's left eye started twitching, again.

"Dad," he continued. "Are you saying that I've got to pay for all the wrong that you and my granddad did, all because you don't want to man up? Is that why you hide behind that robe; because you're scared of some unfair God?"

"Junior, it's not like that, son!"

"So how is it, Dad?" he asked angrily. "Now all I have to do is humble myself before God, and sell my son out like you're doing me, and everything will be kosher bit, huh?"

"Junior, listen for one minute, son. Now that Jesus has died on the cross, the sin I committed fell on him. He paid the price for us all! But if you don't humble yourself before Him and repent, and accept for yourself what Jesus has done at the cross, then my sins could be passed on even until the third or fourth generation of my family. Please son, hear me out and...."

"And what ... Dad? Submit to a God and possibly sell my son out like you've done me, when my son, won't have a clue why he is being punished? No, I'm not gonna do that, Reverend Carl Simmons, Sr.," he spoke sarcastically. "Cause if that's how you roll, then you ain't my family." His eye was twitching more than ever now.

"Junior, please!" he said through tears as he reached out toward his son.

"Junior?" sounded Coldblood angrily. "At least I know now, why you sold Mama out. As of now, I am no longer your son, so tell God to pass your sin on to somebody else. I've got enough problems of my own. I am my own family, and my name is Coldblood; not coldhearted." Then he walked out of the church, as his dad sat in the pew crying and pleading intensely before God to save his son.

Suddenly, a woman walked in from the back of the church. She had long pretty hair, and must have been about 40 years old.

"What did you do, Carl?" she asked emotionally. She had been listening all the time.

"I'm losing him," he cried. "I had to tell him because I didn't know what else to do."

"It looks like you drove him away," she added. "Carl, I don't think this is what Stephanie had in mind when she said for you to save her son."

"Don't lecture me about my son and my wife!" he yelled. "I'm doing the best I can and you know that!" The woman acted as if she wasn't touched or moved by his words.

"I hope you know what you're doing, Carl." Then she walked away.

"I'm trusting you, Lord, to help me," he prayed silently. Then he heard the whisper, *"The Curse Must Be Broken."* Rev. Simmons paused, calmly looked over his shoulder then continued on his way like nothing happened.

Chapter 8

Early that Sunday morning, Cherlene, Jennifer, and Donna, met at I-HOP for brunch. Normally, they would catch the train to meet, but today they were off so Cherlene picked them up in her Camry. Being in the fall season, it was a very rainy day, as the girls talked and ate.

"So, Jenny," started Cherlene. "I hear that you met someone at work the other day." Jennifer sharply turned and looked at Donna who was playing the innocent role, like she didn't know what was going on.

"You just couldn't keep your mouth closed for one day, could you?" said Jennifer. "Dee, you make me so sick, sometimes...you really do!"

"I'm sorry, Jenny," she said calmly. "But it was such good news because you are so quiet and never seem to be man hungry like Cheryl and me."

"Ok Ho! Speak for yourself! I've got a man," Cherlene said defensively.

"Oh you mean Terry?" asked Jennifer. "I hear that Terry ain't the only one rocking your bed these days."

"What?" remarked Cherlene. "What are you talking about?"

"Aw come on, Cheryl, I ain't stupid! Besides, his number is locked in your cell phone, and he left a message on your answering machine at your job the other day," stated Jennifer. "Who is he?" Cherlene was shocked and puzzled that Jennifer knew and began to be a little embarrassed.

"Jennifer," she spoke with a smile. "I am shocked but very impressed. I will tell you everything, but first, you've got to tell me how you knew." Donna started clamming up and twisting her hair around her finger.

"Last week at work, did you let anybody use your cell phone?" asked Jennifer.

"No, I never let anybody use my......" She stopped speaking as she thought about it, then she turned to Donna. "You know...you are a sneaky little ho. When you stopped by my job, you told me that you had to use the bathroom but..."

"Cheryl, I did!" yelled Donna as she cut in. "Honestly, I did!"

"Dee, the only way you could've checked my cellphone and my answering machine is that you had to go into my office when you were supposed to have been pissing. Now tell me that I'm lying?" Dee just sat there twisting her hair around her finger while Cherlene was looking astounded, and Jennifer was laughing.

"She can't help it, Cheryl. The girl ain't been laid but once in her life and he was a nerd with a pole that he didn't know what to do with. As soon as he touched her, he started moaning and skeeting like a water hose and called it sex. Dee still don't know what happened. She got wet and thought the dude pissed on her. She had no idea that the guy never got it in and it was just bad sex." By now, Cherlene was dying laughing with Jennifer.

"That ain't funny, y'all," said Donna with a long face.

"Yes hell it is, Dee," laughed Cherlene. "You get in both of our business, and you tell everything. It's about time we get to talk about you, don't you think?" Cherlene and Jennifer were laughing so hard, Donna couldn't help but to finally laugh with them. Then as they calmed down, Cherlene asked, "So who is the lucky guy, Jenny?"

"No, you first," replied Jennifer. "You've already got yours. I'm just hoping to get mine, so you go first."

"His name is Clint Turner and we just went out on a date. That's all."

"That's it, Cheryl?" asked Jennifer. "One date? How did you meet him?"

"Ok, it's your turn, Jenny," pushed Donna. "Who is this mystery man?"

"I met him at work last week, and his name is Mitch Stewart. We're going on a date this Friday," blushed Jennifer.

Chapter 9

At the GBI (Georgia Bureau of Investigations) headquarters in Cobb County, agents were preparing for a big bust scheduled for that Sunday afternoon.

"We've got a location on 17 guys from 4 different gangs and we need to move now," commanded Chief Agent Jonathan Lewis.

"This is Agent Benny Dixon of the GBI," he spoke into the transmitter.

"All local police and SWAT teams in Cobb, DeKalb, Clayton, Fulton, Henry, and Gwinnett, prepare to move in on my orders." The counties radioed in to confirm their readiness.

"Ok," spoke Agent Dixon into the radio. "Let's do it boys!"

GBI operations had been tracking gang activity over the past year and now have enough information and evidence against certain members to put them away for a while. Their intel believe that today, being Sunday and raining, would be the best day to strike because most gang members are home resting or watching football on TV. They were right, as they rounded up 15 of the suspects they had under surveillance.

As Coldblood walked the street heading to his apartment, he was thinking about the conversation he had earlier with his dad. He began to have an uneasy feeling that maybe some of that stuff was true. Coldblood had a 5 year old son across town, whom he loved very much, but his mom didn't want him affiliated with a lifestyle such as Coldblood had. Just as Coldblood loved his son, he knew that his dad loved him and thought he was doing the right thing by turning to God.

"I'm not ready for that life, yet," Coldblood thought to himself. *"I've still got things I've gotta do—scores to settle and money to get."* Suddenly, as he looked ahead, he saw a cop with a gun peeking around the corner of the building. Then he saw another... and another!

He recognized right away that it was a raid, and they seemed to be targeting his building!

"Are they after me?" he wondered. Coldblood ducked out of sight and watched the GBI raid his building. Suddenly, as fast as they ran in, they came running out with a guy in cuffs, almost dragging him to the police van.

"Hey! Hey!" the man shouted. "What did I do? What did I do?"

"Carl Simmons you have the right to..."

"Who?" The officer stopped quoting the rights.

"Where's your ID?" asked the officer boldly.

"I don't have no ID, man!" yelled the man. "My name is Dexter; Dexter Billingly! What do y'all want with me?" Another officer walked up and showed the arresting officer a picture of Coldblood, and said,

"This is not him; we've got the wrong man."

"Why are you in the apartment of Carl Simmons, Jr.? Are you a member of his brotherhood, too?" asked the arresting officer.

"Man, what are you talking about! I am a law biding citizen visiting a friend," yelled Dexter! "What are you locking me up for?"

"Central, run a check on a Dexter Billingly," the officer spoke to his dispatcher. Within minutes the response came back that Dexter was clean. "How do you know Carl Simmons Jr.? Where can we find him?" Dexter knew he didn't have to answer the questions.

"Man, are you gonna arrest me or not?" The cop gave him a hard stern look then, let him go.

"You tell your friend Carl, aka Coldblood, that we know about him and it's just a matter of time until we get him, if the 'gods' don't get him first." Then he walked away.   The "Black-gods" were a local gang that hated the "Demon-bloods" and had it out for them.

As Coldblood watched the police drive away, he knew that things would not be the same as long as he stayed on the run. He was glad that his friend Dexter didn't get into trouble today. He knew Dexter would stop by, but he was surprised to see Dexter there so early. He wanted to holla at Dexter after the cops left but he knew that was too risky. He decided to go visit his baby mama until things cooled down. He would talk to Dexter later.

As Coldblood sat on the transit, he couldn't help but to think about the conversation he had with his dad earlier. It was really starting to occupy his thoughts now. Plus, he had no money, no job, and now he was on the run with little or no help. As he went on to D'Amica's, his son's mother's place, he wondered what he would say.

****

Meantime back at the GBI Headquarters,

"We've got 15 of the 17 on our list, so that's not bad," spoke Agent Blake Bishop.

"Yeah, we're missing Carl 'Coldblood' Simmons Jr., of the Demon-bloods, and Carlton 'Hookman' Hooks, former hit man of the Black-gods. That's the third time the Hookman has slipped through our fingers. We have to tighten up on him fellas," said Agent Benny Dixon. Then Chief Jonathan Lewis came in.

"Ok guys, what do we know about these two guys that we missed today?" he asked.

"We know that the Hookman has about 30 places he could be at any different time; any different county," spoke Bishop. "He's got about 28 kids all over the place and still making more. Apparently, he's been hooking his wad everywhere and that's why he's so hard to find."

"Bishop, you may want to do a blood test on your kids," joked Dixon. "The Hookman might have you paying for something that ain't yours," they laughed.

"Now that may be so," responded Bishop. "But we know Hookman ain't hooked your girl, yet, because she's still busy banging the precinct. She hadn't gotten to the criminals yet, so Hookman is still waiting in line."

"Girls! Girls!" yelled Chief Lewis. "Can we get back to the issues here?"

"Yes Sir," said the men.

"Dixon, what do you got?" asked Chief Lewis.

"Carl Simmons Jr., aka Coldblood, has a 5 year old son across town by a D'Amica Taylor so he may be there. Also his dad, Carl Simmons Sr., is the pastor of a Baptist Church right here in Cobb County. Other than that, Coldblood don't have a whole lot of places he can be because 85 percent of his brotherhood is dead or arrested, and the rest have practically vanished."

"Ok Dixon, checkout Coldblood's Dad and his girlfriend, along with anything else you can find. We don't want to wait till this guy gets desperate and start hurting people for money so that he can survive, so let's find him.

As for you Bishop, please get me something on this, Hookman. Hell he might be hooking my wife for heaven sake!" Then Chief Lewis walked away with the other agents being puzzled about his last comment. They knew that the Chief's wife was so ugly, that the Hookman would have to be desperate to even look at her.

"I get it," said Agent Bishop. "I know why the Chief said that now."

"Ok, why?" asked Agent Dixon.

"Cause men around here is always talking about how great their wives are. Therefore, the chief wants everybody to know that his wife is attractive, too." Dixon nodded in agreement as they walked away.

Chapter 10

As Coldblood neared D'Amica's apartment in Decatur, he began to creep and peep to make sure the coast was clear. He knew the cops would also be looking for him there and at his dad's place. He also knew that he wasn't safe at either place, but he just needed somewhere to clean up and spend the night until he could think and get himself together.

"Who is it?" answered D'Amica when her door buzzed.

"It's me; let me in," asked Coldblood.

"Me, who?" she questioned.

"Meca, it's important baby; let me in, please?" After a few seconds, she released the door-lock and allowed him to come up. Then she met him at the door, and blocked it.

"What are you doing here?" she asked bossily.

"Come on, Meca, stop playing. Hell I have business here cause I got a son here. Where is he anyway?"

"He's in the tub. What do you want Blood? I told you to never show up here without calling first, now why are you here?" Coldblood humbled himself and answered:

"Meca, I need a place to stay just for the night... please... please?" he begged as she was about to snap. "I'm hot, right now, Meca, and I need to lay low for a minute. I promise I'll be in the wind first thing in the morning, as soon as I get myself together. Please Meca, just one night." About that time, little Shaun, Coldblood's son, came running out. Coldblood stepped around her and met his son.

"Daddy!" he yelled as he jumped into his dad's arms.

"Hey Sport, how've you been?" responded Coldblood.

"Slopp bought me a new iPod; want to see it?"

"Oh yeah?" questioned Coldblood. "Who is Slopp?"

"That's Mama's new boyfriend," he answered while getting his iPod. Suddenly, Coldblood's left eye started twitching as it does when he gets angry and wants to tear up something.

"Don't start no sh..." D'Amica whispered as she saw his eye twitching. "Shaun! Say good night to your dad and go on to bed," she continued.

"Dad, will you tuck me in?"

"Yeah Son, I'll be there in a minute," he uttered as Shaun walked off. "Are you banging another man up in here over my son?"

"Coldblood, don't start with me!" she demanded. "If that's what you came here for then you can get right back on the street!"

"Ok! Ok!" he said humbling. D'Amica also calmed down.

"And no I am not banging anybody in front of my son! If you would have taken care of things like you were suppose to, you wouldn't have to worry about that!" Suddenly, the door bell buzzed again.

"Are you expecting company?"

"What's it to you? I want you out by morning, Blood. Now go tuck your son in. Then you can sleep on the couch." D'Amica headed toward the door and pressed the button on the intercom.

"Who is it?"

"It's me, Slopp," came the man's voice. She and Coldblood looked at each other as he got up and went to tuck in his son. As Coldblood entered the room, he heard D'Amica release the door lock for Slopp to come up.

"Hey Sport! How's my favorite guy in the whole world?" Coldblood asked with a smile.

"Fine," responded Shaun. "Daddy, I will be six on my birthday. What are you gonna get for me Daddy?"

"Well, I don't know, but I'll think of something before then."

"Mama says that you're in trouble and you may have to leave for a while."

"She did? Hmm? Wonder why she told you that?"

"Don't know," he said as he humped his shoulders. "So are you in trouble Dad? Are you gonna leave?"

"If I have anything to do with it, I'll be right here for your birthday," he said while playing with Shaun. "Now you lay on down and go to sleep, son. I'll see you soon, ok?"

"Ok Daddy," said Shaun as he slid under the covers. Shaun sat up in bed and stretched his arms as wide as he could. "Daddy, I love you this much!" Coldblood hugged him.

"I love you, too, son; more than anyone in the whole world. Now go to sleep." Shaun laid down as Coldblood turned out the light and shut the door behind him. Then he stood at the door listening to D'Amica and Slopp as they talked. They were still standing at the front door.

"We're supposed to be together tonight, baby," Slopp pleaded. "What's up? At least tell me what's going on."

"Coldblood is here," she hesitated. Slopp being a solid 250 pound bench presser, did all he could to keep his cool.

"So are you getting back with him after all he's put you through? What about us, Meca?"

"No, no, it's not like that, baby, I promise you. Just give me until morning and this will be all over," she begged as she kissed him. D'Amica was a 5 feet 9 inch tall, thick, very beautiful, white girl, with long black hair. She was enticing and smelling good as she pleaded for Slopp to trust her.

"I just don't trust this guy, Meca. Why does he have to stay here? Why can't we just get him a room or something?"

"Because he is in trouble and I need to find out what's going on," she replied.

"Hell he don't have to stay the night for you to know that!"

"Slopp, please! I think he needs me right now, and I need you to trust me," she spoke seriously. "Besides, he is my son's dad." Slopp paused.

"Ok baby, I hope you know what you're doing!" She kissed him then he left.

"I'll call you tomorrow," she said as she shut the door behind him. Coldblood entered the room and sat on the couch. D'Amica sat beside him. "What's going on, Blood?" she asked. "Why did the GBI come here looking for you today?"

"What? When?" he asked being shocked!

"A few minutes before you came up," she replied. "So why do they want you? What did you do?"

He hesitated. "I don't know, Meca; at least I'm not sure. It's been so hard lately trying to keep my head up. A few times, me and the fellas' .... did some things."

"Some things like what?"

"We took some things from some people...shot up a few places."

"So you've been robbing and hurting folks again... huh?" she spoke angrily. "These were not local cops, Coldblood, they were GBI. What's up with that?"

"We got around a little bit because we couldn't stay in the same place. It was too hot so we had to move around," he said. Suddenly, in anger, she slapped him and started hitting and fighting him as she spoke.

"What am I to tell my son about his dad when you're locked up?"

"Stop Meca!" he yelled as he tried to block her punches.

"You bastard! He is really looking forward to you being here for his birthday next week, and now the only way he may see you is in jail!" Coldblood grabbed her and held her to prevent her from hitting him anymore.

"Meca, I'm sorry, baby; I really am."

"Let me go!" She snatched away and went to her bedroom as Coldblood stayed on the couch. A couple of minutes later, she came out dressed for bed, while carrying a pillow and a blanket. She laid them on the couch next to Coldblood; he could see that she was crying. As she walked away, he jumped up and caught her just outside of her bedroom door.

"D'Amica," he spoke softly and kindly as he grabbed her hand. She stopped to listen. Then she laid in his arms, with her voice trembling through tears.

"Coldblood, I don't know what to do anymore. Your son thinks you're the greatest man on the planet and he tells all of his little friends that." Coldblood wrapped his arms around her and hugged her.

"Baby, you and that boy in there will always be the loves of my life and you know that."

"Then why did you leave us and treat us this way? We need you," she cried. Coldblood is now feeling the pain of abandonment, as he wipe her tears and kisses on her face.

"Meca, you know I had to go because of my lifestyle. But it's time to change now, and I promise I will make things right for you and little Shaun. I just need to know that you will be there when I do." They were hugged and standing face to face, but D'Amica never responded as she stared into his eyes.

Then in the heat of the moment, a deep passionate kiss found its way between them. After the kiss, they just stood there looking at each other like animals in heat; not saying a word. Then she took his hand, kissed it, and said,

"I'm expecting you to be gone by morning. Good night, Coldblood." Then she closed her bedroom door between them. Coldblood knew she still loved him, and he was about to make his way into the bedroom to satisfy his curiosity. As he reached for the doorknob, he heard a click from the other side as she locked the door. He paused then went back to the couch for the night.

He became very restless as he tried over and over to sleep, but he couldn't. He kept hearing cars outside that caused him to get up and see if it were the GBI looking for him. Time and time he went in and looked at his son, as he thought about his lifestyle and all the things his dad had shared with him.

"Could it be true?" he wondered. *"Can I pass my lifestyle on to my son, even if he knows nothing about it?"* Suddenly, while looking in on his son, he heard a voice behind him whisper,, *"The Curse Must Be Broken!"* Coldblood quickly looked back then carefully made his way to the living room, wondering if his mind was playing tricks on him.

"I'm hearing things," he thought. As he continued to think about his life and his son, he went to his son, spoke a few words to his sleeping body, then left. As he walked passed D'Amica's bedroom door, he started to knock and say goodbye. But he changed his mind, and just left in the middle of the night. D'Amica like Coldblood, had never been asleep as she heard him leave.

Chapter 11

A few weeks later, early one Thursday morning, Jennifer walked half-naked through her kitchen to fix a snack. As she is standing at the countertop, a tall, husky guy comes up behind her and wraps her as he kisses on her neck.

"Will I see you again soon?" asked Jennifer as she turned to face him. Then she jumped on him, wrapped her legs around him, and kissed him as he sat her on the countertop.

"You can see me anytime you want to, Sweetie," he smiled. "But I've got to go and I think you do, too, don't you?" Mitch asked while checking his watch.

Mitch Stewart was the guy that Jennifer met a few weeks ago while at work. She and Mitch had been dating a few times, now Mitch had spent the night and she was happy. Mitch was a pilot for the airlines so he was always on the go. Jennifer really liked him and hoped that this may be the father of her children some day. As Mitch kissed her and headed for the door, her phone rang.

"Jenny, why are you home?" asked Donna. "You were supposed to meet me for coffee this morning. What happened?"

"Mitch is what happened!" she said with excitement.

"Oh my God!" said Donna. "Don't tell me that he...."

"Yes, he spent the night!" added Jennifer, cutting in.

"Oh you blessed bitch!" Donna exclaimed. "I want to hear all about it!"

"I'll tell you everything later, but now, I've got to get dressed and get out of here. Have you talked to Cheryl this morning?"

"Cheryl worked late last night so she's home sleeping in. She'll be at work by noon today," said Donna.

"Then we can meet tonight after work. Call Cheryl and tell her."

"Ok," said Donna. "I'll call her now."

Seconds later, Cherlene's phone rang. But Cherlene was in no position to answer it. As Clint sexually pounded her from behind, screams and moans made it hard for her to hear the phone.

"Aren't you gonna get that?" moaned Clint as he stroked.

"Oh yes! I'm getting it...I'm getting it!" moaned Cherlene as her third orgasm came. As she and Clint fell over in exhaustion, the phone stopped ringing.

"Cheryl must be deep sleeping," Donna thought. *"I'll call her later."*

Cherlene and Clint lay next to each other breathing hard, as Clint dozed off to sleep, and started snoring. Cherlene jumped up and checked her caller ID. She had a feeling that it was Jennifer or Donna so she pushed speed dial and Donna's phone rang. Donna was at work but she recognized the number coming through.

"Hi, Cheryl! Guess who got laid last night?"

"Oh God!" said Cherlene as she sat up in bed. "Please tell me that you have been humbled and now we can all have some peace!"

"No, silly... not me. It was Jenny! Mitch spent the night with her!"

"That blessed bitch!" Cherlene sighed. "Why couldn't it be you!"

"I know, right! Well God hasn't smiled on me like that, yet. Sometimes, I don't think he's smiling at all because I can't even get a man to talk to me. So getting laid anytime soon is out of the picture. Anyway, Jenny wants to meet today so she can tell us about it."

"Ok, I'll be there," said Cherlene. "Gotta go."

"Wait a minute!" screamed Donna into the phone. "I thought you were off until noon? So where've you gotta go so early?"

"Jenny ain't the only one blessed in the family." Then she hung up and left Donna standing with her mouth opened.

Cherlene didn't have a man problem at all. She could basically get any man she wanted, but she didn't love any of them; she loved sex. Lately, her sex drive had been very high and she didn't know why. She was screwing Clint when she could, and Terry anytime she wanted to.

Terry was still in love with her and wanted to marry her but Cherlene wasn't ready. Besides, her career was going great, right now, and she didn't want to be tied down to a commitment.

As a matter of fact, all the girls had promising careers and they were very happy. But secretly, they were all starting to experience things in their lives that they were too ashamed to talk about, and it was changing them for the worse.

Especially, Cherlene, as she jumped back into bed and snuggled up to Clint, who was sleeping. Just as she touched him, she heard the whisper, *"The Curse Must Be Broken!"* Cherlene flinched and quickly looked about as Clint turned over from his nap, grabbed her, and kissed her deeply. Within seconds, he had penetrated her again, and she was moaning in ecstasy.

Chapter 12

Jennifer caught the bus and was on her way to work. Today was the last Thursday of the month, which is when her job conducted inventories and re-ordering for all departments. Everyone would be very busy today including herself.

Jennifer was about a quarter mile from her job, once she got off the bus. So instead of waiting for a connecting bus for 25 minutes, she could walk the distance in 5 minutes. She didn't have to be at work for another 30 minutes, so she took her time walking and window shopping. As usual, she dressed very nice and conservative, but she liked walking in her sneakers and wearing her backpack.

"What a lovely blue skirt!" she thought while staring through a ladies store window. *"I want to find out who makes that, because that looks like the last one."*

Then she went into the store to check out the sexy blue skirt. She was only there a second or two, plus, the store employees were busy stocking and didn't see her walk in. So she just checked the label and was on her way again.

"I need a pry bar and a small glass cutter," requested a customer at the hardware store where Jennifer entered. She had passed this store many times and hardly even noticed it. But today, she wanted to browse.

She was intrigued to learn how many of the tools and gadgets worked as she saw customer after customer test them and talk to the store clerk about them. To her they seemed like toys. Therefore, like a child in a toy shop, she began to experiment with many things and to learn how they work. Before she realized it, she had spent 20 minutes in the hardware store.

"My God! In 10 minutes, I'll be late for work." As she hurried out of the store, she stopped at the fruit stand to get some fruit for lunch. But when she reached for her purse, she remembered leaving it on the counter next to where Mitch has sat her earlier this morning.

"Shoot!" she exclaimed. "No purse, no ID, no money!" Then she continued on her way to work.

"Rough night, huh?" asked Michelle, her co-worker and friend. "Never seen you late before, and I was beginning to wonder if today would be the day."

"Girl, I was window shopping and I lost track of time," said Jennifer. After she clocked in, she dropped her backpack and checked around her department. Then she went to talk to Michelle.

Jennifer and Michelle were hired around the same time and had become friends as well as departmental managers. Jennifer managed lingerie and women's clothing while Michelle managed jewelry and sometimes house wares.

All departmental managers were crossed trained so they could easily work anywhere in the store. But Michelle, like Jennifer, was a glamour girl and loved showing off what she knew about jewelry and ladies wear.

As usual the ladies commenced to do their inventories and to re-order and replace shelf items and hangers with new clothing and underwear. As noon approached, Michelle had an appointment and was about to leave.

"Michelle, can you loan me a couple of bucks? I ran out and left my purse this morning, and I don't have money for lunch."

"Sure, Jennifer, here's a twenty. Get it back anytime," she smiled. Being glad to help, she went on her way.

It was before noon, so the store wasn't opened to the customers, yet. Jennifer decided that she'd better change her sneakers before she stepped to the food court because ladies always watched each other, and she knew they would be watching her. Besides, she loved her job and she wanted to represent it like the professional she was. So she went to her backpack to change her shoes and to freshen up a bit. As she opened the backpack, she was stunned!

"What the hell!!!" she wondered in amazement. Inside her backpack was the sexy blue skirt she had seen down the street. Lying beside it were two apples, an orange, some nuts, and a funny looking gadget from the hardware store.

"How did this happen?" She was so shocked that she closed the backpack, then ran out of the store and back down the street where she had seen the blue skirt in the first place. As she stood there looking through the window at the rack, the skirt was gone!

"How could this be?" she wondered! Then she made her way back to work... worried.

As Jennifer sat at her job wondering about the skirt, the fruit, and the hardware, she also thought about the night she had awakened out of her sleep at 2 o'clock in the morning. She thought about how she felt when she saw the beautiful clock on the counter of the store. She remembered feeling the same way when she saw the skirt. She was confused and wondered if the two incidents were somehow related.

Suddenly, out of nowhere, came the whisper, *"The Curse Must Be Broken!"* Jennifer looked around, but no one was there. For the first time in her life, Jennifer was feeling like she needed a strong drink.

****

It was almost noon, and Cherlene had lain in bed a little too long. Clint had already gone, and left her sleeping as he usually does. Cherlene didn't mind him leaving like that because, he was just a friend helping her to fulfill her needs. She didn't want the love-mushy stuff, and neither did Clint. "Bem-bam, thank you, ma'am, or thank you, sir," is the way she saw it, and they were OK with it.

As she hurried about and was leaving, she opened her door and found Terry about to knock.

"Terry, what are you doing here?"

"I called you last night and got no answer. Then I called your job and they said you were there, but you were busy.

Then I called your job again this morning, and they said that you weren't in, yet."

"So why didn't you just call my cell?"

"I did, but you never answered." Cherlene checked her cell phone and saw that Terry had called her twice this morning, but she had placed it on silent to prevent it from disturbing her while she was with Clint.

"I'm sorry, Terry. Dee has been calling me so much, that I put my cell on silent so I could sleep."

"I miss you, Cherlene," said Terry with a look of passion in his eyes.

"Terry I..." Suddenly, before she could finish her sentence, Terry pushed her against the opened door and kissed her deeply. She gently pushed him away and said calmly, "Terry, don't do that. Let's talk tonight, ok?"

Again before she could complete her words, Terry forced her hands tight to the door, and kissed her again. Except this time, he slid his lips to her neck, then to her breast, and finally raised her dress and licked right through her panties. Afterwards, he stood up to her face and pressed his body against hers.

"I need you, Cherlene." In an instant, she felt her body twitching to be held and sexed as she hissed, then wrapped her arms around Terry and kissed him. He picked her up and carried her back into the apartment and made love to her.

Twenty minutes later, Cherlene was back to rushing as she was when Terry stopped her.

"Cherlene, can we at least talk a minute?"

"Terry, I'm sorry, but I'm late for work. Will you please get dressed and drive me. I promise that we'll talk tonight." Terry got dressed and drove her to work. Though she loved her job, it had been a long morning and she was a little disoriented as she ran in and tried to do her work.

"Ms. Tullis," said one of the workers. "I think you forgot to balance the ratio for today, because we've got too many students in one classroom."

"Ok, let's find the class that's short and combine...."

"Ma'am, no classes are short today; they're all full," she said cutting in.

"Alright, alright!" Cherlene said in frustration. "I will join the class as the second teacher to make sure the ratio is balanced, until we can get a teacher."

"Ma'am, its lunchtime and we don't have enough milk to..."

"Damn it!" Cherlene yelled as she hit the desk. "Can I have a moment just to think without you dropping the world on me?"

"Yes, Ma'am," the worker said calmly. "But we still need the milk, right now." Cherlene knew the girl was right and needed the milk, now. Cherlene also knew she was the only one that could go get the milk, and that's why they didn't have it.

Because of her intricate sexual activities, Cherlene had completely overfilled one of her classrooms with students, and forgot to pick up the milk needed for the center to meet the feeding requirements for the state of Georgia. This was a serious violation of the states requirements and could cause the daycare to be shut down, if the state found out.

"How could I let this happened?" she thought as she desperately tried to figure her way out of it. Just as before, she heard the whisper, *"The Curse Must Be Broken!"*

Cherlene nervously jumped then shouted, "Who are you... and what damn curse?" She cautiously looked around as she listened, but the voice was gone. After a few minutes she called her worker back in. "Tell the teachers we will be a few minutes late feeding lunch, today." Then she picked up the phone and dialed.

"Terry, are you busy, right now? I need you to be here in 20 minutes." Though Terry was not a certified worker, he still had the experience to hold a classroom together while she went to get the milk.

Although this was the first time Cherlene had ever done anything like this, it wasn't her last. Because of her strong sexual activities, she began to leave many things undone that she could normally do without thinking.

Eventually, Terry and Clint were not the only ones she was having a desire for. She tried desperately to control it, but the urges were too strong. She was slowly losing herself, and she didn't understand why.

At evening around 8:30 p.m., the girls met at Joseph's Coffee Shop to talk.

"This has been one heck of a day," complained Cherlene.

"You too, huh?" agreed Jennifer.

"Well, it couldn't have been too bad," added Cherlene. "I heard that you had company last night, and y'all saw the sunrise together."

"Yeah, that was a change for me, wasn't it? I'm a little ashamed but hey, it was worth it."

"Hey guys!" exclaimed Donna as she quickly walked up. "I've had a great day! Isn't that wonderful?"

"Oh Lord, here we go," joked Cherlene.

"Oh Lord!!! Oh Lord!! Hmm...? Cheryl is that one of the phrases you screamed when you're in bed with Terry? Or is it with Clint? Tom? Dick? Harry? Bob maybe?" joked Donna.

"One more word and I'm gonna deliberately forget that I love you," Cherlene said while sipping her coffee.

"Both of you are packing so why don't you just count six paces and have at it?" suggested Jennifer. "I promise I won't interfere."

"Packing? I'm not packing anything. She's got a handgun, but I've only got mace," said Donna.

"Then I guess you better hit her with it quick before she pulls the trigger," joked Jennifer.

"Dee, you could just shut up," added Cherlene.

"I get the feeling that you two had a bad day," said Donna. "How is that? Both of you spent the night with a man, yet, you have these long faces, and you want to make me feel bad because I had a good day. Both of you are pathetic and I want no part of you, today." She turned to walk away.

"Dee!" shouted Cherlene. "You're right and I'm sorry."

"Yeah, me too," added Jennifer.

"But Cheryl, why do you always have to make jokes whenever I say something lately... like you're hating on me or something? All I said was *'I've had a great day.'* Then you come back with, *'Oh Lord, here we go!'* Cheryl please tell me what did you mean? I wanna know!" demanded Donna.

Donna stood awaiting a response as Cherlene became saddened and lowered her head... not looking up... not saying a word. Jennifer being the smart one, knew Cherlene and Donna better than they knew themselves. She watched Cherlene's reactions, then started to speak.

"Dee, Cherlene loves you a lot more than you know."

"But why does she treat me like this?" asked Donna.

"Because you're innocent and we're not," added Jennifer. Cherlene started to get fidgety now.

"What do you mean, Jenny? Cheryl what is she talking about?"

"Dee, you are pretty and young and vibrant. Ain't that right, Cheryl?" Jennifer spoke forcibly. Cherlene slightly nodded. "And you're smart and still have a brand new life ahead of you, with the chance to get any man you want, right Cheryl?" Cherlene nodded again, but this time she dropped a tear, and Donna saw it.

"Most important of all, Dee, you are a free thinker, and you're not tied to any obligation or habit. Plus, you say and do exactly what you want, when you want, and that makes you a beautiful free spirit, isn't she, Cheryl?" Cherlene nodded again and turned her face as the tears fell.

Jennifer continued. "On the other hand, instead of Cheryl just being our sister and our friend, she's scared because she feels like she's got to be a mother to us as well, and she is slowly starting to lose herself, aren't you Cheryl?

Dee, you feel free and you are, but Cheryl feels bound and confined. Cheryl doesn't hate you, Dee... she wants to be you, don't you Cheryl?" Cherlene didn't respond as she loudly wept, openly. Donna is shocked and goes over to comfort her.

"Cheryl!" started Donna. "I don't understand why you want to be like me, cuz I'm a nobody. You're smart and can figure things out, but I get confused when I try to tie my shoes. That's why I don't buy shoes with strings.

Cheryl, I'm sorry if I'm a burden but you really are like a mom to me, and I don't know what I would do with myself if you weren't. I need somebody to look up to and I wouldn't want it to be anybody but you.

I love you so much, Cheryl and I need you to keep me straight when I'm wrong. I will do anything you tell me and listen to anything you say, but please don't make me feel small when you talk to me, ok?" Then she pinched Cherlene's arm, hid behind Jennifer, and jokingly said, "or I will kick your old motherly ass!"

"Ok," replied Cherlene. Then they all hugged and laughed about Donna's last comment as Cherlene dried her tears. "Dee, I'm sorry, I really do love you like a daughter, please don't ever forget that." Donna being playful, slowly leaned her face to Cherlene's face, paused for a minute, and just stared. Then with her thumb and forefinger, she pinched Cherlene's cheeks and said,

"I love you too, mama-bitch." All three girls fell out laughing.

Donna not only had a good day, but she had made it a good day for them all. For the moment, Jennifer and Cherlene seemed to forget about their earlier episodes as they concentrated on the love they again shared.

Then as usual, Cherlene took over: "We've lost something, girls, that tonight, Dee helped us to find again. When we were younger, we had more fun, more laughter, and we shared everything."

"Cheryl, we didn't have anything then. Now we have lives, apartments, responsibilities, and men. Ok, most of us got men," joked Jennifer while looking at Donna.

"Ok, so what do we need to do?" asked Donna.

"Well, when we were in our first apartment, we made decisions together, we planned everything together, and we were much happier with each other. Now we just call each other and meet occasionally to talk. That's not enough," said Cherlene.

"So what else can we do?" asked Jennifer.

"We need to visit each other more at home and at work. We can take turns cooking for each other, and even spend the night at each other's apartment."

"Uh, excuse me!" interrupted Donna. "What are we to do while you and Terry and all your studs are with you in your bedroom? I don't want to hear that!"

"Since when?" asked Jennifer. "That's all you use to want to hear."

"Ok, I've grown up a bit, so answer the question."

"When the girls are together, no men will be invited," said Cherlene.

"Ooooh! Cheryl, are you sure about that?" they asked as they looked at each other. They knew that Cherlene had a few men and was always with one or allowing them to come over.

"Ok! ok! I get your point!" fussed Cherlene. "Maybe we can double-triple date or something. Anyway we'll work that out later because it's not the important thing. The important thing is us coming back together as family, ok?"

"I can go for that," said Donna.

"I like it," replied Jennifer. "If you guys only knew!"

"So here is the bottom line. Like the musketeers, it's 'all for one' and 'all or nothing' or something like that."

"Yes!" shouted Donna then Jennifer. "But, I think that's *'all for one'* and *'one for all.'* "

"Whatever, Jenny! Unless we all agree, we will buy no land!"

"Yes!" they continued.

"We will purchase no house or home!"

"Yes!"

"We will marry no man!"

"Yes!"

"We will bare no children!"

"Yes! Yes! Yes!" they screamed. Exactly nine months later, Jennifer and Donna were holding Cherlene's hands, while she was on the delivery table screaming and giving birth to Terry's daughter, Makeda.

Chapter 13

Coldblood had no idea where he was going, nor what his next move would be as he walked the streets of Atlanta. It had been almost a year since his troubles began, and things seemed to be getting worse. From his dad, he learned that his mother was shot and killed in a drive-by by his rivals, the "Black-gods," and his dad was a former gang member. Plus, he learned that he may be cursed, for the things that his dad did, and so may be his son.

Also, his brotherhood in the area had been completely disbanded by the law, and police were looking for him on every corner. He didn't know if the charges they had against him were major or minor, but he felt that he couldn't afford to get caught now. The only person he could depend on and trust was Dexter, who was being watched by the GBI just as much.

Now, his money was gone, and he had worn out his welcome with everyone he knew. From city to city, Coldblood traveled, and from shelter to shelter he lived. He could've easily resorted to robbery, burglary, or stealing, but he couldn't afford to draw attention to himself. So he found a place to hide his guns, then he sold the last bit of jewelry and other items that he carried, so he could buy food.

Finally, using a false name, he joined himself to a small labor pool that sent workers out daily to odd construction jobs. He barely made enough money to buy a room for a week, and to get food.

"Gentlemen," began the supervisor at the labor pool. "From the way things are looking, there won't be much work around here after tomorrow. Especially, for you guys who've only been here a week or two. So if I were you, I'd be making plans to go somewhere else." Coldblood knew that he was right back where he started. Then he heard some of the men talking:

Homeless Man #1- Life is hard. But a real man will make it no matter how hard it is.

Homeless Man #2- I agree, bro. Especially, if he stay close to God and depend on Him to see him through.

Homeless Man #1- I don't know about that, partner. How come God's letting us go through this, if He's so straight?

Homeless Man #2- God fixes things in his own time. He is the daddy, and we are His children. Since when do children get to tell their daddy what to do? Most good dads know what their children need, and he will give it to them, when the time is right.

Homeless Man #1- How *righter* does the time need to be? Man, look at us! It's over with. Prisoners live better than we do, and they've committed a crime. So what's God waiting on.

Homeless Man #2- Well, why don't you ask him?

Homeless Man #1- Ask him? You mean, pray?

Homeless Man #2- That's right. He may not answer when you want him
to, but He will give you an answer. And elieve that His answer
will be right on time.

Coldblood couldn't help but think about his son and his dad, as
he listened to the guys talk. He had been raised in a good home, and he
knew that God was real, but had allowed the cares and riches of life to
choke away his trust and understanding.

"Why did you let my mom get killed?" he asked God while
looking up. "My mom believed in you and so does my dad, and look what
it's gotten them. You are some kind of father, man, if this is the way you
treat you kids." Then being angry he said, "Well, I am not gonna treat my
son like that. As of right now, I'm gonna make things good for him!"

Then Coldblood quickly went to get his weapons. Afterwards, he
noticed that he only had one full clip, and a few rounds. He knew that if
he made the wrong move, those rounds could be gone in seconds.

"What do I do?" he wondered. He wanted to rob a local store or
even a home or two, but he knew that the chances of him being seen and
caught were very high. Even if he didn't get caught, the GBI would
automatically step up their search for him and he didn't need that, either.
Finally, after a couple of more days of searching for work and hiding, he
had expended all that he had. Coldblood humbled himself, and went to
the phone.

"Hello?" answered the voice on the phone.

"I need your help," Coldblood said calmly.

"I'm on my way," said the voice. "Just tell me where you are and
I will be there as soon as I can." Coldblood knew he shouldn't say exactly
where he was because the GBI may be listening, and may follow anyone
he called.

"Remember where I got into my first fight? Meet me there in an
hour."

"Ok," said the voice.

An hour later, at about 8:30 that fall season night, Rev. Carl
Simmons slowly pulled into Mosley Park on Martin Luther King Jr.
Drive. Coldblood watched from the distance for about 10 minutes or so
to see if his dad were being followed. Finally he made his way to the car
and got in.

"How've you been, son?" Rev. Simmons asked.

"I'm fine," he said without looking at his dad.

"Where to?" Coldblood just stared out of the car window, but
said nothing. Seconds later, a tear streaked from his eye and down his
cheek. Rev. Simmons cranked the car and drove away. "It's gonna be
alright, son. It's gonna be alright."

That night, at Rev. Simmons home in Smyrna, Coldblood slept like a baby for the first time in months. But Rev. Simmons hardly slept at all as he continually watched over his son, and prayed. Many times he heard the whisper, *"The Curse Must Be Broken!"* and he was startled by it every time. The next morning Coldblood woke up early and had breakfast with his dad. Finally, the silence was broken.

"I'm not here to stay, Dad."

"I know that, son. That's why I've prepared some things for you." Coldblood saw this tote bag over in the corner of the kitchen as his dad spoke. He went over to it, and opened it.

Inside the bag, he was surprised to see two .40 caliber pistols, one AK-47, plenty of bullets, smoke bombs, bandages, a first aid kit, 2 small crow bars, flashlights, and many other small items. But the thing that caught his eye the most was a black leather jacket with a black leather baseball cap, with the encryption... "Black Sheep."

"We didn't originally start out to be involved in gang activity, but that's what it soon led to. Black Sheep, who were like the NAACP, concern Black Clergy, and other activist groups that opposed white supremecy, were trying to be civil about their business, but the Klan and other hate groups wouldn't let them be.

Eventually, the Sheep had to find a way to protect themselves because the law was on the side of the Klan. So, some of the unauthorized Sheep kinda went undercover to handle things that needed to be handled, so that the Sheep could still function for the people without allowing the organization to be stained. This undercover group only involved a few, so it's existence wasn't known by the main body, and therefore was never sanctioned.

As time went on, the unsanctioned group began to grow and eventually set up an administration for themselves. That's when they became known as 'Black Wolves.' The Black Wolves soon lost focus of what they were really suppose to be about and quickly evolved to what we know today to be a street gang called, 'Black-gods.'

As I told you before, my mother was a drunk, and I never knew my dad. So when D-Lo and Hookman came along and made me feel like the man I longed to be, Big, the leader, accepted me into the affiliation and I became a member of the family. At the time, it was the best thing that ever happened in my life.

D-Lo and Hookman were both ruthless killers and had no mercy on anyone--women and children didn't matter since neither of them had sisters or brothers. As they taught me the ropes, they stole, killed, robbed, beat, raped, and took whatever they wanted whenever they wanted and brought it back to the brotherhood. We were all like brothers and Big was like our dad.

Shortly after I met your mother, she was so pure and innocent, that I didn't want her to see me in the light of what I was really about.

Eventually, I started pulling away from D-Lo and Hookman, and hiding all my weapons, and devices. Though I hid them, I couldn't bring myself to get rid of them. Even when I became a minister in the church, I couldn't bring myself to depart with these weapons. Now, I think I know why.

Son, two choices are presented to you here, today. Me, your father, who now represents the Almighty hand of God, who is ready to deliver and save you... or the way of the devil, who will kill you and cause you to be lost, which is represented by that bag over there. I love you son, and I won't stand in your way regardless of your decision.

But please understand that if you choose that bag, then there is nothing else I can do for you. I tried to tell you before that Jesus has already paid the price for my sins, yours, and your son.

But if we don't accept what he has done, then the sins will possibly be passed on until the third and fourth generations. We can all be saved, son, if you will only believe and accept him, right now." After a short pause, Coldblood said,

"Mom accepted him, Dad; look what it got her."

"But son! No man knows the mind and will of......"

"I'm taking the bag, Dad!" he shouted cutting in. Then they just stood staring at each other for a minute. Afterwards, Rev. Simmons walked over to the window and looked out.

"What is it?" asked Coldblood as he joined him at the window. They saw two GBI agents sitting in a car watching the house. Coldblood suddenly panicked and was about to leave.

"I've got to go, Dad!" he said as he rushed about.

"No, no, you don't, son," he spoke assuredly. "Those men have been watching the house for months now, and they follow me everywhere I go."

"What! You mean you were followed when you picked me up?"

"Relax, son. They didn't see me nor did they follow me. They have no idea that I can drive my car out of my backyard and right through the neighbor's driveway onto the back street. Plus, they don't even know it's my car because it's still in the member's name who donated it to the church.

As usual, the Agents are expecting me to walk out front, and hop into my blazer, while they follow me around town and to the church. That's exactly what I'm gonna do, son. Today won't be any different than what I normally do." Rev. Simmons put on his coat, and started to leave.

"Today, I have plenty of church members I need to visit, and many things I need to see about at church. I doubt very seriously if I'll be home before 10 o'clock tonight. Sometime after dark, take the car, and be on your way.

The neighbors are pretty nosey so you better wait until then. The key is on the table, and there are some clean clothes in the closet. The car is full of gas and gets pretty good mileage, plus there is a cell phone and $300.00 cash under the seat. It's all I could get my hands on since you called me."

Coldblood was really shocked about all his dad had said, but was now feeling better about his relationship with him.

"You knew that I would choose the bag, didn't you, dad?"

"I was hoping you wouldn't, son, but you are my son, and I wanted to be prepared anyway. Besides, when I was your age, I had the same choice to make, and well... I made it."

As they stood there staring at each other again, Coldblood felt a love once again that he used to feel when he was near his dad as a kid. His dad really loved him and everything that his dad was doing now proved it. He knew that his choice was hurting his dad, but he felt that this was the only choice to make at this time.

"I have to go now, Carl Jr.," he said as he headed to the door. "I have a friend in Killeen Texas, one in Aurora Colorado, and another in Felton Delaware. I've alerted them that you may be coming. Their information is also under the seat with the money and the maps. You can go to them if you like, or you can go wherever. But wherever you are, and whatever you decide to do, please don't tell me. I don't want to know where you are nor what you're doing."

As Rev. Simmons was about to break into tears, he said, "You have my blessings, son. And may God be with you and keep you." Then he walked out his door, and waved to the GBI Agents parked across the streets. They waved back then followed Rev. Simmons as he drove away. Coldblood looked on.

As Coldblood sat thinking about all that just happened, he was feeling better about his life again. His dad, the very person he blamed for all his failures, was the same one that had given him peace of mind and hope again.

He still didn't know where he was going or what he was going to do with his life, but whatever it was, he was hoping that he turned out to be a good dad for his son, like his dad was trying to be for him. He knew that he had a rough road ahead which, in the end, would bring him new life, so he decided to rest until time for him to leave.

While resting, he saw his mom's bible and decided to read the scriptures that his dad had read to him, earlier. When he opened the bible, he saw that she had highlighted those same scriptures along with others that related to them. Then a scripture in Isaiah chapter 45 caught his attention. It was verses 4, 5, 6, and 7:

> *4For the sake of Jacob my servant of Israel my chosen, I have even called you by name. I have named you though you have not known me.*

⁵I am the Lord and there is no other apart from me; there is no God. I will strengthen you though you have not acknowledged me.
⁶That man may know from the rising of the sun to its setting that there is none besides me. I am the Lord and there is no other.
⁷I form the light and create the darkness. I make peace and create evil. I the Lord do all these things.
.

"*Why would God create evil?*" he wondered. "My mom really believed in you and so does my dad. "Maybe you are a good God," he spoke out loud. "But if you want me to believe in you, then help me to understand all this stuff in this bible, and why you let that happen to my mom.

You said you created the evil that did this to her, and others so I don't understand things about you, God. But for my mom and dad's sake, I'm gonna try; no promises, but I'll try." Then he went to sleep.

At church, Rev. Simmons locked his office door from inside then entered a code on the alarm keypad in his office. Behind his desk, the bookcase immediately slid open and he entered a secret stairway that lead below his office.

"Rosa!" he called out as he knocked on the door before him.

"It's open," she answered. She was standing by the mirror combing her long pretty hair. "What is it, Carl?" There was a pause.

"Junior chose the bag," he moaned. Then she walked over to him and hugged him as he burst into tears.

"Come on now, Carl; you knew he would do that. You did it, so why wouldn't he?"

"I know, I know," he cried aloud. "It's just different when you see your own child putting himself in harms way like that." Rosa released him and picked up the Kleenex box. Then she handed it to him.

"You know it could be worse, Carl," she added. "You could have been forced to just walk away from your own child like I did."

"But I feel like that's exactly what I just did."

"No you didn't, Carl. If he chose the bag, then he walked away from you. All you did was get out of his way."

"So how did you handle it, Rosa; leaving your child and all?"

"It wasn't easy," she said as she sat down. "But I didn't have a choice if I wanted to save her life."

When Rosa was younger, she once had a family that she loved dearly. But once she became an undercover Agent for the FBI, her marriage fell apart and her husband was threatening to divorce her and file for full custody of their 8 year old daughter. She knew he would have won, because her job kept her away for months at a time. She couldn't even speak with her husband or her daughter for weeks and she knew that no judge would side with her in a custody hearing.

Then to make matters worse, she was given a major undercover assignment that would cease all family contact until the case was resolved, which could take months or even years. But at the end of the assignment, Rosa had been promised a permanent leave of absence with pay, if she made it out alive. It was the offer of a lifetime, and you had to be good to even be considered for such an assignment. Rosa tried to reason with her husband, but he wouldn't hear of it.

When Rosa accepted the assignment and started her training, her husband filed for divorce and full custody of their child. She signed the paper and walked away. If she had tried to see her family again while undercover, a lot of bad things could have happened, and her family's lives may have been in danger. Then one night, her cover was blown and she was shot and left for dead in the river, where she escaped to.

In case she made it out alive, the mob made her a target for every known hitman in the country. To keep her family from harm, she never tried to see them again. She knew that eventually she would be killed, so she decided that she didn't want to be hidden on some island or foreign country where she couldn't even relate. She decided to die at home....in her own land instead.

"Do you ever think about her?," asked Rev. Simmons.

"All the time," she replied. "That's all I do, when I'm not praying. I could've found her years ago but I decided against it. I'm sure she has a wonderful life somewhere."

"I've never asked you about your work, but what kind of case is so worth taking, that you just walked away from your family?"

"Come now, Carl. I was young, energetic, and new to the Bureau. No case is worth trading your family for; I know that, now, and I regret it. But at the time, I thought that it was the chance of a lifetime to be placed in the big league against men like Holloway."

"Is it he that you were after.... Holloway? But you didn't get him. What happened?"

"My cover was blown and he got me instead." She lifted her blouse and showed him all the bullet marks in her body. Rev. Simmons was shocked!

"Holloway is one of the world's most renowned masterminds of all times. It will take Sherlock Holmes and all his brothers to out think him. Holloway mastermind's crimes that they haven't written laws against, yet. So, how will they even convict him if they did catch him?" she commented. After a few moments of thought Rev. Simmons spoke again.

"Thank you for what you're doing for Junior, right now, Rosa. I know what he's done is wrong and it's hard on you to just dismiss it like that, but I am grateful and thank God for you."

"I'm not doing it for him, Carl, nor you, so don't thank me. I'm doing it for Stephanie. She gave her life in your stead, hoping that you would save her son. So for Stephanie's sake, I'm giving you a chance to save him."

"I pray to God that he doesn't get involved with Holloway," said Rev. Simmons.

"Eventually, Carl, if the Bureau doesn't get him, Holloway or the grave will. Holloway will train him, pay him, and protect him if he needs it," she assured him.

"God will protect him, if he will just hear his word," said Rev. Simmons.

"Well, I hope that God's on it because he's running out of time and hiding spaces."

"I guess you would know, huh?"

"Been there--done that, Carl! That's why I stopped right here. After a while, you start anticipating death--a bullet, a knife, a bomb, or just being hit by a vehicle." she added.

"I pray that he never gets to that point," he said.

"Like I said, been there--done that! As Rev. Simmons left, she prayed, "Lord, am I gonna see my child again before I die?" Then came the whisper, *"The Curse Must Be Broken!"* Rosa listened, then, slowly started back combing her hair like she was expecting that answer.

****

Later that night, about 9 p.m., Coldblood cautiously made his way to the car. He didn't know what life held for him, but he didn't want it depending on what was in that bag. At 10:15 p.m., when Rev. Simmons came home, he saw that the bag was still there. So he checked the house to see if Coldblood was still there, but he was gone. Then he looked inside the bag to see if the contents were still there. To his surprise, he found a note that read;

> *"Take care, old man; hope to see you, soon. This is your bag; not mine. Your son... Carl Jr."*

Rev. Simmons became weak in the knees and teary eyed as he cried and shouted,

"Thank you, Lord!! Hallelujah! Thank you, Lord!!"

Chapter 14

While Coldblood contemplated his direction, he drove near D'Amica's place hoping to see his son. He had no plans to go inside nor to interfere in his son's life, but he was just hoping to see him. After awhile, he saw the apartment lights go out, so he drove away. Shaun was seven years old now and Coldblood had missed his last two birthdays. He didn't know when he would see Shaun again, but he was determined somehow to be a better dad.

While traveling west on Glenwood Rd near I-20, he suddenly noticed two suspicious looking vehicles approaching him. As the light flashed inside the rear car, he saw the face of someone he knew: it was Q'Ball.

"What the hell is Q'Ball up to?" he asked himself. Q'Ball was the Bookie and *pick-up* man for many huge business operations. He didn't deal in small time, so Coldblood knew something big was about to go down. As he watched, the first car turned into the Chevron Station on the left side of the street. The car that Q'Ball was in, backed into the Texaco on the right side of the street and turned out the lights. Coldblood quickly turned onto the side road next to the Texaco. He parked, then sneaked behind the dumpster near where Q'Ball was parked. Then he heard...

"If your boss doesn't deliver this five hundred grand by morning, things could get bad for a lot of people," said Q'Ball.
"Look Old School! Don't worry about that," the young driver replied. *"If D-Lo says that he will deliver, then he will deliver!"*

"D-Lo?" thought Coldblood to himself. *"My dad's enemy and the reason my mom is dead!"* As his anger subsided, his eye started twitching and he reached for his pistol. Suddenly, he felt a gun barrel touch him on the head.

"Don't move," said the voice. "Give me the gun." Coldblood slowly handed it over. "Now quietly get up." As Coldblood stood, he hated himself for having stopped.

"I should have kept going," he thought.

"What are you doing here, Coldblood?" sounded the familiar voice.

"Dex?" whispered Coldblood as he looked into the gunman's face. "What's this all about, Dex?"

"That's what I was about to ask you. I was getting gas at the Texaco when I spotted you in your dad's car, so I quickly followed you. What's going on, here?" he asked. Dexter and Coldblood had become pretty close during their time in the brotherhood. But Dexter had a family, now, and wasn't as involved as he use to be. Nevertheless, he still knew the game.

"That's Q'Ball in the car with some other cat," whispered Coldblood.

"Q'Ball?" whispered Dexter. "You mean big-time 'pay-master' Q'Ball?"

"Yeah, and I think he's about to make a move for D-Lo of the Black-gods."

"Word on the street is that the Black-gods have something big going down this weekend," started Dexter. "But D-Lo got burned to a crisp in his girl's apartment many years ago. Why do you think he is still alive? Hookman runs the operation, now. At least that's what the word is on the streets."

"The guy in the car with Q'Ball commented about D-Lo having to deliver five hundred grand by tonight. There's another car parked over at the Chevron that these two guys are waiting for. I wouldn't be surprised if Hookman or even D-Lo is in that car."

"So what are you planning to do, man? We can't fight these guys; they are too big."

"I don't know," paused Coldblood. "But, it was also D-Lo or Hookman that put out a hit on my dad, but killed my mom, instead."

"What?" asked Dexter surprisingly. "Are you sure about this, man?"

"Yeah, I'm sure. My dad told me the whole story."

"Ok, Blood. So what are you gonna do, right now, with 2 guns against fifty?" About that time, another vehicle pulled into the Chevron yard. Two men stepped out of the first vehicle and waited.

"That's Hookman with the silver cane," whispered Dexter. "I don't recognize the other guy; could it be D-Lo?" Suddenly, the man wearing the shades nudged for the Hookman to go over to the vehicle that just drove in.

"That's definitely D-Lo," said Dexter. "Nobody orders the Hookman around but D-Lo, so that's him!" Coldblood's eye started twitching as he replayed in his mind the day his mother was killed. His moment had arrived and now he could get D-Lo and Hookman while avenging his mother.

Suddenly, two more men stepped from D-Lo's vehicle and joined him. As Hookman went over and opened the door of the latest arriving vehicle, a beautiful, brown skinned, young woman, stepped out with two body guards by her side. She motioned for D-Lo to step into her vehicle and he did.

While D-Lo was in the car with the woman, one of D-Lo's men went inside the store to check things out. He had no idea that the store clerk had been watching everything and was hiding a shotgun under the counter. He had already called police and reported suspicious activity.

When D-Lo's man saw the shot gun in the mirror, he quickly went for his gun, but the store clerk was too fast for him, and blew him away. Suddenly, all the men outside started firing at the store clerk through the glass. The guy with Q'Ball jumped from the car and ran across the street to help. As the sirens came, D-Lo quickly stepped out the car and handed him a briefcase.

"Get this back to the Q'Ball and get out of here!" he ordered. Hookman and the other men were now in a shoot out with the police as the two vehicles somehow managed to maneuver from the Chevron station and leave. Two police officers were wounded but the store clerk was dead.

After the young man ran back to the car with the briefcase, he was about to enter the car when he suddenly felt the bunt of a pistol knock him out....cold. While Coldblood was hitting him, Dexter was on the passenger side taking out Q'Ball. Then they took the briefcase and sped off.

Chapter 15

While the detectives were investigating the scene of the shooting, Agents Randy Hardy and Benny Dixon drove up and flashed their badges.

"What do you have, boys?" asked Dixon.

"Two blues down, one dead store clerk, and one dead bad guy," responded the detective. "The store clerk called 911 and reported suspicious activity in the parking lot. Obviously, he was right. Witnesses say there was a meeting of some kind with black and white guys in suits. Then they heard shots being fired into the store at the clerk, after the clerk shot and killed the bad guy."

"Anything taken from the store?" asked Hardy.

"Nope," said the detective. "Apparently there was a meeting between two car load of goons and the store clerk tried to play hero, and got himself killed."

"So the bad guys were not shooting at each other, but sounds like they were shooting at the store clerk for killing their man," figured Dixon. As Hardy walked around the scene, he saw drops of blood.

"Where were the two cars parked that met?" he asked. The detective identified one of the spots very close to where the blood was found.

"Hmm? According to the angle of the blood splash, the store clerk may have hit another one before they got him. Other than that, this seems like a typical shooting with no motives. There was no robbery or hate groups, but just a store clerk who got in the way of some bad guys doing business," said Hardy. "So why does Chief Lewis want us to get involved with a normal local police case so badly?"

"I don't know," remarked Dixon. "Let's call in and ask him." Agent Dixon used his cell phone to call Chief Lewis. "Say Chief, what particularly is it that you expect us to find here? We're at the crime scene, but it seems pretty cut and dry."

"Well, its not that cut and dry," commented Chief Lewis. "I was told that plenty of shooting went on out there, tonight, and blood may have been flying. I have reason to believe that one of our undercover operatives may have been in one of those cars. Are you getting the picture, now?"

"Got it, Chief!" responded Dixon. "And we're on it."

"What's up?" asked Hardy.

"We had an operative in one of those cars." They quickly ran inside and commenced investigative checks on the dead man that the clerk shot. Then they had CSI run checks on all the blood samples that were found in the yard of the store to see if they could find a match. They knew that if one of their agents were in the car, and had gotten hit by the store manager or the police, that he could possibly bleed to death or could be in trouble with the mob that had him.

"Chief," said Dixon on the phone again. "Can you give us any info at all about our guy?"

"No, I can't," yelled the Chief. "But what makes you think, it's a guy?" Then the chief hung up. Dixon and Hardy paused and just looked at each other.

"To all local units in the Atlanta Metro area, this is Agent Benny Dixon of the GBI. Please monitor all hospitals in your area for the next 12 hours to see if any victims are brought in with gunshot wounds. Do not approach the victim; I repeat; do not approach the victim, but call my office immediately and have medical to hold them at your location. Dixon... out!"

Chapter 16

It was about 11:30 p.m. that Friday night as Coldblood trailed Dexter through the back roads of Decatur. Eventually, Dexter pulled into the parking lot of Club Scores on Wesley Chapel Road. Coldblood quickly jumped from his car and went to Dexter's car so they could talk. The briefcase was locked, but if it carried what they thought it did, then they were rich,,,,, or so they thought.

"It doesn't look that hard to open," said Dexter as they checked the case.

"Man, I can't believe this," said Coldblood as he smiled and stared at Dexter. "What a break! I was down on my last leg then this just fallls into my lap."

"Our lap, Bro," added Dexter. "We couldn't do this without each other. Plus, things have not been so peachy for me and my family lately, either. Olivia's been giving me straight hell about the bills and the house needs." Suddenly, Coldblood heard the whisper,, *"The Curse Must Be Broken!"* He quickly pulled his pistol and pointed it as Dexter did the same. As the two men stood back to back pointing their weapons and watching, Dexter asked,

"What's up, man?"

"Did you hear that?" asked Coldblood. "Somebody whispered." Dexter slowly lowered his pistol and turned to Coldblood.

"What are you talking about, Blood? Ain't nobody out here but us." Coldblood was puzzled, but he knew Dexter was right as he, too, lowered his pistol.

"Ok, Dex. We can talk about all of this in a minute. But we need to get out of this parking lot and somewhere private, don't you think? Plus, we need tools... a crowbar or something so we can open this case."

"I have tools in the back, but where can we go? We can't go to my house," said Dexter. "But we need to move kinda fast. D-Lo ain't gonna just lay down about this, so we need to handle it and make plans."

"Isn't there a Super 8 down the street? Let's get a room."

Leaving Coldblood's car at Club Scores parking, Dexter drove to the Super 8 motel and purchased a room while Coldblood stayed with the briefcase. Afterwards, they got the tools from the trunk and cautiously went to the motel room. After struggling to get into the briefcase, they opened it to find exactly what they had hoped--bills paid, rent made, grocery for the house, money for the family, and relief for the brothers. The briefcase contained five hundred thousand dollars, all in small bills.

"What a break!" they thought. After they happily counted and divided the money, they began to talk.

"I just thought about something, Blood. What if somebody saw us tonight? We could be in a lot of trouble, man."

"Who saw us?" questioned Coldblood. "Please don't get paranoid on me now, man."

"I'm just saying that we need to consider it."

"Ok, what do you have in mind?" asked Coldblood.

"We've got to hit the streets and find out what the word is before we just start spending."

"I don't have time for that," replied Coldblood. "I'm already packed and on my way out of town. I've got GBI on my back, remember? Besides, this is the same sucker that did my mom and ruined everything for my family, so I really don't give a damn if he doesn't get a dime back." Suddenly, Coldblood heard the whisper again..."*The Curse Must Be Broken!"*

"But Blood, what about your family? Your son?"

Coldblood just stood there being stunned for a moment. He knew that Dexter was right and they had to check out the word on the street. Because if it is said that he and Dexter were connected to this hit in any way, D-Lo would come after their families, if he couldn't find them.

"Damn!" Coldblood shouted while hitting the wall! "Ok, what's your plan, man?"

"Let's hide the money and lay low for a few days, while we check things out. If we just start spending and paying things, that will be the first giveaway and I think this D-Lo is no fool. We've got to lay low and function as normal," reasoned Dexter.

"Dex, I'm really feeling you on all that; I really am. But, I can't stay around here, right now, or things are gonna be bad for me, anyway. So while you lay low and check things out, I'm taking my cut and heading north. You'll know where I am if things change.

I'll hold onto the money just as it is until I hear from you, and know that all is well. But for now, I have to go. If GBI get to me now, what D-Lo do won't matter anyway. So, my brother, please understand, that I've got to go." Dexter didn't like the idea of being alone and having to check things out, but he understood the position that Coldblood was in.

"Blood, I know you wanna help me and I do understand your situation. But if word gets back to D-Lo about what happened here tonight, you know I'm a dead man. I don't care where you are nor what you're doing, but if D-Lo comes after me and my family, I want your word that you will be there for me, Blood. Please tell me that."

"I promise that if it comes to that, then to hell with the GBI. I will be there for you, brother, just like I know you will be there for me." Then they embraced as Dexter said,

"Demon-Bloods!" Then Coldblood said,

"To the end!" Then they departed. As he drove, Coldblood really wanted to say goodbye to his son, Shaun. So he reached under the seat and took the cell phone that his dad left him and started to dial. After he thought about it, he hung up and decided to wait.

"Hello?" answered D'Amica, but no one was there. Meantime, he pulled into a nearby hotel and stayed the night.

Chapter 17

"Aahhh!" screamed D-Lo in anger as he entered his hide-a-way.

"Bastard shot me!" he yelled as blood dripped from inside of his coat. It wasn't a serious wound, but because it was in his side, the blood continually dripped. "Go get me a bottle," he ordered. One of his men went into the club area to get him a bottle of whiskey. D-Lo was an investor of the Night Club on Old National Hwy., where he was currently hiding out.

"Sit down and let me take a look at it," said Hookman. Hookman helped him to take off his coat and shirt, then got a towel and wiped the blood from D-Lo's side. "What the hell is this? Is this what you're making all that noise about? Hell, it ain't even a flesh wound!" continued Hookman.

"My old lady cut into me more than that when I'm banging her, and you're doing all this crying about a scratch? You're getting soft, D-Lo. I hope you don't ever get in bed with a real woman, cause she's gonna tear your soft ass up." About that time, Brenda, the pretty, brown-skinned, woman, that met them at the Chevron, came hurrying in.

"D-Lo! What the hell happened back there at the meeting? Who started the shooting?" she asked. "Everything could have been ruined, and we would never get the rest of the money. What happened?" After she paused, she saw the blood drip from D-Lo's side. "Oh my God! You've been shot!" Then she went to work trying to clean the wound and patch him up. "So, is somebody gonna tell me what happened back there?"

"Just a trigger happy store employee," said Hookman. "That's all."

"That's all!" she exclaimed. "Well, that's enough! Our client has become very skeptical about our operations and wants assurance that things are fine before he releases the rest of the money."

"What?" loudly asked D-Lo! "I'll talk to him. Meantime, let's get ready to make the next run." Suddenly, Q'Ball and his driver walked in.

"Boss," spoke the driver nervously. "We lost the money!" D-Lo jumped up and put a one hand choke hold around the driver's neck, while Hookman stuck a pistol in the driver's mouth.

"You sure picked the wrong day to be joking about my money," said D-Lo angrily. Then the Hookman, slightly pulled the gun from between his lips and said,

"What you say next, will determine whether it's your last breath or not, so breathe easy, son. Now where is that money that you were supposed to protect with your life?" Q'Ball had both hands up as the driver spoke.

"When D-Lo handed me the briefcase, I ran back to give it to Q'Ball like he told me to. Except as I got back to the car, somebody jumped from behind the car and hit me, I swear. When I came around, Q'Ball was knocked out and the money was gone!"

"That's it?" asked D-Lo. The driver nodded quickly being afraid. "Did you see his face or anything about him?"

"Boss," he answered nervously. "With all the shooting and police coming up, it all happen so fast till I didn't see nothing. I was just trying to get the money to Q'Ball, and get the hell out of there." About that time D-Lo looked at the Hookman, and the Hookman pulled the trigger and blew the drivers brains out.

"Uh!" screamed Brenda being in shock to see what had just happened. Then D-Lo walked up to Q'Ball and started talking.

"Q, you know the importance of that money being delivered into the right hands tonight. You've done this for 30 years now and never lost a dime. What the hell happened, Q'Ball?" Q'Ball, being the vet that he is, spoke calmly as he eyed Hookman. He knew that the Hookman would soon kill him if he showed any sign of weakness, so Q'Ball spoke firmly.

"The kid told you the truth, D-Lo, but it wasn't just one man; he had help. Because as soon as I heard the thump that took the kid out, someone from my side of the car opened the door and took me out. We didn't see anybody man and that's the truth."

After a pause from all in the room, everybody wondered if the Hookman was gonna drop Q'Ball like he did the driver. But Q'Ball, like the Hookman and D-Lo, had been around for a very long time and knew the ropes. Plus, Q'Ball had become a very known trusted Bookie for many bosses and operations.

D-Lo and Hookman knew that if they pulled the trigger on Q'Ball, they would have a lot of questions to answer from the other Bosses. Besides, Q'Ball was so good and trusting for keeping everybody's books, they never considered anybody ever taking his place. So they hesitated, because they needed Q'Ball to help them get things back on track, and hopefully to help find out who had robbed them.

"Damn!" shouted D-Lo. "What a hell of a time for this to happen. That first shipment will be arriving in a few days and we've got 50 counties to supply. Somebody better find my damn money!" he yelled as he hit the desk. Then there was a long pause. "Get that body out of here, man!" Two men dragged it out.

"You know, the more I think about it, the more it seem like a set up to me," said Hookman. "The only one who knew the money would be there is us, and the one who brought it, Mr. Holloway himself. Do you think that bastard got us?"

"Yeah, but nobody knew that the money was going across the street but you, me, the kid, and Q'Ball. As nervous as that kid was, he had nothing to do with it. Q'Ball's moved a hell of a lot more than five hundred grand at one time, so why would he go for this chump change, tonight? That only leaves me and you, Dawg," stated D-Lo. "And I don't take my own money." After a pause and the two men stared each other down, Hookman eased his hand out of his inner coat pocket and slowly pulled a long hook blade.

"Dawg, I've been with you a long time. Don't know nobody else, and don't have no place to go. You are the only family I've known every since I was 13. We've been together 30 years and we ain't never crossed this bridge. For you to even let something like that slip between your lips, means that we must be at the end of our road. You've left me no place to go except across that desk and on your ass." Just as Hookman jumped toward D-Lo, D-Lo quickly tossed the gun from his belt, then raised both hands above his head and shouted,

"Wait!" He knew Hookman and he knew that if he had kept that gun on him in any way at that moment, Hookman wouldn't stop coming and cutting until they both were dead. "Wait! Wait! Hookman!" he shouted. With the blade in his hand, the Hookman hesitated because he expected to be filled with bullet holes by now. With his hands still held high, D-Lo walked right up to Hookman and spoke.

"Please forgive me for what I just did. I know that you didn't have anything to do with the missing money, tonight. But I had to put it out there like that because...hell man, you ain't cut nobody up in over 10 years and I miss you." D-Lo slowly lowered his hands.

"I know that I can trust you more than I can trust my own mama. But somebody out there tonight got my money and I don't know who. What I needed to know right here, right now, is....if you are still the same ruthless SOB I know you to be, that once we find them, you will let nobody live that had anything to do with the missing money.

I wasn't trying you up, my brother. But I was attempting to make you madder and stronger for what I need you to do. You already know that every since Big did what he did to me over 25 years ago, you've been the only family I've got and trust. I love you, man, and I would never try you up like that if I didn't believe in you.

But if you don't believe me, and think that we are at the end of the road, then I don't want to die by nobody's hand but yours." Then D-Lo raised his hands again and said, "This is how much I love and trust you, man. My life is in your hands." After a long staring pause between the two, Hookman put the blade away.

"You know, you really need to find another way to make me stronger cause you had me all messed up. All I could think about was people who need organs and I was about to donate all of yours," said Hookman.

"I've never known you to do anything less than that when somebody crosses you, and I'm not expecting less now. Brother, we've been crossed and whoever did it, don't need to live." By now, Brenda and the other men in the room are all calmed again.

"Whew!" Brenda sighed. "Y'all sho' know how to scare a sister. So D-Lo, what the conclusion? What are we gonna do about the pick-up, which is what the money was for?" she asked. "And how do you want me to handle Mr. Holloway, our investor?"

"Shut up! Let me think a minute," growled D-Lo. "I'll deal with Holloway myself. Meantime, Hookman get some men on the street and see who's suddenly got money to spend or is paying off debts. I get the feeling this is someone we know that hit us, but I didn't think any of them were that stupid."

"Now that I think about it, there is absolutely no way anybody could have known that Q'Ball and the kid would be in that spot, at that time. Therefore, somebody had to be watching us the entire time," said Hookman.

"Q'Ball, did you see anybody at all?" asked D-Lo.

"I'm telling you, man, that as bullets were flying, I was ducking and didn't see anything."

"Ok," said D-Lo. "Let's go to the streets and see what's up. Brenda-girl set up me another meeting with Holloway. I need another five hundred grand.

"Ok," she said. "I'll set it up." Brenda eased out and drove off being undetected.

"Lastly, it's time to go back to the old ways...hit a few people...sting'em a little and stir up some things just to see who holla," D-Lo told Hookman. "Let the men have a little fun for a while and see where it leads."

"I can handle that, Boss," spoke Al, one of his men. Then they left as Cheese came in with the girls and D-Lo smiled. For the next few hours, D-Lo and Cheese partied with the girls as they ate, drank, and smoked.

Chapter 18

Coldblood was sleeping hard when housekeeping came to the room.

"Get up, get up!" smiled the lady as she opened the door and peeped in. "Sir, are you staying another day?" Coldblood groaned as he looked at his watch.

"Dag, is it after eleven, already?" Then he speedily got himself together and went to his car. After he pulled into a fast food drive-thru for breakfast, he headed to D'Amica's place to say good-bye to Shaun. It was Saturday morning and Shaun usually stayed home alone while D'Amica went to work at the Beauty Shop. Coldblood was hoping that today would be no different. As he pulled near her building, he saw her boyfriend, Slopp walking to her door.

"What happen to you last night?" she asked as she met him.

"I told you I was busy, D'Amica, so don't start trip' in cause I'll go on my way. Now are you going to work or not?"

"Do you call yourself staying away because you don't want to help pay my rent this month?"

"Look," he argued. "I told you the night you put me out and let yo' baby daddy stay here, that I wasn't paying nothing else."

"I explained that to you, and you said you were ok with it," she defended. "Slopp don't act like this. You know I need that money and..."

"If you're going to work, then get in the car or I'm leaving," he cut in. D'Amica angrily got in the car and they left. Coldblood eased to the door and rang the bell. Nothing happened. He knew that Shaun had been taught to stay away from the door while he was home alone. Shaun heard the bell, but he was watching cartoons and ignored it.

"Hey Sport," said Coldblood on the intercom. "It's me, your dad. Open up."

"Dad!" yelled Shaun as he quickly buzzed Coldblood in. "I knew you would come back for me Dad!"

"So, what'cha doing, Sport?"

"Just watching cartoons. Mama went to work. She'll be gone all day so you can stay here if you want! We can play games on play station."

"Yeah, I guess that would be kinda fun, huh?"

"Yeah, Dad, cuz Slopp can't play that good. I beat him all the time, whenever he and Mama ain't arguing."

"Oh! Yeah? So what do they argue about?"

"Lately, all they talk about is money and bills and stuff. So Dad, are you back at your apartment now? Can I visit sometimes?" Coldblood kinda laughed and played with him for a minute.

"That's kinda what I want to talk to you about." Then he looked over at the table and saw the box of Cheerios. "Wait-a-minute! Is that what I think it is?"

"Yep!" smiled Shaun. "It's the same box you sent to me. Want to eat some with me?" Coldblood couldn't believe his eyes. About a year ago, he bought Shaun a box of Cheerios, and drew a big smiley face on one side of the box. That same box was sitting on the kitchen table.

"Every time Mama buy me cheerios, I take them out of the box, and put them in this box that you got for me. Want some?" Then he poured cereal in two bowls; one for him and one for his dad as they ate together.

"Sport, I have to go out of town for a while, and I don't know when I will be back."

"I know," said Shaun. "Mom told Slopp that you were on the run."

"She did, huh?"

"Why are you on the run, Dad?"

Coldblood hesitated. "Son, I did some things that I probably shouldn't have done, and now I've got to answer for them...and I will. But, right now, I need to get away until I'm ready. Then, I'm coming back for you and we will be together, forever, ok Sport?" Shaun happily nodded ,,, "Yes".

"So where are you going, Dad?"

"I don't know, yet, but you better believe that when I get there, you'll be the first to know." Then he wrestled Shaun to the floor and began to tickle him until he laughed to tears. After a few minutes, Shaun just locked himself into his dad's arms and held on.

"I love you, Dad." Suddenly, Coldblood heard the whisper ,,,, *"The Curse Must Be Broken!"* He quickly placed his hand on his pistol and looked around.

"I love you too, son, but I have to go now." Then he took four fifty dollar bills from his pocket and placed it under the lamp. "Tell your mom that's for her and I'm sorry, Ok?"

"Ok," said Shaun. Then Coldblood wrote his cell phone number on a piece of paper.

"And this is for you so don't give it to anybody else. Anytime you need to call me, you just call and I will answer, Ok?" Shaun nodded then happily put the number in his pocket.

"Bye Dad," he waved as Coldblood left.

Chapter 19

Jennifer, being in her underwear, kissed Mitch goodbye as they stood in the doorway of her apartment. It was Saturday afternoon and Jennifer had to go to work. Over the passed week or so, Jennifer had come to understand that she had a problem taking things, that didn't belong to her. Sometimes she knew she took things and sometimes she didn't.

Although she loved the feeling it gave her while she was in the act, it was like an addiction or an obsession and she was being driven more and more to take things everyday. She had learned a lot about tools and how to use them in case she needed to break into a place to get what she needed. She became familiar with store's security alarms, and closing times, as well as security cameras.

She was slowly becoming a professional thief and kleptomaniac. Many nights she found herself sneaking from apartment to apartment within her building just for the thrill of it. Eventually, she learned to climb buildings and walk rails as she leaped from balcony to balcony and ledge to ledge. Wearing her black tightly fitting tights, she had become a night wrangler, rounding up things that peaked her interest.

As she dressed for work today, she prepared herself for the job ahead of her during the night. She had seen a children's store while on her route to work and she needed clothes for her niece, Makeda. She wanted to see if she could enter the store after hours, deactivate the alarm, and take what she needed. Then she would jog about 10 miles home or ride the bike she stored at work.

Jennifer left her apartment thinking about what she had become. She wasn't proud of herself, but this had been the only thing that settles her and gives her peace of mind. She even reasoned with herself that she wasn't hurting anybody so it was alright. But what she failed to realize was that it was for these same reasons her dad was shot to death and her mom went to prison; she never saw either, again. Now, she had become her parents seven times over and she couldn't see it.

"Hi, Jenny," said Michelle as Jennifer strode in.

"Hey Michelle. Your *'knock `em dead'* perfume is smelling loud girl!" As usual, Jennifer went to put her backpack away and to change her shoes. Then she checked her register and looked around to make sure all things were in order.

"Something funny is going on in the main office upstairs today, and we were not invited," whispered Michelle.

"Oh?" questioned Jennifer.

"Yeah, there is a meeting with some of the departmental heads and district owners. They've been in there about 20 minutes now."

"What do you think it could be about?" asked Jennifer.

"I don't know, but I'm sure we'll find out soon enough." Jennifer began to think this may be her opportunity to see just how good she was at sneaking and peeking. She decided to see how close she could come to the main office and listen in without being caught. As she started the challenge, she was noticed by the security guard.

"Good morning, Ms. J." he friendly spoke. "Nice day today, huh?" he continued with small talk.

"Hi Jimmy.... Yes it is a nice day. How's your family?" she asked.

"Everybody's fine, Ms. J., and yours?"

"Fine, thank you, Jimmy. I'll tell them you asked." Then she hurried on her way. She knew she couldn't get any closer than she already were without drawing special attention to herself. She and Michelle really wondered what that meeting was about and now they were stressing over thoughts about it.

"I'll be right back," Jennifer told Michelle. "Cover for me." Within minutes, Jennifer had picked up her backpack, walked through the mall and nearly filled it with stolen items: Candy bars, toys, cosmetics, jewelry, clothes, towels, underwear, medicines, food--you name it, she took it. So far, she had not been seen. Just as fast as she slipped away, she came back feeling much better and relaxed again.

"You seem calmed," said Michelle.

"I am," replied Jennifer. Then she heard ,,, *"The Curse Must Be Broken!"* Jennifer looked about and wondered if Michelle had heard it, as she tried to hold her composure. Suddenly, she felt the urge to vomit so she took off speedily for the ladies room. Just as she reached the toilet, dizziness settled in and she threw up all over the toilet seat. Michelle was close behind her.

"Oh my God! Are you sick?"

"Not that I know of," replied Jennifer. Then Michelle calmed down.

"That could mean only one thing then."

"What's that?" Jennifer asked.

"That you're pregnant."

Jennifer quickly looked at Michelle in disappointment. Then she cried, "No! No! Michelle please, not now!" Michelle made her way to Jennifer and hugged her.

"Sorry, girlfriend. But I'm sure that you're very pregnant or very sick. And there's only one way to find out," said Michelle. Jennifer just laid in her arms and cried again. After they bought a home pregnancy test, Jennifer learned that Michelle was right; she was pregnant.

Chapter 20

"Girl, did you see Usher last night at the awards?" Nicole asked excitedly. "He took`em up through there!"

"Yeah, I saw Usher, but I saw Mariah, too," said Tameka.

"Mariah, who?" questioned Melody and Adrienna.

"Girl, here we are talking about men, and you talking about some Mariah Carey," said Adrienna.

"Either you have all the man you can handle or either you're gay. Now, which is it?" asked Melody. The girls were quiet as they stared at Tameka while waiting for an answer.

"All y'all go to hell," said Tameka as the girls laughed. The girls were all beauticians in a Beauty Shop in Riverdale, GA. They often joked and talked about each other and others while preparing for the customers of the day. Today was no different, as they locked in on Tameka. But about a mile away, another conversation was taking place.

****

"Slopp, I'm not with him, anymore, and you know it. Why do you keep trip`n when you know that I'm with you?" begged D'Amica.

"Look, I ain't trying to hear that, right now," he responded as he drove up to the Beauty Shop. He stopped the car, got out, then went to open the door for D'Amica. As the girls in the shop saw Slopp drive up, they commented as they usually does.

"Hey look!" Melody said while pointing. "Here comes Miss Thang, y'all." Suddenly, she took the broom and stepped outside the shop like she had to sweep the walkway. That way, she could listen. Adrienna ran behind her and acted like she was about to clean the outside floor mat, while Tameka did the outside windows. They didn't normally take it to this extreme, but lately Slopp and D'Amica had been arguing a lot about all kinds of stuff, and they wanted to listen.

"I need money for my rent and light bill," said D'Amica as she stepped out.

"Are we back to that again?" asked Slopp impatiently. "I've already told you about that so why don't you quit aggravating me, 'cause it ain't gonna happen." D'Amica was very angry as she just stood staring at him. He stepped closer for a kiss but she just stood there.

"Oh, it's like that, now?" he said as he backed away and went to get in the car.

"Pick me up at 8 tonight!" she yelled behind him. Slopp drove away.

"What's up, Meca?" spoke Adrienna. Adrienna, like most women, was into male watching and she knew what was up. But she and Nicole were a little more laid back than Melody and Tameka. Melody was the oldest but Nicole was the boss. Both acted like mother figures as long as they were talking sensibly. Otherwise, all the girls in the shop acted the same.

This day, Adrienna saw hurt in D'Amica's eyes so she hugged her as she greeted her. But Melody was a different story.

"See, that's what's wrong with y'all white women. When he stepped up for a kiss, I would have told him to kiss my ass. That's why I don't mess with no tight-ass men."

"Let it go, Mel," said Nicole while walking up. "I could see the tears in her eyes all the way from the back." As Nicole hugged D'Amica, she burst into tears. "Hush girl. I know what you're going through, and trust me when I tell you that it'll work itself out," comforted Nicole.

"He knows that we haven't been doing a lot at the shop, and I need his help," cried D'Amica. "Now, he wants to cut me off because I had to talk to Shaun's dad."

"Talk to him? Is that all you did?" asked Nicole.

"Hell, we heard that he spent the night," mocked Melody. "Might have even tapped that ass." D'Amica suddenly looked toward Adrienna because she is the only one who knew about Coldblood spending the night with her.

"Ooooh!" said Adrienna. Then she embarrassingly sped back inside.

"Mel, you may as well go, too, cause you're making things worse," ordered Nicole.

"How am I making...." Nicole put her hand up like a traffic cop stopping traffic. Melody shut right up and went inside.

"Well, did you?" asked Nicole.

"Did I what?" yelled D'Amica. Nicole just stared at her with her hands on her hips. D'Amica dried her eyes and said, "He just spent the night because he had nowhere else to go." Nicole looked at her in disbelief as D'Amica hastily walked inside.

****

Meanwhile, back at Perimeter Mall;

"Sir, we have checked and run double checks and the figures are the same," concluded Carol, the sales managers. "Our profits are not down; it's just that thefts have increased. In every department with the exception of major appliances, thefts have increased by fifty percent compared to where it was six months to a year ago."

"Which means that we can't sell what we don't have," responded the CEO. "Which also means that profits would seemingly decrease." After a long moment of silence, the CEO left his desk and headed to the security video room. "Please come with me, Carol," he ordered. They entered the security room and began to watch the camera, for a minute.

"Now, I can see why we can't catch the thieves," he said. "The cameras don't shift fast enough and maybe the thieves know that. Why don't we, Ms. Carol? I want better cameras doing more coverage of our stores. We can't afford to have thieves homesteading us like we are some kind of free pick. I want this done by the end of the month, before our next stock date, is that clear?"

"Yes Sir," she assured. "Very clear, Sir."

****

It was about 3:30 p.m. as Coldblood traveled North on I-75, being not sure of his destination. He mainly just wanted to get out of Georgia before he got caught by the police. He should have left more than two hours ago, but he had things in his old apartment that he needed. Therefore, he carefully made his way there and found them. Management had already evicted him and new tenants had moved in. So, Coldblood broke in and found the valuables he had hidden there. Suddenly, his cell phone rang.

"Hello?" he answered. It was Dexter.

"Blood, where are you?" he sounded panicky. Coldblood slowed down to talk.

"I'm on I-75 North, just about to pass the Cartersville exit. Why? What's up, Dawg?"

"Get off and spend the night in Cartersville," Dexter warned. "You got major problems up ahead." Coldblood didn't waste any time turning onto the exit. Dexter continued, "I just got word from a friend that there are major roadblocks ahead of you; like they're looking for something."

"Or someone," added Coldblood.

"Maybe so," continued Dexter. "But I don't think this have anything to do with you. When she called, she made it seem a lot more serious than you or I. Anyway, I don't want you to get caught up in it, so just chill where you are for a while."

"Good looking out, Dex. I'm already off the road. I'll be in touch. Later, man."

Coldblood still had payment stubs with the fake name while working with the labor pool. He hoped that he could use them to help him get a room. He knew he couldn't use his own name, and he had to be careful about showing his face in this unfamiliar town. So he covered himself as much as he could and entered a small unfamiliar motel.

"How can I help you, sir?" asked the short fat desk clerk.

"A room for one, please," he answered. "Non-smoking, if you have it, but it really doesn't matter."

"For one night, that'll be $30.00 plus tax." Coldblood took the room. It had a lot of old furniture, but it was clean and the door secured well. He immediately fell asleep.

****

Back at the Beauty Shop, D'Amica had closed her station and was waiting for Slopp to pick her up. It was 8:30 p.m., and everybody was gone except Nicole. Slopp was late and the last bus was about to come to that area for the night. She tried to call Slopp numerous times, but she always got his voice mail. She knew he had dumped her, so when the 8:50 p.m. bus came, she got on it.

Business had been slow lately and D'Amica was barely making enough money to occupy her space. She was really counting on Slopp to help bail her out until things got back to normal. Now, she was really concerned, and didn't know what to do. As she got home at 10 p.m., Shaun excitedly met her at the door.

"Mom!" he yelled. "Guess what? Dad stopped by today!"

"He did?" she asked being shocked. She knew that Coldblood was in trouble and she thought he'd be long gone by now. "Did he say what he wanted? Why didn't you call me?" she asked.

"He just wanted to see me before he left town. He's gone now," said Shaun. D'Amica's spirit settled when she saw the disappointment in Shaun's eyes.

"Did he say where he was going or when he would be back?"

"No," answered Shaun. "But he did leave you something." Shaun happily ran to the lamp, got the money, and handed it to her. "This is for you, Mom." She surprisingly took the money.

"Thank you, Baby!"

"You're welcome, Mom," he said gladly. Shaun was already in his pajamas as she said,

"It's time for you to be sleeping now, Shaun. Plus, I'm tired. Let's go to bed, ok?"

"Ok, Mom," he slowly said. Then she hugged and kissed him as he left. D'Amica was still shocked that Coldblood had stopped by, plus, he had left her money. She knew the call that came through a couple of days ago was from him, so she checked her phone to see if the number was still there. It was, as she started to dial, then she stopped.

"What am I to say?" she wondered. Then she put the phone away. She was still in love with Coldblood, but she didn't want him to know. She didn't like his lifestyle nor did she want Shaun to grow up like that. Plus, in the past, Coldblood had put the brotherhood before her and his son when she really needed him. But lately, he was showing signs of a changed man. Especially, by coming to personally talk with Shaun, and leaving her a few dollars in her time of need.

"Well, I guess I should tell him 'thank you,'" she reasoned as she dressed for bed. So she got her thoughts together and dialed. Coldblood had awakened and saw the number in his cell phone. He assumed it was Shaun.

"What's up, Sport? It's a little late for you to be up, isn't it? It's passed eleven o'clock." Then he heard whisper, *"The Curse Must Be Broken!"* He looked around the room, but nothing.

D'Amica calmly interrupted, "Hey Coldblood." For a minute he was speechless and shocked as he eased down on the bedto sit.

"Meca, baby, I can explain," he quickly started talking. "I know you told me not to come over like that, but I had to say good...."

"Coldblood," she slightly yelled. "It's ok." Then they were quiet again for a minute like two high school kids not knowing what to say.

"Is everything alright?" he asked. "Is Shaun ok?"

"Yes, everything is ok. Shaun is sleeping."

"I guess he gave you the number, huh?" grinned Coldblood.

"No, I got it from my caller ID when you called and hung up the other day."

"Oh," he replied. Then they were silent again for a minute.

"Thanks for the money. I really need it," she spoke softly. Suddenly, Coldblood's voice rose as he asked,

"Slopp, or whatever his name is...is helping you, isn't he?"

"I think he's gone, Coldblood, and I have to do this by myself, again." She spoke softly. After a short pause, Coldblood could hear her sniffing tears in the phone. His heart went out to her.

"Meca, I can be there in an hour if you will wait up for me. Will you?" After she sniffed a few tears, she calmly answered,

"Um-hmm." An hour later, Coldblood was at her door and she let him in.

It was a very peaceful night for Coldblood and D'Amica as they made love through the night. Early that Sunday Morning, they laid in bed and talked about Coldblood's situation and D'Amica's as well. Coldblood told her everything that had happened.

"Meca, I am so sorry that you have to struggle like this. I promise I will be back soon and help you get on your feet so we can take care of our son."

"Yeah, but what am I gonna do right now, Coldblood? We have to live and eat, and I hardly got a job. Promises are not gonna keep us until you get back from... wherever," she responded gently.

Coldblood thought about the money he had stolen from D-Lo and the promise he made to Dexter. He knew it wasn't right to break his promise, especially, because they had a good reason for making it. Now, Coldblood was thinking that his son and his mom needed money and this was a good reason to break it.

"Hold on, Meca." He quickly ran to the car. Then he came back and handed her a hand full of money. "This should hold you and Shaun until I get back. But now I need to go, baby, before Shaun wakes up." D'Amica was shocked as she took the money and kissed him good-bye. It was about 5:30 a.m. when Coldblood sped away. D'amica laid on her bed for a minute then she got up and counted the money. He had left her $10,000. She picked up the phone and dialed.

"What's up, baby?" answered Coldblood. Then she spoke softly.

"Coldblood, you promise?"

"Yes baby, I promise I will come back for you and Shaun as soon as I get settled. Meantime, don't do anything different, and just go to work as usual."

"Can't you at least let me know where you are going?"

"I'm not sure, Meca. Besides the less you know, right now, the better for us both. If something goes down and you can't get me, call Dex."

"Ok," she said gently. "Coldblood... I... I..." She wanted him to know she loved him but she was still afraid. So she said... "I want you to keep your promise and hurry back, ok? We'll be waiting."

"Bye, Meca," he said. Then he hung up.

"Mom, was that Slopp?" asked Shaun as he walked in. "I think I dreamed that dad was here. Why did Slopp leave so early?" Suddenly, D'Amica got a hand full of the money that was on the bed and threw it on him and screamed. They playfully laughed and hugged.

Chapter 21

That Sunday morning, just before daybreak, Cherlene lay restless in her bed trying to get that last bit of sleep. Little Makeda, her daughter, was almost a year old and had kept Cherlene up most of the night. Since Terry was the father of her child, she was allowing him to come by more and Clint less. Nevertheless, she was seeing them both about the same amount of time.

Clint, who was a heavy-equipment operator, often saw her at her job or in his apartment. Currently, Terry was working out of town with his electrical company and would be back in a few days. She thought about calling Clint as she felt her need for sex starting to overwhelm her.

Suddenly, little Makeda let out a loud cry; Cherlene jumped up and comforted her in her crib. Then she went back to sleep. Cherlene knew this may be a bad time to call Clint, but she did it anyway. Within minutes, Clint was there. It was like he was expecting her call. He quickly went in to her, had sex, and was gone as fast as he had come. Now, Cherlene was feeling better, so she dosed off to sleep. Then she began to dream:

"Uh, uh, uh," sounded her mom as Melvin sexually pounded her.

"Mommy," yelled little 7 1/2 year old Cherlene. Just like before, Gladdis and Melvin turned sharply to look at little Cherlene, but they never stopped having sex.

"Go back to bed, Cherlene. Mommy will be there in a minute," Gladdis said while embracing Melvin and still having sex.

"Mommy, Mommy! Come with me! Come with me!" yelled Cherlene. Suddenly, Melvin and her mom, Gladdis, laid motionless and sharply looked at Cherlene.

"Girl, are you crazy?" fussed her mom! "Do you know how good this is? Can I have a little fun without you bugging me?" Gladdis and Melvin went back to having sex, as little Cherlene watched. Then like an evil being, Gladdis turned to Cherlene and said,

"Cherlene, do you want me to stop?" Cherlene nodded, "Yes."

"Then break the curse, Cherlene...break the curse! 'The Curse Must Be Broken!'" she screamed. Cherlene suddenly awakened and sat up in her bed. When she looked at Makeda's crib, little Makeda was now standing in the crib watching her. Then to her surprise, Clint nakedly walked out of the bathroom and laid down on top of Cherlene and started kissing on her.

"Am I still dreaming?" Cherlene wondered, as Clint tried to penetrate her. Immediately, Cherlene looked around at little Makeda who was still watching. Therefore, she begin to push him away. But Clint started forcing her as little Makeda happily started clapping.

"Clint, get off of me!" she screamed and screamed as he struggled to take advantage of her. Cherlene was crying powerlessly as she watched little Makeda happily watching her being raped.

"Yeah!" laughed little Makeda, as Clint penetrated Cherlene and she screamed.

Suddenly, Cherlene awaken and sat up in bed as before. Except this time, she saw Makeda still sleeping and there was no Clint. Cherlene laid in bed on her back thinking about the dream. Then slowly, she lay on her side, folded herself up into a ball, and cried hysterically. She knew she had become just like her mom.

Chapter 22

It was about 8:30 that Sunday night as stores began to close. Jennifer too, started to close at her job. Earlier in the week, she had scoped the places she had planned to hit and tonight was her night. But first, she wanted to hit this baby shop in the mall where she worked.

She loved her little niece, Makeda, so she often bought her nice things; even more than Cherlene or Donna. So just before 9 p.m., Jennifer eased away and quickly picked up a few items from the baby store. She had become so good at it, they never knew she was in the store, as they closed and she sneaked her way back out.

About 10 p.m. that night, Jennifer entered a small electronics store and took the needed equipment that would fit into her bag. Then she went to her car that was parked in the distance and emptied the bag.

Tonight, she was stepping up her game. She had been watching art and painting shops, jewelry stores, and even office buildings, which she had planned to break into this very night. For the first time, Jennifer put on a black masked skull cap as she broke into the building at an office park. She wasn't looking for anything in particular, but she was just enjoying the fun of doing it and seeing what she could see.

Copiers, phones, file cabinets, computers, chairs, desk, lamps, and lots of things, challenged her mind and ability, but she chose not to bother anything just yet. After awhile, she left the building, got in her car, and was on her way to her last stop for the night.

It was about 1 o'clock in the morning as Jennifer parked near the train station in Clayton County. There were a string of stores she had planned to hit over time, but she would get started tonight. Her first stop was this antique shop where she had seen many items that interested her. As usual, it was very simple for her to get in.

After she got what she needed, and was out of the building, she thought she heard someone in the distance. When she checked, she saw three men literally destroying the doors and windows of the stores they went into. Like her, they were burglarizing the neighborhood. She quickly escaped and made her way to her car. This was the first time she had seen anything like this, and she freaked out; she was so scared that she couldn't even drive nor start the car. So, she just sat there until she calmed down.

After awhile, something inside her changed, and she found the courage to go back and see what the men were doing. Within minutes, like a spider, she was on top of the building observing them. This time, she only saw two men going in and out of the stores.

"What are they doing?" she wondered. The men seemed reckless as they took minimal items and placed them by the door. Suddenly, a black van rolled up with the lights out. *"Ah! The third man!"* she thought.

"I need to get closer." Jennifer maneuvered closer so she could hear what they were saying.

> "Guys, just take a few items here and a few there," ordered Al, the lead man. "D-Lo said to just hit'em a little just to shake up things so folks will start talking. We're not trying to put them out of business."
> "I ain't trying to put`em out of business," said Booley. "I just need everything I'm taking, that's all."
> "Ok fine," continued Al. "But break up the place a little and let's get out of here before the cops show up."

"These are not thieves," thought Jennifer as she listened. *"That's why they don't look professional. They are just some kind of mob guys looking to shake things up in the neighborhood. Wonder why?"* she continued. *"They must be looking for money, or payments from business owners."* Suddenly, Andre, the third guy, approached Al with a small black bag.

"Al, look what I found hidden under the counter of the African Dress Shop." Booley quickly stepped to them to see.

"Diamonds!" yelled Booley. "Man, we are rich!"

"No, we are not," said Al. "Obviously, Mr. African Man got some kind of smuggling going on, and it may not be a good idea to interfere with him, yet. Leave the diamonds. That way he won't know that we know what he's up to, until we get ready to hit him big."

"Al it's a lot of diamonds in this bag and I don't think D-Lo will be happy about us leaving them, when we can use them to get paid, now. Plus, we can still deal with Mr. African Man, later."

"Now that I think about it, you're right, Dre," said Al. "Let's keep the diamonds." Jennifer saw Andre place the diamonds on the seat of the van when he opened the side door. Then she had an idea!

"Ok, let's wrap it up boys. Pick up this stuff, and let's get out of here," ordered Al.

As the men started breaking things in the shops, Jennifer quickly ran to her car and got items she needed. When she saw Andre set the bag of diamonds on the seat of the van, something energized her into believing she could steal them.

So she hurried back on top of the building, where she saw Andre preparing to load stolen items into the van. That's when she would make her move. She didn't know why, but she had become so inspired by the challenge and it was driving her. She knew that if she could pull this off, it would be the accomplishments of her life.

"Ok," she whispered. *"You can do this Jenny! You can do this!"*

On a strong fishing line, she placed about four hooks all tied together at the end. Then she tied sufficient weight onto the line so she could move it at will, and even spend the line if needed. She laid down on the building with only her head and arms extended enough to swing the line into the side door of the van.

As Andre bent to pick up the items, Jennifer tossed the line and it landed right on top of the bag. As Andre stood and walked toward the van, she slightly yanked the line and forced the bag of diamonds from the seat. Andre looked around as he thought he heard something. Jennifer, now holding the line still, ducked from the edge of the building in fear.

"Oh my God!" she thought nervously. *"Did he see me?"* She had never been so scared in her life, but she couldn't stop. Andre hadn't seen her nor had he missed the bag of diamonds that was gone from the van. As Jennifer started reeling the bag of diamonds to the roof, she peeped over the edge so she could see how to grab them and run. Just as she did, Booley saw her image in the darkness.

"Hey!" he sounded, as the bag reached the roof. Andre and Booley pulled their weapons and fired where they saw her, but Jennifer was gone.

"You idiots!" shouted Al. "Put those pieces away!"

"The diamonds, Al!" shouted Andre. "Someone on the roof took them!" The men were astounded as they heard the sirens approaching.

"Let's get out of here. We'll deal with this later," rushed Al. Then they left.

****

Jennifer was now safely back into her apartment as she paced the floor and frantically talked to herself like a crazy woman.

"What the hell were you thinking, Jenny?" she whispered! *"What were you thinking? They had guns, Jennifer! They had guns and you could have been shot and killed!"* Again she heard, *"The Curse Must Be Broken!"* Then she sat on the floor in the corner in the dark and cried fervently.

"I'm sorry, Momma!" she said sorrowfully through tears. "Now I know, Daddy; now I know! I couldn't stop myself and I almost got killed! Daddy, I'm so sorry....I'm so sorry; now I understand," she continued. "Now, I really understand."

While she was crying and agonizing about all that had taken place, she begin to feel a pain in her side. When she checked herself, she found a deep cut in her side, plus, a small piece of her knitted pull-over had been torn off.

"Oh my God! I must've hit something as I was coming down the wall." She had been wearing gloves and a masked skull cap to hide herself, but now, it was possible she had left something behind....her blood. While she thought, she suddenly begin to feel sick to her stomach.

"The baby!" she thought again. *"Did I hurt the baby?"* Jennifer had almost forgotten about the positive results she and Michelle discovered about her pregnancy. *"I've got to stop this! Soon, I'll have a child to take care of. What will Mitch think? What will Cheryl and Dee think? What will my child think?"*

As she undressed and stepped into the tub, she heard a voice behind her say, *"The Curse Must Be Broken!"* She paused, quickly looked back, then sat in the tub as she had done earlier, and began to cry.

****

As D-Lo's men headed back to the hide-a-way, they talked.

"Hey, do you think we should tell D-Lo about the diamonds?" asked Booley.

"You mean tell him about the diamonds we don't have and don't know who got them, don't you?" asked Andre.

"If y'all gonna be that stupid to tell D-Lo about diamonds you don't have, then go right ahead," responded Al.

"What diamonds?" said Andre and Booley.

Chapter 23

"Ok girls, come in and sit down," ordered Chief Agent Jonathan Lewis to the other agents. There were 6 agents entering the briefing room to include agents Blake Bishop, Benny Dixon, Randy Hardy, and three others.

"What's this about, Chief?" asked Hardy. "Why all the urgency?"

"If you'll hold your skirt a minute, you'll know," replied Dixon.

"As most of you know," began the Chief. "A little while ago, we raided the city in search of gangsters and bad guys that was heading up about 50 percent of the crime in our fair state. Our operatives identified 17 criminals that could be directly linked to the Mastermind that we've been trying to get to for years now."

"Mastermind? Who are we talking about, here?" asked Bishop.

"Gentlemen, that is none other than, Yoder Holloway," replied Chief Lewis.

"Holloway himself is not directly involved in much of the illegal activities around the state; he's too smart for that. So what he does is find where the goods are--drugs, weapons, chemicals--then he trains lead men and teach them how to sell the goods, and later to move them.

He also sets the prices and decides how much of the money goes to each person or group. He can do this because he is the one that loans the money to them, so they can get started. Once he gets all of his money back, he then get a cut from the sale. So you see, he's not directly involved with illegal operations. But he does train the criminally minded how to do better at what they do. Then he loans them money to do it, for a very hearty fee.

"Sounds like a full proof plan to keep him from behind bars to me," said Dixon.

"Well, by taking down the criminals that he trains, we can put him out of business, fast, in our state," continued the Chief. "Other states are thinking the same thing and that's why we are also working with the FBI to bring down Holloway. When we arrested and indicted 15 major hitters almost a year ago, word is that Holloway's operation got crippled. We had learned of 17 in this state and 7 of them were right here in the metro area. We got all of them except two –Carlton Hooks, better known as 'the Hookman,' and Carl Simmons Jr. better known as 'Coldblood,' both believed to be right here in the Atlanta metro area. Both of these were gang affiliated at one time, but sources lead us to believe that the Hookman may be more involved now in smuggling illegal weapons all over the state."

"That may explain why he's got so many kids," spoke Bishop. "He's everywhere."

"Also, now we know why it's been so hard to catch the Hookman and its not because he's everywhere. But it's because he is not the lead man. He have someone else calling the shots for him; someone we missed because we thought he was already dead. His name is Derrick Logan, aka, 'D-Lo.'"

"What? The D-Lo is still alive?" asked Dixon as he snickered.

"Not only is he alive but he's been very instrumental in planning and helping the Hookman to distribute weapons and drugs. The Hookman and D-Lo are both ruthless killers, but D-Lo is also a thinker....a planner. Hookman doesn't think about it; he just does it. We've been chasing the Hookman based on how he thinks, when we should have been chasing him by the way D-Lo thinks.

We never knew how D-Lo thinks because we didn't know he was alive. A while ago, during the shoot out in Decatur at the Chevron, we found blood and matched it to Derrick 'D-Lo' Logan. That's when we learned that he was alive, gentlemen, and in the midst of things.

Once our main office knew that we knew about D-Lo being alive, they felt they better advise us they had planted one of our undercovers, right smack in the middle of D-Lo's operations, so we wouldn't mistakenly blow their operation and ruin what they've been working on for years now."

"So how long have our undercover been working with D-Lo?" ask Hardy.

"To my knowledge, a long time now," said Chief. "Before you toss a lot of questions at me that I can't answer, let me introduce you to the only agent that's been able to get close to D-Lo, and Holloway without being killed."

"What...you mean he's here.....now?" asked Hardy! Suddenly, Brenda, who had been with D-Lo, walked in .

"Gentlemen," said Chief Lewis. "I'd like to introduce you to Agent Elisa Smith." All the men stood and clapped as Elisa walked in.

"Good morning, gentlemen," smiled Elisa. "As you've been told, I've been working undercover on this case for some time now. Currently, we are closer to Holloway through D-Lo than we've ever been, due to covert operations. D-Lo have gotten careless a few times since being involved with Holloway, so Holloway will be forced to cut his losses with D-Lo, or financially back D-Lo at a very risky distance."

"What do you mean, 'risky distance?'" asked Bishop.

"Once Holloway trains his leaders, he normally allows them to set up and manage their own operations even though they are using his money to do it. He never gets directly involved. Once profits are made, Holloway collects at a very safe distance, through offshore cash accounts.

Since dealing with D-Lo, Holloway has currently invested ten million dollars and have yet, to see a return on it. A few weeks ago, just as

Holloway personally hand delivered five hundred grand to D-Lo, D-Lo lost it within minutes of delivery."

"What do you mean, he lost it?" asked Dixon.

"D-Lo's bookie was hit and robbed immediately after D-Lo left the negotiation table. D-Lo never saw a dime of that money and it was like Holloway just gave it away," she said.

"Now you're thinking that Holloway have lost so much money by dealing with D-Lo, that he's about to help handle D-Lo's operations himself until he gets his money back?" asked Chief Lewis.

"Bingo!" Elisa said. "When D-Lo lost the last five hundred grand of Holloway's money, he asked Holloway for another five hundred g's to continue the operation. It was then that Holloway asked D-Lo to provide him with a list of all the clientele that wanted merchandise."

"Because Holloway is so worried about his money, is he thinking about delivering the merchandise to the clients himself?" stated Hardy.

"That's what we believe," said Elisa.

"Which means that Holloway has to sign contracts and get directly involved with drugs and illegal shipment and sales of weapons," stated Dixon.

"Right again, agent," said Elisa.

"So what happens to D-Lo and his crew?" asked Bishop.

"We have enough evidence to put D-Lo and his crew away for good," answered the chief. "That is, unless Holloway gets upset and puts him away first."

"And what about Coldblood, Carl Simmons Jr.?" asked Bishop.

"Simmons has been lying really low, lately, and we're not sure of his whereabouts anymore. But he doesn't seem to be tied to D-Lo or Holloway in this case," said the chief. "It's believed that Simmons is tied to a couple of dead gangsters found in the park over two years ago, but we can't prove it, anymore. The only witness we had, suddenly had a change of heart about testifying after she found Jesus and was counseled by her pastor."

"What church does she go to?" asked Dixon.

"Yeah, who's her pastor, that he counsels her against testifying?" asked Hardy.

"She attends a Cobb County Church in Smyrna," said the chief. "Her pastor's name is the Reverend Carl Simmons Sr. ....Coldblood's dad." The agents in the room all got quiet and shook their heads.

"Gentlemen," started Elisa again. "In order for D-Lo to find out who hit him and took the five hundred grand, he has resorted back to some of his old ways, when he was an active gang member. The other day, I saw Hookman Hooks shoot and kill an unarmed man in cold blood."

"Now what?" asked Dixon. "Will he start robbing people, and stealing and destroying property and all that, like gang members do?"

"He's gonna do whatever it takes, so be on the look out for his activities," warned Elisa. Suddenly, an officer walked in and handed the chief a print out.

"I've got to get back before I'm missed, so let's wrap this up," said Elisa.

"As a matter of fact, D-Lo's already started," said the chief. "Last night a string of stores were hit from electronic shops, antique shops, office parks, and other areas. Evidence discovered at one of the stores, places D-Lo's men at the scene of the crime in Clayton County.

But it seems like D-Lo has recruited some new blood to assist him. CSI found evidence of blood and skin on one of the building's overflow drains that was burglarized last night. They believe it to be a woman's." Suddenly, the agents looked at Elisa. She humped her shoulders and said,

"Not mine, I was locked-in last night. Don't know anything about it."

"Why does CSI think that one of the perpetrators is a woman, chief?" asked Bishop. "Blood and skin could be anybody's; even a man's."

"Because the blood and skin was found on a small black piece of women's clothing," he answered. Again, all the agents looked directly at Elisa, who was wearing all black, and looking very sexy. This was their chance to check her out.

"What?" she yelled. Dixon started checking her to see if her clothes were torn. She quickly turned and playfully shoved him away. They all laughed.

"Ok men," started the chief. "It is our goal to wrap this case up as soon as possible because we think our time has come. I want all agents to comb the streets and use all your resources to monitor D-Lo's moves because he's our link to Holloway.

Also, get somebody out to that church and talk to the lady that won't testify against Simmons. Elisa, we've got to leave the rest up to you, for now. That's it, ladies! Let's do what we do and put the bad guys away." They all stood and walked out.

"Agent Shelby and Castleberry, hold on please," said the Chief to the new agents. "Look guys, I want you to take the lead on these thefts and burglaries around town, because I don't think they are all linked to D-Lo. Find out what you can. Also, I've got a reporter or someone that keeps calling me from the papers. Can you handle that for me?"

"We've got you, chief," they said.

"Thanks, fellas."

Chapter 24

Early that Tuesday morning, Donna rushed to her desk and proceeded to plan her day at work. Between her untiring efforts and a few night school courses, Donna, like Tenisha, was now an assistant journalist, helping to develop the story instead of just typing them.

Tyler saw Donna speeding to her desk. "Morning Donna," he said. "Why are you in such a hurry? I bet you've got a lead!"

"Yep, I do," smiled Donna while sitting. "Harry, could you get me a cup of coffee, please?" Tyler just stared at her then he turned to get the coffee. "Wait, Tyler! I'm sorry," apologized Donna. "I shouldn't have called you that. I promise I will quit it as of right now," she added.

"Well, I guess it's ok," said Tyler. "Everybody around here calls me Harry, so I guess I shouldn't expect any different from you."

"Yes, you should!" encouraged Donna. "We are friends and you should expect better of me. And if you want me to call you by your name, then that's what I'll do. Now Tyler, get your ass over there and get me some coffee." They both laughed as Tyler went to get the coffee.

Tyler was the closest friend to Donna in the office and they really trusted and helped each other to complete their work. Tyler Johnson was his real name, but he was kinda geeky, wore glasses, cute, and was a little skinny like Harry Potter. Therefore, everybody at work called him "Harry."

Tyler had gotten used to being called that, but he really didn't like it when Donna did it. He had a slight crush on her and wanted her to like him for who he is, and not make fun of him. He was a year younger than Donna but he was an excellent assistant layout editor for the pages of the AJC. Everybody adored him; well, almost everybody.

"Hello, Harry," said Tenisha. She had seen Tyler and Donna at the desk earlier and she knew something was up by the way Donna rushed in.

Tenisha was a very tall, sexy, young, Caucasian woman, who had done her best to torture Donna and her sisters since high school. Now, Donna and Tenisha were work associates in the same department of the AJC. Tenisha had currently cornered Tyler in the break room in an effort to get information. As she leaned closer to Tyler, she placed her hand in his chest.

"Harry...I mean, Tyler," she said enticingly. "Would you like to hang out with me this morning? I want a chance to show you that we can be friends, Harry...I mean, Tyler. Then you wouldn't have to be a *coffee fetch-boy* like you are for the assistant geek girl," she uttered while speaking of Donna.

"Talking about your mama again, Tenisha?" sounded Donna as she stood behind Tenisha. Although Tenisha was bigger, Donna was not afraid of her and Tenisha knew it. Donna was kinda geeky, sometimes, but she was humorous and welcomed a good fight.

Tyler often found himself being a pawn between Donna and Tenisha, but he was ok with it. Because when it was over, he always got a lot of attention from the other girls, who often wondered why Tenisha and Donna fought over him so much.

"Aw, don't get your panties all tangled up, Geek Girl," said Tenisha as she checked her make up. "Don't worry, I'm not gonna do your boyfriend on the floor."

"I know; that's not your style to get all deep, down, and dirty. That's why I will become a journalist and you will be still assisting, because you don't want to get deep, and dirty with the stories."

"Geek Girl," smiled Tenisha. "With looks like this, why do I need to get down, deep and dirty. Unlike you, I just wait until the story comes to me."

"Silly me," joked Donna. "I should know better than to try and compete with that. Because of a certainty, you body will take you places that your brain never will."

"Oooh!" growled Tenisha. She was so angry as she stood toe to toe with Donna like she wanted to choke her. Then she just hurried back to her desk, and logged into her disk journal.

"I don't think that went to well," said Tyler. "I've never seen her that angry before."

"Don't worry about it, Har...Tyler," she paused. "I enjoyed every second of it, so just be happy for me." Then they went back to work.

"Tyler," whispered Donna. "Have you been keeping up with the raids and thefts going on in the city, lately?"

"Yeah, but that's not your story," he spoke.

"Well, it is now," she said while showing him the story.

"How did you get that?" he questioned! "That story was supposed to get to the Chief Journalist and I know you're gonna get in trouble about it!"

"Tyler, are you gonna help me with this or not?" she pressured.

"Ok, what have you got?"

"For the past week or so, I've been snooping around the police and GBI to learn more about what they are working on. I've got some excellent leads," said Donna. "Turns out, these same leads are related to the police raids, thefts, and burglaries, that's been bombarding the news lately."

"Donna," cautioned Tyler. "That's a huge story! Are you sure you're ready for that? If you mess this up, it could mean a whole lot of trouble, Donna!" Suddenly, Donna heard Tyrone Rogers, the editor, talking to the Chief Journalist.

"Did you get that story I dropped on your desk, yesterday?" Tyrone asked.

"No, what is it about?" asked Mr. Golden.

"I'm not sure because the boss handed it to me and told me to drop it off to you. Something about gangs and thefts and that sort of thing, I think." said Tyrone as he walked away.

Mr. Golden immediately started looking toward all the other journalist and assistants because he knew that one of them had stolen his story. He had been around a while and he was very familiar with how the game works. Donna quickly tucked the story away as Mr. Golden approached her desk.

"Ms. Banks," he started. "Did you take a story from my desk within the last two days? Please don't lie because I'll find out if you are."

"No Sir, I did not," she lied. Tyler looked on from where he was standing. "But I did see Ms. Tenisha Cuyler approach your desk yesterday afternoon as I was leaving," Donna continued. Tenisha had placed some papers on Mr. Golden's desk, but Donna knew Tenisha didn't take the story because she had it. Mr. Golden angrily stormed toward Tenisha as the entire department looked on.

"Ms. Cuyler!" he yelled angrily. "Where is the story you took from my desk?" Tenisha was shocked and confused. "Don't try to deny it!" he raged on. "I know you took it because you were the only one seen near my desk yesterday when I left. Where is the story?"

"Sir, I assure you I didn't take anything from your desk: Honest, I didn't!" she pleaded, as everyone watched.

"Ms. Cuyler," he fussed. "I know how people like you operate! You'll sell your own mother out to get a story in the big league! If I find out that you took this story, Ms. Cuyler, you will have hell to pay! From now on, I will be watching you!" Then he sputtered away, mumbling. Donna was smiling as Tenisha glanced in her direction. Tenisha knew immediately that Donna had taken the story. Again, she was so angry as she stormed to the ladies room. Suddenly, Donna's phone rang, as Tyler came near.

"Hello?" she answered.

"*Ms. Banks,*" said the voice. "I have some photographs of the men that may be tied to the story you are working on."

"Excellent!" shouted Donna. "Can you fax me a copy, now? I'll get the hard copy, later."

"Check your fax," said the voice. "They should already be there by now." Tyler went to the fax as Donna signaled him.

"Thank you," said Donna. "I'll be in touch." Then she hung up. As Tyler brought the photos to her, there were 17 pictures, to include the Hookman and Coldblood. Donna immediately went to work.

Donna felt proud of herself because this story could possibly boost her career and put her in the big league if she did it right. She couldn't see the many lies, manipulations, and deceptions, she was using because it was all part of the game to excel. After a while, Donna headed to the ladies room. She was surprised to see Tenisha still there since Mr. Golden had checked her.

"So!" started Donna. "Is this the 'Glamour Girls' new office now, so that she can watch herself in the mirror while the story come to her?" Tenisha leaned against the sink counter but was briefly silent.

"I have never done anything to you, like that," she said in tears. Tenisha seemed genuinely hurts as Donna looked on, but Donna wasn't buying it.

"In high school," continued Tenisha, "I messed with you a little bit and even now we go at each other, but I have never done anything to jeopardize your life or career. I could have been fired out there, today, for something I didn't do. Why do you hate me so much, Donna? What did I ever do to you?" she cried.

"Ah suck it up, Tenisha, cause I ain't falling for it! The first chance you get to slam me and get ahead, you wouldn't hesitate to seize the opportunity. So why shouldn't I look out for me? Just like you, I'm getting to the top anyway I can. So I suggest you strap on your gloves tighter, because I'm in the ring to stay," convinced Donna. Tenisha was so hurt, she just stared then walked away.

Suddenly, Donna started feeling a rush like she had just won the match in a political arena against her toughest opponent. She was on a high as she paced the bathroom and joyfully talked to herself. Then her joy started turning to bitterness and resentment as Donna wondered what was happening to her. Then she heard over and over again in a still small whisper,

"The curse must be broken...... the curse must be broken.... the curse must be broken...." Eventually, it was so loud, Donna covered her ears and screamed.

Chapter 25

"Nicole, this is a drag," said Tameka. "I've done two heads in four days! I won't be able to afford my space in a minute."

"I'm sorry, Tameka, but we're all going through the same thing," answered Nicole.

It was about noon as the girls sat around the Beauty Shop awaiting for customers to walk in. Business was slow because most of their customers had moved away, or gotten married and moved on.

"Ladies," started Nicole. "There are plenty of heads out there needing to be done, but you've got to get out there and beat the bushes."

"Damn, Nicole!" replied Melody. "How much more beating the bushes can we do? Nobody has money, right now. We know the heads are out there, but what are they gonna pay us with. Besides, I don't see any money in your chair, either, so what bushes are you beating? Whereever they are I need to stay away from those bushes because they ain't working for you,." The other girls hesitated to respond because they knew that Melody could be coldhearted sometimes. But Nicole was their boss and they respected her.

"Look, I'm just saying that sometimes you have to put forth extra efforts in order to get what you want," continued Nicole.

"Nikki, where are your efforts?" scolded Melody. "Why do you keep saying that, when you ain't got nobody, either?"

"Just because you don't see anybody in that chair, don't mean that I haven't made plans to have my needs met."

"What kind of plans do you have, Nicole?" asked Adrienna. "I need to make some plans, too." While they were talking, a taxi pulled to the door and stopped.

"Ok, girls, here we go," said Nicole. "Somebody's about to get lucky, today." As they continued to talk, D'Amica walked in being full of smiles, like everything was right with the world.

"Meca, see who that is getting out of that cab," said Melody. Melody was talking and paid no attention as D'Amica stepped out of the taxi. The other girls had seen all and were shocked. D'Amica was walking tall, plus, she was energetic and upbeat as she spoke.

"Hello, ladies! Lunch is on me, today." She opened her bag and handed out food for all. Nobody said a word as they just stared at each other.

"How are you doing?" smiled D'Amica. Nobody answered. Instead, they just stood there holding sandwiches and staring at each other like they had seen a ghost and was scared to move.

"Meca, did you hit the lottery or something?" asked Tameka.

"No girl, don't be silly. I sure wouldn't be here if I did." They paused again.

"You got a new job, didn't you?" asked Adrienna.

"No, Dreena!"

"You ain't fix' in to die, are you?" questioned Melody.

"No! No! No! What's wrong with y'all?" asked D'Amica. By now, Nicole had taken all she could take.

"What's wrong with us? You're asking, what's wrong with us?" spoke Nicole! "D'Amica, today is Tuesday, and you came in here smiling and stepping high with grocery for everybody, when we know you're broke. Plus, you didn't even show up yesterday cause you said you had something to take care of. For the past few weeks you've been fighting with your boyfriend about money and him not helping you to get on your feet, while you cry on our shoulder.

Finally today,... Tuesday... at 12 o'clock... you come strut'in your sassy ass up through here like you've struck gold and you ask what's wrong with us? D'Amica! What in the hell is wrong with you?" It had been a long time since they heard Nicole speak like that---matter of fact, they had never heard her speak like that, but they were feeling her as they awaited answers.

"Ok, ok!" said D'Amica. "I can't tell you what happened, right now, but I promise I will." All the women went in an uproar because they wanted answers. Nicole quickly did the hand thing and everybody silenced.

"What do you mean, you can't tell us? Why the secrecy?" asked Nicole.

"Nikki, if I could, there would be nothing I'd rather do than tell y'all what happened, but I truly can't, right now. I didn't hit the lottery, I am not rich or nothing like that. I got blessed a little bit, and I am just.....happy."

"You sold that ass, didn't you?" asked Melody.

"No Mel! I didn't. Can y'all just be happy for me, right now? I promise to tell you everything when I can." After another brief pause, Nicole spoke:

"Yeah," she smiled. "I guess we can be happy for you, Meca. It's good to see you being alright." Suddenly, the girls tore into the sandwiches as they laughed and talked. After awhile, all the girls were quiet and hanging out at their stations. Adrienna, being the closest friend to D'Amica, kept wondering about the secrecy. So she just stared at D'Amica while standing next to her. D'Amica read her thoughts and smiled.

"No, it was not Slopp," said D'Amica.

"Coldblood!" whispered Adrienna. D'Amica said nothing, but just smiled.

Chapter 26

About six months later, Cherlene, Donna, and Jennifer, attended a job fair in the ball room of a local hotel. They were not looking for new jobs, but Donna's job had sent her there to do a story, and the sisters came with her.

"Jenny, I'm so proud of you," said Donna as she rubbed Jennifer's pregnant belly. "In two more months, 'pop goes the weasel!' Then I will be an aunt for the second time."

"Yeah, I just wish her dad would be around to help me after she is born," said Jennifer.

"Maybe he will if he can get away from his wife and child, in England," said Cherlene, as she played with Makeda.

"Jenny, do you still want him around, even after you found out that he has a family?" asked Donna. As Jennifer paused, Donna asked, "You still love him, don't you?"

Cherlene cut in. "Dee, the most important thing, right now, is that we are all here for each other, and we are about to be some hellafied mothers. Nobody will be better than us, right Jenny?"

"Right!" smiled Jennifer as they gave each other a high five.

"So Dee," continued Cherlene, "If you want a piece of this motherly action, then you better find a man to help you to be fruitful and multiply."

"Who?" screamed Donna!

"What about Tyler? He wants you," smiled Jennifer. Donna frowned. Then speaking of Cherlene, she said,

"You know what Jenny? You didn't even have your baby, yet, and you're already acting like the mama-bitch over there." They laughed.

"Dee, I'm just saying that he is a man who likes you. Why don't you give him a shot."

"Tyler is my friend; not my stud. I have to go. Bye Keda!" she yelled playfully. "I'll be back in a minute." Cherlene was back in night school, so Jennifer started helping her to study.

****

Meanwhile, upstairs in that same hotel, another conversation was about to take place.

"Um baby, you feel so good," moaned Melody while having sex with Hookman.

"That's what I do, baby," said the Hookman. "I make people feel real good, or real bad; ain't no in-between." After the sex, they lay in bed and smoked a joint.

"Carlton, are the folks still looking for you?"

"What've I told you about calling me that?" he scolded.

"Carlton, that's still your name every since I've known ...." He grabbed her by the throat and choked her...to silence.

"Don't get stupid, Mel," he ordered. "You're pretty good in bed, but you've got a bad mouth, so that makes you bad all over!"

"Ok! ok!" she mumbled. Then he tossed her out of the bed by her throat. Melody wasn't scared as she sprang back onto the bed and hit him. Then she snatched the joint from his lips and smoked it. He was about to slam her down but he knew he didn't need another dead body associated with his name, right now.

"You're pushing your luck, girl, and today is your lucky day."

"Carlton, I need some money. Can you help me?" He just laid there quietly ignoring her.

"OK HOOKMAN!" she emphasized. "I really do need some money. The Beauty Shop is barely keeping us going for the past six months and we've been all struggling."

"So why don't you get another job, baby?"

"Cause it ain't that easy," she continued.

"Then come work with the Hookman."

"And do what, Carlton?" He looked at her body then said,

"Oh Hookman got some work for you, baby. Just get with the Hookman."

"Come on, Carlton, be serious, now. Are you gonna help me?" Hookman reached for his pants, and slid out the bed. After he put them on, he pulled a ball of money and handed Melody three $100.00 dollar bills.

"Carlton, I need one more," she yelled. He just looked at her bitterly with no intentions of giving her anything. "Please, Carlton! This way I can pay Meca back the $200.00 I borrowed from her, and pay my utilities; please, Carlton!"

"Meca? I heard that name before. Ain't she one of the girls you work with?"

"Yeah, she's a white girl and a good person. She's like family to us all," said Melody. "That's why everybody wants to give her the money back."

"So she loaned all y'all money? Is her family rich or something?"

"No, it's nothing like that. She ran into a little change and loaned a few of us a small piece to help us out, like family do. So are you gonna give me the money or not?" Hookman was thinking about Meca and the money she had loaned as he handed Melody another bill. Then he kissed Melody and asked;

"Who is Meca's family... her boyfriend?"

"Why?" asked Melody angrily. "Do you want to be with her, now? You men are such damn dogs, and I can't..."

"No, no, baby," he interjected. "It's just business, that's all. Who's her man?" Melody calmed.

"I don't know him, but I just know his name is Slopp."
Hookman's mind begin to turn as he thought about the money that was
stolen from them at the Chevron that night.

"Could I finally have a lead?" he wondered. He pulled his cell
phone and dialed. "Hey Al," he spoke into the phone. "Grab a couple of
the boys and meet me at the spot. Something's come up and we need to
talk." Then he hung up as Melody lay in bed, listening.

"What kind of business do you have with Slopp?" she asked.

"Oh, it's probably nothing, baby, but I've got to go check it out,
anyway. So how much money did you say Meca loaned you?"

"She loaned everybody two hundred apiece. Why?"

"And it's about 5 of y'all that work that shop, right?" asked
Hookman.

"Ok, so what's that got to do with you, Carlton?"

"Probably nothing, baby, but I've got to check on something. I
may stop by your shop to visit you a little later on, ok? I have to go, now."
She waved and he was out the door. He didn't want to take a chance of
being seen in the elevator, so he took the stairs.

****

"This has been an excellent job fair," stated Donna to one of the
marketers. "We need to have these more often." Suddenly, Hookman
came walking suspiciously out of the stairway and Donna saw him. His
face was partly covered, but she saw enough to know that it was the same
guy whose picture was plastered all over her desk. Hookman cautiously
left the building and walk into the crowd, with Donna stumbling to see
him and where he was going. She quickly ran past Cherlene and Jennifer
as they looked on and wondered.

"Dee!" yelled Cherlene. "What's wrong? Where are you going?"
Donna stopped and turned around.

"It's nothing," she said. "I thought I saw someone, that's all."

"Ok then," started Cherlene. "I'm gonna go in a minute because I
need to get home and finish studying for my upcoming exams." Then she
paused. "What's wrong, Dee?"

"Are you ok?" asked Jennifer.

"Yeah! Really, I'm fine. Hold on a minute. I'll be back." Donna
darted back into the hotel lobby where the Hookman came through and
started looking around. She didn't know what she was looking for, but
she knew that something was there. So she quickly took her camera and
kept it handy.

"What were you doing here, Carlton Hookman?" she asked
herself. *"Were you in a meeting? Hmm? Maybe you have a room here. I
know you wouldn't put it in your name even if you did,"* she thought. *"So
what were you doing here?"*

Since the job fair was about over, the lobby traffic was lightening up and she could easily see suspicious persons. But everybody looked like suspects. Suddenly, the elevator door opened, and Melody hurried toward the exit door.

"Gotcha! Hookman!" she exclaimed. "Sex! A woman! That's why you were here!" She quickly began took snap shots of Melody as she walked away. Cherlene and Jennifer saw her and came running.

"Who is that woman, and why are you taking her picture?" they asked.

"This could be the biggest story of my career!" sighed Donna. "Hold on! I'll be right back." She ran to the hotel desk clerk, with Cherlene, Jennifer, and Makeda behind her.

"Hi, my name is Donna Banks and I'm a journalist for the Atlanta Judicial Chronicle. Would you mind if I asked you some questions?"

"Yes Ma'am, how may I help you?" She pulled her camera.

"Have you seen this woman before?"

"Hmm? Her face looks familiar," he said.

"I just saw her exiting the building about 5 minutes ago," said Donna. "Is it possible that she was a guest here?" The desk clerk immediately went to his computer.

"Now that you mention it, I think she is." Her info soon pulled up on his computer screen. "Ms. Melody Watson, room #223."

"Yes!" yelled Donna. "Can I please have a key?"

"Sorry Ms. Banks, but I can't give you that," the clerk said. Donna handed him a twenty. Moments later, Donna, Cherlene, and Jennifer, were in room #223 looking around while Donna took pictures.

"What exactly are we looking for, Dee?" whispered Cherlene. Donna just stood and looked weird.

Chapter 27

D-Lo and Elisa entered the hide-a-way at the club, when Chesse - one of his main watch dogs - approached him.

"Hey Dawg, I need a word with you, man."

"What's up, Cheese?" asked D-Lo as he stepped away from Elisa.

"Look Bruh, a couple of cops stopped by here, earlier, snooping around and asking questions."

"What kind of questions?"

"Questions about you, Dawg; wanted to know about your car and your work."

"Why did they come here, I wonder?" asked D-Lo.

"That's what I was thinking about," said Cheese. "I don't think it was coincidental that they picked this place."

"I don't either," replied D-Lo. "That means somebody's talking."

"That's the second time that's happened, Dawg. It's time to check the people that's close to you. Are you sure everybody's clean, man?" D-Lo just looked at him angrily, then walked away... wondering. Elisa followed him as they went to the back and sat.

"Is everything alright?" she asked.

"Why wouldn't it be?"

"I don't know. You looked puzzled after your little meeting with Cheese a minute ago."

"Nothing to worry about," he said. Then he quickly snatched her into his arms. "Are you ready to please D-Lo again, baby? It's been a long time now." She was surprised, but didn't resist.

"I'm always ready to please you, D-Lo, but that's not what you pay me for." Then he forced her against the wall and pressed himself against her.

"I know what D-Lo pay you for, Baby Girl; to do whatever D-Lo wants, when he wants."

She spoke carefully now. "I thought we agreed that certain things will be bad for business?"

"I decide what's good or bad for the business!" he yelled. Then he started necking her and rubbing her vagina. She knew she had no choice but to make love to him if he wanted her but she was looking for a way out of it.

"Think! Elisa think!" came her thoughts. As h continued, her mind went back to when she was 14.

Elisa's Memories #I

Young Elisa walked the streets of Atlanta from school one day when a gang of Latinos cornered her.

"Hey, hey! What' s up, black beauty?" *said Arroyo their leader. Elisa was afraid and didn't respond. She wanted to run, but there were many of them and she was too scared. So she walked on and said nothing. Within minutes, they had pushed her down and was tearing her clothes off, right on the side of the road. They hit her and scratched her neck until she became bloody. Suddenly, as one of them laid on her, young D-Lo and his gang showed up and fought against the Latinos. By the time they finished cutting and stabbing each other, only D-Lo and Hookman was left standing. Elisa was so scared, she froze up and couldn't talk.*

"Where do you live?" *D-Lo asked her. Elisa just stood trembling and staring at him, being all bloody. He eventually got her home safely. Two years later, the same gang that rescued her, robbed, beat, and killed, her dad one night, as he was coming home from work. Elisa watched and cried. Her mom had already left her when she was 10. Now D-Lo, who had once saved her, was also the leading man that killed her dad.*

Elisa swore that she would revenge her family from the violence of gangs. Once she became an experienced Agent, and was asked to go undercover to catch Holloway, she had no idea that she would soon be at the right hand of D-Lo.

Some years later, as she and two other young ladies sat at dinner with Mr. Yoder Holloway, men he had trained came to meet with him for business. Time and time, Mr. Holloway would introduce one of the women that he trusted to be the mediator between himself and the new clientele he previously trained. Suddenly, D-Lo walked in.

"Derrick," *he greeted.* "Please pull up a chair."

"Holloway," *greeted D-Lo.* "What have we here?" *speaking of Elisa. She knew who he was, right away, as she supressed her anger and tears. A moment later, she excused herself to go to the ladies room, where she broke down and cried and almost blew her cover. When she returned to the table, that's when her life changed, again.*

"Derrick, this is Brenda Lewis," *started Holloway.* "From this day forward, the only way we will contact each other is through her, unless otherwise changed. She is the only one I will trust because I've trained her as well. However, you are responsible for her safety and well being, as well as her financial stability. She's yours to use how you see fit, as of this moment." *Elisa was mentally shattered! But as an agent, hold-it-together, is what she had been trained to do in moments like these. Therefore, she held it together.*

"I can't help but to think that I've seen you somewhere before," *said D-Lo.*

"Well, I'm not from around here," *she answered.*

"So where are you from, Baby Girl?"

"I'm from a little town called, Albany," *she said. After all the small talk Elisa left with D-Lo, to avoid suspicion. She had been living with Mr. Holloway for over a year now, so she had no other place to stay. She knew she was in trouble.*

On the other hand, D-Lo knew that if Mr. Holloway had recommended someone, then he had checked them out, thoroughly. Elisa had been undercover for over a year, and only made contact with the Agency one time, due to Holloway's security restrictions. Because of this, Mr. Holloway was known for taking good care of his girls.

"So, Baby Girl, you belong to the D-Lo now," *he smiled.*

"Yep! Guess so," *she responded.* "I'm all yours."

"You do know that from now on, you are with me, or in the grave," *he added.* "You can never go back to Holloway or anywhere else until I say so. Is that clear?"

"Clear enough," *she answered. Within two hours, she was in D-Lo's place with D-Lo having sex with her. She laid on her back and took it, and cried.* "I came here to do a job; hopefully, to help you to get rich," *Elisa started.* "But is this all you're gonna need me for.. Sex?"

"You're gonna do whatever I tell you to do!" *he shouted.* "Now get dressed! We've got some people to meet." *For months after that, she tried to accommodate his needs. Night after night, he would take her to bed against her wishes. Eventually, he started having other women, as he got tired of Elisa, and never bothered her sexually again .... until today.(End of Elisa's Mem #I)*

Elisa stood pinned to the wall with D-Lo rubbing and kissing all over her.

"Think, Elisa, think!" *quickly came her thoughts. "You can get out of this!"* Suddenly, the Hookman came busting through the door.

"Damn, man!" yelled D-Lo. "Can't you see that I'm busy?"

"I think I got a lead on who took the money," said Hookman. D-Lo quickly pulled away from Elisa. She had been spared by Hookman.

"What've you got, Bruh?"

"Some girl at a Beauty Shop; broke as hell, suddenly got money to lend and she didn't hit the lottery."

"Wait a minute, man! You think some broad bumped me off for five hundred G's?"

"Of course not," answered Hookman. "But maybe somebody she knows did; a brother or boyfriend."

"So what's the plan, brother?"

"I've got the fellas finding out what they can about her then we'll go from there. This may be nothing or it could be everything," said Hookman.

"Check it out and let me know. But be real discreet about how you handle this," cautioned D-Lo.

"I always handle my business, man, but why the special warning?"

"Cops were here today asking questions."

"Here?" questioned Hookman. "That ain't no coincidence D-Lo! Somebody's talking too much!"

"Either that or we have a snitch!" said D-Lo. Hookman looked surprised.

"Aww hell nawl, man!" he yelled. "This is bad, D-Lo! This is real bad! You got any thoughts, man?"

"I got an idea," said D-Lo. Elisa just watched and said nothing.

"Baby Girl, call Holloway and set up a meeting. We need to talk." Elisa stepped into the room to call Holloway. Afterwards, she took a chance and called Chief Lewis.

"Agent Smith?" he was surprised. *"You're taking a mighty big risk! Are you ok?"*

"Shut up and listen!" she whispered. "My cover may already be compromised, but for now, I am ok. However, there is a young hair designer and her family who may be in trouble."

"What's her name?" asked the chief.

"I don't know," whispered Elisa. "But she's been spending and loaning money and now D-Lo wants answers! Find her quick because something is going down soon and ...." Elisa hung up.

"What's her name?" yelled the chief into the phone, but Elisa was gone because D-Lo walked in. "What's her name?"

"Is everything ok with Holloway, Baby Girl?"

"Everything is set up. He'll meet you tomorrow night," she answered suspiciously.

"I've got to go handle something, so get your coat. But don't worry, we'll finish our business later," he said. Then he left and Elisa followed him.

****

"Ma'am, can you give me your full name?" asked Agent Hardy to the lady at Rev. Simmons's church.

"Reda Monts," answered Rosa. "Reda Mae Monts is my name."

"Ms. Monts, will you please tell us what you saw from your home the night the two gang members were murdered?" asked Agent Hardy.

"Look, I told you that I was mistaken. It was only a couple of kids playing that I saw. As a matter of fact, those same boys were playing on my porch after the killing that night."

"Do you think they saw anything, Ms. Monts?" asked Shelby.

"If they did they didn't say anything to me. Been so long, I can't even remember their names."

"Thank you Ma'am. You have a nice day." Then they walked away.

"She's clearly got selective amnesia," said Shelby. Rosa just watched them then continued sweeping the church doorsteps. She knew they were still trying to get her to testify against Carl Sr.'s son, Coldblood.

Chapter 28

Later that night, the Hookman sat at a table with babes in a local night club. After awhile, Al, Booley, and Big Jake, walked in and sat with the Hookman.

"Is this the spot?" asked Hookman.

"Yes, this is the spot," said Al. "I'm told he comes around on Friday nights."

"Ok, break it down to me one more time so I'll know what I'm dealing with," instructed Hookman.

"They call him, Slopp, because he's a big, nasty dude who don't care about nothing or nobody. His real name is Eugene Harris and he works at the tire shop on Campbellton Rd.," explained Al.

"This cat ought not to have a lot of money, right?"

"Not if he works at a tire shop," said Al.

"Ok, let's wait and talk to him." A couple of hours later, Slopp showed up with a girl on his arm while yelling,

"Hey! Hey! Night Crawlers! Tonight is your lucky night! Slopp is in the house just for you. All drinks are on me!" The Hookman immediately stood with a very mean look.

"This don't look good," whispered Al to Booley. Hookman quickly dialed D-Lo.

"I think I may have a lead to your money."

"Bring him in and let's talk to him," responded D-Lo.

Moments later, Al, Big Jake, Booley, and the Hookman, were dragging Slopp's lifeless body, along with the girl, into an abandon building. Slopp was unconscious and so was she. Both their clothes had been removed.

"Tie 'em up and sit them in chairs facing each other," instructedd Hookman. "Then wake 'em up." Slopp and the girl were shocked when they opened their eyes.

"What the hell is going on?"yelled Slopp. He immediately rebelled as he used his weight in an attempt to destroy the chair and free himself. Al and Booley punched him in the face but he continued to struggle. Suddenly, Hookman pulled his revolver as Al and Booley stepped back.

"Just chill a minute, brother," said Hookman calmly. "We just want to ask you a few questions then, we are gonna let you go."

"You think I'm scared of you 'cause you have a gun?" fussed Slopp. "You better shoot me cause when I get free, you're gonna wish you had!"

"Ok," said Hookman. Then he shot him in the foot.

"Aahhh!" screamed Slopp. But he still tried hard to free himself and fight back. As Andre entered, the girl was so afraid, she couldn't speak as she cried and shook like a leaf.

"What did you find out about the girl, Dre?" asked Hookman.

"She's clean," answered Andre. "Just a date looking for a good time." Hookman nodded as Big Jake quickly punched her and she passed out. D-Lo slowly walked in.

"What do y'all want?" yelled Slopp.

"To ask you some questions," said D-Lo. Booley and Big Jake carefully slid brass knuckles onto their hands. "Back there in the club, you bought everybody drinks.. where did you get the money to do that?"

Before Slopp met D'Amica, he was working at the tire shop when a jack gave way, and a car fell on his knee. It had been a few months since he filed his worker's comp lawsuit, but today, it had paid off, twelve thousand dollars. But Slopp, being arrogant and proud, didn't tell D-Lo that.

"It's my money and I've earned every dime of it," said Slopp. Booley and Big Jake slammed the brass knuckles into his jaw. Slopp almost passed out.

"Back at the club you would have easily spent $500.00 on drinks, tonight. I don't know of a tire shop that pays that kind of money. So now I'm gonna ask you again, where did you get the money; it's a simple question?" asked D-Lo.

"If I had pulled it out of your ass, you'd know where I got it from, but I told you that I worked for it; I've earned it!" yelled Slopp. By now, Booley and Big Jake had completely disfigured his face and he could hardly speak.

"Last chance, brave heart," said D-Lo. "Where did you get the money?"

"I ..... I ..... earned ..... it," mumbled Slopp.

"How did you earn it?" yelled D-Lo! Then D-Lo stopped the beating and talked to him again, calmly. "Somebody stole five hundred G's of my money and I'm just trying to get some of it back. Do you have my money, son?" Slopp painfully whispered,

"My ... money."

"Do you know where 'MY MONEY' is?" D-Lo yelled angrily. Hookman lifted his weapon as Slopp attempted to answer the best he could.

"If .... if .... it....was... up .... your .... ass ..." Suddenly, Hookman pulled the trigger and blew a hole in Slopp's head. Two shots had been fired so the police were there quickly as D-Lo and his men ran out. The girl awakens to see Slopp's lifeless body and she screamed.

Chapter 29

"Ma'am, did they say what they wanted?" asked Dixon.

"No," she answered hysterically. "They just kept saying they wanted to ask me some questions."

"Did they ask you any questions?"

"No. Some guy walked in and the next thing I know, I was out cold. The next thing I saw was him, when I woke up." She pointed to Slopp's body.

"Ma'am, can you take a look at these pictures and tell us if any of these men were here tonight?" asked Bishop. As she checked the pictures, she identified Hookman, Al, Booley, Big Jake, and Andre. "Thank you, Ma'am, we'll be in touch." The men walked away.

"So what do you think?" asked Dixon.

"This is certainly D-Lo and the Hookman's M.O.," answered Bishop. "The girl said that his name was Eugene Harris, but they call him Slopp. They kidnapped them from a local club outside of town. Agents Shelby and Castleberry are there now asking questions."

****

"Does Slopp come here often?" asked Castleberry.

"Every weekend," said the bartender. "He was here earlier tonight with some new chick."

"Does he have a regular girl that he comes with?" asked Shelby.

"Slopp has a girl, but nobody is regular with him because of his short fuse: Don't take much to get the guy worked up. Why all the questions? Is he in some kind of trouble?"

"No," answered Shelby. "He's dead. Tell us more about this girl he has that's not a regular."

"Well, her name is D'Amica or Meca or something like that. I've seen her in here a couple of times and she seems to be a sweet girl; does hair or something like that."

"You wouldn't know where she lives, would you?" The bartender checked his mirror where he sometimes allows customers to leave their business cards.

"Here's her card. Today is your lucky day."

****

A few minutes later, Agents Dixon and Bishop approached D'Amica's building.

"Yes?" she responded to the buzzer.

"Ms. D'Amica Taylor?"

"Yes?"

"Ma'am we are agents Dixon and Bishop of the G.B.I. and we'd like to have a word with you." D'Amica came to the door. When the agents saw her they were surprised. They had forgotten they talked with her over a year ago.

"Ms. Taylor," spoke Bishop. "You've become a very popular person within the past two years."

"Oh yeah?" she spoke. "I remember y'all, too. Is this about Coldblood? Cause I don't have a clue where he is."

"No Ma'am, we would like to ask you some questions about another friend of yours. His name is Eugene Harris."

"What? Slopp?" she sounded. "What did Slopp do?"

"Were sorry, Ma'am, but we found Eugene's body tonight in an abandoned warehouse," answered Dixon. "We were wondering if there is anything you can tell us that may help us to find out who did this." D'Amica was slightly in tears, but she remained calm.

"I've only seen Slopp a couple of times over the past six months and he didn't tell me anything about any trouble he was in."

"Were you guys dating?"

"No, he broke it off about six months ago. Since then, I don't know what's been going on in his life."

"Ma'am, have you ever heard the names of Carlton Hooks called the Hookman, or Derrick Logan called D-Lo?"

"No, who is that?"

"That'll be all, Ma'am; thank you for your time. If you think of anything at all that might be helpful to us, please give us a call." D'Amica took Dixon's card and they left.

"The world is really getting smaller, Dix," said Bishop. "How strange it is to run into the same woman in two different cases. I could understand if she were a suspect, but an innocent? Now that's strange."

"I agree. We'd better keep a closer watch on this one," added Dixon. "Things ain't always as pretty as they seem."

Chapter 30

It was a Friday morning as Jennifer was home preparing to go to work for her last day before her maternity leave starts. She was due to be at work by noon. After today, she would have one month until her child came. A sonogram has already revealed that she would have a girl, so Jennifer was leaning toward naming her Audrey.

Four months after Jennifer knew that she was pregnant, Mitch was seen on TV, by Donna, with his wife and child being recognized as one of the safest pilots of the American Airways. During his next visit to see Jennifer, she immediately kicked him out. By now, Jennifer had become one of the best professional thieves in the state. But her activities had been at a minimum due to her pregnancy. As she prepared for work, her phone rang.

"Hello, Cheryl; what's up?" she answered.

"Jenny I need a favor. I've changed my mind about leaving Keda at the center while I attend night school and I want you to keep her."

"Cheryl you know I would, but what happens to her if I go into labor?"

"Then I will put her in the center. But, right now, I don't trust a few of the new teachers to take care of her when I am not around."

"Ok, I'll do it. When do we start?"

"Well, that's another thing," continued Cherlene. "I'm gonna ask you something and I want you to think about it. Will you consider moving in with me until you have the baby? That way, we can look after each other and I won't have to wake Makeda at night when I get home from class."

"Cheryl, I love that idea but what about Terry....and Tom, Dick and Harry?" Jennifer joked.

"Jenny, please, don't start with me. Besides, I'm the boss so until this is over, it's you, me, Keda and... Oh! Have you concluded on a name for your baby girl, yet?"

"Yeah, I think I'm gonna name her, Audrey."

"Then until this is over, it'll be you, me, Keda, and Audrey." said Cherlene. "We can move you this weekend."

"Sounds like a plan. I've gotta go to work, Cheryl. Talk with you later." As Jennifer hung up the phone, Donna drove up and blew the horn. For the past two months, Donna drove Jennifer to work and home again because of her pregnancy.

"Hi, Dee." Jennifer wobbled to the car and stepped in.

"Hi, Jenny." Jennifer tried to sit comfortably as Donna laughed.

"What?" asked Jennifer.

"I'm just still not used to seeing you like this," smiled Donna.

"Well, hopefully soon, your time is coming."

"Do you really think so, Jenny?" Jennifer detected discouragement in her words. "I'm saying, I don't even get a man to flirt with me or talk or even look at me."

"Men ain't all that so don't let *not having one* decide how you're gonna be as a person."

"That's easy for you to say. Look at you; all swollen with some guy's child inside you."

"Yeah, and look what it's gotten me," complained Jennifer. "Now I'm about to be a single mom. Let's talk about this later, Dee. Tomorrow, I'm moving in with Cheryl until I have the baby. That way, I can also keep Keda while Cheryl finishes school. You come over and we can all stay together and talk through the weekend."

"Ok, cool," said Donna as she pulled to Jennifer's job. "See you this evening."

"Thanks Dee, I'll see you, tonight."

"Bye." Donna drove off as Michelle came running to greet Jennifer.

"Hi Jenny, Jenny, Jenny!" smiled Michelle as she rubbed, Jennifer's stomach. "Today is the last day I get to see you here until you're holding little Audrey in your arms. "

"Yeah, I guess so," smiled Jennifer. After being at work for a couple of hours, Jennifer heard Michelle questioning some young woman who apparently had stolen something.

"What is it that you put in your coat?" she asked the woman. "Do you want me to call security? Because if I do, you will go to jail! Now show me what you took from my counter." The woman was afraid as she lifted a necklace from her pocket and handed it to Michelle.

Jennifer entered the counter area behind Michelle and quickly pocketed a more expensive, more beautiful, necklace than the one the lady had stolen. The woman looked desperately in need of help and Jennifer knew that she took the necklace just to sell it.

"I should call security anyway," continued Michelle. "What do you think, Jenny?"

Jennifer approached the woman and pretended to be checking her. Then she slipped the more expensive necklace into the woman's pocket and said,

"Nah just let her go; no harm done. We have the jewelry back." The woman was shocked as she sped out of the store. She was puzzled by what Jennifer had done.

Chapter 31

It was about 9 a.m. Friday morning when Elisa awakened.

"Where am I," she wondered. Everything looked strange as she sat up in bed and yawned. It was secluded but where she slept was very nice. Yesterday, D-Lo had her to set up a meeting with Holloway, and for the first time, she was not invited. Instead, she was told to go with one of Holloway's men while D-Lo and his guys handled some business during the night. She knew they were looking for the young hair designer whom she had notified the Chief about, but she had no idea that they had killed Slopp. While traveling with Holloway's man the night before, she was told that the hide-a-way at the club was hot, and they needed to relocate.

"Where are we going?" she asked.

"To one of Mr. Holloway's spots," came the reply. At first, she was a little afraid that her cover was blown and he was going to kill her. She had almost pulled her weapon when the man spoke again. "Your boss, D-Lo, must be very well liked, because Mr. Holloway never allows anyone to stay at his private place where you're going." Elisa slowly removed her hand from her pistol. The driver sounded sincere and didn't seem to watch her in any way. She knew he could possibly be disarming her mentally and he was doing an excellent job.

"So why am I going there?"

"Don't you know? You have to take that up with your boss." Elisa was puzzled and didn't know what to do. But she knew she had come too far with this case to just give up now.

"Well, I guess we'll just have to see then," she said.

Later on into the night, she knew that her life was not in danger, but D-Lo was relocating because of the heat that was on the previous hide-a-way.

Mr. Holloway and D-Lo had completely trusted her for years now, but it was a rule that no one was to ever be left alone unless authorized by Holloway or D-Lo. In all the time she had been on this case, she had only been allowed to venture alone, twice. Each time she had reported in personally to her headquarters.

Last night, as she entered the new hide-a-way, it seemed small from the outside. But once inside, it was quite spacious and very comfortable. She was surprised to find Q'Ball living there. The man, who had driven her there, took the bedroom next to hers. She had slept very well as she freshened up and walked to the kitchen to find something to eat.

"What's up, Baby Girl?" spoke D-Lo who was sitting in the living room chair with a bottle in his hand. Elisa was startled.

"Where did you come from? I didn't see you there," she said calmly.

"Don't worry, Baby Girl, cause I see you, though."

"Oh, my goodness! Here we go again," she thought. She was dressed in a nice blue night gown with a matching robe, which was open in the front. She knew that D-Lo was about to sexually assault her, but she was hoping that she was wrong. As she opened the refrigerator door, she felt his hand on her butt, then he slid it around and between her legs.

"I told you we have some unfinished business, and I'm about ready to finish it up," he smiled. Elisa was furious but she contained her anger.

"Lord, this is the man that killed my Daddy and even sperm his semen in me night after night when I didn't want it. Why Lord, why me?" she prayed silently. Suddenly, Hookman and two men walked in, and D-Lo backed away. Elisa quickly went to her room and got dressed. She could hear them talking.

"I'm still wondering if we got the right guy," spoke Hookman. "I get the feeling that we made the right connection, but something is still missing."

"Didn't you say that you got only one last night?" asked Q'Ball. "There had to be two that hit us that night. There's no way one man could hit the kid, then move to my side of the car that fast and hit me."

"You're right," said D-Lo. "He had a partner."

"We have to visit the girl," said Hookman. "She knows what's up."

"Not so fast," ordered D-Lo. "We'll get to her in time. We've waited this long so a few more days won't matter. Meantime, place a couple of the boys at the funeral and see who shows up. Also, find out who stands to get paid insurance money from his death. We can also get some of my money back that way."

"Funeral? Death? Insurance?" wondered Elisa. *"Who did they kill?"*

"This is a nice spot," said Hookman as he looked around. Elisa walked in.

"I need to go pick up a few things." she said.

"Like what?" asked D-Lo."

"Things! Food! and what-nots for this place. If I'm gonna be living here, I need those things." After a pause D-Lo walked to her and whispered,

"Whatever you need to get yourself ready for D-Lo, you better get, because your ass is mine as soon as you get back. Take her to get what she needs, Q'Ball." They went to the van and left.

Chapter 32

A week had gone by since Jennifer took off for maternity leave and moved in with Cherlene and Makeda.

"Keda, how would you like to take a bath with Aunt Jenny this morning?" asked Jennifer. "Your mom is rushing about so much, till she just don't have time for us."

"I'm sorry," said Cherlene. "But I'm almost late for my study group. I'll make it up to you guys later, though... I promise." Then she was out the door! Cherlene was only weeks from becoming a certified teacher in the state of Georgia. Her exams had started so she took a few days from work to study and prepare for her finals and the teacher's certification. Normally, she was having sex at least once a day, but she was excited and hadn't had sex in weeks.

Jennifer, on the other hand, couldn't wait to have her baby so she could resume her nightly activities. She didn't want a child in the first place but being around her niece, Makeda, had helped her to love her own. She knew she would be a good mother after watching Cherlene for almost 2 years, now. She was desperate to get back into the world and continue her life, but her stomach had grown so big. There were times when she wanted to move little things when she went out, but her stomach often drew a lot of unwanted attention, when she didn't know that people were watching her. She was careful not to touch anything, but many times it just happened.

"Come on, Keda. It's time to take our bath." Makeda was a very energetic child who looked just like her mom. Terry, her dad, didn't live with them but he often came over to see her and to be with her mom. Lately, Terry had been working out of town and was home only a few days at a time. This was working out good for Cherlene because she didn't have to be so careful about being with other men when she had the time.

Donna, on the other hand, was really becoming a force to be reckoned with at her job.

Like Tenisha, she was very beautiful and could easily pass for a supermodel. Plus, she was very smart and learning well how to manipulate others in order to get what she wanted. She didn't trust anybody except her sisters and Tyler, but many times she was a little bit overly ambitious. As a result, Donna was becoming very selfish and her views were often one-sided. Currently, Donna and Tyler rode together in search of the Beauty Shop. Donna felt that she was hot on the trail of Carlton "Hookman" Hooks, so she wanted to talk to Melody Watson, whom she had seen at the hotel that day.

"Tyler, I'm telling you that she was with him in that hotel."

"Why are you so sure?" asked Tyler.

"Because me and my sisters went up to her room when she left and it smelled like straight ass! She had been having sex and the only man that was up there was the Hookman!"

"But how do you know it was him?"

"Because I never forget a face! His face has been all over the news and in police precincts and it is also on my desk. I could never mistake that face!"

"Well, I hope you're right, because we're here at the Beauty Shop."

"Ok," Donna said excitedly. "Just pull to the curb over there." She fixed her hair and makeup then asked, "How do I look?"

"Donna, you're going into a Beauty Shop. I don't think you're suppose to look good on your way in," Tyler joked. "It's what you look like when you come out that matters." By now, the ladies in the Beauty Shop were peeking through the windows.

****

"Who is she?" asked D'Amica. "She looks like a model or something."

"I doubt that," injected Adrienna. "Because she's in our hood."

"And what's wrong with our hood?" asked Nicole.

"We're broke as hell," laughed Tameka. "Ooh! Ooh! Wait-a-minute y'all! I think she's coming in here!"

Donna left the car and was coming toward the shop. The girls in the shop scrambled to their areas and acted busy as she entered.

"Good morning," greeted Nicole. "Honey, you don't look like you came to get your hair fixed. So how may I help you?" Donna knew right away that she was busted. Tyler had warned her that she would be a dead give-a-way because of her dress and her hair, but she wouldn't listen. Now, she stood frozen while looking stupid and feeling uneducated about how to respond.

"Uh, excuse me for a minute!" Donna sped back to the car where Tyler was and jumped in.

****

"What happened in there?" asked Tyler.

"Oh my God! I have never felt so stupid!" cried Donna. "I froze up."

"You did what?"

"Tyler, I completely froze up!"

"Donna, what's so different about them that you and your big mouth can't handle?"

"You're right," she said after thinking about it. "But they seem so calm in there; really cool and down to earth. I could feel the experience as soon as the one lady spoke to me and I didn't know what to say. She would make a heck of a journalist because she seems very wise."

"In other words, she read you like a book, so you tucked tail and ran, didn't you?" joked Tyler.

"Aw, shut up!" she scolded.

****

The women in the Beauty Shop were puzzled as Donna abruptly left and they watched her through the window. Nicole was more inquisitive, but the rest were hysterical and comical.

"Damn... she *strutted* in here, but she *popped* right out," laughed Tameka.

"So, does that make her *Sally Struthers* or *Mary Poppins*?" joked D'Amica. "Who was that woman?"

"More like the young Ms. Daisy," whispered Nicole while watching Donna. "She's out there talking with her driver now."

"Nicole, I like that," laughed Adrienna. "You've got jokes with your old school self! Except Ms. Daisy had a black driver; that dude is white." They continued to peep and joke while wondering what would happen next.

****

"O.K., I'm going back in there!" said Donna boldly. Then she unbuttoned her top button, loosen her blouse, and attempted to look raggedy. Finally, she took her hands and rambled them through her hair like she was washing it, until it looked terrible. "So, how do I look, now?" Tyler was so shocked as he just stared at her.

"You look..." he paused... "like a story... that I'm sure Tenisha would take pleasure in writing." Donna grabbed her purse and quickly marched back inside the Beauty Shop while the girls inside scrambled back to their chairs as usual.

"Hi," smiled Donna. "It's me again." The girls were looking stunned.

"We never knew who you were the first time," smiled Nicole. "Oh! I'm sorry. My name is Donna Banks."

"Ok, Ms. Donna Banks. How can I help you?"

Donna hesitated. "Can you do something with this?" pointing to her hair. Nicole just shook her head and smiled.

"Come on over here, Ms. Banks, and sit down. Let's see what we can do." Donna sat in Nicole's chair while they small talked. Donna really enjoyed listening to the girls joke about men and life. It was a feminine but really cool environment, she thought. She knew she had to break away from her personal feelings and focus on the business at hand.

"I see that you have an empty chair over there," said Donna. "Does this mean that all the girls are not here today?"

"That's Mel's chair," answered Nicole.

"Mel?" questioned Donna.

"Yeah, short for Melody," answered Tameka. "She's off today handling some..." Nicole quickly gave her a look and Tameka hushed. Donna knew that Nicole had silenced Tameka. Nicole was wise, so she knew Donna wasn't there to get her hair done.

"Why do you ask?" continued Nicole. "Are you interested in doing hair?"

"Oh no!" laughed Donna. "I just saw your empty chair and wondered who was missing in this wonderful atmosphere you have here. I really like it."

"Thank you, Ms. Banks."

"Would you call me, Donna... please? I'm not used to being called, Ms. Banks, unless someone is yelling at me."

"Ok... Donna... thank you," said Nicole. "We'd like to think we have a family atmosphere around here because it tends to make our customers feel right at home. And home is where everybody wants to be."

"I guess nobody wants to be home, today," Donna said. "There's no one here." Tameka and Adrienna laughed, but Nicole and D'Amica didn't feel the humor in her words. Nicole yanked her hair. "Ow!" yelled Donna. D'Amica chuckled.

"So... Donna... what are you really doing here?" asked Nicole.

"I came to get my hair done," she lied. Nicole just stared at her. "Hey, have you seen the news, lately?" Donna attempted to change the subject. "This Hookman guy is a real predator. What do you all think about it?" Everybody just kinda mumbled.

"Don't really know what to think about it," answered Nicole. "Just somebody's son gone bad."

"Hmm? Wonder what Melody would think?" Donna slid it in. The question made her look transparent as everyone gave her a stare.

"Do you know Melody?" asked Tameka.

"No, I don't, but..."

"Then why do you *'wonder'* what she thinks about somebody she doesn't even know?" asked Adrienna while cutting in.

"Well, I didn't mean it like that," defended Donna.

"So how did you mean it, then?" asked Tameka. Donna started fumbling her words.

"You're up to something, Ms. AJC," said D'Amica. "Why don't you just come clean and tell us what's up?" Everybody stood waiting as Nicole spoke.

"That ought to just about do it, Ms. Banks. Your hair is fine now."

"Donna... please call me, Donna."

"No, we call our friends and family by their first names but you, Ms. Banks, have to learn how to be a friend first. That'll be $35.00 for the do." Donna paid her. "Have a nice day, Ms. Banks." Then they started talking to each other like she wasn't even there.

****

Meanwhile, Cherlene is at the library studying to take the biggest exams of her life. She's been in night school since shortly after the birth of Makeda and the big day has come. She had passed all of her exams and now she's preparing for her teacher's certification. Suddenly, she heard the whisper... *"The Curse Must Be Broken!"* She quickly looked about.

"Hello, young lady," spoke a strange voice. "Mind if I join you?" Cherlene looks to see a 6 foot 3, well-built, 250 pound hunk. She pretended to ignore him.

"If you're looking for the study group, they're on the other side."

"Then why are you over here?" he asked.

"Because I thought I could group study but I can't. I do better alone..."

"Or maybe with just one other person," he added while cutting in. "I have the same problem and that's why I'm not with a study group." Cherlene knew she needed to be alone, but it had been weeks since she'd gotten that close to a man-- especially one as fine as this one.

"Okay, you can sit for 5 minutes. But if it doesn't work out, do you promise to leave?"

"I promise," he assured. "My name is Michael Byrd; friends call me 'Big Byrd.'"

"Ok, Big Byrd, have a seat; I'm Cherlene." Big Byrd took a seat. Then he and Cherlene began to talk about the certification exam and what was expected of them. After they studied for a few hours, they began to just talk.

"So do you like family?"

"Love family," answered Cherlene. "I have two sisters and a daughter and we're all very close. What about you?"

"I don't have any family around here but I do have a son that I love very much. He's only 3 years old."

"Where's his mother?"

"She died giving birth so I'm a single parent."

"Oh, I am so sorry. So who keeps your son while you are at work or school?"

"He lives with my mom in Mississippi where I am originally from. His name is Cedric; C-Lo for short."

"What was his mom's name?"

"Her name is Patricia but I called her Pat. She was an excellent woman. We were gonna be married as soon as C-Lo was born but..."

"I understand," said Cherlene as she began to tell him bits and pieces of her life. Back at the apartment, Jennifer and Makeda were playing hide and seek when suddenly, she began to have labor pains.

"Aahhh!" Jennifer's water broke so she knew her moment had come. She made her way to the phone and called Cherlene as she screamed in pain.

"Hello Jenny," answered Cherlene. "Is everything okay?"

"Uh!" cried Jennifer. "She's coming! Audrey is coming!"

"Ok! Ok! I'm on my way!"

"Call Dee!" yelled Jennifer.

"Ok!" screamed Cherlene. Then she turned to Byrd. "My sister is having her baby and I have to go! I'd like to see you again, sometimes, but for now I have to go!" As she ran to her car, she called Donna, who had just left the Beauty Shop. "Jenny is having the baby!" she yelled. "Meet us at the hospital!"

"Oh my God!" screamed Donna. "Let's go, Tyler: Hurry! Jenny is having the baby!" Tyler sped off and they all met at the hospital. Jennifer delivered a very healthy 7 ½ pound girl. Her name is, Audrey R. Sweet.

Chapter 33

The next day after Audrey is born, Donna happily strode across the floor of her job.

"I am an Auntie .... again!" she yelled.

"That's great, Donna," smiled her editor and the rest. Tenisha just stared at her for a moment. Then she went over to Donna's desk.

"You seem happy?"

"I am very happy," replied Donna.

"Then I am happy for you, too," answered Tenisha. "Congrats on your niece!"

"Thank you, oh most evil one!" replied Donna. "Now you can scoot back to your desk because there is no story over here for you to steal," she added. Since the ladies room talk, Donna had been really hard on Tenisha. So hard, she couldn't see that Tenisha had become afraid of how far she would go to hurt her. Therefore, Tenisha tried to be her friend but her ambition blinded her eyes and she was treating most people the same way she treated Tenisha—bad or indifferent! But Tenisha wasn't giving up.

"Donna, why is it that you always think I am after something..."

"Because you are!" Donna yelled while cutting in. "That's your way, Tenisha, and you will never change! When we were in school, you and your posse stole my lunch, you took my sister Jenny's shoes, and you held Cherlene down and took her panties. Then you gave them to the boys in the science class for experimenting. I don't trust you, Tenisha. So get out of my face!"

Donna was used to Tenisha having some really strong words to come back with because that's just how they did it. But this time, Tenisha just walked away. As a matter of fact, ever since Donna made Mr. Golden believe that Tenisha stole his story months ago, she hadn't fought Donna since. This was a wake-up call for Tenisha and it changed her life. Tenisha had a good heart and it was beginning to show. The truth was also beginning to show about Donna.

"I think I'm gonna print a story about all the hard-working moms who are daily giving birth to babies while the men just run off and do whatever," yelled Donna.

"Who wants to read about that?" responded the editor.

"Oh you would be surprised, Sir! You would be surprised!"

"But Donna," started Tyler. "Don't you think it would be better for a working mother to help you with that story? You are not a mom so you are a bit out of your league... don't you think?"

"Okay, Tyler, so who do you have in mind to help me?"

"How about Tenisha?" Donna was surprised and stared at him.

"Harry Piss-Poor-Potter!" she exclaimed. "I thought you were my friend!"

"Donna, I am your friend, but Tenisha has been trying to be your friend, too. She doesn't like fighting with you, Donna. Can't you see that?"

"So she's gotten to you, huh?"

"Nobody's gotten to me, Donna, but you need to let someone get to you. I love you, Dee," he said. "If I didn't I wouldn't be telling you this." Then he walked away. Donna angrily marched over to Tenisha's desk. Tenisha was busy and didn't see her coming.

"Ms. Cuyler," spoke the editor to Tenisha. "Here is a story about quite a few Cobb county thefts that's taken place over the past few months. Most malls and shopping centers seem to think they've had a sudden increase in thefts and want to talk to someone about a story," he continued. "Many of the business owners have met and all decided to increase security in one way or another. The interesting thing is they all see a pattern and believe that these thefts are being done by a group or one hell of an individual. I think this will be quite a story when they catch this guy. Do you want it?"

"Yes Sir, I want it." said Tenisha. He handed it to her and walked away. Then she saw Donna.

"So, Glamour Girl..." started Donna. "You just don't quit, do you?" Tenisha was confused as Donna paraded around her desk like a prosecuting attorney.

"What are you talking about?"

"You know damn well what I'm talking about so, don't play stupid!" accused Donna. "You can pull the wool over everybody's eyes in this place, but you can't fool me and you never will. In school, Dapp was the only boy that had interest in me and you took him. Now, you know that Tyler is my friend and somehow you've managed to make him believe that I am the bad guy," she continued. "Evil one! Believe me when I tell you that I will stop you. Somehow, I'm gonna bring you down if it's the last thing I do!" Then she sped off with Tenisha being more confused.

"That was really, really big of you, Donna," Tyler said disappointedly.

"What?" asked Donna while standing like she was innocent.

"Yep! You really told her off this time. Fact is, you were the only one in school that didn't know that Dapp was gay- he liked men!" Again Donna felt stupid as Tyler walked away and she heard... *"The Curse Must Be Broken!"* Donna flinched, looked about, and innocently walked back to her desk.

Chapter 34

"My Lord!" said Melody. "What did I do to get to see you twice in one month? Normally, you don't show up but twice a year or so, and then it's in a motel. So, what's up? Are you sick or something? Or am I just that good?"

"Aww Baby, I was in the hood and thought about you, so I dialed you up," said Hookman.

"I'm not used to you calling me and taking me to lunch. Hell, when you want me, normally, I am your lunch," she joked. "I can handle this, though. It's been a long time since anybody treated me like a lady."

Hookman was so bothered by the mistake they made by killing Slopp, that he couldn't rest. It seemed that Slopp may have been innocent, but Hookman had enough experience to know that he was on the right trail. He wanted to confront D'Amica, but D-Lo had told him to be patient and stay away for a while. He had never gone against D-Lo's wishes and he wasn't about to start. But he couldn't rest and he needed answers. Therefore, he called Melody and invited her to lunch, so they could talk. He couldn't afford to be out in the open so he had her come to a local club where lunch was being served.

"Go ahead and place your order, baby. You know the Hookman's got you." Melody blushed.

"Carlton, are you trying to become a gentlemen or something? So tell me the truth, Carlton, what's this all about?"

"I wanted to ask you a few questions about something you said, that's all."

"Questions about what?"

"You said that your friend Meca loaned everybody in your shop a few bills, is that right?"

"Yeah, so what's this about?"

"Nothing baby, it's just that I have a good friend that's interested in her and he wants me to find out what I can about her," said Hookman.

"Well, she ain't rich if that's what your friend is thinking," defended Melody. "I told you she was just blessed with a few dollars and that's it. She needed that money because she's a white girl with a black son and nobody was gonna help her."

"So how old is her son?"

"Shaun is about 8 or 9 years old. But tell your friend he don't have to worry about that. Shaun is a good kid and loves his dad. If your friend wants to talk to Meca, Shaun won't be a problem."

"I stopped by Meca's boyfriend's funeral and I didn't see her there," said Hookman. "Why didn't she take her son to his dad's funeral?"

"What? Is Coldblood dead?" she sounded.

"Is that his name, Coldblood?" asked Hookman. "You told me his name was Slopp." Hookman reached into his pocket and pulled an obituary. "It says here that his name was Eugene 'Slopp' Harris. Who in the hell is Coldblood?"

"Coldblood is Carl, Jr. That's Meca's baby daddy—not Slopp. Why would you be at Slopp's funeral? Did you know him?"

"I met him once before he died," smiled Hookman. Melody looked shocked then she placed her hand over her mouth.

"Carlton! You killed him, didn't you? You killed Slopp? Why? What did he do?"

"Evidently, he or this Coldblood, Carl Jr. fellow, took something that didn't belong to them."

"Carlton, what did they take?"

"I've a better question. Where can I find this Coldblood guy? Seems like I've heard that name before but I can't remember where."

"Coldblood is just like you... running from the police. What did he take, Carlton?"

Hookman stood and laid a $20 bill on the table. "I've got to go, baby. You've been a big help. Tell your friend, Meca, that my friend will probably be holl'in at her, soon." Then he left. Melody sat and finished her lunch while she thought about all that was just said. She was slowly putting the pieces together.

"So that's where Meca got all that money," she thought. *"Either Slopp or Coldblood stole it and gave it to Meca. That's why she couldn't tell us where she got it. But it had to be Coldblood that gave her the money because she had broken it off with Slopp. That's why she kicked Slopp out and let Coldblood spend the night. A smart white ho!"* spoke Melody out loud. *"Hell I would have done the same thing."*

****

Meantime, Hookman had made it to D-Lo and they were talking.

"Carl Jr. or Coldblood," said Hookman. "That's his name."

"Coldblood?" whispered D-Lo. "I've heard that name. But are you positive she said that this ... Coldblood's name, is Carl Jr.?"

"That's what she said, man. Do you know him?"

"I don't know him, but if it's who I think it is, I know his old man, Carl Sr."

"Carl Sr.? Why does that sound so familiar? I know of that name," whispered Hookman.

"Yeah, you do know him," smiled D-Lo. "His name is the Reverend Carl Simmons, Sr., better known as..."

"Lo-Down!" Hookman cut in. "Aahhh!" he screamed. He became filled with anger. Then D-Lo spoke.

"Time for us to enter the house of the Lord, brother. I told you to be patient."

Chapter 35

"Money doesn't fix everything, Kris!" shouted Davina as she threw a glass at him and it hit the wall.

"Maybe it doesn't," Kris shouted back. "But you keep spending it like it does and I'm only asking you to lighten up a little – cut back on spending. What's wrong with that?"

"I am not cutting back on shit!" she shouted. "I am here all day keeping your house, while you meet with... God only knows how many women for lunch every day. I'm lonely Kris... are you listening? I need something to do. So don't tell me to stop doing the only thing I am doing and doing well!"

"Davina, you are just drunk, so why don't you relax and..."

"Kris! Listen to yourself," she cut in. "Yes! I am drunk! Until today, I haven't had a drink in 25 years! That ought to tell you something, Kris! I need more than to just sit at home every day and house sit! I was a good anchorwoman until you ... until you... this is all your fault, Kris." She threw a glass at him.

"Davina, stop that!" he shouted. "Our daughter will be here any minute now to bring Nela. You shouldn't let her see you like this because she won't understand! Please calm down and let's clean this mess before she gets here!"

"You know what? I think you have a point," she said calmly. Then she picked up the phone and dialed.

"What are you doing, Davina?"

"I think it's time our daughter understand everything that's going on in this house, then we will see if she still loves her daddy like he's a god or something."

"Davina! Put that phone down!" He started toward her, but she threw another glass at him and he fled behind the couch.

****

Meanwhile, Tenisha was home with her three year-old daughter, Nela. She was preparing for work that morning while also preparing to drop Nela off at her moms. Nela, like normal, was still sleeping.

"It's time to see Grandma," whispered Tenisha. "Come on, baby, wake up." The phone rang as Tenisha was about to leave. "Now who could that be?" She checked the caller ID then answered. "Hey Mom, I know I'm a little late, but Nela and I are just leaving."

"Good!" shouted her drunken mom into the phone. "Cause when you get here, your 'do-right' daddy has something to tell you!"

"Mom?" Tenisha asked surprisingly. "Are you okay? You sound funny. Have you been drinking, Mom?"

"Yes, Tenisha, I am very drunk!" she said while throwing another glass.

"Mom, where is Daddy?"

"He's over by the couch. I keep trying to hit him, but he keeps ducking away. Maybe I'll be out of glasses in a minute and he won't have to." She laughed then threw another glass at him. Then she yelled, "Say hello to your daughter, Kris!" Tenisha could hear her dad in the background.

"Good morning, Tee! Everything is fine, baby!"

"Oh my God!" sounded Tenisha. "Are you guys fighting? Mom, stop throwing glasses—I'm on the way!" Tenisha grabbed her bags, snatched up Nela, and quickly ran out. She only lived a few miles away from her parents, who lived on Old Milton Parkway off Georgia 400. As she drove, Nela awakened.

"Mommy!" yelled Nela. "I wanna go there!" Nela was pointing to a billboard she saw with circus animals. The circus was in town and she was excited about seeing the animals. "Ponies, Mommy!" she continued. "Ponies!"

"I know, baby. Mommy was hoping Grand mom could take you, today, but I'll have to see." Nela was a very good child and Tenisha was an excellent mom. But Nela was born not knowing her father.

Tenisha was a very popular girl in high school and college. She was such a beautiful young lady that girls and guys alike just flocked to her feet. Being raised in an arrogant home, Tenisha was arrogant as well but she had a heart—a good heart. She loved helping others even though sometimes she made them feel like crap.

During her first year in college, she fell in love with a junior, who was also the quarterback and captain of the football team, at the University of South Carolina (USC). Shortly after she started her freshmen year, she became pregnant with his child.

While she was pregnant, Rubik, the father, became engaged to another girl and denied ever having slept with Tenisha. She was so hurt and embarrassed that she left USC to go home and be near her family while her baby was born. She never went back to USC nor heard from Rubik again.

After Nela was born, Tenisha attended a local college to get her degree in communications and journalism, while her mom kept baby Nela. Tenisha's parents were very arrogant, but she had never known them to have serious arguments nor to get drunk. She had seen her dad with a glass a time or two at business luncheons, but he hardly touched it. Today, as Tenisha opened the front door to her parents home, all that was about to change.

"You bastard!" shouted her mom as a glass came flying across the room at her dad.

"Hi, Tee, Honey!" yelled Kris. "Guess your mom had a little too much to drink," he said while dodging her attacks.

"No! I've had a little too much of your bull!" she screamed as she threw another glass. Tenisha and Nela stood in the doorway being shocked at what they saw. Suddenly, when Kris saw that she had to go to the cabinet to get more glasses, he ran and grabbed her, forced her back to the couch, and slung her onto it.

"Daddy!" yelled Tenisha. "What are you doing? Don't handle her like that!"

"Oh, there's a lot about your precious Dad you don't know," started Davina. "Go ahead and tell her Kris!" Tenisha was puzzled as she stood silently waiting to see what her dad had to say. Her eyes went back and forth from her mom, whom she had never seen drunk or act like this before, to her dad, who stood silently looking guilty as sin. Her dad was her idol, but now, she was wondering what he had done so bad that her mom no longer wanted to worship him.

"Daddy?" asked Tenisha as she and Nela sat and cared for her mom. "What is she talking about?" Kris became fidgety and attempted to avoid the conversation as he prepared to leave for work.

"I have to get to the bank," he said. "Tee, you can see for yourself that your mom is just drunk. I've got a nine o'clock meeting this morning and I have to go." He put on his jacket, hugged and kissed Tenisha and Nela, then left.

Again, Tenisha was shocked. She had never seen her dad walk away from her mom without kissing her cheek or saying goodbye. Her mom was still crying as Tenisha stood and looked all through the house at the broken glass, whiskey bottles, dirty dishes, and unmade beds. She had lived here for years as a child and had never seen her home like this. She really didn't know what to think as she called her job and requested to take off for the day. Then she sat down next to her mom.

"Mom?" There was only tears and silence for a few minutes. On the end table was her parents' high school yearbook. Nela picked it up and started turning the pages. Davina sat up and joined her as Tenisha just kinda went along.

"Grandma!" yelled Nela as she pointed to the pictures.

"No baby, that's not grandma," said Davina. "That's Mary Ann, and that's Susie, and that's Carolyn, and that's Nancy, and Buddy and Virginia, and..."

"Janice," cut in Tenisha. "And that's Ebony, and Markus, and Sherri, and Carlos, and Darius, and Nedra, and Randi and Pamela, and Curtis, and Candi and Jerome, and Naomi, and all the friends that Grandma went to school with. Who is she, Mom?" Tenisha had been reading the names below that matched each picture. But when she got to one certain picture, the name had been scratched out. "Who is she?"

Davina just sat and stared for a moment with tears swelling in her eyes. Then she stood and walked around.

"You know, it's lonely here every day having to stay at home and keep house while your father goes out to do…'God only knows what' every day."

"What's going on here, Mom? Is Dad cheating on you?"

"No no, it's nothing like that. At least I hope he's not. It's just that sometimes it gets hard sitting around the house, when you know you gave up a good career and could have been doing more," her mom continued. "Your dad goes out every day meeting new people and enjoying life while I'm sitting around just getting old…older."

"Mom, is that what this is about? Have you and Dad talked about this?"

"Your dad doesn't have time for me anymore, Tenisha, and I'm getting dried up inside."

"Mom, that's not true. You're still very young and Dad loves you very much."

"Then why isn't he listening to me when I talk to him? We've been fronting this marriage for years so he could uphold his image as a successful banker and caretaker. But he doesn't give a damn about me anymore…just his damn clients, some of which are very beautiful," added Davina.

"Is that the part that has to do with the lady in the book? What's her name, Mom? Is Dad seeing her or something?"

"No, no, no!" said Davina calmly. "It's not that. Her name is Keisha Milledge and we were high school friends for a while. That is, until your dad, who was dating me, had a crush on her and started flirting with her like I wasn't even around.

Eventually, we left high school and everybody went their way. Keisha and I wanted to do TV so we majored in communications and broadcasting. During my junior year, I became pregnant with you and had to dropout. Keisha and I were enemies by then, and hardly spoke. She decided to continue her career and become a news anchorwoman on TV, just as she planned. I became a housewife. Kris, who majored in business and money management, promised he would marry me and take care of me and my child for the rest of our lives and he has." Then she started to cry again. "But Tenisha, I'm lonely because he doesn't give me attention anymore, and I don't know what to do."

"Okay Mom, okay," said Tenisha as she hugged her mother. "We'll talk to Dad and we'll get through this."

"Grandma!" yelled Nela as she turned the page and saw Davina's high school picture.

"Oh! She got it right!" laughed Davina. "How did she know?"

Chapter 36

That morning, Cherlene is home preparing for her private graduation ceremony that will be held at the daycare where she works. She passed her teacher's certification exams and will be submitting her resumes to the public school system where she hopes to teach. It's a very high day for Cherlene as she and Makeda prance around the apartment singing and playing in their underwear. Suddenly, the phone rings.

"Hello," answers Cherlene.

"Hi Baby. Congratulations on passing your certification exams," said Terry.

"Oh," groaned Cherlene. "You're not gonna make it to the graduation, today, are you?"

"I'm afraid not, Cheryl. Matter of fact, I won't be home until after the weekend."

"Daddy! Daddy!" screamed Makeda. "Wanna talk to Daddy!"

"Okay," said Cherlene as she handed Makeda the phone. Makeda was 3 years old now and she loved her dad very much. Terry's electrical company had been working out of town a lot over the past year so he hadn't seen a lot of Cherlene or Makeda. But whenever he was away, he would always call and talk to his daughter.

****

Meanwhile, Jennifer, who had given birth about a month ago, is home exercising as she prepares to go back to work. She works her body hard doing pushups, pull ups, and all kinds of callisthenic exercises. She runs daily on her treadmill and while pushing little Audrey in her stroller. Jennifer loves her child and is getting used to being a mom, but she really misses her work, especially her extracurricular activities of the night. She knows that it will still be a while before she can stalk the night again but she is preparing anyway.

****

Donna, on the other hand, is really becoming a good assistant journalist and is expecting a promotion soon. She's currently working on one of the most tremendous stories in the state, and all of her superiors are applauding her. Tyler walks over and hands Donna a prototype of the newspaper layout of her story.

"Donna, you did well; you really did well."

"Thank you, Tyler," smiled Donna. Then she read the headlines of the main story.

Gangs/ Gangbusters On The Rise!
By Donna H. Banks

This was her first big story as she read over the prototype.

"She is really doing well with her work, lately," said Mr. Golden, the chief journalist.

"I know," agreed Mr. Rogers, the editor. "She is very proud of her work and puts a lot of effort into it."

"On the other hand, Ms. Cuyler isn't doing too bad, either," added Mr. Golden.

"She's not a chaser like Ms. Banks, but the stories she writes are really captivating and draw readers. Ms. Banks takes the attention-getter stories and prints them better than the average journalist. But Ms. Cuyler can take the unknown story and make it popular and good reading for the public."

"Again, you're right," said Mr. Rogers. "In a little while, you're gonna need to promote one of these ladies and they're both qualified for the job... even though, Ms. Cuyler has seniority. You've got a tough decision on your hands, right now. I'm glad it's yours to make and not mine."

"Where is Ms. Cuyler, by the way?" asked Mr. Golden.

"She called in this morning and asked for the day off; some kind of family thing. I told her that I would pick up her slack."

Chapter 37

Its inventory Thursday as Jennifer heads to work. She dropped Audrey off at the daycare early so she can get to work by 9 o'clock, and start her first day return on a high note.

"Yeah!" said Michelle and a couple of other ladies as Jennifer walked in. "Congratulations again, Mom, and it's good to have you back. It's been so boring around here with no one to talk to, if you know what I mean."

"I know what you mean," laughed Jennifer. Many of the other ladies that worked there were younger and not so smart. Many times they couldn't even hold a conversation with Jennifer or Michelle because of intellectual differences. Now that Jennifer was back, Michelle was full of smiles and Jennifer understood why.

"My, my!" said Jennifer. "Look at all the new inventory and fashions!"

"Girl, you've missed so much! But don't worry cause I've already done a lot of your work so you will have time to chill, check things out, and talk this morning. I've missed you so much," smiled Michelle.

"Shell, what time did you get here, today?"

"I've been here since seven this morning."

"Michelle, you are such a good friend. I am so glad to know you," smiled Jennifer as they hugged.

"I know you want to attend your sister's graduation party, so I've already told the boss that we were taking an extended lunch period today, but we would make up for the lost time at the end of the day."

"Thank you, Michelle. It's friends like you that makes work fun."

"Well, I gotta go. I have to do housewares today. I've got a new 'Ms. Thang' over in jewelry being trained. She's okay but watch her though. She gets a little side tracked sometimes. See ya in a bit."

"Okay, see you later," laughed Jennifer. *"Man, it feels so good to be here again! I didn't realize how much I miss you all,"* she said quietly to the merchandise.

All morning long Jennifer smilingly completed her work while working with her new assistant. There were 4 new girls and the experienced employees had to train them. After a while, Jennifer was alone as she wondered around the mall just checking things out.

"My goodness!" she thought. *"Look at all the new stuff!"* Before she knew it, she was wearing a small pouch around her waist and carrying a nice looking handbag, neither of which she had purchased. She remembered seeing them as she walked but couldn't remember where she saw them.

Inside the pouch, she had stolen expensive pens, earrings, and other jewelry. The handbag was still empty but it was very nice. It was approaching 2 o'clock, which is the time Cherlene's graduation party was schedule. So Jennifer hurried back to work before she was missed.

After she was back, she began to fill her handbag with lingerie, cute blouses, and other clothing for herself and her sisters. She had given them a lot already, but to her too much was not enough. Jennifer was so happy to be at work again and she was having a really good day.

"Hey Jennifer," said Michelle. "It's about time to go; are you ready?"

"Yep! I'm ready and I'll drive." Jennifer took her things and they left.

****

Meanwhile, back at Tenisha's parents' home, Tenisha and her mom had just finished cleaning the house of all the glass and fighting.

"Mom, get dressed; we have to go."

"Go where?" asked Davina.

"We have to go check out this daycare center I've heard so much about," said Tenisha. "I want you to start doing other things during the day so I'm placing Nela in a daycare center for a while." Her mom was surprised.

"No, Tenisha, I couldn't do that to you or to precious Nela." Tenisha picked up a glass and positioned it like she was gonna throw it at her mom.

"Mom, you know how effective this is better than all people. Don't make me start slinging glasses at you, now get dressed." Her mom was embarrassed as she laughed. Then she went to get dressed. Tenisha took out her disk, inserted it into the computer, and began to type.

"Dear diary, today for the first time in my life, I saw my Mom drunk and throwing glasses at my Daddy, while he ran and hid....

Chapter 38

Cherlene was at the daycare enjoying the company of many parents who had entrusted their children to her care. Cherlene had practically built the program at the Childcare Academy and was very proud of herself. But now that she was a certified teacher, she felt that it was time to move on to the classroom of higher learning.

"Hey Cheryl!" yelled Donna as she excitedly ran in. In her hand she had a gift. "I'm so proud of you, Cheryl." Then they hugged. "When I take over the world, I'm gonna be just like you because you're my she-ro, girl!"

"Dee, I love you so much, but you need to calm down."

"Honey, I need a man to calm me down. You know any volunteers? Here I am—a free spirit, ready and willing," said Donna. As Cherlene turned to friends and introduced them to Donna, Jennifer and Michelle came walking in. "Hey Jenny!" yelled Donna as she excitedly hugged her.

"Dee, stop that!" whispered Jennifer. "You're acting like we haven't seen each other in months and we just spoke this morning." Michelle was laughing.

"Can't I love you, Jenny? Michelle, is it wrong for me to love my sister so much? Huh? Huh? Now come on, Jenny, baby! Show me some luv!"

"Okay! Okay!" smiled Jennifer as she hugged Donna. Then Donna pinched her butt. "Ouch! What did you do that for?"

"That's for acting like you don't love me!" Donna was about to pinch her again but Jennifer was smart and quick as she caught her hand.

"Dee, if you pinch me again, no matter what the reason, I'm gonna deck your ass right here, right now! Now go write a story about that!" said Jennifer as she pushed her away.

"My God," started Donna. "What is the world coming to when sisters can't trust each other. I was just gonna move the little bug that's about to bite you on your butt." Jennifer quickly turned her butt to Donna and panicked.

"Get it, Dee! Hurry up! Get it off!" Donna, who had now outsmarted Jennifer, took her time, smiled at Michelle, then grabbed a nice handful of Jennifer's butt and squeezed it. Then she took off through the crowd. Jennifer turned around slowly because she knew she had been set up. Michelle was laughing with tears.

"Michelle," smiled Jennifer. "That's my sister; lovely as a flower, more humorous than a comedian, and smarter than a computer, but she really needs a man... bad."

"Hi Jenny, Hi Michelle," greeted Cherlene.

"Hi Cheryl." They handed her a gift. "Congratulations on your accomplishments," continued Michelle.

"Thank you, ladies. So Jenny, how's your first day back at work?"

"Uh, I didn't realize how much I've missed it. I love being back to work, but I also want to see my baby. Is she sleeping?"

"Yes," said Cherlene. "So is Keda, but you can go take a peek."

"Cheryl, I'm not gonna stay because I've got a hot item on the press," said Donna. "But I'd love to celebrate with you later."

As Jennifer and Michelle went to see the babies, Donna headed toward the door. Suddenly, this 6 foot 3 inch tall, hunk of a man, is standing in the door looking around. Donna froze with a stare as did Jennifer and Michelle from inside the center.

"Wow! Who is that?" asked Michelle.

"I'll give you one guess," said Jennifer. Suddenly, Cherlene came running to him and hugged him.

"Hi Byrd, I'm glad you made it because I wasn't sure you would. Come; let me introduce you to my sisters." Donna and Jennifer, who were still watching, met Cherlene and Byrd in the middle of the yard where they were celebrating. As Cherlene introduced them, she made it clear who Byrd was with.

"Ladies, this is 'Michael.' 'Michael' came to see 'me' today, because 'Michael' and 'I' are going out, tonight. Michael, these are my sisters, Jennifer and Donna, and this is our friend, Michelle," continued Cherlene.

"You can call me, Byrd," he smiled. "All my friends do."

"Good to meet you, Byrd," they responded.

"I have to get back to work, Byrd," rushed Donna. "It is really nice to meet you," she said while frowning at Cherlene. As she got near the door, she looked back at Cherlene who was watching her, gave Cherlene the finger, and walked out. Cherlene knew she was jealous.

"Cheryl, I'd love to stay but Michelle and I have to get back, too," said Jennifer.

"Okay, Jenny, I understand since it's your first day back to work. We'll talk later."

"Okay, bye," they said. Then they left. Donna had already left the parking lot and was on the road as she passed Tenisha.

"That was Tenisha," she spoke to herself. *"Wonder where she's going?"* Then she saw her turn into the parking lot of the daycare center. *"I wonder what she is up to now!"*

"Tenisha?" spoke Jennifer with a questionable tone. She and Michelle met Tenisha, Davina, and Nela, at the door as they were leaving. Jennifer couldn't help but remember the time in school when Tenisha allowed her posse to take her shoes and made her walk home barefoot. Jennifer wasn't afraid of Tenisha, but like Donna, she just didn't trust her. "What are you doing here?" Jennifer asked.

"Do you work here?" asked Tenisha.

"No, but Cheryl does...well, she used to. Today is her last day."

"So are you guys old friends?" asked Davina.

"Mom, this is Jennifer, an old school mate. Jennifer, this is my mom, Mrs. Davina Cuyler."

"Pleased to meet you, Ma'am. This is my friend, Michelle." Michelle shook their hands as Cherlene came to the door. She was surprised to see Tenisha.

"Whoa!" she said as she froze in her tracks. "Tenisha?" Like Donna and Jennifer, Cherlene's mind went back to high school.

"Look guys," started Tenisha. "Those days are gone. I'm not that person anymore. Can we just let go of the past and start over? Word of mouth and the business world says this place has an excellent program for small children, and I'm looking for a place to care for my child. That's all." For a moment, all the parties stood speechless and unmovable as they stared at each other. Suddenly, Tenisha reached down, picked up Nela, and turned to walk away.

"Tenisha!" shouted Cherlene as she ran behind her. "Wait a minute." Jennifer quickly grabbed Cherlene and whispered,

"She is still terrorizing Dee at work. Don't you let her bring her child here with our children!" Cherlene moved Jennifer's hand and smiled. Then she walked to Tenisha and said,

"We were all a wild bunch, weren't we? Let's see if our kids can be better friends than we've been." Then she hugged Tenisha and said, "My name is Cherlene, and yes we do have one of the best childcare centers in the state. I know you'll like it. Welcome to the Childcare Academy and Learning Center. Come on, let me show you around." Tenisha, who was almost in tears, felt a lot better now. Even Jennifer humbled herself because she could feel that Tenisha had changed.

"Who would have thought?" commented Jennifer as she drove back to work.

Chapter 39

It was about 3:30 pm that Thursday when Jennifer arrived back to work.

"Jennifer Sweet, please report to the main office. Jennifer Sweet, please report to the main office," came the voice over the intercom. Jennifer didn't waste any time as she hurried to the management office.

"Come in, Jennifer, and have a seat," said her supervisor Ms. Carol. "Congratulations again on becoming a mother and welcome back to work."

"Thank you, Ma'am."

"I suppose you're wondering why I called you, so I'll get right to the point. Over the past couple of years, our profits have been down due to thefts. It would appear that in one year's time, thieves walked off with thousands of dollars worth of merchandise, just from our department store alone." Jennifer got nervous as Ms. Carol continued.

"Other stores and shopping centers in this area have noticed an increase in theft as well. Therefore, while you were on maternity leave, all of the local business managers in the area met and agreed to have a very sophisticated security system installed within a mile radius of the mall and inside every business or store within that radius."

"Are you saying that the old system has been removed and a new system is in place?"

"That's exactly what I'm saying, Jennifer. The new system was activated 2 weeks ago, and it's very sophisticated and very well hidden from the eyes of would-be thieves. Since it's activation, we've caught three thieves in two weeks that we normally wouldn't be able to catch." Jennifer's heart skipped a beat. "Come walk with me through the store and I will show you how everything works." Jennifer was so scared, she could hardly walk. She knew there was a high possibility that she had been seen on camera earlier, stealing from various stores.

"What am I going to do?" she wondered. *"I can't go to jail! My baby! Oh God help me!"* she pleaded silently.

"Normally," continued Carol. "Monitors in the security room are manned and watched to protect our inventory. Then when a thief is seen, he is captured on the spot and locked up. But with the new system, it scans and records the face and image of the perpetrator, then review camera images to see how many times this thief has visited the stores in the area over the entire month. So when he is caught, he is not only banned from the store where he was caught, but he may be restricted from buying or selling in the entire area where our security system is set up, especially if he has stolen from more than one store."

Jennifer knew she was in trouble and thought that Carol was just walking her through the process before having the police place her under arrest.

Carol continued. "This morning, the security technicians were experimenting with a new device, so the regular alert system is off until tomorrow morning. But all thefts that took place today will be seen on camera by management in the morning," continued Carol.

"So are you saying that the security tapes of today will not be seen until tomorrow?" asked Jennifer.

"That's right," explained Carol. "Then we will resume as normal. Now let me show you where many of our new cameras are hidden." Carol took Jennifer to many areas that Jennifer would have never guessed cameras were hidden. Many of which Jennifer knew she had been and taken items; within the jewelry counter, at the top of many steel poles of clothing racks, behind mirrors, in mannequins, toys, shelves—cameras were everywhere!

"Finally, there's one other place we want cameras," said Carol. "We want all of our department managers to wear one while they work. It's in this little broach," she smiled as she pinned it on Jennifer. Then Carol pulled a little remote from her pocket. She punched a few numbers, and Jennifer heard the broach beep. "Now it's activated," said Carol. "Again Honey, welcome back to work." Carol went back to her office.

Jennifer panicked! She knew she had a major problem. By morning, not only would she be out of a job, but she would be in jail! She knew that many times when she stole things, it just kinda happened and she wouldn't know about it until it was done. She knew she was a kleptomaniac that was about to be exposed. So she went to the ladies room, sat on the toilet and stayed there. After about 20 minutes had passed, Jennifer heard Michelle looking for her.

"Michelle!" yelled Jennifer. "I'm in here!" Michelle entered the ladies room and saw Jennifer sitting on the toilet,

"What's going on, Jennifer? Why are you just sitting there?"

"Michelle, I don't feel so good."

"What happened? Is it something you ate?"

"I don't think so, but I think I need to leave for today. Can you cover for me?" It was about 4:30 p.m. so Jennifer had a couple of hours to go before she was to take off.

"Well, I will try, Jennifer. Do you need a doctor? Come on, let me help you up?" As Michelle reached to help her from the toilet, Jennifer noticed Michelle's broach for the first time. She became even more disturbed, but she remained quiet.

"Will you turn this in for me, Michelle?" She handed her the broach.

"Of course. You go on home and get some rest. Maybe you came back to work too early. Better call your doctor," advised Michelle.

Jennifer eased out to her car, and sped away from the area for at least two miles out. Then she sat in her car and began to think. Suddenly, she heard it again .... *"The Curse Must Be Broken!"*

"How do I break this damn curse!" she yelled. Then she sat and cried.

Chapter 40

While D-Lo and the Hookman drove the streets of Atlanta, D'Amica was walking, shopping, and paying her bills. She had done an excellent job of budgeting and spending her money. Between her job and the money that Coldblood had given her, she had been living a decent life again. Now, her money was almost depleted but she was happy.

All of her bills were paid, and Shaun had everything he needed. Plus, some of the girls at the shop still owed her a few dollars, but she wasn't worried about them. Over the years she had been there, they had proven they were a family. Just like they counted on her, she knew she could count on them when she really needed them.

As D'Amica finished running her last errand for the morning, it was nearing 1 o'clock. She was scheduled to be at work around that time so she knew she would be a few minutes late. D'Amica searched her purse for her cell phone.

"Hello Meca," answered Nicole. "The fact that it's almost one o'clock and you're calling tells me that you're gonna be late."

"Only about 20 minutes, Nikki; I'm almost there! Have my customer to just hold on."

"Okay, I got you girl. Just come on." Twenty minutes later, D'Amica's bus dropped her off at the Beauty Shop. D'Amica could've taken a taxi but she spent only what she needed to when she needed to.

"Okay Meca, I'm out of here," rushed Nicole as she grabbed her sweater. "You are in charge and I'll see you at 5 p.m., when folks are getting off."

"Whoa! Where are you going?" asked D'Amica. "Where is Melody?"

"You're not the only one who has other things to do, Meca, and it's my turn. Melody had things to do, today, and will meet me here at 5 p.m. to help pick up the slack. You can carry things 'till then so have at it." Then Nicole left Tameka and Adrienna with D'Amica in charge.

As usual, things were very slow this time of the day because most women were at work. Only those who had schedule appointments came by and that wasn't many.

"So Meca," started Adrienna. "How's your love life?" D'Amica thought she was talking about Coldblood even though they hadn't talked about it in months.

"I don't have a love life and you know it, Drenna."

"Drenna met somebody," smiled Tameka.

"Ah!" said D'Amica. "That's what she really wants me to know! Who is the guy? Is he cute? Tell me all about him, Drenna!" Suddenly, the phone rang. "What's up Mel?" asked D'Amica. A week had passed as

Melody struggled to forget all that Hookman had revealed to her. She was really becoming concerned about D'Amica.

"Child, I've got something to tell you!" she yelled into the phone. "You are about a slick sister, you know that? I will be there at 5 so don't you go anywhere 'till I get there."

"Bye, Mel," said D'Amica. "She didn't want anything. So, Drenna... start talking." Adrienna started telling about her new boyfriend.

****

As Reverend Carl Simmons Sr., worked around the church, he didn't notice the black van pulling into the church yard. It was about 3 p.m. and normally the working members came by to help set up when they got off from work. So he was there alone. When he walked past the podium, he noticed a silver coin caught under it. So he got on his knee and slightly move the podium to picked it up. Suddenly he heard the whisper, *"The Curse Must Be Broken!"*

"Reverend Carl Simmons Sr.?" came another voice while he was bending down.

"Yes, how can I help you?" he asked without looking up.

"Or shall I call you, 'Lo-Down,'" smiled D-Lo as he sat in a pew. Rev. Simmons recognized the voice and slowly stood up.

"I don't go by that name anymore," he said cautiously. "Service starts at 7 tonight so you brothers are a few hours early."

"Cut the crap, Lo-Down," ordered D-Lo. "We're here on business."

"Look man, we made a deal after you killed my wife—if I didn't testify and tell all I know, you would leave me and my family alone and let us serve the Lord. Now what are you doing here?"

"Well, Lo-Down, my good preacher, the deal was good until one of your family members decided to serve himself instead of the Lord."

"What are you talking about, man?"

"I need to speak with your son, Coldblood—or do you call him Lo-Down Jr.?" they laughed. Hookman just stood looking and listening. He knew he was looking at the only man who could be as ruthless as he and D-Lo were, and he didn't trust him. He knew that the Lo-Down he knew would never allow a robe and a cross to stand between him and what he had to do.

"Why do you want Junior?" he asked. "What has he done?"

"A while back, somebody robbed me for five hundred big ones. Since then, your boy's baby mama has been living high on the hog. We need to talk to Coldblood to be sure about our conclusions, before we go after the girl. Somebody hit us, and it wasn't no broad, Lo-Down. Where is Coldblood? We just want to talk to him."

"Look D-Lo, Junior ain't here and hasn't been here in months. He's on the run and you know it. Matter of fact, when he left here, he was so broke, I gave him 200 bucks and my old car," he explained.

"So where did his baby mama get the money she's been spending?"

"I really don't know, but she and Junior broke up a long time ago."

"I hope you're telling me the truth, Lo-Down, because if you're not, this will change everything. Your little heaven here will be the first thing I send straight to hell. Now, if you don't mind, I still want to talk to your son. Where is he?" D-Lo demanded.

"I don't know where he is. When he left here I told him to never come back, and he hasn't."

"Then you don't have a problem with me going after the girl, do you?"

"She's got my grandson, D-Lo, and that's my family. Please man..." Rev. Simmons was now pleading hard.

"Please what?" yelled D-Lo angrily! "Just let her spend my money? You know me better than that, Lo!" Suddenly, as Rev. Simmons stepped toward D-Lo in another effort to plead for D'Amica and Shaun, the Hookman reached for his pistol, with the intent to make the preacher back up. But before he could pull it out, he heard a click under Rev. Simmons robe and saw what seemed to be a sawed off shotgun pointing in his direction.

"Whoa, Lo-Down!" said D-Lo cautiously with his hands up. Then he motioned for Hookman to do the same. Hookman lifted his hands. "This ain't the time nor the place, Lo. I don't want any trouble but only what's rightfully mine."

"What kind of preacher carries a sawed off shotgun under his robe?" asked the Hookman angrily.

"One who is ready in and out of season to answer for what he believes. Now get out of my house before I do you a holy sprinkling."

"Same ol' Lo-Down," said Hookman. "You haven't changed."

"Ok Lo-Down," said D-Lo as he backed away. "If what you say is true, then nothing will change as long as you stay out of my way. Have a good day, Reverend. May God bless you!" Rev. Simmons broke into tears as D-Lo and Hookman left.

"Please forgive me, Lord!" he cried aloud. Rosa, who had been listening, stepped from the back and watched D-Lo and Hookman leave. Then she stared at Rev. Simmons quietly.

****

It was 5:15 p.m. as Nicole came rushing into the Beauty Shop.

"Wow!" yelled Tameka. "My... how time does fly when you're telling lies. I'm out of here y'all. I have been here all day."

"Yeah, me too," said Adrienna. "I'll see you tomorrow, ladies." Then they left. D'Amica's cell phone rang.

"Hey Shaun," she answered. "What's up?"

"Mom, what time are you coming home tonight?" Nicole cut in.

"Meca, why don't you go on home? Things are slow today and Mel will be here in a minute to help me handle it." D'Amica nodded then went back to the phone.

"Shaun, I will leave here in a minute, but I have to stop at the store. I'll be home by 7:30," she said.

"Ok Mom, see you then. Bye." D'Amica wanted to catch the next bus which was already coming, so she laid her cell phone in her chair while she put on her coat and got her bag. Then she quickly ran out and left her cell phone in the chair.

****

As Rev. Simmons sat at his church thinking about D-Lo, Coldblood, and all that was just said, he picked up his phone and called D'Amica to warn her. There was no answer as her cell phone just rang. Nicole was busy and didn't see it vibrating. Rev. Simmons didn't know what to do but he knew he had to do something or D'Amica and Shaun might be in trouble. So he picked up the phone again and made the one call he didn't want to make.

"Hello Junior?" he spoke into the phone. "Son, we've got trouble." After he hung up from talking with Coldblood, he looked around and saw Rosa standing and staring at him like a super hero. She was wearing black tights from head to toe, with two silver glocks mounted on her side. Then she heard... *"The Curse Must Be Broken!"* Rosa ignored it.

"Do I need to go save Stephanie's grandson, Carl?" she asked. "Just say the word."

"And blow your cover; give up your life? No! This is not your fight. Let God handle it."

Chapter 41

Melody rushed about while shopping in the mall. It was near 5:30 p.m. so she was late for work, as she dialed her cell phone.

"Hello Mel," answered Nicole. "I guess you're on the way, huh?"

"Yes Nikki, I will be there as soon as the next bus arrives."

"Okay Mel, I'll be here." All week long, Melody had been wondering about the conversation she had with the Hookman while at lunch with him. She knew that Hookman had issues and now she was questioning herself for even dealing with him. She had known him since high school and they used to be a couple. Now, they were just bed partners. She knew that Hookman had done a lot of bad things but he had never discussed any of it with her. However, everything he said lately led her to believe that he killed Slopp, plus, her friend and co-worker, D'Amica, may also be in trouble. Many thoughts were racing through her mind as she boarded the bus and headed to the Beauty Shop. Nicole was busy straightening the shop as D-Lo and Hookman walked in.

"Can I help you, gentlemen?" she asked as D-Lo walked to her. Hookman locked the door and pulled the blinds. Nicole didn't know what to think but she knew this wasn't good.

"Hello, my good lady," smiled D-Lo as he sat down in a chair. "We're here to see Meca."

"Meca, who?" Nicole answered. D-Lo didn't waste any time as Hookman walked near.

"Maybe my man here can help you to remember her." Hookman grabbed Nicole and slammed her face hard on the countertop. Nicole fell to the floor in pain. She quickly stood and pleaded for her life.

"Please, mister. I ain't got no money and Meca ain't here. Take anything else you like, please."

"I want Meca," said D-Lo. "Where is she? Where does she live?" Nicole knew that if she told them, D'Amica would be in trouble. She knew if she didn't tell them then she may die.

"I don't know where she is," lied Nicole. Suddenly, Hookman grabbed her throat and punched her face like he was a boxer. Then he slung her across the room against the chairs and table until she fell. Nicole was crying and pleading for her life as Hookman beat her mercilessly. Suddenly, D-Lo saw the business cards on the mirrors.

"Whoa, Brother; just hold on a minute!" Then he took each girls card.

"We will beat you to sleep, then go after every one of these and do the same to them before day break, until we get the right one. Now, which one is it gonna be?" Nicole's eyes glanced over at D'Amica's card.

"So, it's D'Amica," said D-Lo. "Ms. D'Amica Taylor," he read. Then he searched on the counter near her chair until he found her address. He nodded to Hookman, and Hookman knocked Nicole out...cold. Then they left. As Melody stepped off the bus, she was surprised to see the shades pulled and the lights still on.

"Has Nicole left?" she wondered. "Nikki!" she screamed as she dropped her bag and rushed to Nicole. Nicole slowly stood, being badly bruised and beaten. "Who did this, Nicole? I'm calling an ambulance."

"No," she said. "I'm okay. They're after Meca! Call Meca and warn her!" Melody dialed D'Amica's cell phone. Suddenly, she heard it buzzing from the floor where it had fallen while Nicole was being beaten.

"She left her cell phone!" shouted Melody. "We've got to warn her somehow!"

"Call her house phone!" said Nicole while taking care of herself. Shaun was listening to his headphones and didn't hear the call, nor did D-Lo and Hookman as they unplugged the phone cords. Then they locked Shaun in the closet and waited for D'Amica to come home. Melody dialed 911, but the automated recording pissed her off and she hung up.

"I have to go!" she shouted to Nicole. "Meca is in trouble!"

"Go! go!" waved Nicole. "I'll get 911 but you try to catch her." Melody immediately flagged a taxi and sped across town to D'Amica's.

Chapter 42

It's about 7:30 p.m. Thursday as Cherlene is home with Makeda and keeping Audrey.

"Your mom is a little late," she said while holding Audrey. "Maybe I should give her a call to see what's up, huh?"

"I know her number, Mommy!" said Makeda. "I'll call her!"

"Maybe she's stuck in traffic or something so let's give her a few more minutes. Then we'll call her, okay? Meantime, I'm gonna fix your bath water so you can take a bath, young lady." After Cherlene fixed the water and Makeda was in the tub, the phone rang. "This may be your mom calling now. Hello?" she answered.

"Hi Cherlene, this is Byrd. Are we still on for tonight?"

"Only if we can stay in. My sister's a little late picking up Audrey and Makeda is already preparing for bed. I will even cook for you, if you want."

"Staying in would be even better," he said. "But I've kinda got some things to do early in the morning so why don't I just pick up some fast food on the way over. That way I get to spend more time with you."

"Oooh! I like the way you think," she flirted. "Give me until about 8:30. Makeda will be asleep and I'm sure my sister will be here by then."

****

At 8:30 p.m. that night, Jennifer was still sitting at the bar thinking and drinking coffee, while trying to figure out what was she going to do. She knew her life was over, and she didn't know how to tell her sisters. So she just sat there... thinking.

****

At 8:45 p.m., Makeda was asleep as Byrd knocked at the door. Cherlene opened it while holding Audrey who was still wide awake. Then came the whisper... *"The Curse Must Be Broken!"* Cherlene hesitated then continued.

"Hey girl," he greeted her with a cheek kiss. But Cherlene didn't move from his path because she wanted more. So she moved her lips to his, and deeply kissed him. She had been missing sex and she was in the mood since everything was over concerning her exams.

"Wow!" smiled Byrd. "I like the way this date started already!"

"Come on in and let's eat; I'm a little hungry," she said. As they ate, they talked while Cherlene gently flirted with him to let him know that the moment was right. It didn't take Byrd long to get the message as he kissed on her and rubbed her body.

****

At 9:15 p.m., Jennifer was still sitting and thinking about her situation.

"I have to try!" she thought. *"I have to try to get into that security room and remove those disks before morning. It's the only chance I've got!"* Jennifer knew what she had to do as she finally dialed Cherlene.

"Cherlene, I'm really sorry but something has come up and I need your help."

"Okay, what's wrong, Jenny?"

"Nothing's wrong, but it's just something I have to do. Can you keep Audrey, tonight? I'll pick her up in the morning, if it's okay?"

"Sure, Jenny, you got it. See you tomorrow, Sis. Bye." Jennifer hurried home to prepare for what she was about to do.

****

Terry, on the other hand, was only minutes away as he drove back to the city. He had talked to Cherlene this morning while thinking he had to work out of town all weekend. Normally, he would've, but they experienced major equipment failures and the men were released to go home until it was fixed again.

"Hmm, it's only 9:45 p.m.," he thought. *"Cherlene is still up. I think I'll surprise her and stop by before I call it a night."*

****

"Well, there's my cue," said Cherlene as she hung up with Jennifer. "It's time for you to go to bed little lady." Therefore, she took Audrey to her crib, but Audrey started crying when Cherlene laid her down. So Cherlene brought her back to the couch where Byrd was waiting to be with her. As they flirted, Cherlene could see the bulge in his pants and she wanted him all the more. After they kissed and made out a little, she again took Audrey to her crib and laid her down. Audrey began to cry. Cherlene started playing with Audrey while bending over her crib. Byrd, who was watching her nice buns through her dress, couldn't take it anymore. So he went into the room where Cherlene was playing with Audrey, and started rubbing on her butt. As he took his fingers and fondled her, Cherlene hissed.

"Uhh! That feels so good," she moaned. Then without warning he pulled her panties aside and grinded his penis in her. "Wait! What are you doing?" He kept his hand on her back to keep her bent over while he grinded her. Cherlene didn't want it this way but it felt so good, she didn't want him to stop.

As she moaned and hissed and made faces, little Audrey thought Cherlene was playing with her so she laughed herself to sleep. As the front door opened, neither Byrd nor Cherlene heard Terry coming in, while Byrd sexed her. Terry heard her moaning and stepped around the corner to see: Byrd saw him and stopped.

"Who the hell is this?" asked Byrd! Cherlene was surprised to see Terry, whose anger was beginning to boil. She was embarrassed as she looked for words.

"Get the hell out of here, man," said Terry angrily.

"I ain't going no where, playa; you leave! Hell, I'm busy right..." Before Byrd could finish his words, Terry attacked him like a wrestler and they began to tear up the place.

"Terry, stop!" yelled Cherlene as she grabbed Audrey. Terry had Byrd bent over the couch and was beating him in the back of the head with his fist.

"So you like it from behind, huh? Then I'm gonna give it to you the way you like it!" yelled Terry. Eventually, he got the best of Byrd and beat him all over the furniture. Cherlene, who thought Terry, was about to kill him, ran between him and Byrd to prevent Terry from hitting him with the vacuum cleaner.

"Stop it, Terry...stop it!" she yelled. Terry lowered the vacuum cleaner and paced in anger. "Go! Go!" she rushed Byrd. "Come on, get up! You have to go!" Byrd, being half beaten to death, slowly stood and left. "Terry, what is wrong with you? Why did you do that? You don't own me, Terry!"

"This is what you do when I'm away working, huh?"

"Terry, we are not married, I can do what I..."

"Whose fault is that!" he yelled loudly. Audrey started crying and Makeda walked into the room.

"How many men do you bring in here over our daughter, Cherlene? How many?" She tried to change the subject.

"Terry, if you would have just called before you came by, this would not have happened." After a moment, Terry reached in his pocket.

"You gave me this key, Cherlene." He held up a key. "The last time we were together, you gave me this. I kinda thought it meant something." While they were talking, they heard a noise at the door. Suddenly, the door opened and it was Clint. He also used his key that Cherlene had given him. Terry's anger turned to pain as he gently threw the key back to Cherlene, who was embarrassed and began to cry.

"You've got too many of us putting keys in the same hole, Cherlene. Just like you, it's just a matter of time before the hole will be worn out." Then Terry left.

"Daddy, Daddy!" yelled little Makeda as she ran behind him. Cherlene caught her at the door and pulled her inside.

"Maybe this is not a good time," said Clint.

"No! Wait!" said Cherlene as she grabbed his arm. "Don't leave me alone, right now! I need to talk; just give me a minute." Clint closed the door while Cherlene went to take care of the kids.

After Cherlene put Audrey to sleep and tucked Makeda in again, she was walking back to Clint when she heard the whisper ... *"The Curse Must Be Broken!"* Then she ran into the bathroom and silently cried to prevent Clint from hearing.

"I don't want to be cursed," she cried. "Mommy, what's wrong with me? Why am I like this?"

Clint sounded beyond the door, "Cherlene, where are you, baby?" Suddenly, she felt her body pulsating; wanting to be held by Clint.

Then she screamed in anger... "Damn you, Mother! I've done nothing wrong, so why am I cursed? Damn you, Mother!"

"Babe, are you OK?" asked Clint who stood outside of the bathroom door. Cherlene quickly dried her tears and opened the door. "I thought I heard you yelling; are you OK?" he asked. "Are you OK?"

Cherlene said nothing as she sunk into his chest and deeply kissed him, like she missed him so much. After the kiss, she stepped loosened her dress, and let it drop to the floor. Clint took her to bed and gave her everything she needed for the night—sex .... sex .... and more sex.

Chapter 43

Nicole tried continually to connect with 911 while the taxi raced Melody to D'Amica's apartment. Nicole never said who had beaten her and wrecked the shop, but when she mentioned D'Amica's name, Melody knew. She also knew that D'Amica could be in a lot of trouble, as the taxi sped through Atlanta.
****

"What was that 911 call about?" asked Donna. They were sitting just outside the city listening to her new scanner and trying to find a story.

"It was nothing," chuckled Tyler. "Just some woman whipping her husband."

"Cool!" laughed Donna. "Let's check it out; it may be a story."
Tyler drove away.

****

As Coldblood's plane landed, he quickly made his way through the airport and grabbed a taxi.

"Mr. Taxi driver, I will give you $100.00 dollars if you can safely get me to Candler Road in 20 minutes."

"You got it, brother. Now buckle up," warned the driver. Rev. Simmons had told him all that was happening as Coldblood raced to D'Amica's and his son. He tried calling but got no answer.

"Where is everybody? Lord if you're there, I need your help," he prayed. Then he called Dexter.

****

As D'Amica opened the door to her apartment, Hookman snatched her inside and forced her to sit in a chair.

"What's up, Meca?" said D-Lo. "No need to worry. I just want to ask you a few questions. If you answer them right, then everything goes back to normal."

"Who are you? Where is my son?"

"Ah! ah! ah!" pointed D-Lo. "I'm the one who will be asking the questions, okay?"

"Mom! Mom!" screamed Shaun from the closet where they had locked him.

"I'm here, baby! Are you okay?" She was forced down as she tried to get up.

"I'm in the closet, Mom!"

"I'm D-Lo and this is the Hookman. Maybe you're heard of us?" D'Amica knew exactly who they were because Coldblood told her everything before he left.

"I've never heard of you," she lied. "What do you want with me?"

"You've been spending and lending money around town. So where did you get so much money?"

"I don't know what you're talking about," she lied again.

"Here we go again," said D-Lo. Suddenly, Hookman slapped D'Amica so hard, she almost blanked out.

"Mom!" she heard Shaun yell as she began to cry.

Chapter 44

Meantime, like a thief in the night, Jennifer had dressed the part and was moving about like a night crawler in the mall area near her job.

"I have to get those disks," she thought. *"And I have to do it tonight or I'm doomed!"*

Jennifer knew there were cameras everywhere—inside and out. Therefore, she moved about each building like a spider clinging to whatever she could until she got to her job's building. Within minutes, she had used the gadgets in her backpack to loosen the small unit on the roof so she could go through the air duct. Once in the duct, she was surprised to be blocked by a wire mess that extended across the passageway.

It wasn't easy, but she eventually cut the entire duct and made her way through. She used the air duct to travel as close as she could to the security room before she attempted to come below the ceiling. She knew she would only have minutes to get out once the alarm sounded. With her face and body being completely covered, she wasn't worried about cameras identifying her. Now, as she rested high above the cameras on the suspended ceiling, she was right over the security room.

"Air duct too small; can't continue through it," she thought. *"Hmm, a glass window? Probably safety or Plexiglas —won't be easy to break. Hmm, double bolted lock with alarm on the steel door ... opening out. Definitely can't go that way."* She was almost out of options then something caught her eye.

"Wait a minute! A raised floor! The security room is a raised floor with cables and cords underneath it. I have to find a way to penetrate the wall below the raised floor, and I will have time to get the disk and get out," she thought.

Then from the top of the wall she could see that it was built with a 12-inch thick cinderblock covered with a layer of sheetrock. Now, she knew that the raised floor idea was out.

Eventually, she decided to use the one and only option she had— throwing her body through the window. She used her mini binoculars to look through the window to study the equipment. Then she tied a rope to the bar joist and her body to the other end of the rope.

Finally, she swung with full force and threw her feet into the glass window. Seemingly, it didn't move. She knew she had triggered the silent alarm, by now, so she used the rope to swing into the glass until it gave way.

She was in a lot of pain from throwing her body into the glass, but she knew she only had a minute or two before cops would be there. She took the disks, and quickly erased all she could from the hard drives and back-up programs then she sped toward the front door.

Chapter 45

"Please, Mr. D-Lo, let my son go, please?" begged D'Amica through tears.

"Where did you get the money, woman?" shouted D-Lo.

"I made it at the Beauty Shop where I work."

"Okay, if you insist." Then he bent her arms behind the chair and held them while Hookman punched her in the face and stomach. She was hurting so bad, she could hardly breathe.

"Where is Coldblood? Did he give you the money? Where is he?" shouted D-Lo.

"Nobody gave me any money," she moaned. "I don't know where he is." Then they slapped her and punched her until her eyes began to roll back in her head. They picked her up and threw her on the furniture until her flesh tore and her limbs broke.

With Shaun yelling for his mom, they threw her on the floor and kicked her in the chest and back. After they felt she had had enough, they sat her back in the chair, with her face and body being completely disfigured.

"Are you ready to talk now?" asked D-Lo. D'Amica could hardly sit straignt in the chair as they spoke to her. Her face was swollen and her shoulder and hip, broken. Her ribs were cracked from the beating and she was bleeding from a serious concussion. She could hardly speak or see, but in her weakness, she stayed strong. "Where is my money?" yelled D-Lo! "Is this how you want to die?"

"I...don't...know...where...yo...money...is." D-Lo was so angry!

"Get the kid!" he ordered. D'Amica tried desperately to sit up straight and talk as she saw Hookman reach for his gun while heading toward the closet.

"Wa...wait!" she whispered painfully. "I'll talk." She struggled through tears to speak as drool and blood slid from her swollen lips.

"Did Coldblood take my money?" yelled D-Lo!

"Yes," she whispered.

"Where is the rest of it? Do you have it? Where is Coldblood?" he asked in anger. Suddenly, Shaun kicked the closet door open and ran out.

"Run Shaun, run!" she shouted out. As Hookman started to shoot Shaun, D'Amica with all her strength, in all her pain and broken body, grabbed Hookman and wrestled with him until she was beaten into a coma and pushed back into the chair. D-Lo tried to catch Shaun as he ran out but Shaun was gone. Donna and Tyler were again parked and listening to their scanner as Nicole finally made the 911 call.

*"Unit 321, DeKalb P.D. Possible assault and battery at
2571 Candler Road Apartments. Suspects are identified as*

Derrick 'D-Lo' Logan and Carlton 'Hookman' Hooks. Possibly armed and dangerous, use all precautions. All units in the vicinity provide back up. Unit 321, do you copy, over."

"Dispatch, this is Unit 321, Radio. Please provide information on the victim, over."

"Unit 321, victim is possibly Ms. D'Amica Taylor, a white female in her mid twenties, with an 8 year-old son, over?"

"Unit 321 clear...out." Suddenly, another call came through from another dispatcher.

"Unit 127, Fulton P.D., silent alarm alert near Perimeter Mall at the Macy's department store. Burglary in progress, suspect possibly armed, proceed with caution. Units in the vicinity provide back up."

"Wow! Did you get all of that?" asked Donna, who was listening to the scanner. "Hurry, let's go." By now, all police in the area had heard the dispatchers and were responding to the calls.

"Go Tyler," screamed Donna as they raced behind the emergency medical vehicle. "Wherever they go, we go!" Tenisha who was also listening to her scanner at home quickly grabbed her bag, little Nela, and left.

****

"We got to go, Bro.," said D-Lo as he heard the sirens approaching. Shaun was on the street yelling and waving for help as police arrived. D'Amica was still slumped in the chair. She was so badly beaten and disfigured that it was hard to tell whether she was dead or alive. The police and medical team entered the apartment to witness her last breath as the twitching in her body came to a halt, and she died.

****

Melody sprung from a moving taxi but is embraced by officers to prevent her from entering the crime scene.

"Let me go! Let me go!" she screamed as Coldblood's taxi approached from a side street.

"No! No!" he whispered as the coroner rolled a stretcher into the building. He wanted to see what was up, but he knew he shouldn't be seen or he would be locked up. So he left the taxi and hid behind a vehicle near the crowd.

****

"Donna, don't forget extra film!" yelled Tyler as she left the van.

"Just park and come with me!" she yelled as she entered the scene.

****

"Look around for anyone that looks suspicious," said a detective to his partner. "Sometimes the assailant never leaves the crime scene, but stands back and watches."

"Hey!" responded the partner. "Check out the sister in the black tights looking like a ninja!"

As they walked toward her, Rosa smoothly maneuvered through the crowd. Then, just as she was suddenly seen, she suddenly disappeared.

"Did you get a good look at her?" asked the detective.

"No, I couldn't see her face, that well. Looked like she had her mouth covered."

"Wonder if she's connected to the crime?" asked his partner.

"Ain't no telling. When D-Lo and Hookman's involved, anybody can be a victim or a suspect."

****

Rosa moved with the ease of a Navy Seal night crawler as she tracked D-Lo and Hookman from the scene of the crime. She eventually corners them on a dark distant street and silently made her presence known.

She quickly kicked Hookman into the brick building and stunned him into dizziness as he dropped. Then she took D-Lo's pistol and dodged his fist as she skillfully maneuvered around him and kicked him until he fell to his knees. As Hookman revived, he pulled his pistol, but she pulled D-Lo between them and shoved him into the Hookman. When they looked up, just as she came ,...she was gone.

****

Coldblood peeped through the crowd and saw Melody in tears as the coroners rolled out a covered body. His eye twitched as his anger grew.

"No! No!" cried Melody as she identified D'Amica's body. Then she turned and hugged Shaun to prevent him from seeing his mom's disfigured body.

"Whew!" whispered Coldblood. "Thank you, God, for sparing my son. I am so sorry about Meca. Why couldn't you save her, too?"

****

Hookman ran into the street at a traffic light, pointed his pistol. "Get out, woman; get out!" He and D-Lo took the car and sped away.

"Aahhh..." growled D-Lo. "What in the hell just happened back there? Who was that ninja bitch and what does she want with us?"

"Don't know," muffled Hookman. "But the Hookman aimed to find out. Can't wait to meet her again."

****

"Where have you been, Rosa?" asked Rev Simmons angrily. "I told you to let God handle it!"

"The girl's dead, Carl," said Rosa as she slowly walked to her hide-a-way. Rev. Simmons was so shocked by her words that he was afraid to say anything else as he followed her like a puppy to see what she would say next.

"Don't worry, Carl. Your son was there and your grandson. Both are safe for now, but it ain't over, Carl." He rested with a sigh of relief and thank the Lord. Then Rosa stripped naked and headed for the shower. He quickly turned and walked out as he heard ... *"The Curse Must Be Broken!"*

****

"Ma'am, can I speak with you for a moment. I'm Donna Banks with..."

"I know who you are," said Melody in tears. "You're the one that came snooping around the shop looking for me the other day. What do you want?" Donna changed her tone.

"I'm so sorry about what happened to D'Amica. Can you tell me a little about what's going on here?"

"Excuse me, Ma'am," injected Dixon. Donna stepped aside. "Son, could you see the men or your mom from inside the closet?"

"No, but I could hear Mom crying when they hit her," said Shaun.

"Did you get a good look at the men before they locked you in the closet?"

"Yes." Bishop showed him a picture of D-Lo and Hookman. "Is this them?"

"Yes," said Shaun.

"Thank you, Son." Then they turned to Melody. "Ma'am, will Shaun be staying the night with you? We may need to ask him more questions."

"Yes," she said while hugging Shaun.

"We have your address, Ma'am; here's my card," said Dixon. "If you can think of anything else to tell us, please give us a call."

As Nicole drove up with Tameka and Adrienna, they ran to Melody and Shaun and burst into tears. Donna and Tyler slowly walked away.

After awhile, when things calmed down, the girls loaded up with Shaun and drove off. Shaun suddenly looked saw Coldblood watching him from between parked cars.

"Dad! Dad!" he screamed. "Stop, Aunt Nicole! Stop the car!"

"Boy, what is wrong with you?" As she stopped the car, Shaun jumped out with Melody running close behind him as he went to where he saw Coldblood.

"Come on, Shaun, your dad is not here," said Melody. All the girls came running to see but there was no one there. Coldblood had escaped into the night. Nicole pondered Shaun's words and actions as she drove away.

****

After Jennifer found the disk back at Perimeter Mall, she knew the alarm had been triggered, but she had no way out except through the front door. She couldn't get back to the roof before she would be caught by cops. But if she could get across the parking lot, she would be home free. So she hit the door and ran for her life. As she neared the end of the parking lot, she met a police cruiser. She quickly diverted but ran into another and another until she was completely surrounded. As she threw both hands up in obedience to the police officers, she saw Tenisha take her picture. Jennifer burst into tears.

Chapter 46

It was about 4:30 a.m. that Friday as Tenisha came rushing into the building to prepare her story for the morning papers.

"Bobby! Bobby!" she called. "I need you to help me layout this story!" Bobby was surprised.

"Are you sure you don't want Harry? He's on his way and will be here in a..."

"No, Bobby! I need you for this one!" Tenisha knew that Tyler (called Harry) was too close to Donna and could possibly prevent her from printing the story about Jennifer in time. She wanted this story written and laid out for the paper before Donna or Tyler could get to work that morning.

"Bobby, this is an important story and it's kinda personal. I need you to diligently stay with me on this until the layout is done and ready to print."

"Okay," said Bobby. Then he started preparing himself.

Bobby, like Tyler, was also an assistant layout man, but he was slow. Tyler could often complete two or three columns to his one. Normally, Tenisha despised him because of his slowness, but today she was treating him like he was the man. As they were working, Donna and Tyler came rushing in.

"Big story!" said Donna as she waved her notes while walking by Tenisha's desk. "Big, big, huge! So whatever you have, Glamour Girl, put it on the back page, cause I'm taking the front!" Then she and Tyler rushed into Mr. Golden's office and talked to him as Tenisha watched and continued to print.

She wasn't sure what Donna had but evidently Mr. Golden thought it was big because he gave her the go ahead to print it as front page news. Tenisha didn't trip because her story was also big and she didn't care what page it got printed on. She was tired of Donna continuously bashing her and she hoped this story about Jennifer would shut her up.

"Ms. Cuyler!" yelled Mr. Golden. "Would you come in here a minute?"

"Yes Sir," yelled Tenisha as Donna passed her.

"He wants to tell you to stay out of my way," smirked Donna as she and Tyler went to work.

"Ms. Cuyler, what are you working on for today?"

"Sir, I was on the scene when police caught a thief tonight in the mall."

"And?"

"Well Sir, if memory serves me right, Perimeter Mall has been one of the main areas reporting theft increase and this has become a really big deal to them."

"Continue," said Mr. Golden. Tenisha handed him the photos of Jennifer.

"Sir, the person or thief that's been ripping them off is one of their employees."

"You don't say!" said Mr. Golden as he looked at the pictures. "She's cute, too. Looks like I've seen this girl before."

"You have, Sir," continued Tenisha. "She's Donna Bank's sister, the one who recently had a baby." Mr. Golden was so shocked, he couldn't speak: He just stared. He had planned to tell Tenisha to give Donna the right-of-way to the front page, but now, he was speechless.

"Sir, I know that Ms. Banks has a big story and wants the front page, but I will be happy with just a corner of it if that's okay with you." Mr. Golden still didn't respond as he stared from Tenisha to Donna. "Sir, I'll take that as a 'yes,' " smiled Tenisha as she walked out of his office.

"What is she smiling about?" said Donna as she and Tenisha watched each other. "It doesn't matter. Whatever she has is not bigger than mine." Then both girls went back to work as Mr. Golden just sat in his office and stared.

****

It was about 5:30 am as Cherlene and Clint lay snuggled in her bed. Jennifer, who could make her call at anytime, sat in a cell at the police station wondering what she would tell her sisters and the world.

"Where did you hide the disk, Jennifer?" asked the detective at the police station. "We know you took the security disk from the store. Why?" Jennifer said nothing.

While running out of the store, she knew there was a chance of not making it out safely. So she quickly stashed the disk in the only place she could think of where it would be safe if she were caught.

"Silence is not gonna make it any easier on you. Store managers in that area have spent a lot of money to catch you and I'm sure they will want to put you away for a long time. So think about that while you're being silent." Another detective was also working on Jennifer's case, as her personal information came up on the computer screen.

Detective 2 - Whoa! This is interesting!
Detective 1 - What is it?
Detective 2 - She's not just a thief, but this chick is an
                employee of this same mall. Both
                detectives just kinda looked at Jennifer in
                silence as they thought.

Detective 1 - Hmm? Looking at the way she entered
        the store tells me that she is a pro
        and has done this type of thing before.
        But she didn't take anything, as far
        as we know, except the security disk.
        There's something on that disk she
        doesn't want to be seen. We need to find
        that disk.
Detective 2 - What are you hiding, Jennifer? We're
        gonna find out. It's just a matter of time.

Jennifer had never felt so bad in all her life. As daybreak approached, she knew her sisters would be looking for her, if they weren't already. So she reached through the bars that held her captive and picked up the phone.

****

At the Atlanta Judicial newspapers, Tenisha had finished preparing her story and was awaiting Donna to set up hers. The articles had already been laid out, but Tenisha was stalling because she didn't want Donna to see Jennifer's pictures before the paper was printed. Donna was diligently working as Tenisha stared at her.

"She think she's hot shit," thought Tenisha to herself. *"She and her sisters paraded around high school like they didn't have a worry in the world- always leaning and depending on each other like they owned the world."*

Tenisha's envy was starting to come out. She became teary eyed as her mind went back to the many times she went home from school wanting a sister to talk to or depending on her like Cherlene, Jennifer, and Donna, depended on each other. Tenisha knew that she had been envious of them. The more she thought about her own jealousy, the more she dreaded having to print this story that she knew would change their lives. Donna could even lose her job as a result of it and Tenisha didn't want that. Tenisha was truly reconsidering printing the story.

"What's the matter, Glamour Bitch?" said Donna when she saw Tenisha's long face. "You look like you've lost your job. Maybe you will when you print that... whatever-it-is story." Then Donna laughed and went back to work. Tenisha was furious, now, and decided to pull out all the stops. It was time to bring this to a halt!

****

As Cherlene's head hung off the side of the bed, Clint sexed her while she moaned, scratched the covers, and screamed in ecstasy. Then the phone rang.

"I have a collect call from... say your name, please..." said the recording. Jennifer stated her name. *"Will you accept the charge?"* Cherlene was shocked as she accepted the call. Clint was getting dressed as he heard Makeda call for her mom. Audrey was still asleep.

"Jenny, where are you? What's going on?" asked Cherlene. Jennifer spoke softly.

"Cheryl, I'm in jail."

****

As Donna and Tyler were completing the last detailed layouts of her story, Donna's phone rang.

"Jenny is in trouble!" yelled Cherlene.

"What kind of trouble?" asked Donna. "I'm really doing an important story, right now, and..."

"Jenny is in jail, Dee!" yelled Cherlene. "Now get your ass down to the Atlanta police station, right now, and bring money. She has a fifty thousand dollar bond!"

"What!" yelled Donna. "Oh my God! I'm on the way!" Then she hung up.

"Tyler, please finish this layout and print it. Everything's good so I have to go. My sister Jennifer is in trouble!" Then she grabbed her bag and ran out. Tenisha knew what was happening and that it would be a while before Donna returned."

"Tenisha," called Tyler. "I need the rest of your story and picture for the printer. Are you ready?" Tyler and Donna had been so busy until neither had read the story that Tenisha laid before them. As Tenisha brought Jennifer's picture and placed it in the designated spot of the layout, Tyler took notice and began to read the story. Afterwards, he stared at Tenisha while being in total shock. Tenisha stared back as if to say,

"Yeah, that's right! Now what?" Then she pulled her disk from her bag and began to type, "Dear diary..."

Chapter 47

It was do or die as Cherlene rushed about to handle things on Jennifer's behalf. All of Cherlene's experience came into play as she talked to a bail bondsman while getting Makeda and Audrey ready to go. She also called her job and made preparations to drop the babies at the daycare.

Finally, after all was done, she headed to Atlanta's city limits to rescue Jennifer. She was truly a business woman in spite of her personal problems. As she arrived at the jail, she saw Donna's car and knew she was waiting inside.

"Cheryl, they won't let me see her!" screamed Donna.

"Ma'am, we're almost done with her processing. When we are finished, you can talk to her," said the cop at the desk.

"Sorry, I'm late," rushed Cherlene. "But I had to drop the kids off and call..."

"Whoa, Cheryl!" started Donna, "I know you have good reason for being late; no problem. Just tell me that we're going to get Jenny out of this." Cherlene started crying.

"I don't know. I don't even know what she is being charged with. She just said that she was locked up and has a fifty thousand dollar bond."

"Fifty thousand!" whispered Donna. "The guy at the desk said we only need five thousand."

"That's right," said the bondsman as he walked in. "Your sister is charged with burglary, breaking and entering, theft, and damage to property. She has a fifty thousand dollar bond which means that if you pay me ten percent of that and sign the papers, we can get her released until her trial date."

The girls were stunned by all they were learning. They quickly collected their thoughts and came up with the money. After about an hour had passed, the girls saw Jennifer being moved into a holding cell where they could talk to her.

"Cheryl, there's Jenny!" screamed Donna as she picked up the phone. "Are you okay, Jenny? Are you hurt?"

"I'm not hurt, Dee," said Jennifer. Her eyes were red from crying. Cherlene took the phone.

"Jenny, it's okay so don't worry. You'll be out of there in a minute and we're gonna get you home. Audrey is at the daycare so don't worry about anything." Cherlene was doing her best to console her but Jennifer soon burst into tears. So did Cherlene and Donna.

****

It was about 8:30 am when all managers of the Perimeter Mall were called in.

"The new security system automatically dialed my home once it detected an intruder last night. I've been here with the contractor since 5:30 this morning and he has assured me that all will be back together by noon," said the CEO. "I have some disturbing news and that's why I called all of you in.

Apparently, one of our employees has been stealing or allowing thieves to take from the stores in this area. Because of this, Ms. Jennifer R. Sweet will no longer be employed here. She was arrested last night for breaking into this very mall and attempting to demolish our security system so that thefts can continue." Michelle's mouth opened in awe as they heard their CEO speak.

"I don't know who else besides Jennifer was involved in this, but obviously there are others because she took the security disk of the last two days and the police can't locate them. Investigators are searching now because she could have hidden the disk here in the store.

People," he spoke angrily. "This type of activity will not be tolerated in this store! I've asked the investigators to interview all of you to find out if you were involved in any way with Ms. Sweet or her actions here last night. The investigators are currently waiting in my office.

Effective immediately, all employees are suspended until they have been questioned by the investigators and satisfaction by them is achieved. Michelle Lane, why don't we start with you? Step into my office, please." Michelle hesitantly entered.

****

While Cherlene and Donna waited for Jennifer to be released, they were surprised to see Byrd walk approach the officer at the desk being banged up with his arm in a sling.

"May I help you, sir?" asked the officer.

"Yes, I'm here to file charges against a group of gang members that assaulted me," said Byrd. Cherlene and Donna were surprised and were about to confront him when a slim, very pretty, young woman with a little boy, came in and stood beside him.

"Sir, hold on a moment while I finish this up then I'll file your report," said the officer. Cherlene and Donna stopped dead in their tracks when they saw the woman. Then Cherlene decided to introduce herself.

"Hi," spoke Cherlene to the woman. Byrd turned and looked at her in shock. "Would your name be Patricia or Pat by any chance?"

"Yes, it is," greeted the woman.

"I bet this is your little 3 year-old son, C-Lo, right?" continued Cherlene.

"Yes, and this is my husband Michael. Do we know you?"

"I know your husband quite well," smiled Cherlene. "You see, before my boyfriend, a gang of one, kicked his ass all over my apartment, your husband, Michael, or is it Big Byrd, had me bent over my niece's crib screwing me pretty deep.

I have to admit that he was pretty good, but of course you would know that since you didn't die giving birth to little C-Lo here, like he told me." By now, Donna is confused and Byrd is nervous as Cherlene continues.

"So if you're here to file charges, the gang member that kicked his ass just happened to be my baby's daddy." Then she turned to the officer and said, "Officer, I was the only eyewitness when this man got his ass beat and he started it, when he put his penis in me." By now, Byrd's wife was very angry while staring at him. Donna was trying to keep from laughing while Cherlene stood beside Patricia as both of them stared at Byrd.

"Sir," said the officer. "Do you want to press charges or not?" As Jennifer came into the lobby from the back, Cherlene and Donna ran to her and hugged her. When they entered the parking lot, they saw Byrd lying and pleading with his wife, Patricia, who jumped in the car with her kid and left him standing there.

"Isn't that Big Byrd?" asked Jennifer. "Who was that he was arguing with?"

"Trust me, Jenny," laughed Donna. "You don't want to know."

****

At the mall, police are all over the stores while managers are still being questioned. Michelle had been questioned already and was not a suspect to any of Jennifer's misdealing or thefts. Many of the store employees were talking openly about the situation as Michelle listened.

> Employee #1 - *Man, I bet her house is straight! Ain't no telling how long she's been stealing. Hell, I'm jealous 'cause she didn't let me in on it.*
>
> Employee #2 - *Wonder what's on that security disk they're looking for?*
>
> Employee #1 - *Only she knows, but I hope they don't find it. Then maybe she can come back and get something for me.*
>
> Employee #2 - *Do you think the disk is still here in the store?*
>
> Employee #1 - *Sure it is! They say they caught her in the parking lot but she didn't have the security disk. They already searched the departments where she worked and didn't find it. That only means it's in somebody else's.*

As Michelle pondered their conversation, she began to think. She knew Jennifer better than anyone in the store and wondered if Jennifer had stashed the disk in a place she knew of. So she sneakily began to search the area where she worked; she found nothing.

She was about to give up when she decided to just stand at the counter where Jennifer always stood whenever she came by to talk. As she did, she saw the disk wedged between the wooden panels where the jewelry cabinets comes together. Michelle got nervous and headed to the bathroom to think.

"I know that's the disk," she said. "I know that's it!" Michelle was nervous, but she went back to work, leaving the disk where she saw it.

"So," spoke one of the detectives. "I hear you know Ms. Sweet pretty well."

"Yeah, and I told the investigators all I know," replied Michelle.

"Being the kind of person she is, where do you think she would hide something like a disk or security tape?"

"Maybe in her department," said Michelle. "All of this is a surprise to me."

"I'm sure it is," he continued.

"Will she go to prison?"

"That depends on what's on that disk. But unless we get more evidence, she could get a year or two--maybe even probation and a fine but it's hard to say. But if we can prove that she is the reason why the stores have lost profits over the past 2 or 3 years, then she will get more time and probably have restitution to pay, along with a fine. That's why owners want us to find that disk. Are you sure you don't know where it is?" he asked again.

"I told you this is all new to me and you are welcome to look around." The detective looked like he didn't believe her, then he walked away.

Later that day, when the search was over, Michelle saw that the disk was still there. She knew cameras were everywhere and even her broach was recording everything. Suddenly, Michelle saw someone in the store she recognized. It was the woman she and Jennifer caught stealing a necklace about a month ago. Michelle took a pen and paper and covered it with her hand while she wrote a note. Then she approached the woman.

"Can I help you, Ma'am?" The lady was surprised but remembered Michelle.

"Look lady, I don't want no trouble. I am just in here looking for the lady who was with you that day I came in here. She saved my life and I wanted to thank her. Is she working today?"

"That's a likely story. Please do your shopping, Ma'am, and I will see you later." Then Michelle dropped the folded note so the young woman could see her. After Michelle walked away, the woman picked up the note and read it.

> *"We did you a favor one day. Now my friend is in trouble and she needs your help. There is something lodged between the counters over there. You'll know it when you see it. For my friend's sake, take it if you can, and destroy it. Be careful; cameras are everywhere."*

The woman looked at Michelle, smiled, then gladly did her thing and got the disk. Afterwards, she headed out of the store and went her way.

Chapter 48

"We're running out of time, men," fussed Chief Lewis. "Derrick 'D-Lo' Logan cannot go but so far. Somebody have to have seen something; he's too big. Anybody as big as he is can't just disappear. The murder of this young hair stylist is just too much. For now, we have to forget about Holloway and nail D-Lo and Hookman before they cause a panic in the city. Now get out there and find them!" he ordered. As the men started to disperse, a fax came though and Hardy picked it up.

"Chief, check this out. It's a picture of Jennifer Sweet sent from the local Atlanta P.D. Says that she's a positive match for the blood sample found at a burglary with D-Lo's men about a year ago."

"What's the story on her?" asked the chief.

"Last night, she was caught breaking and entering at Perimeter Mall where she worked. Currently released to her family on a fifty thousand dollar bond," said Hardy.

"Yeah, I read about that story this morning," added Castleberry.

"You two stop by as soon as you can and check her out. Find out what's her connection to D-Lo or Hookman," said the Chief.

****

Meantime, D-Lo and Hookman made it safely back to their hide-a-way. D-Lo is furious as he paces the floor and speaks.

"This whole thing has gone terribly wrong!" he murmured. "Two people have been taken out and we still didn't get the one who took my money. Now, my name is out there and the folks will be stepping up their game to find me.

Aahhh!" he screamed as he turned over the table, and hit the wall. "Why are y'all standing around watching me? Go do something! Get me something on Coldblood and whoever helped him to take my money! Now get!" A couple of the men went outside to the car while some stepped to other rooms and made phone calls.

"Lo-Down was packin' a shotgun under his robe when we visited him," said Hookman. "What makes you think he didn't help Coldblood?"

"If he had helped him, he would have never allowed us to get that close to him. He would've blown our brains out the second he knew it was us," said D-Lo. "Besides, I think this must've been someone younger...a partner. Check around. Everybody has somebody they depend on and Coldblood ain't no different."

"What about that ninja bitch?" asked Hookman. "Think she was with him?"

"Aahhh!" screamed D-Lo again as he kicked over furniture. "I don't know who that was, but I need you on this one. Don't kill her though, because she's mine."

"What happened?" asked Elisa. "What does she look like?"

"Why? Do you know something?" asked D-Lo.

"Well, Mr. Holloway used to talk about a special friend that hurt him once...a lady he thinks he killed but he's not sure."

"Then why are you talking to me?" yelled D-Lo! "You should be talking to Holloway! Now get on it!" Elisa slowly moved toward the cordless phone and picked it up. She was trying to be careful because she knew whatever happened to D-Lo earlier, that night, had him in a rage. Suddenly, he grabbed her and threw her across the couch as she fell to the floor. Then he quickly ran to her and put his hand around her neck.

"I don't like the way you're moving, right now, Baby Girl. Neither do I like the way you look at me when I talk to you." Then he threw her in the bedroom and onto the floor. "Now make the damn call like I said and hurry up!" Then he threw the phone and hit her with it.

Elisa felt ashamed and embarrassed as she tried to force herself to remain calm. But her facial expressions gave her away. D-Lo came running into the bedroom where she was and slammed the door behind him. Then he slapped her down to the bed.

"You're acting like you want to try ol' D-Lo, Baby Girl! What's up? You wanna try me? Come on," he smiled. Elisa couldn't resist. She got into her stance and waited for him to attack. For the first time, she was ready to fight him. As he swung at her, she ducked, then kicked him hard in his side and backed away.

"That was pretty good," laughed D-Lo. "Who taught you that? Let's see what else you got." He swung at her again and she ducked. Except this time, he kept swinging until he eventually hit her in her gut, then in her face until she bled. Just like he did D'Amica, he was throwing her all over the room with no mercy. Elisa felt herself dying as she cried out in desperation and fell to his feet.

"D-Lo, please don't kill me!" she cried heavily. "Please D-Lo, I'm sorry." By now, Elisa was down on her knees with her head bowed to his feet pleading and crying for her life. "I was wrong D-Lo and I won't do it again." she begged. "Just tell me what you want me to do. Please just tell me what you want me to do." Elisa was crying serious tears, now. She was in pain all through her body, and she was dizzy. She felt herself crying out to God for help because she was scared and bleeding from her head and her body.

"Get up!" yelled D-Lo. "I should've killed yo' ass for trying me like that! I still just might! Let's see how you act this time. Now get in the bathroom, clean your face, then make my phone call!" he demanded.

While limping and in tears, Elisa quickly jumped up and struggled her way to the bathroom. She was moving as fast as she could while D-Lo watched her. She was so scared, she just quickly cleaned the blood from her head and face then hurried back to the bedroom to make the call to Holloway. Just as she started to dial, D-Lo slowly took the phone from her hand. Being afraid, she quickly placed her hands to her face thinking he would hit her again.

"No, no, Baby Girl; it's all good. Put your hands down and come here." Elisa was afraid, but she knew she had to go to him. "Don't worry, you're safe now. But I want you to listen to me. Take your time, go in the bathroom and clean yourself up. You are a beautiful woman and D-Lo wants you to stay beautiful, okay?" She nodded as D-Lo hugged her. "Just don't be trying me because I will kill you and replace your ass in a heartbeat. Now go look good for D-Lo."

As Elisa headed for the shower, she felt safe again but her head was hurting. She stood behind the door in the bathroom thinking about her dad and her mom she had lost when she was a kid. She didn't even know of a distant cousin or friend she could talk to.

D-Lo was all she had and he had just proven to her that he would kill her without a second thought. The beating she just took was causing her to lose sight of the agency and the real reason she was there. Elisa now feared for her life and living was all that mattered to her. She especially didn't want to die by the hand of the same man that killed her dad.

After she showered and cleaned up, she had lumps, knots and bruises but she was beautiful again. She was still in a lot of pain, and her head hurt. D-Lo was enticed by how beautiful she was in her nice robe after taking a beating like that. So he followed her into the bedroom and closed the door.

"Come here, Baby Girl," he said while standing against the door. Elisa hurried across the floor and stood to his face smelling like a perfumed factory. "Damn, Baby Girl, you smell so good!" he spoke while rubbing her shoulders. "You know we do have some unfinished business... so are you ready for the D-Lo?"

Elisa was hurting and her headache was getting worse. But this time, she knew she had to play the role, whether she wanted to or not. So she made up her mind to do it right. She faked a nice smile and kissed D-Lo deeply. Then she dropped her robe and exposed her body as she pressed against him. She was forcing herself to be in the mood for her life's sake.

Finally, she took his fingers and started to massage her clit, as she hissed and moaned. D-Lo had never seen her like this before and he was so enticed. Of the many times he'd had sex with her, she never acted like she wanted him. But today was different, and he felt her passion. He picked her up, carried her to the bed, dropped his pants and penetrated her.

"Uh!" she moaned as he slid inside her. "Oh D-Lo!" she screamed louder and louder as he rocked her. "Yes D-Lo, baby, that's it!" she continued as D-Lo pounded her over and over again.

She screamed his name even after he released while she pretended she had been sexed so good and couldn't help herself. Little did D-Lo know that the phone was also on the bed when he first penetrated her, so she screamed his name repeatedly to prevent him from hearing her dial 911.

****

"Hey Chief," started Hardy. "We did some checking on Jennifer Sweet, and it turns out that she has two half-sisters all living in Cobb County. All three have respectable jobs and seem to be well-known by the people they worked with. I know that Jennifer's blood was found at a crime scene where D-Lo's men were spotted, but something's missing. I don't see her as being a part of D-Lo's club."

"Maybe it's coincidental," added Castleberry. "Maybe they just happen to hit the same spot in one night."

"Maybe," continued Hardy. "Let's talk to Jennifer and see what she knows about D-Lo and that night." Suddenly, Chief Lewis gets a call on his cell phone.

"What?" he answered. "When?" He took a pen and wrote an address, then he hung up. "Okay guys, here we go! We just got a 911 of a young woman screaming 'D-Lo' into the phone while making love to him or being raped."

"Did we get the address?" asked Dixon.

"We got it!" said the chief. "Let's go. I want everybody in on this one. It may be nothing, but I want to be prepared." Then he handed an officer the address. "Get me a SWAT team to this location and a negotiator on standby. We can't focus on Holloway anymore, because this D-Lo guy is hurting too many people. We have to bring him down!"

Chapter 49

"Dex, I called you many times when I left the airport and got nothing," said Coldblood. "Where were you, man? I expected you to pick me up! What happened?"

"Olivia is what happened," started Dexter. "Olivia really started trip' in when I told her I was picking you up. She thought I would be killed if I went with you so she threatened to leave me if I met you."

"So why didn't you just call me and tell me?"

"Blood!" he sounded. "It wasn't that easy. You know how Olivia can get and she got really crazy," said Dexter.

"She beat that ass, didn't she?" chuckled Coldblood.

"You got jokes, man, at a time like this." Coldblood had finally got in touch with Dexter and they were driving to see Rev. Simmons at the church. It was still early morning but Coldblood knew he'd be there. Because of the night's previous events with D'Amica, GBI were busy and no longer watching him. Rev. Simmons met them at the front door as they got out of the car.

"Hello, Dad," said Coldblood.

"How are you, Rev. Simmons, Sir?" followed Dexter.

"Hello, Junior... Dexter. I'm sorry we have to meet under such gruesome circumstances. Are you boys okay? Come on in and let's talk."

****

Meanwhile at Melody's, Shaun tried to call Coldblood all during the night, but there was no answer. As he ate at the table with Melody the next morning, Nicole walked in and they began to talk. Shaun took out his phone and dialed again. This time, Coldblood answered.

"Hello! Dad?" spoke Shaun. "Where are you? I saw you last night."

"I saw you too, Son."

"See Aunt Mel! I told you I saw him!"

"Yes, you did," said Melody. "And I'm sorry I didn't believe you."

"Dad," started Shaun as he went back to the phone. "They killed Mom, Dad."

"I know, Sport. How are you doing?"

"I guess I'm okay. Aunt Mel says I have to stay with her for now. Aunt Nicole is here, too. Everything seems kinda funny. When are you coming to get me, Dad?"

"I'm coming as soon as I can, Shaun," Coldblood assured him. "But you know what I'm going through so be patient, OK?"

"I know," Shaun spoke disappointedly.

"Sport, I want you to stay with Melody until I can get everything fixed. And do what she tells you, okay?"

"Dad, are you gonna come see me before you leave?"

"Yes, I will be there today... in a few hours, but let me speak to Melody." Shaun handed Melody the phone. Nicole quickly stepped up and snatched it from Melody's hand. "Hello, Melody?" started Coldblood, "I know we have never really talked and don't know each other, but I thank you for what you're doing for Shaun."

"Coldblood, this is Nicole," she said. Then she walked away from Shaun. "Don't worry about your son; we will take care of him."

"Thank you, Nicole. D'Amica chose her friends well."

"D'Amica was family to us, and so is Shaun. But I need to tell you that Shaun hasn't shed a tear since everything happened and that concerns me. I really think you need to see him as soon as possible."

"I understand," said Coldblood. "I will see him, soon." Then he checked his caller ID. "Can I get you at this number?"

"Yes, but this is Melody's number. I will have Shaun text you my number and you can call either of us when you're ready to come by."

"Good enough. I promise I'll be there as soon as I can. Tell Shaun I will call him later. I've got to go now."

"Coldblood, please take care of yourself. This boy really needs you now." As they hung up, Melody started fussing.

"Nikki, why in the hell did you do that?" she shouted. "You just took the damn phone and did what you wanted to! You always have to be in charge of..." Nicole suddenly put up the hand.

"Melody, as usual you're not thinking. You, of all people, don't need to be talking to that boy's daddy, right now."

"And why not?" questioned Melody.

"Because you're sleeping with the man who killed his son's momma. Word is that Coldblood don't play. And when he finds out about you, Meca may not be the only beautician lying in the morgue." Melody got quiet and began to panic. She knew Nicole was right.

****

"So what are you gonna do, Junior?" asked Rev. Simmons.

"Dad, you already know this... D-Lo and Hookman better than I do. You know they will not rest until they find me and kill me. Which means, everybody I know and love is also in danger. I have to kill' em, Dad."

"Son, no you don't!" begged Rev. Simmons. "You can take Shaun and leave now. I can take care of myself!"

"Dad, I know you can, but your time is over and this is my time now. I'm already running from the law, so I'm not gonna run from gangsters, too. What kind of life is that to live?" stated Coldblood.

"Junior, all I'm saying is that you should give God a chance to help you."

"Dad, don't start that! I'm not stopping God! He can step right in and handle this whenever he wants to. Shaun made it last night, but God didn't seem to care about saving D'Amica, did he? Look Dad, I came out here to see if you will still let me borrow the bag. Shaun is safe for a minute and I've got to get to D-Lo and Hookman before they get to him, again."

"Junior, you're making a big mistake, son!"

"Dad, can I have the bag or not?" Rev. Simmons paused.

"It's at the house."

"Thanks, I'll be in touch. Let's go Dex." They started to leave.

"Junior, remember what I told you about that bag?"

"Yeah, I know, Dad. You can't help me anymore because it's the devil's bag, and you represent God." Then they drove away as Rosa eased from the back.

"You heard?" asked Rev. Simmons.

"Every word," she said. "You know the boy is right, Carl. I just hope that things work out right for him." Rosa had her glocks under her coat as she prepared to leave.

"Wait a minute!" said Rev. Simmons. "Where are you going? It's the middle of the morning! You'll be seen!"

"Carl, I'm a big girl and I'll be alright. Besides, I just got a tip from my sources that D-Lo's hide-a-way has been located and it's not too far from here. I want to be there when they raid the place just in case I run into some familiar faces."

"You think that either Holloway or his men may be nearby, don't you?" asked Rev. Simmons.

"D-Lo has become a liability and Holloway may try to save him." Then Rosa covered herself in her shawl and she was gone.

****

Coldblood and Dexter headed to Rev. Simmons' home to pick up the bag that Coldblood rejected a few months ago. Dexter decided to make a few calls so he started with his brother, Terry.

"Hello, Terry?" said Dexter.

"Yeah Dex, what's up?" groaned Terry.

"Man, you sound bad! What's up with you?" asked Dexter. Terry was quiet for a minute. "It's about Cherlene again, ain't it?" Dexter knew that Terry was madly in love with Cherlene because they had talked about it. "Terry, that girl is gonna really hurt you, someday," said Dexter. "I wish you could just let her go before that happens." Terry just paced the floor. Then he angrily spoke into the phone.

"Why are you calling, Dex? What do you want?"

"Remember what I told you about me, Coldblood, and the money? Well, they know who we are, and now it's us or them," said Dexter.

Terry calmed. "Oh my God, Dexter! This don't sound good. What do you want me to do?"

"Well, I wanted you to know that we're going after them and you may need to protect yourself. Second, please talk to Olivia if I'm not home in 24 hours," said Dexter.

"I got it," said Terry. "Be careful, man. I'll holla..." After they hung up, Terry sat thinking about Cherlene and the events of the previous night. "Dex is right," he whispered. "It's time to let her go. I'm a better man than this. But I have to take care of my daughter, and I will."

Chapter 50

Elisa laid in bed under D-Lo with her body twitching and her head pounding.

"Something is wrong," she thought. Elisa didn't know that the beating she took before sex had damaged her organs. She had internal bleeding in her body and fluids were draining in her head. As the pain worsened, Elisa's body began to lock up and she couldn't speak. All she could do was slightly moan and shake.

As D-Lo lifted from bed and headed toward the bathroom, he saw Elisa slightly twitching and smiled, thinking he had done a great job of sexing her. Little did he know that Elisa was slowly dying. Seconds later, the twitching stopped and she passed out. D-Lo had gone into the bathroom.

Hookman and the men were in the building when D-Lo began to toss Elisa in the bedroom. But after the sex started, they walked outside and just hung out in the yard.

Many of the expensive buildings and residences in Austell were at least a quarter mile apart and had lots of land around them. Such was this place where Holloway allowed them to hide out. It was a nice ranch-type property with a barn and old stable but no animals. It also had a porch, a very nice yard with trees, and a small pond. After the men thought the sex was over, some of them headed back inside.

As Hookman walked back onto the porch, he thought he saw something move within the trees. He did! It was a man with a rifle! Hookman had enough experience to know it wasn't just any man as he heard strange sounds coming from around the property.

"Raid!" he screamed as he ran toward the car. He knew he didn't have time to do anything but yell and run before the police would be all over them. As he sped the car toward the pond, about 30 GBI gunmen raced into the house yelling and throwing smoke. D-Lo was in the bathroom when a tear gas canister came flying though the window. By the time he got to his weapon, Agents were fast upon him. None of D-Lo's men fired a shot before they were arrested.

"He's getting away!" yelled an officer. "Fire at will!" Bullets from everywhere cut into the vehicle as Hookman sped away. Within seconds, Hookman had driven out of the line of fire and was speeding through unfamiliar territories. After the SWAT team and police secured the building, officers found Elisa and knew she was hurt.

"Officer down! Officer down!" yelled Dixon. The medical team quickly rushed in and began to treat her on the spot.

****

As police vehicles pursued Hookman, they got lost and confused by the many back roads that led through the property. As he drove though the trees, Hookman, too, was lost, but he knew he had to get as far away as he could. So he just kept going as fast as he could.

"Get me a chopper!" yelled Chief Lewis into the telephone. "Damn it! Hooks is on the run again! Except this time, I want him caught!"

Police were no longer in sight as Hookman tried to figure his way out of danger. So he stopped the car, turned off the engine, then stepped out and listened to hear if there was a nearby road or neighborhood in his path.

As he listened, he heard what sounded like many feet running toward him but he didn't see anyone. Then he heard the sound of someone on foot quickly speeding through the bushes and bouncing off of tree limbs, but he couldn't tell what direction they were coming from. All he knew was that they were coming fast and coming toward him.

"What the hell?" he thought as he pulled his revolver. As he jumped back into the vehicle and started the engine, he heard a loud swooshing sound of someone flying though the air and landing on top of his vehicle. He pointed the pistol and shot though the roof. Before he could get off a second shot, his door opened and he found himself flying through the air as two strong hands snatched him from the vehicle. He went one way and his pistol went the other. After he hit the ground and shook himself, he was surprised as he turned to see!

"Ah! Ninja Bitch!" he smiled as he took his stance to fight. Rosa said nothing as she circled him like a lioness about to strike. "I don't know what your beef is with me, Ninja Woman, but it all ends here!" Then he took out his knife and attacked her. She easily evaded it, then, slapped him hard—twice. He growled, and attacked her again. This time, she somehow interlocked his arm holding the knife, around her arm, and started a series of slaps, punches and kicks, all to his face and head, until he fell to the ground; now his nose was bloody.

"You didn't have to take that child's life. She was just a young girl trying to make it," said Rosa.

"She took my money!" yelled Hookman as he attacked her again. This time, Rosa diverted the knife and it flew away through the air. As Hookman repeatedly swung at her, she blocked, punched, ducked, kicked, slapped, and wrestled him until he was badly beaten and bloody. Then she kicked him into a tree and almost broke his back.

Hookman could hardly move now and he felt beaten. She advanced toward him for the finale, but Hookman suddenly pulled a second pistol and fired. She ducked, maneuvered, and ran, as he fired shot after shot until he emptied the clip. But as fast as Rosa had come – she was gone. When Hookman saw a chopper overhead, he drove the car into the trees then went on foot until he made it to a nearby neighborhood.

"Who is it?" asked the woman as she opened the door. "Oh my God!" she screamed when she saw Hookman pointing the weapon at her.

"Who else is here, lady? Speak up!"

"No one!" she responded. "My husband's working and the kids are in school! What do you want?"

"I want you to shut up; now come on!" Hookman stepped inside and closed the door behind him. Then he forced the lady through the house as he checked it out. "What kind of car do you have?" he asked.

It was early Friday morning so no one was out as Hookman forced her into the garage and into the trunk of her car. Then he drove to the highway and on to safety. A few minute later, Hookman had parked around the corner and was on foot to Melody's apartment.

"Yes? Who is it?" asked Melody as the door buzzed.

"It's me, girl; let me in for a minute." Melody ran to the window to see with Shaun trailing behind her.

"What are you doing here, Carlton? I told you to never come to my house unless I invited you."

"Come on, girl; stop playing," he begged. "The heat is on and I need to lay low for a minute." By now, Shaun saw it was one of the men that hurt his mom so he ran inside the closet and dialed his phone.

"Hello, Dad?"

"Shaun, I told you I will be there as soon as I can. But I've got something to do then..."

"Dad, he's here! One of the men that hurt mom is here, talking to Aunt Mel!"

"Carlton! Why did you do that to Meca? Why? You know she didn't do anything wrong. Now you think I'm gonna let you come up in here? I'm calling the cops, Carlton!"

"Bitch!" he yelled as he pointed his weapon toward her. She quietly screamed and ducked away from the window. Then she saw him running away.

"My dad's on the way," said Shaun.

"What! Did you call him?"

"Uh huh! And he's gonna get that man! That's the man that hurt my mom!" Melody panicked and picked up the phone.

"Nikki," said Melody. "I need you to come back. Please hurry, Nikki, I'm scared."

"What's the matter?" Nicole asked.

"Carlton just left and Coldblood is on the way!"

Chapter 51

"Aahhh!" screamed Rosa as she laid on her bed back at the church.

"Rosa, I told you not to get involved, but you are so hard-headed!" said Rev. Simmons. "Now look at you! You've gotten yourself shot!" Rosa was on her bed screaming in pain from being shot as Rev. Simmons did his best to take care of her. "I don't know what I'm doing, Rosa! You need a doctor!"

"No, Carl!" she screamed. "I'll help you! Aahhh! Help me take my clothes off!" As he helped her strip down to her underwear, she had a bullet lodged in her side next to her breast and she had a wound from a bullet that cut through the side of her butt. Rev. Simmons didn't want to remove her bra and panties, but because of the wound locations and the blood, he had no choice. He struggled to patch the wound on her hip then he covered her naked bottom. Afterward, he cleaned the wound in her side and prepared to remove the bullet.

"Rosa, are you still with me?" he asked. Rosa was moaning with pain and feeling weak. She had lost a lot of blood and could hardly stay awake.

"Carl! Listen! If I pass out and you don't know what to do...call...call...Chief...Chief..." Rosa passed out and Rev. Simmons panicked.

After he did what he could, he picked up the phone and dialed. "Myrtice," he phoned. "I need your help. Are you busy?" Myrtice, who managed a foster care home not too far away, was also a member of his church. She wasn't a doctor or nurse, but she often gave testimonies about how she dressed wounds and cared for the young boys at her foster home because she couldn't afford the medical costs. Plus, back in the day, he had helped her to get out of a really tight spot and they had become friends.

"Hi, Rev. Simmons," she responded, "I guess I can break away a minute before the kids come from school. Are you at the church?"

"Yes, Myrtice, I am. Please hurry! And bring your first aid kit!"

"Oh my!" she said, "I don't like the sound of that!"

****

Shaun saw Coldblood and Dexter from the window and met them at the door.

"Dad! Dad!" he yelle as he hugged him and pulled him into the building. Coldblood and Dexter had their hands on their pistol. Melody met them at the door.

"Hi, Coldblood," she said in tears. "I'm so sorry about Meca—I really am."

"I know, I know. Are you alright in here?" He and Dexter looked around. "Shaun said that D-Lo was here and..."

"No, it was Carlton."

"Carlton? Who's Carlton?"

"The Hookman. Carlton 'Hookman' Hooks," said Melody. The men looked at each other surprisingly.

"Dad, that's the man that put me in the closet while they hurt mom."

"What was he doing here?" asked Coldblood. "What did he say?"

"He was here to see Aunt Mel," said Shaun. Melody was in tears as Coldblood's eye began to twitch. Then he grabbed Melody and slammed her to the wall.

"Melody? What's going on? What do you have to do with all this?" By now, Nicole had parked and was rushing in.

"Coldblood, I didn't know he was gonna hurt her," said Melody. "I really didn't know!" Then with one hand, Coldblood grabbed her by her throat and lifted her up on the wall.

"You better start talking, lady, before I ..." Suddenly, the front door burst open and Coldblood and Dexter pointed their pistols; Nicole stopped in her tracks.

"Please let her go, Coldblood," said Nicole as she slowly walked toward Melody. "We know you loved Meca, but we loved her, too. She was our sister. Please, let her go and we will tell you what we know." Coldblood let Melody down and they told him what they knew about Carlton, D-Lo, and all that had happened.

"It's not safe for my son to stay here, so he's going with me." Shaun's face lit up. Coldblood was still very angry as he called his dad.

"Yes Son, I understand and I can help," said Rev. Simmons while looking at Myrtice work on Rosa. "I have just the place where little Shaun can stay."

****

It was getting late as Hookman pulled into an alley behind the club.

"Get out!" he told the woman after he opened the trunk. The lady nervously stepped out.

"Please don't hurt me, Mister. I have a family and..."

"Shut up, woman, and quit all that crying. This is your lucky day. I ain't gonna kill you if you be quiet and do what I say. Now climb up there and get in that dumpster." The lady looked surprised but she did it. As she lowered herself into the dumpster, Hookman hit her with his pistol and knocked her out. Then he covered her with garbage.

"Lady, if you make it, then you make it. If you don't, then you don't. But I really don't give a damn." Then he left.

****

Things were calmer with Coldblood after Nicole and Melody explained how Hookman and D-Lo got to D'Amica.

"Again, thank you for taking care of Shaun. I'm sorry things have to be this way." Then as he was leaving with Shaun, Dexter's phone rang; it was Terry.

"Man, I am really having a hard time," said Terry. "Can you stop by?"

"Yeah, I can. I'll see you in a few," said Dexter. "Blood, it's my brother. I need to go see him now. I know you have problems, but my brother does too."

"Do you need me to help you?" asked Coldblood.

"No, it's nothing like that. I just need to be there for him, that's all."

"Okay man, go!" said Coldblood. "I'll take a taxi or something."

"Can I help?" asked Nicole. "I have a car."

****

Rosa was resting peaceably after Myrtice removed the bullet and patched her up.

"I don't know what I'd do without you, Myrtice," said Rev. Simmons. "God sure knows where to place his angels. Thank you so much!"

"Don't thank me, Reverend! She's not out of the woods, yet." Suddenly, Nicole drove up with Coldblood and Shaun. "This must be little Shaun whom you told me about?" asked Myrtice. "Looks like a good kid."

"He is, Myrtice, he is. But we have to save him from our past."

"I understand," said Myrtice. "To keep it legal, I'll process the necessary paperwork then we can go from there."

"Sounds good. Now come and let's meet Shaun and his father."

"Myrtice," moaned Rosa as she awakened. "Thank you." Myrtice smiled then went out to meet Shaun.

Chapter 52

It was evening at GBI Headquarters as they finalized their reports.

"Man, this has really been a busy day," said Chief Lewis. "Can't wait to get home." The agents just kinda looked at each other. Then Shelby whispered,

"Man, if I had to go home after a hard day's work and sleep with a woman who complains like the chief's wife, I think I'd commit a crime and lock myself up." They all snickered.

"What's the joke?"

"Nothing Chief," said Castleberry. "It's just that last night at the crime scene, a couple of local detectives claimed they saw a lady ninja in the crowd. Boy, those guys must be desperate for some action."

"You know for a brief moment, I could have sworn I saw Carl 'Coldblood' Simmons Jr. in the crowd," said Bishop.

"Was he wearing black tights like a ninja women then just disappeared?" asked Castleberry. "Seems to be a lot of that going around."

"Okay men, listen," said the Chief. "As you know, we have D-Lo behind bars and a *'for sure'* grand jury indictment, but it's not enough. We can put him away but we can't tie him to Holloway. Gentlemen, we have to get something on Holloway before D-Lo's trial and put them in bed together. If we can't, then we have wasted years of undercover work because we can't use anything that we have on Holloway."

"Chief, how's Agent Smith?" asked Dixon. "Do doctors think she'll make it?"

"She'll make it," added the Chief. "But we don't know what her condition will be. She's had brain trauma as well as severe internal bleeding. Until we can talk to her, we don't know what to decide about the undercover mission."

"You don't get to decide anything," said a strong voice through the door.

"Who are you?" asked Bishop!"

"I'm FBI Special Agent Walter Dennard, and this is my partner Agent Ruby. We're in charge or Special Operations and Agent Elisa Smith is working under our jurisdiction."

"What do you mean 'is working?' The lady's in a coma," said Hardy.

"We are aware of that, agent, but sources tell us that since D-Lo's arrest earlier today, Holloway has been searching for Agent Smith, because he didn't hear about her being busted in the raid. You guys slipped on this one. If he doesn't find her soon, he will know she's an operative and have every hit man in the country trying to kill her," said

Agent Walter. "We've got to make her whereabouts known or not only do we eventually lose Agent Smith, but we will never get this close to Holloway again."

"Wait a minute, Walter! Are you saying that we have to put her out there so Holloway can decide if she is a target or not?" asked the Chief. "Man, that's suicide! She is in no condition to defend herself if Holloway's goons come after her!"

"It's a risk we have to take."

"You mean it's a risk she has to take, if she chooses to, don't you?" asked the Chief.

"You're right, Chief! That's why we have instructed the doctors to wake her up." The men in the room got loud and started talking. "Chief Lewis, we didn't come here to get your approval, but we came hoping that you want to be there when we wake her up. Now what's it gonna be?" demanded Walter. Chief Lewis grabbed his hat in anger, and left with them.

****

"Carl Junior, it's good to see you again," said Myrtice. "It's been a long time. I've heard about your troubles and I'm glad I can help. Shaun will be safe here. The only visitors we get are social workers bringing kids or taking them away."

"Thank you so much, Ms. Myrtice. I don't know how I can ever repay you," said Coldblood.

"Dad, why do I have to stay here?" begged Shaun.

"The building is divided into two parts—one for the boys and one for the girls. The only time they can come together is in the kitchen and when preparing for school. Boys are not allowed in the girls building and vice-versa. We house 4 boys to a room. Shaun, this is your room and this is your bed. Now I'm gonna go and let you two men talk. If you need me just holla." Then she left.

"Dad, why can't I go with you? I won't get in the way! I promise!"

"I know you won't, Sport, but you know about my situation. Plus, I have something I need to deal with and you need to be safe while I do it."

"Are you gonna get those men that hurt Mom? You're gonna kill them, aren't you?"

Coldblood hesitated. "When we do wrong son, sometimes we have to answer for what we've done. I don't know how to answer your question, Shaun, except to say that I'm not gonna just do nothing when I know that someone is out there trying to take my life or the life of the ones I love."

Coldblood hesitated again then settled in his spirit. "I have to go, Shaun, because it's not good for you or me to stay around here. I'm not sure when I will be back but I am coming back—I promise. Meantime, do what Ms. Myrtice tells you and she will take care of you. Don't talk to anybody about our family situation and try not to hang out with guys that will get you in trouble. You still have your phone, right?"

"Yeah, and I have your number, too!"

"Good, I'll be in touch with Ms. Myrtice to make sure you have everything you need. No matter what you need, just call me any time – day or night okay?" Coldblood looked out of the window and saw Nicole driving up.

"Your ride is here," said Myrtice. Shaun wrapped his arms around Coldblood and began to cry. Coldblood, too, dropped a few tears as he hugged him back.

"I've gotta go, son. Remember, call me any time, okay?" Shaun nodded then ran to the window to watch Coldblood leave.

"Where to?" asked Nicole. She saw the tears in his eyes so she quietly waited.

"Nicole, you've been great and I really appreciate it. But I..." Nicole cut in.

"You need a place to stay, don't you?" Nicole was very wise and Coldblood could feel her motherly spirit each time he talked with her.

"Yes, I do Nicole, but I'm not asking to impose on you. Just help me get somewhere to lay low and do what I do for a minute. I've got money," he said.

"Don't worry, I think I know a place." Then she drove off.

****

"Look guys," started the doctor. "This is a long shot. Even if I can wake her, she may not even know who she is or is able to speak. She has a lot of internal damage and massive head trauma. Waking her may even cause more brain damage than she already have. I've attached a beeper to her finger if she can't talk. Therefore, she'll only be able to answer yes or no."

"Okay," said Agent Walter. "Let's do it, Doc."

"I don't like this," said the chief as the doctor administered the drug to Elisa. She slowly started to move then she cried out in pain. The doctor quickly administered a pain killer as she calmed and slowly opened her eyes.

"Ms. Smith," started the doctor. "There is a button attached to your right index finger because you may not be able to speak. If you understand what I'm saying then press the button three times." Elisa tried to speak but couldn't. Then she hit the button three times.

"Good, good," continued the doctor. "Now, there are some gentlemen here who need to ask you some questions. To answer them, press the button one time for 'yes,' and two times for 'no,' okay? Press it now if you understand." She pressed the button once. Agent Walter and Chief Lewis stepped forward. Elisa recognized them and started to cry.

"Hi Elisa," spole Walter, calmly. "We have a situation and we need your advice. As you know, you're the only agent that's gotten this close to Holloway and remained safe. So far, your cover is still intact. But, because of the raid we just had and captured D-Lo, Holloway is looking for you to bring you back within his operation. Do you understand so far?"

Elisa pressed the button... 'yes.' "Good," Walter continued. "If Holloway doesn't find you and know what's up with you, he will eventually put a hit on you because of what you know about his operations.

Elisa, one way or another, you're going to have to deal with Holloway until we bring him down. The question is, do you want to deal with him while on the run for the rest of your life, or do you want to take a chance and go back in as an operative?"

"Agent Smith," cut in the Chief. "You don't have to do this. The Agency has hidden plenty of operatives who are living good lives in other countries and even in this one. Elisa you can have a life again, if you want out!" he pleaded.

"Agent Smith, we have to decide now because, tomorrow will be too late," added Walter. "If you want us to let Holloway find you so you can get back in, then let us know now. Or, if you want protection, also let us know." Both men stood awaiting Elisa's response. As she attempted to speak, blood gushed from her mouth and she began to cough vehemently. The doctor called for the nurses as they rushed to her bedside.

"Please, Agent Smith, give us an answer!" yelled Agent Walter.

"Can't you see she's dying, man! Leave her alone!" fussed Chief Lewis. Suddenly, through struggles, Elisa pushed the nurse and doctor away and stared at Agent Walter and Chief Lewis. Everybody was puzzled. Then she hit the button once and fell asleep.

Elisa was currently being cared for in a private hospital where the Agency normally protected their operatives and special agents. But now, she would be moved to Piedmont Hospital where Agency doctors would still care for her, but Holloway would also be able to find her.

"Walter, please don't do this!" yelled Chief Lewis as they left the hospital. "She didn't know what she was saying, man! She's too young for this! Don't give her life to Holloway!"

"It's her decision, Chief, now let it go! She's going back in—end of story!

****

It was after dark as Nicole drove up to the back of her shop and went in with Coldblood.

"I've been at this shop almost 5 years and I've only used this door twice," said Nicole. "I don't think the girls even know it's back here." Nicole entered the building then walked into a small room just off the back door. The room was empty except for an old disassembled bed with a mattress, lying in a corner.

"Nicole, this is perfect," said Coldblood.

"Nikki."

"What?" asked Coldblood.

"My friends and family call me Nikki, for short," she said.

"Ok, thanks Nikki, this is perfect. I should only need it for a few days."

"Take as long as you want to but just don't disturb the customers during the operation hours. There are plenty of chairs in the shop and you can even move one of the TVs back here until work starts. I'm usually the first one here, so I'll talk to the other girls. I think the old bed works fine and there is a blanket and a small refrigerator out in the shop near my station. Make yourself at home."

Then she hugged him and said, "Meca was our family. I know what you're trying to do but please be careful. Shaun will go crazy if he loses his mom and dad during this time."

"Thank you, Nikki. Meca chose her friends very well."

"I have to go," said Nicole. "I'll see you later." Then she handed him a key and left.

****

That night, Terry was visiting his brother Dexter and Olivia at home.

"I'm really gonna take your advice and let her go," said Terry. "I've had enough."

"Man, you've been chasing that girl ever since you were 17," said Dexter. "That was 10 years ago! Just take care of your child, man, and move on." Suddenly, the evening news aired and D-Lo, Hookman, and D'Amica, were the top story.

-Dexter, Terry, and Olivia, glued to the TV.

-Coldblood watched in anger from the Beauty Shop.

-Shaun, who was supposed to be asleep, watched while Ms. Myrtice slept in her chair.

-Rev. Simmons, being home on his knees praying, lifted his head in time to see.

-Rosa watched from the church as she changed her bandages.

-Nicole, Melody, Tameka, and Adrienna, watched while

talking to each other on the phone.

-Cherlene, Jennifer, and Donna, were curled on the couch at Cherlene's watching it together.

-Tenisha watched from her parents' doorway as she was about to leave; they were arguing.

-Elisa laid in a coma while having bad dreams about D-Lo and her life.

-D-Lo watched from a private jail cell while working out and planning to escape.

-Hookman watched while strangling a couple in North Carolina so he could hide out in their home.

-Holloway was having a party on his Yacht--he didn't care about any of it.

Chapter 53

Donna and Jennifer stayed at Cherlene's place since the day Jennifer was released from jail.

"I need to work, today," said Donna. "I've been so busy over the past 24 hours that I forgot to read my own story. I'm going to get a paper, so I'll know what's up when I get to work."

"I've got to go to work today, too," said Cherlene.

"Cheryl, today is Saturday," said Jennifer.

"I know, but I wasn't there yesterday and I want to do some things in my new classroom and talk with a few teachers who also said they'd be there today. You should come with me, Jenny, instead of sitting around here. By the way, Dee, there is a newspaper at the front door that I haven't had a chance to get, yet," said Cherlene. Donna went to get the paper.

"Cheryl, I think I want to go home today. I have some things I need to do as well," said Jennifer.

"Jenny, you know you don't have to do that," added Cherlene. "You can stay as long as you like. Keda loves having you around."

"Thanks, Cheryl, but it's time for me to go. Life goes on and I've got to deal with my own problems." Cheryl stopped and hugged her as Donna came in reading the paper.

"Oh my God!" said Donna. "That's what Tenisha was smiling about yesterday morning when she left Mr. Golden's office! Look at this!" Donna was looking at Jennifer's picture in the column that Tenisha wrote. "Oh! I'm gonna get that bitch!" she screamed. "I'm gonna..."

Cherlene snatched the paper and looked at it. Jennifer never looked up because she knew what they were reading. After Cherlene quickly glanced at the article, she turned to Donna.

"Dee, sometimes you let your mouth overload your ass!" Then she nodded toward Jennifer.

"Oops! Sorry, Jenny. It just bothers me that Glamour Bitch wrote that story and placed your picture there. She didn't have to do that."

"Dee, would you have done any less if you had a chance to get back at her?" asked Cherlene. "I don't think so. Have you thought that maybe she wrote that story because she knew it would get to you more than it would Jenny?"

"But that's ludicrous!" shouted Donna.

"Is it, Dee? Look at you, and look at Jenny. You're the one about to blow a fuse, right now. Just like you told me to lighten up on you, maybe you need to lighten up on Tenisha. Cause you can be just as much of a Glamour Bitch as she can!"

"Cheryl, how can you say that about me?" sounded Donna! Then she heard the whisper, *"The Curse Must Be Broken!"* Donna pretended she didn't hear it.

"I'm just saying that maybe you need to take a look at yourself, Dee." Donna was mad as she grabbed her things and headed toward the door.

"That's it, Cheryl! You've crossed the line by comparing me to her! And just think that I wanted to be more like you! You really don't know me, Cheryl. And I surely don't know you!" Then she slammed the door as she left.

"Yeah, I would say it's time for me to go home," said Jennifer.

"Jenny, I am so sorry," pleaded Cherlene.

"Don't worry about it, Cheryl. I'll see you later." Jennifer grabbed Audrey then she left.

****

Tenisha was at work finishing a few things when her mom called.

"Mom, are you and Dad fighting again? What caused it this time?"

"Cause he's a pompous ass!" Davina screamed into the phone. "He's too stubborn when I try to reason with him, and he won't talk to me!"

"Mom, are you drunk again?"

"Yes, I am! Now write that in your paper and sell it!"

"I'm on my way, Mom." As Tenisha got to the lobby, she met Donna coming in.

"You just couldn't resist, could you?" scolded Donna. "Why are you so out to ruin my family?"

"Well, the way you've been using people around here to get what you want, and taking stories from people desks, hmm? It seems to me that stealing just runs in your family, Donna. Nobody made Jennifer do what she did. I just printed the story. I'd love to chat but I've gotta go." Tenisha quickly ran out. As Donna walked onto the work floor, she could feel the tension in the room as all eyes were on her.

"Isn't this a great day?" she spoke loudly. "And it's gonna be a great day at work, too!"

****

Later, as Tenisha walked into her parents' place, Davina met her at the door.

"He's upstairs getting ready for work like everything is just fine." Tenisha acted like she did't hear or see her as she quickly gathers Nela's things. "What are you doing?" Davina asked.

"Mom, you only keep Nela one day now, which is today, Saturday. And you can't even do that without starting up with Dad and causing me to leave work. It's getting old, Mom! I'm out of here!" She grabbed Nela and left. Kris came downstairs and looked at Davina.

"Now look what you've done. You're really starting to disgust me, Davina." As he walked out of the door, she threw a glass behind him.

****

"Hello, this is the Law Office of Carlos, Jerome, and Curtis. How may I help you?"

"I'd like to speak to Mr. Jerome, please," said Jennifer.

"Jerome Bateman speaking, can I help you?"

"Yes, this is Jennifer Sweet, returning your call."

"Yes, Jennifer! Thanks for getting right back to me. I'm afraid I've some bad news since our conversation yesterday. Can you come in and let's talk?"

"No, I'm not feeling good, so just give it to me over the phone."

"Very well then. It appears that many of the community business owners are trying to make a statement about people who steal from their stores. They have convinced the D.A.'s office to move your trial date to Tuesday, which is only 3 days away."

"What?" she whispered. "Will I go to prison?"

"Normally in a case like this, the DA will recommend 5 years to serve 18 months on probation which means you normally do time on paper. But in this case because you were an employee of the business community that suffered, I'm afraid the D.A. is recommending that you do hard time. So it's possible that you may spend some time in prison."

Jennifer started to cry. "I can't go to prison," she sniffed. "What will happen to my baby?"

"Because this case has been moved up on the calendar, I may be able to keep you on the streets a while before you go to prison," said Jerome.

"How much free time can you get me before I have to leave?"

"The courts can grant up to a year depending on the circumstances. We're scheduled to be in court on Tuesday at 1pm so be there on time, ok? Then we'll take it from there."

"Ok." said Jennifer. After they hung up, Jennifer burst into tears.

****

As Tenisha entered the job floor, Donna sat at her desk like an animal ready to strike. She stood and walked toward Tenisha only to see Nela trailing behind her. Donna automatically disarmed.

"Hi, young lady," said Donna. "You must be Nela. My name is Donna."

"Hello, Donna," said Nela. "Mommy says that you don't want to be her friend."

"She did? Why did she say that?"

"I don't know. She cries sometimes."

"Did your mommy tell you to tell me that?"

"No."

"Nela, go sit over there," pointed Tenisha. "I'll be there in a minute."

"That's low even for you, Tenisha. Why would you turn your child against me?"

"Did that sound like I turned her against you, Donna? She used the word *'friend.'*"

"We'll never be friends, Tenisha, and you know it, so don't try that crap with me!"

"Ms. Banks!" yelled Mr. Golden. "Please step into my office for a minute!"

"Yes Sir." Donna sped into his office.

"Ms. Banks how are things at home? You know, with your sister, Jennifer?"

"We had a minor setback, but things are fine, Sir. Thanks for asking."

"There's nothing minor about it, Ms Banks, so please don't pretend with me. I know that you and Ms. Cuyler don't see eye to eye on hardly anything, and that's your business when you're not here. But when it comes to the work around here, both of you are assets and I want to see more harmony between you.

Starting immediately, I would like to see both of you finding a common ground around here that makes me happy or I will only recommend one of you for promotion! Is that clear?"

"Yes Sir," she nodded. "Very clear, Sir."

"That'll be all, Ms. Banks!" Donna nervously walked out and gave Tenisha the finger.

Chapter 54

Nicole came in to the shop early Saturday morning as she usually does, and started preparing to do business. Saturday is one of their busiest days but the first customer doesn't arrive until 8 a.m. Nicole is usually there by 7 a.m. and the rest of the girls arrive before 8 a.m. Coldblood was still sleeping and didn't hear the girls as they came in one by one.

"It seems funny knowing that Meca ain't coming today," muffled Adrienna.

"I know, right?" added Tameka. "Nicole, we ought to at least wait until after the funeral before you lease out her space."

"Yeah, I can go for that," added Melody.

"Look y'all," started Nicole. "Ain't nobody doing nothing around here until after things cool down a bit. But if Meca had her say so, she would want us to do business as usual, especially, if there were somebody who needed her space. But I promise that we won't advertise her space until well after the funeral if this makes you feel better." They all nodded in agreement. Suddenly, a Fed-Ex delivery man entered the shop with a flat package.

"Got a delivery for Ms. Nicole Griffin.... is she here?"

"Yes, I'm Nicole."

"Please sign here, Ma'am." Nicole signed. "Thank you! Have a good day!"

"Damn Nicole, you didn't ask any questions! You just signed the paper," said Melody. "You could have signed for a bomb!" Nicole opened the letter and the girls were quiet as she read, silently. "So what does it say, Nicole?"

"Some lawyer telling me that my dad is dead, and they want to pass on to me his personal belongings." The girls began to chatter.

"Let me see that!" shouted Adrienna. After she read the letter, she put her hand to her mouth in surprise and stared at Nicole; "I'm sorry, Nikki; I didn't know." The other girls were curious as they read the letter then apologized.

"It's okay," comforted Nicole. "I never knew him, anyway." The letter read,

"We, the law firm of Buddy & Virginia, represent the penal system to include the Department of Corrections for the state of Georgia. We regret to inform you that 4 days ago, while serving a life sentence, your dad, Mr. Pete Lockhart, died in prison of a massive stroke. After searching through his personal belongings, we found information with you as his sibling; but no address or forwarding information. It was only through IRS that we are able to locate you. The

shoebox containing your father's belongings will be stored in our office
for 3 months after receipt of this letter then we will dispose of them if
you haven't secured them to your person. We are sorry about your loss.
Please forgive us for the delay."

Signed, Buddy.

"So, Nikki, are you gonna go get it?" asked Melody. "It may be full of money." Nicole just stood there thinking.

"Come on, Mel ... get serious," started Tameka. "My brother is in prison and he told me they only have a small wall locker, and most of the stuff in it belongs to the prison. Men in prison don't have anything and that's why they need family and friends to send them money."

"But Nikki, don't you want to know about your dad?" asked Adrienna.

"What is there to know? He's gone now," said Nicole.

"Girl, you are so right," stated Melody. "Hell, he didn't contact you when he was alive and now that he's dead, that shoebox may be full of bills."

"Mel, why won't you just shut up, sometimes?" spoke Adrienna. Suddenly, the girls heard the toilet flush in the back and they all froze in silence. Then Melody spoke again,

"Oh, hell naw! Meca better not have her ass up in here because that's too quick. Hell, she just died 24 hours ago!" The girls were very nervous.

"Calm down, ladies," said Nicole. "It's just a friend." They all looked astonished.

"Shaun's dad, Coldblood, needs a place to lay low until he leaves town in a couple of days, so I'm helping him out. And we are gonna be quiet about this, aren't we ladies?" Nicole forcibly demanded. They nodded in agreement.

"Poor Shaun, losing his mom and his dad," said Tameka. "It must be hard on him."

"I'm believing that everyone here will be at Meca's funeral on Monday, so let your customers know we will be closed until 4 pm," instructed Nicole. "Reschedule all appointments until then." Coldblood walked out from the back.

"Morning ladies," he said.

"Morning Coldblood," they spoke in unison while staring. Coldblood felt a little odd.

"Uh...Nikki, can I talk to you a minute?" Nicole went with him to the back room. "Are they okay, with this?" he asked. "They're looking at me kinda weird."

"That's just how we are," she laughed. "Everything is fine."

"Okay, I'm going out for a bite. I'll be back in a minute." Then he left. The girls smiled at Nicole as she came back in smiling.

"What?" she asked as they stared at her.

Chapter 55

Agents Dixon and Bishop sat in their car at D'Amica's burial site, watching to see who would show up at the funeral. Coldblood knew they would be there, so he attended the service from a distance.

"Ashes to ashes-dust to dust,"

preached Rev. Simmons as they lowered D'Amica's coffin into the grave.

"For if we believe that Jesus died and rose again, even so them also which sleep in Jesus will God bring with him...

Shaun sat in the midst of the girls that worked at the Beauty Shop with tears in his eyes. He wondered how would his life be after today. He really didn't want to live with Ms. Myrtice, but he knew his dad was doing what he thought was right.

...for the Lord himself shall descend from heaven with a shout," continued Rev. Simmons, *"... with the voice of the archangel and the trumpet of God, and the dead in Christ shall rise first!*

D'Amica's older sister, Nancy, was also sitting beside Shaun and the girls on the front row. Nancy lived in Ann Arbor, Michigan with her three kids and hardly kept in touch with D'Amica. Since D'Amica didn't have life insurance, Nancy exhausted her savings just to make the trip, and provide a proper burial for her sister.

Nancy was in her first year of college when their parents were killed in an automobile accident. D'Amica was a senior in high school. Neither knew how they would provide for themselves after their parents' death, so they survived however they could.

One weekend, D'Amica got with friends and drove to Atlanta to attend 'Freak-Nik' weekend. She met Coldblood and never went back to Michigan. Nancy and her boyfriend Jessie, stayed and kept their parents' home.

...wherefore comfort one another with these words."

As Rev. Simmons ended the funeral. All parties, stood to leave.
"I'm glad my sister had you to love her," started Nancy. "And I'm even more happy knowing that you will keep Shaun so he doesn't have to go into a foster home. Thank you all so much!"
"Meca was our family and that's the least we can do," said Nicole.

"Well, my plane leaves in a couple of hours so I will head to the airport from here. Take care my nephew, Shaun," she kissed him. "And please call if there is anything I can do."

"Take care," they all said. "And have a safe trip." Then Nancy was gone.

"She seemed really nice," said Nicole.

"Honey those three kids have broken her down," said Melody. "That's why she can't take Shaun with her. She can't handle him."

"I'm a little confused about something," whispered Tameka. "Since when are we taking care of Shaun?" she asked as they walked to the car. They knew that something was being planned and Nicole hadn't told them.

"Ladies, we will talk about that later," quickly spoke Nicole. "But, for now, let's get home and relax, and get Shaun to his grand-dad's, Rev. Simmons." Nicole drove away with them being puzzled; knowing they shouldn't talk in front of Shaun.

****

Meantime, Donna was out to lunch with Tyler eating when Terry approached them.

"Oh, hi Terry!" greeted Donna as she hugged him. Then she introduced him to Tyler. "Tyler is the layout man for the paper at my job."

"Assistant layout man," Tyler corrected her.

"Terry is the dad of my niece, Makeda. Remember her?"

"Oh yeah, Cherlene's daughter!" remembered Tyler.

"Yeah, that would be the one," said Terry sarcastically.

"I hate to eat and run," said Tyler as he laid a bill on the table. "But I have some things I need to do. Sorry Donna, I'll see you at work." Donna stood with her mouth open as Tyler quickly left.

"Can you believe he just did that?" she sounded! "I'm gonna get him for that when I get back!"

"Look at it on the bright side," said Terry. "He did pay his half for the lunch."

"Yeah, I guess so," said Donna. "So do you wanna join me?" Terry had seen Donna from across the street, and had every intention of approaching her to talk about Cherlene and why she had treated him this way. But as they talked, she was so lively and free spirited that his spirits were lifted. Not once did he even mention Cherlene! Instead, they laughed and joked with each other like old friends. Both were feeling a whole lot better than when they came.

"So, what are you doing later, silly woman," laughed Terry. "Wanna catch a movie?"

"Oh, my God! Did you just ask me out!"

"Did I do something wrong?"

"No! Oh no!" Donna sounded excited. "It's just that men don't do that to me. So why did you?" Donna placed the palm of her hand on her chin, then smiled and stared at Terry while waiting for his answer. Terry was shocked.

"Because you're stupid, like that," he laughed. "You are so stupid!"

"Ok," she shouted. "If I'm so stupid, then why do you want to go to a movie with me?" Terry was speechless for a moment. Then he realized why Cherlene and Jennifer were always explaining things to Donna that she should have known.

"I'm not calling you stupid, Donna. It's just a figure of speech which means that you're crazy, funny, exciting, humorous, and fun to be around."

"Oh! Now I get it! So why didn't you just say so, silly. Thank you. Nobody ever said that to me before. But I don't know about going out with you. Cheryl may not like that." Terry's face changed and he remembered why he came to talk to Donna in the first place. Donna noticed the change.

"Terry, I'm sorry. I shouldn't have said anything about that, but Cheryl is my sister and she told me what happened. I really am sorry."

"It's nothing to be sorry about. Cherlene's been dissing me since high school, and I didn't want to believe it. Well, I gotta go, Donna." Terry left walking as fast as Tyler had done. Donna, who was feeling bad, ran behind him.

"Terry! Wait! I have an idea!" she shouted as she latched onto his arm. "We are friends right?" Terry stared and wondered where was she going with this. Before he could answer, she made a monster face and started moving her body in a weird kinda way.

"Donna, what are you doing?"

"I'm trying to cheer you up," she said as she did the face and body thing again.

Terry laughed aloud then said to himself, *"This has to be the damn nerdiest fox on the planet. She is so dingy, but good."*

"See, I made you laugh! Wanna hear my idea?"

"Yes, what is it, Donna?"

"Ok, why don't you come home with me, friend, then I can call my sisters to come by while we all watch a DVD."

"Uh, I don't know, Donna." frowned Terry. She did the face thing again and Terry laughed. "Ok, you win, but don't blame me if things don't go like you expect them to."

"I won't," she said. "Cross my heart and hope to die!"

****

It's after dark and the girls had gone home from the Beauty Shop. Coldblood was resting while watching TV. Suddenly, he hears the door opening so he points his pistol in that direction. He is surprised to see Nicole carrying a basket of food. When she saw the pistol, she stopped and tilted her face to the ground.

"I'm sorry," she said. "Just thought you might want some company." Coldblood quickly hid the pistol behind him.

"I'm sorry, Nikki; please come in," he welcomed. Nicole sat the basket down and looked around.

"I like what you've done to the room," she said. Coldblood had gone to the family store down the street, and purchased a few small items he needed to make himself comfortable.

"Thank you. What's in the basket?"

"I brought some of the food the women at church cooked after Meca's funeral." She opened the basket and the aroma seized his nostrils.

"Wow! That smells good," he smiled. "I'm hungry, too!" Nicole smiled as they ate and talked about many things. They were really starting to feel each other but Nicole changed the subject.

"Coldblood, why are you on the run? Don't you want to make things right for your son?"

"Yes I do," he said. "To tell you the truth, I don't even know why I'm running. I just know that the police are after me. Is that crazy?"

"Then why don't you call them and find out?"

"It's not that simple!"

"Why not?" she asked. Coldblood paused then stood.

"Because in the world I'm from, you just don't do things that way!"

"Maybe it's time to leave that world behind, Coldblood; move on to a new world... a new life." Coldblood felt pressured as his eye twitched.

"Why are you bothering me with this?" he asked angrily! "It ain't your business anyway!"

"I see," said Nicole. She stood up to leave and Coldblood grabbed her.

"Look Nicole, I'm sorry. It's just that no one has cared about what I want since my mother died and you're putting pressure on me."

"That's because I care," she said calmly. "And I care about what happens to your son." As Coldblood stood before her, he was confused as Nicole's warmth and passion reached out to him. In the heat of the moment, he leaned and kissed her. She slowly pushed him away as their lips separated.

"I think I need to leave now," she said as she turned to go.

"No please, don't go; not yet! I'm sorry about what just happened and it won't happen again." Nicole just looked at him. "I promise," he added.

"Tell me about your mom," said Nicole. They talked for another hour or so then Nicole left and went home. During the night they both laid thinking about the kiss.

****

It was about 8 p.m. as Terry stopped by to see Donna.

"Hi," she said, "Come on in! I didn't call my sisters, yet, because I wasn't sure if you would change your mind or not. You didn't seem too sure of yourself earlier today. So have a seat, and I'll call them. Meantime, be picking out the movie you want to see."

****

Jennifer was asleep with Audrey lying next to her in bed. After she talked to her lawyer, she didn't want to see or talk to anybody, so she turned out her lights, and turned off the ringer on the phone. She would listen to her voicemail later and decide whether she would talk or not.

****

"Hmm?" said Donna. "Jenny's not picking up, nor responding to my messages. I've left 4 messages since I've been dialing. You think I need to go by there?"

"With the things been happening in her life, I can understand if she just wants to be alone. That's exactly how I've been feeling lately, so I can relate to her," said Terry. "I really don't know why I came here anyway."

"Oh!" said Donna. "Well, don't move yet. Let me call Cheryl."

****

Makeda had gone to bed as usual, prior to Donna's call. Meantime, Cherlene and Clint were in the bedroom bumping and grinding to soft music, with Cherlene in her night gown and Clint in his boxers.

"Hello, Dee," answered Cherlene. "What's up?"

"Hey Cheryl; what'cha doing?"

"Do I need to spell it out for you, Dee?" Donna knew she had company.

"Oh," said Donna. "I was just hoping you could come over for a while and let's watch movies together."

"Bye, Dee," Cherlene hung up. Donna just stood looking stupid.

"Don't worry about it, Donna," said Terry. "Let's watch something."

"What?" she asked.

"Anything! Just don't worry about anybody else. Let's have fun all by ourselves!"

****

A few hours later as Donna and Terry began to laugh and have fun; Cherlene and Clint were deep under covers having sex. She had no regrets that Terry was gone because Clint gave her exactly what she needed, without trying to get her to do what she didn't want. Cherlene was slowly losing herself, but she couldn't see it. *"The Curse Must Be Broken!"* came the whisper. It has become so faint that Cherlene hardly heard it as she whorishly indulged in activity with Clint.

****

By 10 p.m. Audrey was awake and crying for food, so Jennifer took her and fed her. While feeding, she listened to her voicemail and heard her lawyer reminding her to be in court by 1 p.m. tomorrow. Jennifer stopped the machine and began to cry. She hugged and kissed Audrey then she pleaded to the Lord.

"Lord, please help me this once, please! I know I don't go to church and all that but I don't ask you for anything. So I'm asking you now, Lord, to please help me! I don't want to go to prison; I don't want to leave my child!"

After a few minutes, Audrey was sleeping again and Jennifer went to the answering machine.

"Ms. Sweet, this is Kris Cuyler, the manager at the bank. Ma'am, we have some information that you may be interested in, if you would come by. Please give me a call or stop by at your earliest convenience. Thank you."

"Hmm? Wonder what that's about?" she thought. *"Some information I may be interested in? I'll call them in the morning."* She listened on.

"Hi Jennifer, this is Michelle, I really don't know what to say. Anyway, I was just thinking about you and Audrey. See you later. Bye." Afterwards, she heard Donna's voice over and over again; she ignored it.

"Wonder how Michelle is? Maybe she found the disk. Maybe I should call her."

****

As Michelle left work and entered her car that night, she was startled by a visitor.

"Uh!" she jumped as someone tapped her car window. The woman whom had taken the disk was standing outside her car. Michelle rolled down the window.

"Sorry to scare you," said the woman. "But since we are friends, now, I figure its ok."

"What do you want?" asked Michelle.

"I know you said for me to destroy the disk, but I didn't. Neither did I see what's on it. I was gonna destroy it, but when I saw your co-worker's picture in the paper, I kept it and decided to bring it back; here it is." She handed Michelle the disk. "She may need it one day." Then the woman went her way and Michelle was speechless.

****

Finally, back at Donna's, she and Terry had eaten and laughed so much, they fell asleep on her couch.

Chapter 56

It was 5 a.m. as Nicole tossed and turned in her College Park Apartment. It had been a long time since a man took interest in her, so that kiss from Coldblood had her a little awaken and shaken.

"What's wrong with me?" Nicole asked herself. "I'm acting like a nervous school girl at 27 years old! Come on, Nikki, get a grip! That kiss wasn't all that," she tried to convince herself. Suddenly, Nicole got dressed, and headed to the Beauty Shop. She couldn't get her mind off of Coldblood and his kiss, and she was heading to work a whole hour early because of it.

"What are you gonna say to him, Nikki?" she talked as she drove. "You're the wise one, Nikki, with all the right answers, so how come you're so nervous?" Nicole didn't waste any time as she jumped from the car, and ran into the Beauty Shop looking for Coldblood.

"Coldblood?" she called as she opened the door to his room and peeped in. Coldblood had packed his carry-on bag, and left. Nicole's heart sank. She didn't know what to think.

"Maybe he went to see Shaun or his dad and I can catch him there," she thought. Then her conscience began to get the best of her. *"Nikki, why are you chasing a man? You haven't done that since you were in high school. Besides, this man is wanted by the police and he can't even stay around here. What's so special about him, that's has you acting this way?"*

As she pondered these thoughts, she began to settle in her spirit and come back to reality. She closed the door to where Coldblood had stayed then went on with her work.

****

It was about 9 a.m. as Coldblood taxied to his dad's church. He had gotten up early after tossing and turning about his situation with Shaun, his son.

"The Curse Must Be Broken!" came the voice as he rode on. He knew that his dad normally arrives at church around 9 a.m., so he had been waiting at a nearby coffee shop since 6 a.m. that morning. During the night, he just couldn't sleep and the kiss to Nicole didn't help any. Now that D'Amica was gone, Coldblood was thinking of playing a more significant role in Shaun's life, and changing his own.

"Maybe it's time to leave that world behind.... and move on to a new world –a new life," echoed Nicole's words in his thoughts. Coldblood knew he wasn't ready to give up everything he was into, but it was time to make some changes.

As the taxi neared the church, Coldblood saw his dad step from his car, and walk toward the church. Rev. Simmons also saw him and waited for him as he stepped from the taxi.

"Well, this is a surprise," said Rev. Simmons. "Wasn't sure if I would even see you again. Glad I did. I see you have your bag, so are you leaving?"

"I've got to find Hookman before someone starts to recognize me. Besides, it's just a matter of time before your GBI friends start checking on you again."

"You're right, son, so what brings you by?" Coldblood paused.

"Dad, I want to make some changes in my life for Shaun's sake, but I don't know where to begin." Rev. Simmons smiled at him, hugged him, then said,

"You just started son... you just did. Come in let's talk." They went inside the church and talked. Rev. Simmons told him of the many trials and tribulations he faced as a father, while he was young. He told his son what God requires of a dad, and a man, and showed him scriptures in the bible.

"Junior, a young boy always has someone he idolizes, and Shaun idolizes you. So it's very important he knows that you are trying to make things right in your life. You have to help him to see that the things in your past are bad, so he doesn't go that way. Before your mother died, you idolized me. I did my best to show you the way of the Lord, but you rebelled. Now, I think your eyes are open."

"I still idolize you, old man," smiled Coldblood. "I'm just not ready for your life-style, yet."

"Don't wait too long, son, because time is running out. I'm proud of you, son, and I know your mom would be proud of you, too," smiled Rev. Simmons.

"Dad, was Mom happy? I mean, was she really happy?" This was the first time Coldblood actually wanted to just talk about his mom since she died. Rev. Simmons knew it was time to open up to him.

"Junior, I want you to meet someone. Reda, can you come in, please?" He knew that Rosa was listening as she came around the corner. Reda was the name she was known by at church. He wasn't ready to tell who Rosa really was.

"This is Reda Monts," he introduced. "She has been around our family since before you were born. Reda and your mom were close friends." Rosa was dressed like a cleaning lady which is the role she played around the church.

"Hello, Carl Jr.," said Rosa. She moved slowly because of her gunshot wounds from Hookman. "Yes I knew your mom very well. Some even say we were like sisters." she added. "But Stephanie had too much class and she was very spiritual."

"So how come I've never heard of you, Ms. Reda?" asked Coldblood respectfully.

"I was around when you were young, but I had a different life then, and didn't get to see many people around home."

"Were you some type of traveler or something?" asked Coldblood jokingly.

"I know it sounds funny but yeah, I was something like that, at the time."

"So what can you tell me about my mom?"

"That you made her very happy. She loved you more than you will ever know; made your dad quit his old ways for your sake or she threatened to leave him."

"But what she didn't understand, son, is that she didn't have to threaten me to make me do right by you. All she had to do was help me to understand the will of God, because I loved you enough to do right by you anyway," said Rev. Simmons. "Now you need to understand God's will for you and Shaun, just like so many others need to do in this world."

"Dad, I want to find out about my charges, and I've even considered turning myself in. But how do I do that with guys like D-Lo and Hookman on the loose? They will kill me, you, Shaun, and everybody else that's close to me!"

"Don't underestimate the power of God, son," said Rev. Simmons. Then he looked at Rosa. "You'll never know when the Lord will send an angel to watch over you, and he always does it on time." Coldblood saw the look between his dad and Rosa, and knew there was more to that statement than his dad was telling.

"Carl Jr.," started Rosa. "If your mom were here right now, she would tell you to trust the Lord, and listen to your heart. What you are going through is bigger than you, me, her, or anybody you know. You see, we daily wrestle against principalities, against unseen powers and rulers of darkness of this world, and spiritual wickedness in high places," she continued.

"In order to defeat the real enemy that hunts you and your son, you can't do it with your mind nor your weapons, but you must have the mind of God, while you are wearing His armor."

"Ok, hold up, Reda! You're starting to sound like Dad, now. I'm not trying to face the devil or the Lord, right now. But I need something practical to help me save my son and myself from the police, and the people that are after me. How can you help me with that?" asked Coldblood as they stared at each other.

"Carl Jr., I have some friends who can help me to learn about your charges. When I find out, I'll let Rev. Simmons know, and he can tell you."

"Thank you, Reda," said Coldblood. "I'd really appreciate that."

"I've learned from these same friends that Carlton Hooks is on the run, and headed somewhere up the east coast, while struggling to survive. You and your son are safe," she added. Coldblood was shocked.

"What kind of work did you say you do?" Rosa just looked at Rev. Simmons and walked away. Then she spoke,

"Even the pentagon has maids and janitors, son, and we all have eyes and ears." Then she was gone. Coldblood just kinda stared at his dad, who was pretending to be reading the bible. He knew there was more to Reda than he was led to believe.

****

It was near noon and Jennifer was mentally preparing for court. She knew that today, she could possibly be going to prison.

"Oh! Call the bank!" she remembered. She picked up the phone and dialed. "Hello. May I speak to Kris Cuyler, please?"

"This is Kris Cuyler, how may I assist you?"

"Sir, this is Jennifer Sweet. You left a message for me to call you."

"Yes! Yes! Jennifer," he sounded. "I am happy to inform you that our bank will be merging with the largest bank in Georgia, in ninety to one hundred and twenty days. Therefore, we have been trying to renew those accounts with $200.00 or less, in their savings."

"I'm not a customer at your bank, so what does this have to do with me?"

"Apparently, about 20 years ago, your father opened this account with only $10, but we have not been able to locate him. However, your name is listed on the account as a co-signer and beneficiary, and...."

"This account was opened 20 years ago and it's only accumulated an additional $190.00?" she yelled.

"Well... yes... I'm afraid so Ma'am," cautioned the manager. "You see Miss..."

"You keep it, Mr. Cuyler!" Then she slammed the phone down. "Here I am about to go to prison, and he wants me to worry about 200 bucks, that belongs to my dead Dad," she said angrily. She started cussing and fussing to herself as she continued preparing for court. Suddenly, the doorbell rang. She opened it to see Cherlene and Donna standing there. She immediately burst into tears... again.

****

Noon had passed and all the girls were at work at the Beauty Shop.

"Nikki, you've been kinda quiet all morning. What's up with you?" asked Melody. Nicole said nothing as she continued to sweep her area and clean up hair.

"Have you thought about getting your dad's shoebox?" asked Tameka. "Aren't you curious about what's in it?"

"No, I'm not," answered Nicole. "Like Mel said, it's probably a bunch of bills anyway." The girls were stunned. They never expected to hear words like that come from Nicole. She was always positive about everything and always wanting to give everybody a chance.

"What's wrong with you today, Nikki?" asked Adrienna in a compassionate tone. "Are you feeling ok?"

"I feel fine," she said. "Just do your work and don't mind me." Now they knew something was wrong for sure.

"Where is Coldblood?" asked Melody. "He's been asleep all morning."

"Is he even back there?" asked Tameka. "I haven't heard him moving around as usual." Suddenly, the girls stared at Nicole as she stared out the window. Nicole saw Coldblood getting out of a taxi and her heart skipped a beat.

"Hello, ladies," he greeted as he came in. Nicole came alive as they all greeted him back. The girls couldn't help but to recognize it. "Nicole, can I speak to you a minute?" Nicole stepped outside the door with him as they looked through the glass storefront.

"It looks like Shaun is gonna be okay for a minute, so I came to say goodbye, until later. D-Lo is locked up and Hookman is running for his own life."

"It's been really good to know you. I'm sure you will be a good dad to your son." Then she stretched her hand and he shook it.

"Thank you for everything, Nicole. You've really made this trip bearable for me and my son. Thank you so much."

"It was nothing; I enjoyed it," she answered. He waved through the window at the other girls and they all waved back. Then he got into the taxi and left. Nicole went back to her station being the same as she was, before Coldblood drove up.

"Where did he go, Nikki?" they asked. "Will he be back for Shaun, soon?"

"I didn't ask," she said. "That's his business." Suddenly, a taxi came screeching to a halt right in front of the shop as the girls watched in wonder. Coldblood slowly walked in, went up to Nicole, and kissed her deeply. Though she allowed him to kiss her, she never touched him nor raised her hands from by her side. The girls were speechless and motionless. After the kiss, he pulled away and spoke:

"I'll be back as soon as I can, Nikki. I promise that...." Nikki did her usual by raising her hand like a police officer to hold up traffic.

"Please don't make promises you can't keep," she said. Coldblood took her hand, pulled her close to him, and deeply kissed her again. This time, she held him back. After the kiss, he spoke again.

"I said, I'll be back as soon as I can, and 'I PROMISE' that I'm coming for you!" This time, she dropped her head and chuckled as she responded.

"Ok." Then he hurried out and left. Nobody moved nor said a word as Nicole smiled and said, "Ain't y'all ever seen a kiss before?" The girls, who were all stunned by what they saw, became very excited.

"Whoooo!" they sounded as they made fun of her.

"Did you see that?" joked Tameka. "She put up that stop sign, but Coldblood ran right through it and wrecked her!" Nicole tried not to laugh.

"I sho' hope you brought some more panties," added Melody. "Cause we know what happen to those you have on. Hell mine even got wet and I didn't kiss anybody!" Nicole was laughing now.

"But here's the part that got me!" added Adrienna. "When he first pulled on her tongue, she tried to keep her hands by her side, like she didn't feel him yanking on it. But when he went back up through there and yanked it the second time, her arms flapped like a puppet while Coldblood was pulling her string!" For the rest of the evening Nicole was happy. So happy that she decided to leave work early and just enjoy life, while shopping.

****

"All rise," ordered the bailiff. *"The Honorable Judge Carol Phillips presiding."* In addition to Donna and Cherlene, Tenisha and Michelle were also at Jennifer's trial hearing. Jennifer's lawyer talked to the sisters outside the courtroom before her case was called.

"The DA wants to sentence you to 5 years to serve 2 years, as I explained to you," said her attorney. "But I've negotiated for 18 months with no time left on paper. Do you want it?" Jennifer and her sisters talked about it for a moment then asked,

"Will she have to go now?"

"I'll see what I can do," said her lawyer. After talking to the DA, he said, "You'll have 90 days from today to report back here at court to start your sentence." Jennifer then stood before the judge and was sentenced to serve 18 months in prison—sentence to begin in 90 days. Donna frowned at Tenisha, realizing that she was only there to finish her story.

"Jennifer, can I see you a minute?" asked Michelle. They walked away. "I'm still your friend, Jennifer, but I'm confused. Please talk to me later, ok?" Jennifer nodded as Michelle handed her the disk. Then they burst into tears, and left.

Chapter 57

"Doctor! Doctor come quickly!" screamed the nurse as she yelled down the clinical corridor. "She's awake! She's awake!"

It had been a little over 3 months since Holloway's men entered Piedmont Hospital and taken Elisa's sleeping body in the middle of the night. Once Holloway knew where she was and her condition, he waited until Piedmont doctors stabilized her, then stole her away to Nurnberg, Germany, to one of his private clinics.

FBI agents were watching and tracking her as Holloway's men took her, but lost track of her signal once they lifted her away in a private helicopter. FBI knew that Holloway would have scanned for bugs and tracking devices so they never placed one on her body nor her hospital bed. But they placed cameras and other devices within a 1 mile radius of Piedmont, hoping the devices could be their eyes and ears until a car could intercept them and follow them. It didn't work.

Within minutes after Elisa was taken away, she was placed on a copter, which took her straight to Holloway's plane. Ten hours later, she was landing in Germany at the Nurnberg Airport.

"She's awake, Sir!" screamed the nurse. "Please, come quickly!" Elisa sat up on the side of her hospital bed after being in a coma for over 3 months.

"Where am I?" she wondered. Her jaws were tight and her body felt a little stiff from the bed. *"Chief Lewis.... Special Agent Walter.... hm? They're here somewhere,"* she thought. *"What happened to me? Why am I here? Where's D-Lo and the guys?"* she continued her thoughts. As Elisa attempted to stand and walk, she fell to the floor as the nurse and doctor rushed to assist her back to bed. "Um... ma.... duh," said Elisa as she tried to speak.

"Brenda," said the doctor. "You cannot talk, right now, so don't try. Your brain was traumatized so badly that it's used all its strength just to survive. Therefore, it temporarily separated itself from all part of your body that didn't need its immediate use—your legs, your arms, your mouth, your eyes, and your ears to a certain degree. If you understand me, press the button once that's attached to your hand."

Elisa pressed the button. "Good," he said. "You are in no danger of losing your normal abilities, but you have to be patient and re-train your body to respond to your brain, ok?" Elisa pressed the button. "Good, very good! Now, I'm going to give you a sedative to help you to sleep until we're ready to run more tests on you." As the doctor started to inject her, Elisa frowned and pressed the button twice.

"I don't think she wants it, doctor," said the nurse. He injected her anyway and she fell asleep.

****

"What in the world happened here?" screamed Donna as they approached Joseph's Coffee Shop. They were surprised to see their favorite coffee shop remodeled and under new management.

It had been more than a month since they met. The outside tables were different, and the front of the building was more colorful. Plus, the business name on the sign out front was changed from Joseph's Coffee Shop to J.J. Coffee Shop. Inside, the seating was almost the same but the counter area had been changed. The place definitely needed a face lift and it was looking very good as the girls walked in.

"Excuse me," said Cherlene. "Who are you and where's Joseph?"

"Yeah, and where's Pamela the waitress, and Curtis the cook?" asked Donna.

"Ah, the million dollar questions for the past week," responded J.J. "I am my dad's son Jaden Joseph, and I now own the place. Pamela, the waitress, will only be working part time because she started back to school today, to finish her degree in business management. Curtis, the cook's wife has taken ill, and I'm not sure when he will be back. My dad, James Joseph, sold me the place because he thinks he's gotten too old to manage it anymore. Meantime, he is away in Hawaii deciding if he wants to come back while I run the place by myself. I take it that you ladies come here often, do you?"

"Yes, my name is Cherlene, and these are my sisters, Jennifer and Donna. This is our friend, Michelle."

"It's good to meet you. What can I get for you?" The question kinda shocked them because Pamela and Curtis always knew what they wanted, whether it was morning or evening. They gave him their orders then they sat down.

"The place does look better," added Jennifer. "But how is he gonna manage it all by himself?"

"I know what you mean," said Donna. "The line is getting longer already and it's still very early." J.J. was fumbling with his pen while taking orders, but no one was preparing nor serving them.

"We came here to talk before we head to work," said Cherlene. "And we have a very important issue to talk about, so let's do it. How are you feeling about this, Jenny?"

"Oh I feel fine; I really do. The past two months have been tough, but I've pulled myself together and I'm ready for what lies ahead."

"You certainly sound a whole lot better, and you're looking better, too," said Michelle.

"Ok guys," pushed Jennifer. "Let's do this so I can start my day and you guys can go on to work."

Jennifer's 90 days were almost up and she was preparing her mindset for prison. She had exactly seven days from today and she would be on her way back to the county, where they would send her to prison for 18 months.

Donna agreed to keep her apartment and Cherlene was to take care of Audrey. Jennifer's car would be placed in storage, and Michelle agreed to keep money on her books as needed until she was home again.

"I think that just about covers it," said Cherlene. "We can talk about other stuff later tonight." Suddenly, Jennifer's phone rang.

"Hello, Jennifer? This is Kris Cuyler down at the bank. I'm sorry to bother you again, but I wanted to check with you one more time about your dad's account and safe deposit box, before we complete our merger. After that, it will be out of my hands."

"What safe deposit box?" she asked. "You never said anything about that!"

"Jennifer, if you will recall, you hung up on me before I had a chance to."

"Ok, I'll be there today." Then she hung up.

"Is everything alright, Jenny?" asked Donna.

"Yeah, just a past account I have to take care of. Hey! Where are our orders!" As they looked at J.J., he was really struggling to satisfy the customers.

"Where's Joseph?" shouted a customer. "And Pamela?" shouted another. "And Curtis!"

"I have to go," said Cherlene. Donna and Michelle left as well, but Jennifer just sat and waited for her mocha. Many frustrated customers were leaving, but Jennifer went up to the counter where J.J. was microwaving a Danish with his back turned.

"Hey J.J." When Jennifer called his name, he quickly turned to answer her, but his elbow accidentally tipped the jar of spoons. Jennifer was so fast and smooth, she caught the jar and the two spoons that fell, before they hit the floor. J.J. gave her a look that said,

"I can really use a hand, right now." Jennifer didn't even ask. She walked behind the counter, put on an apron, and took over the grill. It was 7 a.m. when she started and she cooked and served tables for the next few hours as J.J. assisted her. Because of her previous experiences with her hands, she could move things lightning fast, while coordinating many things at one time. Before 10 a.m., she had the entire coffee shop back to running normal and the customers were satisfied. J.J. walked over and took her hand.

"You are an amazing woman!" he said. Then he knelt on one knee, kissed her hand, and asked, "Will you marry me?" Jennifer knew he was joking, but she was flattered.

"Ok," she played along. "But I don't come cheap. I'm a high maintenance kinda gal!"

"As long as you help me manage this coffee shop, you can have whatever you want," he said. "At least help me part time until I hire another." Jennifer knew that he was serious now.

"J.J., I can't. Besides I'm leaving in a week."

"Ok, help me for one week, then you can help me again when you get back. How long will you be away?" Jennifer was feeling pretty good about her day, and had totally accepted what she was about to go through. She didn't want to spoil it by hiding behind words. But J.J.'s question almost sent her to tears.

"J.J. in one week, I will be going away for 18 months and I'm not sure if I will be back." J.J. sensed discomfort in her words and saw discouragement on her face. He knew that whatever it was that she was about to go through was difficult for her.

"For what you have done here today, I will always be in your debt. Please tell me how can I help you and I will do it," he pleaded. "Just say the words."

"I did something bad, now I have to pay for it. I'm going to prison next week."

"Oh, I see," he spoke softly. After a pause, he spoke again. "Now you have to go for 18 months to take care of it, is that right?"

"Yes," she answered uncomfortably.

"For what it's worth, you will always be welcome to work here anytime you want to, and I mean that." Jennifer smiled.

"That means a lot, J.J. Thank you."

"As a matter of fact, you can choose any position you want, and I promise that it will be waiting for you when you come back. Will you think about it, tonight, then let's talk in the morning here at the coffee shop?"

"Ok," Jennifer said. "It was kinda fun; I've gotta go. I'll see you tomorrow." As Jennifer left J.J.'s Coffee Shop, she was feeling a lot better about herself than she's been over the past 3 months since her trial. She knew how hard it would be to get a job with a prison record but she had managed to land one before she left. It wasn't the kind of job she wanted but it was fun and she knew that J.J. would treat her fair. She happily strolled to the bus stop and took the bus to the bank, thinking about the goodness she felt while helping J.J. to keep his shop open. An hour later, Jennifer walked into the bank.

"I'm here to see Kris Cuyler, please."

"His office is over there," pointed the teller. When Jennifer saw him, she thought he looked familiar but she couldn't remember where she had seen him before.

"Hello, Mr. Cuyler? I'm Jennifer Sweet." She handed him her ID.

"Ah! Jennifer please have a seat, and I will prepare the necessary paperwork for you to close your father's account and reopen another if you like. Meantime, let me take you to your safe deposit box."

"Sir, my dad died about 20 years ago, and I don't think he left me a key."

"I'm sorry to hear that....about your dad. Now, because of our upcoming merger, special keys have been made and may be purchased over the phone from our main office, for $10.00. You pay me the $10.00, then we'll call the main office and they will give you the combination to open the slotted lock where your key is located."

"Ok, whatever," said Jennifer as she handed him the money. "Just do it." She took the key to box #28 and opened it while Mr. Cuyler prepared her paperwork. There were only 3 things in the deposit box, but Jennifer was surprised by what she saw. She quickly took the items, and ran out of the bank. In her hand she had a bag of diamonds, an envelope, and a funny looking key, or amulet.

"Jennifer wait!" yelled Mr. Cuyler. "I need your signature!" He was too late—Jennifer was gone!

****

Twenty-four hours after Elisa was put to sleep, she awoke to find herself tied down. Her arms, feet, neck, and waist, were all strapped to the bed. Suddenly, she heard a familiar voice in the room.

"Hello, Brenda," said Mr. Holloway. "You've been sleeping a long time. I have some questions for you that can't wait. Normally, you would be administered a drug and observed by a lie detector. But since you can't talk, I guess I'm gonna go on my own instinct. We still have a way to tell if you are lying," he added. Suddenly, doctors and nurses came in and connected monitoring wires to her head and her body.

"You know how this works, Brenda. Just press once for yes and twice for no. Three times if you don't know. Here we go. Were you at the house when D-Lo and the boys got hit?" She pressed 3 times. "Where were you when D-Lo and the boys got hit?" She pressed 3 times. "Did you know that D-Lo and the boys got hit?" She pressed twice.

Holloway asked her many questions but she answered "No" or "I don't know" to all of them. She really didn't know because she had passed out when it all happened. She couldn't even remember dialing 911 because her head was hurting so bad as D-Lo pounded inside her.

"Ok," spoke Holloway to his men. "Prepare her for training. I'll have to finish this when she can talk. There're some things I need to know about D-Lo's operation and I think she can help." Then he left as the doctor took over.

"Brenda, I have some news for you, now. But after I tell you, you must remain calm or I will put you back to sleep, understand?" She pressed once. "Ok Brenda here goes. You have been in a coma for over 3 months." Elisa started to cry. "And you are slightly over 3 months pregnant."

Elisa's eyes widened as she tried to wiggle and talk. She had only had sex with D-Lo and there was no way she was having his baby!

"Please, Brenda, be still or you will go into shock!" yelled the doctor. Tears flooded her face as she struggled. The doctor administered a sedative and she passed out.

****

Jennifer was home with the items she took from the bank. She wasn't sure about the amulet key looking thing, but she knew that it was something important. The next item, a small bag of diamonds, was a twin set to the diamonds she had stolen from D-Lo's men one night, and that really baffled her. But the thing that shocked her the most, was the contents of the envelope and it's writing. Inside the envelope were two beautiful identical necklaces. On the outside of the envelope was written;

> *"For my two beautiful daughters, whom I love with all my soul;*
> *Sarah Griffin-8 years old and Jennifer Sweet-6 years old."*
> *From Dad*

Jennifer had just learned that she had an older sister!

Chapter 58

"Today's the big day," thought Jennifer. Seven days had passed since she learned about the amulet key, the diamonds, and that she had an older sister. She was still baffled about it all, just as she was when she first discovered them, so she hadn't told her sisters.

"J.J., I really appreciate all you're doing for me," she said.

"Don't worry about it, Jennifer. I love the way you work. I promise that a job will be here when you get back if you need it." Donna and Cherlene came driving up while they talked. "Well, that's my cue," continued J.J. "I know that you and your sisters will hang out today until you have to leave. Plus, I need to check out this new girl you brought, to see if she will work out. I just hope she is half as good as you are."

Jennifer and Michelle had recommended Susie for the job. Susie was the one that Jennifer and Michelle let go when they caught her stealing. She also helped Michelle get the disk out of the mall and back to Jennifer. She waved at Jennifer as Donna and Cherlene walked up. "Take care, Jennifer," said J.J. "I wish you the best."

"Ready Jenny?" said Donna. Jennifer nodded. "So where to?" They drove to downtown Atlanta where they met Michelle. Then they just kinda hung out and enjoyed each other until about noon.

"Hey guys, I need to go to this bank for a minute."

"Ok Jenny," said Cherlene. "Where to?"

"It's this little bank in West End Atlanta, on Lee Street. I need to talk to someone there." The girls wondered why Jennifer had business at a small bank in West End Atlanta, but didn't ask any questions. Neither had they asked her anything about why she stole things. They knew that when the time came, Jennifer would talk.

"I'm glad you came back, Jennifer," said Kris at the bank. "Would you like to renew your account?" There were very few words between Kris and Jennifer as the girls watched. After Jennifer signed the papers, she was escorted to her box.

"I'll be back in a minute," she told the girls. They looked on and wondered as Jennifer placed the items in the safe deposit box.

"This bank will be closed in a couple of weeks," said Kris. "But all of our boxes and accounts will be moved downtown to our new main office. You will be able to access everything from there as you did here. Thank you for your business." He shook her hand and they left.

At 1 p.m., the girls hugged Jennifer as she turned herself in to the County jail in Atlanta.

****

"Come on, Brenda! You can do it!" said the nurse. Elisa had been in physical therapy all week long since her last encounter with Holloway.

Her body was slowly loosening as she struggled to walk but her words were still muffled. She never thought she would see the day when taking one step would be so hard. But she was determined to get herself together again no matter what the struggle or pain. She cried and fell many times while in physical therapy but she always bounced back.

"This girl is serious," said one of the men watching her on the monitor.

"Yes she is," added Holloway. "She reminds me of someone else I once knew. Continue to push her and get her talking again. I need to ask her some questions." Elisa fell to the floor as Mr. Holloway left the room. Again, she burst into tears.

Two weeks later, she could stand and move down the rails on her own. Her lips could form words but she still had problems sounding them out. Within another week or so, she could walk and move her arms very well and could whisper certain words. A month later, she walked with a crutch and was beginning to pronounce her words again.

A few months later, Elisa gave birth to a 7 pound baby boy that was removed from her presence immediately after birth. There were no outcries; no pleading; no gestures. After she gave birth, the nurses assisted her, took the baby, and left. Elisa just rolled on her side, and cried....and cried.....and cried a very painful, sorrowful cry.

A few months after her therapy had ended; Elisa was boarded on a private plane and flown to parts unknown.

Chapter 59

Jennifer was cuffed and shackled as she rode the van to the Metro State prison for women.

"I've had bad luck all my life, but I never thought I would end up in prison," spoke the woman sitting next to Jennifer. "I was just trying to teach my kids how to swim. I would never hurt them."

"What happened?" asked Jennifer.

"God destroyed the world with water the last time," she started. "Just in case he decided to do it again, I wanted my children to be able to swim right through it. So I put them in the tub one by one to teach them how to hold their breath. Guess I held them under water too long." Jennifer was stunned to hear what she was hearing. She was detected there were mental issues involved so she calmed herself.

"I'm Jennifer."

"I'm Janis."

"So how many kids do you have?"

"I had 4," responded Janis.

"How many did you drow .... How many did you try to teach to swim?"

"All 4 of them," smiled Janis. Jennifer was stunned again.

"You drowned all four of your children? So why are you smiling?"

"Because I know they've gone to a better place, and won't have to worry about the next flood that God sends." Then Janis started humming and smiling. Jennifer didn't know what to say as she looked around at all the stone faces in the van.

"Ok girls," said the prison guard. "You're here." After Jennifer finished her shower and was given her prison clothes, she was escorted directly to her counselor's office.

"Inmate Sweet," spoke Counselor Francis. "I don't want any trouble out of you. Is that understood?"

"Yes, Ma'am."

"I know who you are, and I know all about you. You have 18 months to serve and you will not be transferred." Jennifer didn't like her tone but she was careful not to show any displeasing signs or gestures. "I understand that you worked in a clothing department store before you decided to steal every damn thing."

That pissed Jennifer off but she said nothing. "After your processing, you will be working in Clothing Issue, Monday through Friday, is that clear?" Jennifer had been told where she would work even before she knew where she was to live. In the office next door, she saw another girl cleaning it and ear hustling while Counselor Francis spoke.

"Your full name is Jennifer Ramona Sweet, is that right?"

"Yes, Ma'am." As the counselor finished processing Jennifer, the girl working next door, slowly made her way out of the office, and quickly back to the cell block. Then she approached Helen and whispered.

"Are you sure?" asked Helen.

"Positive," said the girl. "I'd bet my life on it!" Helen, a thick, 5 feet 6 inch tall white girl, is the dorm orderly and prison bully. She wasn't all that big but she was tough, and solid. Because she wasn't that educated, girls often took advantage of her until she started beating the crap out of them, and making them eat her vagina.

"So where is little Ms. Sweet, now?" asked Helen.

"She's at the counselor office, but I'm sure she will be here soon."

Meantime, Counselor Francis was sitting with her back to Jennifer while fussing and processing Jennifer's personal information into the computer. By the time she was done, Jennifer had stolen many items from her desk, just to piss her off. Pens, pencil, staple pullers, rulers, paper clips, white out,--you name it, Jennifer had stolen it on her first day!

As she walked into her assigned cell, she saw this white brunette about her size, but a little thicker, standing at the back of the cell watching as she entered.

"Hi, I'm Jennifer." The girl said nothing but just kinda stepped between Jennifer and the bunk that Jennifer was about to place her property on. Jennifer stepped back and turned to the other bed. The girl quickly jumped in front of her again.

"You can't just walk in here and put your property down in my house," said the girl. Jennifer was confused. "Either you're gonna pay me or do something before you get on a bed in here." Jennifer wasn't scared because she had expected something like this. But she was more confused because she was told by the counselor, that money was contraband, and would get her hole time, if she were caught with it.

"I don't have any money," started Jennifer.

"So what do you have?"

"Just my bed stuff and some clothes, and pen and paper stuff."

"Oh you have more than that," smiled the girl as she observed Jennifer's butt and breast. Jennifer couldn't believe the thought's that were entering her head.

"Does this girl want to have sex with me?" she asked herself. Suddenly, she felt the girl's hand touch her shoulder. Jennifer dropped the bed cover and sharply turned to face her. As she did, the girl slapped her extremely hard across her face; Jennifer slapped her back.

Within seconds, they were tied up, wrestling, pulling each other's hair, and tearing up the place. Neither was winning when they both fell on the bed exhausted and drained of energy. As the girl sat up, Jennifer was about to tackle her again.

"Wait!" shouted the girl. "I'm too tired to go on; you can have any bed you want—I don't care." After a pause, Jennifer let her defenses down.

"Which one have you been sleeping in?" she asked.

"I've been sleeping in both of them, depending on how I feel." Jennifer picked up her things then took the other bed. "I'm Eboni," spoke the girl.

"I'm Jennifer."

"I know who you are," said Eboni. "Everybody knows that you're Sweet, right? Jennifer Sweet."

"How does everybody know me, already? I don't know anyone here."

"You'll know soon enough," said Eboni. "You'll know soon enough." Jennifer and Eboni became friends in a very short time, as they talked all night.

"Why did you act all tough when I came in? I can tell you are not like that," spoke Jennifer.

"It's just what we do. You never know what a person is about when they come in. The best way to know is to challenge them in one way or another. Then you will quickly find out."

"Does everyone do that when someone comes?" asked Jennifer.

"Oh yes. They may not all fight, but in one way or another, they will challenge you until they find you out, or break you." Suddenly, Jennifer heard what seemed to be a small struggle a few cells down. Then it was quiet and she heard moans.

"What's going on, Eboni? Was that another fight?"

"Nah! That fight was over before she ever entered the cell. Remember that motherly pretty thing that came in with you? Well, they put her down in Helen's cell. When you heard the struggling, Helen had her by the throat and was slamming her down. Then when you heard the moaning, Helen was sitting on her face." Jennifer knew she was talking about Janis.

****

Meantime, on the 7th floor of the county jail, D-Lo had been released to mingle in the dorm area.

"Hey Brother," began D-Lo. "Are there any of the brotherhood in here?"

"That depends on what you're looking for, pops."

"I'm looking for the 'gods.' "

"Yeah, we're up in here," spoke the young man. "We're in here deep, old school. What's up?"

"I'm D-Lo, little brother. I need to make a statement." When the young man knew who D-Lo was, his whole demeanor changed and he seemed nervous.

"We heard that you might be coming, man, but I didn't know it was you. How can I help you, Mr. D-Lo?"

"I told you I need to make a statement. I need a weapon."

"Hold on a minute." The young man stepped away and left D-Lo in a corner while he talked to another guy. Soon, he came back and handed D-Lo a knife, better known as a shank. D-Lo tucked it then stood and stalked the room. As he expected, men started to talk about him being there... stalking them.

"Hey, what's up, man?" asked another guy. "Do you know me or something?" D-Lo continued to stalk but said nothing. Eventually, the guy became enraged and headed toward D-Lo.

"Hey, what's up, old ass man? You're looking like you want to try me or something. What's up?" Suddenly, D-Lo pulled the shank and stuck the guy in his side numerous times, until he fell down bleeding and lying in his blood. Many of the guys became hysterical and feared when they knew who D-Lo was. After a few minutes, the guards rushed in and apprehended D-Lo, who had tossed the shank.

Within minutes, every inmate in the county jail knew what happen on the 7th floor. D-Lo was known all through the jail in Atlanta.

Chapter 60

"Candi, these are the girls you'll be working with," said Nicole as she introduced her crew. "Ladies, this is Candi Monts, our new stylist."

"Hello Candi," they responded. Candi, like D'Amica, was white with beautiful brunette hair. She was about 5 feet 7 inches tall, thick, sexy, and had very beautiful skin.

"Candi, where are you from?" asked Melody.

"I am originally from Columbia, South Carolina, but I've lived in Atlanta since my son was born 4 years ago."

"D'Amica had a son, too," added Adrienna. "His name is Shaun."

"I heard about D'Amica and all that happened," said Candi. "I'm so sorry for your loss. I know she was a good person."

"Yes, she was," added Tameka. "She knew how to treat people and to take care of her customers. So I hope you represent her chair well and..." Nicole put up the hand and Tameka hushed.

"Candi, I'm sorry about that. Listen ladies, Meca is gone and I hate it just as much as you do. But this is Candi's chair now and her clientele. Candi is younger than us but we have to give her a chance to represent herself. We must show her what we know." Then she turned to Candi again and said,

"They're good girls but they just miss Meca, that's all. You'll be ok. Just do what you do and ask questions if you need to, ok?"

"Girl, you have a 4 year old son—how old are you?" asked Melody.

"I'm twenty-one."

"Twenty-one!" shouted Melody. Then she looked at Candi's body and responded. "I guess I can see why a brother wanted all that ass. But girl, have you ever heard of 'the morning after?' It is a brother that got you, ain't it?"

"No, he's not a brother; he's white," smiled Candi.

"So he's got some money then, huh?"

"Mel, why do you have to stereotype everybody?" asked Nicole. "White men aren't the only ones who have money."

"They're about the only ones that have good money," added Tameka.

"What is good money?" asked Adrienna. "I've heard of good and bad money, but money is money."

"Drug money ain't good money," said Tameka. "That's how my brother got in trouble and went to prison. So you see, all money ain't good."

"The money that Judas received for betraying Jesus was called blood money," added Nicole. "That's according to the good book. So Tameka's right; all money ain't good money."

"Look honey, if it's green, spendable, and mine, then it's good," said Melody.

"Wasn't it something about some bad money that got D'Amica in trouble?" asked Candi. The room slienced.

"Who do you think you are, to talk about her like that?" fussed Tameka. "You don't know her!"

"I'm just saying!"

"You need to just mind your own business!" continued Tameka.

"I'm sorry! I didn't mean anything by it."

"Tameka," spoke Nicole. "You were the one who said that all money wasn't good. Candi just helped you prove your point. So why are you upset?"

"Cause, cause...."

"Cause your ass just don't know what to say... that's cause!" added Melody. They all laughed.

"Nikki, did you get the shoebox, yet?" asked Adrienna while trying to change the conversation.

"Now look who's minding my business!" spoke Nicole.

"Nikki, come on with the evasive talk," scolded Melody. "Did you get the box or not?"

"What box?" asked Candi.

"None of your damn business!" shouted Melody, Adrienna, and Tameka simultaneousl, as they laughed again. Suddenly, Nicole grabbed her sweater and headed out.

"Candi, you are fitting in just fine."

"Nikki, where are you going?" questioned Melody. "You didn't tell me that you had to go anywhere."

"I have something to take care of; I'll be back, soon. Meantime, Candi you are in charge until I get back." Then Nicole walked out... laughing. The girls were surprised—even Candi. Candi knew what Nicole was doing, so she released a sudden chuckle then dropped her head. Melody looked at Adrienna and Tameka, then sped toward Candi.

"Oh no you didn't just laugh at me up in here! I will stomp a mud hole in your white ass!" Candi jumped back, put up both her hands like a cobra, and hissed! Adrienna and Tameka grabbed Melody and held her back. Then they stood and looked at Candi, who was still standing in her defense mode.

"I like you!" laughed Adrienna as she took Candi by the hand and led her outside so they could talk. Melody and Tameka were even more surprised at Adrienna.

****

Nicole almost forgot that she was to pick up the shoebox today. Her 3 months deadline has passed but the law firm granted her an extension.

"Hi, I'm Nicole Griffin, and I'm here to pick up a package."

"Yes, Ma'am. Mr. Buddy has been expecting you," said the desk clerk. "Please have a seat." In a few minutes, the attorney entered with a large shopping bag.

"Ms. Griffin, would you step into the conference room with me, please?" Nicole followed him and signed a form releasing the law firm of the package and its contents. "Thank you, Ms. Griffin. I'm sorry this worked out this way. My condolences to you and your family. You can sit here as long as you like to view the contents."

"Thank you," she said. Then he left. Nicole opened the bag and took out the shoebox. In the shoebox, she found a watch, a bible, some reading glasses, a book entitled, "The Cosmic Conflict," and a letter written by her mom. As she picked up the letter to open it, a picture of a young lady fell to the floor. It was a newspaper clipping of a beautiful young woman with long pretty hair. She looked black but Nicole wasn't sure because it was a newspaper clipping in black and white. But as Nicole watched her eyes, she saw something there that connected her.

"Who is she?" she wondered. *"A girlfriend? A sister? Hmm? Maybe she's just a fantasy that prison guys have,"* she continued. Then she decided to open the one thing that undoubtedly connected her to this man as her father. It was the letter from her mom. It reads:

"Hello Pete, I was surprised to get your letter, but glad to know you are ok. Especially after reading your letter, telling me how you almost died from multiple gunshot wounds in your back. God is so good. Now to your letter:

When Nikki was conceived, I received the best gift that any mother could ask for. But that same night, you took something that was not yours to take and I've had a hard time dealing with that. I don't know what else you want from me.

When you disappeared, I didn't know what to tell my child about her dad. Now that I know where you are, I still don't know what to tell her so I won't tell her anything, until you come. If you love her as much as I believe you do, then give her a chance to enjoy you on this side of life. You'll be happy to know that she's pretty, very wise, and wants to have her own beauty salon some day. Please come home to her, Pete, because she needs you in her life.

Finally, I want you to know that I didn't like how you handled things that night but for our daughter's sake, I forgive you. But I'm asking you to please don't write back unless you are writing to your daughter, and hopefully you will have more to offer her than you in a prison cell. But if you write to her now, and she wants you in her life, I will support her. So long Pete—I'm praying for you.

God bless you,
Gerry

After Nicole finished reading, she had tears in her eyes. She loved her mom but from this letter, she knew that her dad loved her, too. She knew it was time for her to talk to her mom as she left the lawyers office.

"Hello Mel, this is Nikki. I'm gonna reschedule my clientele for today but there are two that I need to have styled. Can you cover them for me? I won't be back today."

"Yeah sure, Nicole, I've got your back. Is everything ok?"

"Yeah, yeah don't worry. Everything's fine. I'll see you in the morning; bye."

****

Back at the Beauty Shop, Melody looked concerned as she hung up.

"That was Nikki," she said. "She just took off for the rest of the day without saying why." The other girls looked concerned, too.

****

Nicole reached into the shoebox on her front seat, and placed the picture of the woman on her dashboard.

"Who are you, Ms. Lady?" she softly whispered. *"What can you tell me about my dad?"* Then she picked up the phone and made another call. "Hello, Mom? I was just checking on you. I'm on the way."

Chapter 61

A few months had passed and Jennifer was well on the way in her prison lifestyle. She rose early every morning, ate breakfast then headed to her laundry detail. Officer Nettles, her detail officer, was a tall skinny white guy from Alabama, therefore everybody called him, "Bama."

Bama was nerdy and very smart, so he managed the laundry department very well. But he wasn't an authoritarian, and the girls often took advantage of him when his supervisor or other officials were not around. Bama didn't care because the girls loved being around him, and they took pride in their work.

Of all the girls that worked for him, he liked Jennifer the most, and often let her handle special laundry projects, that kept her from working too hard. Jennifer would laugh when the other girls made fun of him but she never made fun of him. She treated him like the nice young man that he was, and Bama liked that.

In a short time, Jennifer learned to handle herself very well, and to win the respect of the other girls. But the one thing she couldn't stop doing was stealing. Whenever the desire came over her, she tried to fight it, but Jennifer was a thief.

"The Curse Must Be Broken!" she heard many times, but she was learning to accept it as a part of her life. She couldn't resist the urge to take things so she started stealing things the girls needed, and bringing it to them. Because of Bama's liking for her, Jennifer could persuade him to let her move all through the prison. Sometimes, he even escorted her places as long as it wasn't getting him or others into trouble.

No matter how much good Jennifer did she still had enemies and they often challenged her.

"Hey Sweet!" yelled Helen while in the dorm one day. "You're sho' putting in a lot of time at the laundry, lately. What's up? Bama tapping that ass?"

"What's it to you, Helen, if he is!" sounded Jennifer.

"I just happened to notice that your pants are getting tighter, that's all. I may want to tap that ass myself, sometimes."

"Helen, some of us are real women. You know... we like to feel the wood, grinding, and hitting deep. Ooops! My bad. You've been so active making other girls suck on that cow tongue between your legs, till you don't know what a real man feels like, do you?" Some of the girls began to laugh and make fun of Helen.

"That's good, Sweet! That's real good! But in case you hadn't noticed, ain't no real men in here, and can't nobody satisfy the girls like I can. I'm the man up in here."

"Helen, you ain't no man. You just look like a man, that's all." Helen angrily grabbed Janis and left as all the girls laughed and pointed.

"I don't think that was a good idea," said Eboni. "She's gonna retaliate you know."

A few minutes later, as Jennifer and Eboni headed to their cell, they walked by Helen's cell only to see her holding Janis down and grinding on her face. When Helen saw them, she slammed the door and finished the job. That night, Jennifer and Eboni laid in their cell and talked.

"Jennifer, you should be careful how you talk to Helen because she has many friends who will sneak up on you and hurt you—even in the laundry," said Eboni.

"So what should I do, Eboni? Just let her have her way like Janis did so she can turn me out?"

"No, I'm just saying be careful, that's all."

"Thank you for the advice, Eboni! You got anymore?" Jennifer spoke angrily.

"I'm not your enemy, Jennifer. But I do see many girls come and go because of women like Helen. She's never getting out so she's miserable and wants you to be, too."

"I know you're right, Eboni," said Jennifer pausing. "I'm sorry I snapped at you."

"Don't worry about it, Jennifer. You're not a man—you just look like a man." They both started to laugh. "Oh she's gonna get you for that one; you can count on it!"

"Yeah but meantime, Janis is the one suffering," said Jennifer. Suddenly, they heard the doors lock as the guards rushed to Helen's cell, along with the medical team.

"I will kill yo' stankin' ass!" came shouts from Janis.

"I don't know what happened to her!" lied Helen. "She just jumped up out of the bed and tried to attack me with a shank!" Evidently, Janis had had enough of Helen's sexual abuse and had snapped.

"Take her to medical and check her out," said the guard.

"This happens about every other month or so," said Eboni. "Helen always play the innocent role while another victim goes into isolation."

"Well, that's good for Janis," added Jennifer. "At least she's out of there."

"Yeah, but in a couple of days, someone else will take her place and the abuse starts over again. Do you have any sisters, Jennifer?"

"Yeah, I have two wonderful sisters—Cherlene and Donna. Plus, I learned just before I came here, that I have a half sister by my Dad. Her name is Sarah."

"So how would you feel if Cherlene, Donna, or Sarah, had to go through what others are going through with Helen?" Jennifer sparked up.

"Oh I would love for Cheryl to be over there! She would beat Helen's horny ass! And Donna would talk her to death! She would be so confused when Donna finished with her, she'll tap out and beg to be isolated!"

"I see that you love your sisters," smiled Eboni. "What about Sarah?"

"Yeah, I do love my sisters but I've never met Sarah. I only learned that she existed about a week before I came here. I don't know if she is dead or what. Nor do I know where to start searching for her."

"So how did you learn that she is your sister?"

Jennifer began to share her story with Eboni about all that happened since she lost her dad and mom, until the present situation.

"So Cherlene and Donna are not your blood sisters, but is there a chance that Sarah is?" asked Eboni.

"Yeah, I guess so."

"Did you ever hear from your mom, again?"

"No, I haven't. I figured she did her prison time, was embarrassed, and just left me. She and my dad were birds of a feather—always on the move. After my dad died and she went to jail, I guess she figured that I was in the best place to be cared for. She never came back and I never tried to find her. What about you, Eboni? Tell me about you."

"Six months and a wake up!" shouted Eboni. "I'm going home!" After Eboni told Jennifer about her life, they fell asleep.

The next morning before going to detail, Jennifer and Eboni were at the chow hall eating breakfast. Eboni saw Helen walk behind Jennifer and just stand over her. Helen had gotten there so fast that Eboni didn't have time to warn Jennifer before Jennifer spoke:

"Sniff! Sniff!" did Jennifer. "Do you smell that? Smells like straight cow shit!" Jennifer looked around and ducked just in time to avoid being hit by Helen. Helen wasn't slow but Jennifer was quick as a good boxer, and could move like the wind, when she wanted to. She wasn't all that of a fighter, but she had learned to use her limbs like a spider while moving and adjusting her body to avoid contact. Helen was forcing her to use her skills as she maneuvered all through the chow hall to avoid Helen's attacks.

As Helen started to run out of energy, Jennifer remained strong and began to toy with her as the girls laughed. Jennifer had never felt so good as she slid under tables, and tied Helen's shoestrings together, or quickly maneuvered behind Helen and pinched her butt among many other things that made the girls laugh. Jennifer was really astounded by her ability to move and do some of the things she was doing. To the girls, she looked like a superhero, but to her, it was child's play.

"On the floor! On the floor, now!" yelled the security guards as they ran in. Helen and Jennifer were placed in isolation for 30 days.

While there, Jennifer completely forgot about Helen and wondered about her new found abilities to move and do what she did in the chow hall.

"What in the world is happening to me?" she wondered.

Suddenly, she heard something she hadn't heard in a long time.

"The Curse Must Be Broken!" came her dad's voice.

When she heard this, she understood why she was able to do what she did. It was a part of her ability to be a master thief. As she burst into tears, she screamed,

"Why don't you help me!!!" Jennifer fell to her knees while crying a hard cry.

"Jennifer?" came a small voice. Jennifer thought she was hearing things again. "Jennifer, I'm here," said the voice again. This time Jennifer recognized it.

"Janis, is that you?"

"Yeah, I'm here, next door to you. I saw you come in. Are you alright?"

"No, Janis, I'm not," she cried. "I think I'm going crazy."

"No, you're not crazy, honey. That's what those demons in your head want you to think. You wanna know the best way to get rid of them; to get them out of your head?"

"How Janis?"

"Just take yourself over to the toilet, stick your head in it as deep as you can, and just keep flushing it and flushing it, until the demons are all gone and you hear nothing. I had four of them bastards and I drowned every one of them. You can do it, too. Jennifer just burst into tears again for she knew that Janis was mentally insane and had shared with her the real reason why she drowned her four kids,,, she thought that they were demons.

Chapter 62

As Nicole pulled into Hardwood Court in Jonesboro, she sprung from the car with the shoebox in her hand. She was surprised to see her mom, Ms. Gerry Griffin, standing in the doorway awaiting her arrival.

"Mama! What are you doing? You didn't have to wait out here for me!"

"When you called, I knew it was time to get a little fresh air before you came." Ms. Gerry looked at the shoebox. "You don't shop for them kind of shoes so I guess those belong to your father." Nicole was shocked.

"Mom you knew? Did the lawyer tell you?"

"No, you did when you called a few minutes ago. I could hear it in your words. I guess he's gone, huh?" Nicole pulled the letter and handed it to her mom.

"I need to know, Mama." After Gerry took the letter and looked at it, she handed it back to Nicole and took her seat.

"Your dad wasn't a bad man, Nicole, but he was just roguish as hell—would steal anything. I think that's how he ended up in prison. Anyway, we were young; all of us were really, really, young. Your dad wanted me, but I was in love with June Bug. I was 18 and your dad was 21. But June Bug was 24 and a big time businessman all over the city. I had known your father since high school and I really liked him a lot. He would chase me and bring me things and make me laugh but I wasn't in love with him. Your dad knew that I would be faithful to him if he could only get me to sleep with him. So he tried and tried but I wouldn't give in because I didn't love him like that.

While me and a few friends were at the Varsity one day, this smooth talking, suit wearing, baby face, lover boy, came in and stood right next to me as he placed his order. I wasn't sure if he saw me so I kinda made sure he did, if you know what I mean. He wasn't just nice and gentle, but his words were captivating and heart felt. No one had ever talked to me like that before. We started dating and I fell in love right away. Your father kept stalking me and telling me that I was involved with a bad man, but I didn't want to hear it.

Then one night, June Bug told me that he wanted me to go with him on a boat ride, but he had to make a business stop first. I was thrilled that he asked me, and I knew this would be the night I would lose my virginity. But to my surprise, everything changed for me on that night."

Gerry's Memories I

"Pete, will you please leave before he comes! He will be here any minute now and I don't want him to see you!" said Gerry as they stood on the porch of her mom's house.

"I promise that nobody will see me, Gerry, but I don't like this guy and I know he's not good for you."

"But you are good for me, right? You steal everything that ain't tied down and you could go to jail at anytime. I don't want a man like that!"

"Listen, Gerry. All I'm asking you to do is find out what kind of business he's involved with before you go away with this guy. I just don't want to see you hurt, that's all." Suddenly, a black limo pulled up and June Bug jumped from the car.

"Hey baby, you look ravishing! Are you ready?" Gerry was sure Pete was still standing there and had been seen as she started to explain. But when she looked to where he was standing, he was gone. "Are you ok, baby?"

"Yes, I'm fine," she said. But she knew Pete was nearby as they drove away. So she kept looking back while in the limo to see if she saw his car.

"Where are we going, June Bug?"

"I told you that we are going on a boat ride, a few miles outside the city."

"No, you said that you had a business stop first."

"Oh that!" he said. "We won't be long; I promise you. I have to make a quick stop on Fulton Industrial at one of our warehouses."

"As we drove into this industrial area, we drove behind a building where there were many tractor trailers and huge canisters like a shipping yard or something. But the driver didn't take us all the way in.

'Wait here, Gerry. We'll be back in a flash,' said June Bug.

I'm already a scary person and that night I was more afraid than ever: Seem like I heard all kinds of scary noises as I waited alone for over 30 minutes. After a while, I had to use the bathroom really bad. So I got out the car and stumbled in the direction I saw June Bug and the limo driver go. When I peeped around the corner, I saw two other men counting out something to June Bug as he dropped it in a small, dark cloth bag. It looked like marbles or something but I was too far away to tell. After they finished counting, two more guys came out from hiding with machine guns.

'It's a set up!' yelled June Bug. Then all 4 men pulled out guns and started shooting. I was screaming and too scared to move, as I saw them kill each other.

'Aahhh!' I screamed as somebody grabbed me and pushed me against the huge canister.

'Shhh!' said Pete. 'I told you this was a bad idea. Stay here until I check things out!'

I was so scared I couldn't even talk. I was shivering with tears and I wanted to go home. Before, I realized it, I was standing against *the canister where Pete left me, with pee running down my legs; I knew I was only moments away from a nervous break down. I saw Pete go to where the dead men were and pick up the small bag, and what looked like an amulet or something, then he hurried back to me. As he rushed me to his car, another car with two gunmen sped around the corner, and stopped right where we were standing. I was shaking so bad and crying that I couldn't keep quiet. Pete forced me tighter to the canister and covered me with his body the best he could so that I couldn't be seen or heard. I closed my eyes and begin to think on my church and the goodness of the Lord, like my mom told me to do when I get in trouble.*

First Gunman-Aw man! This is not good! Mr. Holloway won't like this!
Second Gunman-Go check the bodies to see if they got the merchandise!

After they checked the bodies, they came running back to their car. I assumed they were looking for the small bag and the little shiny amulet key thing that Pete had taken. With Pete still covering me and keeping me safe, one man got back in the car they came in, but the other one got in the limo and took it. My face and body was pressed hard against the canister as I heard them drive away. I was so thankful for Pete being there that night until it didn't matter what he did or said to me. I just wanted to stay in his arms.

'Sniff! Sniff!' sniffed Pete. 'Geraldine! What did you do?' I had urinated on myself and he was smelling it, but I was still too scared to say anything.

'Baby, you're all wet! Ain't no telling how long we will have to stay here in order to be safe, so you'd better take them wet clothes off,' he whispered.

With his body still pressed to my backside, he lifted my dress and slid my wet panties off. Next thing I knew, he opened my legs a bit, and I felt him inside me doing his thing. When he finished doing his business in me, he became the caring, loving, heroic, man, that he was when he first showed up that night. He took me to his home, bathe me, nurtured and cared for me, until I was calm again, and could go home. Your dad never did touch me sexually, again, but he came to check on me everyday to make sure that I was ok. Nine months later, after that night with your father, you were born. He loved you so much." (End of Gerry's Mem #1)

"So Mom, according to what you just told me, I wasn't supposed to be born. I was a mistake," said Nicole.

"No baby, you wasn't. I was the one about to make the mistake. God knew that on that night, I was planning on giving up my virginity to the wrong man. So he sent the right one along and everything worked out just like he planned it. You were born to the right man—no mistake." Nicole laid her head in her mom's chest.

"Mama, whatever happened to you and Daddy?"

"He kept begging me to marry him and let's be a family just like God told him, too. But I was stubborn and upset because of the way he took advantage of me that night and I wouldn't submit to him. Plus, he was too darn roguish and wouldn't stop stealing. I was scared that he was gonna get himself killed one day, and I didn't want to face that. After you were two years old, I began to see just how much he really loved you, and I wanted that for you. So I made up my mind to tell him I'd marry him on your third birthday. You and I waited for him, but he never showed. Five years later when you were almost 8, he came to see you. But I told him that if he was gonna just disappeared again, then don't interfere with your life. He left and the next time I heard from him, he was in prison."

"Is that when you wrote him this letter?"

"Yes. Your dad loved you, Nicole. But he couldn't be still nor keep his hands off of stuff."

"Well Mom, I'm glad he put his hands on you or I may not be here."

"Baby, I couldn't have said that better myself." Gerry hugged Nicole and they smiled.

"Oh Mama! Let me show you something else!" Nicole reached into the shoebox and pulled the picture of the girl from the newspaper clipping.

"This was also in the box. Do you know who she is?" Gerry put on her glasses and looked thoroughly at the picture.

"I don't know, but she's pretty though," commented Gerry. "Maybe she's just a fantasy or something. I've heard that guys in prison do that." Gerry turned the picture over and saw the printed ink.

"Hey, this is a newspaper clipping or it's from a magazine. When you're not so busy, maybe you ought to visit the newspaper place and ask about it."

Chapter 63

The 30 days of isolation were over as Jennifer and Helen were released within the population of inmates. Jennifer used her isolation time to pray and learn about herself. She also wrote letters to her sisters and friends. Helen used her time trying to figure out how she could get back at Jennifer without facing more isolation time. Both women had lost their assigned cells and would be sent to a new one. Jennifer had also lost her detail, but hoped she could get it back. She needed to find a way to talk to Bama.

"Hi, I'm Carolyn," said the girl waiting as Jennifer walked into her new cell. "Girls around here call me Cal, for short."

"Man, I hope she doesn't grab me," thought Jennifer. Carolyn was big, tall, and black. She spoke easy but she was very big; weighing about 400 pounds.

"I'm Jennifer and it's good to meet you, Cal." Jennifer quickly walked out of her cell and went toward her old cell to find Eboni.

"What's up, girlfriend?" said Eboni as they hugged. "So how did you like the hole?"

"Uh, it was a piece of cake," bragged Jennifer.

"Ok, you wanna go back?"

"It was also the worse piece of cake I ever tasted," they laughed.

"So what cell are you in now?"

"I'm with a big girl named Carolyn."

"Oh she's cool. She came from probation detention and is on her way home. Believe me, she doesn't want any trouble," said Eboni.

"Ok, so what's the word on the compound?"

"I think you already know that Helen and her goon squad is planning to do you. So you better be careful and watch your back. But you have friends, too, who are also enemies of Helen, so it may not be all bad." Suddenly, Helen walked into the cell block and into her new cell. Within seconds, Jennifer and Eboni heard fighting. Just as fast as it started, it was over.

"Who is in there with her this time?" asked Jennifer.

"It's a new girl—only been here about 3 days."

"Why don't they do something about her? They've gotta know."

"Yeah, but who is gonna tell? If you tell, then one of the gang members will come after you for being a snitch. You just have to fight your way through."

"Chow call! Chow call!" yelled the floor officer. Many of the girls were glad to see Jennifer back. They remembered the show she had given them in the chow hall before she went to isolation and they were talking about it.

"You're in my seat, bitch!" spoke Helen to Eboni who was sitting across from Jennifer. Eboni got up as Helen sat down and began to stare at Jennifer. Jennifer stared back as everybody watched.

"So how long are we gonna do this, Helen, huh? My grits are getting cold, and staring at you don't make my breakfast taste any better." Then Jennifer started eating very peaceably. "You don't scare me, Helen, and I'm ready to go back to the hole at anytime, are you?" Helen said nothing. "That's what I thought. Oh by the way! Are you gonna eat your cornbread?" mocked Jennifer. All the girls started laughing again.

"Sweet." yelled the officer. "You're needed at laundry. Let's go!" Jennifer was happy because she knew that Bama had requested for her to come back. All the girls at laundry clapped as she walked in.

"You are on probation, Jennifer," said Bama. "You cannot get into anymore trouble or I may not be able to get you back again, ok?"

"Yes Sir, Mr. Bama, Sir," mocked Jennifer as she saluted him. "Bama, you left me in the hole for 30 whole days and not once did you come to see me. What's up with that?"

"We told him he should go," said one of the girls. "But he wouldn't."

"I wanted to come but I didn't trust Helen's goons. They may have lied and got me in trouble."

"So you were scared, huh?" added Jennifer. "Bama, pull your pants down and let me check your balls. I think mine are bigger than yours and I don't even have any," she joked.

"Ha! Ha! Jennifer," said Bama. "That's real funny."

"I'm just kidding, Bama. I know how devious Helen and her crew can be." For the next few hours, Jennifer worked in the laundry then she headed back to her cell. As she went on, she noticed that the girls weren't speaking to her as usual, and they were all looking like something was wrong.

"What's going on, Cal?" she asked. "Why is everybody so quiet and staring?" Cal said nothing but just rolled her eyes toward Eboni's cell. "Is something up with Eboni?" Jennifer ran to Eboni's cell but Eboni had been moved.

"Where's Eboni?" she shouted but no one answered. Then she ran to the floor officer and asked her.

"She was moved to the infirmary about two hours ago."

"Why? What happened to her?"

"Nobody knows," said the officer. "She was found laying on the floor of her cell, all stuck up and bleeding." Jennifer took off toward the infirmary.

"Can I speak to Eboni Little for a minute, please?" she asked the nurse.

"No one is to speak with Inmate Little until the investigation is finished; Warden's orders!" said the nurse.

Jennifer, being angry, headed back toward the dorm. She knew that Helen and her posse had hurt Eboni but nobody would talk. Helen just stood in her doorway smiling as Jennifer rutrned, but Jennifer gave her a very serious look.

An hour later, the girls heard kicking, grunts, and punches, sounding within Jennifer's cell. Within the little 5'x 8' cell, Jennifer was speeding from wall to wall, kicking and punching her homemade punching bag, while dropping and rolling to do push-ups and other calisthenics all at the same time. Jennifer was working out like she was getting ready for a main events bout. She was already quick on her feet, lightning fast with her hands, and could toss her body under and above things like she was swinging on a rope. Now she was hitting and kicking, squatting, and jumping, to add to her orchestra of newly acquire skills because... she was mad! She was beyond mad—she was furious! The peaceful, smart, young girl, who once ran and hid behind the door while Cherlene and Donna fought, was gone! Jennifer was not the same person she was when she was at home, and she didn't care to be. Helen and prison life had accessed the beast in her, and she was about to bring him out. She didn't know how she was able to skillfully master the techniques that infiltrated her, but she welcomed them. For Jennifer was no longer just a thief, she had become a survivor and a fighter! She was angrily preparing to go after Helen!

Chapter 64

"Thank you all for attending our luncheon and awards ceremony today!" announced Mr. Golden. Donna, Cherlene, and Tyler, stood across from Tenisha and her parents as they waited the big moment. Today was the day Mr. Golden would announce to the executives, who was new, who would be awarded, and who would be promoted. Both Donna and Tenisha had received written notices of a mandatory attendance so they knew their names would be called for a promotion or an award.

"Look at her standing there like she is so innocent," commented Donna. "Given the opportunity, Tenisha would cut my throat and take all the glory for herself."

"I don't know, Dee," commented Cherlene. "After having seen how she worked with the Daycare center, she seems different—like a changed person."

"Oh no you didn't just defend her again, after all she's done to you!"

"People change, Donna," said Tyler. "Tenisha is really trying to be a good person to all people—including you. Why can't you see that?" Donna got angry.

"That bitch printed a story about my sister, Jenny, and put her picture in the paper for all to see. She didn't have to do that. To me, that was worst than the crime Jennifer did."

"Dee, I think you are taking this a little too far. Why all the hatred?"

"It's not hatred, Cheryl; it's competition. We're both trying to get to the top by any means necessary and she proves it everyday. If she had the opportunity, she'd hit me with a bat and push me in front of a moving truck; I just don't trust her." *"The Curse Must Be Broken!"* came the whisper, but Donna tried to ignore it.

Cherlene was surprised to see Donna acting like this but Cherlene was also smart. She knew that Donna wasn't really like this, therefore, there had to be something else driving her to act this way.

"I need you now, Jenny," thought Cherlene. *"This is your specialty—to discern what's really going on with Dee."* Then her mind went back to the day she chased Donna around the apartment because Donna wanted to move out. *"That's it!"* she thought again. *"The pain inside me and Jennifer came out that day, but Dee is still holding her's in! She's hurt about her parents leaving and is channeling all her anger toward Tenisha!"* Cherlene knew she was right, but had no clue what to do about it.

"Mom, please stand up straight!" whispered Tenisha. "People are watching! Why did you have to take a drink today of all days anyway! You knew I wanted you here today, so why couldn't you just stay sober for one day!"

"Because of your bastard father over there," argued Davina. "Look at him—standing there like he's so righteous and respected by the world. But I know your sins, Kris!" she yelled. "Your sins will find you out!" People in the crowd looked around as Tenisha kinda dropped her head.

"My wife's had a long morning," smiled Kris as he addressed the crowd near him. "Davina, please contain yourself for our daughter's sake," he whispered as his cell phone rang. "I have to take this." He walked away and answered. "Hello?"

"Hi Kris," said the soft voice. "It's me." Kris paused for a minute.

"Keisha? Keisha Banks? When did you get... So how are you?" Keisha Banks was the one girl in college that could make Kris turn cartwheels, at anytime. He was in love with her then, and had feelings for her even now.

"Yes, I'm out Kris," she said. "I'm out of prison and I have nothing. I need to see you."

"Sure Keisha, where can I find you?"

"I'm at the same place you took me that night in room 328. I'll be here all day Kris. Please come by."

"I'll be there in a couple of hours." He hung up and walked back near Davina and Tenisha.

"Normally at this time," started Mr. Golden. "We only promote one person to the position that I'm about to announce. But God has smiled on us and sent to the AJC, two of a kind, that's proven worthy to excel as journalist.

One, have learned to feel the needs of the community and that's how she chooses what she writes about. Then she writes with compassion as she places herself in her stories and causes the readers to want more of her. Then she just keep on coming—exploding with informative compassion.

On the other hand, our second choice have not been with us as long as our compassionate one but she is a tiger; a go-getter who will stomp a hole in Godzilla if that's what it takes to get to the truth. She knows how to exploit a story and find the missing elements that sends her readers in awe.

Both, our compassionist, and our tiger, get along well with others, while performing a cut above our expectations. They're young... pretty... smart .'pretty,' ..... did I say pretty, yet?" Some laughed. "They're both very good friends and make a fine addition as Journalists to our AJC Team.

Ladies and gentlemen, let's hear it for our two new journalists, our compassionist, Ms. Tenisha Cuyler, and our tiger, Ms. Donna Banks."

The crowd cheered and applauded as Tenisha and Donna accepted their certificates as journalists, from Mr. Golden.

"This concludes our ceremony," announced Mr. Golden. *"Please enjoy your luncheon."* Tenisha walked to Donna and extended her hand.

"Congratulations, Ms. *Tiger go-getter*," smiled Tenisha. Donna hesitated then said, "Thank you, Glamour Bitch. Congrats to you, too."

"So how does it feel to be a 'Tiger?'" smiled Kris as he shook Donna's hand.

"Actually it feels pretty good," smiled Donna. "Where do I know you from, Sir?"

"I was the bank manager in West End Atlanta, but we just merged with our sister bank. I'm Kris Cuyler."

"Now, I remember!" shouted Donna. "My sister, Jenny, opened an account at your bank a while back! I may need to talk to you!"

"My my," laughed Kris. "You sure don't waste any time, do you? You really are a go-getter. But I have to run, so just stop by the bank at any time and I'll see what I can help you with."

"Oh I might just do that." Kris looked at Davina, hugged Tenisha, then said goodbye as he sped off.

"Congratulations, Tenisha," said Cherlene. "It's good to see you again, Ms. Davina."

"Thank you, young lady. You and your sister are so pretty."

"Thank you, Ma'am. Well, I have to get back to work," said Cherlene. "It's strenuous work being a teacher, sometimes."

"Maybe one day we can sit down and develop a story about your compassion to teach," said Tenisha. Cherlene was pleasantly surprised as she looked at Donna. Donna gave her a skirmish grin.

"That would really be nice, Tenisha," remarked Cherlene. "I look forward to telling you my story, in the near future."

"Uh, before you go, can I have a word with you?"

"Sure, Tenisha, what's up?" They walked away to talk. A few feet away, another conversation began to take place.

"So you're little Donna, huh?" greeted Davina. "Congratulations on your promotion."

"Thank you, Ma'am. I know you must be proud of Tenisha."

"I am, but I want to tell you something. He called her a pussy cat and you a tiger. But you girls are not as different as you may think, you'll see."

"My God!" thought Donna to herself. *"I will never be anything like Tenisha, and she's nothing like me! Is this woman drunk?"* Before Donna could finish her thought, Davina burped and Donna smelled the

alcohol on her breath. *"That explains it,"* she thought again while smiling.

****

"So, Ms. Compassionate Journalist, what's on your mind?"

"Cherlene I have something to ask you so I'll cut right through the chase. When we were kids, I did some horrible, unforgettable, things to you and your sisters. I told you on the day of your teacher's certification that I was sorry and I meant it." Tenisha was in tears, now. "I really meant it, Cherlene. I truly am sorry." Cherlene hugged her.

"Ok, Tenisha. I know where you're going with this and I think it'll soon pass, if you can hold on a little while longer."

"But why does your sister hate me so much? What can I do to help her understand that I'm not like that anymore?"

"Listen, Tenisha. The problem is not you; it really isn't. It's deeper than you or anything you've done. You just have to trust me on this one, so please just continue to be the person you are and it'll all work out, soon."

Chapter 65

Shortly after Kris drove onto Cobb Parkway, he turned into this motel where Keisha was expecting him. She saw him driving up so she stood in the door.

"Hello, Keisha," he smiled. "You look different. Good, but different." Kris didn't know whether to shake her hand or hug her. She slowly wrapped him and hugged him.

"Prison has a way of changing a person, Kris. Plus, I'm about 20 years older now. You still look the same. So how've you been?" she asked. "Are you still with Davina?"

"Yeah, unfortunately."

"You don't sound happy. Are you guys having problems?"

"No, no, nothing like that," he said. "She's just still struggling to let go of the past."

"What! All these years, and you mean she still manages to think about me? I guess I was a force to be reckoned with, huh?"

"Yeah, we were something back then," added Kris as he sat on the bed. "I would have given anything to have you, Keisha,,, anything!"

"I know that, Kris, I know. But those years are gone and we can never get them back. Besides, I'm here for a different reason now."

"What is it, Keisha? Just name it."

"Kris, I don't have a life anymore. I'm fresh out of prison and I don't have anything."

"Ok, I'll find a place and put you up until you're on your feet again."

"No, no Kris, I can't let you do that. I don't want to mess up your life any more than I already have. I just need to know if you will loan me some money, until I can pay you back."

"Sure, Keisha. How much do you need?"

She hunched her shoulders. "A few hundred, I guess. I have nothing, Kris, so I'll take whatever you can give me."

"If you will come by the bank, I have an account with a couple of thousand in it. I knew I was saving it for something so it's all yours." Keisha kissed his hand .

"Thank you, Kris. You've always been too good to me."

"I saw your daughter get a promotion today," added Kris. "A *Tiger'* they called her. She picked up exactly where you left off. She's a pretty little thing. Don't you want her to know that you are ok?" Keisha paused for a minute then changed her tone.

"Kris, you've always been straight up with me, even when I did you wrong and treated you like shit. So now, I'm gonna be straight with you, and I hope you don't hate me for it." Keisha stood then yelled,

"Bettie, come on out!" The bathroom door opened and a thick woman with long blonde hair, about Keisha's height, came walking out.

Then she and Keisha embraced and deeply kissed, while Keisha squeezed her butt.

"Kris, this is Bettie and we're in love," smiled Keisha. Kris just stared at the two beautiful women.

"I understand," he smiled. "I wish you both the best." Keisha followed him outside to his car as he prepared to leave.

"So, you will stop by the bank, won't you?" said Kris.

"Yes, tomorrow morning first thing," she said. Then she grinned, hugged Kris, and kissed him deeply.

"Uh!" sounded Kris as she grabbed his butt. "But I thought you were a hom...."

"Yes Kris, I am! But when I saw those nice buns bouncing under your jacket, I thought I'd just get one for the road." Then she smiled and left. Kris was flabbergasted as he entered his car and chuckled.

Chapter 66

A few days had passed since Jennifer last saw Eboni. She was determined to see her again because she had made up her mind to go after Helen and her posse, even if it meant risking her life.

"Bama, I need your help."

"What's up, Jennifer?"

"I have to see my friend, Eboni, who is in the infirmary. She could be going home any day now and I need to talk to her."

"Ok," said Bama. "I'll let you know in a bit if I can help." About an hour later, Bama told Jennifer that he needed her to stay over and help pass out supplies to the inmates in the infirmary. She knew this was her break.

"Hello, Eboni." Eboni sat up in bed and laughed out loud. "Here's your soap, toothpaste, and toiletries, Ma'am," smiled Jennifer.

"I knew your crazy ass was coming—one way or another," laughed Eboni. "I'm glad you walked in here and was not carried in like me. So what's up with you, Sweet?"

"Oh, just checking on you, inmate Little," she joked. "Eboni I need to know what happened. I've heard all kinds of stuff but I want names. Who did this to you?"

"Stop trip'n, Jennifer; you already know. Cowards caught me with my back turned and stuck me in the side with something. After that, Helen and her number one just beat the hell out of me and stuck me up. Doctors say I'll go home from here so I'm safe now. It's you I'm worried about."

"Oh don't worry about me, kid. I've planned to do a bit of sticking on my own."

"What are you talking about, Jennifer? Are you going after Helen?"

"Yep! I'm gonna give her a taste of her own medicine, and I know I can do it."

"Jennifer, I have something to tell you. I wasn't gonna be the one but I think you need to know.

Like you and me, many girls come to prison with only a few months to serve. Then when they get a taste of this lifestyle, they change and find themselves doing years instead of months, or caught up in a revolving door that keeps bringing them back. If you go after Helen and win, you will become known as some type of champion, and other kinds of Helens will be coming after you. Before you know it, your family and friends will no longer be your primary reason to live, but surviving prison life will be. Because once you take out Helen, you will get a name. With that name will come shanks, drugs, pills, sex, homosexuality, wheeling, dealings, and a whole lot of scary ass inmates who will depend on you to protect them. That will become your life! Your mom got caught up in this same trap!"

"What did you say?" asked Jennifer. "Did you say my mother?"

"Yes Jennifer, your mother, known as 'Mad Margit,' was here."

"Eboni, when? Why didn't you tell me this before?" Jennifer was about to get angry and emotional.

"Calm down, Jennifer! I'm your friend, remember? But if you gonna act up, I'll lay my white ass down and leave you wondering."

"Come on, Eboni, please don't do this to me!"

"I see now that you get too emotional and that's why I didn't want to tell you this before. Officer!" she yelled. "Officer!"

"Ok! Ok! Eboni, I promise I'll calm down," begged Jennifer. She was sure that Eboni had gotten mad and was gonna have her kicked out.

"I'm ready for a smoke break now!" yelled Eboni. "Inmate Sweet have volunteered to roll me out!" Jennifer helped Eboni to her wheelchair after security opened the door to her room.

"Scared you, didn't I?"

"Yes, you did," laughed Jennifer. "Thank you for that."

"I told you, I'm your friend. That's why I want you to hear what I'm about to say and take heed to it.

Like you, your mother came here with 18 months to serve. Here it is 20 years later, and I hear that your mother is still here."

"Is she here at Metro?" asked Jennifer.

"No, I mean here in prison. I've only been here about 18 months, but she was the talk of the place when I came. The talk only died a few months before you came. But once you came here, it only took about 30 seconds for the whole place to know that Mad Margit's daughter was here."

"That's how you knew who I was when I came in your cell."

"Yes, and that's also why I challenged you like I did. We all needed to know if you were as dangerous as your mother, Mad Margit. Besides, Helen and her posse had warned me that if I didn't challenge you, I would be in the infirmary or the morgue before sunrise the next day. They never expected us to become friends---I didn't either."

"So tell me about my mom. Where is she now?"

"I don't know where she is now. Some say she's at Pulaski. I just know they say she's a mean bitch, and nobody messes with her."

When Margit first came to prison, she was pulled into a cell like most new girls and turned out. Except back then, once they turned you out, girls would claim you as their own then trust you explicitly to sexually handle their bodies. So when they wanted you to give them oral sex, they laid on their back, and allowed you to do what you do. Well, Margit decided that she had had enough. So that night when it was time for her to go down on her mate, she cut off her clit with a pair of scissors she had stolen from medical. After she cut off her clit, Margit lost it and used the same scissors to stab the girl more than 30 times until she was dead. Everybody's been calling her 'Mad Margit' every since. She was placed in the hole for two years, and given a life sentence for what she did. Seven years later, when Margit went to her first parole hearing and learned that they wasn't gonna let her out, she decided to live up to the name, Mad Margit, by going after any and everybody she thought was a problem. Many times she won but sometimes she lost---she didn't care. She was just mad as hell. A few years after that, Helen showed up on the scene and immediately started slamming girls and having her way. A few days later, the word was that Helen had put a hit out on Mad Margit; claims the girl that Margit killed was her sister. That same night, they transferred Mad Margit to another camp; nobody knows where.

       Jennifer, if you go after Helen, you could end up in prison for life just like your mother. Somebody has to stop this train of prison events that just keep coming back around. Why not you, Jennifer? *'The Curse Must Be Broken!'"*

       "What?" Jennifer turned sharply toward her. "Why did you say that?"

       "Why did I say what?" asked Eboni. "Why are you looking like that? Are you ok?"

       "I gotta go," said Jennifer. Then she took off back to her cell, where she cried and cried until she fell asleep.

       "Mail call! Mail Call!" was the sound that woke Jennifer a few hours later. It was dark so mail call was a little late.

       "Jennifer Sweet!" sounded the officer. "You've got mail!"

       Almost a year had passed since Jennifer was incarcerated, and she had only received a card form J.J. and letters from Michelle. Every month, Michelle faithfully sent money and updated her of certain current events. When Jennifer went to get her mail, as usual, it was from Michelle. Each time Michelle wrote, Jennifer happily laughed and smiled as she read her letter. It was like she wasn't in prison as Michelle's words connected her to the outside world again. Cherlene was taking care of Audrey and Donna kept her apartment, so she was ok with them not writing that much. Besides, she could call them anytime she wanted to. But Michelle's letters had become special to her because they gave her comfort and peace.

       When Jennifer finished reading her letter, she always wrote back, immediately. Today would be no different.

       "Hi Michelle," she wrote. *"I've never told you this but before I came here, I learned that somewhere out there, I have a half sister named Sarah. I'll tell you about that later. Today, I learned that my mom was here at the same prison where I am. She's gone now. They called her 'Mad Margit!' "*

Chapter 67

More months had passed and Eboni had been released. Between Eboni's last words and Michelle's letter, Jennifer had peace again, so she avoided Helen and her goons. Helen still tried to do her thing to uphold her image, but it was getting harder; prison was changing. Many girls had gone and new ones came. But the new girls were younger, wiser, and more rebellious when Helen and her goons came at them. Like gang members, the young girls teamed up and saved each other from the likes of Helen. Jennifer mostly kept to herself when she wasn't at detail talking with Bama, but even there, most of the girls were new.

"Why do y'all call him 'Bama?'" asked one of the new girls. "Can he really *Bam it* like that? Here Bama! Bam this!" Then she shook her butt in front of him as she screamed, "Bam! Bam! Bam!" They all laughed.

"He's called Bama because he's from Alabama," smiled Jennifer.

"Oh! I get it now," said the girl. "But I still want to know if you can bam it, Bama?" She started flirting and rubbing on herself to entice him as the girls looked on. Bama was very shy and had never been laid in his life. So he was fidgety and trying to ignore her.

"Leave him alone!" smiled Jennifer as she pleasantly pushed her young friend away.

"Ooooh!" screamed the girls. "We know whose man that is now!"

"No wonder he always keep her around when we're finished," joked another. "Cause he's gonna *bam* that ass after we leave!" Then they all started singing;

"Go Bama! Go Bama! Go Bama! Go Bama!" Then over at the table, one of the girls spoke more seriously once the girls were quieted.

"Yeah, I hear that Bama ain't the only one that wants to tap that ass," she said. "Helen wants it, too, but the word is that you're running. What'cha scared of, Sweet? Can't you handle your own?" The girls just listened.

"Time to go!" shouted Bama. "Everybody out! Jennifer stay a minute."

Jennifer knew that it was just a matter of time and she would have to face Helen. The place was small, and a gal could only run so far.

"Jennifer, we have two going home tomorrow, and three transferring out tonight," explained Bama. "Plus, we have four arrivals tomorrow."

"Wait-a-minute Bama!" she screamed. "I don't process arrivals and transfers and all that. I just get their bed stuff and their clothes ready. I don't want to stay here tonight, Bama! Please let me go."

"Ok, but I need you to help me tomorrow when the arrivals get here, so make plans to stay." Jennifer sped off and caught up with the other girls. She didn't want to walk alone because Helen had eyes everywhere. That day, she made it back safely to her cell and on through the night.

The next day was an easy day because many of the officers, including Bama, had to go away for a class. Another officer substituted for Bama during the arrivals processing so Jennifer skipped out on it. She went back to the dorm and chilled for the rest of the evening. Later she decided she would go into the TV room to watch a movie.

"Hey Jennifer," came a whisper over her shoulder. "Helen is rounding up her girls. I think she saw you come in here." Then Jennifer noticed that everyone was slowly walking out one by one and the movie was just starting. So she quickly left and headed to her cell.

"It's just a matter of time, Sweet," said Helen as she walked by. "Just a matter of time." Jennifer knew that the only reason they hadn't come up in her cell is because Cal was so big, and they really didn't know what she would do. Cal was a sweetie, but she was strong as an ox and they knew it. Jennifer was a short timer now and only had a few months left to serve on her sentence. So to avoid trouble, she stayed in her cell whenever she wasn't at detail.

"Jennifer Sweet ... Visitation!" yelled the officer. It was Sunday and Jennifer was anxiously awaiting to see her sisters and Audrey, her daughter. This would be their third and final visit before Jennifer would be released in a few months.

"Mommy! Mommy!" screamed Audrey as Jennifer came through the vistiing room doors. Donna jumped to her feet and hugged her with Cherlene and Makeda trailing close.

"Oh Jenny look at you!" stated Donna. "Girl you've got muscles and... look at your skin! You are so pretty! Isn't she, Cheryl?"

"I have to say, Jenny, that you're looking pretty good," added Cherlene.

"I guess so, because Audrey hasn't stopped staring at me since I walked through the door," said Jennifer.

For the next few hours, the girls and kids ate, laughed, and shared, about their life experiences since Jennifer had been away. Then as their visit neared an end, Jennifer announced new enlightenment.

"I have something to tell you guys and I hope it doesn't change who we are as a family."

"What! Jenny why would you even think that?" asked Cherlene. "No matter what you say to us, we will always be sisters because that's who we are."

"Yeah, I agree with Cheryl," said Donna. "We are family, forever... no matter what."

"Ok, here goes. Before I went to court, I got a call from this bank telling me that my dad had left me a couple of hundred bucks and a safe deposit box. When I went to check it out, I found something in the safe deposit box that shocked me. Inside, was a small bag of diamonds, probably worth thousands, a funny looking amulet key or something, and an envelope with two identical necklaces. All of the stuff is well and good but it's what was written on the envelope that reeally got me." The girls were focused on Jennifer's every word.

"What did it say?" asked Donna.

"It read,

'For my two daughters, Sarah Griffin-8 years old, and Jennifer Sweet-6 years old, whom I love with all my soul.'"

"Oh my gosh, Jenny!" shouted Donna. "So you have a blood sister out there somewhere!"

"Do you know anything about her?" asked Cherlene.

"No, I don't know anything because I didn't have time to look for her. Maybe she's gone or married, or even dead; I don't know. But I do want to know as much as I can about her if you will help me."

"I'd love to help you find her, Jenny," said Donna.

"Jenny, you only have a couple of months and you'll be free. Why don't we just wait and look for her together?" suggested Cherlene.

"That will be fine, because I know you're busy now. But that's only half the story." The girls locked their attention on Jennifer again.

"I've always thought my mom just left me when she got out of prison. I found out a little while ago that she never left me. She is still in prison after all of these years."

"What?" asked Cherlene. "Is she here?"

"No, she's not here, but she is somewhere, and I want to find her."

"Wow!" said Donna. "A new sister and a mom!"

"How do you feel about all of this, Jenny?" asked Cherlene.

"Well, I'm kinda anxious and excited, but due to circumstances, I am also a little confused and wondering."

"I'm so happy for you, Jennifer," smiled Cherlene.

"Visitation is over!" came the announcement. "All inmates to the rear, please!"

"I love you, Jenny," said Donna and Cherlene as they hugged her and left.

Jennifer felt really good as she headed back to her dorm. Her mind was completely out of prison as she thought about her daughter and her sisters. She couldn't wait to be released within the coming months as she hummed her way to the dorm. Little did she know that she was about to get the surprise of her life!

Chapter 68

Donna was home at her computer, running a search for Sarah Griffin, Jennifer's older sister.

"My Lord!" shouted Donna. "There must be hundreds of Sarah Griffin's in the United States! Look at all these names! Ok, let's narrow it down to Georgia and see what happens. Aha! That's better! Only 35! Now let's narrow it down to Atlanta Metro area. Yes! Only 14! Time to make some calls! I wonder how it feels to know you have a sister out there somewhere. Jenny must be really excited!"

****

"Hello?" answered Tenisha.

"You better get over here and talk to your father before I kill him!" phoned Davina.

"Mom, I'm not gonna to be a referee whenever you and Daddy fight! Besides, if you'd quit drinking so much, you wouldn't argue all the time. Now go deal with it, Mom!" Tenisha hung up and went to fix Nela some food. Within minutes, the phone rang again. Tenisha checked the caller ID then answered.

"Mom! It's Sunday morning for God's sake! Go to church or something!" As Tenisha was about to slam the phone down, she heard her dad.

"Honey! Honey! It's me, your father!"

"Dad, what is she doing now?"

"Honey, I've never seen her this bad, so you'd better get over here."

"Ok Dad. Just let me speak to Mom." Kris handed Davina the phone.

"You're taking his side and you don't know the half of it," cried Davina. Davina was drunk and in tears but still arguing. "You don't know what he has done to me!" she cried continually. Tenisha calmed before she spoke.

"Mom, give me two hours, ok. I promise I'll be there and we'll talk. Don't do anything foolish, ok? Just leave Dad alone and I will be there as soon as I can."

"Well you better hurry because he ain't got long before I call the cops!"

"Don't call the cops, Mom. I'm on my way, Ok? Bye Mom." Tenisha was tired. The drama between her parents was ruining her life and she didn't know what to do about it. Neither her dad nor her mom would give her details about why they fight so much. But today, Tenisha knew it had come to a head and somebody had to talk.

Two hours later, Tenisha and Nela entered the front room of her parents' home. Davina was laid out drunk and asleep on the couch.

Tenisha just looked at her and left her there. She went into the backyard where her dad was working. Little Nela went to the refrigerator to find a snack.

"Dad, what really happened to her? Why is she like this?"

"You know your mom. She is just drunk that's a...."

"Dad, you always say that and she always accuse you of hurting her. Neither of you ever tell me what's going on, but you always call me when you fight. So Dad, please tell me what I need to know."

"It's just life, 'T,' you know; couples go through things. But if they hang in there long enough, things will work themselves out."

"Tenisha!" yelled Davina. "Is that you out there?" Tenisha walked into the room where her mom was sitting on the couch.

"Hi, Sweetheart. I didn't hear you come in. I've been waiting for you."

"Why, Mom? What can I do for you other than put you to bed? Dad can do that."

"No!" yelled Davina. "He can't touch me ever again!"

"Why not, Mom? What has he done so bad?"

"Ask him; he knows." Kris came into the room then headed upstairs.

"No! No! Kristopher Cuyler! Don't you go up those stairs! Your daughter is asking you a question and she deserves an answer!"

"Davina, why don't you just go to bed and sleep off the booze. You'll be..."

"Don't patronize me, Kris!" Davina jumped from the couch and stood strong toward him. "Yes, I may be drunk, but I'm not too drunk to recognize when you are trying to make me look bad in front of our child! You come down here this minute and talk to her! Or so help me God, if I don't divorce your ass and take everything you've got!"

"Divorce?" screamed Tenisha! "Dad!"

"Keisha, calm down!" yelled Kris.

"Aha!" yelled Davina angrily. "Did you hear that? He called me by that bitch's name!"

Davina reached on the table, got her glass, and threw it at Kris.

"Mom, stop: Nela is watching!" yelled Tenisha. Nela was eating a carrot and playing alone. Davina sat on the couch and folded her arms like a pouting angry teenager, while she waited to see how Kris would respond. "Dad, you called her Keisha. Did you know you did that?" Kris was surprised. The name Keisha had slipped out in the heat of the moment, and he knew he had to explain now. "Is this about Keisha Milledge that Mom told me about?" Tenisha lifted the high school year book and turned to the page where the name had been ripped away. Then she held it for them to see.

"Mom, I thought you said Dad wasn't seeing her?" Davina looked at Kris. He was sitting in the chair with his head down.

"You better start talking, Kris, or I will," demanded Davina. Tenisha was patiently listening as she watched her dad. He was struggling with whatever it was that her mom was forcing him to say. Little Nela came and got the yearbook while nibbling her carrot stick.

"Tenisha, honey," started Kris slowly. "I love you with all my heart. I've dreaded this day for so long, but I don't see how any of us can go on without a clearer understanding of why we are even here." Davina was boiling on the inside. She stood and paced while Kris attempted to explain. "During my college years..." Davina cut in yelling,

"He fucked that bitch!" Suddenly, she burst with tears and ran upstairs. Tenisha watched her dad slump into a very sorrowful cry then she ran upstairs behind her mother while Nela watched.

"Mom," said Tenisha. "I'm so sorry." Tenisha sat on the bed beside her mom and wrapped her arms around her.

"I'm ok, baby. I'm sorry I yelled out like that."

"It's ok, Mom. You've been hurt, and I guess Dad never fixed it with you."

"Oh, you don't know the half of it!"

"So where is Keisha now? Is Dad still seeing her?"

"He better not be!" laughed Davina. "Keisha went to prison almost 25 years ago—got caught up in some kind of scandal with drug dealers and bad businessmen."

"So why are you worried about her now? Has she come back in Dad's life?"

"Not as far as I know," said Davina. "Even if she did come back, Kris wouldn't get involved with her because it may tarnish his image."

"Mom, I still don't understand why you are so upset about it now. Has something new happened since 25 years ago?" Davina stood up.

"Come on, let's go back downstairs and let your father finish his story. I promise I won't butt in or blurt anything out." They went back downstairs. Kris was still sitting in the chair looking sorrowful.

"Dad, I need you to finish telling me what happened when you were in college."

"Well, your mother has told you most of it." Davina stood and started to yell but Tenisha grabbed her.

"Dad, I want to hear it from you. Mom has promised to let you talk but you've got to talk, Dad." Davina calmly sat, tilted her head to the floor, and waited.

"As I said, during my college years, I managed to get a little wild and made some bad choices. Your mother and I had planned to get married right after college but everything got screwed up, thanks to me."

"Mom told me that she got pregnant with me during her sophomore year, but where does Keisha come in?" asked Tenisha. Davina took over.

"Kris knew I loved him and was faithful to him. He even assured me that he loved me back, and we would be married. At that same time, Keisha, his high school crush, had decided she would marry Antwaun Banks, whom everybody just knew would become some big white house politician one day.

Keisha didn't love him, but she decided to marry him for the ride... the name... because she was ambitious and wanted to get to the top in any way that she could. But your father didn't know that she didn't love Antwaun and wouldn't be faithful to him, so he decided he'd better get her and run off to some motel with her, before Antwaun got all the goods.

Since Keisha and I were no longer friends, she wanted to make sure I knew she had humbled my future husband before I did; I was hurt. Kris denied it of course, but every time they were around each other, it was written all over them. I noticed it, and Antwaun did, too." Davina started to cry again, so she ran upstairs and laid down.

"What happened after that, Dad?"

"Antwaun had been chasing after your mother for years, just like I had been after Keisha. But she remained faithful to me as she promised, until she was certain that Keisha and I had slept together." Davina came back and listened while she sat on the stairs with Nela.

"Then what? Did Mom start dating other guys?"

"No she didn't. She still remained faithful to me and herself. But she was so hurt by Keisha and I, that she wanted us to feel her pain.

So one night when Keisha and I were together, returning from the library, we saw your mom watching us from her room window. Next, I saw Antwaun walk up to her, remove her clothes, then he made love to her while she watched us, watching them." Kris and Davina both started to cry.

"Before I slept with Keisha, I was a virgin and so was your mother. So she thought it was only fair that since I gave my virginity to the woman chasing me, that she give hers to the man chasing her." Both Kris and Davina were crying aloud now.

"He made me do what I did, and I am so ashamed," cried Davina.

"Davina," begged Kris. "I saw the look on your face that night he made love to you, and I knew I was the one hurting you and I'm so sorry. Please forgive me, Davina. I never meant to hurt you like that. Please, please forgive me." Tenisha started to cry with them, too.

"Kris, I forgave you right after it happened. But I needed to know that you really loved me. You spent more time with her than you ever did with me—even till the day Antwaun took her away. From that day until now, I've been wondering if you really love me."

"Oh my God, Mom!" cried Tenisha. "You've been carrying that pain with you for over 25 years!"

"Davina, I am so sorry," said Kris. "And yes baby, I love you. I've always loved you more than life." Kris went to Davina and embraced her as they all cried... together.

****

"Ok! That's it!" sounded Donna. "I've made the last call of all the Sarahs in Atlanta, and most of them are elderly, or married to a Griffin. Sarah could be anywhere in the whole world! Well Jenny, I've tried! It's on you now!" Donna just sat at her computer, wondering what she could do next.

****

The next day after work, Tenisha couldn't wait to get to her mom and talk. She had talked briefly with her mom this morning while going to work and things seemed fine. But because of the intensity of the situation between her parents on the previous day, she wanted to see her mom face to face and talk. So after work, she picked up Nela from school and went directly to her Mom's where she was scheduled to meet with a gymnast to discuss Nela's future.

"Mom!" yelled Tenisha. "Where are you?"

"I'm here, honey! I'm coming!" Tenisha opened the door and walked in but Davina was cleaning off the patio after having watered her plants. Then she came running in, dressed like an around the house worker being all happy, jovial, and sparkling.

"Hello, my favorite women in the world!" she said excitedly. She hugged and kissed Nela, and did the same to Tenisha. "Aren't you off a little early today?"

"Yes, I wanted to beat the heavy traffic. Mom, you seem happy today," smiled Tenisha. "And very... sober. You look really good, Mom."

"I feel really good, daughter! So how was your day?"

"Well to be honest, I've been thinking about you and Daddy all day."

"I am fine, as you can see, and I'm sure your father is, too. He called about an hour ago and said he would be here immediately after work today."

"He did?" shouted Tenisha. "It's been a long time since Dad came straight home after work. He normally have more work to do."

"Well, its been a long time since I've given your father a reason to come directly home after work." Davina started smiling and shaking her hip.

"Mom, you didn't!" shouted Tenisha. She smiled hard with her hand to her mouth.

"Oh yes we did, twice; last night after you left and this morning after breakfast. I was his dessert. He called at lunch time today and asked about Viagra. I told him that he didn't need it but he said he wanted me to ride the pony like...."

"Mom!" shouted Tenisha. "I'm happy for you and Dad, but please: Spare me the details."

"Grandma," said Nela. "I want to ride the pony."

"Baby," smiled Davina. "When the time is right, I'm sure you will ride all the ponies you want to."

"Mom!"

"Well its true, Tenisha! Oh stop being a saint! I'm sure you've ridden a good pony or two, yourself. You're not the only one with a good saddle, you know."

"Mom! Whatever! Just wait a while before you start talking like that around Nela!"

"Mommy, Mommy! I want to ride the pony!"

"Nela, Sweetie, there is no pony right now. I will try to take you to the circus so you can ride soon, ok? Now look in Grandma's refrigerator. I'm sure she has some good carrots for you to eat, while we wait to meet your new teacher." Nela ran to the refrigerator.

"I didn't know she loved carrots like that," said Davina. "She hardly ate them when I cooked them."

"That's because she likes them raw, Mom. It's her favorite food." Davina looked surprised as she looked at Nela and Tenisha and wondered.

"Mom, yesterday you didn't tell me much about this Antwaun fellow. I didn't want to ask in front of Dad because I didn't want to make things worse."

"There's nothing to tell. He was chasing me but I was in love with your dad."

"If you were so in love with Dad, then why did you sleep with Antwaun even that once?"

"Have you ever been hurt, Tenisha?"

"Rubik left me barefoot and pregnant for another woman, remember? Mom, you of all people know what I went through."

"Times were different when I was in college, Tenisha. Self respect meant a lot to us back then, and your father and Keisha had taken mine. The whole campus knew that he and Keisha were sleeping together and I wasn't doing anything about it. I felt that I was losing him to her so I did the only thing I knew to save face with myself."

"I'm sorry, Mom. It must have been really hard on you. I'm sorry Daddy put you through that."

"What's done is done. Besides, it's all over now and I feel a lot better that you're here to help me and your father through it." Suddenly, Nela came running and jumped into Davina's arm. Davina playfully caught her but couldn't help but notice the carrot in Nela's hand and how she kept eating on it. Tenisha was turning the pages of the high school year book.

"Mom, how come there is no picture of Antwaun in your yearbook?"

"That's because he went to Sandy Springs High and we went to Dunwoody High. Keisha met him at a high school football game one night and that's how we got to know him."

"Mommy, there's a car coming into the yard!" sounded Nela.

"It's probably just your new teacher. Come on, let's go meet her."

Like her Dad, Nela is very athletic and loves sports and gymnastics. Therefore, Tenisha decided to talk to a gymnast about Nela's future, while hoping that her daughter would become an Olympic star someday.

"Yes, this is very possible," responded Ms. Bayer, the gymnast. "She is still very young and now is the right time for her to enter our school. Until she is nine years old, she can continue to live with you, as we train her. But after that, she must come to live with us until her training is completed."

As Ms. Bayer continued to explain the program, Davina was intrigued by the way Nela and Tenisha kept nibbling on the carrot sticks.

"Ms. Bayer, you have been very informative and helpful. I will call you soon with my decision." assured Tenisha as she escorted the woman out. Upon her return, Davina asked,

"Tenisha, honey, what is Nela's blood type?"

"Hers is Ab negative; the same as mine-which is the rarest in the US. Why do you ask?"

"It's just interesting to see a child her age that love vegetables like that so it makes me curious, that's all. Do you know her father's blood type?"

"I think he is an O positive or something, but who cares. Me and my baby are 'blood' and that's all that matters. Mom, I've gotta go. It's almost rush hour and I don't want to get caught in it even at a short distance. Tell Dad I love him and I'll call him later."

"You better wait until tomorrow! I think it's going to be a Viagra nighter!"

"Mom, that's disgusting! Bye!" After Tenisha drove off, Davina ran to her computer, and engaged site after site on Google about blood types and genetic engineering. She was astounded by what she found. An hour later Kris came home being all jovial and kissed her.

"And how is my Queen, today?" smiled Kris. "After he kissed her, he headed to the shower while happily whistling along the way. Davina fixed dinner and set it on the table while Kris yelled from the shower, telling her about his day. He continued to happily talk all through dinner.

"Davina, you haven't said much since I came in. Is everything ok?"

FROM GENERATION TO GENERATION

FROM GENERATION TO GENERATION *"The Curse Must Be Broken!"*

"Yes, everything is fine," she smiled. But Kris could tell that something was up.

"Are you sure honey? You mean the world to me, and I will do anything to make you happy; just name it."

"Kris, would you mind if we could... do the pony thing another day? I'm more exhausted than I anticipated."

"Oh sure, baby, I don't mind at all. Another time is fine!"

"Thank you, Kris. I'm gonna shower and go to bed. I'll see you in the morning." Davina left the table; Kris was confused.

William C. Lewis.   Page 261

Chapter 69

Jennifer was happy as she left the visiting room that Sunday. Little did she know that Helen had laid an ambush for her as she came back to the dorm. Before Helen and her girls could strike, there came another surprise.

"Bama!" yelled Jennifer. "What are you doing here today? You don't work on the weekends, so what's up?"

"I have some work I need to do before tomorrow and I need your help," he said. "So let's go." At first Jennifer wanted to rebel, but she knew that Bama had been really good to her. Plus, she really didn't have anything else to do anyway.

"Ok, Officer Bama Nettles, Sir!" she joked. "You win, Sir! Where to, Sir?" As they walked, Jennifer noticed they were walking the long way to the laundry, when they could have been there a few minutes ago.

"Bama, what's going on? We never go this way?"

"I thought I'd change it today, so I would have more time to talk to you. By the way, Eboni left this for you." He handed her a note with a number on it. "A couple of days ago I told you to work with intake on processing. But when you saw that I wasn't here, you didn't help the officer."

"Bama, please don't start that! I always do whatever you tell me as long as its my job! Why would you have me do somebody else's work that I know nothing about?"

"I was trying to help you, Jennifer, because I know your situation. But I couldn't just come out and tell you what was going on because I would have gotten in trouble."

"What are you talking about, Bama?"

"This is not only a permanent camp but it's a diagnostic center and court is also held here. Sometimes, the parole board meets inmates here as well. The other night when I told you to stay, the parole board had planned to meet with a very special inmate, whom you would have gotten to meet face to face had you stayed and helped. That inmate's name is Margit Sweet, your mother." Jennifer was shocked.

"Bama, why didn't you just tell me? Did she leave already?"

"I couldn't tell you because that would have been a security breach. Margit was supposed to ship back out after her hearing but they made her a sleeper until tomorrow. She's still in isolation for now." Bama and Jennifer were only seconds away from the isolation area.

"Bama, you have to take me there; please Bama." After she spoke, she saw laundry buggies around the corner with sheets, blankets, towels, and other laundry items needed for inmates.

"Inmate Sweet, I need you to help me issue these supplies to the inmates in this isolation area. Do you understand?"

Jennifer smiled. She knew that everything Bama was doing was for her. She could have seen her mom two days ago, had she followed Bama's instructions. Now, he had come to work on his day off, stocked buggies, and moved them to isolation, just so that she could see her mother. At that moment, she didn't know whether to kiss him, or just thank him.

"Bama, thank you so much. I don't know what else to say."

"Maybe you need to say it to your mom."

"Does she know I'm coming? Does she know I'm even here?"

"She's a little doped but she knows."

"Why is she doped? What did they do to her?"

"Jennifer, you don't have much time. Go talk to your mother." Jennifer was a little nervous as she approached her mother's cell. What would she say? She hadn't seen her mother in 20 years. She was only 7 years old when her mom left. Now, Jennifer was almost 28 and wondered how her mom looked.

"Hi, Mom," she spoke as she peeped through the glass on the steel door. Margit smiled and came near the door.

"Hello, little girl, how are you?"

"Do you know who I am?" asked Jennifer.

"They tell me that you're my daughter, but my Jennifer is 7 years old." Jennifer burst into tears. Then she heard the whisper, *"The Curse Must Be Broken!"* Jennifer paused.

"I've missed you so much, Mommy," cried Jennifer. Suddenly, Margit came alive as if she was overpowering the medication that had her relaxed.

"Jennifer! Is that you?" she yelled. "Ah, Jennifer! You are so beautiful; please come closer."

"I'm right here, Mom! I'm right here!"

"I went to a parole hearing and they won't let me come home, Jennifer. They say I'm a threat to society." Margit started crying. "I think I'm going to die here, Jennifer." Suddenly, the medication took over. "I have to rest now." Margit left the door and went to her bunk. Jennifer just watched her through tears.

"She sounded so much different when she came a few days ago. When the parole board set her off for another 7 years, she snapped and threatened to kill them all. So they had her drugged until she transfers out," said Bama.

"Where is she going?"

"I won't know until tomorrow. We have to go now, Jennifer." Bama looked sad as they pushed the buggies back to laundry.

"Thank you, Bama," said Jennifer after they went inside the laundry facility.

"I know I'm not supposed to say this but you're a really good friend and I hope I can pay you back someday." Then she walked near and kissed his cheek. Bama became nervous as he looked around and acted like a scared child. Jennifer laughed as she walked away. When she got to the door of the laundry facility, she paused and looked back at Bama. Then she smiled and said, "Aw what the hell!" She slammed the door shut, pushed Bama to the floor, and made love to him. Bama was never the same again.

Jennifer laughed as she hurried back to her cell. Until now, Bama was a virgin and Jennifer enjoyed the feeling she had while being with him. It made her forget about her mom, Helen, and prison, while feeling like a school girl again. Once she reached her cell, she saw Cal preparing to go to the shower.

"That's a big girl," said another to a friend. "Have you seen the towel she wraps in when she goes to the shower? It's the same size as her blanket and it still don't cover all of her ass."

"Jennifer, I'm going to the shower now," said Cal. She took her medication, then wrapped in the towel, with parts of her butt still showing. All the girls laughed. Jennifer was in the cell with her back turned as Cal walked away.

Suddenly, Helen and her crew rushed Jennifer and attempted to beat her and stick her with a shank. But Jennifer was too fast and caused the girl to miss.

Cal, who was only a step or two away, saw them and came back to help. She used her body to smash one girl to the iron rail, then the one with the shank, dropped it and ran. That left Helen and Jennifer in the cell alone to fight.

As Cal blocked the door, Helen and Jennifer slung each other from wall to wall while fighting like gladiators. They were both about the same size but Jennifer was faster and hitting harder.

Soon, Helen started wearing down but Jennifer kept going strong. This was the moment she had been waiting for. Helen was finally beaten and laid out on the floor.

Now that the moment had arrived, Jennifer planned to give Helen a taste of her own medicine but she couldn't go through with it.

When Cal saw Helen stretched out on the floor, she backed into the cell, stood over her, removed the towel, and allowed her 400 pounds to come crashing down on Helen's face---butt first!

"Ooooohh!" shouted the girls when they saw Helen's face locked between Cal's butt cheeks. "That's nasty!" As Helen struggled to get up, Cal burst into laughter over and over again. Everyone laughed with her.

"Cal!" yelled Jennifer. "Why are you laughing?"

"Ha! Ha! Ha!" laughed Cal. "Every time she struggles, she blows between my cheeks and it tickles, Ha! Ha! Ha!"

Minutes later, security took Cal, Jennifer, and Helen, with her crew to isolation. A few days later, Jennifer was taken to disciplinary court where she would get hole time.

"Inmate Sweet," sentenced the judge. "You will be given 30 days isolation with 30 days store restriction, 30 days phone restriction, and 30 days of no visitation. However, for the welfare of the institution, and for your safety, you will remain in isolation after your restrictions are served, for the duration of your original sentence."

Chapter 70

"Where are you going so early?" asked Kris.

"I have a lot of errands to run, today, and I want to get an early start. But I should be back before you get home," responded Davina.

"It's no problem, honey. I'm just glad to see you venturing out. Have fun, and I'll see you tonight." Then Kris kissed her and headed to work. Davina quickly rushed to her car and left.

****

"Why good morning, Tenisha!" smiled Donna as she walked from Mr. Golden's office. "How are you today, Ms. Compassionist?" Tenisha knew that she was up to something.

"I'm fine, Donna, thank you, and you?"

"Oh, I'm just as good as a hot apple pie, honey!" Donna went to her desk as usual.

"Ms. Cuyler!" called Mr. Golden. "Red Cross is here!"

"Uh, Red Cross, Sir?"

"Yeah, Red Cross! Aren't you covering the story on them? Well, they're in the parking lot and they want us to be the first blood donors. I figure since you are covering the story, you can also donate blood on behalf of AJC. Now get out there; they're waiting!" Tenisha angrily stared at Donna as she prepared to leave.

"That's why you spoke so friendly to me," thought Tenisha. *"You set me up, again."*

"That's your kind of story, Ms. Cuyler," laughed Donna. "We're so proud of you."

"I'll go with you, Tenisha," said Bobby. A while back, Tenisha had given Bobby a chance to compete against the exuberant Tyler Johnson, when she printed the story about Jennifer. He saw what Donna had done and thought this would be a good time to help Tenisha out.

"Tenisha, have you read the local Dunwoody paper, recently?"

"No Bobby, I haven't. Why? What's interesting about it?"

"About a week ago, I read a very interesting article about an ex-news anchorwoman who was released from prison. You may want to check it out." Bobby walked right past the Red Cross Mobile and headed to the fruit stand.

"Where are you going, Bobby? Aren't you gonna give blood?" Bobby threw up his hands and kept going.

"Get the Dunwoody paper, Tenisha!" he yelled. "It was dated a week ago today!" Tenisha felt abandoned and betrayed again.

****

"Thank you for seeing me on such a short notice, Marcus. I really need this information, or I wouldn't have driven this far today."

"Being a Warden has its perks. Besides, I never could say 'no' to you, Davina. How's Kris these days?"

"Still at the bank being Kris. He's been good to me, Marcus."

"That's good to hear, Davina. Ok, here comes the physician's assistant now with the info you need. Davina checked the file then burst into tears.

"Davina, what's wrong? Are you ok?"

"I'll be fine, Marcus. I have to go now. Thank you for the info."

****

After Tenisha finished her story with Red Cross, she went to her desk and accessed the Dunwoody paper online.

"What are you looking for, Tenisha?" she wondered. *"This better be good, Bobby, or I'm gonna... wait a minute!"* Tenisha began to read:

"Ex-Television news and anchorwoman, Keisha Banks, was released today after serving a 20 year prison sentence. Twenty years ago, Keisha and her husband, Antwaun Banks, were arrested and indicted after GBI agents went undercover to catch public and state officials, involved with drug dealers, and other businessmen for personal profit or gain. Today, Keisha is a free woman. Her husband still remains behind bars here in Georgia."

"Oh my God! Does Bobby know about my parents and Keisha?" Tenisha panicked! "How could he! He's not as old as I am!"

"Hello, Mr. Golden, Sir! This is Ms. Cuyler. I have a family matter that just came up, so I'm gonna take off for the day," she phoned.

"Did you get that Red Cross story?" he asked.

"I got it, Sir. It will be printed tomorrow."

"Good, Ms. Cuyler. I knew we could depend on you. Have a good day?" Tenisha hung up then dialed again but she only heard the answering machine.

"Hello, Mom? Pick up the phone; I know you're there. I'm coming over right now, because we need to talk!"

****

Davina slowly entered her home in just enough time to hear Tenisha say,

"I know you're there. I'm coming over right now!"

Davina went to the kitchen, got a bottle of gin, and begin to drink... again. Thirty minutes later, Tenisha arrived at her parents home.

"Mom!" yelled Tenisha. Tenisha opened the door and went upstairs. She found Davina laying on her bed, soaked in pee and drunk asleep. She picked up her phone, again, and dialed.

"Dad? You better come home right away. Something is wrong with Mom."

"I'm on my way Honey; stay right there!"

****

Jennifer had completed her hole time, but she was still in isolation. She had less than a week to serve on her sentence and she would be free again. For 18 months, she'd missed out on life and entered a world she hoped to never see again. Suddenly, the head nurse and the warden came to her cell.

"Jennifer," started the nurse. "I got your tests back today, honey, and you're 2 months pregnant."

"Who is he, Sweet?" asked the Warden. Jennifer was so shocked by the news, that she didn't even hear the Warden. "I have the power to keep you here and force you to do a DNA test, Inmate. Now who is the daddy of that baby?"

"Ma'am, this is my baby. Please just let me go home and take care of it. I promise that you won't hear from me again."

"You can take care of your baby all you want. But I still want the man who's behind this pregnancy."

Jennifer knew she couldn't tell, even if they kept her longer. She was the one that forced Bama to have sex with her so she didn't want to ruin his life. A few days later, Jennifer's family awaited her at the front gate, where she was escorted and released.

****

"What's wrong with her, Doc?" asked Kris.

"As far as I can tell, she's just drunk."

"So why won't she talk? She just keeps bursting into tears every time I speak to her," said Tenisha.

"Physically, your mother is fine. But I think something happened that caused her mind to lock up. I would get your mom to see another doctor, if you know what I mean." Suddenly, Davina spoke out.

"I'm not crazy, Tenisha! Please don't let them put me away!" she begged through tears.

"No one is putting you away, honey; I promise," added Kris. When he tried to touch her hand, she pulled away and hugged Tenisha, whom was sitting on the bed next to her. Kris started pacing.

"Ok, Mom, why won't you talk to me? I have to know what's wrong before I can help you." Davina just burst into tears again.

"I think my work is done here," said the doctor.

"I'll walk you out," said Kris.

Tenisha paused. "Mom, Dad's gone now. Is there something you want to tell me?"

"Yes," said Davina. "Give me my bottle back or get out!" Tenisha handed her the bottle. Davina drank from it until she fell asleep.

Chapter 71

"Jenny! Jenny! Jenny!" screamed Donna as Jennifer walked through the release gate of the prison. Donna ran to her.

"Mommy! Mommy!" yelled Audrey as she ran behind Donna.

"Hi, Jenny," smiled Cherlene. They hugged her with smiles and joy as they loaded in the car, and headed home.

"Cherlene, thanks for leaving the clothes inside," said Jennifer. "I needed that."

"Uh excuse me!" yelled Donna. "Cheryl isn't the only one in this family who thinks of things!"

"What! You Dee? I am surprised and blessed! You even got the right size! How did you know? Thank you so much!"

"You're welcome," smiled Donna. "Just don't forget this if I ever go to prison, God forbid."

"So Dee, tell me... have you gotten laid, yet?" asked Jennifer.

"Um uh," gestured Cherlene as she nodded toward Audrey. "You may want to talk about that later; too many ears are listening, now."

"Aren't you the perfect mother and teacher!" said Jennifer.

"Yes, I am. You'll be happy to know that I'm planning to get my certification to teach high school, soon. I want to try my luck with the older kids."

"Good for you, Cheryl," responded Jennifer. "I'm proud of you."

"So Jenny, have you decided what you're going to do now?" asked Donna.

"Yeah, I'm thinking on a few things, but the jury is still out concerning them. Right now, I just wanna get some real food and spend the rest of the day with my child."

"That sounds like a good idea!" said Cherlene. After they finished eating at Applebee's, Jennifer went to her apartment where she spent the rest of the day with Audrey. The next morning, Jennifer drove Audrey to kindergarten and talked with her teacher. Then she headed to J.J.'s to check on her job.

"Ah!" yelled Jennifer as she ran and hugged Michelle. "I am so glad to see you!"

"I was hoping you'd be here," smiled Michelle. "I had a little time before I went to work so I decided to stop by. You look good, Jennifer. So how are you?"

"Michelle, your letters really helped me to be ok. I never would have made it without them. Thank you so much for being a friend." Then they embraced again. "I love you so much."

"Is that my star employee, back from the dead?" joked J.J. "Hi Jennifer, it's good to have you back."

"Hello, Jennifer, remember me?"

"Of course I remember you, Susie. How can I ever forget?"

"I wish I could forget her," said J.J.

"I heard that!" yelled Susie. "He's just kidding, Jennifer. I'm the best thing that's ever happened to this place... besides you of course."

"She really is," added J.J. "Thanks again to you. I'd marry her if I could."

"Wait-a-minute, J.J. I recall you proposing to me just before I left. So Susie has bumped me off, huh?"

"Sorry, kiddo, but she's what this place needs. I'm thinking about turning the management over to her completely." Jennifer was shocked with pleasantness.

"Are you serious? I never would have guessed it! Congratulations, Susie!"

"Thank you, Jennifer."

"I have to go," said Michelle. "Jennifer we'll talk later, ok? Bye guys."

"So, are you here to work or what?" asked J.J.

"I haven't decided, yet, J.J. The store seems to be doing fine, aren't you?"

"Yes, thanks to Susie. I have to admit that I didn't think I'd find anyone as good as you, but Susie even has a way with the customers that I just love, and so does most of them."

"Here's your coffee, Sam," said Susie. "You need to do your wife a favor and drown yourself in it!"

"See what I mean," laughed J.J. Jennifer chuckled.

"J.J., I love it! Give me two weeks and I'll let you know, ok?"

"Two more weeks won't hurt me. I look forward to your answer."

"I'll see you later, guys. Bye!" Jennifer headed downtown to find the new bank that managed her safe deposit box.

"Ms. Sweet," said the assistant manager. "Your new box number is #83."

"Thank you, Sir. Is Mr. Cuyler in today?"

"Yes, Ma'am, but he had an early luncheon. He'll be back shortly after noon."

"Thank you," said Jennifer. Then she went to her box and all the contents were still there. Plus, she had added the bag of diamonds she took from D-Lo's men 2 ½ years ago.

She took the diamonds, the amulet key, and the envelope with the necklaces, and left. She immediately went home and accessed all the major jewelers and diamond suppliers she could find in her computer. Then she spent the rest of the day calling them and learning about their business operations.

"I never knew these stores were so simple," thought Jennifer. Prison had changed her. She was not only a thief and a good one, but she was also a con and a fighter.

Taking risk had become a way of life for her as she studied the building layouts of all the stores she visited, along with the buildings security, the personnel, and the surroundings. Every where she visited, she learned her route of escape before she even formulated the plan.

She was an intelligent thinker, had a sharp eye, could clearly hear three or more conversation at the same time and converse with them, and was fast and very light on her feet. All her senses seemed to have magnified to the third power as she was beginning to smell, touch, hear, taste, and see, from a three dimensional perspective all at the same time. She didn't know why this had happen to her but she welcomed it. She thought that it was simply... a gift.

Finally, as Jennifer saw the many vendors on the street at the Five Points Station, she decided to test herself. She studied her entire surroundings, watched and waited for a certain crowd, then met them as she passed the street vendors.

When she walked through the crowd, she only wore jeans and a long sleeve black blouse. But after she walked through the crowd and passed the vendors, she had 2 men wallets, a skull cap, 3 CD's, and a sandwich, which was all being carried inside the handbag that she took from one of the vendors. Also, she had an umbrella, a bracelet, a watch, a small knife, and some lip gloss, inside the jacket she was wearing, that she took from one of the racks. Afterwards, she turned to look back at the crowd and they were moving as usual, with the vendors still doing their thing.

Jennifer got on the train and went back to her car. She was now ready to execute her plan. She had thought about everything while she was in prison, and now it was time to bring it to past.

"Hello, Cheryl," called Jennifer. "Can I stop by and see you, today?"

"Sure, Jenny! Do you mean here at school or later tonight?"

"Come on, Cheryl! You and I know that you love getting your freak on during your time off, so can we do this today?"

"You didn't have to be so blunt about it, Jennifer. But I do have some plans for tonight. My last class is at 2 o'clock today. Then for an hour, I have homeroom. That'll be a good time for us to talk."

"Good, I'll see you then," said Jennifer. At 2 o'clock, Jennifer walked up to Cherlene's classroom door. Cherlene came out and they went to the teacher's lounge.

"Cheryl, girl, this is definitely you. You seem to fit into this environment so well."

"Thanks, Jenny; I love this work. As it gets easier, I want more of the challenge. That's why I'm trying to move to the high school classes. I have to go back to school, but I'm ok with that? I think I'm built for this. What about you, Jenny?"

"I'm still trying to find myself on that one."

"I hope you don't wait too late, Jenny. We're getting old," smiled Cherlene.

"I know, I know, so don't remind me."

"So, what's on your mind, Jennifer?"

"I want to thank you for keeping Audrey these last 18 months that I've been away. You're like a second mom to her and I appreciate it."

"More like an old grandmother," commented Donna as she entered.

Jennifer was surprised. "Dee, What are you doing here?"

"She called right after you did, Jenny, and I told her that you were coming by. Is it a problem that she's here?"

"Cheryl, don't be ridiculous. We've been doing it like this since we were kids, right Jenny?"

"Well, I kinda needed to talk to Cheryl," frowned Jennifer. "But..."

"Oh!" Now Donna was surprised. "Excuse me! I'll le..."

"Dee, I'm kidding!" laughed Jennifer. "Now sit your butt down before I grab ya!"

"Oh!" said Donna, again. "You got me then, Jenny. I had all kinds of thoughts circling in my head and I didn't know which one to grab. So what's up, guys?"

"Both of you guys have been the best and I really shouldn't ask you for anything more. But Cheryl, I'm hoping that you could keep Audrey for 2 more weeks until I get on my feet." Cherlene looked puzzled.

"Jenny, keeping Audrey will never be a problem, but I'm more concerned about you. What's going on, Jenny?"

"All I need is a couple of weeks and ..."

"That's bull, Jennifer!" shouted Cherlene. "When are you gonna talk to us about what's going on with you? We deserve to know."

"Cheryl, It's her business so just let it g..."

"Shut up, Dee! Well, Jenny, are you gonna talk or what?" Donna got nervous and quiet because it had been a while since she'd seen

Cherlene in a rage like this. For years, Cherlene had been their strength and they respected her as such. But, something was about to change.

"Cheryl, please don't push me. Like Dee said, it's my business, so are you gonna keep Audrey or not?" Donna was even more afraid after Jennifer spoke.

Jennifer was the smartest, but she was always afraid to stand up to Cherlene, especially when Cherlene was right. Today, they stood like two lioness about to rip at each other. But Cherlene was about to show why she was the glue that held them together.

"So it's your business, huh? Was it just your business when you got locked up in an Atlanta jail, Jenny? You called me at 4:30 in the morning and forced me to get Keda up and out. Was it just your business when you left here for 18 months while I cared for your child and Dee kept your apartment?"

Cherlene was angry, but Jennifer was angrier that Cherlene had thrown these things back in her face.

"That's right, Jennifer, I said it," she continued. "I said it because you need to know that my concern for you didn't stop there. I took the time to learn about prison life weeks before you got there, so I could know what you were up against. After you were there, I called there every single day for a month, just to make sure you were safe. You think I don't know that you went to the hole, Jennifer--- twice for 30 days? After you went to the hole the first time, I made sure you had some protection when you came out. That big girl, Cal or Carolyn that was in your cell, was not there by coincidence. I did that for you! I know you think you're some kind of tough girl or something, now that you've beat down some prison bully. That's why you're standing there being all swole up, like you're tough," fussed Cherlene.

Jennifer started to disarm and clam up. Donna was frozen.

"I guess you want to beat me up because I'm telling you the truth," she continued. "Ok, Jennifer, here I am; go ahead—take your best shot and see if I don't stomp your ass!"

"No, Cheryl, I... I don't want to do that," stuttered Jennifer. She had stood up like a lion, but Cherlene had broken her down to a pussy cat.

"Cheryl, I'm so sorry; I didn't know," pleaded Jennifer. But Cherlene wasn't letting it go.

"Why do you need me to keep Audrey, Jennifer? When are you gonna talk to me and tell me what's going on?"

Jennifer got tongue tied because she hadn't expected this. Cherlene was only a few months older than Jennifer, but she had made it clear that she was the caretaker of this family.

"I... uh... I..." hesitated Jennifer. She was stuck with her words like a fly caught in a web because she couldn't tell Cherlene what she needed to hear. "I... uh... I'm... uh... I'm... pregnant." Jennifer was nervous while Donna stood in awe. *"What in the hell did I say that for?"* thought Jennifer. *"What's wrong with me?"* she continued. *"Why am I feeling so scared of her?"* Jennifer was so nervous that she couldn't even look at Cherlene so she just stared at Donna.

"You're pregnant?" questioned Cherlene angrily. "You're pregnant?" Jennifer nodded, "Yes! Two and a half months now."

"So you got pregnant while you were in prison?"

"Yes, Cheryl yes!" yelled Jennifer as she burst into tears. Cherlene just stood there shaking her head angrily. Then she calmed and said,

"I'll pick up Audrey from kindergarten tomorrow." Then she walked out. Suddenly, she came back in and stood before Donna and said,

"If you ever put me through any of this shit like she has, I will bust a cap in your ass!" Then she was gone again. Donna walked over to Jennifer and hugged her.

"Guess I had that coming, huh?" said Jennifer.

"Wow!" responded Donna. "I didn't even know Cheryl could get that pissed!"

"Me either," said Jennifer. "Prison was easier than dealing with her."

"Yeah. I'm glad she's our sister or she might have busted a cap in my ass a long time ago!"

Chapter 72

The next day, Donna and Tenisha sat at their desks thinking about all the drama that's happened over the past week. Tenisha had learned that her parents, whom she idolizes, were living with scars and wounds from their past that were bleeding into her future. As a result, her mom had become an alcoholic, her dad was stressing, and she was wondering what Bobby Moore, one of the layout men, knew about her family's problems. He had told her to read a Dunwoody paper about Keisha Banks being released from prison and she had. But she couldn't understand how Bobby tied into all this. She knew that she would have to talk to him, soon.

On the other hand, Donna had just learned that Jennifer was keeping secrets from them and Cherlene knew it. She found out that Jennifer was pregnant again, but by some guy at the prison. Finally, she recognized that Cherlene wasn't only their sister, but she was like the mother they never had. Cherlene didn't play, and she had checked Jennifer and threatened Donna.

"Why doesn't a loving mom, fresh out of prison, want to keep her own child?" thought Donna. *"Jenny's up to something... but what?"* Donna passed Tenisha's desk while on her way to the bathroom.

"Good afternoon, Glamour Bitch," spoke Donna as she passed. This was not uncommon for Tenisha to hear because Donna walked by and said it everyday for over 3 years. Sometimes she said it each time she walked by which were many times a day. But today, Tenisha had had enough as she followed Donna to the restroom. Donna was at the mirror fixing herself.

"Donna, could you please not do that? I don't like it when you call me that."

"What, Glamour Bitch? But that's who you are. Don't you want people to know you?"

"Donna you are so childish..."

"Whoa! Hold on, Glamour Bitch. You've picked the wrong girl, wrong day, and wrong time to air out your personal feelings. I've got a lot going on in my life, right now, and I really can't handle you in addition to it, so please... leave!"

"As I was saying, you are so childish to run around calling people names. Just a few weeks ago, we both received honors as professionals, who I quote *'get along well with others.'* Donna when are you gonna start living up to that standard?"

"As long as you're here, Tenisha... never!"

"See, that's childish! You're still stuck in your high school days and we've been gone from there for over 10 years!"

"And you're still a bitch!" added Donna. Tenisha became angrier.

"I know what your real problem is, Donna. Me and both your sisters have kids, which is evidence that we can get a man. But you can't get a dog to sniff that little ass of yours, huh?"

"OK, Glamour Bitch, that does it!" Suddenly, Donna grabbed Tenisha by the throat and Tenisha grabbed her the same. Then they screamed at each other while turning around and around in the middle of the floor.

"Let me go!" screamed Donna. "You're gonna put bruises on my neck!"

"You first!" yelled Tenisha. "You're gonna make me break my heels!"

The truth is that neither girl was really fighting the other because they thought they would break a nail, or a shoe heel, or maybe cause a run in their stockings. They were so much alike that neither wanted to move from the middle of the floor, in fear of falling against the sink or door and scarring their skin or damaging their outfits. They were doing more screaming and yelling, than fighting.

Neither noticed the entire AJC staff peeping through the door at them until they were near done.

"Both of you in my office, now!" screamed Mr. Golden. They went in as the staff made fun of them.

"That was pathetic!" he scolded. "If you two had fought, it may have been easier to deal with, but you just screamed at each other while pretending to be fighting. What is this really about, ladies?" Both were afraid of what the consequences might be so they played it off.

"We're fine now, Sir," said Tenisha. "We were just playing around."

"Yes, we're fine now, Sir," agreed Donna. Mr. Golden just stared then shook his head.

"After today, I don't want to see anything like this between you two, is that clear?"

"Yes sir, they answered."

"Both of you take the rest of the day off and go relax. By the end of the week, I want a story from each of you with 100 words or more, telling all the good things you like about each other, and don't lie!" said Mr. Golden. "This story could determine your future here at the AJC."

Donna and Tenisha went back to their desk to get their things. Tenisha slowed around as Donna angrily raced out of the building.

Tenisha wasn't happy about her role in what just happened and she was feeling the pressure.

Tenisha felt that now would be a good time to have a sister or a close friend to talk to about her problems, but there was no one. Even the one person she used to talk to about everything was drunk and wouldn't talk to her. As she left the building, she felt herself sliding into depression.

"Ooops! Excuse me!" said Cherlene as she bumped Tenisha at the door. Cherlene saw tears in Tenisha eyes. "Are you ok, Tenisha?" After a moment, Cherlene hugged her and walked her to the park bench nearby.

"You want to talk about it, Tenisha?" After a pause Tenisha spoke.

"It must be nice to have sisters to talk to, sometimes."

"Yes it is," smiled Cherlene. "But you know our story, Tenisha. We haven't always been sisters."

"You mean the foster care thing where you grew up? But you still had each other, and now you all are closer."

"Yes we are," added Cherlene. "But sometimes I think they want to get rid of me because I'm a bit overbearing and overprotective. You have a mom and a dad. Sometimes, I feel like I'm the only mom we've got, so I protect them."

"That is so wonderful, Cherlene. You are a great person. I wish things had been different between us in school. Did you and your sisters ever know your parents?"

"We all knew our parents. But we lost them while we were so young and never had a chance to know a lot about them. So, me and my sisters learned about each other instead. Tell me why were you in tears back there, Tenisha." Tenisha hesitated.

"I'm a little ashamed, but I think I can tell you about it. Me and your sister just had a fight." Cherlene jumped up and looked around for Donna's car.

"Don't worry; she's ok. It wasn't really a fight. Besides, you just missed her. We were both told to take off for the rest of the day and to write this story about how much we love each other by the end of the week." Cherlene was first startled when she heard that they fought. But now, she was laughing.

"I think that's a good idea," laughed Cherlene. "Maybe you two will stop fighting each other and find a way to get along."

"Cherlene, I really don't want to fight with her. I want to be her friend, just like you and I are learning to be."

"If you want to be her friend, then why did you put our sister's picture in the paper? We understand that it was your story to write. But when you put her picture with it, that exposed Jennifer to the world, along with us. Friends don't do things like that to each other."

"Yeah, that was bad, huh?"

"Yes it was. I've gotta go now," said Cherlene. "Tenisha just keep trying, ok?
I think you're gonna be alright, but I will talk to Donna. If I can help more, then just call me. I'll be glad to be a friend."

"Thank you, Cherlene. You have really help to make my day."
Then they hugged, and left. Tenisha had a couple of hours before picking

FROM GENERATION TO GENERATION *"The Curse Must Be Broken!"*

up Nela from school. So, instead of leaving she went back to her desk and logged onto her computer.

"Cherlene Tullis... moved into foster care in September 1981... Hmm? Limited info there," said Tenisha. "No way to know her parents. Let's try Jennifer Sweet. Ok, here we go... Hmm? Same thing... moved into foster care in March 1981. She was there before Cherlene was. Let's see about Donna Banks... moved into foster care in June 1981... Hmm? Jennifer went first, then Donna, then Cherlene. No prior info."
Tenisha was so impressed by Cherlene's candor, that she wanted to know more about what she and her sisters went through to be placed in foster care. But the computer only revealed their entrance into foster care, and bits and pieces about them after that.

"Hey, Tenisha," sounded Bobby. "Did you find the story in the Dunwoody paper I told you about?"

"What story was that, Bobby?" She was testing him to be sure she read the right story.

"The story about Antwaun and Keisha Banks, silly. I thought you would have jumped all over that one." She was concerned now, and sure he knew something about her dad and Keisha.

"Bobby, what is it that you know about them other than they went to prison?"

"Well, the same hour they were arrested, my dad was the officer driving the second car that picked up their daughter, Donna."

"Donna who, Bobby?"

"Donna Banks, your co-worker!" Tenisha froze with her mouth opened.

Chapter 73

Jennifer was home putting the final touches to her plan.

"I have to do this right," she thought. *"Or I will end up having my baby in prison. Plus, I can't let Audrey and my sisters down."* Then she picked up the phone and dialed. "Hello, Eboni! I have the diamonds. Are you ready?"

"Ready as I'll ever be," she answered. "I sure hope this is worth it."

"Me too, Eboni. So where should we meet?"

"Meet me in Lawrenceville, Ga, on Pike Street at the Pawn Mart. Then we will go from there!" An hour later, Eboni and Jennifer met in the parking lot at the Pawn Mart.

"Oh my stars! Jennifer, these are beautiful!" said Eboni excitedly as she saw the diamonds. "Come on, let's go inside and see what you've got."

"Eboni!" shouted a handsome dark haired gentleman in his late forties. "Long time--no see!"

"Hello, Andrew," she greeted him with a smile and a hug. "It's good to see you again, too."

"I was very happy to get your call, Eboni, and to know that you were coming by."

"It's not a social call, Andrew. Me and my friend here need your expertise. This is Jennifer." They greeted each other with a shake.

"So what can I help you with?" Jennifer handed him two diamonds, each about the size of a marble or bigger. Andrew pulled out his Lupe and checked them.

"Are you a gemologist?" asked Jennifer.

"I used to be before I went to the slammer and lost my credentials. Now, I'm better than a gemologist," he smiled. As he viewed the diamonds, Andrew's smile changed to a more serious look. "Where did you get this?"

"Is that good?" asked Eboni.

"Good, is not the word that fits this diamond. Come, my ladies, let's step into the back where the sun is." They went outside as Jennifer watched Andrew check the diamonds over and over like he was looking for something specific. She was very curious as she watched.

"So, Andrew," she questioned. "If 'good' is not the word, then what is?"

"The word is cubic zirconia or fake!"

"How can you tell?" asked Eboni.

"First of all, it was kinda hard to tell for sure. That's why I came out into the sun light. A diamond is rated by five C's—Clarity, Color, Carat (weight), Cut, and Cost.

The color spectrum of light determines the color and cost of a diamond. A good diamond is also identified by three colors—rose or pink, canary yellow, and clear or blue. The clearer or bluer the diamond, the more it's going to cost. But a fake diamond like this is full of many bright unreal colors.

Most of the time, this is a dead give-a-way. But somehow, the blueness in this diamond was so excessive that it was covering the bright colors; like someone was deliberately trying to hide them. But the sun helps to determine the true colors of a diamond.

These are fakes; sorry." Andrew handed the diamonds back to Jennifer and she placed them back in her bag. Then she opened the bag her dad left in the safe deposit box and handed Andrew a diamond from it.

"Here, check this one," she asked. Andrew did his thing with his Lupe. Then he headed outside with the ladies and checked it again.

"Jackpot!" he said. "These are real." Andrew and the ladies went inside into a little room where he had a gem scope.

"These diamonds look identical to the others to the naked eye but they are very different through the gem scope. Plus, the cut is a little different in the real ones.

"So what's a diamond like this worth?" asked Jennifer.

"This diamond's clarity is about a C1 or C2. Therefore, it is easily worth five hundred thousand

Jennifer and Eboni gasped for air. "That's five hundred grand a piece," said Andrew.

A few minutes later, Jennifer and Eboni were sitting in the car, talking.

"Are you sure you want to go through with this, Jennifer? We could end up back in prison or worse."

"We're both ex-convicts, Eboni. Do you want to work a dead-end job for the rest of your life? I have a kid already and one on the way. If for nothing else, I have to try just for them." Then she heard the whisper, *"The Curse Must Be Broken!"* but she ignored it.

Chapter 74

"Jesus!" shouted Tenisha. "Donna Banks! Antwaun Banks! Keisha Banks! Why didn't I put it all together!" For the next hour or so, Tenisha worked her computer and made phone calls until she found the information she needed to confirm what Bobby had told her. She had just learned that her dad and mom had had sex with Donna's mom and dad... what a mess!

"Hello, Dad?" phoned Tenisha. "I need to talk to you... right now!" A few minutes later, Tenisha was at a restaurant talking to her dad.

"You knew, didn't you, Dad?"

"Knew what, honey? Did your mother tell you something?"

"No, Dad! I'm talking about Donna Banks! I saw you talking to her at our promotion luncheon. You knew she was Keisha's daughter, didn't you?" Kris was caught off guard and not prepared to answer.

"Well, honey I... uh..." he stuttered.

"What else are you not telling me, Dad? Does this have to do with why Mom have shut down? Does she know?"

"I don't think so, honey. She never mentioned it. Tee, I'm sorry for not telling you but I didn't think it was important."

"Dad, Donna is my worst enemy!"

"What!" he sounded. "You seemed to get along at the luncheon! What happened?" Tenisha got really angry now.

"Dad, I want you to find out what's wrong with Mom and I want you to do it soon." Then she left to get Nela; Kris shouted behind her.

"Honey, I love your mother. What else can I do?"

"Just fix her, Dad!" she shouted. Then she was gone.

****

Jennifer and Eboni were dressed for bed as they discussed their plan to get rich.

"It would be so much easier if we could just sell them," said Jennifer.

"These jewels are hot---the ones you took and certainly the ones your dad took because they are worth millions," said Eboni. "He left ten diamonds in a safe deposit box identical to ten fake diamonds you took from a group of goons. You better believe that somehow, those diamonds are connected and somebody is looking for them. That's why your dad never sold them.

"My Dad was killed 20 years ago. Do you think someone is still looking for these diamonds?" asked Jennifer.

"If they were mine, I'd never stop searching for them, so I would say 'yes.' Jennifer you have ten of these at five hundred grand each.

That's 5 million dollars! Why would anybody stop looking for that?" After they laughed and talked a while, they laid down and went to sleep.

A few days later, Eboni, being dressed as an eloquent business woman, walked into the diamond jewelers store that Jennifer had told her about.

"Hello," she spoke. Eboni looked glamorous and rich as she wore one of the fake diamonds on a ring, another three on a bracelet, but a real one on a chain around her neck.

"Those are beautiful matching stones," said the store owner. "I couldn't help but to notice them."

"Yes, my Dad left them to me before he died," spoke Eboni. "I love my jewelry, but I can only wear five at a time, because they are so heavy."

"Ma'am, I don't mean to pry, but how many do you have?"

"My Dad left me 10, so I have 5 more just laying around the house, showcasing. I've been thinking about selling them, but they are from my dad."

"So if you decide to sell, what kind of money are we talking about?"

"Why don't you tell me, Mr." She took off her necklace and handed it to him.

"Williamson! Kenneth Williamson, Ma'am. You can call me, Kenneth, but my friends call me, Swole." Kenneth was a big muscular white guy who obviously worked out.

"The name suits you, Mr. Swole."

"No, Ma'am. Just, 'Swole,' please."

"Ok, Swole. My name is Nadiellka Bishop. My friends call me Nadie." Swole was using his Lupe to check the diamond.

"So, you own 10 of these, huh?"

"What do you think, Swole? Still interested in my stones? Just out of curiosity, what would you pay for such a stone?" She could tell that Swole was excited about whatever he saw in his Lupe.

"A few thousand for each, I guess."

"A few thousand, huh?" she smirked. "Hmm? For a 28 carat, clear Marquis diamond, with a clarity rating of a C1 or C2, that's almost flawless, Swole, I am afraid that a few thousand each... won't do."

"Ok, lady, you got me," he smiled. "I guess you know your diamonds."

"I also know a cheap hustler or a con, Mr. Swole, and right now, you fit the description of both."

"I ain't no con, lady. I make an honest living and do good business."

"So, how much for the stones, Mr. Kenneth; the truth this time."

"The stones are easily worth five to eight hundred grand a piece, but I don't have that kind of money."

"Who does?" Swole started checking her out.

"I might know somebody, but I haven't seen you around these parts before. Where did you say you were from?"

"I'm at the penthouse of the Marriott Marquis downtown, Mr. Kenneth. If your friend is interested, have him bring me five hundred thousand for each stones or I will take my business elsewhere."

Then she left. Meantime, Jennifer had broken into the store from a rear entrance and wired the place and the phone, so she could monitor the calls.

"Hello," phoned Swole. "Let me talk to Mr. Holloway."

"What do you have, Swole?" asked Holloway.

"I think I found something you've been looking for, Sir."

"What's that, Swole?" "Remember those little 'Marquis' you lost some years ago? "I think I just found them." Jennifer had monitored the call from the car while using her ear piece when Eboni got in.

"So who did he call?"

"Some dude named, Holloway," answered Jennifer. Eboni dialed the phone.

"Hello, Andrew? It's Eboni. What do you know about a Yoder Holloway?"

"No one knows where he lives because he claims residence everywhere. Most of the time, he stays at the Waverly or on his yacht out on Lake Lanier. Eb, I don't know what business you have with Holloway, but you better be careful."

"Thanks, Andrew, I owe you a lot. I promise you will hear from me soon." Eboni and Jennifer went back to her apartment where she set up equipment that would monitor Swole's Jewelry Store and phone calls.

Eboni was a communications specialist who helped two criminals in her past to set up and rob an armor truck while she monitored their route and communications to their main security office. They got away with the robbery and lived well for 3 years. They died later in a police shoot out after one of the robber's girlfriend caught him cheating on her and she went to the cops. They couldn't prove that Eboni had anything to do with the robbery but she was given 18 months to serve in prison because phone records tied her directly in contact with the men while the robbery was in progress.

Eboni was teaching Jennifer what she knew as they became a new team of criminals. After they set up the jewelry store, they went back to Jennifer's apartment and checked the monitors.

"The call Swole made was to California. It connected to Holloway then diverted to a restricted number and location," said Eboni. "We've got less than 24 hours to figure out where Holloway will stay and get monitoring set up. He'll be here by then."

"Eboni, I'm a little nervous about this. Are you sure we can't just sell them to him then move on. We can use fake names. People do it all the time."

"Jennifer, don't kid yourself. These diamonds are stolen. Once they surface again, whoever owned them will be looking for the seller, or the person that found them, and they will not be nice about it. Now if you want to stop this, tell me now. Otherwise we have work to do."

"So what's our next move?" asked Jennifer.

"You need to find out what you can about that yacht on Lake Lanier and his residence at the Waverly. I'm gonna monitor Swole and deal with it accordingly."

Eboni went to work on her computer as Jennifer left to find out what she could. About 6 hours later, Jennifer walked in as Eboni monitored a meeting at Swole's store.

"Who is this chick?" asked Holloway. "Did you check her out?"

"Yes Sir, I did. So far, she seems clean. It's all right here in the computer," said Swole. "See for yourself."

"Nadiellka Bishop from Charlotte, North Carolina," read Holloway. "What is she doing here?"

"I didn't ask, Sir. She was kinda sharp and seemed to know her stuff. I didn't want to get too deep and scare her away, so I got her info and called you."

"How did she get the jewels? Did she say?"

"Says her dad left them when he died?"

"So, who was her dad?" asked Holloway. "I need to know how this woman got connected to my stones. Is she fed or what? See if you can find anything about her dad in that computer." Eboni panicked! She had been feeding information to Swole's computer, but now the question about her father had caught her off guard.

"Oooh! Oooh! Your dad, Jennifer! Quickly tell me about him!" Jennifer began to say what little she remembered as Eboni processed it into the computer.

"Here it comes, now," said Swole. "Pete Mott Lockhart,,, petty thief,,, born and raised here in Atlanta. Shot dead while robbing a pawn shop off of Candler Road in Decatur over 20 years ago."

"Hmm? How would a petty thief end up with 10 million dollars of my diamonds?" questioned Holloway. "Did she say anything about the amulet key?"

"No, Sir. Maybe he didn't know what he had. Could be your lucky break, Sir."

"You did good, Kenneth. Set up a meeting with her for tomorrow." Holloway turned to one of the two men with him.

"Go to her suite and learn what you can about why she is here. Locate the diamonds if you can. Meantime, I'm going to the bank. You know how to reach me." Holloway and his men left.

Eboni and Jennifer hurried to the Marriott before Holloway's men could get there. Eboni quickly used her charm to divert the desk clerk while Jennifer acted on behalf of the hotel and mislead Holloway's men.

"Did you have a chance to check the guest register to see who is really in the penthouse?" whispered Eboni!

"Yes, no one was there. So I registered Nadiellka Bishop and got you this!" Jennifer handed her a key card to the penthouse door.

"Damn, you're good!" smiled Eboni. Eboni went upstairs while Jennifer went to find Holloway's guys.

As Eboni hurried toward the elevator, she stole a suitcase from the pile that the bellboy was loading onto his cart.

When she made it upstairs, she peeped inside the suite and saw Holloway's men rambling. She closed the door then loudly walked down the hallway toward the suite so they would know she was coming.

Then she went into the suite, put her suitcase on the bed, and learned where the men were hiding.

Afterwards, she went into the bathroom and closed the door behind her. Her plan was working as she heard the men tipping out while she was in the restroom.

Seconds later, Jennifer came rushing into the suite, pointing a gun and yelling.

"Eboni! Are you ok?" Eboni was shocked.

"Where did you get that?" whispered Eboni.

"I took it from the man in the elevator as he came in," said Jennifer.

"Man?" questioned Eboni. She motioned for Jennifer to be quiet. Then she took the gun and cautiously searched the suite. Suddenly, the other man ran out, but Jennifer attacked him and tripped him to the floor. Eboni quickly pistol whipped him until he passed out. They stood looking at each other in wonder about what to do next.

"This wasn't part of the plan, Eboni. What are we gonna do now?" Eboni paused and paced. Then she picked up her phone and dialed.

"Hello, Andrew. We have a problem. I need your help." Thirty minutes later, Andrew showed up at the hotel with a huge trunk and checked in. He took the trunk to the penthouse and placed the man inside it, whom the girls had gagged, covered his head, and tied up. Then he hit him in the head again, and knocked him out. Holloway's men came back looking for him. By then, he was gone.

"This is the Marriott," spoke Jennifer into the special phone that Eboni had wired. "How may I direct your call?"

"To the penthouse, please," answered Swole.

"Mr. Kenneth, Ms. Bishop left a cell phone number for you to call her. That number is 770-987-5432."

"Hello?" spoke Eboni as Swole dialed back.

"Nadie, this is Swole. Can we meet tonight? 8:30 sharp at my place?"

"I'll be there, Sir. Thank you for calling." The final stage had been set. The girls knew that it was now or never as they sat in Jennifer's apartment and thought.

"So what are you gonna do with your half, Eboni?"

"I'm out of here, forever," she said. "Georgia will never see me again! What about you?"

"Haven't quite decided, yet. I have a family here and a child on the way to think about," said Jennifer. *"The Curse Must Be Broken!"* came a whisper. Jennifer heard it and knew what it was. Then she picked up the phone and dialed. "Hi, Cheryl."

"Jenny, are you ok?" asked Cherlene. "Where are you?"

"I'm out... trying to handle a few things, Cheryl. Just thought I'd check in with you, since I've been gone a week already. Is Audrey awake?"

"No, the kids are sleeping, but you can call back in the m..."

"Could you wake her, Cheryl... Please?" Cherlene paused and wondered. She knew that Jennifer would not ask her to wake Audrey unless it was serious.

"Sure, Jenny. Hold on a minute." Audrey came to the phone and Jennifer talked to her for a few minutes.

"I love you, Audrey, and don't you ever forget that, ok? Go back to bed and I'll see you soon. Let me speak to Aunt Cherlene."

"I love you, too, Mommy. Bye." Audrey handed Cherlene the phone and went to sleep.

"Cheryl, I am so sorry about everything. I love you so much. Tell Dee..."

"I know, Jenny, I know," cut in Cherlene caringly. "Is there anything I can do to help? Jennifer, please tell me; you know I'll do it if I can."

"You're already doing it, Cheryl. Hopefully, I'll see you soon. I've gotta go now. Bye."

Cherlene sat by the phone and for the first time, she prayed. Then she heard something she hadn't heard in a long time. *"The Curse Must Be Broken!"* came the whisper. Cherlene didn't fight it. She just laid on her couch and wondered.

****

At 8:30 that night, Eboni showed up at Swole's to meet with Holloway.

"Ms. Bishop," greeted Swole. "This is the gentleman I told you about, Mr. Holloway."

"How do you do, Ms. Bishop?" introduced Holloway. "It's nice to meet you!"

"Likewise, Sir. Do we have a deal or what?"

"Can I see the stones, please?" asked Holloway. Eboni pulled the five stones from her briefcase. Holloway checked them. "Kenneth tells me that you have 10 of these. Where are the other five?"

"Do you have 5 million dollars tonight, Sir?" asked Eboni. Holloway motioned for one of his men to bring the money. Eboni counted it to her briefcase. Then she reached inside her bra and pulled out the necklace, the bracelet, and the ring, and handed it to Holloway. Suddenly, Holloway's two men pulled their weapons.

"Ms. Bishop," smiled Holloway. "Surely you didn't think I would allow you to walk out of here with 'My' diamonds, and 5 million dollars of my money, did you? You don't know very much about business, Ms. Bishop." Eboni quickly cuffed herself to the briefcase and locked it.

"I go where this money goes," she said forcibly. Suddenly, one of Holloway's men whispered,

"Hey Mr. Holloway! There's a cop outside heading straight for us!" Eboni quickly burst through the door and walked toward the police officer with Holloway's men on her trail.

"Hey! What's going on here?" asked the officer as he reached for his revolver. The men shot and blew him away while Eboni ran to her car.

"Please, Mister, don't kill me, please?" she begged as they caught her. "Here's the key to the cuffs. I'm taking them off and you can have the money back!" She quickly released the cuffs and tossed the briefcase toward them. They shot her numerous times as she fell to the ground. Then they grabbed the briefcase and ran.

"Hey! Where is that cop we shot?" asked one of the men.

"I don't know," said Popo. We'll worry about that later. Let's get out of here."

Meantime, Holloway placed the diamonds in his pocket and made his way through the back door. As he walked out, he met Jennifer being dressed like a night assassin. Before he could think, Jennifer attacked him, wrestled him into the wall, took the diamonds, and she was gone. Holloway and his men quickly met up at his yacht; Holloway was furious.

"I've lost the diamonds, again. I think we were set up," he said. "Did you get the money and the girl?"

"The money's right here, Boss, but we had to take out the cop and the girl."

"Open the briefcase," ordered Holloway. One of the men shot the lock off. When he opened it, it was full of paper. Holloway slowly walked over to Popo and pulled the gun from his sports jacket. "How long have you been with me, Popo? Twenty years? Thirty?"

"Every since you were in college, Boss." He was a little nervous as Holloway pointed the pistol to his head.

"So, you know me pretty good, right?"

"Yes Sir."

"And you know what happened here tonight is unacceptable, right?" Popo was very nervous as Mr. Holloway lowered the gun to his genitals.

"Yes Sir, Mr. Holloway."

"Don't you ever think I won't kill yo' ass and run my own operation. What happened here tonight made us look like amateurs. That bitch took my jewels and now she's got my money! I'm sure she has the amulet key, also. Now find her soon, or that's yo' ass. Am I clear?"

"Yes Sir, Mr. Holloway." Holloway handed him the gun and said, "Now get out of my face." Popo left.

****

Meantime, at the Pawn Mart in Lawrenceville, Jennifer, Eboni, and Andrew, were counting their money.

"Two mil for you, Eboni, two for me, and one for you, Andrew, as agreed," counted Jennifer.

"Whooo!" they sounded.

"That cop idea, along with those bullet proof vests, was what's up!" shouted Eboni.

"Andrew you looked like a real cop, too. When I burst through the door, Jennifer you switched that briefcase so fast, I thought you missed. Girl, you are good!" An hour later, Popo met Swole leaving his store and put a bullet through his skull.

****

The next morning while at Cherlene's, Jennifer received a phone call.

"Where are you?" asked Eboni.

"I'm at my sister's place. I'll give you directions." A few minutes later, Eboni and Andrew drove up to Cherlene's place. Jennifer was wearing a maternity dress.

"My! My! My!" laughed Eboni. "I would have never pictured you like this!"

"Cheryl, this is my friend, Eboni, and that's Andrew in the car." Cherlene shook Eboni's hand and waved at Andrew.

"I get the feeling that I have you to thank for bringing my sister back," said Cherlene. "Thank you so much." Then Cherlene went inside.

"So where are you off, too?" asked Jennifer.

"Well, I can't stay around here. Holloway has seen my face," said Eboni. "Guess I'll follow my dream to travel around the world; I'll start in New York."

"Andrew going with you, huh?"

"Nah, he's got other plans. He knows that before sundown, Holloway will have Atlanta swarming with men in search for me. So he's just making sure I get to New York and safely settled in."

"It's been nice knowing you, Eboni. Please take care of yourself."

"You too, Jennifer." Then they hugged. "Take care of those babies!" she yelled as they drove away.

Jennifer got in her car and drove to the bank. She opened her safe deposit box and placed her money inside. Then she took the two bags of diamonds, sat them on top of the money, and left.... smiling.

Meantime, as Eboni rode away, she felt something in her jacket. She checked her pocket and found two clear diamonds the size of a thumb marble.

"Which is the fake, and which is the real one?" read the note attached to them. Eboni smiled and held them up to the sun. Then she shouted,

"Jennifer! I love you, baby! Whoo-hoo!"

A few months later, Jennifer gave birth to a healthy baby boy. She named him, Pete, after her dad, but Audrey called him, Dent, because he had a small sunk in his head. So, Pete Sweet was Dent.

Chapter 75

"Hello, Meca," started Nicole as she stood at D'Amica's gravesite. "I know it's been a minute since I've been here, and I'm sorry. But I know that you are ok. We have a new girl at the shop and she is doing pretty good; her name is Candi. The rest of the girls are still the same---just trying to make it from day to day. Anyway, I was thinking about you and thought I would stop by. I haven't heard anything from Coldblood or Shaun so I don't have anything to tell you. But when I leave here today, I promise that I will check on Shaun to see how he's doing. Take care, Meca. See you later."

It was Sunday about 3p.m. as Nicole drove to see Shaun. It was a spring day and the weather was nice.

"Well, Well! Hello baby," greeted Myrtice. "You kids grow up fast these days. They must be putting fertilizer in your shoes or something, and you look so pretty!"

"Thank you, Ma'am," smiled Nicole.

"How's your mother? Missed her at church last week. I guess she missed me today, huh?" she laughed. "Old bones ain't what they used to be, so I stayed home, today."

"Yes, Ma'am," answered Nicole. "That's the same thing Momma said last week. That's why she wasn't at church."

"Pray for us, child!" Nicole laughed. "You are so pretty. What brings you by?" asked Myrtice.

"I came to see Shaun. Is he here?" Myrtice's countenance changed.

"He's around here somewhere," she mumbled.

"Is something wrong, Ms. Myrtice?"

"The boy stays in trouble ---won't mind either. Them school teachers always calling here telling me how he's ruins their classes and not doing his work. I'm bout sick of it, but I promised his dad I would take care of him, and I will. But that boy needs his dad while he's still got a few youthful years left. He's 11 years old now and bad as hell! He's wearing me down, baby. Can you talk to him?" Nicole found Shaun around the corner playing with some friends.

"Aunt Nicole! Aunt Nicole!" he shouted. Then he ran and hugged her.

"How are you, Shaun?"

"I'm good, Aunt Nikki! Do you want to talk to my dad?" he asked excitedly.

"Maybe in a minute, Shaun, but I want to talk to you first, ok? Come on let's walk and talk." Shaun waved to his friends and walked away.

"How are your grades, Shaun?" Shaun dropped his head.

"Not so good," he said. "Nobody helps me when I don't understand."

"Are you saying that Ms. Myrtice won't help you, Shaun? I know better than that."

"She tries to help me, but she gets confused and sometimes she falls asleep while we're studying. Most of the time she is too busy, so I just leave." Nicole knew this was a problem and Shaun needed help.

"Ok Shaun, I understand. But you still have to keep studying on your own and with your friends. Have you talked to your teachers about this?"

"They don't listen to me. They just say I'm bad." Nicole had a worried look now. She didn't know what else to say.

"I think I will talk to your dad, now. Can you call him?" Shaun pulled out his cell phone and dialed.

"Hello, Dad? Aunt Nikki's here! She wants to talk to you!" Shaun ran to play with his friend while they talked.

"Hi, Coldblood, how are you?" phoned Nicole.

"I'm good, Nicole. It's good to hear your voice. How've you been?"

"Things are alright for me, but I'm not so sure they are ok for your son."

"Are they after him? Have you heard from D-Lo or..."

"No, it's nothing like that. He's not doing good in school. From the sound of things, he's creating other problems, too. It's not his fault, Coldblood. He needs his dad---he really needs you."

"Oh," answered Coldblood. "What can I do, Nicole? If I come there, they will lock me up and he still won't have a dad. If I bring him here, they will use his whereabouts to find me and he still won't have a dad. What am I to do?"

"Coldblood, I don't know, but somebody better do something or he may end up in the very same mess his father's in right now. Well, I have to go. I'll check on him when I can, but that's all I can do."

"Nicole, thanks for calling," said Coldblood. "Put Shaun back on the phone." She handed Shaun the phone then she left wondering how she could help.

A few days later, Shaun was involved with a group of boys throwing rocks at a homeless man sleeping under an overpass on I-20. Shortly after that, he was chased by a convenient store owner for stealing. Eventually, Shaun started cutting class to hang out at the game room. He stayed in his classes just enough to stay in school, so he wouldn't be placed into juvenile. Finally, he started fighting and getting involved with older guys that were selling drugs and vandalizing small communities.

When Shaun reached age 13, he started vandalizing his school and stealing from his teachers. He was a bully's bully, and his justice was only for himself. Many times he would ride the bus across town just to steal from convenient stores. He stole homework from other students, cheated on exams, sexually harassed girls, created rival between football players and cheerleaders, and played teachers against each other.

When he was age 16, he was with a group of guys that broke into the school after hours. They convinced one of their young girlfriends to hang out with them, and she did. After they were alone with her in the school, they strapped her to a chair, and began to hit her and sexually abuse her until she cried.

Shaun watched as his anger began to build and he didn't know why. Suddenly, he grabbed a broom stick from a corner and began to beat the boys ferociously.

Of the four boys involved, two had major concussions, and ended up in the hospital, while the other two suffered broken limbs and fractured ribs.

Because the girl claimed that she was afraid for her life and that Shaun had rescued her, the charges were dismissed against him. Later that day, while Shaun rode the bus and walked the streets, he found himself sitting on the steps of his old apartment home--crying-suffering--wanting something---needing someone---For the first time since she died, Shaun cried for his mother.

Chapter 76

A few years had passed within the Atlanta Metro Area since many of Shaun's troubles began. Shaun, now 16 years old, walked the streets of Smyrna in the neighborhood where he lives.

He barely has passing grades in school and doesn't care to do any better. He hardly talks to Coldblood anymore and just lives the life that's satisfactory to him. He has become a terror to the streets and a danger to himself because there's no one to help him guide his thoughts, or take responsibility for his actions. Suddenly, another streak of bluish colored ice appeared in the heavens as a huge ball of fire also appeared and followed it toward the earth. Meantime, Cherlene, Jennifer, and Donna, are close again, though they still have their individual problems. Jennifer still searches for her half sister while Tenisha wish she had one. Donna still competes with Tenisha at work while Nicole endeavors to learn about the picture found in her dad's shoebox. D-Lo is in prison for life while Hookman and Coldblood are still on the run. Davina is in AA while Rosa is still in hiding. Finally, there's Elisa, who is still undercover, but is training to be a personal bodyguard for Yoder Holloway.

"Uh! Uh!" struggled Elisa as she trained in Germany while being suspended by ropes and cables. She had a separate cable attached to each of her limbs while they suspended her 8 to 10 feet above ground---pulling her in 4 directions. Plus, she had many other ropes attached to her waist, also pulling her in all directions. Elisa struggled to escape the confines of the cables and ropes but she was not successful.

"Damn it!" screamed Holloway. "Get her down!" Then he walked away angrily. They loosened the ropes and Elisa fell to the floor. Since Holloway started this training years ago, many have had their arms or legs snatched from their body because of the tension of the ropes or cables. Some had survived and become his personal agents watching over his affairs, but only one had been powerful enough to beat the cables and come down on her own. Holloway fell in love with her and later put a hit on her when he learned that she was a cop. He's been looking for another to beat the torture cables every since.

"Hey! Hey Brenda!" whispered the voice. Elisa was laying on the floor of the warehouse, suffering. "It's gonna hurt a while---I've been there," came the voice again as Elisa gasped for air and kept her eyes closed.

"I'm Sherri, and we will be roommates. Come on, get up." She helped Elisa up and gave her some water. Elisa was still suffering as she opened her eyes and sat. "Don't try to talk," continued Sherri. "Your body is in too much pain so just listen to me. He's gonna bring you back to these cables week after week until he's sure you can't defeat them. Each time there will be even more tension on the ropes and cables; so much that it will snatch your arm or leg right off your body if you're not strong. You have to be a very unique person to survive this so..."

"I am unique... uhhh!" screamed Elisa. When she tried to talk, she felt massive pain in her gut and it caused the rest of her body to hurt.

"I told you not to talk," ordered Sherri. "Your muscles, your veins, and all inner organs, have been stretched and forced out of sorts— even your vocal cords. You must give them a few hours to readjust or you may damage yourself even more than you already have. Now, if you understand me, nod and let me know." Elisa nodded. "Good. I'm gonna pick you up and walk you until you can do it yourself. Afterwards, I will put you in the shower and then to bed, ok?" Elisa nodded again. As Sherri lifted her, Elisa screamed and tried to lay down, but Sherri held her up with special padding wrapped around her body. She knew that everywhere she touched Elisa's body, it would hurt. Therefore, she padded her body so Elisa could partly endure the touches.

"Uhh! Uhh!" screamed Elisa as Sherri walked her about.

Chapter 77

Rosa, being dressed in her sexy tights, trains in her underground home beneath the church. Like a warrior ninja, she jumps, kicks, and punch swinging bags, while running up the side of walls, avoiding and deflecting darts, tossed by a machine. She have mastered the art of karate, Tai Kwon Do, Kung Fu, kick boxing, and hand-to-hand combat, while combining them to develop her own style and methods. But most of all her gifts are... endurance... and speed. She can move like a leopard, and leap like a deer, while attacking and disarming her challenger like a ninja assassin. Her hands, arms, and head, can weave like three cobra snakes to sting you, while her blows are powerfully used to subdue, or render an opponent harmless. After training in her one thousand square foot underground space, Rosa took her shower, then rested on her couch. Suddenly, she heard something upstairs in the church.

"Who could that be?" she thought as she checked the time. *"It's 11 o'clock at night!"* She picked up her weapons and eased to the door.

"Lord, I need you more than I've ever needed you before," she heard. "I know that you have forgiven me of my sin, but Lord please help Carl Jr. Help him to know you and to listen to your Spirit and be obedient." Rosa went back to her couch and sat down.

"Carl is praying for his son," she said. Then she began to think about her family and things she has done, as she heard the whisper.... *"The Curse Must Be Broken!"*

Rosa's Memories I
"How did the job search go, today?" asked Rosa.

"Not to good," responded her husband, Eric. "But I managed to find a few odd jobs and I started one today."

"Honey, have you thought about changing your line of work?"

"And do what? Jobs are lacking in all fields, right now. It's not just in real estate."
Eric had been laid off from his real estate job, and was resulting to remodeling small home projects for friends and others who were still trying to look out for him.

"Eric, If we are going to get ahead, things have to change soon."

"Don't you think I know that, Rosa? Please don't rag on me. I'm doing the best I can. Things will change, soon." Rosa fixed him some food then put on her coat to leave. "Where are you going?"

"We're short handed at the precinct and my boss is allowing some of us to work extra hours a week. I'm going in ---we need the money."

"Don't do this, Rosa!" he yelled angrily. "Its not about the money and you know it! You never want to leave that damn job!"

"Eric, please don't start that. Yes, I love my work, but we need the money, also."

"Rosa, I need you, too. Please don't go; stay home tonight... please."

"I have to go, Eric. I'll see you later tonight." Then she left.(End of Rosa's Mem #I)

"Rosa! Rosa are you here?" called Rev. Simmons as he interrupted her thoughts. "You seemed to have been in deep thought," he said as he peeped in. "Are you ok?"
Rosa gave him a look of sadness. "Oh Lord," he sighed. "I guess I'm not the only one who needs to pray right now, huh? What's bothering you, Rosa?"

"I threw away my marriage and ruined my family, Carl." She started to cry. "What was I thinking?" Rev. Simmons sat beside her and she laid her head in his lap.

"Shh... shh child," he comforted. "God knows your pain and he will heal your hurt. But if you need to talk, I'm here, too."

"I loved my husband, Carl, I really did. But one night I made the biggest mistake of my life, when he needed me and I left home."

"Tell me what happened."

"Eric was having a hard time finding work. We argued about it one evening, then I left and went back to work, when I should have stayed home."

Rosa's Memories II

"Ah! You changed your mind, huh? Told you that you'd be back."

"Jonathan please, no 'I told you so's... please." She sat at her desk near Jonathan.

"I'm sorry, Rosa, I didn't mean it that way. Are you ok?"

"No I'm not! Eric and I had a fight again."

"Oooh! That's not good," he said. "It's really tough out there, right now. You need to lighten up on the guy."

"I know, but he keeps going around in circles and I'm ready to move on."

Suddenly, Jonathan heard one of his favorite songs on the office radio. He turned it up, snatched Rosa from her chair, and danced with her in his arms.

"What you need, my dear, is a break to get away from the norm of things. You've been doing extra work everyday for almost 2 months and you need to let go and live a little." Rosa smiled and enjoyed her dance, but she was a little nervous.

"Stop this, Jonathan! We have a case to work on. Where is everybody, anyway?"

"We are the only two working over tonight. This shift is so short handed, every one else is on the streets. So we have to also manage the store, honey." Suddenly, he whirled her and caught her in his arms. Rosa laughed and felt good and enticed by it. She really liked Jonathan and he loved her.

As they worked into the night, they kept thinking about each other and the dance. Jonathan wanted her and he wasn't doing a good job of hiding it, though he tried. She kept finding herself with wondering thoughts, and couldn't focus on her work. She decided to get up and get some air to clear her head. So did Jonathan as they met on the side of the desk. Once they stood face to face, like two animals, they smelled each others scent, and never left the very spot. Within seconds, she was jacked on the desk with Jonathan making love to her.

"Unit 327 Atlanta P.D. zone 1, Officer in Bowen Homes Apartments need assistance in a neighborhood gun fight. All available units please respond," came the call.

"That's right around the corner!" said Jonathan. *"And there are no available units near Bankhead but us!"*

"We have to go," said Rosa. They fixed their clothing and responded to the call. (End of Rosa's Mem #II)

"So did Stephanie know about this?" interjected Rev. Simmons.

"Stephanie was my best friend; of course she knew! Jonathan and I never got together like that again, but a permanent damage had been done."

"How?" asked Rev. Simmons. "Did your husband find out?"

"It was worse than that! Jonathan and I knew we made a mistake and we didn't do it   again. So nine months later, why would I think that my newborn child was anybody's other than my husband's?"

"Oh my God, Rosa! What happened?"

"Eric and I loved our newborn daughter and things were fine. About six months after our child was born. Eric was out of work again. So without my knowledge, he decided to sell his sperm to help this unknown couple have a child."

Rosa's Memory III

     "Hello! This is Avery University Clinics, Dr. Perry. Can I speak with Eric Smith, please?"

     "Eric is not home, but I'm his wife. What's this about?"

"*Sorry, Ma'am, but it's a personal matter and I need to speak to your husband,*" *said the doctor. Rosa immediately went to the clinic, flashed her badge, and threw her weight around until she got answers.*

"*Detective,*" *said the doctor.* "*Mr. Smith came in voluntarily to have his sperm cells checked. As you know, guys with good sperm are paid a fee for their services.*"

"*What!*" *yelled Rosa.* "*Eric was selling his sperm?*" *Rosa became sad. She knew that her husband had gotten desperate to support his family. She loved him all the more when she heard what he was doing, but the doctor had more news.*

"*I called to inform him that he is generating dead sperm cells and we cannot use him as a donor. Sorry.*" *Rosa was startled.*

"*How long has he been like this?*" *asked Rosa.*

"*As far as we can tell, all of his life,*" *said the doctor.* "*Something's in his system killing the sperm cells before they are released. He can never have kids.*" *Rosa went to the bathroom and cried. (End of Rosa's Mem #III)*

"Lord Rosa!" said Rev. Simmons. "What did you do? Did you tell Eric?"

"I talked to the doctor, showed him my child, and explained the situation to him. I gave him the cash to pay Eric, that day, and he had compassion on me. I've been living a lie every since." She started to cry as Rev. Simmons hugged her. "Carl, I've been so miserable! I don't even know where my child is!" Then she cried herself to sleep on Rev. Simmons lap.

Chapter 78

Rosa was awakened the next morning by the ringing of her private cell phone.

"Yeah?" she answered.

"The Serpent surfaces," came the voice.

"When and where?"

"The Western Peachtree Plaza in Buckhead, in the ballroom 9:30 p.m." Rosa checked her wardrobe. A few minutes later, she was working out... again.

****

"Wow!" said Susie. "Those are so beautiful!"

"They are for you," said Jennifer. She handed Susie a pair of silver earrings as she strapped on her apron to work.

"Oh I love these, Jennifer! Thank you so much!"

"Anything for my partner in crime," smiled Jennifer.

"What! You stole these? Jennifer why? You don't have to do that anymore. I thought that's why you came to work here, so you can enjoy life without having to worry about making money."

"I am enjoying life, Susie. Aren't you?"

" Yes I am, but I choose not to steal anymore. Especially, since I have a good job, thanks to you." Jennifer watched her in wonder.

"Susie, don't you get the urge to do it again... ever?"

"No Jennifer, I don't. I did it because I was broke, almost homeless, and I needed money. Jennifer, you have more money now than you'll need for life. Especially, with the investments you've made with J.J. Soon, you'll have a string of coffee shops all over the south, so why are you stealing?"

"I can't help it, Susie. It brings me a peace of mind; connects me to my parents again, I guess."

"Do your sisters know?"

"They don't know that I'm still doing it, but they know," said Jennifer. "We don't talk about it. You are the only one I've talked to about it."

"Do they know that you are rich as hell and still sitting on 10 rubies worth millions?"

"It's diamonds, Susie, and it only 9 of them. I gave one away, remember?"

"Diamonds, rubies, who cares," said Susie. "They both make you rich!"

"Susie, I need your help."

"Of course, Jennifer, what's up?" Jennifer hesitated.

"I need you to go with me somewhere tonight ---a private party and banquet."

"What am I gonna wear to something like that? Besides, why aren't you going with Marquis, that new stud of yours?" Suddenly Jennifer handed her a shopping bag. Susie pulled out a beautiful black evening gown.

"Lord have mercy!" said Susie. "Girl, you will knock`em dead in this!"

"It's not for me, it's for you," added Jennifer. Susie was speechless at first.

"Wait-a-minute! Tell me what's going on here, Jennifer. First the earrings, and now the dress. What's next... shoes?" Jennifer handed her a pair of black silver-laced shoes that matched the earrings and the gown. Susie stood speechless... again.

"I really need you to watch my back tonight, Susie, and all you have to do is be there and talk to me."

"Ok Jennifer, I'd be pleased to accompany you. What time should I be ready?"

"About 9:30 or so; I'll pick you up."

"I'll be ready," smiled Susie.

"Good, but you might want to know that I'm going to rob the place."

"What!" screamed Susie. "Oh no! Not me! I ain't going! I can't do it!"

"Susie, all you have to do is talk to me, while I do what I do," begged Jennifer.

"Why me, Jennifer? I have a good life here, and you're trying to get me locked up!"

"Susie! Listen! I'm lonely and I feel like I'm starving to death. No one understand my need like you because you've been there."

"No I haven't. You're trying to get me to go there!" she shouted.

"Just this once, Susie."

"No!"

"I promise that you will have fun!"

"Jennifer, No!"

"The dress cost $1200 dollars, the shoes were $500, and they're all yours."

Susie paused to process what Jennifer had said.

"Plus, the earrings," added Jennifer. "They cost more than the dress and the shoes put together, and they're all yours, if you go with me tonight."

"The dress, the shoes, and the earrings---you stole them, didn't you?"

Jennifer didn't answer. She just stood looking embarrassed.

"So you want me to go with you to some party where lots of people are so you can steal, and you want me to wear all stolen stuff!"

"All you have to do is talk to me, Susie, and enjoy yourself."

"How am I to talk to you while you're stealing or whatever?" Jennifer pulled out a beautiful silver necklace to match the earrings, and handed it to Susie.

"The earrings have a built in receiver, and the necklace has a transmitter at the end of it."

"Hot damn!" yelled Susie. "I ain't never been a spy before!"

"I promise it will be fun, and you will be absolutely gorgeous while doing it."

****

"This is the captain speaking. It is currently 7:15 p.m. and we will land at the Atlanta-Hartsfield –Jackson Airport shortly. Please fasten your seatbelts and brace for descent."

"Ok Ladies," spoke Anitra." This is your first practical training assignment so don't blow it. Mr. Holloway will meet lots of guests and you will not say a word even if you are spoken to. You may nod, bow, or execute whatever he tells you to, but only talk to me through your transmitter; you got that?"

"Anitra, I've worked for Mr. Holloway before," said Elisa. "I know how I'm suppose to be." Anitra smiled and leaned toward Elisa.

"When you worked for Mr. Holloway years ago, you were his young hussy slut that he passed from client to client as his investment," she started. "Now that you're a used whore, your stock's declined and that account is now closed. You are his personal protector now so wipe that pretty off your face and toughen up!" Anitra walked away.

"I'm gonna stomp her someday," said Elisa.

"You'll have to get in line," responded Sherri. "Even the men want to stomp her, too."

"Did you find out where we are going?"

"One of the guys said that we are going to a hotel somewhere in Atlanta."

"This is my home," said Elisa. "I'm surprised he's allowing me to come back here."

"I've learned that he has a motive for everything he does," said Sherri. "Sunday, he has another meeting in New York that we also have to attend. I wonder if these trips are related."

"Did you see the two 21 year olds with him as we boarded?" asked Elisa. "One will be dropped off here tonight as another man's property, and the other will be dropped in New York. That's what he did to me. I never saw it coming. The man he gave me to, killed my dad and got me pregnant."

"That's horrible, Brenda. Where's your child now? What happened to him?"

"I don't know." Elisa dropped an angry tear. "He took it away as soon as it was born. I don't even know if it was a boy or girl. I knew I couldn't keep it so when it was born I refused to look at it; I just cried."

"I'm sorry, Brenda, but that's his way. As far as I know, Holloway doesn't allow people that are close to him, to have family or even close friend attachments; he says it creates too many problems for his business. Therefore, we learn to depend on each other... trust each other, while building our lives around him."

"So what's your story, Sherri? Did he pawn you off, too?"

"No, I was never one of his girls like you. I'm told that my dad, whom I never knew, was one of Holloway's main men. He died a few years ago, while saving Holloway's life. Before he died, he confessed to Holloway about my existence and made him promise to look out for me. At the time my mom and I lived in Vineland, New Jersey, and all was well. But immediately after my dad died, my mother was killed in a car crash, while drunk at the wheel. Afterwards, I lost my job and desperately tried to get other work, but no one would hire me. That's when Holloway popped up and rescued me, or so it seems."

"Do you think foul play was involved?" asked Elisa.

"My mom didn't drink, and her brother, the only living relative I had, mysteriously disappeared after being faithful in visiting my mom and me for years. Foul play?" commented Sherri. "What do you think?" Elisa and Sherri sat on the plane having long faces, and wondering how they could get back at Holloway.

"We're here girls," said Anitra. "Now do your jobs!"

****

As Jennifer entered the Western Peachtree Plaza hotel in Buckhead, she saw the many eloquent guests checking into the private dining area.

"Testing one, testing one, two, three," said Susie into the mic.

"Susie, what is it?" whispered Jennifer.

"Everything is so quiet out here so I checked the mic to make sure it's working."

"Susie, be quiet, and just wait in the car!" whispered Jennifer. "I'll tell you when to move."

"Don't tell me to be quiet! You told me to talk to you," argued Susie. "That's why I came!" Susie was very nervous.

"Can you be quiet for now, Susie? I'm trying to get you in!"

"Are you in, yet?"

"No! Susie be quiet!" Susie sat in the car and waited.

****

Rosa entered the lobby of the Peachtree Plaza hotel while walking behind a couple. No one noticed her as she pulled the name badge from her pocket and pinned it onto her chest. As she neared the doorway to where the dinner was taking place, she stopped an employee and brushed powder onto his shoulder, while pretending to be brushing it off.

"Young man!" she said. "What have you gotten yourself into? Go clean this up immediately before you serve any of our guests!" The young man read her badge:

      Ms. Queen Harper
      Western Peachtree Plaza
      District Manager

"What are you staring at young man?" she said to the door registrar. "Now, do your job! Watch your guests!" The employee was a little confused as Rosa walked into the dining area like she owned the place, but they dared not stop her, thinking they may be reprimanded or lose their job.

****

Jennifer roamed the floor area until she met one of the servers for the guests. She followed her down the hall, then hit her over the head with a small wooden statue that she took from a lamp table.

"I'm sorry," she said. She pulled the unconscious employee in a nearby room and took her clothes, and identification. Then she hurried inside the dining area. "I'm in," she whispered.

"Well, I'm coming in, too," said Susie. "I'm tired of sitting out here."

"No Susie! Wait until I get you approved!" Susie had already left the car.

Jennifer hurried to find a place to change back into her evening dress without being noticed. Just after she changed and made it to the door, Susie walked up. Jennifer tried hard to see the names on the guest list but the registrant had it closely guarded.

"Hello, Ms. McClinton," greeted Jennifer as Susie walked up. Jennifer caught a glimpse of the McCl on his clipboard and guessed that it was McClinton. "I am so glad you made it!"

"Mrs. Tonya McClinton?" asked the registrar.

"Yes!" shouted Jennifer as she grabbed Susie and sped inside.

****

"Hello Vanard," greeted Holloway as he entered the ball room. "How's Ruth?"

"She's right over there, why don't you ask her yourself," he smiled. Rosa saw Holloway the minute he entered, therefore, she prepared to kill him at her earliest opportunity. She thoroughly observed his surroundiings and knew that Elisa and Sherri were following close behind him while Anitra trailed him at a distance. She once had the same position as Anitra, and even shared Holloway's bed, so she knew his game better than anyone. She saw Holloway and his two young girls sit at a table, while Elisa sat at another table on his left and Sherri to his right.

"I feel sorry for them," whispered Elisa. *"They are in hog heaven as long as they are by Holloway's side and don't know this very night, they will be pawned away."*

****

"Ok Susie," instructed Jennifer. "Look through this crowd and tell me what you see?"

"Money!" she whispered. "I see lots of money in here! I'm kinda nervous, Jennifer. What do you want me to do?" Jennifer was smiling like a little girl, who had just found her many best friends, and she wanted to mingle with them all.

"Help me to see the things they have hidden," said Jennifer. They stood and stalked the crowd as everyone mingled and greeted each other. Some were sitting and some were standing.

"Ok," started Susie. "Dude over there with his hand in his pocket is holding onto his room key; his valuables are there. Dude over there has a huge bank roll in his upper jacket. You see home girl over there,,, she's packing *(speaking of Rosa)*. And see the sister with the big boobs, they ain't all boobs," continued Susie. "She has credit cards stashed in there, too."

"Ok, my turn," smiled Jennifer. "See the guy talking with the chick in the blue; he's got a box of breath mints in his inner jacket. See the woman with the huge purse, she has family pictures she wants to show off. And see the guy at the table with the two young ladies *(speaking of Holloway)*, he has a document in his vest pocket for someone to sign."

"What!" screamed Susie. "That stuff you just mentioned is worthless!"

"It's not about the money, Susie. It's about the challenge! The game!" smiled Jennifer.

"Did you bring the bags?"

"Yeah, one is at our table, over there."

"Ok, here we go," said Jennifer. "Watch my back as I go through the crowd. If you see anything or anyone getting suspicious, holla and head for the door."
Jennifer started weaving and mingling with the guest while lifting money, wallets, pictures, documents, gum, breathe mints, credit cards, asthma pumps, keys, and anything she could find. Then she would drop it off in the bag, and start over again.

As she maneuvered she heard, *"The Curse Must Be Broken!"* but she had learned to ignore it.

****

"Look at that bastard!" thought Rosa. *"He took my whole life and caused me to be separated from my family. Now I have nothing, and I'm in hiding for the rest of my life, because of him. Tonight it ends. I know one of his three watch dogs will get to me, but not before I get to him!"*

Rosa slowly moved through the crowd while watching Anitra, Elisa, and Sherri. She knew that she would only get one chance to get to Holloway, and she had to do it right. She had a split in her evening gown where she hid her small pistol. Her intent was to shoot him between the eyes, then fight her way till death, if she had to. Twenty feet away! Seventeen feet away! Fifteen! Twelve! Suddenly as she reached for her gun, she felt a quick tug on her dress, and the gun was gone! Jennifer had swiped it!

"What the h...!" She looked up just in time to see Jennifer's backside heading in Holloway's direction. Without thinking she made a quick jolt to catch Jennifer, but Elisa intervened and grabbed her.

"Hold on, Ma'am!" said Elisa. They stood staring each other down. Suddenly, Rosa heard, *"The Curse Must Be Broken!"* Rosa knew she had to escape before Holloway turned to see her face, so she forced Elisa's hands away and headed for the door. When she saw Anitra approaching, she quickly pulled her veil over her mouth and nose, then exchanged a few blows with her as she ran out. Anitra ran out after her.

****

"Jennifer, something is wrong," called Susie. "We'd better get out of here!"

"Already ahead of you," radioed Jennifer. "Get to the car! I'll see you there!" Susie saw that the bag was gone; Jennifer already had it.

"Damn, she's good!" laughed Susie. Then she left.

****

Holloway met Anitra at the door when she returned.

"Did you see her? Who was she?"

"I didn't see her face," said Anitra. "She had it covered. Brenda you grabbed her. Did you see her face?"

"No I didn't," said Elisa. "Like you said, she was covered."

Chapter 79

"Go, Susie Go!" shouted Jennifer as she approached the car. Susie didn't want to drive away too fast because she didn't want to look suspicious.

"What the hell happened back there?" asked Susie! "There was this one woman who seemed to have snapped---started fighting right after you passed her, then she ran out! What did you do? Was she following you?"

"I don't know," answered Jennifer. "I didn't see her. When I heard the commotion from the crowd, I knew something was up so I dipped. But man that was fun! Whoopee! Yeah!" she shouted.

As they entered the main street, they heard a small running sound with loud panting. Suddenly, with a loud crash, something landed on the trunk of the car. Susie looked in the rear view mirror in wonder.

"Oh God, it's her!" screamed Susie.

"It's who?" asked Jennifer. By then, Rosa was on top of the car as Susie began to weave across the road. But Rosa was so experienced, she still managed to hold on and reach through the passenger side window toward Jennifer. Jennifer was almost as swift as she blocked her hand before she could latch onto her. She saw Rosa glance at the bag in the backseat and knew that Rosa was about to go for it. By the time Rosa could turn her body and reach to take the bag through the back window, Jennifer had already made it to the backseat. When Rosa grabbed for the bag, Jennifer laid on her back and kicked her completely off of the car, as they sped away.

"Oh hell, Jennifer!" shouted Susie. "What have you gotten me into?"

"That heifer is good!" smiled Jennifer. "She still got the bag!"

****

Rosa stumbled back to her car after being banged and bruised up.

"Ha! Ha!" she laughed. *"That little petty thief heifer is pretty sneaky! Quick too! She obviously doesn't work for Holloway or I would've been dead the moment she stole my gun. How could I let someone steal my gun?"* she wondered. *"Am I losing it? Am I getting too old? Who was the girl that grabbed me? There is something about her eyes. I should have broken her neck but I couldn't move. Why not? I need to know."*

****

A while later, back at the Western Peachtree Plaza motel, the dinner was ending.

"Calvin, it's been good doing business with you," said Holloway. "Now I have a gift for you." Holloway turned and looked at one of the girls sitting with him at the table. Elisa knew what was about to happen.

"Calvin, this is Afia. From this day forward, the only way we will arrange our business is through her, unless I change it. I've trained her and I trust her. Without her we have no business. Therefore, you are responsible for her safety and her well-being, as well as her financial stability. As of this moment she's yours to handle as you will, but you must take care of her." The girl was shocked as she spoke.

"But I don't know him, Mr. Holloway; I can't go with him."

"Afia, we are all family in this business. Trust me ---you'll be ok."

"But you just said that I belonged to him," she cried. "You never told me that you would give me away to a stranger, that I don't even know!" Holloway signaled to Anitra and she stepped forward.

"Don't cry, Afia," she said. "You can go with me, tonight, and think about it. Come on, let's go." Elisa and Sherri thought it to be strange when Anitra pacified her, but they said nothing.

"Calvin, this is Cindy. The same rules apply as did Afia," said Holloway.
Cindy, the other girl was shocked, but hesitantly went with Calvin. The next morning, Afia, the girl who rebelled, was found dead in the hotel dumpster with a broken neck.

Chapter 80

"Anitra killed that girl!" whispered Elisa as they talked in their room.

"You don't know that!" whispered Sherri. "Don't jump to conclusions!"

"So, do you think the girl just jumped into the dumpster and died?"

"Of course not," answered Sherri. "I just don't know if Anitra killed her."

"Jesus!" panicked Elisa. "That's what would have happened to me had I rejected D-Lo the night that Holloway introduced us!"

"Ok! I've heard enough!" demanded Sherri. "You're panicking over something you're not even sure about. Let's talk about something you do know about. That woman you grabbed last night---who is she?"

"I don't have a clue, Sherri. Why do you ask me that?"

"Because you lied when Anitra asked you did you see her face. Her face was not covered and you stared directly at her and she stared at you. So why did you lie?"

"I don't know, Sherri. As I stood there looking in her eyes, I felt like I knew her---there was something about her eyes."

"I don't think it's a coincidence that she was there with us at that moment. She was after something and that's why she ran out. Plus, the way she exchanged blows with Anitra, tells me that she is a professional. Are you sure you don't know her?"

"Yes Sherri, I'm sure!"

A few hours later, Holloway, Anitra, Sherri, and Elisa, were back on Holloway's private plane heading to New York. Holloway had another 22 year old girl by his side.

****

Rosa sat in her hide-a-way logging onto her computer.

"Where are you? I know you are out there," she whispered.

"Knock knock!" said Rev. Simmons. "Rosa I'm coming in! What are you doing?"

"I'm just searching for some information." Rev. Simmons saw her at the computer.

"You're looking for your child, aren't you? You swore to never interfere in her life after you left her. So why are you torturing yourself?"

"I just need to know if she is ok, Carl, then I'll leave it alone."

"What's her name?"

"Her name is Elisa, and she was so beautiful. I just need to know what happened to her after I left and her dad died." Rev. Simmons pushed the switch and turned the computer off.

"Rosa, are you sure you want to do this?" At first, Rosa just stared at him. Then she took his hand, led him to the couch, and laid over in his arms as they sat.

"Carl, after I left my family, my daughter was forced to grow up fast. She became the woman of the house at 10 and she knew it. Five years after I left and traveled the world with Holloway, we came to Atlanta to handle some business. Holloway took up residence here and I was here for two years, off and on. I decided to contact Eric. He was still single and glad to see me. For a while, we met in secret places while trying to maintain my cover, and to work with Holloway. When Eric and I first started secretly meeting, things were great. Then we started arguing more and more each time we met.

Rosa's Memories IV

"What we're doing is not fair to our daughter," said Eric. They finished making love and were in bed, talking. "Rosa, she doesn't even know you are alive. She thinks you're dead!"

"Eric, you know that I stay away for her sake as well as yours. The people I'm involved with are very dangerous and I can't take any chances when it comes to you and our daughter."

"Rosa, we can't meet like this anymore because, Elisa doesn't deserve this. Why don't you come home to us; give up this life of secrecy and abandonment?"

"Eric we've been over this many times. Why are your bringing this back up?"

"Because I love you and need you here. Elisa needs you, too."

"Eric don't do this! Don't make me feel like I'm abandoning you and my child, especially when you know I have to stay away just to protect you!" Eric was quiet then he stood and got dressed.

"When I was seventeen," started Eric. "My friends, Reggie and Maria, who were also about my age, were seeing each other. Maria had a very strict dad and everyone stayed away from him. After a few months, Maria got pregnant. In order to protect Reggie, she lied and told her dad, that I was the father. It was a big mess. My mom eventually got involved and demanded a DNA test. At first, I was happy because I knew that my name would be cleared. But the doctor's found something in my blood that made them want to run more tests. Not only did they prove that Maria was not pregnant by me, but they also found that I had a permanent medical condition called Testicular failure, and I would be sterile during my lifetime." Rosa was shocked and started to cry. Now she understood what he was telling her.

"Eric, I am so sorry. It only happened one T..." Eric cut in.

"Elisa is my daughter and I love her----that's the bottom line. I'm going home to my daughter, Rosa. After this night, please don't

contact me again, and certainly don't contact her. Promise me that, Rosa! That's all I want!"

"I promise," she nodded in tears.

"Take care of yourself, Rosa. I hope you have a good life." Then he left.(End of Rosa's Mem #IV)

"Rosa, I am so sorry," said Rev. Simmons. I can only imagine your stress, all these years. How old is your daughter now?"

"She's thirty-two and a half. Her birthday is February 19. After Eric left me that night, two of Holloway's men entered the room where Eric and I met. They beat me and cuffed me to the inside of their vehicle. They drove me near the park where Eric was walking through, and had this gang of guys to kill him while I watched. That night was the last time I saw Eric or my child. Later, Holloway tortured me in efforts to make me tell him who Eric was, but for Elisa's sake, I didn't. After that, Holloway killed everyone in his operation who worked alone, except me, because he was in love with me. So any possible chance to communicate with my daughter or the agency was over and I was completely in Holloway's care. I gave up on life and seeing my daughter until now. Carl, please! I have to find her!" Rev. Simmons stood and took Rosa back to her desk. Then he turned the computer back on.

"Rosa, I hope this works out for you and your daughter. As long as you stay faithful to the Lord and obedient to Him, He will help you to find her." Then he kissed her forehead and left.

Rosa diligently searched for information in her computer. Her sources were limited after Eric died, so she couldn't find much info about her daughter.

"Mango Circle, Bowen Homes. Hmm? John Carey Elementary School."

Rosa started to reminisce as she read the computer screen about her days with Elisa as a child. *"Here's another---Oak Forrest Apartments at Glenwood and Moreland. Hmm? She left and went to Simpson Valley Apartments F4, on Simpson Road where she attended Washington High School. Wow! My baby went to Washington!"* she smiled.

"Ok, here we go. Finally, here's something about her adult life! Ah! She had a house! 1911 Hardwood Ct. in Jonesboro, Ga. Good Rosa, good! You're doing good! Last known address- no other information available. What... Is that it?" Rosa started to pace the floor and think. *"What happened to her?"* she asked herself. *"There is no deceased record that I know of, so she's not dead; maybe she got married."* Rosa went back to her computer but she couldn't find anymore information that would help her to find her daughter. After a while, she sat and prayed.

"Lord, I don't know your will for me. I don't even know who I am anymore. But I want to make up to my daughter before I die. I am sorry for all the wrong I've done, and I want to do something for my

daughter. Help me to get back on track. Please help me---I really need you now." Then she heard, *"The Curse Must Be Broken!"*

"Then help me to break it!" she sounded. *"Whatever it takes, I'm ready."* Rosa grabbed her coat, and she was gone.

Chapter 81

"I don't belong here!" shouted Davina. "I need to talk to my daughter you bastard! Leave me alone!"

"Davina, please calm down!" whispered Kris. "I just came to check on you, but if you don't calm down, they will make me leave!"

"You need to leave! You call Tenisha right now, Kris, or so help me God I will di...."

"Yeah yeah, I know you will divorce me and take everything I got. I've been hearing the story for the last 5 years, Davina. When are you gonna sober up so we can get on with it!"

"You insensitive bastard!" she yelled. She looked for something to throw but there was nothing. Therefore, she sat on her bed being angry. "Kris, I need a drink."

"Lay down, Davina. Tenisha will be by soon." Then he left.

Over the years, Davina had gotten worse and was drunk everyday. She had bladder control problems and she cried a lot, but she still would not tell anyone what drove her to this madness. Therefore, to keep from putting her in a mental institution, Kris and Tenisha sent her to AA.

"I don't belong here, Kris!" she shouted as he left.

****

Rosa walked into the Lincoln Cemetery on Westview Dr. and Simpson Rd.

"Hello, Eric. I guess this is a surprise, huh? I know you didn't think you would hear from me again, but I need to talk to you. So how are you, Eric? I won't stay long but I wanted to tell you that I need to break my promise. I've stayed out of our daughter's life for over 20 years just like you asked. But I think she needs me now, Eric, and I'm going to find her---Lord knows I need her. I am so lonely, Eric, and I'm starting to hate my life. Anyway, that's it. Take care and maybe I'll even see you soon. I love you, Eric... Bye." Minutes later, Rosa was in her car making a call.

"Hello, this is Special Agent Rosa Smith. Connect me to the director's office."

"FBI Chief Special Agent Walter Dennard speaking. Who is this?"

"Walter, this is Rosa. I'm coming in."

****

"Hmm? There goes the Glamour Bitch!" said Donna. Tenisha walked to her desk as Donna watched.

"Tenisha has really mellowed over the past few years," said Tyler. "So why do you keep calling her that name?"

"Because I don't like her and I don't trust her," said Donna. "It's all just a front. She's like a pet snake. At any given time, she will change and bite you."

Donna and Tenisha just stared at each other from desk to desk. Donna shot Tenisha a bird, so Tenisha bent over with her butt toward Donna, then sneakily patted it. At first Donna seemed raged, but soon she smiled.

"What are you smiling about you, little slut?" thought Tenisha. *"Your mother was a slut, and I know that it's just a matter of time before it comes out of you. Oh, how I wish I could tell you about your whorish mom. But because of my friendship with Cherlene, I won't. Maybe I'll write an article about her and leave it on your desk!"* Tenisha began to smile back when she thought of leaving an article on Donna's desk.

"What are you smiling about, Glamour Bitch?" thought Donna. *"If you only knew my thoughts, you'd wipe that smirk off your face."* Donna saw Tenisha in her mind with a missing front tooth, wild unkempt hair, and wearing rags for clothes, as Mr. Golden scolded her for writing a bad story. Suddenly, both their cell phones rang and they left.

****

"Agent Smith, you've been off active duty for almost 10 years," said Agent Walter. "Plus, your cover was compromised because you became personally involved with the very target you were supposed to bring down."

"Sir, I am aware of my failures, Sir, but you know that I did my job better than any other agent, in spite of my involvements. Plus, I gave up my family and my life just for that assignment. All I'm asking for is a chance to go active again, and prove my loyalty to the bureau." Agent Walter stood and walked to where Rosa was standing at attention.

"Rosa, let's talk plainly. You know there are hits on your life if you ever surface again. It will affect your family and friends if you come out of hiding."

"Walter, I'm willing to take that chance," begged Rosa. "I really need this."

"Rosa, you're 50 years old and ..."

"And I'm still the best field agent this bureau has, if you'll give me a chance." Walter hesitated then extended his hand.

"Welcome home, Agent Smith; we've missed you."

Chapter 82

"Hi, Jenny!" greeted Donna. "I can't believe that you beat me here today."

"We have a new girl working at the coffee shop this week. I thought I'd give her a chance to show what she knows, so I took off for a few days."

"A few days, huh? Must be nice," added Donna. "I have to take leave days just to clean my apartment." Donna and Jennifer met for lunch at Applebee's on Cobb Pkwy. Suddenly, Marquis and Terry walked up from different directions; Marquis arrived first.

"Hey, Donna," waved Marquis. Then he hugged and kissed Jennifer. "How's my girl today?"

"I'm just fine," smiled Jennifer. "How are you today?"

"Better now, that I'm with you." Marquis and Jennifer had been dating for a few weeks.

"Hey!" smiled Donna. "You guys sound a little serious. I think this may grow into something special."

"Hey guys! What's for lunch?" yelled Terry.

"Terry!" greeted Jennifer. "This is a face I haven't seen in a while. How are you?"

"I'm good, I'm good. What about you guys?"

"We're fine, Terry," said Donna. "Come sit and eat with us."

"Terry," started Jennifer. "This is Marquis, my boyfriend. Marquis... Terry."

"Good to meet you, Terry."

"Terry is our niece's dad, and a really good friend to the family," added Donna. "And right now, he's gonna buy my lunch because I treated him the last time," she said as she punched him.

"Ok, Donna, I get it," said Terry. "You don't have to beat me up and take my money. I'll gladly pay. So, Marquis, what kind of work do you do?"

"I sell insurance. What about you?"

"I'm an electrician. I've been working on a couple of major projects out of town and haven't been around for a while, but I'm back now."

"Have you visited Cheryl and Keda since you've been back?" asked Jennifer.

"Of course I have."

"And?"

"Jennifer, if you're asking if Cherlene and I are back together, the answer is no. That chapter in our lives is over, and we've moved on."

"I'll believe that when I see it," smirked Donna.

"So Jennifer, how's Audrey and Dent?"

"Both are fine and doing good in school; thanks for asking, Terry."

"What is this I hear about you having a half sister somewhere?"

"Yes, that maybe true," she responded. "Her name is Sarah, but we haven't found her, yet. Nor do we know what she looks like, but the search goes on."

"Good luck with your search," said Terry. "I hope she's found soon, and is all you hope for."

"So is there another 'Ms. Right' in your bed these days?" asked Donna.

"Dee, stop that!" demanded Jennifer! "Don't ask a man that! It's not your business. So, Terry, do you have another girl?"

"Whoa! Didn't you just tell Dee not to ask a man that?"

"No! I told her not to ask a man who's in his bed. Don't be evasive, Terry; do you have a woman or not? It's a simple question!" Terry knew that he was being trapped and interrogated as he attempted to answer.

"No, I don't have a woman in my life except my daughter. I've been too busy with work to have a woman, until now."

"Maybe that's my problem, too," said Donna. "Maybe I'm too busy or something because I still don't have a man."

"Why that's crazy," said Marquis. "You're a very attractive young lady."

"I am?" smiled Donna. "Tell me about it!" She stared into his eyes. Terry felt relieved because the pressure was off of him. He knew how direct these girls could be and he didn't like getting caught in their cross fire. Marquis was fairly new to it as Jennifer and Donna stared at his every word.

"Well, you're very beautiful, and charming, and sexy and..." Jennifer kicked him on his foot. "She's not as sexy as you, baby."

"Jenny, you party pooper!" joked Donna. "You probably hear him telling you stuff like this all the time. Couldn't you let me enjoy this moment?"

"No Dee, go get your own." Terry was laughing and enjoying them arguing. After lunch, Donna spoke up.

"I've just moved into a new apartment. Anybody want to see it?"

"That's my cue," said Jennifer. "I have to go to work."

"Liar Jenny! You told me that you took off already. What about you guys?"

"I really do have to get back to work," said Marquis. Donna quickly hugged Terry.

"Please Terry, come with me; I need some help! I'll even pay for your lunch... again?"

"Ok Donna, let's go!" he groaned. "I know I'm going to regret this." They all said their good-byes and left.

Chapter 83

Tenisha drove to the AA Recovery Campus in Atlanta. A few years ago, she lived a secluded life being sheltered and overly protected by her parents, even after she gave birth to Nela and moved into her own place. Recently, things had changed and she had become the guardian for her parents. The stress of working with Donna, plus, the strain of being a single mom to a young girl, was teaming up on her. Finally, for the past five years, her mom had slipped into a drunken stupor and she didn't know why. As she pulled into the parking at the AA Center, she began to cry.

"Lord, I don't know anything about you, and sometimes I don't even want to know. But people say that you can fix anything. I don't even know what I did to get things this messed up in my life, but I am asking you to help me fix it. I need my life back; I need my mother. Please help me." Afterwards, Tenisha went inside.

"You did this to me, Kris," started Davina as she talked to herself. She had her back turned to the door as Tenisha walked in. "You took my whole life when you screwed that whore in my face." Tenisha ran over and smelled the cup Davina was drinking from.

"Mom! Why are you still drinking? How did you get alcohol in here?"

"It's been an ongoing problem with her," said Olive, the nurse. "You're the one spending the money to keep her here so we've tried to accommodate you. But, she fights, she rebels, she gets booze somehow, and she never takes her pills. Ms. Cuyler, your mom is becoming a threat to the other nurses that work here. I saw you come in and decided to tell you that she must change now, or she will be sent home next week." Tenisha sat down and just stared at her mom. She was speechless as the nurse walked out.

"All of this is Kris' fault. He should have never brought me here!" yelled Davina.

"What is dad's fault, Mom? Is it Keisha? Is it you sleeping with Antwaun? Dad didn't do that ---you did! Mom, why do you keep holding onto this? It's ruining everything!" She started to cry. "I need my mom back." Davina hadn't seen Tenisha cry like this since Rubik broke her heart in college. Davina was speechless.

"Mom, why don't you trust me?"

"I do trust you, baby," she comforted. "You are the only one I can trust in this whole world."

"When you and Dad told me about your college years with Keisha and Antwaun, I felt your hurt and I thought you were gonna die. But you pulled through that same day and I was so proud of you. You seemed to let it all go. But, the next day, I found you drunk and waddling in piss, and blaming Dad again. This time, he doesn't even know why. What happened, Mom? Why won't you talk to me? Nela asks for you, your friends call for you, and Dad put them off. Please Mom, tell me something. I don't know what else to do."

"Your Dad put us both in this mess and now he just..." Tenisha snapped! She leaped from the chair, put her hands around her mom's neck, and slammed her into the wall while yelling.

"Don't tell me anymore that you being here is my dad's fault! It's your fault, Mom! Dad confessed what he did and he apologized! What more do you want from him? These people are about to put you out and now Dad is welcoming a divorce. Then what are you gonna do, Mom?" Tenisha released her.

"Tenisha..."

"Shut up, Mom! You haven't wanted to talk to me for the past five years, so don't talk now: Listen!" Tenisha's tears began to fall as she calmed and continued.

"Five years ago after I found you like this, you begged me not to let Dad put you away. So I dealt with you for 3 years after that and things got worse; so bad, you forced me to put you in AA. You come out, then you're right back. Well, this is the last time, Mother. You once told Dad that if he didn't talk to me and tell me what I needed to know, that you would divorce him and take everything he's got. I will be back tomorrow, Mother. When I come, either be sober and back to normal, or justify to me why you are putting us through this. Or so help me God, if I don't pack your things myself and have you put away until you come to your senses! Then Dad will divorce you and I will see to it that he loses nothing. Bye Mom, I'll see you tomorrow!"Davina was shocked, but understanding, as Tenisha turned to leave.

"My second choice in college was to be a biologist or to major in chemistry," spoke Davina. Tenisha stood in the door with her back turned and listened. "I was pretty good at it, too. It was fascinating to learn about the elements of nature and about the natural man. When a man and a woman falls in love, there are certain things they overlook about each other, because they want to make the relationship work. Sometimes after they've learned each other, they find that one of them is stronger than the other. Sometimes it's a good match, and sometimes it isn't. That's kinda the way blood cells are, too."

"Blood cells?" Tenisha turned angrily. "Mom, what does this have to do with anything?"

"I'm not drunk, Tenisha. Just listen to me, ok. Once a woman becomes pregnant, the child in her receives separate sources of genetic codes from each parent called Alleles. Alleles are classified as A, B, AB, or O. The child will not be born without having one of these Alleles. However, A and B are the most dominant over O, and AB negative is the rarest in the world." Tenisha's interest peaked because she knew that her blood type and her daughter's is AB negative, and her mom had just mentioned it. "A child will not be born without having one of these Alleles from the donor parents," continued Davina.

"So how does a child choose which parent's blood type he will be?" asked Tenisha.

"A child can't decide nor does the parents," continued Davina. "But the parent with the most dominates Alleles or blood type will also determine the blood type of the child." Tenisha begin to think.

"So, since Rubik is an O positive, and mine is an AB negative, Nela is also an AB negative because my blood is more dominant than Rubik's O?"

"Yes, baby you got it," shouted Davina. She dropped a few tears. Tenisha knew that her mom was finally talking to her. Davina dropped her head, but Tenisha still didn't quite understand.

"Ok, Mom, I get it. My blood is more dominant than Rubik's, so Nela has my blood type. That's even better knowing that Nela will take after me."

"No Tenisha, that may not be true. She has your blood, but that won't decide her character."

"Then tell me what are you saying, Mom?" Davina took Tenisha's hands and they sat on the edge of the bed.

"Honey, other than your father, I've only had sex with one other man in my life."

"Yes, I know---Antwaun Banks." Davina dropped her head again, and this time she said nothing. She felt that she had said all she needed to say as she waited for Tenisha to take the lead. Tenisha sensed that about her mom, but was still a bit confused. Finally, she understood that her mom wasn't talking about her, Rubik, and Nela at all.

"Mom, what is your blood type?"

"I'm a B positive," said Davina.

"And what's Dad's blood type?"

"He's an O positive." Tenisha was puzzled.

"That means that I should be an O positive or a B positive, doesn't it?" Davina nodded.

"If such were the case of your conception, yes." Tenisha stood and walked across the room very nervously.

"Mom, are you saying what I think you're saying?" Davina stood and went to the window as she dropped tears and cried.

"You are a B positive, Dad is an O positive, and I am an AB negative. Are you telling me that..." Tenisha paused, paced the floor then just stared at Davina.

"I am so sorry, Tenisha. I am sooo sorry!" said Davina in tears as she attempted to hug Tenisha, but Tenisha pulled away. Then she emotionally turned from her Mom and asked,

"Mother, what is Antwaun Banks blood type?" Davina didn't answer as Tenisha turned and gave her the most hurtful look she had ever seen. As Tenisha ran to her car, Davina nervously dropped to her knees. Tenisha entered her car and cried a deep... painful... soul screaming cry, of a lost child needing the comfort that only a Mother could give. But her Mother, whom she trusted above all others, had just betrayed her by revealing to her that Antwaun Banks was her real Dad. More than that, Tenisha learned that Donna Banks, the one person who despised her the most, was her sister. She had finally gotten what she'd been praying for, and now she didn't want it. Tenisha was hurting... beyond her pain.

Chapter 84

"Hey, this place is empty!" said Terry.

"That's because I have to paint and clean up and clean the windows and a whole lot of stuff," said Donna.

"This place looks immaculate! Why do you want to change it?"

"It's not my colors, Terry. The colors are loud and I'm a mellow kind of girl."

"Ok, what do you want me to do?" asked Terry. Donna went to the closet and opened it. Inside she had paint, drop cloths, rollers, brushes, brooms, mops, wax, cleaning supplies, and three sets of work coveralls. "There are three sets of coveralls in there. Who had you planned to come by?"

"Those are for me, Cheryl, and Jennifer, or in this case... you and me. Come on, Terry, you ask too many questions when we need to be working."

For the rest of the day, Donna and Terry completely refurbished her apartment. They laughed, played, and had fun, such as Donna never had with a man before. Neither had Terry interacted with a woman in a long time. They were instantly becoming good friends and they liked each other.

"So, Terry, do you ever miss Cheryl being in your life?"

"I think about her sometimes, but our break up was for the best."

"How can you say that when you have a little girl with her? What about your daughter?"

"Cherlene has chosen a different lifestyle than the one I planned for her and my child. My child would have always seen us fighting and disagreeing. What kind of life is that for a child?"

"Well, when you put it like that, I can understand and agree with you. So, do you still love Cheryl?"

"She was my first love so I will always have feelings for her. But my mind is made up and I don't want to be with her anymore."

"What do you want, Terry?"

"I want to finish painting!" Then he rolled paint up Donna's arm and onto her jaw.

"Oh! I will get you back for that!" She chased him through the apartment as they played and grew closer as friends.

****

Tenisha sat in the parking lot of the AA Recovery Campus, crying after she learned that she was not her dad's child.

"Mom, how could you?" she thought. *"How could you hurt me like this?"* After a while, Tenisha went back inside and sat on her mom's bed.

"So, is that why you're here?" asked Tenisha sadly.

"When I found out, I knew my life was over and I didn't know what to do. I guess that's why I'm here because I couldn't tell Kris. Even though I feel like he forced me to do what I did, I couldn't take you away from him. He loves you so much."

"You could never take me away from Dad, Mom. I just wish you had told me sooner, and we could have avoided all of this. How did you find out about this, anyway?"

"I knew Antwaun was in prison, and just so happen that I know the Warden personally, where he is. So I convinced the Warden to let me see Antwaun's medical records, and he did. I saw that Antwaun's blood type was an AB negative like yours and Nela's and I knew the truth."

"But on that day when you and Dad told me about your college years, you seemed ok, afterward. You were even making plans to do your 'ride-the –pony' thing with Dad that night, but the next day everything changed. Is that when you learned about the blood thing?"

"I did learn about the blood types the next day, but what tipped me off was you and Nela, the day before. Nela loves to eat raw carrots and I've seen you nibbling on them a few times. The only person I know that eats carrots like that is Antwaun, and you and Nela made me curious. I did my research the next day and learned the truth. What are we gonna do now, Tenisha?"

"We're not gonna tell Dad, that's for sure," paused Tenisha. "I've always wanted a sister, but I never knew how to tell you. Do you remember the girl that got promoted beside me at the luncheon?"

"Yes, her name is Donna something. Why? What are you saying?"

"Her name is Donna Banks and she is Antwaun and Keisha Bank's daughter."

"Oh my Lord! That means that she's your half si..."

"Yes, Mom, she is my half-sister and my co-worker. Also, I learned today that Dad is not the only one guilty of past sin in his college days, but you are too, Mom."

"Honey, I told you why I did what I did! I didn't want Antwaun!"

"Mom, that's only part of the problem."

"What are you saying?"

"I'm saying that Dad wasn't the only one driven by love for Keisha Banks, but you were, too. That's why things are worst than you even know."

"Tenisha, honey, I'm confused, now. What are you talking about?"

"Keisha Banks was smart, explosive, flirty, spontaneous, beautiful, and sexy, as well as talented, and everybody liked her. You wanted to be her but when you couldn't, you became her enemy. Now, that same hatred has become a generational curse between her daughter and yours. Because of yours and Keisha's hatred for each other, that same curse now resides between Donna and me---we are sisters, yet we are enemies! Dad didn't do that---you did!" Davina was shocked and speechless as Tenisha's eyes filled with tears.

"Honey, I don't know what to say," said Davina. Tenisha continued to fuss as she and Davina painfully embraced the truth about their life styles.

"Mom, stop blaming Dad because you have fallen just as short as he has. He who is without sin, let him cast the first stone. Please stop throwing stones at Dad and let's just move on." Davina paused.

"Ok, Tenisha, you're right. I've been so wrong, and I'm gonna change." Tenisha and Davina sat on the bed beside each other and just thought about everything for almost 30 minutes without a word. Then Tenisha laid her head on Davina's shoulder.

"Too late," said Davina. "I got to pee."

"Mom, is all of this over, now? Are you ok with yourself and Dad and life?"

"Yes baby, thanks to you, I am."

"Can we go home now, cause I really need a drink," said Tenisha. Davina reached under the mattress and pulled out a flask and handed it to Tenisha. Tenisha just looked at her and shook her head. They both giggled.

Chapter 85

For the next few days, Donna and Terry spent a lot of time helping movers and organizing her new apartment. She moved from Cumberland Glen Apartments on Cobb Parkway to Highland of West Village on West Village Place, so she wouldn't be to far from Jennifer and Cherlene.

"Terry, because of you, I haven't had to call my sisters at all and we are almost done. Thank you so much!" She hugged him then patted his butt.

"Dee, what are you doing?" he screamed.

"Aw hush! I've seen Cherlene do that to you many times and you know you liked it."

"Yeah but... that was different! We were..."

"What? Friends? So are you and I," smiled Donna. Terry realized that she was truly innocent in her thoughts so he tried to explain.

"Donna, I've had so much fun with you over the past week. It's really been fun."

"Right! I've had fun with you, too. So why are you trip'n over a little pat on the butt?"

"Because you just don't do that to a man unless you have a personal claim on him."

"So when guys in sports pat each other like that, they have this personal claim, huh? Oooh, that don't sound too good, Terry." Terry did his best to explain but Donna kept twisting his words. Then she grabbed his butt again and ran.

"Donna!" screamed Terry as he ran through the apartment behind her and pinched her butt. Then in fun they had a butt pinching contest as they ended up falling on the floor. Terry laid face to face on top of her.

"Terry, what is that?" Donna felt a bulge in Terry's pants.

"What is what?" he asked.

"What is that I feel against my leg?" Terry quickly stood and walked away.

"What's wrong, Terry? Are you sad?"

"No Donna, you don't understand!"

"I want to understand, Terry; please help me!" He grabbed her and kissed her then he backed away.

"I'll call you later, Donna. Good night." As he left, Donna was speechless.

Chapter 86

"Yeah," answered Hookman.

"This is the D-Lo. What's up?" D-Lo was at Hinton State Prison on a cell phone.

"Took you a long time to finally call, man. A lot of things have changed since you've been gone----almost 7 years now. What's up?"

"It's time to finish what we've started. You game?"

"Finish what, man? Those deals with the weapons have long been dead!"

"I'm not talking about that!" he shouted. "I'm talking about Coldblood, Lo-Down, and that bitch that got me put here. It's time for them to pay. So are you game or not?"

"D-Lo, how are you gonna do something from inside? Besides, that stuff is over with."

"It ain't over until I say it's over!" shouted D-Lo. "Now you're the only family I've got, and you at least owe me this, since you're out there and I'm in here. That's all I ask. I want Coldblood knocked off. Now, what's it gonna be?"

"What do you want me to do, D-Lo?"

"Just stand by for now," said D-Lo. "I'll tell you when to move. Meantime, find out what you can and who all was connected to taking my money. Later."

****

Shaun stalked the streets alone one August morning as he left the foster care home where he lived. He was almost 17 years old and it was the first day of school for his Junior year. Shaun was big like a football player, so most people thought he was a senior or even in college, until they got to know him. Then they would realize that he was nothing but trouble and they stayed away. As he walked to school, he noticed two young kids---a girl and a boy stealing from the fruit stand. He laughed and moved on as the streak of ice and the fire continued toward the earth.

****

Cherlene was home rushing about that same morning for hers and Makeda's first day of school as well. Makeda was going to Griffin High School, while Cherlene was heading to Campbell High School to teach.

"Keda, don't forget to take your lunch from the frig!" yelled Cherlene.

"Ew! Your mom makes you take your lunch? How elementary is that?" said Karla, Makeda's friend.

"I know right," said Makeda. "I always give it away and eat with everybody else. Yes Mom, I got it!" she yelled. "See you later!" Makeda and Karla left. Cherlene jumped in her car, and sped down her street on Winchester Trail.

"Why am I rushing?" she thought. *"I'm way ahead of schedule."* Suddenly, she crashed into the car ahead of her. She jumped out to see the damage.

"Oh, I am so sorry, Sir, are you o... Clint?"

"Hello, Cherlene. It's been a long time." Cherlene smiled and they hugged.

"Wait a minute! Did you deliberately pull out in front of me to get my attention? You could've been hurt or killed!"

"Did it work? Besides, it's only a scratch. So, what'cha doing later on?" Cherlene knew where this was leading to, so she quickly walked away. Clint grabbed her hand and stopped her.

"No, no, Clint! We can't start this again! I'm a high school teacher, now, and I have a daughter that's 14 years old." Clint quickly kissed her and she loved it. Since it had been a while, it felt good. But when he squeezed her butt, she slapped him and ran to her car.

"I'll call you!" he yelled as she sped off.

"No!" she yelled back. Cherlene began to reminisce about the good times she had in bed with Clint. She found herself sitting at the traffic light reliving the moments when a car horn blew from behind her. She threw up a finger and sped off.

"Good morning, class," she greeted as she walked in. "I see that you're all early, too."

"No, Ma'am, we're not," said a student. "Time changed last night and you didn't set your clock; you're late!"

"Guess we know who's going to be our class big mouth, already, don't we? What's your name?"

"Shaun, I'm Shaun Taylor, but you can call me... anytime." Shaun laughed as the ice and the fire continued on its course to the earth.

Chapter 87

"It's been a really busy summer, folks," spoke Mr. Golden. "And a heck of a long day. School kids started today and we need somebody on alert for the gangsters and the shooters. This generation of whacko's are crazy, so we know they will be out there. At the same time, we have the traffic and the road ragers, along with the after school neighborhood drugs and violence. This month is gonna be hot and I need someone covering all these areas."

"I'll take the neighborhood drugs and violence," yelled Donna.

"I figured you would, Ms. Banks. You like to be in the heat of things."

"Sir, I'll take the schools and watch the kids," said Tenisha.

"I was hoping you would, Ms. Cuyler. You and Ms. Banks can both focus on the traffic and work together." Donna looked at Tenisha and snickered. "What was that, Ms. Banks? I didn't hear you!"

"Nothing, Sir! Just had a little itch on my nose, that's all!"

"That lying little slut," thought Tenisha. *"Ok Lord, you helped me with Mom and things are fine again. Thank you. But I think this new problem may be more complex. But, I promise that I will try to love her if she will let me."*

"That's all, folks," ended Mr. Golden. "Now go home and be ready to go on tomorrow!" Everyone headed out.

"Take care of those kids, Glamour Bitch," smile Donna as she walked by Tenisha. "See you tomorrow." Tenisha looked up.

"See what I mean, Lord? If you don't fix this one, then I will... my way."

****

"On tomorrow, I want you to bring a short paragraph; no more than one-half page, telling me about your favorite leader in the world, and why," instructed Cherlene. Then she heard, *"The Curse Must Be Broken!"* but she ignored it.

"What? I thought this was a history class!" yelled Shaun. "Why are we to write about someone who may not be dead, yet?"

"A person doesn't have to be dead in order to have been a good leader and made history, Shaun. Besides, I just want to see where your head is, so write the story."

"You're a weird teacher, Ms. Tullis." Suddenly, the bell ranged.

****

Donna was freshening up her apartment before Terry arrived. She had called and left a message for him to come by so she could cook for him in appreciation for his help. When Terry kissed her, something inside of her changed and she didn't know how to face it. It was her first real kiss and she was afraid to even talk to anybody about it other than Terry.

"Hey Dee," spoke Terry as she opened the door.

"Wow! Look at you!" she said admiring his sports jacket and slacks. "I thought you were a jeans kinda guy. Never seen you like this before."

"Does that mean you like it?"

"Oh, I love it! Come on in. I'm almost done. We can eat in a minute."

"Dee, I must say that I was surprise to get your message after listening to how Cherlene and Jennifer talked about your cooking."

"Yeah, I know right! They say I can't cook, but tonight, you can be the judge for yourself."

"Plus, I was more surprised to hear from you after what I did the other day."

"What! You mean the kiss? Oh that little old thing? Don't let it bother you," she laughed. "I hadn't even thought about it, anymore, until you brought it up."

"Really? That's good, Dee! Cause that's all I've been thinking about."

Suddenly, the oven flooded the kitchen with smoke and the skillet on the stove went ablaze. Donna threw a towel on the skillet, then accidentally snatched the skillet onto the floor while pork chops flew everywhere.

"I see the chops," said Terry. "What's in the oven?" Donna looked sad.

"It was suppose to be a bean casserole with cheese," said Donna. "I guess my sisters are right. I'll never get this cooking thing. So what'll we do now?" Terry checked his watch then headed to the closet where he knew the work clothes were.

"Come on, Dee; get undressed!"

"What?"

"Here, put this on." He tossed her a pair of coveralls. "It's still early so we have time to cook, and I'm gonna show you how to do it. Do you have more chops?" Donna was very excited as she lounged around his neck. She really like him and was happy that he didn't just leave when she ruined the dinner. The best part of the evening was helping Terry prepare the meal. They had a lot of fun. Afterwards, they said good night and Terry left.

Chapter 88

That same night after the first day of school, Shaun saw a couple of young gangsters hanging around a convenient store. Then he had an idea. He knew they were inexperienced and waiting for their leader. So he quickly pulled his hat over his face and walked into the convenient store. When the cashier opened his drawer for a customer, Shaun leaps across the counter and snatched money from the register before the cashier could get it closed. Then he ran toward the gangsters while stripping off his hat and jacket, yelling,

"Gun! Gun!" The two young gangsters took off running just as the store owner ran out, and as Shaun tossed his hat and jacket behind the dumpster. "There they run!" shouted Shaun.

"Did you get a look at them?" asked the store owner.

"No! I thought they were coming for me so I got out of the way."

"Damn kids," said the store owner. "They're gonna get themselves shot."

A few minutes later, when the two young gangsters saw Shaun again, they chased him into a residential area where Shaun hid until he could elude them.

"Whoa! What have we here?" smiled Shaun. "Two young tenderonies and a stud!" Shaun was just outside the wooden fence that surrounded Cherlene's backyard. She had recently bought the place since she became a teacher and didn't believe it to be a neighborhood where stalkers and others existed. Therefore, her rear windows and curtains stayed slightly opened to allow the breeze to settle in.

Shaun saw Makeda and Karla laughing and giggling as they took turns lap dancing Scott, a young boy from their school.

"Hee, Hee! Your turn," said Karla.

"Why can't he dance for us, sometimes?" asked Makeda.

"I can do that," laughed Scott. Scott quickly stood, removed his shirt, and started twirling it while he danced to the music for the girls. They laughed and clapped.

"Keep it down in there, girls," yelled Cherlene as she entered her bedroom.

"My, my, my!" smiled Shaun. "That's what I'm talking about!" He saw Cherlene through her bedroom window as she undressed to prepare for her bath. After Cherlene went to the bathroom, he saw Makeda and Karla sneaking Scott out of the house.

"Good night, Ms. Cherlene," yelled Karla. "See you tomorrow."

"Two sneaky little tender sluts!" thought Shaun. After a while, Cherlene came back to her bedroom wearing only her robe, which was opened. Shaun could clearly see her naked body as he went closer to the view.

All during the day, Cherlene's mind had been on Clint and the kiss he gave her that morning. She was tempted to call him, but she knew that Makeda was too young to experience a man coming into their home for such as this. So she erased the idea from her mind and continued to oil and moisturize her body.

"Oh it's been such a long time since I've had sex," she thought. *"Sure would feel good tonight."* Cherlene began to get a little freaky as she rubbed on herself. Her desire for sex became so strong, she went to her closet and found a gift that was given to her when she passed her teachers' certification, which was a vibrator.

Cherlene was 32 years old and had never needed one until tonight. Shaun watched as she caressed herself in the mood and put the vibrator to work. Cherlene was very good at pleasing her lovers so she pretended she was with them as she worked the vibrator.

"Aw sookie sookie, now!" moaned Shaun. "Freaky baby, freaky!" A few minutes later, Cherlene let out a yell of anger and slung the vibrator hard against the wall. Makeda came running in.

"Mom, are you ok? What was that noise?"

"Nothing baby," said Cherlene calmly. "Just mommy throwing out some trash." She hugged Makeda then they began to play and have fun. Shortly afterwards, the lights went out while Cherlene and her daughter went to sleep.

That night, Shaun was changed forever. He had never seen anything like that before, nor felt his body respond like that. Within the few minutes that Cherlene had worked the vibrator, she had stolen his heart and Shaun was in love.

High in the sky, the streak of ice and the ball of fire continued to speed to the earth.

Chapter 89

The next day, Shaun couldn't wait to get to school and see Cherlene. He even completed his homework which was rare for him. Seeing Cherlene the night before had changed him and he was going to school with a new attitude.

Nevertheless, he still enjoyed seeing certain routine things and people as he journeyed along the way. So he waited near a street corner for a few minutes. As usual, he saw the little girl and boy sneak up to the fruit stand and steal fruit while on their way to school. They were always on time, and they never got caught. Shaun thought it was so funny.

As Shaun headed to school, two unusual things happen that morning. A man, being chased by the police, tossed something in a trash can not far from where he was walking. Shaun went to the trash can and took it just before the police came looking for it. It was a .40 caliber pistol that the man used to rob a liquor store with a few nights before. Someone had recognized him and called the cops.

Shaun tucked the gun in his pants and watched the police drive the man away. As he walked along, he saw this big kid, about 12 years old, ride his bike right into this little four-eyed kid and knock him down. They were just outside of the elementary school as Shaun was passing by. Shaun knew that the bigger kid was a bully.

"Where's my money?" asked the bully. "I told you to bring your whole piggy bank today, so where is it?" The little boy seemed so scared as the bully shoved him around. "Where is the piggy?" demanded the bully.

"My Mom... my Mom took... it to..." The little boy started to pee on himself. The bully didn't seem to care. He emptied the little boys pockets and took his sack lunch. Then he heard a click behind his head. Shaun was pointing the gun at him.

"Let's go," said Shaun. "Both of you." He forced the boys around the building by the trees where they couldn't be seen. "Give me the money and the lunch." The bully gave it up. "Now give me all your other money, too." The bully quickly gave it up in fear of being shot. "Now both of you take off your clothes; even your undershorts." The boys did it and stood butt naked. "Now switch clothes and put them back on; even the undershorts," added Shaun. The two boys were shocked.

"I can't fit his clothes," said the bully. Shaun aimed the pistol at the bully's penis. The bully quickly grabbed the little boy's wet clothes and squeezed in them. When the little boy saw the bully wearing his small wet clothes he laughed so hard, other students came around to see what was happening. Shaun took the bully's ten speed bike and left. He ate the sandwiches along the way as he went to school.

****

"Good Morning, class," said Cherlene. "I want everyone who completed their assignment to hold it in their hand and walk to the back of the class." All the students moved except three. Cherlene checked the students that stood and ignored the ones still sitting. After she was sure the kids standing had done the assignment, she asked them to sit again.

"For those of you who did not do your assignment, you will stay over today for at least one hour or until you complete them, whichever is the longest."

"I have football practice today," said the boy. "I can't stay."

"You can and you will, Sir, or you will be cut from the team," said Cherlene.

"My mom works two jobs and she doesn't have time to wait that long," said one girl.

"Then you should be ashamed of yourself, young lady," scolded Cherlene. "Not only are you old enough to work after school and help your mom, but you should also catch the bus or the train home like many other students, and stop your mom from having to pick you up. Surely, I do not feel sorry for you. So if you are not here at 3:15 today, I will see to it that you become a detention major." When the last girl saw what happen to the first two kids, she just sat down and said,

"Yes, Ma'am, I'll be here."

"Good choice!" said Cherlene. "Now who want to talk about their assignment first?"

"I will," said Shaun.

"Mr. Taylor, I hope you don't disrupt class today because I'm not with it, nor feeling it. Now come up and tell us about your favorite leader." Shaun stood tall and proud as he began to talk.

"My favorite leader in the world is my dad, Mr. Carl 'Coldblood' Simmons, Jr. My dad is a leader of the Demon-Bloods and he don't play! He'll take you out in a heartbeat. Right now, he is still on the run from the cops but I am expec..."

"Hold on, Shaun." Cherlene had just remembered the story from the news a few years ago. "I know your dad is an excellent leader, but I need to discuss your story with you before you tell it. You are not under punishment, but I would like for you to stay over today, so we can talk, ok?" Shaun nodded in agreement.

"Good," said Cherlene. "Who's next?"

At 3:15 when school was over, Shaun was the first student back to see Cherlene. He had been thinking about her all day and couldn't wait for his private time to talk to her. When she asked him to stay over, little did she know that she made his day.

"What do you want to talk to me about, Ms. Tullis?"

"Would it be a problem if I hear the story of the students before we talk? I'll drop you off at home if that will help."

"No, that will be fine. I can wait---take your time." An hour and fifteen minutes later, Cherlene talked to Shaun.

"Shaun, I think I may know a little about your home situation, so would you mind talking to me about it?"

"What do you want to know, Ms. Tullis?"

"You started off earlier today talking about your dad and him being a gangster. Why do you think that's a good thing to talk about?"

"I never looked at it as being good or bad, Ms. Tullis. You told us to write about our favorite leader in the world and my dad is mine. What's wrong with that?"

For the next hour or so, Cherlene learned about Shaun's family situation while trying to teach him about morals, character, values, and choices. Shaun was no idiot because he had made his way to the 11th grade on his own. But he was so enticed by Cherlene and all he knew about her, that what she said about him and his family didn't register to him.

"Shaun, it's getting late and I have to go home, now. Can I drop you off somewhere---maybe home?"

"Oh no, that's ok. I have my bike and I don't live far from here."

"Ok then, I'll see you tomorrow. By the way, thank you for staying over. And I hope that things get better for you and your dad." Then they left.

Immediately after dark, Shaun made his way to Cherlene's backyard and began to stalk her. Cherlene, who is easily sexually aroused, had held strong against her desires for over three years before the surprise kiss came from Clint. Now, every night when she came home, she was out of control, rubbing... feeling... squeezing... poking... and moaning.

For the next few weeks, Shaun followed his normal routine as he fell more in love with Cherlene---school, talk to Cherlene, make trouble until dark, then hide out and stalk Cherlene and Makeda. He even started being nice and attentive in her class and Cherlene took notice. Then he started doing his homework, regularly, although it was mostly wrong. He noticed that whenever he did it wrong, Cherlene would spend extra time with him after school or during her study hall class, just to help him get on track.

Soon, he started getting better grades and Cherlene was proud of him and herself. She was still kinda new at teaching high school kids and Shaun was the first student she took a personal liking to. She didn't see any harm in tutoring him because he showed daily improvement in his grades in all classes, and he was treating her like she was the best teacher in the school. Plus, Shaun had a manly body and mature ways for his age.

Little did she know that Shaun's whole mission was to have sex with her, someday, and he was patiently working toward that goal.

Shaun soon became her favorite student. Therefore, she allowed him to come by her home to help out around the house after school and some weekends. Sometimes, he would see certain teachers at school, or men near her home, making passes at Cherlene or just admiring her sexy body.

At first, he hated it and wanted to hurt the men. Then he realized that each day after Cherlene flirted or talked with one of the men, she'd go home that night, and put on a sex show as he stalked her.

Cherlene had all kinds of gels and sex toys by now, and she was using them to full capacity. Not only was she creating a monster in Shaun as he stalked her night after night, but she would get so engrossed in her sex acts, she never noticed Makeda, her daughter, also heard her moaning and groaning behind the bedroom door late at night.

Eventually, Makeda being curious started peeking through the door as she learned from her mom about sex and self-satisfaction. Night after night, Makeda watched Cherlene, as Shaun watched them both. Meantime, the ice and the fire stayed on its course toward the earth.

Chapter 90

"The Curse Must Be Broken!" came the whisper many times to Jennifer's hearing.

"Susie, you have to help me!" said Jennifer. "I am going crazy!"

"What's the matter, Jennifer?"

"I can't shake these urges. I'm going to do something soon; I can feel it! I need to take control of myself or I know it will just happen!"

Jennifer, who had also bought a house on Foxwood Trail SE in Smyrna, was in her living room talking to Susie about her problem. Jennifer and J.J. were opening a string of coffee and donut shops throughout Atlanta and the south, yet, Jennifer still couldn't shake her desire to steal and take things.

"I have an idea!" said Susie. "I know you're gonna go out and steal everything no matter what I say so why don't you do some good with it, like you did me, when I first met you?"

"You mean, steal for others?"

"That's not exactly what I'm saying," said Susie. "I'm saying that there are a lot of homeless people and others less fortunate than you and I are. Do something to help them. The day I came to the Mall and you dropped that necklace in my pocket, was one of the happiest days of my life.

I'm not a thief, Jennifer, like you keep thinking. But on the day I met you, I was two months behind on my rent and my landlord wasn't allowing me to go for three. Plus, my kids were hungry and I didn't have money for food because I used it to pay the back rent. I needed a total of $1400.00 to pay rent for 3 months and buy food or I had to get out by the next day. You came along and dropped a $2500.00 necklace in my pocket. The jeweler thought he was getting a steal when I told him I only wanted $1400 for the necklace... no more no less.

You made me a happy woman, that day, and I will be forever in your debt. Now, all I'm saying is that you should use what you have as a blessing and don't let it be a curse to you. Use it to help others like you did me, and your light will brighte the night for a lot of people who need you."

Susie's appeal had given Jennifer purpose. For the next week or so, Jennifer, along with Audrey and Dent, visited every mall around the metro Atlanta area—from Shannon Mall to the south, all the way to the Mall of Georgia to the north; from the Stonecrest Mall to the east, to the West End Mall to the west.

Jennifer's basement was full of stolen items from coats, clothes, shoes, food, toys, jewelry, watches, camera's, lap-tops, deodorants, soaps, washing powder, bleach, pots, pans, cookware, ---you name it, she had it. She took most of these things during the day when stores were least expecting her to do it. At night, she did the more timely jobs---some stores opened; some had closed. She took flat screen TVs, expensive jewelry, clothes, and tools.

For some reason, she had no fear as she sometimes set off store alarms just to outrun or out maneuver security guards and cops until their back up came. Then she would disappear into the night. When she came home, Audrey and Dent would always be waiting for her, because they too, were excited about participating in their mom's work.

"Mom, our basement is almost full," said Audrey. "What are we gonna do with all the stuff?"

"We're gonna bag what we can. Then this weekend when you're out of school, we will travel over Atlanta to the homeless and less fortunate areas and give it away."

"Kool!" said Audrey and Dent.

That weekend, Jennifer and her kids did just that. Jennifer disguised herself so that people she helped would have a hard time telling the cops who she really was. Some people even thought she was a guy because she tucked her hair and wore a mustache. To some, she was a clown and to many she was wonder woman behind a mask.

In the event the items were traceable, she made sure that the people she gave them to could not clearly identify her, or her kids, or her vehicle.

Late that Sunday afternoon, Jennifer had distributed most of the items and she was tired. She was almost home when she pulled over to get a paper to see if there were any stories about her thefts. She left her car only for a minute.

When she returned, Audrey and Dent were gone. She looked around and saw them about a block away, sneaking up to a fruit stand, to steal fruit. They had everything precisely timed as Jennifer watched.

"Sneaky little devils," she thought. *"They're too young for this. If I can see them, then someone else can see them, too."* Jennifer didn't know that Shaun already had. Then she heard the whisper, *"The Curse Must Be Broken!"* She drove home being concerned while thinking about what she and her kids had become.

Chapter 91

The bell rang as Cherlene's students started to leave.

"Ok kids," yelled Cherlene. "You have a very important test tomorrow, so please study and get your rest tonight." Everybody left except Shaun as her next class entered. "Shaun, I want you to stay home tonight and study, too. Don't worry about coming by the house today. You've been looking a little tired lately, even though you leave my home in plenty of time to rest."

"No Cherlene," he blurted. "I mean... Ms. Tullis! I can come by! I'm fine... honest!" Cherlene smiled. She knew he had become attached to her plus, he was her favorite student.

"Shaun, this is an important test that will affect your grades if you don't prepare for it. Now promise me that you will go straight home and study, and get your proper rest. Besides, I think I will to get to bed early myself, ok? I'll see you tomorrow in class."

Shaun was angry as he hesitantly left the classroom. He wanted to go home with Cherlene, but she said no. As usual, shortly after dark, Shaun was outside of her window. To his surprise, he saw Cherlene come into her bedroom fully dressed. Then she fell on the bed and slept.

Makeda tucked her in, turned the light out, and was fast asleep, right beside her mother. Shaun went home, being angry. It was late as Shaun checked his room then ran to see Ms. Myrtice in the kitchen.

"Where's Bobby?" he asked. "Isn't it a little late for him to be out in the park?"

"Bobby is 14 years old and like you, he comes and goes when he wants to. You've been a very bad influence on that boy, and I don't like the direction he's heading." Shaun frowned at her and headed out. "He's not in the park!" yelled Ms. Myrtice. Shaun stopped.

"Where is he then?"

"He was picked up in the projects somewhere for selling marijuana along with his buddies. They say they're charging him as an adult," continued Ms. Myrtice. "He has a $10,000 bond and I don't have a dime for that." Shaun was shocked!

"If you had the money, would you go get him out?"

"I suppose so," she said. "I need $1000 dollars to do that, though."

Shaun went to check his funds. Cherlene had paid him almost $300.00 dollars for the weeks he helped her. Currently, he only had about $200.00. He entered the train, thinking... trying to figure out how to get the money. He ended up in Decatur, back on the steps of his old apartment, with his pistol in his hand while talking to his mother.

"I know you would know what to do, Mom, but I don't. Me and Bobby and the other boys don't have anybody to help us. Bobby is in trouble now. I guess it's up to me to help him. Ms. Myrtice doesn't have the money and I have only $200. I need $800 more, Mom. What should I do?"

Suddenly, Shaun saw a man strong arm robbing another man, after hitting him and knocking him out. Shaun followed after the man as he ran away because he knew the neighborhood well.

He saw the man turn the corner, then jump into a car and count the money he had just stolen. Shaun walked up to the window and nervously pointed the gun at the robber. The man could tell that Shaun was nervous as he raised his hands and stepped out of the car.

"You're gonna hurt somebody with that thing, young man. Why don't you just give it to m..."

"Bang!" The gun fired and the bullet scraped the man's jaw.

"Hey! What do you want, man?" yelled the robber. Then he slung the money at Shaun and ran away. Shaun grabbed the money and sat in the car as the heavenly ice and the fire entered the earth's atmosphere. Suddenly, it veiled itself and became a mighty rushing wind.

"$150.00 dollars," he counted. "I need $650 more." When he saw the keys in the car, he started it then banged his way from where it was parked until he learned how to drive it. Soon, he was recklessly heading down Glenwood toward I-20. Twenty minutes later, he was pistol whipping a shopper in the parking lot of the Lakewood Mall while taking his money.

"Only $55 dollars," counted Shaun. Nevertheless, he had found his answer. From malls, to convenient stores, to residential areas, Shaun traveled I-285 pistol whipping men and strong arm robbing them. He had well over a thousand dollars, but he was enjoying the rush he was experiencing when people submitted before him.

Finally, as he sat in the parking area at a Grocery Store, he saw a silhouette of someone walking between the cars toward him. So he slid down in the seat and waited.

"This will be my last one," he thought. *"It's late and I have to see Ms. Tullis, tomorrow."* As the steps came closer, the mighty rushing wind entered him as he jumped out of the car, and started hitting a woman over the head. As she screamed, her voice sounded familiar.

"Mom?" sounded Shaun as he looked into her face. Visions of his mom being beaten flashed in his head. The woman was too scared to move as she sat on the ground begging for her life. All Shaun could see and hear was his mother and what she went through as he jumped into the car and left.

Shaun dumped the car a few blocks from his home, then he beat on the door until Ms. Myrtice got up and let him in. He handed her the money, then went to bed and cried. Shaun knew that he needed help.

The next morning Cherlene noticed that Shaun was absent as the class was given their test.

"Where is he?" she wondered. *"He's never been late for my class."*

At 9 a.m. Ms. Myrtice headed to see the bondsman. Shaun came in at 3:30 a.m. so she decided to let him sleep. All during the day, Cherlene wondered what happen to her favorite student; class didn't seem the same without him. So she decided to find his address and go check on him after school.

****

Meantime, Makeda and her friends were planning a study group for the night.

"My house would be perfect!" said Karla. "Mom is away with her job, and Dad never comes home before 1 o'clock a.m., when Mom is away. I think he's cheating on her."

"So what time should we tell the boys to come?" asked Makeda.

"The later, the better!" said Karla. "That way, we can get our studying done."

****

After class, Cherlene went to the office to find Shaun's address.

"Sorry, Ms. Tullis," said the secretary. "That student has a 'need to know only' address. You must talk to the principal if you're to get it."

"Why is that, Ms. Head?"

"Most of the time there's something in the student's file that shouldn't be made public, like he's a sex offender or a foster child, or something."

"That's it!" thought Cherlene. *"He said his dad is on the run and his mom was killed. He's a foster care child and I bet I know where! Thank you, Ms. Head. Have a good day."* Cherlene went to her car and left.

"Hello, Mom?" phoned Makeda. "Don't forget that I will be studying with Karla for a while today so I will be home later."

"Ok, honey. Don't stay too late. I know you want to pass your exam but you need your rest, too."

"Ok Mom, Bye." A few minutes later, Cherlene pulled in to Ms. Myrtice's Foster Care. Ms. Myrtice was on the phone.

"Son, you said to call if I had any problems, so that's what I'm doing. Your son needs some help. He's been doing things I can't even talk about. So you really need to talk to him. Please, Carl Jr., talk to him or I may have to put him out. He's a bit much for me to handle. I'm too old for this now. Please don't tell him that I told you, ok? You take care, son. Bye." Then she hung up and spoke to Cherlene. "Yes, Ma'am, how may I help you?"

"Ms. Myrtice, it's me, Cherlene Tullis!" Ms. Myrtice was surprised.

"Oh my Lord! Girl, let me look at you! You are still so beautiful. I never thought I'd see you again! How are you?" Shaun awaken when he heard Cherlene speak. Until he looked out the window, he thought he was dreaming.

"I'm fine," said Cherlene. "I couldn't help but to hear your phone call. Sounds like you've got a problem child here. Was that DFACS you were talking to?"

"No Honey, I have an unusual situation with this one," said Ms. Myrtice.

"That was the child's da..."

"Hello, Ms. Tullis," interrupted Shaun. Ms. Myrtice frowned as Shaun grabbed Cherlene's arm and walked away. "What are you doing here?"

"It's nice seeing you, Cherlene!" yelled Ms. Myrtice. "Tell your sisters hello!"

"Yes Ma'am, I will!" she yelled back. "Shaun, what are you doing? Stop handling me like this!"

"What are you doing here!" he asked angrily.

"You weren't in school today, so I came by to check on you. Why are you acting this way?" Shaun calmed down.

"I'm sorry, Ms. Tullis, but can we drive somewhere?" After they got into the car, she drove around the corner and stopped.

"What's gotten into you, Shaun, and why weren't you at school today? Was Ms. Myrtice talking to someone on the phone about you?"

"I don't know who she was talking to, Ms. Tullis. I had a long night and I slept all day."

"What happened, Shaun? You want to talk about it?"

"No I don't!" he yelled "Please, just let it go, Ms. Tullis!" Cherlene paused and stared at him.

"Wanna know how I know Ms. Myrtice?" she asked calmly. Shaun said nothing. "I used to live there." Shaun looked surprised. "I'm a foster child ,too, Shaun, and I used to live there."

"What? You?"

"Shaun, you look like hell. Did you eat anything?"

"No, you woke me up when you came by. I've been asleep all day?"

"Why don't I take you home with me, cook us a meal, and you tell me all about it, ok?" Shaun smiled and said,

"Ok."

****

"Hello, Ladies!" said Jay. "The bad boys are here and the party starts now!" Shortly after dark, Jay, Corey, and Scott, met with Karla and Makeda at Karla's house.

"Look what I got!" said Corey the oldest. He held up a bottle of gin.

"What do you think you're gonna do with that?" asked Karla.

"Just leave that to me," he said.

"Hello Makeda," said Jay. "You about ready to give me that lap dance Scott told me about?"

"Scott! You're so big mouth!" shouted Makeda. A few minutes later, the girls had music playing while Corey was spiking the punch, and Karla and Scott were dancing. "Jay, what do you want to do?" asked Makeda.

"Do you want to dance?" asked Jay.

"Yeah." Jay and Makeda got up to dance as Corey handed them a cup of punch. A few minutes later, Makeda felt the effects of the spiked punch and began to talk. Karla and Scott went into the other room to make out.

"Whoo!" said Makeda as she twirled her hand in the air. Are you ready for that lap dance, now?"

"Oh yeah!" said Jay. Jay and Corey sat down as Makeda drunkenly shook her butt from lap to lap.

"Now, I'm gonna show you how my mom does it." Makeda started rubbing on her hips and her breast while she moaned and licked her lips.

"Uhh! Umm! Oh yes... um hmm," she moaned. The boys were surprised, but very much enticed.

"Am I the only one hot in here?" asked Makeda. Then she removed her blouse and exposed her bra. Next, she fell on the boys and started rubbing on their faces. Within seconds, she passed out in their arms as they started to take advantage of her.

"Listen," said Karla who was making out with Scott.

"Listen to what? Everything is quiet," said Scott.

"That's right... too quiet," said Karla. She jumped from the bed and ran into the living room. Jay and Corey were struggling to get Makeda's clothes off.

"You twirts!" shouted Karla. Then she took a pillow and hit them.

"What did you do to her?"

"Nothing!" shouted Jay. "She just passed out!"

"Corey, you spiked her punched, didn't you? Ok that's it! All of you get out!" Karla put the boys out then called a taxi to take Makeda home.

****

All while Cherlene and Shaun fixed dinner, they laughed, talked, and played. Cherlene felt good knowing that she was helping someone like herself, who had lost his birth mother. It was good therapy for her because Shaun would understand her and she would understand him. She had gotten so relaxed and comfortable with him, that she didn't see any reason to keep her guard up to prevent student-teacher attachment. After dinner, everything was about to change. For dessert, they challenged each other to see who could make the tastiest banana split. He made one and gave it to Cherlene then she made one for him.

"Umm! This is how I will eat yours," said Shaun. Then as he enticingly licked between the two bananas, he noticed Cherlene's change in countenance as she watched. Next, he rubbed both sides of the dish like he saw Cherlene rub her hips, night after night, while licking into the banana split. Cherlene was caught completely off guard as she felt moistness in her panties. She quickly left to go to the bathroom, but Shaun blocked her way.

"Where are you going, Cherlene?" He had her pinned to the wall and was breathing on her neck.

"Shaun, what are you doing? You are 16 years old and I am your teacher!"

"Really?" he said as he slid his finger between her tits. Cherlene slapped him and was about to speak. Suddenly, Shaun slapped her back just as hard and she fell dizzily into his arms. Again, she didn't expect that.

Before she could shake the dizziness, she felt Shaun's hand grab her vagina, under her dress, and his fingers slid right inside. At this point, Shaun had no clue what he was doing, but Cherlene didn't know that. As far as she was concerned he had done everything right to cause her to drop her guard, and now she was melting.

It had been more than 3 years since she allowed a man to touch her because she didn't want Makeda to fall into the same sexual lifestyle as she had. But tonight, as she pulled Shaun into her bedroom, she held nothing back as she sexually indulged him, time and time again, until she had stripped him of all his energy. Afterwards, Shaun was fast asleep.

"Honk! Honk!" sounded the car horn of the taxi.

"Oh my God!" whispered Cherlene. "That must be Makeda. What is she doing in a taxi from being less than a mile away? Wake up, Shaun! You have to go!" He quickly dressed as Karla ran in.

"Ms. Tullis, it's Makeda! She's in the car!" Cherlene ran to the taxi.

"Keda! Keda!" she called. "What's wrong with her, Karla?"

"I think they spiked the punch!"

"What! Help me get her in the house!"

"I'll get her," said Shaun.

"No!" said Cherlene. "Shaun, go home!"

"I can help, Cherlene!"

"No, damn it! Shaun, just go home!" He left angrily as they took Makeda into the house and helped her.

It was about 11:30 p.m. when Karla's dad finally picked her up. Cherlene bathed and cared for MaKeda while Shaun watched everything from the back yard.

"Mom, " said MaKeda.

"Yes baby, I'm here."

"They put something in the punch, Mom; my head hurts."

"I know, Sweetie. It's ok, it's ok." Cherlene stayed in Makeda's bedroom all night, holding her, while thinking about what had happened between her and Shaun.

"Cherlene, how could you do this to your daughter?" she asked herself. "You were so caught up in yourself that you never even checked on your child. I will never forgive myself if something happens to you." Then she heard the whisper, *"The Curse Must Be Broken!"* She looked about and yelled,

"Damn you and your curse! Leave me alone! Leave me alone!" Then she cried while nursing her child.

Chapter 92

"I know it will work man," said Bubba. "I know the officer that drives the perimeter car (P-car) and I know her shift."

"But how do you know that she won't look under the vans," asked Jones.

"I don't. But she doesn't get much attention from men and she loves it when a man flirts with her. When that happens, she smiles and half do everything. That's how we got our packages in. She was working at the back gate when we had a pound of weed, 15 packs of bugler, and 10 cell phones stuffed in a 4 inch pipe as we walked right in with it. All because Big Jeff was telling her how good she looked."

"So when are we gonna do this?" asked D-Lo.

"Ah! The dead comes to life!" said Bubba.

"I just don't have much to say," said D-Lo. "I'm an action man."

"I'm feeling that, brother. Our timing must be just right, but it will certainly happen soon. Are you in?"

"I'm in," said D-Lo. Bubba and Jones walked away and whispered.

"Man you know as well as I do, that only 2 vans gonna go through that gate at on that day; one for you and one for me," whispered Jones. "How are we gonna do this with a third wheel? That's to risky Bubba!"

"You think I don't know that, Brother? Don't worry about it. We need a decoy that day, to give the officers and the administration something else to focus on, while we move. He'll just be one of the dead bodies stuck up on the flat top at breakfast, while we make our move. "Blue was standing by listening as they talked.

****

At 3 a.m., Cherlene is sitting in bed holding her daughter. Makeda had awakened a couple of times during the night and stumbled to the bathroom in agony to vomit. Cherlene couldn't stand seeing her child like this. Near daybreak, Cherlene finally nodded off to sleep about an hour before Makeda woke up. Then the phone rang.

"This is the Tullis residence. Please leave a message at the beep."

"Hello Makeda," spoke Karla. "You didn't call this morning so I don't know what's up. I'm leaving in 10 minutes, and I'll be by. I can't wait to get this exam finished so I can stop pounding this stuff in my brain. See you soon. Bye."

"Oh! Oh!" screamed Makeda. "I've got an exam today!" she jumped from bed and started getting herself together.

"Keda, are you feeling ok?" asked Cherlene. "You don't have to go to school today if you don't want to. I'll call your teacher and we will work it out."

"No Mom! I have to show up, today!" she screamed. "Oh my head!"

"That's it! I'm calling your teacher and cancelling your..."

"Mom, I said *'No!'* Just go cook something! Karla will be here any minute, so I don't have time to fight with you. Please Mom, just help me get ready!" Cherlene sped to the kitchen to fix Makeda some food just as Karla walked in.

"I'm ready! Be there in a second!" said Makeda. She sped to the kitchen and got a glass of juice from the frig. Then she tried to run out.

"See you, Mom!" Cherlene caught her by the book bag and yanked her back.

"Sit down!" demanded Cherlene.

"Mom, I have to go!"

"Sit down right now and eat or you will not leave this house!" Then she looked at Karla. "You too, young lady; sit down!" Karla nervously sat at the table next to Makeda, who was eating fast.

"I don't know what happened last night, but somebody better explain it to me when you come home, understand me?"

"Yes, Ma'am," said them both.

"Mom, can we go now?" Before Cherlene could nod *'yes,'* the girls sprung from the table and were gone.

Meantime, at school, Shaun arrived early. He was excited about seeing Cherlene after being with her the night before. It was an experience he'd never forget and he couldn't wait to see her smile at him.

As he came to the door of the classroom, Cherlene was not at her desk, nor in the room. So he checked the main office and the teacher's lounge but she was not there either. He ran back to the class to see if he had bypassed her somehow. To his surprise a substitute was in her stead.

"Come in, young man, and have a seat. Ms. Tullis is out for today. My name is Ms. Walker, and I will be your teacher until she returns. Open your history book to chapter three and read it. Here are your instructions.

"Where is Ms. Tullis?" asked Shaun.

"I'm sure she will be here tomorrow, sir. Until then, please read your assignment."

"But she doesn't do things like this. She talks to us before class and..."

"I'm sorry, young man, but she's not here today," cut in Ms. Walker. "I'll let her know that you missed her. Meantime, please read your assignment."

"No wonder you're a sub instead of a teacher," said Shaun angrily. "You don't know how to handle people, do you?"

"Well, I can send you to the principal's office and handle that, if you keep talking. Would you rather that?" Shaun didn't answer. He knew that a trip to the principal's office meant one hour of automatic detention after school. He didn't want that because he needed to see Cherlene.

After a few minutes, Shaun couldn't take it anymore. He made up his mind to leave school right after class. Soon, the bell rang for second period.

"Shaun Taylor," called Ms. Walker. "I need to see you a minute please."

"Yeah, what's up?" rushed Shaun. "He knew he had to clear the hallway and the school grounds before the bell rang or security would stop him.

"Walk with me to the teachers lounge, son."

"Ms. Walker, I have to get to class. What's this about?"

"Don't worry, I'll give you a late pass if you need it." Ms. Walker talked to him about his attitude, but Shaun was watching the clock and not listening because he wanted to get away.

"In two minutes, I have to be gone or I won't make it," he thought. Suddenly, when Shaun saw no other teacher in the teacher's lounge, he slightly forced Ms. Walker inside.

"Hey! Shaun! What are you doing? Aahh!" she yelled as Shaun punched her in the face. She lost her balance and hit her head on the corner of the table and passed out. Shaun took off running and left the building. Thirty minutes later, he was knocking at Cherlene's door.

"Who is that?" wondered Cherlene as she sprang from bed to see. *"Might be Keda coming back."* She opened the door and saw only Shaun. "Shaun, what are you doing here? Why aren't you in school?"

"I had to see you, Cherlene." From the way he called her name, she knew she had a problem. "Can I come in?" She let him in so she could try to talk to him.

"Shaun, what happened last night was a mistake."

"No, no, Cherlene, don't say that! I love you and there is no mistake about that."

"Oh Shaun," she groaned disappointedly as she jumped in bed. She was so tired and sleepy that she hardly had energy to talk.

"Shaun, I am your history teacher and you are my student--- that's it! We did something that never should have happened and I'm ..."

"Don't say that!" yelled Shaun angrily. Cherlene became sorrowful but remained strong.

"Shaun, I am so sorry this happened. As soon as I get back to school, I'm gonna fix this. I'm gonna resign if I have to, and move away. This is all my fault."

"Move?" Shaun rubbed her shoulders and she snatched away. "You want to leave me?" Shaun touched her again and she jumped from the bed. "Wait Cherlene, let's talk."

Shaun grabbed her and she hit him. She had forgotten how hard he could hit back as he punched her in the face and almost knocked her unconscious. Cherlene was already in her night gown, so Shaun didn't waste anytime taking his clothes off and climbing in bed with her.

This time, he took the lead and handled her while having sex with her. For the first time in her life, she was not enjoying the pounding penetrating her body. She began to see flashes of her mother being raped as Shaun continually took her against her will. Cherlene began to cry.

****

Detective 1 = What do you think? Does this look like a homicide or accident?

Detective 2 = Hard to tell, right now. But looks like she have a knot on her forehead, too. Which means, that if it was not an accident, somene hit her in her forehead, which caused her to fall backward onto the corner of the table.

Detective 1 = There's nothing here that indicate's anything otherwise. Beside, that bruise looks like knuckle prints. What do you think?

Detective 2 = Same here. Autopsy will tell though. Who found the body?

Detective 1 = English teacher over there, coming to chill out during her study hall. Says, the dead woman is a substitute for the history teacher, today.

Detective 2 = Now that's really odd. I can see why some student may be mad with one of their regular teachers for not passing them or something. But why would someone kill a one-day substitute?

Detective 1 = The school board has shut the school down until tomorrow or Monday. That gives us time to question all the students in the history class.

Detective 2 = Good. Also, let's visit the history teacher to see what she can tell us about any of her students.

****

Cherlene laid in bed beside Shaun as he played in her hair.

"What are we gonna do now, Cherlene?" asked Shaun. "I don't want you to leave." Cherlene was so disappointed in herself. She knew this was her fault so she had to find a way to fix it without ruining Shaun's life.

"Shaun, would you please leave for now, until I've had time to think? I promise I won't leave you."

"We should be together, Cherlene. Where do you want me to go?"

"Just go home for now, and take a bath and clean up. I promise that we'll talk later, ok?"

"Ok, Cherlene, anything for you." Shaun got dressed and left. Suddenly, the phone rang.

"Hey, Cherlene," started Annie, a teacher from school. "You will never believe what happened to your sub today!"

Chapter 93

"Momma come on, and stop talking so much," fussed Nicole. Elder Byrd will be here next week and you can finish talking to him then."

"Child you just brought back memories when you spoke," responded Gerry, her mother. "I remember when I said something like that to my mother and she slapped me blind. I still get dizzy every time I think about it."

"Girl you better hush!" joked Melody. "Your momma's about to snap!"

"Momma it's 2 o'clock already, and you told Ms. Myrtice that you would pick her up by now. She may be waiting outside the church with nobody there," begged Nicole. "Please, let's go!"

"Alright! Alright!" said her mother. They got in the car and left. Nicole, her mother, and Melody, were all members of Pastor Byrd's church on Hightower Road. Service had just ended, and they were on their way to pick up Nicole's mom's friend, Myrtice, from Rev. Simmons's church. Myrtice had invited her for dinner today, and Nicole didn't want to be late.

"Hey girl!" shouted Myrtice to her friend, when she saw Nicole driving up. "I finally got you out of the house and outside of Jonesboro," she laughed.

"Well, next time, you're going home to eat with me," said Gerry.

"What! All the way to Jonesboro? Let me know when in advance, but I'm pretty sure I'll be too terribly sick to make the trip." Nicole and Melody just looked at each other as the ladies told corny jokes and laughed. Soon, Nicole pulled into the Foster care home where Ms. Myrtice lives.

"How's Shaun, Ms. Myrtice?" asked Nicole.

"Child, don't ask! All I can tell you is that he's always into something. But I'm glad that whatever he's into, ain't up in here. He usually comes in pretty late, so I'm sure he's not here now."

"Ok, I'll check on him, later, when I come back."

"Where are you going, Nicole?" asked her mom.

"Momma, I'm going to drop Melody off at her friend's place. I'll be back in a few hours to pick you up."

"Nicole, what's gotten into you, today? First, you got sassy at the mouth. Now, you just want to drop me off like I'm your step child. Does Melody have you doing drugs or something?" Melody was shocked.

"Ms. Gerry, why are you putting me in this! You know I can't tell Nicole what to do! She doesn't listen to nobody but you!" said Melody.

"She ain't listening to me today, either. I figure it must be them cheap drugs she's listening to."

"Bye, Momma; bye Ms. Myrtice," kissed Nicole. "I'll see you in a bit."

"Bye, Ms. Myrtice; bye Ms. Gerry," waved Melody. "Y'all have fun." Then they drove off.

"Don't they grow up fast, Myrtice?"

"They really do, Gerry. I've had so many to come through here that grew up and out. Can't remember many of their names anymore, but I know their faces."

"Myrtice, you're sixty-five years old, now. Why are you still doing this work?"

"What else am I to do, Gerry?"

"Retire, like I have! It's not so bad! These Shaun type of fellas you keep telling me about are getting worse and worse. He doesn't respect your curfew anymore, and the other boys are following his leads. You ain't in shape to be chasing after young men like these."

"You're right, Gerry, but my retirement time hasn't come yet. When it does, you'll know." The women talked about many things over dinner while Nicole was away. They hadn't visited each other in a long time.

"Would you mind if I see how the kids live?" asked Gerry.

"No, come on up and I'll show you their rooms." Myrtice had a section on the wall upstairs of the girls pictures that lived there since she started the business.

"My, my Lord!" sounded Gerry. "Look at all these cuties that have had misfortune!"

"Don't let their faces fool ya; some of them were witches!"

"I'm sure they were. Myrtice it takes a lot of patience to do what you do. I thank God that you are my friend. That way, if one of my grand kids starts acting up, I can send him to you," she laughed.

"Oh yeah, send him on," joked Myrtice. "I ought to have a 20 gauge shotgun by then. That'll keep `em in check." Suddenly, one of the pictures caught Gerry's eye.

"Myrtice, who is this little beauty?" Myrtice looked at the picture.

"Her name starts with a J, I think---JoAnn, Jessica, Janie, Jennifer, Jamila, Jennica, Janis, Jamie---honey, I've had everyone of those girls to live here and I can't remember what name goes to what face, anymore. Why do you ask?"

"Honk! Honk!" tapped Nicole on the car horn. Gerry went to the window and waved for her to come in. Nicole did.

"Nicole, a few years ago, you and I had a special talk about your little shoebox. Do you remember that?"

"Yes Momma, why?"

"Well, when we finished talking, you showed me a picture of a young lady, remember?"

"Yes, I do. I still say why?" Gerry pointed to the picture on the wall. Nicole was so surprised. She quickly searched in her purse for the picture. When she found it, she held it next to the one on the wall---it was a match.

"Momma, I don't know what to say!" said Nicole.

"I don't think your dad stopped making babies after you were born. Who knows! You may even be the youngest; I don't know. But it's obvious to me that you have a sister, somewhere, and she's been living right here under our noses.

Chapter 94

"Marquis, why all the questions, all of a sudden? Are you trying to check up on me?"

"No, I just wanna know where you are during the many nights you just disappear. You always say you went shopping whether day or night, but you never bring anything home."

"How do you know that Marquis? You don't live with me and you hardly spend the night. Do you think that we need a break?" asked Jennifer.

"Are you breaking up with me?"

"I'm really just trying to get you to back off with the interrogation!"

"Ok fine! No more questions!"

"Good," said Jennifer. "Now let's enjoy our relationship and do things together like most couples do. I'd like that, if you don't mind?"

"Don't mind a bit, but I've got to finish up a few policies before tomorrow. Besides, your sisters are on the way, aren't they?"

"No," smiled Donna. "We're already here!" Donna and Cherlene walked up and took a seat, next to Jennifer.

"Wow! I feel really special, right now!" smiled Marquis. "The three of you together like this makes Charlie's Angels look like little girls. You're all breath taking!"

"Jennifer, you have to do something really special for this man tonight," said Cherlene. "He really knows how to make a girl smile."

"I have to go, ladies," said Marquis. He kissed Jennifer. "See you tonight, ok?"

"Call me!" said Jennifer. Marquis walked away.

"Jenny, he's a keeper! You've had him longer than any man that's been in your life," said Donna. "So how are you guys really doing?"

"We were arguing just before you came. Lately, he has all these questions like he's some kind of detective or something."

"You mean like he's checking up on you?" asked Cherlene.

"Kinda, but it's different. I can't quite put my finger on it."

"Maybe he just likes you and wanna be with you more."

"I hope he's not a stalker," said Cherlene.

"Cheryl, why would you think something like that?" asked Jennifer.

"Because that's the first thing came to my mind."

"Y'all know what?" said Donna. "It's been a while since we just sat and talked. Cherlene I don't have a clue what's going on in your life. Please, enlighten me." Cherlene shook her head slowly.

"You guys wouldn't believe it if I told you. Hell, I'm in the midst of the mess and I don't even believe it!"

"What's up Cheryl?" asked Jennifer. Cherlene hesitated sadly.

"I've messed up really bad this time. I don't exactly know how to sugarcoat things so I'm just gonna say it. I slept with one of my students, and now he's in love with me."

"You did what?" they screamed. "Cheryl, how could you?"

"Believe me I didn't want to, but he caught me with my guard down."

"More like your panties down," said Jennifer. "How did this happen." Cherlene told them the whole story about her relationship with Shaun.

"Did he actually rape you?" asked Donna.

"Not exactly, but that's how I felt while he was doing it."

"Cheryl he either raped you or he didn't. Which is it?" asked Jennifer.

"The night before, I willingly gave it up. But the next day when he wanted me again, he kind of forced me but I did it without a fight or struggle. I didn't want him but, I knew I had created a monster from the night before and I needed time to think before I started to fight him. So, I let him have his way."

"Are you alright?" asked Donna.

"Well, it gets worse," said Cherlene. "That day that he came back to the house and we had sex, the school where I work called and said that my substitute teacher for that day had been killed while in the teacher's lounge. Detectives are still trying to decide if it was an accident or homicide."

"What does this have to do with you or Shaun?" asked Donna.

"The only way Shaun could have known that I was home that day is for him to have gone by the school first. When he saw that I wasn't there, he left and came to my house."

"The fact that you are telling us this means that you think Shaun had something to do with your substitute's death. Is that right?" asked Jennifer.

"I pray to God that I'm wrong about this."

"Cheryl, this sounds really messy," said Donna. Cherlene sparked up.

"Ok guys, please don't worry about me too much. I promise I'm gonna handle this, and all will be well. Where is that damn Hooter's girl? I need a drink!" The girls were at underground Atlanta not too far from Donna's job. Jennifer and Donna were really worried about Cherlene and her situation. Cherlene knew it and spoke up.

"Look girls, I know how you must feel about all I've said and I understand your anguish and concern. But remember that I'm a big girl and I can handle my own. I'll be ok."

"Cheryl, this is big!" cautioned Jennifer. "I'm really worried. If this gets too bad, I don't know if I can be there for you like you were for me. Now that I understand what you went through with me, it's hard to measure up to your standards sometimes."

"Would you please leave this alone and tell me about your lives? I promise that I will deal with this uncannily."

"Ok, Cheryl, I hear you," said Donna. "Before I tell you about my little problem, let me say this: You once told me that if I ever put you through... *'tough shit'*... that you would bust a cap in my ass. Does that *'cap busting'* also apply to you?"

Cherlene chuckled and said, "I get the point Dee, and yes it does. But I'm going to do all I can to avoid it."

"You better," said Donna. "Now for my little problem. I have this girlfriend who's been talking to me about this guy she likes. This guy's been supporting her even when her family didn't have time, too. Now she's thinking about going on a date with this guy, but she knows that her family will never approve of it, because the guy used to date another girl in the family and even had a baby by her. This is a really nice guy. What should I tell my girlfriend to do; date or don't date?" Jennifer said nothing.

"Well, if the guy is single and the girl is single, the family should respect their wishes to get together, as long as he and this other girl have broken up. Yes! I say date him and have fun, as long as she don't get pregnant and bring another child in the house by the same man."

"Cheryl, are you sure?" asked Jennifer.

"I'm positive!" said Cherlene. "They like each other and I think they should see where it leads. What do you think Jennifer?"

"I don't know Cheryl. I'm gonna let you and Dee have this one."

"Tell your girlfriend to go for it Dee; I would," said Cherlene. Jennifer looked at Donna blatantly, because she knew that Terry had been helping Donna a lot at her new apartment, and they had gotten closer.

Therefore, she didn't want to side with Cherlene's ignorance nor with Donna's cunningness, so she remained un-opinionated in the whole thing. Whatever will happen, will happen---that's how she saw it.

"So what about you, Jenny? What's happening in your life these days?" asked Donna. "You've been very cunning and sneaky since you came back from you know where."

"How can you call me sneaky, Donna? You sneaky little slut!"

"Jenny, what are you talking about? I am not being sneaky about anything!"

"What are you talking about Jenny?" asked Cherlene.

"Never mind," said Jennifer. "It will reveal itself in time. As for me, I'm just working hard to expand my investments with J.J."

"You never did tell us where you got all the money to do what you did?" said Donna. "And what about your half sister? Sarah, what's her name? Did you just give up on the search?"

"I haven't exactly given up on finding my half sister, but I just don't know where to look anymore. As for the money, I saved it while I was working at the Mall then turned it into investments."

"That's bull!" said Cherlene. "Dee and I came her with truth today but you want to tell us a bunch of bull! We know you stole it Jennifer. Don't forget that we were there when you went to the slammer."

"Cherlene, why is it that you are so smart when it comes to business but you are so stupid when it comes to relationships?" said Jennifer.

"I'm smart enough to kick your butt Jennifer! That's the second time you've called me out since your little prison tour!" Jennifer gave her the finger.

Cherlene was mad as she launched at Jennifer. For the first time since they were teenagers, they were fighting. Cherlene chased her all over Hooters and tried to hit her or grab her, but Jennifer was too fast and exceptionally witty. Even when Cherlene finally caught her and put her in a choke hold, Jennifer masterfully slid out of it. After awhile, it all turned to laughter and they hugged.

Chapter 95

Nicole was more curious than ever as she looked at the picture that night in her College Park home. That Monday before work, she made copies of the picture and posted one of them on her mirror in her shop. She posted a second copy at home, and kept the original in her purse.

"So who's the girl in the black and white on your mirror?" asked Candi.

"Just somebody I hope to soon meet," answered Nicole.

"Hup!" shouted Melody. "Nicole's being evasive y'all! Something's up!" They all took a look at the picture.

"She's pretty," said Tameka. "Is she black or white?"

"What I want to know is who is she?" spoke Melody. "Nikki, are you bringing somebody else up in here?"

"Maybe," smiled Nicole.

"Ok, that's it!" demanded Melody. "Who is she, Nikki?"

"Calm down, calm down everybody, I'll tell you. When I went to pick up my dad's belongings, he had a few small items in the shoebox along with this picture. I'm not sure who it is, but Mama thinks it may be somebody significant to my dad."

"Do you mean like somebody special?" asked Candi.

"Yes, very special," responded Nicole.

"What? Like a wife or girlfriend or something?" asked Adrienna.

"Maybe," answered Nicole. "But more like a daughter." All the girls stopped moving and looked stunned.

****

Sunday night after Cherlene and her sisters talked, she talked with Makeda.

"Keda, please come sit with me for a minute." Makeda came and saw tears in her eyes. She had never seen her mom like this.

"Mom, what's wrong?" she asked. Cherlene hesitated and dropped tears. "Mom, please tell me."

"I can't," said Cherlene. "It's too bad." Makeda got closer to her as she cried. "Your mom did something really bad and I'm too ashamed to even talk about it right now," cried Cherlene. "I just want you to know how much I love you no matter what happens, ok?"

"Mom, you're scaring me. What's wrong? Are you sick?"

"No baby, it's nothing like that. Sick in the head, maybe, but my health is fine."

"So what is it? Will you tell me?" pleaded Makeda.

"I promise to tell you later, but I need you to do me a favor right away."

"Ok, what favor?"

"I need to get away for a few days and I want you to come with me."

"What about school, and your job?"

"You know those things are very important to me," said Cherlene. "So if I am asking you to miss your school, then I have a really good reason." Makeda tossed more questions but Cherlene kept her focus on the importance of her need to get away.

"Ok Mom, I'll do it. When do we leave and where are we going?"

"Where we're going is up to you. We can go anywhere you want to, but we must leave by tomorrow morning."

"Tomorrow!" shouted Makeda. "Mom, what about my friends? Karla?" Cherlene had been patient, but she felt she'd better get a little serious now.

"Makeda, we have to go tomorrow, or there may not be any more friends around here; no Karla, no anybody! Please Makeda, just do this for me."

"Ok, ok," said Makeda as she felt the impact of her mom's words. "Can I tell Karla?" Makeda called her friends to say goodbye and to question them about where she should go with her mom. Cherlene called her school principal and told them she had a family emergency and would be gone for a while. Then she called another teacher friend at Makeda's school, who was also one of Makeda's teacher, and covered for Makeda's absence.

By morning, she talked with her sisters then they were gone. When Shaun realized what had happened, he dropped out of school, and became a menace to anyone who got in his way.

One night, shortly after Shaun left the backyard of Cherlene's home, he went to Decatur and sat at his old apartment building.

"Mom," he started. "I think I'm in love but Cherlene keep acting up."

"She is, huh?" spoke a - would be robber who was now holding his knife to Shaun's throat. "Empty your pockets, man! Hurry up!" Shaun quickly reached into his coat pocket and pulled out his pistol, then fired it.

"Uh!" screamed the *would be robber* as Shaun shot him in the leg. "I'm sorry, man! Please don't kill me!" Immediately, Shaun's anger caused him to fire the pistol numerous times in effort to kill him, but the clip was emptied after the first shot. He then pistol whipped the bleeding man until he was unconscious. Then he threw the gun aside and took the man's knife.

Afterwards, Shaun walked the streets terrorizing all he came in contact with. He could no longer feel the presence of his mother when he called her, and now he needed her help. He had become a menace and Cherlene was his last hope, as he ended up in her backyard... waiting. Cherlene had promised not to leave, but she was gone.

Chapter 96

"Melody, I have to take care of something today," said Nicole. "Please mind the store while I'm gone."

"What time are you leaving, Nikki?"

"Now!" Nicole grabbed her coat and left.

****

It was lunchtime that Monday as Jennifer met Donna at a restaurant not too far from Donna's job.

"Do you think Cheryl is ok?"

"I think she did the right thing," said Jennifer. "This gives her time to think."

"When things messes up, Cheryl always does the right thing," said Donna. "That's her nature—who she is. I love her so much."

"We need her, too, Dee. I don't know what I would have done without her all these years. But, now I am scared for her."

"Me too," said Dee. "What can we do though?"

"Right now? Nothing except be there for her and keep loving her." Lunch had ended so Jennifer was walking Donna back to her job.

"Hey, I have an idea!" said Donna. "Why don't we find Shaun and kill him!"

"That's really good, Dee," smiled Jennifer. "But we can at least learn about him and see what he's like, in case we do have to kill him."

"I like it!" laughed Donna. "Let's plan to visit his school!"

"We will. But first, it's time to pay our foster mom a visit and see what she can tell us." Suddenly, a pigeon flew by and dropped a huge splash of pigeon waste in Jennifer's hair.

"Ah!" screamed Jennifer. "Why me! This is so embarrassing!"

"I'm sorry, Jennifer! What should I do?" yelled Donna. They were so engrossed in Jennifer's situation, that neither of them saw Nicole as she entered the building.

"May I help you, Ma'am?"

"Yes," answered Nicole. "I need to talk to someone about a picture printed in one of your papers." Nicole had the picture in her hand.

"Ok," said the desk clerk. "Is this the picture? What do you want to know?"

"I need to know who this is or when was the picture taken or anything you can tell me." The clerk took the picture and went from desk to desk, but nobody knew anything. Many of the people were out to lunch or out on business.

"Sorry, Ma'am, but no one knows who that is, or when this was taken. Are you sure it's one of ours?"

"No I'm not, but it is a newspaper clip, right?"

"Now that I see it, it does look like one of ours." As the clerk examined the picture, Jennifer walked by with her sweater pulled over her head in embarrassment, while Donna guided her to the bathroom. Nicole glanced at them as they passed, but thought nothing of it.

"Is there a Ms. Donna Banks still working here?" asked Nicole.

"Yes, Ms. Banks is employed here, but she's out, right now. Do you want to leave a message?" Nicole pulled her business card.

"Have her to call me as soon as she can. I would appreciate it."

****

"Oh Jenny! This is bad!" said Donna. "Your hair is a mess!"

"Shut up, Dee, and help me to clean it up! Go find me a towel or something!"

"Ok! Ok!" Donna left and came back with a couple of towels. Then she stood back and watched Jennifer from a distance.

"Aren't you gonna help me?" asked Jennifer. "Now, I miss Cheryl!" Tenisha walked in, looked at Jennifer's hair, then chuckled.

"Glamour Bitch!" shouted Donna. "Just get out!" Tenisha left smiling.

"It will take me forever to fix my hair, again!" sobbed Jennifer.

"I'm sorry, Jenny," said Donna. Jennifer whined and stood looking in the mirror. Suddenly, Tenisha came easing back into the bathroom.

"I told you to get out!" yelled Donna. "Now please, leave!"

"What is it you want, Tenisha?" asked Jennifer. "Are you here to take another picture of me wearing pigeon shit? I don't think that would be appealing to your readers!"

"Jennifer, I'm sorry about the picture thing. I truly am, and I hope you accept my apology," said Tenisha. "The only reason I came back in here is to apologize to you. Your presence here... like this*(pointing to Jennifer's hair)*... kinda caught me off guard, so I laughed. You have to admit that you do loo weird, so I laughed. But, I'm not laughing now; I'm very serious. Please, accept my apology."

"Don't trust her, Jenny!" cautioned Donna. "Once a snake---always a snake!" Tenisha paused then her entire countenance changed as she spoke.

"Donna why do you do this? If you only knew what I've suffered since those high school years, you wouldn't act like this. I'm sorry about my mistreatment of you during that time, but I can't change it! What do you want, Donna? What do you need me to do, to be forgiven by you? Name it and I will do it: What?"

" Ok!" said Donna. "I want you to drop dead, right now! Can you do that?" Jennifer was shocked at Donna's reactions. Donna's words cut through Tenisha's heart like a razor as her tears fell.

"Jennifer," apologized Tenisha. "I am so sorry about... everything. Especially, the picture. If I could take it back, I would." Then Tenisha left.

"Dee, she seemed serious," said Jennifer. "I feel sorry for her."

"Don't fall for it, Jenny! You know Tenisha can't be trusted. Remember what she did to you."

"That was a long time ago and she's apologized----even for the picture! I've never known Tenisha to be an actress and I don't think she is being one today. She meant it and it made me want to reach out to her."

"Jenny, you have proven to be pretty smart in our family. Please don't be dumb enough to fall for Tenisha's tears. I firmly believe that once a Tenisha bitch... always a Tenisha bitch and I will never trust her!" Tenisha stood outside the door listening. Afterwards, she went back to her desk.

"I told you, God, that this problem was impossible," prayed Tenisha. *"I give up. It's up to you now."* A few minutes later, Donna and Jennifer snuck out of the bathroom. Jennifer had a towel across her head as she trailed Donna. As she passed Tenisha, she hesitated and whispered,

"It's ok, Tenisha, I forgive you." Tenisha smiled and whispered back,

"Thank you." Then she opened her computer diary and started to type... "Dear Diary..."

Chapter 97

"Hey baby, do you need a date?" smiled Sandra as she prostituted the streets near Metropolitan Parkway on Sunday night.

"How much?" asked the driver.

"How much you got?"

"I got a couple of dollars."

"A couple as in, a couple of hundred?"

"What!" shouted the driver. "No! I mean about twenty." Sandra got mad.

"Move on, Mister. It cost more than that to talk to a woman these days. Besides, you look married; go home to your wife!" He drove off. Soon another car pulled up.

"Hey baby, are you looking for a date?" She looked at the driver.

"Carlton? Man, it's been so long! Can I get in?"

"Yeah baby, get in and take care of the Hookman." She happily got into the car. "What are you doing out here on the streets?" he asked.

"Can't get a job, and all the men who can take care of me are locked up. I had to do something because everything's getting harder out here. So, what do you do now? How are you making a living and paying for this high gas?"

"Like you say, baby, it's kinda hard out here. I do a little business here and there though. Where are we going?"

"For you... my place." She directed him to Fairburn Townhouse Apartments on Fairburn Road. Hookman handed her a couple of hundred bucks. She smiled and stuffed the money in her bra. "Oh, your 'little business' must be going pretty good," she said. Sandra always had a thing for Hookman, but he never had time for her in the past. She was hoping this may be her big moment so, tonight would be more than just sex for her; she needed his heart.

"Since you're out here on the street, I know you use protection, right?" Sandra pulled condoms from her pocket, showed them to Hookman then tossed them out the window.

"I don't need those for you, Carlton. I want to feel all of you inside me."

As they entered the apartment, Hookman grabbed her, and slid his hand between her legs. She quickly tossed her blouse and dropped her skirt. He picked her up and took her to the bedroom. She had a nice antique bed with a steel head and foot rail; sort of like prison bars, but they were golden in color. Sandra was on her knees holding the foot rails as Hookman made love to her. Suddenly, Hookman's cell phone rang.

"Yeah," he answered.

"This is the D-Lo. What's up, man?"

"You tell me, what's up?" responded Hookman. He sat next to Sandra as she caressed him.

"It's time, man. Within the next few days, I'll be out of here. Do you have a lock on Coldblood, yet?" Sandra rubbed on Hookman while he tried to talk, but he pushed her away.

"I've been checking out Lo-Down and asking questions, but there are no answers. I got nothing. We can always take out Lo-Down and force Coldblood out."

"No, that'll alert too many people and we will have cops everywhere. But you've got options that you're not thinking about. Word is that Coldblood's partner, Dexter, has a brother, so check this out. Who would you trust to look over your family and affairs when you can't?"

"My partner," answered Hookman. Sandra started rubbing her breast on him.

"Right!" said D-Lo. "Kill the watch dog, and it leaves the junkyard vulnerable and wide open! Take out Dexter, and Coldblood will show himself."

"So you think I should get to Dexter through his brother, huh?"

"It's a backdoor and they will never know who hit them, until its too late. But if you go directly after anybody in Coldblood's family, that will send out signals and the folks will be expecting us."

"I don't know, D-Lo. This sounds like a long shot to me." He pushed Sandra away, again.

"You got a better plan? What... to just sneak up on Lo-Down and take him out... is that your plan? You will be locked up or killed within an hour after that. Start thinking with your head, man!" Hookman got mad.

"Since when does the D-Lo talk to the Hookman like he's a child?" asked Hookman. "Don't do that man, cause I'll cut your ass up!" Sandra was annoying now.

"Then stop thinking like a child!" screamed D-Lo.

"Ah!" yelled Hookman as he angrily stood up. "You're doing it again, man!"

"Just make the damn move, Hookman; get to Dexter!" D-Lo hung up.

"Aahhh!" growled Hookman. He grabbed Sandra and slammed her head between the bars on the foot rail. "Stop messing with me when I'm trying to do business!" Sandra's head was stuck and she couldn't get out.

"Carlton, why did you do that!" she yelled. "Help me out of here, Carlton!" He got dressed, took his money back, and left with her yelling at him.

Chapter 98

Detective #1 = If this is a homicide, we don't have any leads.
Detective #2 = Ok, let's call the 1st student and question him.

The Cobb County detectives were at Campbell High School questioning students about the death of the substitute teacher, Ms. Walker. The first student, a boy, came into the teacher's lounge.

Detective #2 = Hi son...
Student #1 = Where did Ms. Walker die?
Detective #2 = *(The Detective pointed)* Over there. *The boy suddenly dashed out of the door running and crying for his mom.*
Detective #1 = I can see already this will be a long day. I'll get the next one.

(Student after student came in but nobody seemed to know anything. But things changed when they called student number 19.)

Detective #2 = What's your name, son?
Student #19 = Smokie.
Detective #1= That's a weird name. Is that your nickname?
Student #19 = No, my name is Smokie Simmons after my granddad.
Detective #2 = Ok, Smokie. What can you tell us about Ms. Walker.
Student #19 = Nothing. She didn't say much except to fuss at Shaun.
Detective #2 = Who's Shaun? What did she fuss at him about?

(Detective # 1 checked his list of students that were present the day of the murder. Then he shook his head to Detective #2 indicating that Shaun's name was not there.)

Student #19 = Shaun is Ms. Tullis' favorite student, so he tried to tell Ms. Walker how Ms. Tullis did things.
Detective #2 = And how did Ms. Walker take it?
Student #19 = She told him to be quiet and do his work or she would send him to see the principal.
Detective #2 = Then what happened?
Student #19 = Nothing, Shaun shut up and that was it. Oh, one more thing! When class was over, Ms. Walker told Shaun to stay and walk with her to the teacher's lounge.

(The detectives kinda looked at each other. A few minutes later, they were in the main office looking at Shaun' picture.)

Detective #2 = *(Talking to the secretary)* Shaun Taylor was not
      present the day of the incident, but a student remembers seeing
      him arguing with Ms. Walker. So why doesn't your records show
      him to be present on that day?
Secretary = We have no way of knowing who is present until the
      homeroom teacher turns in her roster. Ms. Walker was Shaun's
      homeroom teacher, that day.
Detective #2 = Can you give us Shaun's home address?
Secretary = Shaun lives in foster care. Here's his address. *(Detective #1*
      took it)
Detective#2 = Can you also give us the address of the teacher who was
      absent that day? I hear that Shaun is her favorite student. Maybe
      she can tell us more about Shaun.
Secretary = Sure, but she's not home, though. She called in a family
      emergency and took a leave of absence just this morning; didn't
      say when she would be back.
Detective #1 = Is Shaun here in school today? *(The secretary checked*
      the roster)
Secretary = No, he's a no show today. No call in or anything.
Detective #2 = Thank you, Ma'am. Have a nice day. *(The detectives*
      walked out)
Detective #1 = Are you thinking what I'm thinking?
Detective #2 = The teacher---she knows something.
Detective #1 = She knew questions would be asked so she's dodging the
      bullet.
Detective #2 = Let's see if we can find Shaun.

        ****

    "Hello?" answered Myrtice. "Who's calling please?"
    "It's me, Ms. Myrtice... Carl Jr.! I got your message and I'm
calling to talk about Shaun. What's going on?"
    "Oh Carl Jr., I don't know where to begin. So for his soul's sake, I
won't sugarcoat anything. Your son has become a danger to himself and
everybody he's around. I'm afraid if you don't come help him, then the
state will soon bury him, because somebody's gonna kill him."
    "I hear you loud and clear, Ms. Myrtice. I'm on my way as soon
as I can." They hung up and Coldblood dialed Nicole's cell phone.
    "Hello?" answered Nicole.
    "Hi Nicole, its Coldblood. I need a place to stay again. I'll tell you
about it when I get there."

Chapter 99

That same afternoon, Hookman visited many places asking questions about Dexter and his brother, Terry. After awhile, he drove to a nearby club to buy a beer, as they sold lunch. To his surprise, he hear three electricians talking while eating at a table near him.

Terry = It is so good to work locally, again. Now, I get to see my daughter more.
Howard = Yeah, it's been a minute for you, kid. How's Dexter? Is he still an electrician?
Jimmy= *Yeah, how is ol' Dex?*
Terry = Dexter gave that up a long time ago. He's into the big money now (they looked puzzled). Don't ask, or I'll have to kill you!
Jimmy = You're gonna kill us for asking?
Terry = Like I said, don't asked and everybody will be fine.
Howard = In high school, Dexter was one the fastest running backs I've ever seen. Too bad he didn't go pro. I'd have paid to see him.
Jimmy = Lunch's over fellas. Let's get back to the jobsite. We have about two hours of work left for today. We can be heading home by 3:30.

Hookman trailed them back to the jobsite. After work, he followed Terry home to Old Time Village Apartments in College Park, and waited.

****

"Cherlene is away with Keda, and Jenny is with her family," said Donna.
"So what can I do, today? Who can I call?" Donna was driving home talking to herself when her phone rang.
"Hello, Donna. What's up? This is Terry!"
"Oh Terry! I was just thinking about you! What's up?"
"Now that I'm home and don't have to work out of town, I was wondering if you could return a brother a favor, and help me straighten up the place. It's really filthy around here and I can use some company."
"Terry, I would love to help! Tell me how to get there and I'm on my way."

****

Late Monday evening, Jennifer was home talking to her kids while washing her hair.
"Mom, where is Aunt Cherlene and Makeda?" asked Audrey.
"They had to take a trip for a few days. They'll be back soon, though." Dent walked in with a computerized game toy.

"Mom!" yelled Audrey. "Dent's been picking the lock to the basement again!" Jennifer looked at him.

"Dent! What have I told you about doing that?"

"I can't help it," said Dent.

"Mom, he has picked every single lock at his school, and sold pencils, papers, and many school supplies to the High School students next door."

"I can't help it!" yelled Dent again.

"I know, baby," said Jennifer. "And what are you doing, young lady. Dent is not the only guilty one here. You've got a cheerleader's uniform in your room, but you're not a cheerleader."

"She stole it, Mom!" yelled Dent.

"Shut up, Dent!" answered Audrey.

"And why do you have seven different book bags when I bought only one?"

"She stole`em, Mom!"

"Shut up, Dent!"

"Go prepare for bed, kids. We'll talk about this later. I know what's going on, and it's ok. But we need to get an understanding about everything that's happening, ok? Now go!"

****

"Terry, I have really enjoyed being here to help straighten up this filthy place!" said Donna.

"Well it's home and I enjoy it, no matter how filthy it is. Now let's fix something to eat."

"No! It's already 10 o'clock! I have to go home, take a shower, and get ready for work tomorrow!"

"I have an idea," said Terry. "Instead of you being out by yourself this late, why don't I give you one of my big shirts? That way, you can clean up here, eat, spend the night, and be fresh in the morning when you awake. You can even sleep in my bed and I will take the couch."

"Oh that sounds so tempting!" said Donna. "I am kinda tired and don't feel like driving. Do you promise to do no funny stuff?" Terry threw up both hands.

"I promise. I'll feed you then you can sleep."

"Ok, it's a date!"

Donna cleaned herself, ate the sandwiches that Terry prepared then went to bed. Terry's bed was nice and comfortable, but Donna still tossed and turned while thinking about Terry and being with him sexually. Terry did exactly the same thing on the couch. After a while, Donna got up and walked to the couch where Terry was sleeping.

"Terry, are you awake?"

"Yeah, what's the matter, Donna?"

"I'm scared." Terry sat up.

"Scared of what, Donna? What's wrong?"

"I want you to make love to me, but I'm a virgin, so I'm scared."

"You're what?" asked Terry being surprised. Donna turned to go back to bed. "Wait-a-minute, Donna. I'm sorry. You caught me by surprise, that's all."

"Terry, if you don't want to do this, then I understand---no hard feelings."

"I didn't say that, Dee. It's just kinda awkward having to face it this way."

"So how should I have told you, then?"

"Well, that's kinda hard to explain, too," he said. Donna was hesitant, but she was serious.

"Terry, I'm 31 years old and I'm not getting younger. I don't need sex, if that's what you're thinking. I know what love is because my sisters show me that all the time. But, I need a man to make love to me and help me to experience what I'm missing while making me feel like a woman. I don't know anything about that and I want you to show me. I trust you, Terry." She took his hand and placed her other hand in his. "Please take me, and do to me whatever you will... please."

Terry couldn't resist against her approach. Her words had staged the moment as Terry picked her up and took her to the bed. Donna was on a high, even though Terry hadn't penetrated her, yet.

The kissing, the necking, and caressing, sent her to a whole new level of life. Just like she needed, Terry was making love to her and she never wanted him to stop.

After Terry penetrated her, she understood why Cherlene moaned and hissed the many nights she listened to her have sex, when they were younger. As her orgasmic moment approached, she started to lose control. Terry knew he had to explain to her what was happening.

"Just be free, baby," he said. "The best intimate moment God has given you is about to spring forth, so just let it happen!" Suddenly, at her release, she screamed.

"Aahhh!" It was heard all throughout the building.

Chapter 100

The next morning, Donna was happy but she was too embarrassed to look Terry in the face. Terry grabbed her and kissed her and tried to make her feel comfortable. Donna felt aroused and soothed as she melted in his arms.

"What's happening to me?" she wondered. *"Am I becoming like Cheryl? Am I a slut? Oh! He feels so good!"* Terry made love to her again, and again, and again. He turned her in many positions and allowed her to take the lead. Donna was having the time of her life that morning.

Afterwards, she headed home to take her shower and change her clothes. She had a whole new outlook on life because Terry had changed her world and she wanted everyone to know. She didn't realize that someone other than Terry already knew because they had been watching all night.

Shortly after Donna left, Terry left for work, also. Hookman entered the premises to check out the place. Now, all he needed to do was lay low until he heard from D-Lo.

As Donna left the shower in her apartment, her phone rang.

"Hello Dee?" yelled Jennifer. "I need some help!"

"Oh, I'm sure it's nothing, Jenny, what's up?"

"My hair! I think I need a beautician or something." Donna pulled Nicole's card from her purse.

"I think I have just the thing! Meet me at my job. I have to check in then we can leave." Thirty minutes later, they met in the AJC parking lot in downtown Atlanta.

****

"Nikki, me and the girls are kinda concerned," said Melody. "You've been behaving very strange since you got news about this woman in the picture. Are you ok?"

"It's just frustrating not knowing what to do," answered Nicole. "What if I really do have a sister out there somewhere?"

"Yeah, and what if she's rich?" added Melody.

"...And got a brother or a son my age?" smiled Tameka.

"You all are so pathetic," said Candi. "Can't you see this is bothering Nicole?"

"You're the one trip'n," said Tameka. "Nicole know that we love her and we're just talking, right Nikki?"

"Whatever, Tameka. Mel, I'm leaving early again, today," said Nicole. "I have one stop to make."

"What!" shouted Melody. "Nikki, what is going on? How can you afford the gas and keep taking off like this?"

"Mel, be easy," said Adrienna. "We all know that Nikki don't normally act like this, so it must be serious."

"Thank you, Drenna. I can't think of nothing else these days. I think I'm losing my mind." The girls went over and hugged her as she prepared to leave.

****

"We are almost there," said Donna.

"Where are you taking me?" asked Jennifer. Donna handed her Nicole's card.

"To see her. She's good with hair and even better with people. I don't really know her, but I got to visit her shop when I was working on a story."

"My hair is a mess. I hope she has time to do it today."

"Well, we will see," said Donna. "We're here, so park over there."

****

"Hey, look who's getting out of the car," said Melody.

"That's Ms AJC, ain't it?" asked Tameka. "And she's got somebody with her whose head is covered. Y'all know what that means... money!"

"I left a message for her," said Nicole. "I didn't think she was gonna stop by."

****

"Dee, slow down a minute," said Jennifer. "It's full of women in there! You didn't tell me that! I'm to embarrassed to go in there like this!"

"Hello ladies," smiled Donna as she stood in the doorway of the Beauty Shop. Jennifer was still outside with her head covered. *"Come on Jenny!"* whispered Donna.

"Hello, Ms. AJC," said the girls in the shop. Nicole met her at the door.

"I'm sorry about that AJC comment," said Nicole. "I guess you got my message to call me. Thanks for coming by."

"I brought you a customer who really needs her hair fixed today. She's my sister and she's about to drive me crazy with this! I told her not to worry because you would fix her up."

"Why thank you for the vote of confidence, Ms. Banks. So young lady, you should step inside and remove your head dress so I can see your hair." Jennifer kept her hand over her face as she stepped inside.

"Oh, I'm so embarrassed," she whined as she lifted her head dressing and revealed herself. Nicole looked into her face and grabbed her mouth.

"See Dee, I told you it was bad," said Jennifer. "She doesn't want to fix it." Nicole suddenly ran back to her station as all the girls watched in wonder. Then she snatched the picture from her mirror and ran back to Jennifer.

"What's wrong?" asked Jennifer. "What are you staring at?" Nicole handed her the picture. Jennifer was surprised to see the picture of herself and didn't know what to say. But when she looked back into Nicole's eyes, it all became clear.

"Sarah?" whispered Jennifer. Nicole dropped a tear and nodded,

"Yes." Jennifer was astounded as she extended her hand and said,

"Sarah Griffin... I'm Jennifer Sweet... your sister."

"Sarah?" whispered Melody. *"When did she become Sarah?"*

"Jennifer," smiled Nicole. "I'm Sarah-Nicole Griffin, your sister." After they stood at the door embraced, Nicole started to play in Jennifer's hair.

"Can you fix it?"

"Oh, I think I can handle it," assured Nicole. "I've looked at this picture enough to know just how you want it."

"Oh that reminds me!" said Jennifer. "I have something that belongs to you. I will get it to you today!"

"That can wait. Come on let me introduce you to the girls and fix your hair." They all happily introduced themselves. Donna was on the phone.

"Come on, Cheryl! Please pick up!" But she only heard the recording.

"You have reached the voicemail of Cherlene. Please leave a message and I'll call you back."

"Cheryl, please call me, please call me! I've got great news! Jenny found her sister!"

****

"That's the last of it," spoke the lady as they loaded her furniture into the moving vehicle. Shaun was walking by the house on Deerfield Trail as a lady and her husband moved out.

"I'm really gonna miss this place," said the man. "But I already love our new place so let's go honey." They stepped into their car and followed the moving van. Shaun doubled back and went to the back of the empty house and forced the door opened. He checked the place then he laid down and went to sleep.

****

After about an hour, Nicole had Jennifer looking as beautiful as ever.

"So what should I call you---Sarah or Nicole?" asked Jennifer.

"Please call me, Nicole. I haven't used the name Sarah, since my teacher called me that in school. It's too old fashioned so I don't use it unless I have, too."

"Nikki, you are old fashioned," said Melody. "But now that I know you, the name Sarah doesn't fit you."

"Our dad must have liked it, because it's by that name that I knew you existed," said Jennifer.

"I found your picture in our dad's personal belongings a few years ago, after he died, but there was no name with it."

"What do you mean, *'a few years ago after he died?'"* asked Jennifer.

"Didn't you know?" asked Nicole. "Our dad died in prison a few years ago, and that's why they told me to come get his things." Jennifer seemed disturbed. She walked outside to avoid too many listening ears as Nicole followed her.

"Nicole, something is wrong with our information. I clearly remember seeing my dad shot to death when I was 7 years old. How can you say he died a few years ago?"

"Honey, I can't debate with you about any of this. I never knew him at all until I got word from this law firm that he was dead," said Nicole. "But since then, I have learned that Mr. Pete Lockhart, the man in prison, was really my dad. I think you are the one who needs reassuring."

"So how can you be so sure he's your dad, if you didn't know anything about him?"

"I talked to the one person who knew---my mom. Maybe she can help you, too."

For the rest of the day, Nicole rode with Jennifer as they talked and got to know each other. They found each other very easy to talk to, and they were both smart and understanding in many ways. They were quickly starting to act like sisters.

"Mom," said Nicole. "This is Jennifer Sweet, my sister, and the girl I called you about."

"Lord, Lord," said Ms. Gerry. "You finally found each other. It was meant to happen. How are you girls doing? Come on in."

"Mom, can you help us to know about our dad? Did you find anything?"

"I never had to look," she said. She pulled out a letter and handed it to Jennifer. The girls stood together and read it.

Dearest Geraldine:

I'm sorry to come to you like this but as you see, I'm in prison. I was shot and almost killed during a robbery just like you warned me might happened, if I didn't quit. Geraldine, I'm so sorry. In spite of all this, I just learned that the woman I live with was also arrested and has been doing time for a year now. That means that my daughter is out there somewhere and I don't know where. You are the only person I know that can help

me. Please find my child, Geraldine. Her name is Jennifer
Sweet. I'm counting on you.
I'll always love you, Pete

"Mom, you knew!" shouted Nicole. "Why didn't you tell me her name when I came to you? Momma that's the same as lying!" Nicole was shocked as she held onto Jennifer, who was crying.

"Sit down, girls," said Ms. Gerry. The girls hesitated. "I said sit down—both of you!" They did. "Nicole, when that letter came, you were 9 ½ years old. Jennifer, I wasn't sure about your age. My mother had just died, and Big, my bother, was killed shortly after that. Big was the closet thing to a father that I had in this world..."

"...And she was my favorite grandma," continued Nicole. "I remember that now."

"Jennifer baby, I looked for you all I could but my mother's death had me messed up inside. I knew the state had you somewhere, but I didn't know where. It took me quite a few years to get myself together. By then there was nothing I could do."

"When I brought you the picture, why didn't you tell me her name?" asked Nicole.

"I didn't know that was her," defended her mom. "I'd never seen the child. Besides, look at me Sarah-Nicole, I'm crippled and disabled and you're all I have left in this world. I didn't want to tell you something that would cause you to worry even more. After you had calmed down, and we could talk, I had planned to tell you everything."

"Tell me about my dad, Ms. Gerry. Did you know my Mom?" asked Jennifer. For the next couple of hours, Ms. Gerry told the girls all she could remember about their dad.

****

"Terry, it's so nice of you to pick me up, today," said Donna. "Jennifer met her sister Nicole and it was so cool! I'm sure they're talking right now."

"Wow, that must've been something!" said Terry. "I'm happy for Jennifer and her sister."

"Terry, you're passing the exit to my job!" shouted Donna. "I have to get my car!"

"It'll be there in the morning when we come back," he responded.

"In the morning?" she asked. "When we come back?" she asked again. "So are you taking me home now?" she asked a third time. Terry looked at her and smiled. Donna finally got it. After that, all she said was... "Hee! Hee!" They spent the night together.

The next morning when Donna awoke, she called in and took the rest of the week off, and so did Terry. For the rest of the week and all through the weekend, Terry and Donna stayed at her apartment like newlyweds. They only went out to get her car one night and even then they pulled over and had sex on the side of the road. She was uncontrollably falling in love.

****

Like Donna and Terry, Jennifer and Nicole were also changing each other. They hung together every chance they could, and visited each other daily, just to talk. Audrey and Dent took a liking to Nicole unlike how they felt for Cherlene and Donna. They even called her every night to say good night and were very excited to see her during the day.

Neither Nicole nor her mom usually did a lot of laughing out loud because they were more laid back. But Jennifer could be exceptional humorous at times, and caused them to laugh until it hurt.

They also had their differences. Though Jennifer looked black like her dad, her nature was like her mother. When Nicole and her mom cooked soul food, Jennifer and her kids had a hard time getting used to eating it.

When Audrey or Dent were disobedient, Nicole attempted to whip them, but Jennifer prevented it; she believed in time out. Overall, the Griffins and the Sweets were the best thing that happened to each other and both were happier than they had ever been.

Eventually, the girls at the shop started complaining about Nicole's neglect to do little things and properly manage the shop. They noticed the decline in customers and addressed it with Nicole. Nicole heard them, but she was overwhelmingly into her new family to act on it.

The same was happening with Jennifer and her business with J.J. Many of Nicole's clientele showed up after work everyday, while most of Jennifer's ate at breakfast and lunch. Therefore, to fix the problems, Nicole started spending the first half of the day learning to help Jennifer manage her coffee shops, then Jennifer would spend the rest of the day at Nicole's shop learning to do hair, while helping to manage the business.

Nicole and Jennifer became such a team, that Nicole's clientele eventually more than tripled. She was forced to rent a bigger place on Old National Highway and to hire more stylists. Likewise, the coffee shops began to expand for Jennifer and J.J. throughout the metro Atlanta area.

Chapter 101

Nicole drove to Jennifer's at about 11 a.m. Monday morning and ran into the house.

"Are you ok? I was waiting for you at the coffee shop this morning but you never showed. What are you doing here?" asked Nicole.

"I was coming in today, but I changed my mind. I have more important plans so I stayed home to think about them."

"Ok, I understand all that, but your phone still works, right?" Jennifer smiled and hugged Nicole with a really warm hug. "What was that for?"

"Because you have brought a joy into my life I didn't even know was possible," said Jennifer. "Today I want to talk to you about something." Nicole sat down.

"You sound like me when I'm at the shop. So I'm gonna sound like Melody and ask, 'You ain't fix' in to die, are you?'"

"I better not be," smiled Jennifer. "This would be a heck of a day to do that!"

"Why is that?" Jennifer sat down next to Nicole.

"Nicole, I have so much I want to share with you, that I never even thought about sharing with Cheryl and Dee. They are my sisters and I love them dearly," said Jennifer. "But you and I, your mom, and my kids... we have this special connection that I can't explain."

"I can explain it," said Nicole. "Blood is thicker than water."

"That maybe so, but that's not what I was thinking."

"So what are you thinking?"

"Do you believe in generational curses or blessings?"

"Do you believe in Jesus?" asked Nicole.

"I don't know much about Jesus," said Jennifer.

"I don't know much about curses and all that, but I know Jesus can handle them."

"You're making this hard, Nicole, so why don't you just shut up and listen, ok?" Nicole chuckled. "What's so funny?" asked Jennifer.

"You have such a good way with words. Nobody ever told me to shut up and listen before, although I know that many times they wanted to. So what's on your mind?"

"Nicole, I think I'm cursed and so are my kids."

"Really now? Explain that?"

" I don't think the curse is on just me and my kids, but it's on Cherlene, Donna, the girls at your shop, your mom, and even you."

"Whoa pony!" Nicole put the hand up. "You're bucking just a little too much, now. So tell me what you're talking about."

"Ok! Cherlene's mother was a prostitute. She loved sex and died in bed while having sex. Now, Cherlene is just like her mother; she never stops having sex. Donna can be so self-centered making things all about her. She doesn't think I know, but her parents were the same way. Dee can be selfish as hell."

"So what's that got to do with me and my mom, or even you and your kids?" asked Nicole.

"Well, our... yours and my dad was a thief."

"So! I'm not!"

"But I am," said Jennifer. "And so are both of my kids. We're all kleptomaniacs."

"Whoa!" Nicole stood up. "I mean... are you serious?" Nicole sat back down.

"I'm very serious, Nicole."

"Am I safe? My place, my business, you know... me?" Jennifer smiled.

"You're safe, Nicole and so is everything about you," said Jennifer. "Although what I have is uncontrollable and permanent, I've learned to recognize the urges and to curve them into a less damaging way."

"Less damaging, huh?"

"Yes, less damaging," repeated Jennifer. Suddenly, Jennifer reached behind her and revealed Nicole's watch.

"How did you get that? That was on my arm!" fussed Nicole. Then Jennifer showed her a button she cut off of Nicole's sweater.

"What! You cut off my button?" Nicole was surprised. Finally, Jennifer handed her the small role of money she took from Nicole's pocket.

"Nicole, when I hugged you, I took all those things and you didn't have a clue. Lastly, if you hadn't sat down when you did, your skirt would've fallen to the floor because I also unzipped it in the back, and you're not wearing a belt." Nicole was slow to speak but she finally did, as she zipped her skirt.

"Huh!" started Nicole. "This is interesting. Seems like you have accepted your curse and you're dealing with it."

"I think that's the key," said Jennifer. "To accept it and deal with it accordingly."

"Well, 'if' I had a curse, then that maybe the case---to accept it and deal with it," said Nicole. "When you started this conversation, you spoke of generational curses and blessings. You can have the curse if you want to, but I have the blessing. I do believe things, good and bad, can be passed on because the bible says they can. But if we put our trust in the Lord, and in the power of His Word, then even a curse can be a blessing. I might be cursed and so may be mother, but we will never know because we are too busy trusting God, and enjoying our blessings!"

"Ok! Ok!" said Jennifer. "If that's how you want to look at it, then go ahead!"

"That's not how I look at it, Jennifer, that's how it is! I don't want to live a life that I have to 'curve' and be 'less damaging.' I just tell Jesus about my problems then leave them there. Ain't no curving, no less damaging, and no curse. It's just me and Jesus with all of my blessings.

I quote: *'As a man thinketh, so is he.'* If you *'thinketh'* you're cursed, then you are. I *'knoweth'* I'm blessed therefore, I am. Change your thinking and you might find a blessing, too." Jennifer paused and thought for a minute. This was the first sermon she had ever had, and Nicole wasn't hesitating to give it to her.

"So how did you get to be so wise, Nicole?"

"The same way you got to be so smart; God did it, and it's our blessing. Now, give me my watch, my money, and my button back! And if you take anything else, I'm gonna *'bless'* you out!" Jennifer laughed and attempted to hug Nicole. Nicole pulled away. Jennifer chuckled again--- Nicole smiled.

"Nicole, I know you just beat me down with your words, but what I don't know is, why do I feel good about it."

"Maybe it's because you hear me saying to let God deal with your curses and you focus on your blessings and how you can please God."

"I think that's what our dad did before he died. His focus was on us, his girls, which were his blessings, and not so much about his own life and the things he was going through," said Jennifer. "He was shot, sick, and in prison, yet, he never asked either of us for a dime. I know how it is. I've been there."

"Were you in prison?" asked Nicole.

"Yes, for 18 months. It's hard to do prison time without family support so I can understand what our dad went through. I had Michelle and my sisters but Dad had no one." Jennifer stood up. "Come ride with me," said Jennifer. "I have something to show you." They got in the car and left. A few minutes later, they walked into the main bank downtown.

"I have... We have a safe deposit box at this bank, with complimentary blessings from our dad. Here is your key I had especially made for you. There are only two keys---I have one, and now, you have the other."

"What about Cherlene and Donna?" asked Nicole. "Don't they have keys in case something happens to you?"

"They don't even know this box exists," said Jennifer. "I've never talked to them about my habits or problems, neither about this box. At first, I didn't know why I didn't want to tell them; especially since I love them so much. But now, I know these things were meant to be shared with you."

"So what's in the box?" asked Nicole. "I'm anxious!"

"Well, you'd better get a hold of yourself, because, though this box holds a lot, it is the little things that will help you to know what we meant to our dad. Come on... let's see if your key works." Nicole placed her key in the slot and turned it. She opened the box and couldn't believe her eyes. The box was full of money!

"How much is this?"

"Two million dollars," answered Jennifer. "It's a million a piece for you and I. At first, I thought I needed this money to live so I started spending it. Then, I learned how to use my curse... ok, my blessing, to my advantage, and my returns have been great! Especially, with the coffee shops!

Therefore, every dime that I took out of this box, I put it back, shortly after we met. This is our box---not just mine." Nicole was blown away by Jennifer's words, and all the money in the box.

"Can I touch it?" she asked.

"Nicole, the only way you will truly feel our dad's love for us, is for you to physically examine everything in the box. Please go ahead; it's yours, too."

Nicole took the crazy looking amulet key in her hand and looked at Jennifer. Jennifer indicated to her that she didn't know what it was. Next, she took out the two bags of diamonds and observed them. "I'll tell you about those in a minute," said Jennifer. Finally, Nicole saw the envelope, and read it.

> *"For my two beautiful daughters whom I love with all my soul. Sarah Griffin-8 years old and Jennifer Sweet-6 years old... from Dad."*

When Nicole read the envelope and saw the necklaces, she could no longer stand to her feet as she weakened and declined toward the floor; Jennifer held her up. They stood there holding each other until Nicole could contain herself again. Then they dried each others tears, and put on their necklaces. Nicole locked the box, and they left.

Chapter 102

"First Block/Big Yard!" yelled the guard at Hinton State Prison. Many of the men went to the big yard that morning.

"Guess who's gonna be at the gate in the morning?" asked Bubba.

"Is it our Big girl?" asked Jones.

"That's right. It's time to do this, man. Tomorrow about this time, we could be well on our way to freedom." He turned to D-Lo. "Are you still down, man?"

"I'm down with the lick," said D-Lo. "When and where?"

"In the breeze way at the cross gate after the 5 a.m. count," said Bubba. "Word is the vans may be rolling a little late in the morning because of lack of staff. They'll be near the gate just as K-Building goes to chow. That's when we will make our move."

"I'll be there," said D-Lo. Then they separated.

"You know what you have to do, right?" asked Bubba.

"I'll handle it," said Jones. "I wouldn't miss this trip for the world, man."

"Good! Hit him at G-Building then make a dash. I'll be waiting."

****

"Umm!" kissed Donna as she laid naked next to Terry.

"You are such a beautiful girl," said Terry. "I don't understand why you've been alone all this time."

" Why didn't you want me?"

"Because I was with Cherlene and you know that."

"It doesn't matter," she said. "Just come over and make love to me." Suddenly, her phone rang.

"Hello, Jenny. How's Nicole?"

"Everybody is fine," answered Jennifer. "And you?"

"Oh I'm great. I decided to take off for a few days because I haven't had a vacation in years."

"Have you heard from Cheryl?" asked Jennifer.

"No, but I called and left her a message. She hasn't called back."

"Is Terry with you?" Donna hesitated.

"A... yeah, he's right here. What's up?"

"Dee, do you think that's a good idea? What would Cheryl say?"

"Jennifer, you were there when Cheryl said to go for it."

"But she had no idea that you were talking about you and Terry. What about Makeda?"

"Makeda's a big girl, Jenny. Things like this happen all the time. Besides, Cheryl has enough problems of her own, right now, than to be thinking about me and a man she doesn't want. Suddenly, Donna heard the whisper, *"The Curse Must Be Broke!"* Donna became very frustrated but tried to hide her expressions from Terry.

"I'm just trying to caution you, Dee, that this may blow up in your face."

"Ok, you've made your point. Bye Jenny!" Donna hung up as her frustration turned to anger.

"What's up with Cheryl and Makeda?" asked Terry. "Are they ok?"

"They're fine," said Donna. "Did you come here to talk about them or to make love to me?"

"I came here for you, Donna, but..."

"Ok, then here I am. Take me and shut up!"

****

"What's up, D-Lo?" answered Hookman.

"It's going down tomorrow," said D-Lo. "Is everything in place?"

"I got Terry in my sights. Just say when."

"When! Go ahead; make the move," said D-Lo. "If all goes as planned, I'll see you tomorrow night---2 days at the most. That depends on what happens when I hit the street. I'll call you as soon as I'm out. Later." He hung up.

****

Shortly after dark, Shaun entered the back fence at Cherlene's place to see if they were home, but nobody was there. He thought about breaking in but he wanted everything to be perfect when Cherlene returned. After a while, he went to his foster home and laid down.

"Shaun," said Ms. Myrtice. "Son, things have to change around here. You're coming in too late at night. Can you do better? Are you still in school? Where are you during the day? Are you working?"

"What do you want, Ms. Myrtice?"

"I want you to talk to me, son, and let me help you."

"You're too old, and you can't help me," he said.

"Maybe I can if you will tell me a..." Suddenly Shaun jumped up, slightly pushed her to the other side of the door, and slammed it shut in her face. She walked away.

The next morning he was back at Deerfield Place, his new hide-a-way, watching a small TV that he burglarized from a neighbors home down the street.

Shaun would stay there until he was bored, then he'd walk the streets and terrorize small stores as he took what he needed. Sometimes, he would go by the High School to see what was happening but he would end up at Cherlene's place during the night. He had lost all sense of life as he walked.

****

"K-Building, chow call!" sounded the guard. D-Lo convinced the officer to let him out of G-Building as the K-Building crew went to breakfast. Jones, who was with the K-Building crew, crept behind D-Lo with his shank and attempted to stab him.

"Ugh!" yelled Jones. Blue, who was laying and watching, stabbed Jones over and over until he was bleeding and screaming for his life. The crowd from K-Building ran wild as D-Lo headed toward the breezeway. He arrived just in time to see Bubba lift the fence and roll under the approaching van.

"Where's Jones?" whispered Bubba.

"He didn't make it, man," said D-Lo. "Cops got him back there!" D-Lo slid under the other van as they heard the code 1 come over the radio, followed by a code 2 and a code 3. D-Lo had planted distractions all over the camp.

As the vans reached the exit gate, the big girl officer was so consumed by the activity being called on her radio, she hardly checked under the vans. A few minutes later, D-Lo and Bubba rolled from under the van and sped away on foot to the car that was waiting. Bubba found the key and started the engine.

"Whoo!" he screamed. "We're home free!" As they drove on highway 49, heading toward Atlanta, the daylight started to appear.

"We have to get out of these clothes or we're dead," said D-Lo. "Where are we going, anyway?"

"I'm going to Jonesboro. Where are you going? Did you set it up?" Bubba handed D-Lo the phone. "Here, call your folks and tell them to meet you in Jonesboro." As Bubba pulled on a side road, D-Lo stabbed him in the neck until he was dead. Then he pulled him out of the car and into the ditch. Suddenly, the phone rang.

"Yeah," answered D-Lo.

"Bubba, is that you?" asked the woman.

"I'm sorry, Ma'am, but Bubba didn't make it. They caught him at the gate."

"Is this Jones?"

"He didn't make it either. This is the D-Lo."

"The D-Lo? Who the hell is that?"

"Bubba told me where everything was in case he didn't make it. He said that you have some clothes for me, but he didn't tell me how to get to your place in Jonesboro. I'm sure Bubba will call you as soon as he can."

"Ok, Mr. D-Lo. I'll tell you how to get here."

As D-Lo pulled into the yard, a young woman in her mid thirties came to the door. Suddenly, a guy driving a wrecker quickly pulled in behind him and jumped out of the truck.

"Where in the hell is my brother, man?" raged the driver. "And who the hell are you?" D-Lo quickly shanked him through his ear and the driver dropped to the ground. He caught the girl inside, trying to get to the shotgun, and cut her throat.

          ****

That same Tuesday morning, about 6 o'clock, Terry was sleeping at Donna's when his cell phone rang.

"Hey Terry, this is Jimmy! Wake up, buddy!"

"Jimmy, what do you want? I'm off today," groaned Terry.

"I know! I know!" said Jimmy. "But remember that little restaurant in Athens on Baxter Street near the Pizza Hut, where we were working? Well, they want to pay an electrician 2 grand for a few days work and I got the job! If you help me, we will split it fifty-fifty, but we have to leave now!" Terry was excited.

"Let me get some clothes and I'm on the way!"

"Meet me at the truck," said Jimmy. They hung up.

"What's going on?" groaned Donna.

"I have to go," said Terry. "I have a chance to make some extra money so I'm gonna take it."

"When will you be back?"

"I'm not sure, but I'll call you and let you know." He kissed her then he was gone. Terry rushed to his apartment to change his clothes and pick up his tools. As he opened the door and walked in, Hookman knocked him out... cold.

          ****

"Hello Dex? It's me... Coldblood. What's up, man?"

"Everything is everything, Blood. Ain't nothing hap'n around here, man."

"Good. That way I can deal with Shaun peaceably when I come."

"What's up with Shaun?" asked Dexter.

"I'm not sure, but it sounds serious. I'm on my way."

"Ok Blood. Holla when you get here. I'm here for you, man."

"Thanks Dex. Peace out!"

Chapter 103

Elisa and Sherri had traveled around the world with Holloway and proven their loyalty to him many times over. So far, Elisa never had to do anything to cause her cover to be jeopardized, and she loved that part. There were many times she got lost in the shuffles of Holloway and almost forgot who she was and why she was there. But Sherri's high standards of superb loyalty to her job, helped Elisa to keep her focus as well.

They had become close friends, and Elisa dreaded the day she would have to arrest Sherri. She could tell that the day was coming when this life of secrecy would soon be over. She just didn't know what she would do after that.

"Here we are," said Sherri. "Back in Atlanta again. I know you don't like coming here, so are you ok?"

"I'm fine," said Elisa. "It's not that I don't like coming here because I love Atlanta. It's just I have so many bad memories that I haven't been able to shake yet. I'm working on them though. You have really helped me; thanks."

"You've done just as much for me as I have for you so don't thank me. Just have my back when these damn shady deals go sour. They make me really nervous sometimes---especially when we have to pull our weapons."

"I welcome those moments," said Elisa. "It feels good to make a guy know that I will bust a cap in him, if he crosses the line."

"Girl, you are so gung-ho! That's what I love about you."

"Did you just call me a guns ho?" joked Elisa.

"Well, if the guns fit, ho, then I guess you're a *guns-ho!*" They laughed.

"That was good, Sherri. It's almost noon so let's check the news to see what's happening in Atlanta before we attend the party tonight." Sherri turned on the TV as they unpacked at the Waverly Hotel.

"This is Channel 2 with breaking news. Earlier today, during a mini riot at Hinton State Prison, two inmates escaped and believed to be heading to the Metro Atlanta area.

Both men; Black 'Bubba' Bastard and Derrick 'D-Lo' Logan were serving multiple life sentences for a string of violent crimes. If you see either of these men, please call crime stopper right away---they are believed to be armed and dangerous."

Elisa suddenly lost all sense of focus as she envisioned D-Lo killing her dad, and Holloway making her to become D-Lo's property. In her mind, she began to relive D-Lo sexing her, night after night, while she laid there and took it.

Finally, she remembered the beating she took that sent her into a coma, after he sperm her and got her pregnant. Elisa was becoming emotionally violent as Sherri grabbed her and wrestled her to the floor.

"BRENDA!" shouted Sherri. "Snap out of it!" Elisa did, and stood up. Then she paced the room.

"Look at me, Sherri, look at me! I can't go on like this!"

"You have to calm down! If Anitra sees you like this, ain't no telling what she will do! Now get a hold of yourself!" whispered Sherri. Anitra came rushing in.

"What was that noise?" she questioned. "What are you doing over here?"

"We were just doing a little practicing," lied Sherri. "...getting ready for the party tonight, that's all. You never know when a crazy woman with a scarf over her face will pop up and attack here in Atlanta, so we just want to be ready." Anitra knew that Sherri was mocking her about the last time they were in Atlanta when Rosa showed up.

"Just keep it down, will you? Don't draw attention to yourselves, you idiots!" Anitra left---Sherri shot her a bird.

****

Meantime, Hookman had Terry tied to a chair.

"What do you want with me?" begged Terry. "Is this about money? Please man!"

"You'll know soon enough," said Hookman. "Now shut up or I'll put you out again. Meantime, if you don't want anything to happen to that little tenderoni you had in here the other night, you'll be quiet and do what I tell you: Got it?"

****

Elisa sat on her bed thinking about D-Lo and all the events that had changed her life. The more she thought, the angrier she became.

"Sherri, this may be my last night with you," said Elisa.

"Brenda, don't say that! We can get past this, just like before."

"Not this time, Sherri. After tonight, I'm going after him. I can't live the rest of my life scared and knowing he's out there. I have to face him."

Chapter 104

That morning after Terry left, Donna called Cherlene but got no answer. Then on her way to work she called Jennifer; Jennifer answered.

"Hey Dee! What's up?"

"I've been calling Cheryl all week long and she hasn't returned any of my calls. This is not like her. Do you think she's ok?"

"Dee, what Cheryl did is very serious. The fact that she just left at the last minute, should tell you that she needs this time alone with her daughter. She doesn't want to answer the phone."

"But I need to talk to her."

"Why?" asked Jennifer. Donna paused. "Is this about you and Terry?"

"Well, sort of!"

"Donna, you still don't get it, do you?"

"But I deserve to be happy, too!" yelled Donna. "Cheryl doesn't want him, anymore! You have a man and now you've got Nicole. What do I have, Jenny? All I want is him; Terry."

"Donna I really had planned to chill at home today and do nothing, but we need to talk. Let's meet for lunch at our spot."

"I'll be there at about 1 o'clock," said Donna. She drove on talking to herself. *"What does Jenny know about being alone... she has a man, and Cheryl gets any man she wants."* She was still fussing with herself as she entered her job. *"I can be a good woman for him and Jenny knows it."*

"Ms. Cuyler, come in here, please!" yelled Mr. Golden as Donna walked in.

"Now I have to deal with this heifer all day," thought Donna. She saw Mr. Golden hand Tenisha a story and Tenisha walked out smiling. Donna slowed her pace as she passed Tenisha's desk, hoping to catch a glimpse of what it was. To her surprise, Tenisha had been watching her every move, and was delighted to slam the story topic on her desk so Donna could read it.

"Gala Celebration-Tonight-Waverly Hotel"

Donna stopped with her mouth opened.

"Tonight! No!" she whispered. "Mr. Golden promised me that story, but I forgot that it was tonight! People from all over the world will be there! How could he do this to me and give it to you, of all people!"

"Maybe it's because I've been here, and you've been gone for almost a week doing... 'Lord knows what,' Donna. Nor have you talked to anybody since you've been gone."

"How would you know I haven't talked to anybody?"

"You don't think I would let your boyfriend Harry, over there, spend the night at my place, eat my food, sleep in my bed, and I not suck him dry of everything he knows, do you? Come on Donna. What kind of girl do you think I am?" joked Tenisha.

Donna sharply turned to look at Tyler. He looked up just in time to see Donna's mouth fly opened, and to see Tenisha smile and wave at him. Tyler smiled and waved back, proudly. Donna acted like she wanted to puke.

"Tyler, how could you?" Tyler later explained that he only spent the night at Tenisha's because, during the huge storm on Sunday night, his car broke down outside of Tenisha's apartment just as she was coming home. She picked him up and allowed him to stay until the storm let up, but it never did. Therefore, Tenisha offered him food while he waited. Tenisha's daughter, Nela, was away in school so Tyler went to sleep on Nela's bed.

"Oooh!" shivered Donna. "She's such a conniving bitch!" Donna saw Tenisha reach into her purse and pull out a disk. Tenisha inserted the disk into her computer and started typing.

"Tyler," smirked Donna. "Don't you think it's about time we found out what's on that disk of hers?" Tyler saw Tenisha insert the disk. After she finished typing, she removed the disk and placed it back into her purse. Then she went to the bathroom.

"Now's our chance, Tyler," whispered Donna. *"Go for it!"* Tyler dropped a stack of papers next to Tenisha's desk then pulled the disk from her purse, which was under her desk. He quickly copied it and put it back in her purse, while Donna watched to distract Tenisha if she had to. Donna and Tyler skimmed over the contents of the disk and learned that Tenisha had a DOD---Diary on a Disk!

"Oh my God," said Donna. "Look at all this stuff! It's her whole life's story; all her secrets!"

"I don't know about this, Donna," said Tyler. "Maybe we have gone too far this time."

"Wait-a-minute!" whispered Donna. "What was that I read about a sister? Back up!" Tyler rolled the screen back and they began to skim the page.

> *"...I will never tell the world that I have a sister because she makes me feel ashamed of her. The man who made her was a whoremonger who just happened to get with my innocent mom, also.*
>
> *My mom knew that my dad was whoring around so I don't know why she allowed him to put her in this trap. Mom was torn apart when she found out, and drank for years. It was only recently that our family is starting to be a family again. I*

love my dad dearly and don't know how he could let this happen in the first place.

Now that things are looking up again, I've been thinking about reaching out to my new-found sister to see if we can come together and represent our family. But she acts like a spoiled brat with no regard for other's feelings as she parades the world like the slut her mom was. Nevertheless, I'm doing my best to love her in spite of her ways."

"Tyler! Put it away," whispered Donna. *"Here she comes!"* Tenisha saw them whispering and knew they were talking about her. "I can't believe that her dad cheated on her mom, and made a child! I've heard that he flirts with women at the bank, but I didn't know he went that far," continued Donna.

"I think I'll finish reading this at home," said Tyler.

"I want to know everything," demanded Donna. "Find out who this sister is and why Tenisha is so ashamed of her. I might just put a story together about this."

"Oh I don't know if you should do that," cautioned Tyler. "How will we explain how we got this information? We can get in trouble."

"As long as the information is not erroneous, when we print it, we will be fine. Now get the information and get me a story. I have somebody I need to go see."

****

"Hello, Dad," phoned Tenisha. *"What are you doing for lunch today? I need to talk about something important. It's about a story that may be right down your alley."*

"Since you put it like that, I guess I'm having lunch with my wonderful daughter. Is it ok if your mom comes? She called first anyway."

"Sure Dad," said Tenisha. "I'll see you shortly after noon." Then she hung up.

****

At 11:30 that Tuesday morning, Donna walked into the bank downtown where Kris worked. He saw her enter from across the floor so he met her.

"My, my, my! It's Ms. 'Tiger Go-getter' Banks, isn't it?" Kris shook her hand with a smile.

"Oh, you remember me!" smiled Donna.

"How could I forget such a lovely young lady that reminds me so much of my daughter?"

"Which one?"

"Uh, which one, what?" smiled Kris. "I have only one daughter; Tenisha."

"Oh you sly son-of-a-gun!" smiled Donna. "That's not what I hear, sir. You've been pretty busy with the women making nightly deposits, haven't you?"

Kris' smile broke. He knew that Donna could have possibly stumbled onto information leading to his many infidelities and was after a story.

"Ms. Banks, would you step into my office, please?" They went in and closed the door.

"So, Mr. Kris Cuyler... playboy... tell me about this other daughter you have? It's obvious that your family is ashamed of her, so that's why you keep her in hiding. Where is she, Sir? How old is she now?"

"Listen, you've obviously got some wrong information, Ms. Banks. I don't have another daughter."

"Tenisha thinks so, and I wonder what your wife will say when I talk to her." Donna pretended to leave. "Maybe she will start drinking again, huh?"

"Wait, Ms. Banks!" Donna sat down again. "You said Tenisha knows about this? What did she say? Is that why my wife drank all those years?"

"I'm sure she doesn't talk about it because she doesn't want the world to know about your whorish affairs. But it's out now, Mr. Playboy! Unless you give me what I want, the papers and TV will run wild with this. All I want is an exclusive."

"But I don't know anything!" yelled Kris. Donna stood again to leave.

"Then I guess your whole life is about to change, Sir."

"If Tenisha knows about this, then my life is already over," groaned Kris. Kris had cheated with so many different women in the past, that he really didn't know if he had an illegitimate daughter or not. Tenisha was his life, and Donna had convinced him that Tenisha knew of his infidelity. He was sure this was why Tenisha wanted to meet with him today, to tell him that she knew.

Suddenly, Tenisha entered the bank to take her dad to lunch, so she could talk to hi. She saw Donna leaving her dad's office.

"We'll talk later, Sir," smiled Donna. "Remember, I want that exclusive." As Tenisha walked toward his office, he looked at the gun in his desk and thought about suicide. He had no idea that Donna had the information all wrong!

"What are you doing here?" demanded Tenisha.

"It's a bank, Tenisha; Duh!" said Donna. "People come here for money!"

"You better not be making trouble here, Donna."

"My, my! Daddy's little girl is kinda over protective, isn't she? Chill out, Glamour Bitch! You're causing sweat to ruin your cheap make-up!" Then Donna walked out.

Kris sat in his office watching Tenisha and Donna talk. He couldn't hear what they said but he knew that it wasn't good.

As Tenisha started again toward his office, his heart felt like it was gonna jump out of his chest! The sweat poured from his face as the central air blew on him like a blizzard; yet he sweated and he was so nervous.

When he was younger, Kris lived to prey on weak women day after day, because the love he had at home just wasn't enough. Thereforea he sowed his adulterous seed all over the country in search or contentment.

As Tenisha grew and showed him how much she loved and needed him, his life took on new meaning, and he gladly forsook all other women except his wife. Tenisha had become the love of his life---his main reason to live.

But now, the thoughts of her knowing about his infidelities and believing he had a child somewhere else, had broken his heart. What would he say to her? What could he say to her?

Kris looked at the gun in his desk again as Tenisha came closer. She was so beautiful... so poised and eloquent as she strolled toward him. He felt so blessed to see this smart, beautiful, creature, that God had delivered from his loins. Finally, he closed the drawer shut, and decided to take whatever she threw at him. She was his heart, and he dared not let her see him blow his own brains out. It was by far the worse moment of his life.

As she reached his office door to enter, Kris saw a ray of hope; a spark-like beacon of light, that pierced its way through his office window, and lodged into his heart! It was Tenisha's smile. Kris knew there was a God, and he saw Him in her smile.

"Hello, Daddy." She happily smiled and hugged him. "Are you ready to go?"

"Ah.. Da.. uh... um.. ah... yeah!" stuttered Kris. He turned to wipe the tears from his eyes so she wouldn't see them. "We, uh.. have to wait for your mom."

"Ok," said Tenisha. "What was Donna here about?"

"Oh, just ah... bank business," he stuttered again. Tenisha closed the office door.

"Donna doesn't bank here, Daddy. I thought that you think I am too intelligent for you to toss me an answer like that. So what did she want, Dad? The truth this time."

As Kris stared into Tenisha's eyes, his legs could no longer support his body, no more than the morality in him could support his lies and deception. He was right back where he was a minute ago as he eased into his chair to talk. He turned his face from her as he spoke:

"I haven't been honest with you, 'T.'" Kris was sad. "It appears that my past life have reared itself again and taken its place in my life."

"Dad, stop this long winded crap and just tell me what was she doing here!"

"She told me that you knew already," said Kris.

"That I know what? That I can't trust her?" Kris was surprised and began to settle down.

"When you called earlier, you said you wanted to talk to me about something. What is it you came to talk about?"

"The Gala tonight, at the Waverly Hotel. I was gonna ask you to escort me." After a minute of thought, Kris burst into laughter at how stupid he had been to Donna's inquisition.

"Dad, for the last time, stop this!" yelled Tenisha. "This is not funny! What did she say?"
Kris calmed.

"She mentioned something about me having another daughter, or something, and that you knew. She said that we keep this child hidden because we are ashamed and don't want people to know about my past."

As Tenisha listened to her dad talk, she grew angrier than she had been in a long time. This may even have been her peak. She realized that Donna must have stolen her DOD and read her personal information and she was furious.

"Tenisha honey," continued Kris. "I've done so many really bad things in my past that I'm not proud of, but I've changed now."

"Dad, please stop!" Tenisha was so mad. "I know that you and mom are no saints so please spare me the sermon and benediction! What I want to know is, how could you let Donna just walk up in here and sell you some shit that you know nothing about?" Tenisha walked out as Davina walked in.

"Honey! Where are you going?" yelled Kris. "What about lunch?"

"I'm not hungry!" she responded angrily as she rushed out.

"What about the Gala tonight?"

"Take Mom!" Tenisha was gone as Davina stood in wonder.

"What is going on at this bank?" she asked. Kris burst into laughter.

"God has smiled on me, Davina!" He kissed her. "This is the happiest day of my life!"

Chapter 105

Tyler knew that reading Tenisha's diary at work was too risky of him being caught or seen by the wrong person. So he went home for lunch to read the disk.

"Wow!" he said. "Look at all this stuff!" Tyler saw everything from Tenisha's college years even to the present. He didn't have time to read it all so he read what he needed to help Donna piece together a story. But as he read, something within him started changing.

He read how Tenisha suffered at home being an only child with her dad and mom always on business ventures; how she fell in love while in college, got pregnant, and dumped by the man she was supposed to marry.

He read about her efforts to make things right with Donna for years, and how she really admired them as a family, even though Cherlene and Jennifer were not her blood sisters. He read about Tenisha's parents and the things they went through that affected her life. Tyler read so much about how Tenisha had suffered and her efforts to do good, that he started feeling hate for Donna, whom he thought he loved.

****

It was shortly after one o'clock as Donna and Jennifer met at the coffee shop.

"Ok Dee," started Jennifer. "Tell me what's on your mind."

"I just don't think it's fair, Jennifer, that when I've finally found someone for me, and you seem to have a problem with it."

"What?" shouted Jennifer. "Are you talking about you and Terry? Dee, he has a child by our sister, for peace sake? Don't you even care about that?"

"Terry is a free man and I am a single woman! I have every right to him as Cheryl does. Besides, how can you talk against it when you slept with a married man, and had a baby by him?"

"That was different and you know it, Dee. I had no idea Mitch was married. What has gotten into you?"

"I can ask you that question too, Jennifer. Every since you found Nicole, you've been acting really funny. You even took Tenisha's side over mine when I needed you."

"Dee, that is not true. I only said that Tenisha seemed like she has truly changed. How is that taking her side against you?"

"If she has changed so much, then why is she and her family trying to hide her bastard sister from the public's eye?"

"Tenisha has a sister?"

"Yep!" said Donna. "But she's hiding her and I'm gonna expose her and her family soon." Jennifer couldn't believe her ears.

"Dee, this doesn't sound good. Why don't you just put everything on hold until Cheryl gets back, then, we can all talk about it."

"You would love that, huh? Then you and Cheryl can team up against me and tell me how wrong I am for wanting Terry, and for trying to take my career ahead of Tenisha's.

Frankly, I'm kinda sick of you and Cheryl trying to run my life. I am a woman and Terry thinks I'm a good one. But you and Cherlene treat me like I'm a kid---like my decisions are all wrong about everything . Why Jennifer? You and Cheryl found your own way. Why don't you let me find mine?" Jennifer picked up to leave.

"Dee, I don't know where this is coming from, so I'm gonna just let it go, and maybe we can talk another time. I'll see you later." Donna angrily talked to herself as Jennifer left. Then both girls tried to dial Cherlene.

"This is Cherlene... leave a message and I'll call you back."

"Where are you, Cherlene?" spoke Jennifer. "Dee really needs you now."

"Where are you, Cheryl," spoke Donna. "You can run, but I will find you. I want to tell you something you need to know!" Donna hung up and drove back to work while dialing Tyler. Then she heard, *"The Curse Must Be Broken!"* She was so startled to hear the whisper that she drove off the road and almost wrecked.

Jennifer, also being upset, was desperately trying to calm herself because being upset sometimes causes her to steal. That's how she would regain her peace whenever she became stressed.

"The Curse Must Be Broken!," she heard. As she entered her home, she was so stressed that she snatched the mail from the box and threw it on the table without reading it. Within the mail was her first letter from Margit, her mom, and she never even saw it.

****

Tyler was home reading over the last few segments of Tenisha's Diary on a disk. The things he learned had not only changed his perspective of Tenisha, but he had developed a dislike for Donna.

"Hello Tyler?" phone Donna. "How's it going? Do we have a story?"

"Donna, I can't do this," said Tyler. "Besides, it's not at all what you think." Donna became enraged.

"Why is it that everybody suddenly wants to push or pull against me? Tyler you will get your butt to my office with that information or I will be sure to let Tenisha know how we got it. Is that clear? It's time to print the story!" Then she hung up and drove with the whisper ranging in her ear... *"The Curse Must Be Broken!"*

Chapter 106

"This has gone too far," she murmured. "Messing with me is one thing, but you have gone after my family, you little slut, and it must all end here, today. It's now or never, Lord. I can't take this anymore!" Tenisha angrily talked with herself as she drove back to work. As she neared her job, she saw Donna turning onto a side street also heading toward the job. "Ah! There she is!" Tenisha floored her gas pedal and drove straight for Donna's car.

"Bang! Crash!" sounded the cars as they smashed together. Tenisha rammed into Donna's driver's side rear panel and sent Donna's vehicle sliding across the street. Tyler drove up just in time to see Donna step out of the smashed car. She was a little shaken but unharmed.

"You bitch!" yelled Donna. "You did that on purpose, and I'm gonna see to it that you pay dearly!" Tenisha jumped from her car and ran toward Donna screaming.

"Stay away from my family, you selfish slut, or I will kick your..."

"Bring it on, Tenisha!" yelled Donna. "I've been waiting a long time for this!"

For the first time since high school, they were mad enough to harm each other as their bodies clashed together and they fell. Tyler sprang from his vehicle and separated them while they struggled to get to each other.

"Go!" yelled Tyler to Tenisha. He pointed to the other side of the road where Tenisha's vehicle was stopped. "Go now, Tenisha!" he demanded while holding Donna back.

Tenisha and Donna were a little surprised by Tyler's efforts to take charge. They had never seen him like this before, but they could tell by the authority in his voice, that he had manned up to the task and he meant business

"Tenisha, this is the last time I'm gonna tell you to go. Now get your ass across the street... now!" Tenisha hesitantly turned and walked away. "I read your diary," said Tyler. "I know the truth." Tenisha stopped and gave him a teary-eyed disappointing look as if to say,

"Why?" Then she hurried toward her car being sad and in tears. Suddenly, Donna started shouting.

"That's right, Glamour Bitch! We know all about your secret sister and your whoremonger dad, and I'm gonna write about them!"

"Stop it, Donna!" yelled Tyler.

"No! She needs to understand that we know all about her and her family secret, while she's trying to act so righteous!"

"I said stop it, Donna!" shouted Tyler angrily. "We've made a mistake!"

"It's not a mistake, Tyler!" yelled Donna. "We read it from her own diary that she has a bastard sister! Why are you protecting her?"

"Because she is not hiding her sister," shouted Tyler. "She's trying to protect her and get to know her! Her dad is not the whoremonger, Donna! It's your dad!"

"What!" Donna was shocked as she calmed down.

"She's been trying to protect you, Donna," said Tyler calmly. "Your dad, is also her dad! You are her sister!"

For a brief moment, Donna was stunned speechless. Then selfish thoughts led her to believe that Tenisha had somehow twisted the story in effort to ruin her life.

As her rage increased, she released an eerie, almost evil scream, as she ran full speed toward Tenisha to harm her. Her attention was so madly focused on getting to Tenisha that she paid no attention to the traffic, as a truck met her waistline and sent her flying through the air.

"Aahhyee!" screamed Tenisha as the truck made contact. Tyler rushed to Donna's side, who was out cold. Tenisha while trembling with fear, was afraid to move or look.

"Get an ambulance!" came a yell. "She's alive!" Tyler took over the scene until police and paramedics arrived. Tenisha finally came to herself and went to Donna's aid. When the paramedics arrived Tenisha was sitting on the ground with Donna's head in her lap, nurturing her. After Donna was strapped into the emergency vehicle, the paramedics asked,

"Who is going with her?"

"I am!" said Tyler. Tenisha calmly touched Tyler and said, "No, I am; I'm her sister."

Chapter 107

"Hello, Rosa," spoke one of the agents. "Welcome back."

"Thanks. It's good to be back." Rosa was sitting at the agency's computer looking up information about her family. She wanted to know what kind of life her daughter had and to see if she would forgive her and take her back. Suddenly, Agent Walter came in and Rosa quickly followed him toward his office.

"Agent Ruby," he talked. "Tonight is a very important night. As you know, we've been tracking this guy all over the country and now he's in Atlanta. Somehow, we have to contact our undercover agent and get an update. We need one more set of eyes in there that won't seem so conspicuous."

"Chief," interjected Rosa. "Can I talk to you? Maybe I can help."

"Not now, Rosa, I'm busy!" Rosa stood fast so Agent Walter motioned for Agent Ruby to leave.

"What is it, Rosa?"

"You've been deliberately ignoring me and my request to go back into the field. Why?"

"It's not that simple, Rosa. Things have changed since you and I were out there. There's a string of questions and red tape from here to Washington about why I've even brought you back. They think it's a bad move, Rosa. With the hell that I'm catching because of this huge case we are working on, I'm starting to think so, too!"

"Walter, I'm sorry, but I can't just sit around anymore and wait to die. Please Walter, help me! Let me die doing what I do best... please!"

"Ok Rosa, give me a couple of days to get through this case and I promise I'll send you out... somewhere."

"Thank you, Sir; I won't let you down." She turned to leave.

"Rosa," he paused. "I know you won't let us down. It's just that you became the most distinguished target for hit men all over the world, once you learned about Holloway's operations, and forced him to rewrite his book.

The Agency still believes that some of those hit men are still around. They also believe that the first time you show your face, you'll be dead in 24 hours, and we may not be able to prevent it."

"I know, chief," she responded. "But it's a chance I'm willing to take." As she headed out of the building, her private cell rang.

"Yes?" she answered.

"The Serpent Surfaces," came the voice. Rosa immediately ran out.

****

Jennifer was home with her kids going through the stuff in her basement when Susie called. Donna had gotten her upset so she needed something to do to keep herself calm.

"Hello, Jennifer? What'cha doing?"

"I'm just going through some stuff with the kids. What's up with you, Susie? You wanna come over?"

"Not really. I'm kinda busy myself, but I just wanted to check on you."

"That is so thoughtful, Susie. Thank you. Me and the kids are looking at our nearly empty basement, wondering what are we gonna do with it next, once we get rid of all this stuff."

"What do you mean by *'what'cha gonna do with it next?'* Are you sure you're ok?" Jennifer paused.

"What's going on, Susie? You keep asking me that like I shouldn't be ok, right now, so spell it out," demanded Jennifer.

"It's nothing; I was just ch..."

"...Checking on me, yeah I know! You're lying, Susie, now tell me the truth!"

"It's just that I heard from a friend that there's another one of those big parties tonight, at the Waverly, and I didn't want you to make me go with you, if you were going."

"Susie, do you think that I made you go with me the last time?"

"You are kinda my boss and I didn't want to lose my job. So when you asked, I went," said Susie. Jennifer was surprised.

"I am so sorry about that, Susie. But you are my friend, and I was asking for your help as a friend. Please don't ever think I will make you do anything like that."

"Whew!" said Susie. "That's a relief. I was so scared the last time, especially when that crazy woman attacked us in the car. I was scared for you, too!"

"Well don't be," said Jennifer. "I'm not planning anything tonight except to stay here with my kids. Good night, Susie." They hung up.

Jennifer continued to think about all that Susie said while straightening and cleaning her basement. *"I will personally take Susie a gift tomorrow and apologize for making her feel that way,"* she thought. *"I never meant to make her feel like that."* She continued to work but she couldn't get thoughts of the party out of her head.

"Hmm? The Waverly, huh! I wonder what time?"

"Ding-dong," rang the doorbell.

"Oh!" whispered Jennifer. "Kids let's go!" She and the kids hurried up the stairs to prevent anybody from knowing about the stolen stuff in the basement. When they reached the top, she met Marquis, who was already standing inside the house and heading to the basement door. "Marquis," she smiled. "How'd you get in?"

"The door was unlocked. I ranged the doorbell a few times but no one answered. So I turned the knob to see what was going on." Jennifer looked at Audrey who was locking the basement door.

"Don't look at me!" said Audrey. Jennifer looked at Dent.

"Mom, I locked it!" he said. "Cross my heart and hope to die!"

"Good thing I came along when I did, huh," said Marquis. "Had it been a thief, he could have cleaned you out while you guys were in the basement." They all faked a laugh then Jennifer frowned at Dent again. He yelled,

"But Mom, I did lock it! I promise!"

****

"Hello?" answered Hookman.

"This is the D-Lo. Do you have the boy?"

"I got him, man. Where are you?"

"Not far," said D-Lo. "But things are still kinda hot so I better lay low another day until they kill the dogs. You ok with that?"

"It's cool, man. That'll give me time to get to know this young white thang that stops by every now and then for a little lov'in. I've got your number locked in if I need you: Peace." D-Lo hung up and dialed again.

"Hello, Club Turner!" answered the manager.

"Cheese, this is the D-Lo."

"What's up, man? I saw you on the news, brother. Are you ok?"

"I need some info. Can we talk?"

"I have your number and I'll call you back in a few minutes on my cell."

****

It was an hour after dark as Jennifer and her kids ate supper. Marquis was also eating with them.

"Ok kids, supper is over," said Jennifer. "Prepare for bed." The kids said their goodnights and left. "Marquis, I think I'm gonna turn in early, too, so would you mind?"

"No honey, not at all. I've got a few clients I need to prepare for before I get to bed tonight and this will give me time." Marquis kissed Jennifer good night, then he left.

"The Waverly Hotel," thought Jennifer. She knew what was happening so she didn't try to fight it as she went into the bedroom to say good night to her kids.

"Mom, will you call Aunt Nicole for me and say good night?" asked Dent. "I'm too sleepy." Jennifer smiled and tucked him in. Then she went to see Audrey.

"Here's Mom, now, Aunt Nicole. I'll talk to you later," said Audrey. "Good night." She handed Jennifer the phone.

"What's up, Sis?" asked Jennifer.

"Just saying good night to my niece and nephew," said Nicole.

"Well, I'm saying good night to my sister. Good night, Nicole. I love you."

"I love you, too, Jennifer. We'll talk tomorrow. Good night."

"I love Aunt Nicole," said Audrey.

"I know, Sweetie," said Jennifer. "We all love her. She's such a blessing... and that reminds me. I have to go out tonight, ok?"

"Mom, you go out a lot of nights. I'm not always asleep and I hear you," said Audrey. Jennifer laughed and tickled her.

"Ok, you got me, you sneaky little thing! But tonight is different. I may be out for a while. If I'm not back by morning, call Nicole, ok?"

"Ok, please hurry back, Mom."

"I will, now go to sleep. Good night, baby." Jennifer kissed her and tucked her in. An hour later, Jennifer grabbed her gear and she was out the door. She never suspected Marquis was parked and watching her leave.

****

"Ok, it's time to go, ladies," ordered Anitra. "Mr. Holloway wants us to have escorts tonight and stay sharp. Don't want anything happening like the last time. Now let's go."

"Wouldn't you like to just piss on her face while she talks?" asked Elisa.

"No, but I do wish she'd shut up, sometimes; she's annoying," responded Sherri. Anitra, Sherri, and Elisa, met three of Holloways men at the elevator, who escorted them to the main dining and ball room.

After Elisa and Sherri stepped into the elevator with their escorts, Holloway stepped in with his girls, followed by Anitra and her escort. They knew that the business here wouldn't take long because Holloway had his private party scheduled for midnight on his yacht at Lake Lanier. But something had him spooked, because he doubled the protection as he took his seat at the table.

Chapter 108

Marquis watched Jennifer drive off then he eased to the back door, popped the lock, and snuck in. Walking with his mini camera, he checked the drawers in Jennifer's bedroom and went through her personal belongings. He took pictures of her clothes, jewelry, and anything that had high value to it. Finally, he popped the lock to the basement and went in. He was surprised!

"How in the world could she get all this stuff!" he wondered. He saw nice expensive coats, clothes, jewelry, bed covers, house wares, vacuums, microwaves, radios, flat screen TV's, bicycles, toys, tools, printing equipment, and so much more. Marquis quickly took pictures of everything. As he attempted to leave the basement, Audrey saw him and locked him in.

****

Unlike before, Jennifer picked pocketed one of the guests ID from her purse and walked right in.

"Piece of cake," she thought. She checked things out, laid her plan, and immediately went to work. Her phone was in her car, so she had no idea that Audrey was calling to tell her about Marquis.

****

"Let me out of here, Audrey, or you will be in big trouble!" Marquis yelled. Audrey tried to dial Jennifer again after Marquis told her who he was.

Marquis, an undercover GBI agent assigned to follow Jennifer shortly after she left prison, knew she was a master thief but they wanted catch her. Marquis had made it all the way to her bed, but this was the first time he had any hard evidence that he could make stick. Audrey opened the door to the basement and Marquis showed his badge.

"Where is your mother?" he asked. "Where did she go?" Audrey didn't know. Marquis called in and asked questions.

****

Rosa did her name plate thing and was in the ballroom in a snap. She immediately spotted Holloway, but couldn't see his protectors.

"Where are you?" she whispered. *"You've changed on me, but I know you're here."* Finally, she spotted Anitra and remembered her from the last time. When she saw Sherri, she figured out that they changed

their seating and Holloway had protection on every side now. Nevertheless, she was determined that this night, she or Holloway would die. She wasted no time reaching under her dress to pull out two darts, then she hurled them at Holloway.

Suddenly, she saw Jennifer step between her darts and Holloway while attempting to pick pocket a guest. Sherri's quick eye-to-hand coordination caught one of the darts as the other one grazed Holloway's ear.

Jennifer saw Rosa and wondered if the dart was meant for her. By the time Sherri looked in the direction where the dart came from, Rosa was already floating through the air with a kick of death heading straight for her. The kick only stunned Sherri and knocked her down because Elisa saw Rosa coming and kicked her out of the air, just as she connected with Sherri.

Rosa saw Anitra rushing Holloway out as two men with weapons blocked the door. Jennifer, like Rosa, was now trapped inside.

"Damn crazy woman!" Jennifer thought. *"Why now! Why me!"*

The guests, who were running, were making it hard for the men to shoot Rosa as Elisa approached to fight her. Rosa quickly tossed darts into the electrical sockets, the light switches, and the lights, and the place went dark. She threw Elisa over her back and fled to safety. Then she dropped her dress and revealed her fighting tights that were fully armed with a glock, a knife, and plenty of darts. She went to work whipping everything she touched.

Eventually, only Rosa, Elisa, and Sherri, were left in the room fighting in the dark. When the lights came on again, Jennifer had dropped her dress and was dressed in black tights like Rosa then dove between the two armed men at the door and quickly released their clips and ejected their bullets.

"Oh she's quick!" thought Rosa. *"Just the time I needed."* As Rosa kicked Sherri out cold, Elisa pulled her pistol and pointed it to fire. But Rosa was so quick she touched pressure points to Elisa's wrist and took the pistol. Elisa was shocked as they stared at each other for a brief moment.

"Who are you?" asked Elisa. "What do you want?"

Rosa punched her out then hit the men at the door as she ran out, trailing Jennifer. They almost made it out of the building as cops drove up and flooded the front entrance. Jennifer and Rosa ducked into a corner as cops headed to the ballroom. For the first time, they stood face to face... watching... checking each other.

After the cops passed, Rosa darted out to find another exit, with Jennifer following her. Sherri and Elisa were only a few feet behind them. Finally, Rosa saw an exit off the back dock and sped toward it, with Jennifer being close. Elisa and Sherri were no longer in sight. Rosa burst through the double doors with Jennifer on her heels. By the time Jennifer went through the doors, Rosa was gone.

"Wow!" thought Jennifer. *"Where did she go? She's got to teach me that trick!"*

As Jennifer jumped from the dock and left the hotel, she met cops around the corner that forced her to change directions.

"Oh no! Not this time, Tenisha! No more pictures of me in the papers!" She used her speed to jump cars to out maneuver the police, and to outrun the few that were on foot.

After she made it to Galleria Parkway, she crossed the main road and headed toward the Embassy Suites hotel. Many cops were behind her, but she saw only one car approaching. *"Ha!"* she said. *"Only one car left; a piece of cake!"* The police car stopped just as Jennifer diverted to out maneuver it.

"Jennifer! Wait!" yelled the man's voice. Jennifer kept running.

"Who the hell is that calling my name?" she wondered. *"Voice sounds familiar."*

"Jennifer, it's me, Marquis. Please stop!" Jennifer stopped and turned.

"We know who you are, Jennifer; we've always known! We know about the stores you've hit, and even the people you've helped with it. And we know about the stuff in your basement!" Jennifer was shocked to tears as Marquis approached her.

"Marquis, you ate at my table and slept in my bed. Was it all for this?" Jennifer was hurt as other police officers pulled in. Some were on foot with Elisa and Sherri trailing the crowd. Suddenly, Jennifer reached into Marquis jacket, pulled his weapon, and stuck it to his head.

"So Marquis," she said angrily. "Since you know everything else about me, did you know I was gonna do this? Huh? Did you?"

"Jennifer, please put the gun down. You're not a killer."

"Do you know that for sure, Marquis?" she yelled. "Do you? My mother wasn't a killer either before you put her in that hell hole of prison, but now look at her. She can't ever get out! Let's go, Marquis!" She forced him into the lobby of the Embassy Suites Hotel, then she cried and waited for what would happen next. Elisa and Sherri came up.

"Are they inside?" asked Elisa.

"Yes, but only one of them," answered an officer. "She's holding Agent Marquis hostage at gunpoint. He says her name is Jennifer Sweet. Do you know her? Is she a friend of yours?"

"Brenda," said Sherri. "We'd better go. Our ride will be looking for us."

"No," said Elisa. "I think I know this girl. I'm going in." Elisa ran inside the building where Jennifer and Marquis were.

"Ma'am, hold on!" yelled the cop. "She's got a gun!" Elisa walked in.

"Stop!" yelled Jennifer. "Who are you? Don't move another step!"

"I'm a friend, Jennifer."

"Are you a cop?"

"Yes, but I'm a friend, too. I'm undercover right now, like my mom was when I first met you, a long time ago."

"Lady, what are you talking about?" asked Jennifer. Elisa paused then spoke.

"When I was 10 years old, I lost my mom and I saw my dad killed. I became an orphan just like you. Before my mom disappeared, we were walking down Candler Road in Decatur, when we saw a man run out of a pawn shop and was gunned down, while his 7 year old daughter watched.

Within seconds, that same little girl saw her mom get arrested and taken to jail. That little girl was you. I know that because as you saw your dad shot and your mom arrested, it was my mother that grabbed you and kept you until you were taken away. I stood on the street behind my mother, that day, crying with you because I felt your pain. I was 7 years old then, just like you.

"You're lying," cried Jennifer. "There was no child at that house when I was there. Nor in the car when I was taken away."

"Yes Jennifer, I was there, but I was scared. You cried so hard, that I laid down in the car near the front seat, while Mom held you in the back. I didn't want to see your tears because it hurt too much. After I got home, I hid in my room until you left." Elisa shed some tears.

"Three years later, the same thing happened to me. I lost my mom and I saw my dad brutally beaten and shot to death. When I lost my parents, I remembered how you cried, that day, and I haven't been able to forgive myself ever since. I promised God that if I ever got a chance to apologize to you that I would. Well, here we are... again." Both women were crying.

"I left you alone once to deal with those things you were going through, and I am sorry. But tonight, I've decided not to leave you again. I'm here for you, Jennifer, because we're a lot alike. But what you're doing with that gun is not who we are. I know you have issues, Jennifer; we all do. But you and I have a special gift that helps us to love people and to help them with their issues."

"Shut up!" shouted Jennifer. "You don't know me, so shut up!"

"Yes I do know you, Jennifer, and you know me. When it comes to someone we care about, you know that we can never just *'shut up'* because that's not our way. Just like we care about others, we care about each other, because that's how we're built. So, I know you're not gonna shoot or threaten anybody else here because that's not who we are. We... you and me... are built on love for others and that's who we are." Elisa paused.

"I'm gonna come over and get the gun, then you and I are gonna walk out of here, together, being who we are." Jennifer didn't know Elisa, but she felt her passion and knew that Elisa was right. She thought about Nicole's words as thoughts of the innocent woman she used to be, filled her mind.

"I don't want to be cursed, anymore," cried Jennifer.

"Then come on, honey," smiled Elisa. "Let's claim our blessings, right now." Jennifer handed her the gun and broke into a very emotional cry as Elisa hugged her. As they stood embraced, the wind of strife that was upon Jennifer blew away and vanished as a ray of light suddenly illuminated her. Then Jennifer heard the whisper, *"You... Are... Blessed! The Curse... is Broken!"*

"Come on, Sweetie, and let's make our parents proud!" Elisa handed Marquis the gun and they walked out, together. Jennifer was placed in the police car.

"Oh Jennifer! I have one more question," said Elisa. "The woman that fought with us tonight, who is she and what does she want?"

"I don't know her," sniffed Jennifer. "We just ran into each other a couple of times and that's it. But I have a question for you, too. What is your name?"

"My name is Elisa... Elisa Smith." As Jennifer was taken away, Sherri was confused.

"I thought your name was Brenda Lewis," she said. "Who are you?"

"I am the same person you knew an hour ago, yet, I am someone who really need you to trust me and what I am about to do.

For the first time in years, we're out here; free, all because we chased a woman who is after Holloway. Right now, Holloway believes that we are chasing her, and we were until she escaped. Now I'm asking you to help me, this time, to catch the man that killed my dad and destroyed me and my child. Please Sherri, I'm asking for your help."

"Ok," answered Sherri. "But first tell me your name; your real name."

"My name is Elisa, but that's all you need to know for now. Come on, let's go." Elisa and Sherri left on foot going back to the hotel.

"Wait here," said Elisa. She left Sherri in the parking lot next to the Hotel's van while she ran inside to talk to the manager. Moments later, Elisa had the key to the van and they drove off. Anitra had been watching them from a distance every since they initially started chasing Rosa and Jennifer.

****

"This is Cherlene. Leave a message at the beep and I'll call you back."

"Where are you, Cherlene?" Tenisha asked herself. She had tried many times to call Cherlene and Jennifer after she arrived at the hospital with Donna, but couldn't get them.

"Cherlene, this is Tenisha again. Please call me the moment you get this, thanks." It was well after nine p.m. and Donna was still in a coma. Tenisha patiently waited by her bedside as Kris and Davina rushed in.

"How is she?" asked Kris. "We came as soon as we got your call."

"She's in a coma," said Tenisha. "Doctors say that she can wake at anytime now. She has a broken hip and some internal bleeding, but that's all they know for now. They hope to run more tests when she wakes up." Kris and Davina were dressed for the Gala at the Waverly, but had diverted to the hospital when they got Tenisha's call.

"Have you been able to reach her sisters?" asked Kris.

"No, not yet."

"I'll try to call them later," said Davina. "Is there anything else we can do, honey?"

"No, Mom. Why don't you and Dad go on home and get some rest. I'll be fine, here," said Tenisha.

"Ok, honey," said Kris. "If you need anything at all, just call me, ok?" Kris and Davina left after they hugged Tenisha. After they had gone a ways, Davina stopped.

"Oh, I forgot to get Donna's sisters' numbers from Tenisha. I'll be right back, Kris. I'll meet you at the car." Tenisha saw her come back.

"I had a feeling you'd be back."

"I had to come," said Davina. "What happened?" Tenisha was still a little teary.

"She knows, Mom. She knows that we are sisters." When she found out, she went into a rage and didn't see the truck coming."

"Oh honey, I'm so sorry. Does your dad know?"

"No he doesn't, but he may find out from her. She tried to tell him today, but she got the story twisted and Dad doesn't believe her."

"He must not find out, Tenisha, or it will destroy him."

"I know. That's one of the reasons I plan to stay right here until she wakes up. I have to know her plans." Davina smiled and kissed her.

"You are a wonderful daughter and a good person, Tenisha. I'm glad you're my daughter, no matter who your father is. I love you so much." Davina hugged her then she left.

Chapter 109

"Hello, D-Lo?"

"Yeah, this is the D-Lo."

"This is Cheese, man. I told you I'd holla back so what's up?"

"What can you tell me about Coldblood? Does he have any close family here other than Lo-Down?"

"Remember the girl that got killed a while back, that worked in the Beauty Shop? Well, she had a son by Coldblood."

"Ah! Bingo!" shouted D-Lo. "I remember the kid now! Where is he?"

"I don't have a clue, Bro. But I'm sure one of the girls at the Beauty Shop does. Try Melody—she talks a lot and will tell everything for a buck or two. The Beauty Shop has a new location, though. They are right down the street from us, on Old National."

"Thanks Cheese, I'll holla."

Shortly after 9 p.m. that Tuesday, D-Lo cruised down Old National near the Beauty Shop. Melody was cleaning up as Nicole finished her last customer.

"Child, I can't wait to get home and chill," said Melody. "It's been a long day!"

"Yeah, I'm kinda tired myself," added Nicole. "I may just sleep a little late tomorrow, too." Melody gave her a look.

"Who do you think you're fooling? As usual, you'll be here before noon, and it won't be a soul here for you to work with. Why do you do that?" asked Melody. "Why do you come so early?"

"For your information, I'm eating lunch with my niece, tomorrow, so I won't be here before 2 p.m." said Nicole.

"Ah! So that's why you asked me and Tameka to be here by 11 a.m. tomorrow. You're not gonna be here to open up, are you?"

"Since Wednesdays are our slow days, Candi and Adrienna decided to come late, too," said Nicole? Suddenly, Nicole's cell phone rang and it was Audrey.

"Hello Aunt Nicole? This is Audrey."

"Hey Sweetie Pie, how's it going?"

"I think you need to come by. Mom might be in trouble," said Audrey. "Me and Dent are here, but the police was here, too."

"I'm on my way, baby, just stay in the house, ok?"

"What's wrong, Nikki?" Nicole started rushing to leave.

"I don't know. Audrey said Jennifer is missing and the police have been there. We've gotta go!" As Nicole and Melody stepped to the door, D-Lo met them while pointing a gun.

"Ah!" screamed Melody.

"Ok girls, back up and let's talk. I just need some information and everybody will be fine."

"I'll tell you what I can. Just please don't shoot me!"

"You must be Melody," asked D-Lo. "I was told that I would find you very cooperative, unlike your partner standing next to you. As I recall, she took a pretty good beating the last time I was here, because she wouldn't talk."

"What's he talking about, Nikki?" Nicole looked angry, but nervous.

"This is one of the men that hurt me that same night D'Amica was killed. I guess they never found whatever it is they're looking for."

"D'Amica's son---where is he?" asked D-Lo as he closed the blinds and locked the door.

"Who, Shaun?" questioned Melody. "What do you want him for?"

"Yeah, Shaun, that's him! He's got what I need."

"Who, Shaun?" Melody yelled again. "He lives in foster care---he doesn't' have any..."

"Melody shut up!" yelled Nicole. D-Lo pointed the gun at Nicole.

"See," said D-Lo. "That's what got you beat up the last time." He cocked the gun and put it in Nicole's face. "I don't have time for that, this time, so you best tell me what I need, and tell me now! Where is the foster home that Shaun's in?" Nicole and Melody were afraid, but Melody was also hysterical.

"He's in Smyrna, right off Cobb Parkway at Ms. Myrtice's," said Melody. She quickly grabbed a pen and wrote the address. "He's here!" D-Lo was staring Nicole down as he took the address from Melody.

"You look like you want to try ol' D-Lo, Sister Girl; what's up? D-Lo put the gun away then slapped Nicole to the floor.

"Ow!" screamed Melody. "Please let her go, Mr. I told you everything, I swear I did!" Melody knelt to comfort Nicole.

"Melody just saved your life, Sister Girl, so you ought to thank her. Now get up!" D-Lo forced them into the bathroom in the back, then tied and gagged them. Then he hit them with his pistol and knocked them out.

Chapter 110

Tenisha was still at the hospital with Donna when she saw the breaking news about the Gala, come over the TV.

> *"Tonight at the Waverly Hotel, during the Gala event, guest and foreigners ran for their lives as two attackers ran through the ballroom attacking and robbing guests. One of the assailants escaped, but the other was caught and arrested. She has been identified as would be thief and robber, Jennifer R. Sweet, who was also tried and convicted for the Perimeter Mall thefts, a few years ago. This time if convicted, Jennifer could face up to 20 years. More tonight at eleven."*

"Oh no!" whispered Tenisha. "Donna doesn't need to know this, yet!" She turned the TV off in case Donna woke up. Then she tried to call Cherlene, again, but there was no answer.

****

"What is this place?" asked Sherri. "And what are we doing here?"

"It's a place where D-Lo used to hang out. He has some old friends here who might know where he is," said Elisa. They drove the van to the back of the club, then sat and waited for their chance to get inside, without being recognized.

When they saw someone taking the trash out the back door, they quickly followed him back inside. To Elisa's surprise, the man they followed inside was the one she needed; it was Cheese. He felt the gun behind his head and turned around.

"Brenda!" he started. "What are you...(click)!" He felt Sherri's gun barrel against his genitals.

"Let's go, Cheese," whispered Elisa. "Outside!" They forced him into the van and down the street to the motel where they got a room. Then they forced him into the room, stripped him naked, and tied him to the chair.

"Ladies, y'all don't have to go through all this just to get laid. As fine as y'all are, I'd do it without a fight." Sherri looked at his penis and said,

"Not with that you won't. We have other plans for you that help us to feel better." Suddenly, Sherri hit him in the face and he almost passed out.

"Wait-a-minute!" screamed Cheese. "Why don't you just tell me what you want!"

"Oh, I just want some information," said Elisa. "She is already getting what she wants." Sherri hit him again with an uppercut.

"Where can I find D-Lo, right now?" demanded Elisa.

"What? He's still in prison, ain't he?" said Cheese. Elisa knew that he was lying.

"Ok," smiled Elisa. "The longer it takes you to answer me, the more she's gonna kick your butt. She like to do this kind of thing in her past time." Suddenly, Sherri backed to the wall, then speared her body into Cheese's chest and cracked his ribs.

"Uh! Ok!" said Cheese, "He's in Atlanta looking for Coldblood." Sherri hit him.

"Try again," said Elisa. "Who is Coldblood?" Cheese was in a lot of pain.

"He's... he's the guy that ripped D-Lo off for a lot of money. D-Lo is trying to get it back." Sherri tried to hit him, but Elisa caught her hand. "Look," continued Cheese. "Coldblood's dad owns a Baptist Church in Smyrna on King Springs Road. His name is Reverend Carl Simmons. I'm sure he can tell you where Coldblood is. Honestly, that's all I know."

"You did good, Cheese," said Elisa. "Too bad we can't leave you awake because you might find a way to alert D-Lo that we're coming." Elisa and Sherri beat him to sleep and left him in the chair.

Chapter 111

"Mom, why did we have to come home at night?" asked Makeda. "This seems so weird."

"Until we can find out what's going on, we don't need to be distracted," said Cherlene.

"Can't I even talk to Karla and my friends?"

"Keda you promise to wait until tomorrow."

"That's because I thought we weren't coming home until tomorrow. This is so unfair! I'm a teenager. I live to talk on the phone!"

It was about eleven o'clock Tuesday night as Cherlene and Makeda came back to the house. Cherlene had taken Makeda to Disney World in Orlando, Florida, under conditions that they break all contact until she could deal with the issue at hand. Makeda agreed. Therefore, their cell phones were left at home until they returned from their trip. Makeda couldn't wait to call her friends.

"Wow! Seems like I have a thousand messages and text; Cool!"

"Get ready for bed, Keda. It's gonna be a long day tomorrow."

Cherlene went to her bedroom to listen to her messages. She heard Donna and Jennifer calling the most so she knew that was not unusual.

"Tenisha? Hmm? Wonder what she wants? Ah! Very Good! Jennifer found her sister! Wonder what she's like? Well, I will call them all on tomorrow," thought Cherlene. Then she prepared for bed and slept.

Wednesday morning before day, Makeda woke up and quickly dialed her cell phone.

"Hello, Karla; I'm back!!"

"Makeda, I need to talk to you before you leave here, today. It's important!"

"Ok Mom, I'll be there in a second!" After she got ready for school, she came to the kitchen where Cherlene was calmly sitting.

"What 's up, Mom? What do you want to talk about?"

"The same thing I've already talked to you about, but there's more."

"Mom I get it; you had sex with one of your students. I don't want to hear it, anymore."

"Well, you have to because it's for your good. So sit!" Cherlene knew if word was already out that she slept with Shaun, it would ruin Makeda's life as well, so she explained it to her. "Keda, I love you more than you can ever know. That's the main reason I took you away. I needed to protect you from the very thing you may face today when you get back to school.

"What are you talking about, Mom?"

"I'm talking about your friends and your life. If somehow, they've already found out what I've done, some of your friends will become your enemies and they will hurt your life."

"They won't find out," said Makeda.

"Things like this have a way of coming out when we least expect," said Cherlene. "If you find yourself being attacked today by others, do not try to deal with it. Call me or come home right away. Don't even speak to your teachers about it; just leave, ok?" Makeda was a little nervous because she never heard her mom talk to her like this.

"Mom, are you ok?"

"No, I'm not baby," she paused. "I have to talk to Shaun today and help him get back on course. He can still be a good kid if he will hear me and be able to get past this. But if he can't, then I have to do the right thing and quit teaching; maybe even turn myself over to the authorities." Makeda had not felt the entire seriousness of the situation until now. Suddenly, going to school didn't seem the thing to do.

"I can stay home with you if you want, Mom?" Cherlene hugged her.

"No baby , you need to go and enjoy your life. I can handle it from here as long as I know you're safe. Now go! Karla will be here in a minute."

****

As the sun arose, Shaun couldn't sleep as he tossed and turned in his foster care bed. He decided to get up and do the things he usually does as he went to school. He walked toward the corner where he always stopped, but he didn't see the kids stealing from the fruit stand.

Audrey was still home struggling to help Dent get ready for school. Instead of taking his usual school route, today he decided to go by Cherlene's place before he headed to his private hide out.

To his surprise, he saw a silhouette of a person through the curtains at the front of the house. Shaun took off running and rang the doorbell because he knew she was back!

"Ding-Dong." Cherlene peeped and knew Shaun was there. She made sure she was properly dressed and appropriate before she opened the door.

"Just a minute!" she yelled. She paced and encouraged herself to be the strong, good, school teacher she was before she slept with Shaun, while diligently trying to steer him back on the right course of life. She put on her teacher's smile and wits, then she opened the door. Shaun flopped around her waist and almost pushed her back into the house, but she held her ground.

"Whoa! Shaun!" she said. "It's nice to be missed but this is quite much! Come on, get up! Stand up straight!"

"I've missed you so much, Cherlene!"

"Shaun, my name is Ms. Tullis, so please call me that," she explained.

"Whatever!" he said ignoring her words. "I have so much to tell you!" Shaun tried to step around her and come into the house but she blocked his way.

"Shaun No! Stay right here and talk to me," she demanded.

"Why can't we go in and sit down?" I have a lot to tell you about."

"No! Why don't we go for a walk," she insisted. "Then you can tell me why you're not in school today." She closed her door and stepped out.

"You're not in school so I'm not there, either. The other teachers don't know what they're doing so I've been waiting for you to come back."

"What?" Cherlene was shocked. "Are you saying that you haven't been to school since I've been gone! That was almost two weeks ago."

"What's the big deal? You're back now so I'll go back."

"Shaun, I'm thinking about moving away and teaching out of state," she added.

"That's cool. I'll just move with you, Cherlene."

"That's it!" thought Cherlene. *"I've ruined him. Now I have to quit teaching and just move away."*

"Cherlene," started Shaun again. "I know what you're trying to do and I can help."

"How's that, Shaun?"

"Come go somewhere with me. I want to show you something."

"No Shaun, we are not going anywhere together, anymore..." Then he cut in,

"You want me to go back to school, don't you? Then come go with me and I'll go back to school. I just want to show you something."

"Hmm? This maybe what he need in order to come back to his senses," she wondered. *"But it could be a trick."*

"No tricks, Cherlene, I promise." It was like Shaun had read her mind.

"OK Shaun, I'll go with you on one condition; that you stop calling me by my first name. From now on, I want you to respect me as Ms. Tullis."

"Ok cool. Can we take your car?"

****

Tenisha sat at the hospital with Donna all through the night and on into the morning. Even the doctors were surprised that Donna was still in a coma. But Tenisha had made up her mind to wait as long as it took. Jennifer was in jail and Cherlene couldn't be found. So Tenisha decided to be the sister she always wanted to be.

At the same time, Melody and Nicole were tied up and locked in the bathroom at the Beauty Shop. They awakened and waited for Tameka to find them when she came to work at 11 a.m.

"About one more hour," groaned Melody through the rag around her mouth. "One more hour and Tameka should be coming to work." Suddenly, they hear the shop phone ring and the answering machine come on.

"Hey Melody, if you're there pick up. This is Tameka. Look, I have something that came up and I cannot make it until late today. Please cover for me if you can. And make sure you erase this message. Please don't tell Nicole. Thanks, bye."

"AAAAYYEE!" yelled Melody. "Of all the days, this heifer ain't coming in today! What kind of mess is that?"

"You can look at it in one of two ways," said Nicole. "By Murphy's Law, which says, 'anything that can go wrong, will,' or by God's word which says, 'All things work together for good to them that love God, to them who are the called according to his purpose!' So which is it for you, Mel? God or Murphy?" Melody was shouting mad.

"I say that every damn thing that can go wrong is going wrong!"

"Fine," said Nicole calmly. "I think we could've been shot last night and still left in here anyway. So I'm glad I'm in here waiting to live again, instead of waiting for someone to find us dead. All things have worked for my good---I'm going with God."

****

Hookman was eating Terry's food while Terry sat watching. Terry was still tied to the chair.

"Hey, I'm hungry, man," said Terry.

"Um huh," said Hookman as he kept eating.

"I got to use the bathroom, too." Hookman ignored him.

****

"Where are we, Shaun? Whose house is this?"

"Come on; I'll show you!" said Shaun excitedly. "Come on, get out the car!" Cherlene stepped out and followed Shaun through the yard to the backdoor. Shaun had taken her to his hide-a-way at Deerfield Place in College Park. Cherlene followed Shaun inside and looked around.

"Shaun, this is nice but, whose house is this?"

"Do you like it, Cherlene?" Cherlene saw the realtor's sign laying in a corner and knew that Shaun had moved it from the yard. "This can be our place, Cherlene. Yours and mine if you want! We can move in right now and forget about school and people and all that. Just say the word and we're here!"

Cherlene was so disappointed in herself now. She had been mislead again, and began to doubt her ability to think reasonably.

"No! No!" she whispered. *"This can't be happening."* She started to walk out.

"Wait Cherlene!" Shaun grabbed her and tried to hug her while trying to convince her they should be together.

"I said, No!" Cherlene turned and delivered all her strength into a blow so that he would let her go. Shaun fell to the floor as she ran out and locked herself in her car. Shaun came behind her and stood at the car.

"Open the door, Cherlene."

"Shaun , you need some help."

"Open the door, Cherlene!" he said angrily.

"This is all my fault, Shaun, and I'm gonna do the right thing now but you have to get some help!"

"Open the damn door, Cherlene!" yelled Shaun as he hit on the car.

"No, I said No! Do not come back to my house, Shaun! I don't want to hurt you, but I will. Please give me time to get you some help!"

Shaun picked up a rock and threw it as she sped away. Cherlene knew there was only one way to fix this and she had to do it. She dialed her phone shortly after she drove off.

"This is the law offices of Carlos, Jerome, and Curtis. How may I help you?"

"I need a good criminal defense lawyer," said Cherlene.

"All of our lawyers are criminal defense attorneys, Ma'am. Which one would you like to represent you?"

"All of them! And I need to talk to them today!"

"They are in court today, but they will talk to you this evening at about 6:00 pm; if that's not too late." Can you stop by the office?"

"I'll be there!"

Chapter 112

"Welcome home, Coldblood; I've missed you, man," said Dexter.

"I've been cleaning myself up, Dex. Next month, I'm even thinking about buying a pad for me and Shaun. But I can't stay in Georgia because the laws are so against us."

"Yeah I know," said Dexter. "I've been thinking about leaving here myself, but Olivia don't want to go. She was born and bred here. So where are we going, now?"

"I need to see Shaun, right now. I plan to be on a plane this time tomorrow, headed back to Bridgeton, New Jersey, with Shaun.

Shortly after Dexter and Coldblood left the airport, they pulled in at Ms. Myrtice's foster care home and knocked at the door. Ms. Myrtice met them.

"Hello, Ma'am," said Coldblood. "I'm looking for my son, Shaun Taylor.

"Oh my Lord!" she said. "Come on in, son, and take a load off. It's so good to see you again. So how've you been?"

"I'm fine, Ma'am; is Shaun here?"

"No, I'm afraid not," she said. "I don't know when he comes or goes anymore. He's here 4 out of 7 days and I have no clue where he is when he's not here." Coldblood dialed Shaun's phone, but the number had been disconnected.

****

Candi stood outside the Beauty Shop as Adrienna walked from the bus stop.

"Why are you standing out here?"

"I sho' hope you have a key," said Candi. "Ain't nobody here."

"What!" said Adrienna. "Where's Nicole, and Mel, and Tameka? All of them suppose to be here! Have you tried calling them?"

"I called them, but I only got Tameka. She ain't coming in today."

"Something is wrong with this picture," said Adrienna. "Nikki doesn't do this."

"So do you have a key or not?" asked Candi.

"Girl, I hadn't used my key since we moved in here. Somebody is always here when I come and when I leave. So I took it off my key chain and left it at home."

****

"Nikki, listen!" whispered Melody. "I think I hear somebody! It's got to be almost 5 or 6 o'clock cause I'm hungry as heck. Somebody's out

there, Nikki! Come on; let's scream! Heeelllllppp!!!" they screamed.
Candi and Adrienna didn't hear them.

****

Coldblood and Dexter drove the streets of Atlanta in search of
Shaun and where he might be. They went to parks, clubs, and
neighborhoods projects, hoping they could talk to someone who had seen
him, but they came up with nothing.

****

D-Lo had finally found Ms. Myrtice's place as he sat in the car
and waited for Shaun to come home.

****

Nicole and Melody yelled while Adrienna stood outside trying to
call them on her cell phone.
   "So what do we do now?" asked Candi.
   "I guess we go home and get my key," said Adrienna. Then they
left.

****

"Makeda!" phoned Cherlene. "I have an appointment, but I'll be
home in an hour or so. Please be prepared for bed when I get back and
don't open the door for anyone."
   "Ok, Mom!" It was near dark as Shaun lingered around the back
of the house and watched for Cherlene.
   Then he saw Makeda changing her clothes and getting ready for
her bath. Suddenly, he saw Makeda caressing herself and bouncing on
the bed and sexually playing with herself. Makeda wasn't in a sexual
mood, but she moaned and hissed and did things to her body, because
she had been watching her mother many nights, and was now mocking
her.
   Makeda had no idea that her actions were penetrating the mind
of a 17 year old psycho stalker, who only saw her 33 year old mom
enticing him, instead of a 14 year old school girl just playing around.
   Shaun entered the house and on into Makeda's bedroom without
her awareness. Before she could scream, he grabbed her and slung her
against the wall and rendered her dizzy and slightly unconscious. Then
like he did her mother, he spread her and turned her and had his way
with her as he tore her womb and sexually bruised and abused her body.

Her blood was on the bed, the floor, the dresser, the desk, the wall, and everywhere Shaun took her to satisfy his needs. His final stop was in Cherlene's bed where he pretended she was Cherlene and completely wretched her. When he finally let her go, he left her mentally disturbed and damaged, for life.

****

Detective #1= Hey, we got something back from the coroner on that dead substitute teacher at the high school.
Detective #2= Oh yeah, what'd he say?
Detective #1= The bruise on her forehead was definitely done by a fist or hand blow.
Detective #2= Which means that somebody hit her and caused her to fall and hit her head.
Detective #1= Shaun Taylor is our only suspect, right now.
Detective #2= What about his Houdini school teacher, Cherlene Tullis. Maybe he told her what he did and she disappeared to prevent testifying against him.
Detective #1= So what do you want to do?
Detective #2= Let's go see Shaun and bring him in for questioning.

****

"This looks like the church," said Elisa. "Can you see the name on the bulletin board?"

"Yes, it reads, Rev. Carl Simmons, Sr.," said Sherri. "This is the one."

"Looks like prayer meeting is ending. Let's go talk with the good Reverend." Reverend Simmons saw Elisa and Sherri come in.

"Hello, sisters, can I help you with something?"

"Sir, we're looking for your son, Coldblood. Can you tell us where he is?" asked Elisa.

"Who's asking? Are you cops?"

"We're friends, Sir. We just want to talk to him, that's all," said Sherri.

"About what?"

"Rev. Simmons, Sir," started Elisa. "We're trying to find a man named Derrick Logan and we were told that..."

"D-Lo?" questioned Rev. Simmons. "Do y'all have business with D-Lo?"

"You might say that," said Elisa. "Word on the street is that Coldblood owes D-Lo money and D-Lo may be coming for it."

"Even if it's true, what business of that is yours?"

"Like I said, I got my own reasons for wanting D-Lo," said Elisa.

"Is there a number where I can call you?"

"No Sir, but we can call you if you give us your number," said Sherri. Rosa peeped and saw Elisa and Sherri! She knew them right away. Rev. Simmons handed Elisa his card.

"Call me in about an hour and I may have some information for you." They left and went back to the van.

"That's it for me, Brenda, or Elisa, or whatever your name is," said Sherri. "This has turned out to be a long drawn out personal battle between you and a man I know nothing about. I can't go any further."

"Sherri, I understand. Thank you for helping me this far. I'll take you back to the boat."

"No, no, that's ok," interjected Sherri. "You're on a mission and I want you to succeed. Just drop me off at the train station and I'll call Anitra from there." Elisa dropped her off and they said their goodbyes.

"Good luck, Elisa; take care of yourself. I hope you get your man."

****

"Hello, Carl Jr.? This is your daddy, son; we need to talk."

"What's up, Dad?" Rosa walked in while he talked on the phone.

"Evidently, D-Lo's back in town and he knows you're here. He's looking for you son, so you need to be careful. There were also two nice-looking gals here looking for him, too; one black and one white. Do you have any business with them?"

"Not that I know of. Were they cops?"

"They may have been cops, but they didn't seem like it."

"They're not cops," sounded Rosa. "They work for Holloway."

"Son, I have to go, but I'll call you back." Then he hung up and turned to Rosa. "Do you know those girls?"

"I don't know them, but I've sparred with them a couple of times," smiled Rosa.

****

"Yo, D-Lo," phoned Hookman. "Where are you, man?"

"I'll be there soon" said D-Lo. "I have somebody to pick up that will help us to get Coldblood. Just hold on a little while longer."

"I can't stay here too much longer, D-Lo. Neighbors are getting suspicious and people are coming around. We have to end this."

"We'll end it when I say we'll end it!" shouted D-Lo. "Now, sit tight!" As D-Lo hung up, Hookman became frustrated and decided to take matters into his own hands. He pulled his pistol and walked to Terry.

"I want you to call your brother and get him to see you tonight," ordered Hookman.

"My brother; why? What do you want him for?" asked Terry.

"Pow!" Hookman slapped him hard. "Never mind that! You just better sound convincing when you call him or it will be your last conversation. Do you understand?" Terry gave Hookman the number and he dialed it.

****

Meantime, Coldblood and Dexter were in a nearby park asking questions when Dexter's phone rang. He checked his caller ID.

"It's Terry. He's got women problems and I am sure he is calling to talk about Cherlene. I wish he would just drop that whore. Hello Terry, what's up?"

"Dex!" said Terry nervously. "What are you up to these days?" Dexter was surprised to hear Terry sounding so up beat.

"Terry, are you high? You sound kind of funny," said Dexter.

"No, but I do need to talk to you about something important. Can you stop by my apartment in about an hour?"

"Terry, is this about you and your girl, again? Man, I don't have time for... "

"Yes! Yes!" yelled Terry. "I need to talk to you about my girl friend, Olivia!"

"Olivia?"

"Yes!" shouted Terry again. "I just can't seem to get Olivia out of my mind! I love her so much but she's been trip'n lately. Olivia, is my life man, and I need to talk about it. Please Dex, stop by!" As Terry hung up, Dexter was puzzled.

"What's wrong?" asked Coldblood.

"That was Terry and he wants me to stop by. He says he's in love with Olivia and he wants to talk about it."

"Olivia?" questioned Coldblood. "Your wife?" Both men stood looking confused. "What else did he say?"

"Nothing," said Dexter. "He just hung up."

****

It was after dark when Shaun saw the two detectives talking to Ms. Myrtice, so he stayed out of sight and listened.

Detective #1=Ma'am, we would appreciate it if you would give us a call as soon as Shaun gets in. We just want to ask him a few questions, that's all.

Ms. Myrtice took the card and they left. Shaun assumed they were there because of Cherlene and Makeda.

"How could Cherlene do this to me," he thought. Shaun crept into the house, got his things then eased back out. As soon as he walked outside the house, D-Lo put his pistol to Shaun's head.

"Hello, Shaun," he said. "Remember me? Let's go for a ride." As soon as Shaun got in the car, D-Lo knocked him out and drove away.

****

"Aaahhee!" yelled Melody as Adrienna and Candi entered the Beauty Shop.

"Do you hear that?" asked Candi. "Sounds like somebody yelling." They ran to the back and saw Nicole and Melody tied up in the bathroom.

"Thank you, Jesus!" said Melody. After they untied her, Nicole rushed to the phone.

****

As Rev. Simmons speedily left the church, Elisa followed him. She knew he would lead her to Coldblood, where she hoped to find D-Lo.

****

Cherlene quickly drove Makeda to the hospital. She came home and found Makeda bloody and clammed in a corner of the closet... shaking nervously. She drove with one hand while comforting Makeda with the other.

"You'll be ok, baby. Just hold on. Help is on the way!" The doctors treated Makeda and laid her to rest.

"We'll keep her overnight then you can take her home in the morning," they told Cherlene. "She has some torn tissue but it's not anything time won't heal. However, she will need plenty of love and attention along with psychiatric treatment." Cherlene started to cry.

"Thank you," she said.

Chapter 113

That night at the hospital, Tenisha sat at Donna's side while Cherlene nurtured Makeda to sleep. Donna had been asleep a little past 24 hours as Tenisha tried to call Cherlene, but Cherlene had left her phone in the car during her efforts to get Makeda to the emergency room.

After Makeda was sound asleep, Cherlene laid beside her thinking about her life and all that had happen until now.

"The Curse Must Be Broken!" she whispered. She used the hospital phone to dial Jennifer and Donna but couldn't reach them. Then she kissed Makeda, walked through the hospital kitchen, and left.

****

"Yeah," answered Hookman on the phone.

"It's me," said D-Lo. "I'm outside with Coldblood's kid. Let me in." D-Lo forced Shaun from the car at gunpoint, and into Terry's apartment.

"I thought you would never get here," said Hookman. "Now let's do this and get it over with. I have other business to do today." D-Lo pushed Shaun toward the phone.

"Call your pops, boy, and tell`em you want to see him."

"You don't have to call me, Sport; I'm right here." Coldblood and Dexter entered through the back unexpectedly and were pointing their pistols at D-Lo.

"Dad!" yelled Shaun with his hands being still tied. Coldblood and Dexter didn't see Hookman because he hid behind the door once they stepped in. Terry saw him and tried to yell but he was too late. Hookman hit Dexter and knocked him out, then quickly pointed his gun on Coldblood. Coldblood was about to shoot him until D-Lo spoke.

"Ah-ah-ah!" said D-Lo as he wrapped Shaun by the neck and pointed a pistol to his head. "So you're Lo-Down's Boy, huh? We finally meet! If you're anything like your dad, you can be a dirty muther, and I don't trust you. Tie him up!"

Hookman tied him while Dexter was out cold on the floor. "We wouldn't be doing this if you and your partner hadn't stolen my money," continued D-Lo.

"I took your money," said Coldblood. "But how much have you taken from others that didn't belong to you?"

"It all belongs to me," said D-Lo. "Only the strong will survive in a world that's already destined to be destroyed. Meantime, I am my brother's keeper, so I keep his belongings, his money, and his wife. I take it because it's declared mine by the powers that be. So for those who don't like it, when I take what's mine, I take them out!"

"Is that why you killed my mom? What did she ever do to you?" D-Lo hit Coldblood with his fist. Coldblood's eye began to twitch.

"Don't piss me off, Coldblood. Where is my money? That's all I want then you can go."

"Just like you let D'Amica go when she told you where it was, right?" D-Lo hit him again and starting beating him. Shaun started having flashbacks of his mom, taking a beating as he watched D-Lo beat his dad. Hookman heard someone at the front door, so he went to look. No one noticed Shaun slipping his hands from the scarf that tied them.

"Who do you see out there?" asked D-Lo.

"Dad!" yelled Shaun as he freed himself, and stabbed D-Lo in his shoulder from the back. D-Lo dropped the gun. As Hookman turned his gun on Shaun, Dexter attacked him and knocked the gun from his hand and across the floor to Shaun. Hookman, ran out of the front door and escaped. D-Lo opened the back door to escape, but Elisa was standing there as she quickly latched onto his genitals and squeezed.

"Remember me!" she said. Suddenly, like having a mind of their own, her hands and arms repeatedly slapped him until he was dizzy. Her legs and feet also came alive as she leaped through the air and slammed her knees into the side of D-Lo's head numerous times until he stumbled.

Elisa didn't know how she was able to fight so precisely, but she didn't have time to think about it. She was angry and she just wanted D-Lo to feel the impact of the hatred he'd caused within her.

She was speedily hitting him on every part of his body as the pain caused his body to lock up. Like Rocky, to the Russian, Drago, in Rocky IV, little 5 feet 8, 160 pounds, Elisa, was cutting, 6 feet 9, 245 pounds, D-Lo, down to her size. D-Lo was in a lot of pain as she pounded him, but he was determined to stay on his feet and hit her.

But the knife that was stuck in his back had him at a disadvantage. Elisa didn't care as she wrapped herself around him and head-butted him, twice, while keeping him embraced. Her arms and legs were working rhythmically as she interlocked her hands around his neck and high kicked her knees into his ribs until she cracked them. With D-Lo still having one arm to fight, he clinched his fingers into her face and shoved her so he could hit her. As he swung, Elisa easily avoided it, span around him, then used her elbow to slam the knife deeper that was already lodged between his shoulder blade.

"Uh!" he screamed as he attempted to run out. But Elisa latched onto the knife and pulled him back. "Uuuhhhhhhhhh!" he screamed again as she yanked the knife to remove it, but it was stuck in his bone.

While yanking on the knife with one hand, she was beating him with the other as he screamed because of pain. When she finally released him, D-Lo fell against the wall... beaten, and almost dead. Therefore, with her final effort, she snatched the knife from between his shoulder blade, rammed it between his legs, and cut into his genitals. "That's for what you did to me," she said. Then she straight kicked him in the chest numerous times and cracked his ribs.

"That's for what you did to my dad!" D-Lo used his last few breaths to stumble toward the front door in efforts to get away. Saliva and blood rolled from his mouth as his eyes rolled back in his head. He could hardly walk as he forced his body to move to the front door.

He held to his cut penis with his good arm as he stood in the door being unable to go any further because of pains and loss of blood. Just before D-Lo took his last breath, he opened the door to see the two barrels from a sawed off shotgun, pointing directly at his chest.

"Boom! Boom!" The blast sent him hurling through the air and on his back to the middle of the floor.

"That's for taking away my Stephanie," said Reverend Simmons as he lowered the shotgun. Coldblood looked at his dad proudly as the sirens grew louder. Shaun untied him and Terry. "That coward, Hookman, got passed me before I could fire but his day is coming."

"We'd better go, Dad," said Coldblood. "You don't need to be seen here like this. "

"Junior, I should've dealt with this a long time ago. I'm too old to run now." He handed Coldblood the shotgun, who handed it to Dexter.

"You boys go on," said Rev. Simmons. "Take Shaun and get out of here. Had I faced up to my sin a long time ago, none of this would've happened. All this blame is mine, and I will wait right here and take responsibility for it when those sirens come." Then he looked toward heaven and said,

"Lord, I don't know what my daddy did, or my grand-daddy. But I know my sin, and I'm sorry... I truly am. Stephanie's gone and she left me a son to bear my legacy. Lord, you know how she was. I haven't been right with you, Lord, and I'm so ashamed. But there was no shame in Stephanie's love and worship for you, so I'm asking you, on her behalf, to forgive my sin, and save our son. Please Lord... Please Lord... don't let him have to live with my curse, and my shame. Amen."

Coldblood was speechless as he hugged his dad. He knew that his dad was doing the right thing, even though it didn't feel right at the time. While they were embraced, the winds of strife that were upon them blew away and vanished, as rays of light illuminated their presence.

"The Curse... Is Broken! You... Are... Blessed!" came the whisper as Rev. Simmons broke into a deep heartfelt cry and repeatedly thanked the Lord.

"I'm proud of you, Dad," said Coldblood. "And I'm not gonna leave you here to deal with this alone. I'll find a way out for us, Dad, I promise I will."

"I may be able to help with that," said Elisa. "My name is Elisa Smith and I'm a cop." Coldblood was shocked. "Don't worry; I'm not here to take you in. I'm here on personal business myself. So listen to your dad and get out of here." Coldblood and Shaun hugged Rev. Simmons, then they left.

"I have to go, too," said Elisa while writing a note. "Get this note to GBI Agent Jonathan Lewis and he will help you. You will be hearing from me, again." Elisa quickly left as the cops came.

****

Rosa was alone at her hide-a-way in the church while working online that night. She was desperate to find her child before some hitman found her and took her out.

"Where are you, baby?" she asked herself. *"Mommy's coming if you only let me know where you are."*

Rosa checked references and cross-references of high schools, where her daughter last attended but found nothing.

"Maybe I'm doing this wrong," she said. "If she has a life then she works. Taxes! Everybody pays taxes!" She went online and used her daughter's name to find her work history and career profile. Suddenly, her computer screen went blank. Rosa stood angrily and speechless as she wondered what happened. Suddenly, she knew!

****

Then back at FBI Headquarters.

"Chief!" called out one of the agents. "Someone at a location in Smyrna is attempting to access a file of one of our operatives."

"Shut`em down!" yelled Agent Walter.

"I already did," said the agent.

****

Rosa quickly left the church because she knew she had stumbled onto something that caused her computer to be shutdown. As she drove, she dialed.

"Hello?"

"Jonathan, this is Rosa. How are you?"

"Rosa?" Jonathan was shocked as he sat in his home. "My God Rosa! Is it really you! I thought you were dead! Where are you calling from?"

"I'm in Atlanta, Jonathan. I've always been here."

"I don't understand," he said. "Why didn't you tell me? You know I would do anything to help you."

"Then help me now, Jonathan. Tell me why would the FBI shut my computer down while I conducted a search for my daughter?"

"Ah... well, that means that she has confidential records, and is connected to the bureau!"

"That's exactly what I thought. Who can help me with this, Jonathan? Is it Walter?"

"Wait-a-minute, Rosa. What's your daughter's name?"

"Her name is Elisa Smith."

"Elisa Sm... Oh my God! How could I have been so blind." Rosa heard his tone and pulled over to the side of the road.

"What is it, Jonathan? Talk to me, you bastard! Where is my child?" Jonathan hesitated to answer.

"Rosa, I don't know how to tell you this, but she's an agent... undercover, who picked up where you left off. She's with Holloway." Rosa thought as she heard the whisper, *"The Curse Must Be Broken!"* Then she panicked and sped off.

"Jonathan, we have to get to Holloway's yacht, now! I'm on my way; send help!" Rosa sped towards Lake Lanier where she knew Holloway was having a private party.

Chapter 114

"Man, look at all the police cars!" said Shaun. Dexter drove calmly by the many police cars that headed toward Terry's apartment.

"This is bad," said Terry. "Will somebody please tell me what's going on?"

"Later Terry," said Dexter. "I have a better question. Where are we going?"

"Let's get a room and hold there for a minute," suggested Coldblood.

"We don't need to be seen by anyone, right now," said Dexter. "Not even checking into a hotel. Nor can we go to my place because they will look for Terry and call me."

"Hey, I know a place!" shouted Shaun. "No one knows about it, and we can stay there as long as it takes!"

"Are you sure, son?" asked Coldblood.

"Dad, I'm sure! I go there everyday!" Coldblood spoke to Dexter.

"Ok, let's do it! Tell us how to get there." A few minutes later, Dexter parked at Shaun's hide-a-way on Deerfield place. They eased inside and began to talk.

"What am I to tell police about my place?" asked Terry.

"That's easy," said Dexter. "You've been out of town at work."

"How am I gonna get my dad out of this mess? That's the question!" said Coldblood.

"That lady cop said she would help," said Shaun as he walked around the house.

"I am so hungry," said Terry. "I've been tied up for two days and haven't eaten; I need food, man."

"I have some food," said Shaun. "In there--in the cabinets and the closet." Shaun hurried to the kitchen and started pulling the can meats, breads, pastries, and other items he had stolen from the convenient stores.

As the men indulged themselves, no one noticed the two eyes peeping through the louver doors from the small pantry; stalking... waiting... for the right moment to strike. Behind those pantry doors was an evil; a vengefulness that no one in the residence had anticipated, and it was about to reveal itself.

As Shaun walked past the pantry, the doors suddenly flew open and "*swish!*" Shaun felt the knife, like that of Michael Myers of Halloween, slam between his neck and his shoulders. "*Swiissh!*" two times, "*Swiissh!*" three times, "*Swiissh!*" four times! Shaun's feet were locked to the floor as the same knife stabbed him in the gut, over and over like it was being pumped by a machine.

The blade went so deep that it penetrated out of his back each time it was thrust through his stomach. Finally... "*slice*"... the blade made its way diagonally across his chest, "*Swiissh!*" and across his neck as his throat opened wide. The slash across his throat cause him to spin around and reach for his dad, who quickly made his way toward Shaun in wonder and anger.

"Shaun!" he yelled, but it was too late. Shaun, with his back being turned to the pantry had one more blow to experience before he fell dead in his father's arms.

"Aaaahhheeeyiii!" screamed Cherlene as she slammed the long hospital knife in Shaun's back, through his heart, and out through his chest.

"Ugh!" moaned Shaun. Then she snatched it from his body, raised it above her head, and locked her evil eyes onto her next victim... Coldblood. Before she could strike, Dexter zeroed in on her with Reverend Simmons shot gun.

"*Boom! Boom!*" Both barrels hit her in the midst and locked her to the pantry wall. Cherlene's arms, hands, head, and feet were on one side of the wall, but her butt and her back protruded through the wall, and was sticking out to the other side. She was truly locked into the wall.

"No! No! No!" cried Coldblood as he held Shaun in his arms. Terry, who was afraid, had calmed as he walked to Cherlene's body. He was stunned to see the mother of his child locked into a wall like that, being dead. No words could explain this to him, because he still loved her with all his heart. Then he hurtfully broke into tears.

"What the hell is going on?" shouted Dexter. "We have to go, Blood!"

"Who is that woman?" asked Coldblood angrily. Terry spoke softly.

"I had hoped she'd be my wife, someday. I don't know what she's doing here, or why she attacked your son."

"Terry," spoke Dexter. "I'm sorry, man, but she snapped and I didn't know what else to do!" The men were surprised as the cops pulled in, but they had no where to run. Before they could escape, police cornered them and took them away.

While detectives saw Cherlene's body locked into the wall and Shaun's body on the floor, suddenly, the winds of strife released from their bodies and sped towards the city of Atlanta. As the two winds trailed each other to the hospital where Makeda rested, they entered her and caused her to scream.

"Aaahhyyeeeiii!" Then she leaped from the bed and fell into the corner against the wall being afraid. The nurses sped to her aide, but Makeda had no idea what had just happened.

Chapter 115

For the second night since Donna's accident, Tenisha diligently watched over her, hoping she would soon come around. Almost thirty hours had past since the accident and Tenisha was exhausted. She checked the time and it was almost eleven o'clock.

"Hmm? Wonder if there are more details about Jennifer on the news?" she thought. Tenisha turned the TV on and listened.

'Tonight our top story is about a prison escapee who was killed by a Baptist preacher. An hour ago, police received a call about suspicious activity in Old Time Village Apartments on Godby Road, in College Park.

Upon arrival, police found convicted murderer and prison escapee, Derrick D-Lo Logan, stabbed and shot to death, with Baptist preacher Reverend Carl Simmons Sr., claiming to have killed him. There were no weapons found at the scene of the crime.

However, a few miles away in a Deerfield place residence, Reverend Simmons' grandson, Shaun Taylor, was found stabbed to death 28 times, in conjunction with another woman, who had been nailed to the wall by buck shots from a shotgun, which was found at the scene.

The dead woman have been identified as school teacher, Cherlene Tullis, who is also the sister of convicted felon, Jennifer Sweet, who was arrested for robbery and theft on yesterday.

Reverend Simmons' son, Carl Simmons, Jr., along with two brothers, Terry and Dexter Billingly, were caught at the scene on Godby Road and have been arrested in connection with these crimes.

Police believe that the crimes on Godby Road and Deerfield Place are related. This story is still unfolding: more tomorrow at noon.'

Tenisha stood with her back pinned to the wall while in shock.

"There's no way this could be happening!" she thought. Tenisha had worked with Donna for over ten years, and had some idea how Donna might respond to knowing that both her sisters, Cherlene and Jennifer, had been taken away. For the first time since she had been by Donna's side, Tenisha was afraid of what might happen when Donna wakes up, so she was ready to leave.

****

As Elisa drove away from the crime scene that night, all the pressures... the weight of her troubles since her dad was killed, began to come down on her. She pulled the van over near an overpass and began to cry like a lost child in need of her parents; she had no one.

"Mommy," she cried. "Why did you leave me? Daddy, I don't know what to do! Please tell me what to do; how to be! D-Lo is dead and I'm supposed to feel better now, but I don't." She began to cry a intense passionate cry as she curled on a seat in the van and called out.

"Mommy! Daddy! Please tell me what to do!" After a while, she calmed and just sat... thinking. Then she spoke out loud.

"Daddy, I killed a man today. All these years, I've waited to do that and now, I don't feel any better. Mommy, you have a grandson out there somewhere and I don't even know his name. They took my child, Mommy, and only God knows where he is."

Elisa wiped her tears, got herself together, then sat behind the wheel of the van again, being ready to see Holloway. She knew there was a high probability he would have her shot on sight, but as she sat in the van, she usurped a certain faith and confidence. Then she looked up through the windshield of the van and said,

"I need you right now; I really do and I'm asking for your help. I have a son out there somewhere and I'm asking you, for his sake, to don't let him grow up alone... without a mother... without me. That's all I ask, and I won't bother you again," spoke Elisa. Then she drove off to Lake Lanier.

****

Rosa sped up I-85 toward Lake Lanier to save her child. Her sources had informed her of the yacht party, so she had planned to crash it and attempt to kill Holloway. Now she was crashing it for a different reason---to save her child's life!

Rosa used to be Holloway's leading security person, so when she saw Elisa and Sherri at the church asking questions about D-Lo, on their own, she knew this was a direct violation of Holloway's rules and Elisa and Sherri may be in serious trouble.

"Jonathan, I hope you are on the way with help," she whispered. The she heard, *"The Curse Must Be Broken!"* Rosa hesitated then pulled over and stepped out of the car near the same overpass where Elisa had previously stopped.

"Lord," started Rosa. "I don't have time to even talk to you right now, because my daughter is in trouble and I may already be too late." She started to cry. "I've told you many times I'm sorry for leaving her like I did, and you know I mean it. Well, I can't leave her again, and you promised you'd never leave us or forsake us.

Right now, we both need you. I'm ok with my curse now, because I know it came as a result of my dad and mom leaving me; I left mine, too, but now I'm going back and I need your help and your blessings. Lord, I just want a chance to make things right with my child. Please Lord, help me; right now."

****

Elisa pulled into the parking area not too far from where the yacht was being accessed. All invited guests were picked up from the docks by a pontoon boat which propelled them to the yacht. Elisa knew she couldn't go that way.

"I have to swim," she thought. She began to search the cars to see what she could find that would help her. Soon she saw a dark colored full body swim suit in one of the vehicles. She broke the window and put it on. *"Just what I needed,"* she whispered. *"A little tight---but right!"*

Elisa found a place to ease into the water without being seen. When the pontoon boat came for the next guest, she attached herself to it and made her way to the yacht. She managed to get past the watchman and onto the yacht without being seen. Eventually, she made her way to the lower level to learn what was going on before she revealed herself to Holloway.

Suddenly, she saw Anitra going to a certain part of the yacht like she was on a mission. Elisa followed her. Anitra turned into a small area and talked to two men in black.

"It doesn't matter what she tells you; she cannot leave this room alive," said Anitra. "And do not tear her body. It must look like an accident when she drowns, got it?"

"Yes, Ma'am, we got it," answered the men. Anitra left and went back to the guest area. Elisa made her way toward the men and peeped the area. She saw Sherri... naked and live but strapped to the wall and suspended from the floor by cables that had both her arms pulled apart, and the same for her legs.

"Guys, please don't do this!" Sherri begged. "You know if either of you ever slip he will do you the same way. Please don't kill me!" Sherri had wires like jumper cable attached to her nipples and her two big toes as she begged for her life.

"He doesn't have to know that you didn't kill me. Just throw me overboard and I promise you will never hear from me again." Suddenly, one of the guys turned a switch and Sherri's body began to jolt---she was being electrocuted. After a series of electrical currents were sent to her body, Elisa heard the men ask,

"Where is she? What is she doing and who is she with?"

"I don't know," answered Sherri. "She dropped me off after we chased the woman and I haven't seen her since." Elisa knew they were asking about her.

"I have to help Sherri," she thought. She knew that the men in the room were no match for her, so she quickly stepped in, disarmed the one, and broke his neck. The other guy was a different story. He had his gun on her before she could blink.

"Do you really think you will beat me with a few kicks and blows?" he asked. Then he laid down his weapon and invited Elisa to let's do it. They fought hard as Elisa kicked him and punched him sore. She was fast and evaded his attacks as much as possible, but he was wearing her down.

Elisa was also strong so she hurt the guy in many ways and had him almost beaten. But he was just as determined to kill her, as he swung and hit her and threw her around. After a while he started getting the best of her as flashbacks of D-Lo beating her clouded her mind.

"No! No!" she whispered. By now her ribs were cracked and her ankle was twisted. "Ah!" she screamed. Elisa and Sherri knew they were facing death. Through her blood dripping hair, Elisa saw Sherri struggling to free her hands from the cables.

"One hand free..." she saw. "Two hands free!" Elisa mustered up energy through her pains to force the man to move backwards and onto Sherri who placed him in a sleeper head grip. Sherri held on for life as he almost tore her body by trying to yank her from the strapped wall in efforts to get away.

"Aahhh!" screamed Sherri each time he yanked. Suddenly, she had an idea. "Throw the switch, Brenda!" she yelled.

"What?" whispered Elisa. "No!"

"Throw the damn switch!" yelled Sherri again. Then she pulled the electrical connectors from her tits, hit the man with chops to his throat, then packed his mouth with the connectors, just as Elisa threw the switch. Sparks flew everywhere as the wetness from the man's mouth caused the electrical current to become more intensified as it electrocuted him and Sherri both. The man fell to the floor, but Sherri hung from the wall being passed out.

"Sherri!" shouted Elisa. She loosened the straps and Sherri fell down. As Sherri hit the floor, she grasped for air. Elisa knew she would be ok as the third guy ran in with his weapon drawn. Elisa quickly picked up the pistol near her and fired. The man went down.

"Go!" whispered Sherri. "Go now! I'm right behind you!" As Sherri felt peculiar after the electrical shock, she checked herself and saw openings like gills having developed in her side beneath her underarms. Her body was beginning to change.

"What the hell is this?" she wondered. *"What's happening to me?"* Like a fish, Sherri had four gills, all in a straight line, on both sides

of her body, and they were opening and closing as they allowed air to flow. Sherri became nervous and confused.

Elisa ran out putting bullets in everyone she met as she painfully made her way from the bottom of the yacht. By now, Rosa had dropped kicked the driver of the pontoon boat and was driving it herself directly at the yacht. Rosa like Elisa, was putting bullet in the guys now firing at her. She boarded the yacht on one end being under gunfire just as she saw Elisa surfaced to the deck on the other end.

The guests were all laying on each other on the floor as gunfire zipped all over the yacht. As Elisa stood on the deck looking for a way to escape, three men with automatic weapons evolved from within the yacht and began firing at her. Elisa managed to drop one of them.

"Ugh!" he sounded. But the other two men lodged bullets in her chest, shoulders, and upper body, until she began to wobble uncontrollably, and fell into the water.

"No!" shouted Rosa as she sprinted down the side of the yacht, putting bullet between the eyes of all the many men that attempted to stop her. She was almost at the point where Elisa fell when Jonathan pulled beside her on a security boat.

"Rosa, jump over!" he shouted.

"No! The water Jonathan!" she yelled as she ran. "The water!" she pointed.

"What's in the water?" yelled Jonathan.

"Your daughter!" Rosa, like a flying diver, leaped before she reached the railing and cut through the water like an eel, with Jonathan close on her heels. They grabbed Elisa from under the water and pulled her toward the top. "I've got you, baby!" said Rosa. "I've got you!"

"Sherri," whispered Elisa. "Save Sherri."

"Sherri?" asked Rosa. "Where is she?" Elisa passed out. "Jonathan, we have to move quickly! She's been shot!"

"Let's get her on the boat!" yelled Jonathan.

"No Jonathan!" she demanded. "Swim away from the boat! It's too close to the yacht, and the yacht is gonna blow!"

"What!" said Jonathan. They swam hard to pull Elisa away.

"Mama?" moaned Elisa.

"Yes baby, it's Mama, and you're safe now." Elisa stretched open her eyes long enough to see Rosa, then she passed out, again.

As Rosa held her close, the wind of strife released from her life and vanished into the air. Rays of light immediately illuminated her presence. Rosa felt the blessings of God embrace her and she knew exactly what it was. Then she heard, *"The Curse... is Broken!"*

"Thank you, Lord," she humbly prayed. "Thank you."

Then as she held Elisa close and pulled her to safety, the yacht suddenly exploded and the blast also caused the security boat to explode.

"Oh my God!" said Jonathan. "All those people... gone, just like that. Holloway won't be a problem, anymore, I guess. He just went down with the ship!" Rosa's keen eyes cut through the darkness to see a thin, flat, very quiet motor boat, with Anitra taking Holloway to safety.

"Yeah, you're right," said Rosa. "He went down with the ship." The police and Medical team crashed the scene and rushed Elisa, Rosa, and Jonathan, to the hospital. After they reached the emergency room, Jonathan looked at Rosa.

"My daughter? Do you mean that..."

"Yes, Jonathan," Rosa cut in. "That night at the office." Jonathan smiled and adjusted his pants. As the doctor walked into the lobby, they were afraid to speak.

"She may be out for a while," said the doctor. "She's lost so much blood. We need authorization to do a transfusion. Who's her next of kin?"

"I am!" said Rosa and Jonathan proudly at the same time.

Chapter 116

As Tenisha faced the window looking into the night while trying to decide whether she would leave or stay, Donna opened her eyes and looked around. She saw the empty room with only Tenisha inside. The voice in her head was still ringing... *"The Curse Must Be Broken!"* but Donna ignored it.

"How long have I been out?" Tenisha surprisingly turned to comfort her. "What are you doing here, anyway?"

"Donna, just rest for a minute and all your questions will be answered, ok?"

"No!" said Donna. "It's dark, already, and you didn't even let my sisters know that I am here. Why haven't you called them? And why do they have me strapped to this bed? I want to see a doctor!"

Tenisha became very emotional after hearing all of Donna's questions and burst into tears. Then she ran out of the room being nervous... shaking... trembling... wondering how could she tell someone that hates her so much, all the bad news that's happened to her and her family. Suddenly, she met Davina.

"I couldn't sleep," said Davina. Tenisha quickly grabbed her and hugged her.

"Oh Mom! Why do I have to do this?" she cried.

"You don't have to Tenisha, but I think we're the only family she has now."

"Doctor!" yelled Donna. "Will someone please come and talk to me!" Tenisha pulled herself together as the doctor approached.

"Please doctor," begged Tenisha. "Will you run another test and be sure?"

"I'm sorry, Ma'am, but we've run this test three times and we're pretty sure."

"Do you want me to come with you, Tenisha?"

"No Mom. Just wait for me out here. I may be a while."

"I'll wait here as long as you need me, too," said Davina. Tenisha followed the doctor to Donna's room.

"Hello doctor," said Donna. "I can't be doing too bad, right? I don't feel any pain. So why am I strapped to this bed?"

"Slow down, Ms. Banks," said the doctor. "Just relax." Donna saw Tenisha as she stood behind the doctor.

"What are you still doing here? I thought you left! You didn't even call my..." Tenisha cut in and went into a rage.

"Shut up, Donna, just shut up! Slow down for a minute and listen to the doctor!" Donna got quiet. There was something in Tenisha's voice she hadn't heard before and it concerned her. So Donna gave the doctor her undivided attention.

"Ms. Banks," he started. "Your accident is not life threatening, but I'm afraid I have some disturbing news." Donna saw Tenisha drop a tear then face the door. She knew this didn't look good and she got nervous.

"You're scaring me, doctor. Where is Jenny and Cherlene?"

"Donna," started Tenisha. "Jennifer and Cherlene can't help you now. Do you think I've been sitting with you for two days because I hate you? Donna you are very smart. Now please listen to the doctor then we will talk... please."

For the first time in Donna's life she actually believed she heard compassion in Tenisha's voice. Donna didn't know what to think, so she humbled herself before Tenisha and the doctor, again.

"Ms. Banks, somehow the accident caused your neurological pathway to detour your brain signals to your senses only. Like the rest of us, you can still see, hear, taste, touch, and smell, as long as it's all done above your shoulders."

"What are you saying?" asked Donna. "Plain English, please."

"I'm saying that you are not strapped to the bed, Ms. Banks; you can't move from your shoulders down to your feet because you're paralyzed."

"Aaahhheee!" screamed Donna with tears. Tenisha turned her back to Donna and cried with her. She was still nervous and knew that Donna hadn't heard the news about her sisters yet. After the doctor told Donna about her condition, he left her in Tenisha's care, per Tenisha's request. There was about fifteen minutes of silence as Donna laid slightly weeping, after hearing about her paralysis.

"So is it true?" Donna finally spoke. She was much calmer now, but Tenisha answered nothing. She wasn't sure what Donna was asking her.

"Tenisha, your diary on the disk; is it true? Are we sisters?"

Tenisha hesitantly answered, "Yeah, it's true."

"Please explain it to me," said Donna. Davina stood in the doorway listening as Tenisha explained. Donna laid with tears rolling from her face as she heard the words of Tenisha. Afterwards, there was another 15 minutes of tears and silence.

"So it was my father that you spoke of as a whoremonger in your diary, huh?" asked Donna. "My dad slept with your mother?"

"Yes, that's how it seems," said Tenisha, hesitantly.

"Does your dad know he is not your real dad?" Davina dropped a tear.

"No, he doesn't," responded Tenisha. "My dad and mom are happier now than they have been in a long time, and..." Donna cut in.

"And you'd like to keep it that way, right?" Donna looked at Davina. "Don't worry, your secret is safe." Davina walked to her bedside and said,

"Thank you. Thank you so much."

"Now tell me about my sisters. Why aren't they here?" The question Donna asked was not only one to help Tenisha to grow, but it would also strengthen her to be a better woman.

Neither Tenisha or Davina ever had to tell anyone that their family was gone and never coming back. But today, that burden rested on Tenisha's shoulders as she and Davina sat at Donna's bedside. Tenisha knew that Donna couldn't move, but she felt that when she told Donna about Jennifer and Cherlene, Donna may just jump up and hit her.

Tenisha tried to be strong as she slowly, cautiously, patiently, moved Donna's hand into her own, hoping that Donna would feel her love and goodness, even in the midst of a bad situation.

"Jennifer had another run in with the police," started Tenisha. "It's pretty bad." Donna's tears flooded her pillow, but she said nothing after Tenisha spoke. She understood perfectly well that Jennifer was locked up, again.

"What about Cherlene. Is she still out of town?" Tenisha didn't know how to start, so Davina cut in.

"Since you've been here, a young man entered Cherlene's home and sexually violated your niece while Cherlene was away."

"Who? Makeda?" asked Donna surprisingly. Tenisha looked shocked because this was news to her as well. Donna dropped many tears. "Is Keda ok?"

"Yes, she's ok, for now. I've been sitting with her while Tenisha's been here with you. She's just around the corner in another wing of the hospital."

"Oh my God! Is Cherlene with her? Does she know I'm here?" panicked Donna.

"Donna, I want you to calm down and listen to me very carefully," spoke Davina being motherly. Donna seemingly braced herself as Davina continued.

"After Cherlene brought Makeda here, it appears that she let her anger get the best of her. Instead of calling the police after the guy assaulted her daughter, she went after him on her own." Davina paused and looked sadly toward Tenisha, who was also surprised to hear what her mother was saying.

"I wish there was a better way to tell you this," cried Davina. "But it's not. Your sister eventually found the man that hurt your niece. But in the process of the violence between them, neither one of them made it through."

"What do you mean by *'neither one of them made it?'*" asked Donna. "Where's Cheryl? Where's my sister?" Donna started yelling. "I want to see my sister!"

"Sweetie," paused Davina. "She's gone."

"NOOOOOO!" screamed Donna. Tenisha turned her face away as she felt Donna's pain, again. Davina slowly left the room and went back to see Makeda.

Suddenly, Donna started violently hyperventilating, so Tenisha yelled for the doctors. The medical staff rushed in and learned that Donna had more internal bleeding. After they treated her, Donna was sleeping and Tenisha was alone with her, again.

The next morning, Donna awoke and the doctors gave her a full report of her diagnosis. They didn't know if she would ever be able to walk again. Donna couldn't believe what she was hearing. For days she was speechless in tears as Tenisha, cared for her, along with the nurses.

A few days later, Davina and Kris helped to bury Cherlene. Her only relative present was Makeda. Terry, Dexter, Coldblood, and Rev. Simmons were all arraigned in court at one million dollars bond,each. None of them had the money nor any help, so they remained in jail.

Elisa was still in a coma with Rosa and Jonathan by her side. Doctors had no idea how long it would be before she would revive. During the process, the FBI staged a bogus hit on Rosa and Elisa, and faked their deaths. Elisa remained in a coma, but no one knows where she is.

Shaun's body became the property of the state, therefore he was cremated.

Nicole became a very wealthy business woman who owned hair salons, and coffee shops all over the south. She became the legal guardian of Audrey and Dent, and taught them the ways of the Lord, and how to pray and trust him. They haven't stolen anything since.

While Jennifer was in the Atlanta jail, Nicole often took Audrey and Dent to see her because Jennifer wasn't given a bond. The judge and the mayor thought it to be a bad idea, because she might steal the city.

About a year after Jennifer was jailed, she was sentenced to serve 15 years for strong arm robbery and theft by taking.

Coldblood and Dexter were found guilty of aggravated assault and accessory to murder, and were sentenced to serve 20 years.

Reverend Simmons was found guilty of premeditated murder and barely escaped the death penalty. Due to mitigating circumstances, Terry's trial was delayed. A couple of months after Makeda moved in with Kris and Davina, they learned that she was pregnant with Shaun's child.

One night as Kris and Davina laid in bed and talked, Makeda stood outside the bedroom door and listened.

"Kris, she's only 14 and she's pregnant already. What do you think we should do?"

"Having a baby at such a young age will ruin her life," spoke Kris. "She deserves a chance to live; go to college; see the world. After all she's been through, I think she should abort the baby and end this pregnancy."

"I think you're right, Kris, and I'll talk to her about this tomorrow. I feel so sorry for her."

"Well, this is the best thing for her and the baby," said Kris. Then he kissed Davina and said good night. Davina laid on her back thinking as Kris turned to go to sleep.

"Kris," she spoke softly. "I need something."

"Yes baby, what is it?"

"How's the pony?" she asked. Kris turned towards her.

"He's strong as a horse; Viagra kicked in thirty minutes ago." Davina smiled and turned out the light. Makeda went to her room and laid down.

The next morning at breakfast, Davina talked to Makeda about aborting her baby.

"No, I don't think I would be happy about doing that," answered Makeda.

"Honey, this is your life you're talking about," explained Davina. "Besides, you're only 14 years old. What do you know about being happy?"

"I know it won't make me happy to kill my baby so I'm not gonna do it." Then she ran to her room and cried. Later that day, she heard Davina on the phone talking to DFACS about her situation. As they pressured her to abort, Makeda said,

"No!" Later, she ran away to Felton, Delaware.

****

A few days after Donna laid speechless in the hospital, the doctors finished their test and told Donna she would soon be released. Tenisha remained by her side.

"So what will happen to me now?"

"You're more than welcome to come live with me since Nela is away in Gymnastics training. I promise to take care of you until you decide what you want to do."

"Don't even try it, Glamour Bitch! We may have the same dad, but I will never trust you to be a caring sister," complained Donna. "If you hadn't rammed me with your car, I wouldn't be here even now. This is your fault that I'm like this, and now you think I'm gonna live with you? How stupid do you think I am?"

"Donna, what are you gonna do? How can you take care of yourself?" Tenisha was shocked when an attorney walked into the room, followed by a special care nurse.

"When did you do..." Tenisha was so shocked, she couldn't finish her words as she grabbed her bag and sadly left. Donna saw the hurt and disappointment in Tenisha's eyes as she talked with the attorney before she left.

Chapter 117

"She called again," said Edith. "I told her that you couldn't be better."

"Good," said Donna. "I know she wants to believe I'm doing bad so she can gloat and write about me." Donna had been in special care for four months but Tenisha still called her often to check on her. But Donna still refused to believe that Tenisha had her best interest at heart. "Don't ever tell her anything about me unless it's something good," advised Donna.

"It's your life," spoke Edith the nurse. "I don't care what you tell her."

The truth is that Donna was miserable. She had completely given her life into the hands of some jack-in-the-box law firm, and a family of special care nurses, who provided everything except, special care.

"Aren't you gonna bathe me, now?" asked Donna. "I smell really bad."

"You already know that I bathe you on Fridays; once a week. It's just Monday so stop your bitching."

"But I think I just pooped on myself."

"You better hope Ernestine cleans you up when she comes on Wednesday," complained Edith. "All you do is eat, sleep, and shit. I guess if I cut back on your food, you wouldn't use the bathroom so much and wouldn't need bathing."

Week after week, the special care nurses became worse and worse. Because of Donna's insurance and Cherlene's life insurance policy, Donna had good financial stability to live her life, even with a lawyer and special care nurses. But they were quickly spending her money and not providing the care she needed. Donna had moved into Cherlene's house because it was better suited to handle her than an apartment.

When a contractor was hired to fix the house in accordance to Donna's needs, one of the special care nurses had sex with him on Donna's kitchen table while Donna was forced to watch.

When Donna used the bathroom on herself, they would push her onto the patio and leave her there for hours as punishment. They fed her the scraps from their plates when they ate and they hardly cooked anymore.

They would pay their teenage cousins to clean the house, but they never really cleaned it. They just stayed on their cell phones and made fun of Donna. They used to read letters from Jennifer to her and even write Jennifer back on Donna's behalf. Then they started throwing the letters away and not accepting Jennifer's phone calls.

Donna had her attorney to fire them and hire another special care company, but they were worse. They left Donna in bed most of the times and she was suffering from malnutrition. Yet, because of her hatred and lack of trust toward Tenisha, Donna willingly endured it. Then one Sunday afternoon, the phone rang.

"Hello?" answered the nurse.

"I need to speak to Donna," said the voice. The nurse didn't hesitate to prop the phone into Donna's special bracket so she could talk.

"This is Donna?" she answered.

"Donna, this is Tenisha. How are you?"

"Hey, Glamour Bitch! Are you checking to see if I'm dead, yet? Well, bad news, I'm still here and doing just fine."

"Good, then you won't have a problem with me coming by to see you. I need to talk to you about something important."

"And what pray tell may that be, Tenisha."

"I'll tell you when I get there; I'm just around the corner."

"No!" yelled Donna, but Tenisha hung up. She wasn't gonna take 'no' for an answer this time. She had asked to come by many times but Donna said 'no.' This time Tenisha was desperate and planning to tell Donna she would leave her alone forever and forget about being sisters, or friends.

When Tenisha drove up, she couldn't believe the condition of the house from the outside. The paint looked bad, the windows and doors were broken and dirty, and the whole house looked run down. Tenisha didn't knock, but just opened the racked door and went it.

"Who are you?" asked the country talking nurse watching TV and smoking a cigarette.

"I'm here to see Donna," answered Tenisha. She saw trash, beer bottles, filthiness, dirty dishes, and the furniture was bad. The house needed cleaning and it smelled.

"She's in there," pointed the nurse. Tenisha cautiously made her way through the filth, and into the bedroom where Donna was laying in bed. When their eyes met, Tenisha saw hurt and pain in Donna's eyes like she had never seen before. This was the day Donna dreaded would come more than any day in her life. She never wanted Tenisha, of all people, to see her so down, so helpless; so miserable.

"Why did you come here!" cried Donna. "Get out! Please get out!" Tenisha heard her, but she didn't hear. Tenisha was busy looking around at all the filth. She saw dirty bowls, where the nurses had fed Donna and just left them there. The bed covers were stained and needed cleaning. Donna's face was dirty and her hair was a mess. Plus, the smell in the room almost made Tenisha sick. "Get out, Tenisha! Get out!"

At this point Tenisha no longer heard Donna's words. She was too busy observing the environment and making plans in her mind to clean up the mess.

As she walked closer to the bed, the stench grew stronger. "Please, please, get out!" cried Donna through tears. But like the compassionist, Tenisha just kept on coming. She grabbed the blanket that covered Donna and slowly pulled it back. When Tenisha saw the condition of Donna's body, she grabbed her mouth as she began to puke. Donna was not only lying in a urine soaked bed, but she had opened bed sores with small wormlike maggots on part of her body.

"Ugh!" vomited Tenisha as she ran to the filthy bathroom. After Tenisha accepted the reality of what she saw, she completely lost it! She grabbed the broom standing in the corner and held it over her head as she stared insanely at Donna. Donna was shocked as she saw Tenisha rage into the front room where the nurse was watching TV.

"Aaahhheee!" screamed Tenisha. The nurse turned just in time to feel the broomstick as Tenisha slammed it across her breast. The nurse fell backwards onto the floor. "I want you out of here, now!" screamed Tenisha again.

Being afraid, the nurse hurried out the door and was gone. Tenisha paced the room wondering what she would do next. She knew the only reason this had happened was because of Donna's pride and selfishness. She knew Donna would feel even more destroyed if she let this get out.

"Tenisha!" yelled Donna. "Are you in there? Where's my nurse?" Tenisha slowly walked to the bedroom and stared at Donna. "What're you gonna do?"

"I'm gonna help you, Donna."

"I never asked for your help! I just want you to ..."

"Shut up, Donna!" yelled Tenisha. "Don't you say another damn word or I will cover your head!" As Tenisha dialed her cell phone, Donna was certain that Tenisha was about to tell the world about her situation and even print it in the papers.

"Hello, Mom?" phoned Tenisha. "I need some help. I need a special medically trained person to help me take care of someone, but I want them to keep it hush, hush."

"Honey are you ok?" asked Davina.

"I'm fine, Mom, but I need help for a friend. Can you help me?" Davina figured that it was for Donna.

"You know what?" started Davina. "I know just the person and I'll have her to call."

"No, Mom! I don't want to talk to her over the phone. If you trust her, just send her to this address, right now." Tenisha gave Davina the address then she hung up. Donna and Tenisha said nothing as Tenisha started cleaning the place. An hour later, a car drove into the driveway. Tenisha was surprised to see the nurse that supervised the nurses at the AA center, where she had admitted her mother.

"Hello, again, Ms. Cuyler. Your mom said this was urgent and you needed me." At first Tenisha had her doubts about the nurse, but she knew that if her mom trusted her, so should she.

"Please call me, Tenisha."

"Ok, Tenisha, please call me, Olive," responded the nurse. "So, what's this about that you want to keep it, hush, hush?" As they walked inside, Olive didn't seem too bothered by the filth or the smell of the place. Tenisha took her into the bedroom and uncovered Donna's body.

"I need her taken care of and healed of these sores no matter how long it takes," ordered Tenisha. "I'll pay your fee, but I don't want anyone to know your business here---not even my mother. Do you understand?"

"I got it," said Olive.

"Good, when can you start?"

"I need to start now. She doesn't need to spend another second like this."

"I agree," said Tenisha. "Until we can find a suitable person to care for her full time, I will be your only helper or assistant. Order me as you will and I will do whatever you say."

"Ok then, prepare plenty of warm water and let's get her cleaned up."

For the next few months, Tenisha and Olive fixed the place and stayed by Donna's side until her body was healed again. Tenisha spent her savings and took out a loan to care for Donna, yet Donna still had reservations about trusting her motives.

During their promotion luncheon, Tenisha had been called the compassionist, therefore Donna thought Tenisha was just setting her up to become the perfect story that would boost her career. In spite of her thoughts and un-appreciation for Tenisha, she loved being able to feel beautiful again, and couldn't think of anyone who would treat her as special as Tenisha had, still she didn't trust her.

****

"We, the jury, find the defendant, Terry Billingly, 'not guilty' on all counts." Tenisha stood in the courtroom during Terry's trial and release as she shied away from other reporters and journalists that were completing the story surrounding D'Amica, Shaun, Cherelene, and D-Lo's death. Upon his release, Terry hugged Oliva, Dexter's wife, who had remained supportive throughout his incarceration. Then he saw Tenisha.

"Hi, Tenisha. I hear that you're a big-time reporter, now. I often see your name in the papers: Congratulations."

"Thank you, Terry. I'm glad that things worked out for you, today. What will you do now, after all these months."

"I guess I'll try to find out where my daughter ran off to. Did she leave any clues to where she might be going?"

"No, not a clue, Terry; sorry."

"Shortly after I was locked up, I saw Jennifer in the news and read about Donna in the papers. Have you heard anything from them?" Tenisha paused.

"Terry, I don't know what's up with Jennifer's current situation except that she's in prison. But obviously, you haven't heard that Donna... Donna is being well taken care of." Terry got excited.

"What! You know where Donna is, don't you? Tell me where she is! She may know where Makeda..." Tenisha cut in.

"Terry, I don't think so. None of us knows where Makeda is... least of all, Donna."

"How do you know that, Tenisha? At least let me talk to D..."

"I know that because Donna's my sister, and I take care of her now; she lives with me." Terry was baffled. "Terry, I am so sorry for your lost; I truly am. But there's nothing more me or my family can do to help you. I wish you the best." Then she walked away as Terry yelled behind her.

"Tenisha, I'd like to know how Donna is doing sometimes. Can I at least call you and find out?" Tenisha hesitated then turned and handed Terry her card. Then she was gone.

****

Later that night, a Trailways Bus Liner exited I-75 and entered the city.

"This stop is Atlanta! This stop is Atlanta!" announced the driver as he pulled into the station. Many travelers happily greeted their families as they stepped from the bus. But for the last traveler, there was no one--no family, no luggage, no food, no money, no smiles--only a borrowed quarter and lots of bad memories as she helplessly looked around.

"Uh!" she moaned as she experienced her first labor pain. But no one seemed to care as she painfully struggled to the phone and inserted her last coin. The labor pains subsided, but tears were many as Makeda missed her mother.

Chapter 118

"This is my last day with you, kid," said Olive as she fed Donna at the table.

"Why?" asked Donna surprisingly. "I kinda like having you around. It's the Glamour Bitch, isn't it? Is she firing you?"

"No, she is not," defended Olive. "Why do you always call her that? She's been nothing but wonderful to you. I'm leaving because you don't need me anymore, and I don't feel right draining Tenisha of her money; especially when you don't need my help."

"Olive, please don't leave me alone with her. I'll double your salary if you stay.... please?" begged Donna.

"If you have money, you need to help your sister take care of you. She's accumulated a lot of debt for your sake, yet you still have reservations about her." Tenisha walked in from work while they were talking.

"What's going on, guys?"

"Oh nothing," answered Olive. "I was just saying goodbye to our patient here."

"Tenisha, please don't let her go; I need her!" begged Donna.

"We've taken Olive away from her job long enough ---almost 4 months and it's time to let her go. Besides, I'll be here to help with your needs."

"Well ladies, it's been very interesting and fun," said Olive. "You know where I'll be if you need me. Take care, Donna. You really are in good hands; bye." Then she left.

"So now what?" asked Donna. "Are you gonna write up this wonderful story about this handicap ex-journalist you've rescued from disaster?"

"Donna, after all I've done for you, why do you continue to treat me like an enemy?"

"Because I know you still have ulterior motives like you always have. You're up to something and it will reveal itself in due time." Tenisha ignored her and looked at the bills.

"The only thing I'm up to is bills. I'm up to my neck in them," sighed Tenisha.

Donna knew that Tenisha was financially stressed because she overheard Tenisha talking to her mom on the phone about it, when Tenisha thought she was asleep. She knew that it was time to help.

"Ok, Glamour Bitch," started Donna. "I guess I better help you before you make a mess of both our lives. Take me to the computer and go online." Tenisha hesitated. "Come on, come on!" continued Donna.

Tenisha did as she was told while wondering what was Donna up to. "Now access my bank; enter this account number... #01149911-

3072605." Tenisha did as instructed, and was shocked as she read the screen and the balance to Donna's account.

"What!!" paused Tenisha? "Where did!! How did you get all this money? There's over a million dollars in this account!"

"I'm crippled, Tenisha---not stupid," smarted off Donna. "My insurance and injury claims came to well over 3 million. I turned it over to my attorney the day he showed up at the hospital for him and his special care team to take care of me. But when you stopped them six months later, that also stopped their fees."

"What!" yelled Tenisha. "You paid them nearly two million dollars in 6 months just to be mistreated and get bed sores?"

"Yep! And they milked me like a cow!" exclaimed Donna. "That is, until I froze the account and changed my account number. I still believe you're up to something, Glamour Bitch, but you did get me out of a pissy bed and healed my sores. So, I guess you're the lesser of two evils. I'd rather die by the hand of a known enemy, than by a fraudulent attorney and special care people pretending to be my friends, just so they can get rich."

Tenisha calmed and spoke. "Donna, I am in a lot of unnecessary debt because of you, yet, you call me evil. Had I this money months ago, you would be much better taken care of by now. You can't even feed yourself, yet, you are very selfish toward the one who feeds you. Why, Donna, Why?"

"Tenisha!" yelled Donna. "Suck it up! You have full access to my account unlike my attorney! Transfer the money! Pay your debts! Buy whatever you want to! Just, whatever!" After a long pause of silence between them, Tenisha's cell phone rang. It was Davina.

"Hello Mother, what's up? Is Nela ok?"

"Nela's fine, but we have another problem."

"What's that?"

"Makeda's back and she just called for me to pick her up at the bus station."

Chapter 119

"Makeda!" shouted Davina. "Over here!" Davina met Makeda at the greyhound station, in downtown Atlanta, late Friday evening. She was 8 ½ months pregnant and ready to be delivered as she wobbled toward Davina.

For almost 5 months she moved from shelter to shelter, and with friends until she wore out her welcome and had no place to go. She knew that her baby would be delivered any day now, and she didn't want to have her baby in some alley without any help. So, she hustled and begged for enough money to buy a bus ticket to Atlanta, to the only help she knew.

"Makeda!" shouted Davina again. Makeda walked toward her with nothing in her hands. "Where's your bag, child?" Makeda just stood staring at Davina with weariness in her eyes. Davina pulled her close as Makeda burst into a painful, sorrowful cry.

****

"Your niece, Makeda, is back at Moms," said Tenisha.

"Makeda?" perked Donna. "Is she coming by? I want to see her!"

"No! Not, yet."

"Why not? Why won't you take me to see Jenny or Cherlene's grave site?"

"Because you are not ready for that, yet, and I need you to trust me before you start venturing out."

"I'll never trust you, Glamour Bitch!"

"Then you'll never see your niece or your sisters because I'm not taking you!"

"I hate you, you..."

"Ah! Ah! Ah!" Tenisha pinched her cheek and held a bar of soap to her mouth. Starting right now, I want you to clean your words or I will feed you soap and clean your mouth myself!" Donna got quiet.

Over the next few weeks, Tenisha paid her debt and even bought new clothes for Donna. She had a beautician to do Donna's hair and make up, so that she felt like a woman again. When Donna saw how beautiful she was, she forgot about her distrust for Tenisha, as she laughed and joked like they were friends. This was the first time in Tenisha's life she felt happy while talking and sharing with a sister, like she always dreamed of.

****

"Uhhh!" cried Makeda. "It hurts!"

"Hurry Kris!" scolded Davina. "You're driving like an old man and her water broke!"

"I'm going as fast as the traffic will allow me to go, honey. Just be patient!"

"What traffic?" yelled Davina. "It's 2:30 in the morning!"

"Uhhhh!" screamed Makeda. "It's coming! I feel it!" An hour after Makeda entered The Memorial Hospital, she delivered a healthy 7 ½ pound boy. She named him Lance, which means, "Born of the land."

****

The next morning when Tenisha woke up, she was excited as she ran in to talk to Donna.

"Guess what? I've got some good news, some really great news, and the best damn news that money can buy!" smiled Tenisha. "Which do you want first?"

"Ok. Let's start with the good news," sighed Donna.

"The good news is that Makeda is fine, and so is Lance, her 7 ½ pound baby boy. Congratulations! You are a great aunt!"

"That is really great news!" said Donna.

"No, the really great news is that I'm walking you through the neighborhood today." Donna was happily surprised.

"Are you sure, Tenisha? I want to get out so bad! Can we go see Makeda?"

"No Donna! I said, through the neighborhood. I don't have the right vehicle to properly transport you, yet. But that brings me to the best damn news that money can buy!" Donna got excited.

"Tell me! Tell me!"

"We're moving." Donna paused.

"What? Where? When?"

"Soon," said Tenisha. "I've talked to my dad, and we're gonna have a special house built to accommodate all of your needs." Donna was puzzled and seemed ill.

"Will this new house make me whole again so that I can do things?"

"Come on Donna, you know what I mean. Besides, over the past 4 months, I've seen more of you than I have my own daughter. I miss her and she misses me. This new house will be good for both of us."

"I see," said Donna. "So now that you've gotten your hands on my money, suddenly, you need a new house to do all the things for me that you're already doing. That makes a lot of sense, Glamour Bitch! Why don't you just say you want a new house for you and your daughter? Because that's who it will really be for, won't it?"

"Donna why do you have to twist good things and make them seem bad? I'm so sick of you doing that. This house is fine for you maybe, but not for me. You can stay here if you want, but I'm leaving with or without you and your money. Now what's it gonna be?" Donna just whistled and stared to the ceiling. Then she said,

"Do whatever you want."

About a year had passed since Tenisha built the new house and moved together with Donna. Makeda and Lance also moved in with them to help manage Donna while Tenisha was at work. Many times Tenisha was allowed to work from home when Makeda had to go out.

With help from Donna's and Cherlene's insurance, Tenisha had a special built home with full accommodations for Donna's needs. Donna's air-powered wheelchair moved her around whenever she blew into the tube. The house was built with a ramp at every exit, plus, she had special accommodations to help her escalate her chair up and down the stairs.

Tenisha really wanted things to work between them so she would not allow Donna to see anyone until she learned to trust her and come to depend on her, like sisters were suppose to. She altered her life for love's sake, and had proven many times over that she had Donna's best interest at heart.

Donna had the best that life could offer and she was slowly starting to trust Tenisha to take care of her. But she had hated Tenisha for so long, she still struggled when she tried to talk to Tenisha and show her appreciation.

"What's wrong with you?" asked Makeda as Tenisha entered from work.

"We've got two young new employees who hopes to be journalists some day, so all they do is argue and fight. They make it really stressful when you're working on an important story."

"Hmm? Sounds like two young journalists I used to know," injected Donna. "Glamour Bitch, I was really on your ass, wasn't I? You were no match for me when I wasn't in this chair." Tenisha had had a very stressful day, and really didn't want to hear Donna gloating about the past.

"I have an appointment, so I'm out of here," said Makeda. Then she left.

"Wait-a-minute!" yelled Donna. "I thought you were gonna do my hair?"

"I'm gonna do your hair. Just give me a minute," said Tenisha.

"But I've been waiting all day, and my head is itching. Can you hurry, please?"

"Donna, I'm tired. Plus, I have to cook and I have to run a few errands for Mom today. I just want a little break, that's all."

"But what about me? Who's gonna help me? Cheryl and Jenny would never do this to me. If they were here, they wouldn't just wash my hair, but they wouldn't be ashamed to get naked with me and hold me in their arms, while bathing me in the tub. That's how real sisters do it. Not use some special tub chair like you do when you sit me up and bathe me."

"Donna how would you know that? They have never had to experience you like this," questioned Tenisha. "They may treat you worse for all you know."

"I know how'd they treat me because we love each other like sisters, and there's nothing we wouldn't do for each other. We took the time to learn each other's ways and what we like. They both know that I like being soothed and submerged in perfumed bath water and they wouldn't have a problem helping me to enjoy it like that, even if they had to get in the water with me. Not treat me like I'm your patient or special project! But look at you, Glamour Bitch. Even after a hard stressful day at work, you still look and smell good. I'm pretty, too, and all I'm asking is that you help me to feel pretty, like I am!"

"You're not being fair, Donna. You grew up with Cherlene and Jenny so they know you better than anyone. Please don't compare me to them," demanded Tenisha. "I'm gonna do your hair right now. But I don't want to hear anything else about Jennifer and Cherlene and all they would do for you because they are not here for you now; I am!"

Donna was speechless as Tenisha dressed comfortably then yanked her from her chair. Tenisha laid her on a special plastic knitted lawn chair that she used to bath Donna with, when she was placed in the tub. The bath chair also had special braces to hold Donna in place to keep her from sliding while being bathed.

After Tenisha laid her on the chair in the bedroom, she places a small tub under the chair below Donna's head then she washed her hair.

"Oooooh! That feels so good!" exclaimed Donna. "This should've been done earlier today!" Tenisha was not enjoying Donna's hair at all, as Donna continued to annoy her with selfish comments, in an attempt to make her feel inferior. After she washed and blow dried Donna's hair, Donna's words began to take Tenisha's anger to a whole-nother-level.

"There were times you really surprised me, Glamour Bitch. Although you started at AJC a year before I did, you know I was gonna be chief journalist before you. Yet, you hung in there trying to beat me out. Now, I know that's why you felt you had to ram me with your car. I can't even say I blame you because you had to stop me somehow.

Well, here I am; right where you want me---harmless toward your career progress and can only do as you command. Can you honestly say you're not happy that your greatest competition is out of your way?"

While Donna spoke, Tenisha started thinking about all she had gone through while in college. She was denied love by the man she loved, while he married another, and left her pregnant with his child.

She thought about her parent's troubles and how she had to be a referee then mediator to hold them at bay for more than five years of her life. There were the stresses of trying to maintain stability at her job while some childish, selfish, unknown sister tried to get her fired everyday. Then there were the pressures of being a good single mom, and example for her daughter.

Finally, there was an unappreciative invalid living under her roof, who was doing all she could to make Tenisha feel like she would always be second to her, when all she could do was... talk, and run her mouth.

Tenisha slowly got angry as Donna continued to tongue lash her about her career, and to compare her to Jennifer and Cherlene.

As the weight of the past and present resided on her, she changed and became like a different person. Her eyes turned evil as she yanked Donna's head while combing her hair.

"Ouch!" yelled Donna. "That hurts!" Tenisha paid no attention as the thoughts became more prevalent in her mind. "Ouch! Ow!" yelled Donna again. Tenisha's anger had caused her to grind the comb into Donna's skull. "Tenisha that hurts! Ouch! What are you doing? Ouch!"

"Shut up, you selfish slut!" yelled Tenisha. Then like a subtle most evil one, she stood and walked around the room talking to herself while Donna watched in amazement.

"I just wanted a normal life," whispered Tenisha. "Normal, that's all!" She took a picture of Rubix, Nela's dad, from a drawer and looked at it. "But what did I get? I got a lying bastard who got me pregnant and left me!" She dropped the picture onto the floor and kept walking and talking.

"Who am I?" she asked. "I'm not even my daddy's child? Who is my daddy? I don't even know him so how can I truly know myself. Who the hell am I?" she continued insanely.

"My child will have to ask these same questions, one day, cause she don't know her daddy, either. What will I say? It's a damn curse; that's what it is." Tenisha turned to Donna and continued. "Meantime I've got this selfish, inconsiderate cunt of a sister that I'm forcing myself to be friends with. What is wrong with me? This is not who I am!"

"Tenisha you're scaring me!" said Donna. "Please stop this!" Tenisha ran to Donna's wheelchair, grabbed her shoulders, and talked while staring into her face like a crazy woman.

"Oh now you're scared, huh? Just before you got in that wheelchair you wanted to hurt me all because I tried to be your friend. 'Slap!'" Tenisha slapped her hard, then yelled, "Now shut up, whiny bitch!"

Then she had a thought. "Whoa? Hmm? Whiny Bitch? Yeah, that's who you are. You're a whiny bitch!" Tenisha pointed to herself and said, "Glamour Bitch?" Then she pointed to Donna and said, "Whiny Bitch." Afterwards, she started dancing and singing around the room and saying, "Glamour Bitch! Whiny Bitch! Glamour Bitch! Whiny Bitch! Et cetera, et cetera, et cetera!" Then she ran to the window and yelled out, "We are the 'Bitch Sisters'... Glamour and Whiny!"

Donna started to cry as she watched and listened. She knew that Tenisha had lost it and she didn't know what Tenisha would do next.

"Tenisha?" pleaded Donna. "I am so sorry and so scared. Please don't do this! Please, Tenisha?"

"Oh! So now I'm Tenisha, huh? You've called me a bitch everyday for years, and you've done it 3 or 4 times a day. But now that you are afraid, I'm suddenly Tenisha again, huh? No way---not today! I'm Glamour and you are Whiny! *'Slap! Slap!'* Now, shut up, you Whiny Bitch!"

After Tenisha slapped her again, she stood waiting for Donna to say something so she could hit her again, but Donna said nothing. After Tenisha circled behind her like a lioness ready to strike. she sat behind Donna and started forcibly doing her hair again.

"Tenisha, I'm sorry," squeaked Donna. "Ow!" Tenisha yanked her hair violently while brushing, combing, and insanely fussing. "Ow! Ouch!" cried Donna.

"I told you to shut up, Whiny!" She kept fussing and digging into Donna' hair.

"Ouch! Ouch! Tenisha it hurts! Ouch! Ouch! Ow! Please, Tenisha stop! I'm so scared, right now, and it hurts!"

Then while sitting behind Donna, Tenisha began a series of slaps to Donna's head. *'Slap! Slap! Pow! Pinch! Slap! Slap! Yank! Slap!'* "Now, say something else, Whiny Bitch! Go ahead and try me... I dare you!"

After a moment of silence, Tenisha started yanking her head, again, as she combed it. "Ouch, tt hurts! Please... Ow! Ow! Ow! Ow! Uh! Ow! Please stop, please..." Suddenly, Tenisha ran to the front of Donna and screamed,

"I said shut up, Whiny!" She raised her hand to slap Donna again but this time, Donna screamed and cried out,

"Aaayyiiee! Please, Cherlene, help me! Please Mommy, help me! Mommy please come back!" Her tears were many as Tenisha lowered her hand slowly. "Mommy I need you, Mommy! Please help me! I don't know what to do! I don't know, Mommy... what to do!"

Donna's words and tears were so fervent, they also delivered Tenisha from the madness she was going through. From the grave, Tenisha began to hear Cherlene's words;

> *"Tenisha, the problem is not you. It's deeper than you or anything you've done. Just continue on being the person that you are... continue being you... continue being you..."*

As Tenisha listened to Donna cry, Cherlene's words became clearer now. She understood that Donna had never accepted the pain of abandonment caused by her parents all these years, because she depended so heavily on Cherlene and Jennifer to replace them. Now that

Cherlene and Jennifer were gone, Donna, for the first time since she lost her parents, cried out for her mom.

"Mommy, I need you, Mommy!" continued Donna. Tenisha slowly knelt before Donna and cared for her. She quietly dried Donna's tears while wiping her own.

"Shh!" whispered Tenisha. "It's over now, Sweetie. It's over." Donna stared at her.

"I'm scared, Tenisha. Please don't hurt me again... please?" sniffed Donna. Tenisha held her hand and kissed her forehead.

"I won't hurt you again, Dee, I promise. I'm not sure about what just happened but it's over now." Donna was afraid and didn't know what to think, so she was calm and quiet. Tenisha started to care for her again, and brushed her long pretty hair carefully. Donna could feel her compassion again and welcomed it, though she was still nervous.

After a short while, Tenisha took Donna from her chair and braced her up with pillows on the couch. She wanted to talk and this time she felt that the lines of communications had been opened differently and they may finally move on in happiness. So to make Donna feel more comfortable, like a friend, Tenisha braced her up so they could seem like two sisters talking---face to face.

"Dee, we have both been through hell in our lives---me with my parents, and you without yours. But I have accepted it that we are sisters and no fighting or hatred will ever change that; not even Glamour and Whiny. Let's stop fighting, Dee, please? Just because you're in a wheelchair, doesn't matter to me, as long as you can be my friend and hopefully love me back when I love you. You're smart, funny, and I need you in my life just as much as I know you need me."

"You need me, Tenisha?" questioned Donna humbly. "For what? I can't do anything?"

"You can be my sister just like you were with Cherlene and Jennifer. I promise that I'll be yours back and love you even more than they did in the end. All I'm asking for is a chance. If it doesn't work, I'll do whatever you want me to do and leave you alone."

Donna was a little surprised. All this time she really believed that Tenisha had an ulterior motive and was up to something. But when Tenisha spoke of being a family and needing her, she felt Tenisha's compassion and it seemed right. Donna's peace had subsided, and it was like barriers had been removed from her eyes and heart.

"Ok," said Donna. "I promise to try." Tenisha happily embraced her and started to cry. While they embraced, the wind of strife that was upon Donna, blew away and vanished as a ray of light illuminated their presence. Then Tenisha started kissing all over her face.

"Stop that, Glamour Bi... I mean...Tenisha! That tickles," said Donna. Tenisha laughed then paused and wiped her face. "Tenisha, can I ask you something?"

"Sure, what's up?" Donna was cautious.

"Will you take me to see Jennifer... please, and take me to say goodbye to Cherlene; please?"

After a pause, Tenisha spoke. "I think that's a great idea! Give me a couple of weeks to get myself together and gather information, and we will go. Meantime, I have a surprise for you."

Tenisha stepped into her master bedroom and was gone for a few minutes. When she returned, she was dressed only in her bath robe and carrying another one in her hand. Then she undressed Donna and placed her in the twin robe that she brought in. Donna watched in wonder.

Finally, she placed Donna in her chair and rolled her to the master bath, that was perfumed with pedals and flowers exactly as Donna liked it. She carefully lifted Donna into the huge special made tub, and held her close while she bathe her, and just talked. They both started to feel that this was the beginning of a sisterhood that would never end.

After the exquisite bath was over, and all was well between them, Tenisha carefully lifted Donna to her chair, where she was about to dry her off and prepare for bed. As Tenisha sat Donna in the chair, she suddenly slipped onto the wet floor, and fell backward, with her head about to hit the toilet bowl. As she fell, the look on her face told Donna that Tenisha knew that this fall could be fatal and they both were afraid.

"Aaaiiaah!" screamed Tenisha as the wet floor caused her body to become completely suspended air borne. Because the bathroom was built so big to accommodate Donna, there was nothing close enough for Tenisha to grab onto to keep herself from falling.

"Tenisha!" screamed Donna as she watched Tenisha seemingly falling to her death. As she looked into Tenisha's face, she suddenly saw the face of Cherlene then it changed to Jennifer!

Donna was a quick thinker. She knew that the strength of Cherlene, the wisdom of Jennifer, and the love of them both, were all in Tenisha, as she watched fate about to take away her last sister. Just as Tenisha's head barely made contact with the toilet, Donna stood and caught Tenisha by her arm.

Chapter 120

Almost six years had passed since Cherlene's death as Makeda hung out with her son, Lance, in a neighborhood park.

"Girl, you're only 19, and you have a son almost 6 years old!" spoke Irina. "Aren't you a little afraid he may grow up and just take over your life someday? You're not much older than he is!"

"I didn't have much of a choice," responded Makeda. "I didn't want to abort my baby because my mom taught me better than that. Besides, it doesn't matter how old he is. Children grow up and take over their parents lives everyday. That's why you should have a very special relationship with your children."

"Yeah, but you were raped," argued Irina. "I don't think your mom would've screamed had you aborted him. Plus, you were so young."

"Lance, be careful!" shouted Makeda. Lance and Irina's son, Lil Fella, were throwing rocks at the trees in the park where people were walking. "Stop throwing rocks before you hit somebody!"

"Yes Ma'am," said Lance. Lil Fella continued to throw rocks and laughed when he caused a man to duck to avoid being hit. Irina saw it, but said nothing and continued trying to reason with Makeda about having a child so early as a result of forced sex.

When Lance saw the man duck, he looked back at his mom, because he knew he would be in trouble if he picked up another rock.

"Maybe we should stop throwing and go to the slides," reasoned Lance. But Lil Fella laughed and just kept throwing. Just as Lance turned to walk away, Lil Fella aimed a rock and hit Lance in the head and hurt him.

"Ouch!" screamed Lance. Lance quickly wrapped his hands around Lil Fella's throat and started choking him.

"Lil Fella!" screamed Irina. Makeda and Irina hurried to separate the boys.

"I don't care what you say," fussed Irina. "You should have aborted that bad little bastard! He tried to kill my son!" Makeda being tough like Cherlene responded.

"Your son is the one that hit my son in the head with a rock. Had you been the mother you're suppose to be, none of this would have happened."

"Ok, Makeda," argued Irina. "You're just 19, but you got all the sense! We'll see!"

"Yes we will!" said Makeda. "Because you're 24, and you ain't got no sense!"

While the women argued, Lance saw Lil Fella pick up a rock, and slip it into his pocket. He knew that Lil Fella was about to throw it, but he wasn't sure. Therefore, he set his iPod on the picnic table, sneakily picked up a rock, and cuffed it in his hand. Then he kept his eyes on Lil Fella.

"Let's get out of here, Lil Fella, before this woman pisses me off!" Irina hurried away with her son following her but Lance kept his eye on Lil Fella. After they were about 50 feet away, Lil Fella quickly turned and hurled the rock at Lance. Lance ducked, and quickly threw a rock back. Just as the rock was about to hit Lil Fella, he stepped aside and the rock hit Irina on her butt.

"You little bad bastard!" screamed Irina as she turned and hurried towards Lance. Makeda turned to see what happened.

"Mom, he threw a rock!" yelled Lance. "So I threw one back!"

"He hit me with a rock!" yelled Irina as she reached to grab Lance. Makeda quickly stepped between them.

"Irina," spoke Makeda calmly. "I'd like to think that we're friends. But if you keep acting like you want to touch my son, so help me God if I don't deck your ass and stuff you in that sandbox!" Irina was very mad as she stood toe to toe with Makeda. The boys were also at a face off being ready to fight.

"Let's go, Lil Fella!" she yelled. "This ain't over, Keda!" she said as she left. As Lil Fella was about to walk away, he noticed Lance's iPod on the picnic table, and smiled. Then he ran after his mother.

When Lance looked toward the iPod, he saw it was broken. Lil Fella's rock had missed Lance, but it had hit and broken his iPod. As Lance looked, Lil Fella was laughing and shooting a bird at him. As Lance's anger began to grow, suddenly his eye began to twitch!

In Loving Memory
Of
Myrtice Hixan Roberts
12-22-1948 to 10-1-2012

Because of Myrtice 'Red Velvet' Roberts, I was able to create programs, develop games, and feed entire prison dorms of 96 men at a time, every single holiday while dedicating my own life back to God. Myrtice faithfully sent her financial blessings to help me and others like me even when the system failed us.

Hopefully our book, hers and mine, entitled, "From Generation to Generation," will be published soon. Because of Myrtice's untiring efforts, love, and desire to live the life Jesus talked about in Matthew 25:35-40, I am a blessed man, even in my current situation and so are many others that are with me.

Myrtice was one of the four that engrafted her good fruit into my tree and made me whole again. Praise God for Myrtice and all she has done. Her life and examples are a testament to the great things God has done and is still doing; I pray that on that great day, she'll be presented faultless before his throne.

Until then I, William Charles Lewis, encourage you all to remember my friend, Myrtice Roberts, and the love she shared with the world. Hopefully, it will bless you also to stay in God's care. Thank you, Myrtice. Sleep well; I'll see you soon.

Your friend in Christ,

Charles

About the Author

After surviving the violent projects lifestyle of Americus Georgia, William Charles Lewis completed high school and joined the United States Army. While serving in the military as a Cannon Crewman, he attended the University of Maryland within the Nurnberg Germany location where he received his Associates Degree in Business Management.

After 8 years of military service, William resided in Atlanta where he completed his degree in Drafting and AutoCad at Balin Institute of Technology.

Being already known as a spiritual man, William joined the church and incorporated his management and architectural skills toward building churches and many other commercial projects around Metro Atlanta.

Although he learned and knew the will of God for his life, temptation and spiritual negligence became overwhelming as William openly fell short of his heavenly goal; prior sin of the fathers had him on a direct course to hell!

Finally, after many infidelities, a bad divorce led him to commit heinous crimes that landed him in prison. Since that time, William rededicated himself to God and gave his undivided attention through faith and prayer for God's guidance. When he was least expecting, he heard the call of God... again.

William is the father of three grown children; Charles Antwaun, Jennifer Ramona and Jonathan Lamar. Currently, William and his daughter Jennifer are on the course to alert the world of the generational curses being passed or inherited to their descendants because of past sin of the parents.

FROM WILLIAM:

Even within our fictional novels, the Word of God is real and rebellion against it can be devastating. There's no doubt that I'm a worthless sinner (forgiven) but still sorrowful before God and you. My friends... please take your thoughts off of me... the man... and hear God in the message, before you pass your sin to your children.

Through this generational series, God is trying to help somebody. Think about it... it could be you!

NOVELS BY
LEWIS-SMITH BOOKS

FROM GENERATION TO GENERATION
(The Series)
by William C Lewis / Jennifer R Smith

Book 1	*"The Curse Must Be Broken!"* Available Now!
Book 2	*"A Curse Unleashed!"*	Available Now!
Book 3	*"Evils of a Cursed Son!"*	Available Now!
Book 4	*"A Cursed Daughter's Vengeance!"*	Available Now!
Book 5	*"Saints... Chosen, But Cursed!"* Available Now!
Book 6	*"Angels... Fallen From Grace!"* Available Now!
Book 7	*"So-- & Go-- Remixed! (In Atlanta)"*	Available Now!

THE MATE TRILOGY
BY WILLIAM C LEWIS / JOELYN D MILLER

Book 1	*"The Mate!"*	Available Now!
Book 2	*"The Mate... Domination!"*	November 2020
Book 3	*"The Mate... On Fire!"*	December 2020

Coming in 2021!

"Before The Fall!"

"Unexpected Turbulance!"

Made in the USA
Monee, IL
31 December 2021